ISAAC BASHEVIS SINGER

AVON
PUBLISHERS OF BARD, CAMELOT AND DISCUS BOOKS

DESIGN: *Marshall Lee*

Parts of the first three chapters originally appeared in
Playboy magazine, in a slightly different form, under the
title "The Courtship."

AVON BOOKS
A division of
The Hearst Corporation
959 Eighth Avenue
New York, New York 10019

First Avon Printing, March, 1979

AVON TRADEMARK REG. U.S. PAT. OFF. AND IN
OTHER COUNTRIES, MARCA REGISTRADA, HECHO EN
U.S.A.

Printed in the U.S.A.

TO MY WIFE ALMA WITH LOVE

CONTENTS

AUTHOR'S NOTE TO THE NEW EDITION

The Manor and *The Estate* were written as one book, originally published in Yiddish between 1953 and 1955 in the *Jewish Daily Forward*. The original title was *Der Hoyf,* which means *The Court.* It is only for technical reasons that this work first appeared in English in two separate volumes and at separate times under the imprint of Farrar, Straus and Giroux—*The Manor* in 1967 and *The Estate* in 1969—and I am happy that they are now coming out in one volume under the title of the first part. Both parts were translated into English by my nephew, Joseph Singer, and by Elaine Gottlieb. A few of the chapters were also translated by Herman Eichenthal. The entire novel was edited by Cecil Hemley and Elizabeth Shub before it was sent to Robert Giroux, my editor for almost twenty years, who did the final editing. I dedicate this book to the blessed memory of my brother and master, Israel Joshua Singer, and of my sister Hinda.

I.B.S.
September, 1978

AUTHOR'S NOTE TO THE ORIGINAL EDITION

The Manor was written between 1953 and 1955. As with many of my stories and all my novels (with the exception of *Satan in Goray*, which I wrote while still in Warsaw), it was first serialized in *The Jewish Daily Forward*. Although *The Manor* was published many years after *The Family Moskat*, it portrays an earlier period—the epoch between the Polish insurrection of 1863 and the end of the nineteenth century. It was the era of gas lamps, the time when the Poles had finally become resigned to their loss of independence and turned to a kind of national positivism. Poland now began to emerge as an industrial country; railroads were built, factories were opened, and the cities grew rapidly. The Jews, who until 1863 for the most part still lived in a ghetto atmosphere, now began to play an important role in Polish industry, commerce, the arts and sciences. All the spiritual and intellectual ideas that triumphed in the modern era had their roots in the world of that time—socialism and nationalism, Zionism and assimilationism, nihilism and anarchism, suffragettism, atheism, the weakening of the family bond, free love, and even the beginnings of Fascism.

The Estate, a sequel to and the conclusion of *The Manor*, ends in the last years of the nineteenth century—an epoch when humanism undertook to practice what it had preached for generations. What happened in the village of Jampol, and what was discussed by a small group of self-educated youths in furnished rooms in Warsaw, became the basis of the social upheavals and the terrible disillusions of our present time.

Both parts of *The Manor* were translated by my nephew, Joseph Singer, the son of my brother I. J. Singer; and by Elaine Gottlieb, the wife of my unforgettable friend Cecil Hemley; and a few chapters were translated by Herman Eichenthal. The book was edited by Cecil Hemley, Elizabeth Shub, and Robert Giroux, to whom I wish to express my deepest gratitude.

I wish also to thank the National Foundation on the Arts for the grant awarded me in connection with this work.

I. B. S.

THE MANOR

ONE

I 🏰

After the unsuccessful rebellion of 1863, many Polish noblemen were hanged; others—Count Wladislaw Jampolski among them—were banished to Siberia. The Czar's soldiers led the Count in chains through the streets of Jampol, the town which bore his name.

Though it was dangerous to have anything to do with an insurrectionist, the priest appeared to administer a farewell blessing, wearing his vestments and holding a crucifix. Peasants removed their caps; women wept.

There was great excitement when the Count passed the cluster of huts on the outskirts of the town, where the Jews had only recently formed a community of their own, known locally as The Sands. Since Jampol was still under the jurisdiction of the Church, Jews were not permitted to live in the city itself and had to pay a toll for the privilege of entering it.

The residents of The Sands were astonished by the bearing of the aristocratic prisoner. The Count with his wind-blown white hair and mustache, his jaunty stride, flushed face, and unbuttoned fur coat, with his hat at a rakish angle, seemed as unconcerned as though he were going off to a party.

Some weeks later the town crier, after summoning the people of Jampol with his drum, read out an edict that had come from St. Petersburg. The Imperial decree announced the total confiscation of Count Jampolski's estate except for the land already divided among his former serfs. Countess Maria Jampolska was given six months to vacate the ancestral manor. Eventually it became known that Czar Alexander had deeded the Count's possessions to a duke who was one of his generals.

The Jews shrugged their shoulders: such was the way of the Gentile, where might was right. Calman Jacoby, a Jew of some standing who dealt in wheat and traded with the manor, obtained from the village officials the name of the new lord of the Jampolski manor. Paying a clerk eighteen groschen, he dictated a letter to the duke in St. Petersburg, stating that whereas he, Calman Jacoby, was a trustworthy, God-fearing man and a warden of his community, he ventured respectfully to beg his Excellency to grant him a lease on the manor and all that went with it. Calman concluded with the offer of a generous annual rental.

There was no word from St. Petersburg for some time. Then one day the duke arrived unannounced in Jampol and, settling down at the manor, sent a Cossack to bring Jacoby to him. The Cossack, riding bareback on a small horse, wore a cylindrical cap, a single earring, and carried a leather thong instead of a whip. He led the way at a slow trot, while Calman walked behind. The Sands' inhabitants were close to panic. They feared that false accusations had been leveled against the community and expected retribution, disaster, and bloodshed. Calman's wife Zelda, accompanied by the children, escorted Calman part of the way, wailing as if he had already died. It was rumored a gallows had been erected in the manor courtyard; Calman was to pay for having traded with the rebels.

When Calman entered the manor hall and saw the new master, he prostrated himself to kiss his gleaming boots and plead for mercy. The duke was young, with curly hair and luxuriant side whiskers, and he was wearing civilian clothes. He ordered Calman to his feet. Calman, who could speak some Russian, answered the duke's innumerable questions and the next day returned home with the lease to the manor. Soon afterward the duke departed, leaving Calman Jacoby in charge of the Jampolski estate.

Calman Jacoby's first move was a judicious one. He informed the Countess Maria that she was free to remain at the manor for the rest of her life. Furthermore, he would provide her with horses for her coach and milch cows for her household. He also promised to keep her supplied with wheat, barley, potatoes, groats, and other staples. Calman then came to terms with the bailiff and stewards, though they were known to be drunkards and thieves. Nevertheless, the Jampol peasants resented this Jew, an infidel, who lorded it over Polish soil in the name of an alien oppressor. But at least he did not put on airs. Poland had fought and lost once again. Her finest sons were now being driven into the dismal icy tundras, where the survivors of the 1831 revolt still languished. What did it matter who ruled in the meantime?

Calman Jacoby moved into a cottage formerly inhabited by the manor blacksmith. After nailing mezuzahs on the doorposts he had all his household effects brought in: two sideboards, one for meat and the other for dairy products; the Passover dishes; the everyday crockery; the wardrobes, beds, benches. Calman also had an oak chest, covered in cowhide and braced with brass bands, where he kept his money, articles that were pawned with him, and his silver candlesticks. Since God had denied his Zelda the blessing of a male child, Calman had to save for the dowries of their four daughters.

It was soon apparent that Calman's new venture was a fortunate one. The harvest that year was abundant. After the emancipation of the serfs, much of Count Jampolski's land had been distributed among the peasants, who now had permission to graze their cattle on manorial pastures and cut timber in the Count's forest. However, there were too many hands to work the small individual holdings. Only yesterday these peasants had been slaves who were whipped for their efforts; now Calman Jacoby paid them cash for their work and did not expect his hand to be kissed. He consulted the elder peasants on where to sow seasonal crops, where to plant potatoes, beets, cabbages. From the neighboring gentry he learned of the new threshing machines that were replacing flails. He installed a machine for chopping straw used in cattle fodder. He opened a tavern and a general store in Jampol where one could buy cloth, kerchiefs, shawls, furs, leather, trimmings, iron saucepans, pickled herring, lubricating oil, as well as scythes, sickles, hammers, saws, files, nails. The peasants who shopped at Calman's store or drank in his tavern received a discount. Some paid in Calman's private currency—slips of paper printed in Yiddish and bearing his stamped signature. He granted credit to those who qualified for it, and paid more than the market price for flax, calves, oxen, honey, hides, and other surplus produce, which he exported to Warsaw.

Calman had infringed on the law by opening his shop in Jampol, but the Russian officials looked the other way. The entry toll for Jews was abolished. Jampol was no purer than other Polish cities. Wherever Poles settled, the Jews were sure to follow. Other Jews from The Sands began to acquire sites in and about the Jampol marketplace. Jewish tanners, cobblers, coopers, tailors opened workshops. Polish merchandise now moved freely into Russia. Only on the Sabbath did the Jews of Jampol pray collectively, making up a minyan, or quorum of ten, at a private home; but a synagogue was being planned. A cemetery was needed also, for the Jewish dead still had to be carted to the town of Skarshew, where the burial society charged exorbitant fees.

Calman Jacoby prospered rapidly. Though not yet forty, he was already wealthy. No great scholar, he could just about manage to find his way through some of the simpler parts of the Talmud. Nevertheless, he was esteemed for his piety, honesty, and shrewdness.

He was a man of medium stature, broad-shouldered and straight-backed, with calloused hands like those of a peasant. He had a broad, pitch-black beard, a narrow forehead, beetling eyebrows over a large nose, and a thick bullish neck. Yet his dark eyes were spiritual and kind. Like all pious Jews, he wore long sidelocks and close-cropped hair; his neck, ears, and nostrils were tufted with hair. On the High Holy Days his sonorous voice led the congregation in the afternoon prayer. On weekdays he prayed at the first sign of dawn. His breakfast consisted of bread, herring, and cottage cheese, followed by a long draught of water.

Although Calman employed modern methods in business, he refused to have his household tainted by current fashions. He forbade Zelda to use tea or coffee, and at night he lighted his room with a solitary tallow candle or a wick in a saucer of oil. He dressed like other Jewish merchants, wearing a high-crowned hat and an ankle-length caftan. His trousers were held up by a piece of string.

Zelda, who came from a genteel family in Krashnik, longed for brass doorknobs, carved wooden beds, chairs with cane seats, and other signs of affluence. She would have loved to see copper saucepans and basins hanging on the kitchen wall. But Calman insisted that such luxuries, merely decorative at first, would soon become indispensable. And if it should happen that they could no longer be afforded, debts would accumulate until a man would end up bankrupt.

The women in and around Jampol envied Zelda. But she was dissatisfied. Her father, Reb Uri Joseph, had been a scribe, and her family was noted for its men of learning. Her husband, for all his wealth, lacked refinement. His strength made him clumsy, and he had no idea how to handle a woman as delicate as she. He was stingy about consulting doctors. He wouldn't believe that she was not always up to his carnal demands. In the first years of their marriage there had been frequent quarrels and even talk of divorce. But Calman was not a man to relinquish a woman easily.

It had been difficult to raise the children with Zelda constantly ailing. But, thank heavens, the worst was over. She had help now.

All the daughters assisted in the housekeeping, especially

Jochebed, the eldest, who was already of marriageable age. Zelda also had a maid, Faigel, and a man-of-all-work, Getz. On summer days, she could now sit on a chair on the lawn and have a footstool brought to her, while she read the Yiddish version of some sacred book.

Zelda was gaunt, with a pointed chin, a red, bony nose, and pouches under her bleary eyes. She had withered prematurely. As she read, her bonnet kept bobbing, and she was constantly brushing away the bees that mistook the artificial flowers adorning her hat for real ones. Though she was thankful to the Lord for His mercies, Zelda could not accustom herself to sitting in the fields, in the midst of nowhere. There was no place here where women could worship, no butcher shop, no friendly porch where neighbors gathered. The stream purled on its way, trees rustled, cows lowed; shepherds roasted potatoes over bonfires, sang ribald songs.

Zelda thought about her daughters: they should have friends their own age; they should be getting married—she wanted Torah-studying sons-in-law in the house. She longed for grandchildren. One's own children were born of pain, but grandchildren were sheer profit. With God's help, she would one day be a mother-in-law and a grandmother.

II

The estate adjoining Calman's property belonged to a nobleman named Jan Pawlowski. Before the liberation of the peasants, he had owned three hundred serfs. A widower, he lived alone. Closeting himself in his room, behind locked shutters, he sipped brandy through a straw from a carafe on the table, and occupied himself with an endless game of solitaire.

In his youth, Pawlowski had been involved in lawsuits all of which he had lost. He had been married to a famous beauty who had died of consumption while still young. The abolition of serfdom had left Pawlowski with only fifty acres of arable land, a tract of forest, and a low hill said to contain limestone.

Pawlowski sent his steward, Krol, to Calman with an offer to sell the hill. Calman replied that he had no use for it. What should he, a mere leaseholder, do with a hump of earth wedged between the estates of two strangers? But Pawlowski, who was in debt and desperately in need of money, had persisted. After considerable haggling, Calman bought the hill for a small sum.

It developed that Calman had stumbled on a treasure, for the hill was actually composed of the highest grade of limestone. Calman hired laborers and an expert to supervise the quarrying. A kiln was erected, the lime was dug, baked, and then carted to Jampol. The furnace blazed day and night. The spiraling smoke from the chimney was a sulfurous yellow, which at times turned red with shooting flames, and reminded Calman of Sodom and Gomorrah. The Jews believed that if the fire continued for seven years it would surely bring forth a salamander.

The peasants complained that the Jew was contaminating the Polish countryside, putrefying the air, but the authorities ignored them. Poland, after the insurrection, was full of activity, as if awakened from a long slumber. Workshops sprang up, mines were dug, forests cut down, and railroads built. Polish products, textiles, leather goods, brushes, sieves, sheepskin coats, glassware appeared on the world market. As soon as the Jews were granted permission to reside freely in the cities, the country began to grow.

It was said that Calman had been blessed by a holy man. A building boom was in progress, and his lime quarry yielded immense profits. Scores of Jews and Gentiles earned their livelihood from it. Calman purchased horses and wagons and built a smithy. As if all this were not enough, the Russian government decided to build a railway line through Jampol. The contract was awarded to the Warsaw magnate Wallenberg, a Jewish convert to Catholicism. Since steel rails needed wooden ties, Calman had one of his clerks write a letter for him to Wallenberg offering to provide ties at a cheaper price than anyone else. Wallenberg asked Calman to come to Warsaw to discuss the matter.

On the morning of his departure, Calman brushed his beard, put on his Sabbath gaberdine, polished his boots, and climbed into his carriage. Getz sat in the driver's seat. Calman leaned out of the window to say goodbye to Zelda and the four girls.

"Godspeed!" exclaimed Zelda, bursting into tears. So much good fortune had begun to alarm her. She feared the Evil Eye and, from the holy volumes she had read, knew that riches might portend disaster. She would prefer to live in the poorhouse rather than have the slightest harm befall any of her children, even the chipping of a fingernail.

Faigel, the maid, came out with a chicken, which she had roasted and wrapped in cabbage leaves, to give to Getz. He sat on the box wearing a peaked leather cap and high boots. His little tufts of yellow beard were trimmed. A small mustache sprouted on his upper lip. He had watery eyes, tawny eyebrows, and a nose shaped like a ram's horn. He waved his whip at Faigel familiarly.

"Behave yourself!" Faigel admonished him.

Calman's daughter Jochebed was blond like her mother, with the same narrow face, pointed chin, prominent nose, and freckles down to her neck. Though already eighteen, she was still not engaged to be married. Calman had been so preoccupied with business that he had neglected to find a husband for her. This was another matter he intended to take care of in Warsaw. Her sisters had nicknamed her "the young spinster." It was not easy for Jochebed to think of herself as a rich man's daughter. She still wore frowzy clothes, worked hard, and tended her sisters. On weekday evenings she helped Faigel the maid pluck poultry. On Sabbath afternoons, after the cholent dinner, she read the Yiddish version of the Pentateuch at her mother's side. A fortuneteller had once told Jochebed she would die young and she had never forgotten it. Now, standing back with her mother, she likewise called out, "Godspeed!" and dabbed a tear with her apron.

Shaindel, "the Gypsy," a year younger, stood on the carriage step, to embrace and kiss her father. She had sparkling black eyes, jet-black hair, and a dusky complexion. Shorter than her older sister, she had rounded hips and a large bosom. She loved costume jewelry, earrings, bracelets, and flowers to twine in her hair. Now that her father was becoming rich, Shaindel made a list of things she wanted him to bring back from Warsaw: a necklace, shoes with buckles, hair ribbons, canvas and thread for embroidery, scented soap. Calman promised everything she asked. This daughter brightened his life with her vivacity; she pampered him as if he were a favorite uncle, not her father. Having gone over the list, she added, winking at him, "And don't forget a handsome bridegroom!"

Miriam Lieba, at fifteen, was already half a head taller than Jochebed. With her blond hair in two plaits, her slenderness, her blue eyes, her graceful neck and straight nose, she did not look Jewish. The ways of a wealthy young lady seemed to come naturally to her. She yearned for fashionable clothes, read Polish books, and even had had a tutor from Jampol to instruct her. Rather than share her sisters' bedroom, she preferred a small attic room of her own. Coming forward, Miriam Lieba presented her father with a list of the Polish books she wanted from Warsaw, and kissed his forehead. She affected a remote and pensive air, for she was in the midst of a Polish novel about a countess who had left her castle and eloped to Paris with a violinist.

Tsipele, the youngest, eight years old, with diminutive pigtails, was dark like Shaindel. A pious woman came regularly from Jampol to instruct her in prayers and penmanship. The warmhearted Tsipele could not resist beggars, and whenever one came to the house she parted with all the pocket money she had. Her father, mother, sisters, and even the peasant women were always kissing her. Tsipele asked her father to buy her a doll in Warsaw and a miniature prayer book like one she had seen at a friend's house in Jampol.

On the way to Warsaw, Calman realized for the first time

that he was a man of consequence. Innkeepers fussed over him; salesmen trailed after him. Peasants whom he had never seen before called him "squire" and raised their caps to him. Even the dogs seemed to be in awe of him. It was as it is said in the Book of Proverbs: "When a man's ways please the Lord, He maketh even his enemies to be at peace with him."

Warsaw was so changed that Calman, who had not visited it since before the rebellion, barely recognized it. Streets which formerly had been forbidden to Jews now had many Jewish residents. The town had expanded, buildings crowded each other, and the shops were full of people. The courtyard of the inn where Calman was staying was so jammed with wagons that Getz could scarcely find room for the horses. Everywhere, the wooden sidewalks were being replaced by flagstone, gutters deepened, and new lampposts erected. Across the Vistula, in the suburb of Praga, the sky was filled with writhing smoke from the factory chimneys.

Calman proceeded to Wallenberg's office. Wallenberg was short and stout, had a huge head, mutton-chop whiskers, a crooked nose, dark Jewish eyes. He was dressed in a black jacket, checked trousers, a high collar and broad cravat. Calman presented his credentials. He was the leaseholder of a manor and the proprietor of a lime quarry; he also had a letter from the magistrate at Jampol attesting his honesty. Calman, who spoke the Polish of the peasants, frequently broke into Yiddish. Wallenberg, just as the Russian duke had been, was favorably impressed with Calman. He offered him a cigar, and after detailed negotiations, Calman obtained a contract to supply ties for the Imperial railway, as well as a substantial payment in advance. When they parted, Wallenberg shook Calman's hand and wished him luck—in Yiddish.

On the street, Calman was besieged by a host of beggars— deaf-mutes, cripples, hunchbacks. He distributed alms and was blessed in return. At a kosher restaurant, he and Getz had a city meal: noodle soup, meatballs, applesauce, brandy with egg cake. After dinner, since he was in a hurry and did not know his way about, Calman hailed a droshky, which clattered over the cobblestones among pedestrians who scarcely bothered to step aside. How they escaped being knocked down was a mystery. Porters crowded the streets hauling all kinds of loads; women venders squatted on the sidewalks in front of their wares; students strolled about with elegant young ladies. Mounted police armed with lances patrolled the streets, on the alert for any new signs of rebellion.

Reb Ezekiel Wiener, whom Calman had in mind as a father-in-law for Jochebed, was a follower of the Hassidic Rabbi of Marshinov. He lived in a fine house on Mead Street, and Calman, seeing his brass nameplate at the entrance, was awed by it. The maid who opened the door gave him an insolent glance and told him to wipe his feet on the mat.

The family was expecting him. Reb Ezekiel Wiener, a small, red-faced man with a broad silvery-white beard, introduced his wife, who wore a wig fastened with combs. She was all smiles and her fancy Yiddish was incomprehensible to Calman. The matchmaker was there too, drinking tea and nibbling cake. The prospective bridegroom, Mayer Joel, was a tall, dark-complexioned young man, wearing kid boots, a cloth gaberdine, and a silken vest from which a watch chain dangled. He smiled slyly, twirled his sidelocks, and made witty comments. Taking a sheet of paper from a drawer, he signed his name in Hebrew, Polish, and Russian.

"You may examine him to see how much he knows," Reb Ezekiel observed.

"I'm no scholar."

"Then get an examiner. In Talmudic studies, you'll find him very advanced."

But Calman did not want to waste time in further discussion. At his insistence, a preliminary agreement was drawn up whereby he contracted to provide a dowry of three thousand rubles, all the wedding gifts, and in addition to support the newlyweds for the first ten years of their marriage. The ceremony formalizing the engagement of the young couple would take place at Jampol. Mayer Joel gave Calman a letter for his future bride, which he had copied word for word from a manual of model letters.

The following morning, at dawn, Calman said his prayers and left for home. He found the city and its constant din oppressive. In the chaos and babble, amid such towering structures, a man could easily forsake God and be forsaken by Him. Getz lashed the horses. Once out of the city, Calman sat back comfortably, reflecting. His wealth was increasing, his enterprises expanding—the Lord preserve him from the Evil Eye. Did he deserve it? Perhaps his rewards on earth would be paid for by damnation later. Calman vowed that he would never become like the rich men of Warsaw, inflated with their own importance; he would always remain a humble, unaffected Jew.

The news of Calman's contract preceded him to Jampol. Lumbermen, brokers, job applicants surrounded him the minute he arrived. Fellow merchants suggested that he employ a bookkeeper and a cashier, since he could no longer keep his money in his pocket or in a chest. His business ventures now involved millions of rubles.

While in Warsaw, Calman had been advised by the lime merchants to build a branch line linking his quarry to the railway. This would, of course, cost a fortune, but the banks would not deny him credit.

Locking himself in the back of his store, Calman took out a pencil and wrote down columns of figures. He was no expert at mathematics, but he could add, subtract, multiply, and divide. And he never forgot the old saying: He who lives without reckoning dies without grace.

2 🏰

Calman soon discovered that it is as difficult for a rich man to be parsimonious as it is for a poor one to be extravagant. The house would have to be refurbished for the visit of the future in-laws, for how could such refined people be expected to eat with tin spoons and sit on wooden benches? With a zeal that astounded him, Zelda and the girls began to redecorate the house. Zelda purchased wardrobes, tables, sideboards, chairs, beds, vases, and bric-a-brac from Countess Jampolska, since many rooms at the manor were no longer in use. A craftsman from Skarshew repapered the walls, painters stained the floors. New clothes were needed too, and tailors and dressmakers made coats, gowns, and underclothes for Zelda and her daughters. A fox-lined overcoat with little tails dangling from the inner seams was tailored for Calman, as well as new caftans and breeches. New boots were ordered from Warsaw.

Calman scarcely had time to reproach his family for their prodigality, however, for he went to bed late and was up at cockcrow. He had to supervise reapers and threshers, make sure the meadows were mowed in season, the hay gathered and stacked properly for drying. The peasants needed careful watching, for some of them stole. Innumerable disputes, arguments, and lawsuits developed. Calman was obliged to bribe the court assessor as well as the local chief of police, and to distribute gifts among their subordinates. He was swamped with proposals of various kinds: a Jewish bailiff recommended that Calman distill brandy and brew beer, since the Jampol countryside was especially suited to the cultivation of hops; a sugar refiner wanted him to plant beets. The merchants supplying the builders clamored for more lime than the kiln could produce. Calman now understood the meaning of the Talmudic saying: The more property, the more anxiety.

Nevertheless, Calman had signed a contract, and there was no question of his not honoring it. The railway demanded its wooden ties. To supply them, Calman had bought a tract of nearby forest and the trees were now being cut down. The work went slowly because the lumbermen, a hard-drinking crew, were forever going off on sprees and had to be driven back while in a state of drunken stupor. Moreover, the watchmen were incompetent and timber vanished in large quantities. Calman had to assert himself everywhere. He built a hut in the middle of the forest and took two dogs and a gun along for protection, although he loathed firearms. A man alone in the forest had no other alternative. Ever since the insurrection, gangs of bandits roamed the countryside. Calman also began to ride horseback in order to cover the great distances, and since a long gaberdine was awkward, he adopted a short jacket. To keep house for him in the forest, he was compelled to hire a Gentile maidservant, Antosia, since no Jewish girl would trust herself alone in the wilderness.

The blows of axes, the grating of saws echoed through the woods. The finished ties were carted and stacked along the track of the future railroad. Discarded logs, wooden chips were taken to the lime kiln to be used as fuel. Wherever possible, the pine trees were tapped for turpentine. At night Calman returned to his cabin so exhausted that he slumped onto his crude bunk in his clothes, and Antosia had to come and pull off his boots. On several occasions he missed his twilight prayers, but made up for his dereliction by repeating the Eighteen Benedictions during the evening prayer, first throwing a coat over his gun, so as not to utter hallowed words in sight of a weapon. He stood in a corner, facing east toward Jerusalem, with his forehead resting against a plank, and prayed with deliberation, inwardly translating the words from Hebrew to Yiddish:

"Make us lie down in quietude, O Lord our God, and cause us to rise up to life, and spread out the tent of Thy peace. And ward off Satan before and behind us, and envelop us in the shadow of Thy wings."

While Calman mumbled and sighed, Antosia prepared dinner, boiling water and milk, cooking dumplings, millet, or potatoes, depending on the day's menu. Calman ate no meat on weekdays. He had to watch Antosia closely, and even supervised the milking of the cow, for how could one trust a Gentile to observe the dietary laws? His appetite, stimulated by the forest air, was always ravenous. After washing his hands and saying the appropriate benediction, he sat down, eating slowly and abundantly, swallowing the brimming bowl of milk that Antosia set before him. The chirping of grasshoppers, the cries of birds settling down for the night came through the tiny window. Midges, butterflies, and moths circled the single candle, casting weird shadows and singeing their wings in the flame.

Antosia hovered close by, bringing the saltcellar, more bread, serving cheese or honey. She came from a village near Jampol, and her husband had disappeared while serving in the army. Though still in her twenties, she looked almost forty, had a snub nose, green eyes, a stubby chin, freckles, and ash-blond hair. With no one else to talk to, she told Calman all the details of her past: how her poor dear father had died of consumption; how her sweet mother had introduced a stepfather into the home; how her stepfather had beaten her every evening with a wet rod which she herself had been forced to soak in slops for the purpose. Sitting on the floor near Calman, scouring a pot with cinders, she would relate her story in a plaintive, singsong voice.

"He beat me unmercifully, he did. There was I, kissing his feet, while he kept on whacking me as if I had no more feeling than a cabbage. He was like that—when he started whipping, he couldn't stop. If my dear mother tried to stop him, she got it too. The beast had no pity!"

"Just a murderer," murmured Calman, between mouthfuls.

"Ah, but he could be sweet as an angel, too. When the devil left him, he was as tender as my own father. He'd call me to the table, pinch my cheek, feed me from his own plate. And then he'd smile so lovingly. I forgot all the beatings when he smiled."

"Is he still alive?"

"No. Dead."

"That's how it all ends," muttered Calman to himself. It was futile to offend God; and of what use were earthly riches? What did the Holy Book say? Money is a temptation and a chastisement. Getting up from the table, Calman washed, said the concluding grace, and then, without a pause, began to recite his bedtime prayers. Antosia, shaking up his straw pallet to make it more comfortable, always found a few grains of wheat in the straw and popped them into her mouth. In some ways she was like an animal. Every evening, circling about Calman, baring her teeth in an endless grin, she found things to do to keep her in the cabin, although her bed was in the stable. Night after night, Calman had to endure Joseph's temptation in the presence of Potiphar's wife. But he would not expose himself to damnation. Had not God blessed him with fine daughters and wealth? It was true that Zelda, after each childbirth, had been unapproachable for months on end, that she lived on medicines, had undergone her change of life at an early age, and had long since become frigid. But where is it written that all must go well with a man? Men more pious than he had fared even worse. Calman resolved to assume no further commitments. The manor and the lime quarries were more than enough for him and would support all his children after his death. The forest was fit for wolves, not men.

Soon his meditations ceased. His eyelids grew heavy and closed. A single snore issued from the depths of his body. The next thing he knew, the sun and the twittering birds had awakened him.

II

In Jampol not only Calman but the whole Jewish community was prospering. As the Jews moved out of The Sands, Gentiles moved in. Land for a synagogue had been acquired and the foundations laid, a burial ground had been purchased, and a rabbi had come. Calman had contributed liberally for everything.

Though Calman had sworn not to embark on new business ventures, he became involved in a scheme to revive a half-ruined brickworks that lay on the outskirts of Jampol. The owner had fled to Krakow to avoid paying his sons' ruinous debts. With his assets and cash reserves, Calman could always borrow money at low interest rates, and by acquiring the brickworks he was able to supply not only timber and lime but bricks as well for the new communal projects.

That year Calman and his family stayed in Jampol for the High Holy Days, the New Year and the Day of Atonement. After the services on Simhath Torah, followed by the parade of scroll bearers, Calman invited the worshippers to his tavern. He set out food and opened a cask of beer, a barrel of wine, and a keg of mead. Even the rabbi, Reb Menachem Mendel himself, joined in.

As the feast was ending, Calman pledged himself to build a poorhouse, whereupon four husky, inebriated men hoisted him on their shoulders and bore him in triumph to the site of the synagogue, the rest of the crowd trailing behind. Once there, the men formed a ring and danced, with the children in the center frisking about. The women stood on the sidelines, clapping and laughing gleefully. Members of the Ladies Aid Society of the new Burial Association had brought along a hollowed gourd with candles in it, which they now lit. They tried to place the gourd on Calman's head as a crown, but he refused such a tribute. Zelda protested that it was a pagan custom learned from the peasants, who crowned their newly appointed headmen in that way. Shaindel took the gourd and mischievously placed it on her own head. Immediately, a cluster of young women led her off in state to the rabbi's wife, but it was the rabbi's son, Ezriel, who came to the door. Shaindel, intoxicated by a goblet of wine and crying, "I am the queen of Jampol!" tugged one of his sidelocks.

The next day it began to rain and the rain continued for four days. The foundation of the synagogue became a pool; houses were flooded; the stream that drove the Jampol mill submerged the sluices, and the dam burst. Weeks of freezing rain and snow followed.

Reb Ezekiel Wiener, the future father-in-law, sent a letter from Warsaw to say that it would be a great strain upon himself and his family to travel to Jampol twice, once for the betrothal, and again for the wedding. He therefore suggested an early wedding, to be held on the Sabbath of Hanukkah, and Calman agreed. Jochebed was about to turn nineteen, the age of spinsterhood, and Shaindel was only one year her junior. Calman had inherited from his forebears the principle that the sooner one's daughters are married off, the better.

Zelda hastened the preparations for Jochebed's trousseau. A Warsaw merchant supplied silk and velvet, wool and lace, but the local dressmakers complained that Jochebed was hard to fit. Gaunt and small-bosomed, she had no hips worth mentioning and her hands were rough. Despite the help of the maid, she had continued to knead dough, carry pails of water, bend over the washtub, bake bread, and fuss around with brooms and mops. Jochebed could not outgrow the period of Calman's poverty.

The wedding was a noisy event in Jampol. The bridegroom's family arrived from Warsaw in three covered wagons. The men wore coats lined with fox and squirrel. They walked about puffing cigars and pipes, humming Hassidic melodies, or else were absorbed in abstruse theological discussions. The women were dressed gaily in satin bonnets and fancy wigs, headbands, fur-lined coats, capes, and all sorts of fur stoles and muffs. They smelled of almonds and honey cake, and exuded an air of cosmopolitan vanity. As Calman's small house could not accommodate all the visitors, beds had to be set up in the barn. Soon after he arrived, Mayer Joel, the bridegroom, who was not particularly reticent, went to inspect the cattle in their stalls. Accompanied by his brother, he then set off on a long stroll through the fields, now sown with winter wheat. On their return, the two reported having glimpsed a deer.

The girls in the Warsaw party included not only the bridegroom's sisters, but also first and second cousins, and these young ladies assumed a lofty attitude toward the unsophisticated girls of Jampol. Assembled for the wedding, they strutted about in dainty shoes with singularly high heels, and wore snug-waisted gowns with pleats. Their faces were unblemished and their coiffures in the very latest style. Constantly nibbling cakes and other delicacies, they made sly gibes at the bride and mimicked the country girls. When the dancing started, they paired off, followed the most intricate steps, and called to the musicians for special tunes. The Jampol girls, afraid to display themselves, looked on, astonished. Shaindel, Calman's daughter, was furious at the insolent Warsaw coquettes. Light on her feet, and knowing she danced well, she asked Mirale, the rabbi's daughter, to be her partner. Mirale blushed.

"I don't know the steps."

"You don't have to know them. Come on!"

Placing one hand on Mirale's shoulder, Shaindel encircled her waist with the other arm, and they whirled round and round, their feet drumming the floor.

"Why hasn't Ezriel come?" asked Shaindel.

"Because his gaberdine is torn."

"Then why didn't you mend it?"

Mirale was at a loss for an answer.

"If I had a brother, I'd look after him," said Shaindel. "A litter of girls was all that my mother could produce," she added and laughed uproariously.

The marriage canopy was set up outdoors, on the frozen snow. The younger women, carrying twisted candles, ranged themselves in two rows before it. The frosty air was still. Calman and Reb Ezekiel escorted the bridegroom, who towered above them, out of the house. Striding rapidly along, he glanced furtively right and left. A beard already sprouted on his chin. His eyes were dusky and his velvet cap was perched roguishly on his head. His sidelocks were twisted into tight little horns. The tops of his high kid boots gleamed from beneath the hem of his overcoat. Though a Hassid, he had the powerful physique of a Cossack, and the girls whispered among themselves that he could easily tuck Jochebed away in his belt.

Next Jochebed was led out by her mother and her mother-in-law. Zelda could scarcely walk, her legs were so swollen. The doctors said that, among other ailments, she suffered from diabetes.

Under the canopy the bridegroom stepped on Jochebed's shoe to signify that he was to be the master, and crushed a wineglass as an omen of good luck.

At the wedding dinner, after the "golden soup" course, Mayer Joel expounded briefly on the Talmud, and throughout the feast, while doing full justice to the various dishes and the wine, he recounted miracles attributed to the Hassidic Rabbi of Marshinov. He even managed to discuss a little business on the side. The local guests admitted that Calman had picked a winner. But was that surprising? Money will buy anything—even a seat in Paradise!

3 🏛

In the shed which served as a temporary house of worship while the synagogue and study house were being built, Ezriel, the rabbi's son, each day studied the Talmud, reciting and interpreting the text to himself in a singsong chant. His father wanted him to follow in the family tradition and become a rabbi, and was already instructing him in the finer points of Judaic law. Ezriel wore full Hassidic dress: skullcap, gaberdine, sash, and trousers tucked into high boots. His sidelocks were shaggy and short. Nevertheless, because of his straight nose, blue eyes, thin lips, and longish chin, he did not look like a typical Hassid. His flaxen hair was streaked with gold. Only his high forehead suggested the Jewish intellectual.

Reb Menachem Mendel had long been concerned about the erratic behavior of this slender boy, who was fond of sitting on roofs and climbing up ladders, who liked to chop wood, dig ditches, and who often wandered off for long tramps in the fields. As a child, he had set snares for birds, carved whistles from reeds as shepherds do, and brought home not only cats and dogs, but frogs and other unclean reptiles.

Worst of all, he had begun a long time ago to ask questions that reeked of heresy. Does a live carp suffer agonies when it is scaled and cut to pieces for the Sabbath meal? Why are some people poor and others rich? What was there before the universe? Does a goat have a soul? Was Adam a Jew? Did Eve wear a bonnet? And he was constantly finding contradictions in the Holy Writ, pointing out that in one place it is stated that a man is punished only for his own sins, but in another, that the third and fourth generations must suffer for them; and first the Lord is said to be invisible, then it is written that the elders while they ate and drank saw the Lord. For another thing, Ezriel criticized the prophet Elisha for causing the children to be attacked by bears; the boy felt bitterly reproachful toward King David for slaying Uriah the Hittite, and he wept and blasphemed when he read how Abraham sent his concubine Hagar into the desert with nothing but a jug of water, and how she almost perished of thirst.

Reb Menachem Mendel, descendant of a long line of wise men, could not understand how he had fathered this misfit. He blamed it all on his wife Tirza Perl, whose father, Reb Abraham Hamburg, warden of the Jewish community of Turbin, was an inveterate opponent of Hassidism. Whenever Ezriel misbehaved, Reb Menachem Mendel rebuked his wife, saying, "It's that heathen blood of yours!"

In Turbin, his father-in-law's home town, where Reb Menachem Mendel had held his first rabbinical post, Ezriel had utterly disgraced himself. At cheder he had been unable to get along with other boys, mimicking the teachers, telling fantastic yarns, and playing with girls. It was partly Ezriel's fault that Reb Menachem Mendel had gotten into difficulties with his congregation and had had to leave.

Following his stay in Turbin, Reb Menachem Mendel had spent several years in Lublin as an assistant rabbi. There, though Ezriel had gradually acquired studious habits, he nevertheless had been unable to remain settled in any one yeshiva for long. He would be absorbed in his books for days, but then suddenly he would want to be out, touring all the inns and markets, or exploring Piask, the thieves' quarter. Moreover, he read depraved works, reports of scientific observations and experiments, descriptions of natural marvels, guidebooks to big cities and foreign lands, and accounts of life among savages. He would utter such preposterous statements as that the earth revolved around the sun and not the sun around the earth; that the moon is inhabited by human beings; that stones called meteors drop out of the skies. Once Ezriel brought home a magnet to demonstrate its attraction for nails; another time, he lit a candle, covered it with an upturned tumbler, and explained that the reason the flame went out was lack of oxygen.

His mother, Tirza Perl, though alarmed by his antics, delighted in his knowledge, but Reb Menachem Mendel frowned upon it. Reb Mendel knew the ways of temptation. One began with questions, then one adopted modern styles of dress, and next there was loss of faith, even apostasy. Consequently, Reb Menachem Mendel had accepted with alacrity the rabbinate at Jampol. Enlightened individuals could not possibly inhabit so small a community. Baubles such as magnifying glasses, compasses, and maps would hardly be found there. He observed with relief that, once in Jampol, Ezriel again seemed engrossed in his Talmudic studies. Reb Menachem Mendel was anxious now to have him marry without delay, for when a youth finally has a wife, a dowry, a father-in-law to support him, and children of his own, he settles down.

"We'll be proud of him yet, God willing," he remarked to Tirza Perl. "Jampol is not a den of infamy, like Lublin."

Ezriel, seated at the table, had for several hours been immersed in a chapter concerning forbidden impurities. Now he glanced up, resting his gaze on the curtain embroidered with red eagles and blue deer, on the Holy Ark, decorated with the tablets of the Ten Commandments and flanked by two gilded lions standing with tails up and tongues protruding. Crowding the bookcase were the Talmud, volumes of exegesis, the Cabala, law digests, ethical treatises, and other religious books. No matter how defaced the titles on the backs had become, Ezriel could distinguish one from the other by their bindings. Through the window, he saw a sky full of low-hanging clouds. It was snowing heavily. In the direction of his gaze lay Calman Jacoby's manor, beyond it fields, forests, hills, and still farther Germany, France, and Spain. Then came the ocean, where ships sailed to America. On the other side of the New World was the Pacific Ocean, in which, according to ancient belief, the fiery sun each night immersed itself. Further on were Japan, China, Siberia—and so home again!

The earth is spherical, Ezriel had read, one and a half million times smaller than the sun, which is itself no more than a star among millions of others. But in the Bible the sun and moon are presented as two lamps, and the stars merely as lesser lights. The author of the Pentateuch obviously had not the remotest conception of natural science. That being the case, how could he presume to know the truth about other matters? One must assume, therefore, that the Bible was nothing but a collection of legends and old wives' tales. That being so, why study the books of Holy Writ? On the other hand, how had the universe come into being? Could it have created itself? How had the atoms arranged themselves in order, with summer, winter, day, night, men, women, thoughts, feelings? The worldly books Ezriel had read in Lublin, though they revealed many facts, explained nothing. What was magnetism or electricity? According to the authors, things just happened by themselves. The universe was ruled by chance. But what then was chance? And how did it work?

Ezriel yawned, stood up, slowly raised one arm and then the other, flexing his muscles. Where had he come from? Or his thoughts? How could a sperm cell without will or soul turn into a human being with a mind, heart, joys, sorrows, dreams, love? What a riddle!

The door opened and his sister Mirale stood on the threshold, a shawl covering her head, the toes of her shoes caked with snow. Something must have gone wrong at home because as a rule girls did not enter the men's house of worship.

"What is it?" he cried.

"You're wanted at home. Your future father-in-law is waiting."

"Who?"

"Reb Calman Jacoby. And he's brought a Talmud examiner. You're engaged to Shaindel!"

Ezriel's heart began to pound. He slowly closed his book in an effort to calm himself, resolving not to be too hasty, or distressed if nothing came of the interview. Strangely enough, ever since Simhath Torah, when Shaindel had tugged his sidelock, her face had been in his mind; he had even dreamed of her. Their marriage must have been predestined. Yes, a divine eye keeps watch and a divine hand gives guidance. Slipping into his coat, he made a gesture as if to apologize to the Holy Ark for having profaned it with his doubts.

"After you," he commanded Mirale, since it was considered unseemly for a marriageable young man to be seen in the company of a girl, even his own sister.

II

Calman Jacoby and the Rabbi of Jampol, eager to see their children married, set the wedding date for the Sabbath following Pentecost. Meanwhile Calman invited the prospective in-laws to the manor for the Feast of the New Year of the Trees.

Ezriel and Shaindel, who had exchanged only diffident glances at the betrothal ceremony, by now felt more at ease with each other. It was a family party. At the men's table Mayer Joel asked Calman and Ezriel to accompany him on his next visit to the Hassidic Rabbi of Marshinov. The conversation veered from holy men to Moses Montefiore, from the Rothschild fortune to the bags of gold which certain Polish noblemen had purportedly left in Jewish custody before taking to the forests to fight the Russians.

Reb Menachem Mendel told the story of a dibbuk at Turbin. One night, when a girl went outdoors to fetch a pail of water from a well, an evil spirit took possession of her body. A weird male voice came from her throat. The wandering soul had been a man, a Talmudist of perverse character, who had recited prayers and portions of the Torah backward, starting at the end and finishing at the beginning. He would also wrangle with the sages on difficult points of Judaic law. The bewitched young woman, though ordinarily frail, lifted a rock that three strong men together could not budge. She juggled it as though it were a pebble.

This reminded Calman of his native village, where a corpse had once been summoned to appear before a rabbinical tribunal. The corpse had made a habit of haunting and tormenting his former business partner. The beadle went to the cemetery to summon the ghost by rapping thrice on his tombstone with the rabbi's walking stick. At the tribunal, a corner of the room, partitioned by a sheet, was set aside for the dead man. The judges ruled that the dead man's partner should pay an indemnity of several hundred gulden to the heirs of the deceased, and the haunting stopped.

Mayer Joel, plucking at his fledgling beard with one hand, while with the other he drummed on the table, exclaimed: "What would the skeptics say to that?"

"They'd say it was nonsense!" Ezriel announced, much to his own amazement.

"But people saw it . . . with their own eyes!"

"Saw what? A sheet?"

"The soul is not visible—"

"Science concerns itself only with the visible, with things that can be weighed and measured," said Ezriel, feeling as though he too were possessed.

Reb Menachem Mendel paled and clutched his red beard. Mayer Joel gave his father-in-law a mocking glance. Calman lowered his head.

"Don't you believe in dibbuks?" Calman asked.

"One can't accept the ridiculous."

"Do you believe in God?"

"Of course."

"Well, that's something. At least you believe in God," Calman said.

Shaindel was alarmed. Aided by her younger sister Miriam Lieba, she had been bringing in refreshments, figs, dates, raisins, almonds, cake, various sweetmeats, and mead. With her hair in a chignon, wearing a new dress and a golden necklace, a betrothal gift from Ezriel's mother, she was standing near the table, holding a tray, and listening, delighted that her fiancé held advanced views and was bold enough to express them. He sat there pale, his lips quivering, his ears fiery, his blue eyes fixed upon her. It was she alone who had induced Calman to approach Ezriel through the matchmaker. Every night as she lay in bed she marveled at her infatuation for this young man whom she scarcely knew. Unobserved, she would take the betrothal document from her father's chest of drawers and pore over the signature: Ezriel Babad. It had none of the flourishes of Mayer Joel's hand; there was an austerity about it. His signature seemed to bestride her own. There in the betrothal document, with its ornate border, its gold-embossed *Mazel Tov*, and its Hebrew text, incomprehensible to Shaindel, he and she seemed already united, practically man and wife. Now that Mayer Joel was trying to confuse Ezriel, Shaindel thrust herself forward with the tray.

"Well, daughter, put it down," said Calman. "Don't be shy."

But Shaindel took her time as she set the table with the plates, cups, and saucers handed to her by Miriam Lieba. Let the hot tempers cool! When everything was on the table, the girls still hovered within hearing.

"So you don't believe in the transmigration of souls?" inquired Mayer Joel.

"There's no reference to it either in the Bible or in the Talmud," answered Ezriel.

"Will you accept the authority of Ari the Saint on the subject?"

"Maimonides dissented."

"That's the battle cry of the Maskilim—emancipator's talk!"

Reb Menachem Mendel unclasped his beard. "He's really a good boy, but something of a show-off and nonconformist—takes after my father-in-law, Reb Abraham Hamburg. And he's not behaving maturely."

"Marriage will alter him, please God," said Calman, soothingly.

"The truth is all I care about," Ezriel insisted.

"It is absolutely certain that transmigrating souls exist. The world is full of them," Reb Menachem Mendel reaffirmed hoarsely. "In Izhbitsa, a six-months-old infant fell ill, God help us, and as it died cried out in a voice that made the walls tremble, 'Hear O Israel, the Lord our God!' The doctor, a debauched unbeliever, did penance after hearing that cry. He gave up his medical practice and went to live with a holy man. In time he became a saint!"

Reb Menachem Mendel stopped short. His voice was choked. His right hand tingled with an almost irresistible desire to strike Ezriel. Not only was the young fool mocking the Lord and His works, but he was wrecking the match! Calman would call off the engagement. Reb Menachem Mendel saw himself being forced out of Jampol by an infuriated mob. Recalling the passage, "Thy undoing and thy ruin shall from thyself come forth," he mopped his brow and began to fan himself with his skullcap. Even his sidelocks were moist. Calman suddenly noticed Shaindel and Miriam Lieba.

"You still here? Back to the women's table with you!"

"I haven't brought the jelly yet," said Shaindel.

As the girls withdrew, Shaindel gripped Miriam Lieba's wrist. The engagement was as good as broken, all because that overrighteous Mayer Joel had set himself up as God's own policeman. Shaindel was overcome by sympathy for Ezriel, who had let himself be carried away by his passion for the truth. But she would be on his side. She would plead for him with her father: "I marry Ezriel or no one else—ever!"

In the kitchen she burst into tears. Then she washed her
face in the basin and examined herself in a mirror. Climbing a
stool, she got a long-forgotten jar of currant jelly from the
top shelf and returned to the men's table. A Talmudic debate
was in progress. Ezriel held forth on the Torah, but managed
to gaze directly at Shaindel above the heads of the others. She
glanced at him, blushing as she did so from her neck to the
roots of her hair.

III

Mayer Joel tried to induce his father-in-law to call off the engagement, but Calman did not want to humiliate Ezriel or his
father, the Rabbi of Jampol. Aware of Shaindel's feelings toward Ezriel, Calman made excuses for him. "Who doesn't
speak rashly in the heat of debate?" he argued. Zelda sympathized with Mayer Joel, but Calman reminded her of the saying: "Rather slash parchment than rip paper." Better to have a
divorce than a broken betrothal. Calman had accordingly presented his gifts to Ezriel, including two hundred rubles for the
purchase of a complete set of the Talmud, the works of Maimonides, law digests, and commentaries. Ezriel was to buy the
books in Warsaw himself.

The following day he boarded a sled bound for the capital.
His father still would not speak to him, but his mother and
sister had provided him with food, a change of underclothes,
and other travel necessities. In Warsaw he was to stay with
Mayer Joel's father, Reb Ezekiel Wiener. Despite the campaign of denunciation that Mayer Joel was conducting, he had
presented Ezriel with a letter of introduction to his father requesting that everything possible be done to assure Ezriel's
comfort, and adding a postscript, half a page long, of greetings
to every member of the large family.

The day was a cold one. The sled traveled swiftly on the
hard-packed snow. Icy trees and frozen wastes rushed past,
fields flew by. The thatched roofs of the village houses looked

like white featherbeds. Toward dusk, icy gusts of wind churned up eddies of snowdust. The sky was overcast, but the setting sun filtered through in purple streaks, like blood streaming from some celestial holocaust. The snow turned red. Heaven and earth seemed one, and, looking out, Ezriel was reminded of a description he had once read of the Arctic Ocean. The sled carried three other passengers in addition to Ezriel. Zelig, a glazier, was going to Warsaw to buy a diamond for glass-cutting; a woman named Blooma was traveling to see a doctor about an abscess in her ear; and a girl, Dvosha, an orphan, hoped to find work in the city. Zelig had on a sheepskin cap, a padded jacket, and straw overshoes such as the peasants wear. With his unkempt beard, now encrusted with icicles, and his bristly iron-gray eyebrows, he resembled a hedgehog.

Taking a pinch of snuff from a horn box, he croaked hoarsely: "Call this winter? In the old days we had real winters! Bears froze to death in their lairs. Packs of wolves slunk about the villages, their eyes glittering like candles. One winter, when I was living at Radoshitz, hailstones fell that were as big as goose eggs! They shattered half the windows of Poland, and the peasants screamed that the world was coming to an end.

"Reb Zelig, can you hear that noise?" Blooma broke in, her head swathed in a blanket over her shawl.

"What noise?"

"A rumbling, in my ear, like wheels. I thought it might be the wind. It doesn't stop—like the gnat in the head of the tyrant Titus, curse him!"

"Don't worry, you'll get better. But if you'll take my advice, you'll keep away from the doctors. When you get to Warsaw, go see Feivele Konskelwoler. He has some magic copper coins blessed by the holy preacher of Kozhenitz. Place one of those next to your ear, and the pain will vanish. You know these doctors—they're all too quick with the knife!"

"You don't have to tell me! One doctor thrust a needle into my ulcer! One tells you cold compresses, another tells you hot. But my head begins to tick like a clock the minute I lie down."

"My little brother once pushed a pea into his ear, and did we have trouble getting it out again," chimed in the orphan Dvosha, a thickset young woman who wore a fur vest, and a wool kerchief on her head.

"Are you going to work as a domestic?" asked Blooma.

"That's right."

"Can you cook?"

"I can try."

"Take a tip. Never talk back, just do as your mistress bids. In Warsaw the ladies are always eating, and each meal has a lot of courses. They'll give you plenty of work at the stove. They get their husbands to fuss over them. And they'll wake a maid up in the middle of the night to do the washing."

"Where? At the river?"

"At the river? In Warsaw? Don't be silly! You'll bend over a washtub in the kitchen until you ache. But remember one thing—eat. Eat them out of house and home! My grandmother used to say there was once a wise man who lay face downward three days and nights wondering what keeps people alive, until at last he stumbled on the fact that it was food."

"It doesn't take a wise man to figure that out."

"They'll make you sleep in the kitchen. You'll empty the family's chamber pots. But don't forget to keep a jug of water at your bedside. You'll find it useful if there's a grown son in the house. If he tries to get into bed with you, tell him nicely to go away. If he won't, douse him with water. He'll keep his distance after that. In the morning say it was the cat who overturned the jug."

"You know all the answers."

"Live and learn. I was poor, too, when I was young, and in those days Jews weren't allowed in Warsaw—they turned us back at the gates. Those who entered had to pay a special tax. There was one informer, a Jew himself, who betrayed everyone, but the butchers finally took care of him. When I was a baby, my father died, and my mother didn't last much longer. I stayed with an aunt who was worse than any stranger. On Yom Kippur she'd bless me, but next day the torture began all over again. They married me off to a cobbler who promised me the moon, but he spat blood, poor fellow. When he lost his temper, he beat and kicked me. I bore him three children, but they died young. The last one didn't have a stomach, woe is me. Finally my husband died, and I've remained a widow. Nowadays we have Reb Calman, who never turns anyone away. When it comes to charity, he's almost as good as God. Do you realize, young man, how lucky you are? Your Shaindel has both her head and her heart in the right place—and what a beauty! Dazzling! Yes, I went to your future father-in-law and told him my troubles. He gave me money for the trip and for the doctor's fee, too. What a match—the rabbi's son and Reb Calman's daughter! But why are you going to Warsaw?"

"To buy books."

"Is that so? Very nice! It's your sort, studying holy books, that redeems this wicked world! What good is a woman except to comfort a man? Is it true you don't believe in dibbuks?"

"Who says so?"

"Why, everybody with a tongue in his head, may all their mouths wither. Envy, that's what it is. They want to devour you alive. May the worms get them!"

"Hey, where do you think you're going?" Zelig suddenly bellowed at the driver.

Itcha, the coachman, woke with a start and tugged at the reins.

"Whoa! Back! Back! Where the devil are those nags heading?"

"Caught you napping, eh?"

"Just nodding. You'd better get out, all of you."

"Oh Lord, my legs have gone to sleep," chanted Blooma. "They won't budge!"

Ezriel jumped down and helped the woman out. Under her weight, he sank to his calves in the snow. "The emancipation-ists are right," he thought. "The fanaticism of Polish Jews is too preposterous for words. While the rest of Europe is learn-ing, creating, making progress, they remain bogged in igno-rance. What do these people know of magnetism, electricity, the microscope and the telescope? Who among them has ever heard of Voltaire, Jean-Jacques Rousseau, Kepler, Newton? And what do I know of their theories? Surely not enough. I must study. I must help these people emerge from darkness. Shaindel will assist me." Ezriel scooped up a handful of snow, molded it into a hard ball, and hurled it at the twilight sky.

IV

In Warsaw, Ezriel preferred to stay at an inn, rather than with Reb Ezekiel Wiener. He walked first to Mr. Wallenberg's offices in Krolewska Street to deliver a folder of invoices from Calman. The weather was freezing. Sleds creaked on the icy streets, while their drivers clucked and cracked their whips. Roofs and balconies were laden with snow. Boys in braid-trimmed caps and brass-buttoned coats hurried home, schoolbags over their shoulders. A nun led a file of uniformed girls wearing heavy woolen socks over their stockings. Ele-gant men and women in fur coats and sable caps promenaded their dogs. A beggar played a hurdy-gurdy. All the shops were crowded despite the cold. Horses dropped manure, which steamed in the cold air; chimneys coughed smoke; carts laden with firewood rumbled into courtyards. For the first time in his life, Ezriel saw coal. At Saxony Park, he stopped to look in through the railing. Boys and girls with multicolored scarves, caps, jackets, skirts, and gloves wove dazzling patterns as they skated on the frozen lake, while those who fell scrambled up, laughing hilariously.

Mr. Wallenberg was in conference and Ezriel waited patiently, hat in hand, in a large office watching the bookkeepers work over huge ledgers. Their steel pens glided over the broad pages as they wrote, blotted, figured, manipulating the beads of their abacuses at an uncanny speed. A maid came in with a tray full of glasses of tea for them. Suddenly the door of Wallenberg's private office opened, and a stout, red-bearded general in spurred boots and golden epaulettes stepped out. His unbuttoned coat revealed elegant braided breeches, and a bulging chest loaded with medals. One gloved hand rested on the hilt of his sword. A liveried attendant opened the front door and stood reverently at attention. Wallenberg escorted his visitor to the threshold, bowed, and waited while the general settled himself in his sled. Wallenberg, with his round shoulders, lofty brow, crooked nose, and flabby ears, looked very Jewish. A short, stocky man, he had a head like a pumpkin, dark glowing eyes, black mutton-chop whiskers that, like the curly hair at his temples, were threaded with white. A stiff collar encased his neck, and he wore a medal on his lapel. Turning around, he caught sight of Ezriel and asked in Polish, "Who is he?"

"He's from Jampol, sent by Calman Jacoby."

Ezriel was awed by the splendor of Wallenberg's office with its elegant draperies and parquet floor, so slippery that he could scarcely walk on it. On the walls hung portraits of gentlemen and ladies, and gilt-framed embossed documents bearing impressive signatures and wax seals. The mahogany desk, with its reading lamp and bronze statuette, was covered with papers. The aroma assailing Ezriel's nostrils was a mixture of cigar smoke, leather, and something unidentifiable.

"What is your connection with Calman Jacoby? Are you his son?" Wallenberg inquired in Polish.

"His daughter's fiancé."

"I see. Be seated."

"Thank you."

"Relax. We won't eat you."

Ezriel sat down.

"Now tell me about yourself. Do you study the Talmud?"

"Yes. And other books, too."

"I see you understand Polish—a rare accomplishment for a Polish Jew. Six hundred years in the country and the Jews haven't bothered to learn the language. What will you do after you're married? Go into business?"

"I'm not sure."

"The Jews are an odd lot." Wallenberg's voice boomed. "Time passes them by. Mankind progresses, but they remain as static as the Chinese behind the Great Wall. Of course, I'm talking about the Polish Jews only, not those of Western Europe."

"Naturally."

"I'll be candid with you, young man. I can see you're no fool. I'm no longer a Jew, I've been baptized. But blood is thicker than water and I can't stand seeing the Jews suffer. How can anyone move into someone else's home, live there in total isolation, and expect not to suffer by it? When you despise your host's god as a tin image, shun his wine as forbidden, condemn his daughter as unclean, aren't you asking to be treated as an unwelcome outsider? It's as simple as that."

"Well, what can we do about it?"

"I won't preach, I'm no missionary. But what will be the end of it? Our assimilationists, who call themselves Poles of Moses' faith, believe neither in Moses nor in Jesus. They appear at the synagogue only once a year, on Yom Kippur. Why do they remain isolated? True, they pray to God for the restoration of Jerusalem, but Palestine is a wilderness; the Messiah coming on his white ass, a pretty legend. Contrary to biblical teachings, modern science holds that the earth was created millions of years ago."

"I know. Kant and Laplace."

Mr. Wallenberg raised his eyebrows.

"Now where did you ever hear of them?"

"I've read about their theories."

"At Jampol?"

"No. Lublin."

"And is your future father-in-law aware that you read such books?"

"I don't think so."

"Well, that's interesting. The ice must be breaking after all. What is your father, a merchant?"

"No. A rabbi."

"That is amazing! A rabbi's son! And how do you account for your blue eyes and fair hair? You didn't get those from your Jewish ancestors! We are all products of Europe. What brings you to Warsaw? It can't be this bundle of papers."

"I've come to buy books."

"The Talmud?"

"Yes. But I also want some scientific works."

"On what subjects?"

"Physics, mathematics, geography . . ."

"Go to Swietokrzyska Street. That's where the Jewish booksellers are, and those Jews in their long caftans are the finest bibliographers in Poland. But, on second thought, why waste money? My house is full of textbooks that are not being used. My children have all completed their studies. Isn't it strange that the Lithuanian Jews should have gone in for education, but the Polish Jews have little interest in secular knowledge? The Hassidic movement is to blame for that. The first thing you must do is master Polish grammar. It is absurd to live in Poland and jabber away in a German jargon, and it is even more ridiculous to live in the second half of the nineteenth century and behave as if you belonged to antiquity. The Poles have a religion too, but they aren't totally immersed in it. If I go to one church service on Sunday, I am considered a good Christian, and I don't have to strap little boxes to my arms and forehead every morning or pray all day long. I've traveled through Turkey and Egypt, and even the Bedouin aren't half as savage as our Hassidim. The sons of Ishmael are at least good horsemen. And let me tell you—the ritual baths are unhygienic. We had a rabbi here who delivered his sermons in Polish. What a sensation! But I don't believe in half measures. The Jews must become one hundred percent Polish. Otherwise they will be driven out as in the days of Pharaoh."

"The Poles are themselves enslaved."

"That's another story."

"The strong want to consume the weak," said Ezriel, a little hazy about the relevance of his remark.

"True, I'm afraid. There's a recently published English book that is causing a furor in the world of science. Its theory seems to be that all life is a struggle for survival and that the strongest species win out. . . . Well, drop in again tomorrow and the cashier will have a load of books for you—bring a suitcase if you can. I'm busy today, but next time you're in Warsaw, look me up."

Wallenberg picked up a small bell and rang it. He wore both a wedding ring and a signet ring. Offering his left hand to Ezriel, he remarked, "Courage, young man! We live in a world of progress."

4 🏛

Despite the neighboring squires' advice to the contrary, Countess Maria Jampolska petitioned Czar Alexander to pardon her husband, Count Wladislaw Jampolski. Her plea was that the Count had been carried away by his headstrong nature and that he now regretted what he had done. She, his wife, was ill and humbly begged his Majesty to accede to the Christian charity in his noble heart, and bestow forgiveness on his erring subject. The petition was supported by the governor of Lublin province, to whom the Countess had obtained a letter of introduction. Daily, Maria Jampolska knelt and wept in her private chapel before the image of the Holy Virgin.

In her passionate eagerness, she did something that astounded the Jews of Jampol. She drove to the house of their rabbi, Reb Menachem Mendel, and implored him to pray to God for the liberation of her husband, Wladislaw, son of Wladislaw. A neighbor interpreted, since the rabbi understood no Polish. The Countess then donated eighteen rubles for candles for the synagogue and a small sum to be distributed among the poor.

"All things rest with the Lord," the rabbi told her. But he agreed to offer up a prayer.

And it seemed as though he had actually worked a miracle.

A communiqué arrived from St. Petersburg announcing that his Majesty had graciously consented to issue an amnesty to the banished Count Wladislaw Jampolski, and that the governor of Archangelsk province had been instructed to free the Count and facilitate his journey home. Afterward it was discovered that the Count too had addressed a penitential letter to the Czar, and that the Archangelsk governor had interceded in his behalf.

When the news arrived by mail, the Countess fainted. Her daughter, Felicia, revived her with eau de cologne and brandy, while the nurse, Barbara, a relic with milk-white hair and a red, pock-marked face, unlaced the Countess's corset. After the Countess had dozed off, Felicia decided to write a letter to her brother Josef, who had fled to London after the uprising, and to her sister Helena, who was staying with an aunt in Zamosc. Her younger brother, Lucian, was either still in hiding somewhere in Poland or had perished. A Russian tribunal had condemned him to death *in absentia*, and nothing had been heard of him since.

The cuffs of her sleeves turned back to keep them from being stained, Felicia wrote in an ornate script, a flourish at the end of each word. She rejoiced at the prospect of her father's return; she had lit many a candle before the altar, dropped numerous coins into the charity box, and prayed constantly to God that He might free the exiled Count. Yet her joy was not unmixed, and Felicia felt ashamed before the Lord, who knew one's secret thoughts. Her father had been unkind to her, had called her an old maid, mocked and mimicked her. Felicia feared that after his appalling experiences in Siberia in the coarse company of criminals and Russians, he might prove even more untractable than before. Nevertheless, she implored God to grant her father a safe return, reconciling herself to the indignities he would probably inflict upon her, and forgiving his meanness in advance. Felicia had written only a paragraph or two when she tore up the letter, unable to decide whether she wanted to call Josef "dear" or "my dear." Nothing was as painful for Felicia as making a decision—one reason, no doubt, why she had remained a spinster.

Her father and Lucian were patriots who had risked their lives for Poland, whereas Josef had fled to London. He thought of himself as a philosopher, preached positivism and maintained in each of his letters that only through industry and science, not idle dreams, would Poland be restored. Such ideas, worthy only of tradesmen, had cooled Felicia's feelings toward her elder brother, whom she had worshipped in childhood. Helena, too, was constantly visiting relatives, close and distant, imposing on them, and forming indiscriminate friendships. A new generation had grown up, godless, impudent, selfish. After the 1863 disaster, the nobility had slowly resumed its old way of life. Receptions and balls were being held again, but Felicia was no longer invited to them. The years had passed; her suitors had all become husbands; her friends and her relatives had become distant, acting like strangers. Even the bread she ate was not her own, but the condescending gift of a Jew, Calman Jacoby.

Her father's exile to Siberia, Josef's escape and flight, the death sentence against Lucian had given a tragic significance to Felicia's life. She dressed in mourning, grieved over Lucian, her father, and the lost fatherland. For years now she had nursed her ailing mother and assumed complete charge of the manor house. Though their land had been confiscated, there still remained in the Countess's jewel box strings of pearls, heavy gold chains, diamond-studded combs, golden hairpins. Among the vestiges of their former opulence were delicate pieces of porcelain, silverware, a gold dinner service, a harness encrusted with precious stones. The wardrobes were still packed with furs, silk and satin gowns, petticoats, jackets, capes. Books bound in velvet and silk lined the library shelves. Felicia, not entirely resigned to her fate, felt that, at thirty-three, romance was still a possibility for her. Her luck would surely turn. A "gallant knight mounted on a white horse" might still appear, a touch of gray at his temples, gravity in his gaze, a mature smile beneath his mustache; and at a glance he would perceive her noble heart, the modesty of her soul, her untapped love. A son of the old aristocracy, he would adore poetry and prefer a cottage, a stream, the rustling of the forest, the wisdom of silence. And there would still be time to present him with a son, whom she would name Lucian Juljusz after her vanished brother and her favorite poet, Juljusz Slowacki, who wrote that wonderful song, "I am sad, O God!"

The return of the Count would upset the realities as well as the dreams . . .

Felicia began another letter, then rose and studied herself in the mirror. Her hair, which she wore in a bun, had once been a honey blond, but now it had darkened. Her face was white and narrow and there were bluish shadows under her hazel eyes. She wore black, a high-necked blouse and trailing velvet skirt, onyx earrings, and on her left hand an onyx ring which bore the inscription of the fateful year: 1863.

She went back to her writing. She had childish caprices, sometimes unendurable even to herself. Certain letters of the alphabet appeared sympathetic to her, others odious. Even among the fowl in the poultry yard, she had her loves and hates. It was her tragedy to be incapable of indifference.

Barbara, the old nurse, knocked at the door.

"My dear, your mother's asking for you."

"I'll come right away."

Felicia found her mother with her head propped up on two pillows in the four-poster bed. Two gray strands escaped from her nightcap; her flushed cheeks were crisscrossed with tiny purple veins. Her small nose and thin lips were bloodless above a pasty double chin. Only an extremely perceptive person could have discerned in her the traces of former beauty. The Countess's eyes flickered open as her daughter approached the bed.

"I haven't a thing to wear for your father's arrival, Felicia. You'll have to see Nissen, the tailor."

Felicia was astonished.

"Why, how can you say that, Mama? Your wardrobes are bulging with clothes."

"What clothes? Rags!"

"Father won't be here for weeks yet."

"I don't want to look frightful when he returns. See how gray I am!"

Felicia made no comment. Who would have thought that her mother, old and ill, would still cling to feminine vanity?

"What do you want me to tell Nissen?"

"Bring him here. I shall order new things for you, too. We won't look like paupers when your father arrives."

Felicia's eyes filled with tears.

"I'll do as you say, Mother dear."

11

In the month of March, the quiet of Jampol was upset by the news of the Count's return from Siberia. He had arrived driving a low sleigh, wearing a peasant's sheepskin coat, felt boots, and a broad-brimmed fur hat. He had grown perceptibly stouter. His face was flushed, his eyes glowed with mirth, and his walrus mustache sparkled with icicles. In the sleigh sat a woman in a squirrel coat, with a man's black fur cap on her head, and rugs wrapped around her shoulders and knees. Halting before Calman's tavern, the Count helped his companion down. He removed his fur coat, draping it over the horse, and entered the tavern boisterously, as though already drunk.

Getz, the manservant, happened to be behind the bar when the new arrival called out: "Hey, Jew, how about some vodka?"

The woman, meanwhile, had taken off her fur coat and hat. She seemed to be in her thirties, a brunette with black eyes, dazzling teeth, and a beauty spot on her left cheek. She walked mincingly on high-heeled boots. The townspeople, who had gathered to welcome the Count, stared as the woman rolled a cigarette of thin paper and tobacco, lit it, and began to exhale smoke through her nostrils. She lifted her drink, clinked glasses with the Count, and the two exchanged remarks in Russian.

"Idiots! What are you staring at?" the Count finally shouted at the spectators. "Do you think this is a circus?"

The Count stood up, whispered something to Getz, escorted the woman to Itche Braine's inn, and proceeded on his way to the manor. The Count's family were not expecting him for several days. His wife was asleep; Felicia was reading poetry in the library; Helena, who had just returned from Zamosc, was at the pianoforte in the drawing room. The gate stood open. As the sleigh pulled into the yard, the Count's two hounds, Wilk and Piorun, rushed toward it, yelping frantically. Wojciech, the family coachman, whose duties now included those of butler and valet, came out. Mumbling and damp-eyed, he advanced, cap in hand, toward his master. The old nurse appeared, giggled nervously, clapped her hands, and then broke into loud wails, like a peasant mourning the dead. Helena stopped her music and rushed out in her negligee. Her father, measuring her at a glance, remarked that she had become a beauty. The two embraced. Felicia joined them, and her father kissed her cheeks. She paled: the squire had come home drunk.

"Well, where's your mother?" the Count demanded impatiently.

"Mother's in bed ill."

"What's wrong with her? I'll go and see her."

Still in his hat and coat, tracking carpets with mud, he strode toward the Countess's room. Aroused by the commotion, she was sitting up in bed, flustered, clutching the silver handle of a mirror. The Count halted at the door, momentarily confused. Was that his wife or her mother? In the excitement, he had forgotten for a second that his mother-in-law was dead.

"Maria!" he shouted.

"It is really you," the Countess cried. "Now I can die in peace!"

"Why die? You're not that old!"

Drawing near, he kissed her hair, brow, and cheeks. She grew limp and her face flushed. During the ten minutes the Count spent with his wife, Wojciech unharnessed the horse; Magda, the cook, caught a goose and unearthed a clay-covered bottle from the wine cellar, a relic of the old days. The Count emerged from his wife's room, having removed his overclothes and changed his felt boots for high leather ones. Opening doors, he came upon Felicia.

"Why are you wearing black? No one has died."

"I'll change soon."

"What's that you're reading—more sentimental nonsense?"

"Please, Father, don't speak like that. The author is a distinguished poet, a prophet."

"A prophet, eh? You'd better find yourself a man and get married. Hook the first fool that comes along."

The tears instantly welled up in Felicia's eyes. Her father had indeed grown coarser in exile. Even his boots had a vulgar squeak. He wore a rough black shirt, and a brass watch chain spread across his vest. He resembled one of the Russian secret police who had ransacked the manor in their search for Lucian.

"God in heaven, please forgive him," she mumbled.

"Don't you ever crave a man?" The Count propped one foot on the upholstered seat of a chair. "What do you have in your veins: blood or sour milk?"

"Father dear, please don't start teasing right away. We were praying to God for you all the time."

"It wasn't God but the Czar who granted me an amnesty."

"Please, Father, have pity. Don't spoil the joy of your homecoming."

"An honest-to-goodness old maid, that's what you are. There's no God, and Jesus was nothing but a lousy Jew. The

Apostles made religion a business. Haven't you ever heard of Darwin? Answer me!"

"Father, let me be."

"Don't run away. Man is descended from the ape. For your information, one of our forebears was nothing but an orangutan." The Count laughed uproariously. "Our ancestors perched in trees and caught fleas. That's the undiluted truth. There's more progress in frozen Siberia than in all of your Poland. Vanity. Stupidity. Bah!"

The Count stalked out, leaving Felicia stunned. He still enjoyed shocking her. He had become thoroughly brutal. He drank; he blasphemed; he no longer had any respect for his own soul.

Entering her mother's bedroom, Felicia observed the Countess standing in lacy underwear, while Barbara struggled to fit her into a corset. Felicia quickly closed the door. She turned another knob and found Helena, also primping.

"I beg your pardon."

"Not at all. Come right in. What do you think of him? Isn't he marvelous?"

How Helena's body has matured, thought Felicia. Only yesterday she was a child. How boldly she stands, half naked, without a trace of shame. What breasts, what shoulders, what a complexion, what hair! She will have her fill of happiness—including the share I missed. She is blessed with everything—except a soul!

After exchanging a few words with her sister, Felicia left. Should she discard her mourning? She had vowed to wear black as long as Poland remained subjugated. She was no longer a child. No one could order her about. Though still undecided, Felicia proceeded to her own room, where the new gray gown made by Nissen the tailor hung in an oak wardrobe. Opening her door, Felicia recoiled. Her father lay sprawled on her bed, his boots on, one foot hanging over the edge. He was snoring. Felicia caught her breath and stared at him. What sort of a person was he? What iron nerves! Was she really his daughter? Why hadn't she inherited any of his strength and will?

"Father!"

The Count opened an eye.

"Oh. It's you. I'm exhausted. Starved, too. I've crossed half of Russia. Take off all that black. The Middle Ages have passed. Too much idealism, too much poetry, too much easy patriotism. Smokestacks are what we need in Poland, towering smokestacks spewing smoke; and fertilizer for the fields—mountains of artificial manure!"

5 ⌂

I

Jampol was filled with activity as the railroad line approached. Engineers came from Warsaw with cases of instruments and other equipment. A government inspector with a retinue of minor functionaries arrived and had to be banqueted and toasted with champagne. Calman Jacoby had been granted a loan by the Bank of Commerce in Warsaw and was having the ground surveyed for the spur to the lime quarries. Wallenberg, angered over delays caused by a shortage of ties for the Imperial railroad, wired Calman, threatening to sue for damages and revoke the contract. Calman, besides employing engineers and other skilled workmen, now had the job of procuring rails and freight cars. He had already established an office in Jampol and, because he needed clerks who spoke Russian, had found it necessary to hire Jews from Lithuania.

These strangers, who were beardless and wore Gentile clothes, considered themselves enlightened, but the town found them heretical. One of them, David Sorkess, who had graduated from the Zhitomir Rabbinical Seminary, quoted the Talmud irreverently, smoked on the Sabbath, and wrote poetry in Hebrew. The wife of Shalit, another employee, who came from Vilna, went bareheaded, flaunting orthodox ritual. Ignace Herman, a native Pole who had been an army officer at the time of the insurrection, was rumored to have fought with the Polish aristocrats and was no better than a heathen. They had all become friendly with Grain, the Jampol pharmacist, and spent their evenings at his house drinking tea from the samovar and playing whist. Calman was disturbed because he had to associate with these nonconformists who, the townspeople complained, demoralized the young. Even though he kept accounts himself in the old way, recording in pencil his income and expenses, assets and obligations, the services of clerks and auditors familiar with the Russian language and laws were indispensable to him. Strangely enough, he found that, as a man of wealth, he was now deeply in debt, while as a poor man he had not owed a cent.

During all this turmoil, elaborate preparations for Shaindel's wedding were in progress. Set for the Sabbath after the Feast of Pentecost, it had to be delayed until the Sabbath of Consolation, because her trousseau could not be completed in time for the earlier date. Shaindel, hearing she would have to wait two months longer, wept. Her father, to placate her, held out a ten-ruble note.

"Here, darling, go buy yourself a present."

"Papa, I'm not a child any more."

"Obviously not."

Calman shrugged. His recent wealth seemed to have brought him only complaints. He was forever justifying himself, apologizing, offering bribes, and making promises. Frequently, at night, Zelda woke him to complain of a headache and cramps, insisting he light a candle, apply a heated stove lid to her abdomen, or massage her with vinegar or alcohol. Sitting up with her scrawny neck and wizened face lost beneath an outsized nightcap, she stared into the night, her deeply lined eyes widened by anxiety.

"What good is your money to me?" she would wail. "It won't bring me comfort on earth or grace later. People curse me from envy. If only the children are spared the Evil Eye— may I atone for their sins! God grant them a longer life than mine. What wrong have they done, I ask you."

"What wrong have I done?" Calman countered. "Should I throw our fortune away? It is God's will! What I throw out, others will pick up."

"You think you're a husband? Are you ever here? You're always away. You spend weeks in the forest, night after night. The Lord knows what you do there. You're only flesh and blood, after all."

"You're being silly, Zelda."

"You always were a little coarse. I could have married a scholar. But my mother—may she rest in peace—favored you. What did she see in you? Don't be offended—but you did look oafish. Calman," Zelda suddenly changed her tone, "I don't think I'll last much longer. I get weaker every day."

"Go to the mineral baths—you know I've been trying to persuade you to go. Why suffer here? I want to do all I can for you, but you won't let me."

"Warm springs aren't what I need. I don't want to die away from home. I don't want to recite my last prayer here. I want my children to cry at my funeral."

Yes, Zelda was sick. Jochebed, who was pregnant, was also not well. Her belly had expanded to the size of a drum; her face had grown yellow and blotched. She feared ghosts, longed to eat chalk and eggshells, and still brooded over the fact that a fortuneteller had predicted she would die young. Mayer Joel had hung amulets inscribed with psalms about her room. He had the Book of Raziel ready to place under her pillow when her labor began, and he had written to the Rabbi of Marshinov, enclosing an offering of twenty-five rubles and requesting his help through prayer. Zelda, despite her ill health, had made a pilgrimage to another miracle-working rabbi and brought back a talisman and an amber charm, both said to be potent in the easing of childbirth. In addition to Dr. Lipinski, she had hired a midwife from Skarshew.

Calman was also upset over his daughter Miriam Lieba. Polish books engrossed her. She objected to women wearing wigs after marriage, disapproved of the Sabbath dishes, cholent and kugel, and was forever at odds with her mother. Once when she combed her hair on a Sabbath and Mayer Joel had scolded her for transgressing, she had said rudely, "It's I who'll roast in hell, not you!" Now neither would speak to the other.

Calman's associates and employees were full of complaints. Every office clerk, middleman, and menial laborer had a grievance. Wrangling among themselves, each denounced the other as a swindler. The forest wardens either neglected their duties or were in league with the thieves. Timber vanished; Calman's grain and potatoes were pilfered by the peasants, who also pastured their cattle on his meadows; the millers helped themselves to his flour; the wholesalers falsified weights and measures and padded his bills. Everyone's palm itched. And how could he, Calman, be everywhere at once?

The more Calman thought about it, the more he came to believe that he was the captive and not the master of his fortune. Actually, his wife was right. What good did his wealth do him? His supper still consisted, as it had when he was a peddler, of a dish of buckwheat grits, and he still slept on a bed of feathers, not of gold. The main difference was that while once he had eaten at a leisurely pace, chewing his food thoroughly, now he bolted it down. His afternoon meal had occasionally been followed by a nap but now, try as he might, he could never fall asleep in the daytime. Fortunately the Almighty, blessed be His name, had given the Jews the Sabbath. Business matters were put aside as Friday evening approached. Carrying fresh underwear and socks, provided by Zelda, and the fringed ritual undergarment, he and Mayer Joel would go to the nearest stream to bathe, or sometimes Getz would drive them to the hot baths in Jampol. Returning, Shaindel would welcome Calman with a freshly baked bun and a saucer of cooked prunes. Then, slipping into his Sabbath gaberdine, he would sit down and begin the recitation of the Song of Songs. Praise God, the demons of drudgery had no power over the Sabbath. Zelda and Jochebed would perform the benediction over the lighted candles in the silver and brass candlesticks, in the presence of all the girls, washed, combed, and dressed in their best. Mayer Joel complained that he could not get used to praying without a quorum. Calman vowed that he would erect a small synagogue on the estate, subsidize a quorum of ten pious Jews, provide a Torah scroll, the Talmud, order a Holy Ark and a lectern as well as a laver, menorahs, and an embroidered curtain for the Ark. He would even build a ritual bath, if only Jochebed came safely through childbirth, Shaindel were married, and Miriam Lieba betrothed. Calman did not intend to live his life without purpose, or arrive in the afterworld with nothing but a sack of sins.

II

Calman finally yielded to Mayer Joel's urging that they make a pilgrimage to the Rabbi of Marshinov for the Feast of Weeks. Reb Menachem Mendel and Ezriel were to accompany them, though Ezriel was not particularly eager to make the trip. He would have preferred to spend his time reading the textbooks given him by Wallenberg. He had begun to study algebra, geometry, Latin, physics, chemistry, and geography, all at once. He had also acquired some dictionaries and an atlas in Warsaw. It seemed a waste of time to neglect this store of knowledge in order to visit a Hassidic rabbi, but he could not easily snub his prospective father-in-law.

Calman had ordered a generous supply of butter cakes and buckwheat wafers for the journey, as well as several bottles of wine for the Marshinov rabbi's table. The coach was to start early the next morning, the day before Pentecost. Ezriel, who had scarcely slept that night, packed a geography book and a compass along with his prayer book and phylacteries.

Dawn came early. Calman and Mayer Joel were to stop for Reb Menachem Mendel and Ezriel. Reb Menachem sighed as he dressed. The Rabbi of Marshinov was, no doubt, a great sage, he reflected, but he himself felt more drawn to a different rabbi, the Preacher of Turisk. Unfortunately, Turisk was a great distance from Jampol, and Reb Menachem had gradually drifted from his spiritual home.

The stars were fading. A cock crowed. Despite the unseasonable warmth of the spring, Ezriel felt chilled. Like a shadow, his mother, Tirza Perl, moved about in bathrobe and slippers. His sister Mirale, hair disheveled, lay in bed, lost in a daydream.

"Watch your manners in Marshinov," Tirza Perl warned Ezriel. "What did your grandfather accomplish? One can't defy the world! Thank God you're lucky in your betrothed —don't spoil everything."

"You like to preach, Mother, don't you?" Mirale observed.

"And I thought she was sleeping! Wash up and have a cup of chicory. Don't be jealous, dear, your turn will come, God willing. What do I have left now? Just two darling doves."

Rumbling wheels approached, then halted near the house. Ezriel carried out their suitcases. The horizon glowed and dew glittered on the grass. A solitary worshipper, hugging the bag that contained his prayer shawl, stumbled like a sleepwalker toward the synagogue. Mists rose from the river. The horses stood with heads obediently bowed, as though whispering together. Mayer Joel, his hat set jauntily on his head, was evidently in high spirits. He had had his way. Calman helped Reb Menachem Mendel into the carriage; Getz, chewing a bit of straw, waved his whip. The two older men sat opposite Mayer Joel and Ezriel.

"Please keep an eye on him, Reb Calman," Tirza Perl called out from the doorway.

"Don't worry," Mayer Joel reassured her. "There aren't any bears running loose in Marshinov."

Getz tugged at the reins and the coach started. It passed the marketplace, the church, and Calman's tightly shuttered store. The road to Marshinov skirted Calman's estate. As though undecided whether to ripen or fall early, the green stalks drooped in the fields. A bird, hovering over a grove, flapped its wings.

Shaindel stood, pale and sleepy, near the road, and at her signal Getz reined in the horses. She held out two parcels, one tied with string, the other with green ribbon.

"What's that you're holding, dear? You should be sleeping," Calman said, surprised.

"This is for you, Papa, for the journey."

"Thank you."

"And that's yours," she told Ezriel. They both blushed.

"A good trip!"

"Goodbye."

The coach rolled on. Shaindel's figure receded. Ezriel wanted to wave to her, but felt shy. Calman ran his fingers through his beard.

"What's in those packages, I wonder," Mayer Joel remarked.

"Delicacies, no doubt," Calman said.

"Well, father-in-law, they'll come in handy at Marshinov. There, it's share and share alike. A man may be comfortably asleep at the inn—suddenly some poor traveler will appear to share his bed. That's Marshinov! The rabbi once declared: 'It's easy to profess love for the Lord, but it's not so easy to love a crippled tanner.' One time a Litvak, a skeptic who came only to mock, appeared in Marshinov. The rabbi gesticulates as he prays and this Litvak stood nearby, imitating every gesture. Some of the younger worshippers wanted to strike him, but the rabbi, who knew what was going on, prevented it. Very often petitioners waited days to see the rabbi, but this Litvak was admitted with scarcely any delay, and, strangely, he spent a whole hour with the rabbi. To make a long story short—he became a devotee, and Marshinov, to this day, is his spiritual home. Luckily he settled in Warsaw, or else Marshinov would have become swamped with Litvaks."

"Aren't Litvak Jews like the rest of us?" Reb Menachem Mendel interrupted. "All Jewish souls were assembled on Mount Sinai."

"Yet—"

"At Beltz," Reb Menachem continued, "you see Hassidim from remote parts of Hungary who recite the Gemara in a Hungarian dialect—yet have sidelocks reaching to their shoulders."

"Amazing!"

"The Talmud maintains that the ministering angels do not understand Aramaic. Hebrew is their language," Reb Menachem explained for Calman's benefit. "But the Almighty knows all tongues. Even the Sh'ma can be recited in dialects other than Hebrew."

"Wouldn't the Sh'ma sound a little odd in Turkish?"

Ezriel had felt impelled to raise his voice. He had wanted to break in earlier, to say that the man asleep in his bed might be contaminated by the poor stranger with whom he was suddenly forced to share it; that no one had ever conversed with angels, or ascertained their linguistic gifts—but he had restrained himself. Mayer Joel was always on the alert to embarrass him, probably annoyed that he had been duped into marrying Jochebed, while Ezriel was getting Shaindel. Ezriel turned his gaze to the heavens.

A blazing chariot streamed westward. In the east, the sun rose like a bloody head; birds flocked to greet it. Purple shadows lingered on the plains. It was odd to remember that even while the coach rolled toward Marshinov, the earth rotated on its axis from west to east, revolving about the sun as it had for centuries. Ezriel thought of the laws of gravitation. What caused them? Why must one body attract another? The physics textbook he had received from Wallenberg did not answer these questions. He would have to find a more advanced text.

III

Marshinov swarmed with crowds. Even in Lublin, Ezriel had not seen so many people. Hassidic pilgrims were everywhere, in the House of Worship, in the rabbi's courtyard and garden, and throughout the sprawling marketplace. The inns were jammed and guests slept on straw pallets, or even on the bare floor. Calman just managed to find one room for himself, Reb Menachem Mendel, and Ezriel. Getz found lodging with a local teamster. Mayer Joel found his father, Reb Ezekiel Wiener, with his brother, two brothers-in-law, and an uncle from Lodz, and became one of their party. Reb Menachem Mendel and Calman hastened to the ritual baths. Although Ezriel was urged by his father to join them, he managed to escape. He did not intend to bathe in a pool already used by so many others. He made a tour of the town instead.

The windows of the houses of Marshinov were decorated with cut-outs of doves and flowers, with twigs made of silver and gold paper, on which perched small birds, their heads modeled from dough. And placed at the corners of the windows were always some water flags or reeds symbolizing the granting of the Torah on Mount Sinai. Children ran about everywhere, blowing on their reed whistles. Since Pentecost was a dairy festival, the town was redolent of coffee, chicory, milk, and pastry.

Ezriel visited the synagogue of the non-Hassidic congregation. He wandered about the streets and alleys. Girls promenaded in their best clothes; the men were returning home after visits to the baths. The stores remained open for the poorer customers, who the last minute had managed to scrape together or borrow a few coins to make purchases for the festival.

The aimlessness of Ezriel's tour reflected his unrest and impatience. What's wrong with me? he thought. Why do I feel a stranger here? Were people really so blind to the obvious inconsistencies of their faith? God was Master of the World, and in that world the poor were starving. Although He was presumed to be merciful, He allowed the strong to overcome the weak. How had Wallenberg described it? Yes—the struggle for survival. There was certainly no Gehenna to punish whales who devour small fish. Christian nations, praying to Jesus, devastated their weaker neighbors, and though they preached turning the other cheek, their rulers sent political opponents into exile. And the Jews? God's chosen people remained oppressed and forever exiled. Once it was Chmielnicki, then Gonta or Czar Nicholas; it was either mass murder or harsh decrees. Were those victimized Jews supposed to be atoning for the theoretical sins of their ancestors? Hadn't their prayers and Talmud study been fervent enough? The Messiah had not yet appeared. Would he ever? The Book of Daniel had been ransacked by sages seeking clues for the Messiah's coming in *nutrakon*, the interpretation of initials, and through *gematria*, the study of the mathematical value of letters. It was all a lie. They had based all their hopes on a single book, the product of mortals!

It was time to return to the inn; the sun was setting—he had to get into his holiday clothes. But Ezriel had lost his way. He couldn't even recall the name of the inn. Reversing his direction, he strode past a tailor's shop where a garment was hastily being ironed, past an occasional woman still scrubbing the stoop of her house. Wearing satin gaberdines with wide sashes, fur-trimmed velvet hats, slippers, and white stockings, pious Jews were already approaching the synagogue. What would his father and Calman say if he failed to arrive in time? Mayer Joel would, no doubt, have a great deal to say. Calman might become so angry he would break the engagement. Ezriel stood still, looking to the right and left. The inn must be somewhere nearby, but where? He tried to stop some passersby, but not one paused or answered. Didn't they see him? Were they angry at him? He was hot and sweaty. His eyes had begun to blur. It's my nerves—just like my mother. Everyone thought him healthy, but in reality he was sick, half mad. Ezriel became enraged at his father, at Calman, and at Mayer Joel. Why did they drag him to these wonder rabbis? He didn't believe in them, he was not even sure he believed in God. He again inquired the way to the inn, describing it. This time a man replied, but Ezriel could not hear what he was saying, and the man pointed, first in one direction, then in another, as if to mock him. I don't want to live, Ezriel's mind screamed. I don't want to get married and bring more Jews into the world. Wallenberg is right, it's all madness, all this piety and martyrdom! Perhaps I should run away right now. But where? And what would Shaindel do?

A familiar grief overcame Ezriel, a grief he could remember feeling as far back as the first grades of cheder. All the boys except Ezriel had formed a group. He had remained an outsider. Even the teacher had been suspicious of him. The boys had ridiculed him, called him names, hit him, and at the same time had tried to woo his friendship. The pattern had repeated itself everywhere, in Turbin, in Lublin, in Jampol. Here, even in Marshinov, people were reacting to him with hostility. . . . It must be something in me, he thought. But what—my face, my eyes? Do I seem crazy? He pitied Shaindel. She didn't know the kind of man she was marrying. She had arisen at dawn to give him a package of butter cookies.

"Ezriel!" someone called. He stopped short. It was Mayer Joel.

"Where are you going? Have you been to the baths?"

"Yes."

"I didn't see you there."

"Nevertheless, I was there."

"All right, so you were. Where are you going now?"

"Just walking."

"Have you forgotten? It's time for the evening prayer."

"I must change my clothes."

"There's barely time, it's sundown."

Only then did Ezriel notice that Mayer Joel was already dressed.

"By the way," he asked, unsteadily, "where is the inn?"

"Lost, are you? I thought so. Just like a philosopher."

Oddly enough, Ezriel was almost directly behind the hotel. There was the well next to it, there the steps. How could he have missed seeing it? Still confused, he opened a door leading into a kitchen and was greeted by the screams of a young woman in the midst of dressing. He walked up and down the corridors, trying to locate his room. Finally he caught sight of Reb Menachem Mendel.

"Father!"

"Where have you been? I've been looking everywhere. You shame me!"

"Which is our room?"

"This one."

Ezriel entered the cubicle crowded with three cots. Groping in the dark, he changed his clothes as quickly as he could, and with his father and Calman set out for the rabbi's synagogue.

Services had begun by the time they arrived. The candles in the menorahs were already bent with the heat. A multitude of voices, rising from a forest of satin and velvet gaberdines, issuing out of a wilderness of beards and sidelocks, chanted in refrain: "For He is our life, and the span of our days, and by Him shall we be led day and night."

Ezriel stood apart near the entrance. How familiar these surroundings were to him, yet how remote. Some hidden and hostile force seemed to separate him from the others. He no longer felt himself to be among them; it was their holiday, not his.

He could not stand the heat in the synagogue. He left and joined a group of young men praying outside. The evening air was invigorating. Glowworms sparkled at his feet, above his head stars twinkled and a crescent moon sailed along. I get lost in a small town, he mused, but the stars, racing along for millions of miles, never deviate from their orbits. One comet describes a circuit in seventy years!

Ezriel, who had begun to recite the Eighteen Benedictions, could not continue. God might exist, but these words expressed nothing but a faith in a revelation that never took place and a belief in God's love for the Jews which was their own invention.

IV

"Reb Calman of Jampol, please be seated."

Calman was astounded. How was it that he, an ordinary Jew in a coat of common cloth, had been singled out for such a distinction with a study house suffocatingly full of the rabbi's disciples, many of them venerable ancients, dressed in satin, and with long sidelocks? Inclining his head, he followed the two synagogue wardens to a seat of honor. The chief rabbi sat in an armchair at the head of the table. Short, stocky, round-faced, with a silvery-white fan-shaped beard, he wore a white silk gaberdine embroidered with lilac leaves, and a wide hat trimmed with fur. One sexton brought the rabbi a copper jug, basin, and towel, while another poured water over his hands, after which the rabbi chanted the appropriate prayer. To his right sat his eldest son, Reb Shimmon, whose jet-black beard and dark shining eyes were in vivid contrast to his father's white robe and hair. A younger son, Reb Moshe, known as the Rabbi of Chmielev, a tall, lanky man with a beard scarcely covering the tip of his chin and girlishly long sidelocks, also attended the rabbi. Hassidic devotees surged about the rabbi's table, those in front pressing forward as those behind pushed against them. Calman, who was perspiring heavily, found himself unable to reach his handkerchief to wipe his brow.

The rabbi sliced a white loaf, using a knife with a mother-of-pearl handle. After he had taken a single bite, his followers vied for the rest, crust and crumbs, as the loaf was now sanctified. The rabbi merely tasted each course, taking a sliver of fish, a bite of meat, a spoonful of soup, one stewed prune. Throughout the feast, the rabbi's associates broke into Hassidic songs, the crowd joining in the refrains.

Calman, though he had at first gasped for air and felt that he would perish from the heat, gradually became used to the stifling atmosphere. He marveled at the rabbi's radiance. It was as if the Divine Presence had enveloped this seer. Everywhere around him were wet, clinging gaberdines, black, yellow, and gray beards, eyes glowing with fervor. A spirit of unalloyed rejoicing prevailed. Calman, though the local Hassidic chants were unfamiliar to him, joined in the choruses. He was not alone here, but among fellow Jews united in worship of the Lord. Across the table sat an old man with a furrowed brow. He wore a frayed velvet hat and worn coat. Next to him sat a young man, his head bowed so low that his sidelocks brushed the tablecloth. Piping young voices blended with asthmatic wheezing. All sang one hymn. Together they praised the Almighty for His mercies, prayed not for earthly well-being but for the coming of the Messiah and the abolition of evil, slavery, exile, and that heavenly joy and salvation should exalt the world.

Ah, this is the place for a Jew. It's wonderful here, Calman reflected. One's spirit grows younger. During recent years, Calman had become withdrawn. He had met so many swindlers, usurers, parasites. Now all rancor subsided in him, and brotherly love replaced it. Who am I, compared to these pious men? Just another fellow who happens to have made money, he thought. I'll come back here, God willing. Here is where one finds true rejoicing.

Silence was ordered and there was a sudden hush. The rabbi began his discourse on Holy Writ, his voice at first scarcely audible. The men behind Calman pressed forward, breathing on his neck, tickling him with their beards. Soon the speaker's voice gained volume. The rabbi took his text from the Talmud, which states that even before the people knew the nature of the Ten Commandments, they were prepared to obey them.

"Why should this be considered a virtue?" the rabbi continued. "Isn't is more commendable to listen and consider before plunging ahead blindly? Doesn't the Talmud say elsewhere that the evil servant acts first and asks questions later? There seems to be some contradiction here. According to common sense, is not inaction preferable to deeds whose consequences are unknown? The truth of the matter is that in certain cases action does come before thought. The need for a pilgrimage cannot be explained, for it will not be understood until it has been experienced. Philosophy inevitably begins with doubt, with chaos and emptiness. Thus it is unable to create anything, for what was void to begin with will remain void to the end. Therefore it is written: 'In the beginning God created the heaven and the earth. The earth was without form, and void.' *In the beginning God created*—and only then did He perceive the void. If He had beheld it first, there might have been no creation. When the Almighty gave the Torah to the Jews, He feared that they might first wish to know what it was—for if you argue and think about anything long enough, doubt is sure to arise. This was exactly what happened in the case of Esau and Ishmael, who according to the sages were offered the Torah first, and refused it. But the Jews followed the Lord's way when He created heaven and earth. With them, action preceded deliberation. In the deed, all misgivings were resolved.

"Yet how and when is this principle to be applied? Only in the fulfillment of holy duties. In secular matters and those pertaining to the flesh, it is the opposite course one must follow; one must consider and deliberate first, and only then perform one's duty. It is the evil-doer who first inflicts harm and then asks questions. For wickedness awakens endless questions in man. All doubts vanish in the performance of virtuous deeds. Yet how can one recognize the true spirit of virtue? The answer is: through joy. The man who injures someone is disturbed and full of conflicts. But a good deed is succeeded by inner happiness. For a man who is uplifted, all questions are resolved."

Parts of the rabbi's speech were too abstruse for Calman, but one message in particular seemed meant for him: one must do good and confer benefits without thinking, regardless of motive; but exercise restraint and judgment before injuring someone. "God in Heaven, how true and wonderful!" Calman murmured. The holy man had divined his most secret thought. From now on I shall perform good deeds, be more charitable, assist those who need my assistance, and spend two hours each day studying the Torah. I will be malicious toward no one, and will esteem everyone. Yes. Yes.

After the speech, Mendel the beadle climbed on the table in his stocking feet and began to pour wine for everyone, for the privileged who sat at the table, as well as for those who were standing, and there were no exceptions, not even among the very young men. Calman heard a sexton call out the names of Reb Ezekiel Wiener, Mayer Joel, his son-in-law, and the latter's younger brother. Then suddenly Calman heard, "Wine for Ezriel, son of Reb Menachem Mendel of Jampol."

Calman looked around for Ezriel. The goblet of wine, given by the sexton to the nearest man, passed from hand to hand until it reached Ezriel, standing at the doorway. What a prodigious memory the Rabbi of Marshinov had, thought Calman. He himself was always absentmindedly forgetting the names of his employees, sometimes even those of his daughters, but the rabbi personally honored every man under his roof, young or old. Yet one question still baffled Calman. Why had he been selected for a place of honor? What had he done to deserve it? Was it his wealth? If this were the case, it was probably the work of the rabbi's wardens, not of the rabbi himself. Why should the rabbi need money? An aging man, he was closer to heaven than to earth.

v

During the holiday two young men were proposed to Calman as eligible matches for his daughter Miriam Lieba. One was Jochanan, son of the rabbi's widowed daughter, Temerel; the other was the son of Reb David Gombiner, a wealthy man from Plock. Jochanan's father, Reb Zadock, had been a saint. Even while a very young man, he had fasted two days a week and risen at midnight to pray, and it had been generally predicted that he would one day succeed the Rabbi of Marshinov, whose two sons, Reb Shimmon and Reb Moshe, would be left without a following. But Reb Zadock had died of consumption, which the doctors ascribed to the chilly ritual baths. His widow Temerel, left with two daughters and a son, had never remarried. Like his father, Jochanan had begun at eleven to observe all the fast days, and to perform his ablutions in an icy pool at dawn. His grandfather, the old sage Reb Shmaryah Gad, had once admitted that the sanctity of his grandson surpassed his own. Now sixteen, dark-eyed, with a narrow face, Jochanan was much too small and gaunt for his age. His cheeks were sunken, his sidelocks reached his shoulders, his neck was scrawny, and his Adam's apple prominent. Observers at the ritual bath reported him all skin and bones. On the other hand, scholars called him a prodigy who had memorized the six rounds of Mishnah, and it was even maintained by some that he was already a Cabalist.

Reb Shimmon, who had for many years feared that his brother-in-law, Reb Zadock, might succeed the rabbi, now feared his nephew, Jochanan. And though it was Reb Ezekiel Wiener who was trying to forward the match between Jochanan and Miriam Lieba, it was generally understood that it was Reb Shimmon who was behind it. Jochanan, if he became a rich man's son-in-law, would be less ambitious about the Marshinov rabbinical post, reasoned Reb Shimmon, and also, since Miriam Lieba was rumored to be something of a heretic, she would probably not be too sympathetic toward her husband's becoming Marshinov's spiritual leader.

"Calman, do you realize what a prize Jochanan is?" Reb Ezekiel Wiener asked him. "A jewel! In all Poland you won't find another like him!"

Calman had difficulty accustoming himself to the idea that he might become a relative of the Rabbi of Marshinov. He did not deserve such an honor. It was too much, and he was full of doubts. Fate might be playing a trick on him, raising him up, as the saying went, before knocking him down. He also thought that Miriam Lieba would not care much for this match. She read all kinds of secular books, loved to wear pretty clothing, and Jochanan's religious erudition would mean nothing to her. Who could tell whether they would get along together? Calman feared too that in Jampol men would scorn him for trying to buy his way into the Marshinov court.

He answered Reb Ezekiel humbly: "What should I say? Who am I? A simple Jew, an ignoramus . . ."

"Don't be so modest! Everyone knows Reb Calman Jacoby. Will you call on Temerel?"

"Call on the rabbi's daughter? What am I to do there?"

"She's very anxious to see you. Come, let's go."

To reach Temerel's house, they passed through an orchard where lilac bushes grew among the apple and pear trees. The Hassidim plucked the fruit early in summer, when it was still unripe. The air was fragrant, birds sang, and blossoms drifted to the ground. In the middle of the orchard was an arbor, where the rabbi sometimes sat and instructed his grandchildren. The house—or, as some young wits called it, "Paris"— was two-storied. Reb Shimmon's wife Menuche, herself a rabbi's daughter, managed the household, although the half-paralyzed, aged wife of the old Rabbi of Marshinov was still in command. The wealthy second daughter-in-law, Binneleh, visited Marshinov only for the holidays. Among the women, Temerel passed as a scholar; she received Hassidic visitors and wrote letters in Hebrew.

Calman walked up the red-painted stairs with Reb Ezekiel. Long mezuzahs in carved cases were nailed to the doorposts of the high brass-knobbed doors they passed. When Reb Ezekiel pushed one open. Calman stepped onto the gleaming parquet floor of a drawing room; leather-bound books with gilt edges stood on shelves behind glass, together with goblets, trays, spice boxes, citron holders, and various silver and gold-plated objects. Brocaded draperies hung over the windows, and along the walls stood chairs with purple-tasseled covers.

At a little table, in an upholstered chair, sat Temerel, hook-nosed, with high cheekbones and round birdlike eyes. She wore a silk stole and black bonnet. An open book with a fine linen handkerchief beside it lay on the table, which held a carafe of wine and three glasses.

"A good holiday to you," said Calman, flustered and shy as a schoolboy.

"And to you, Reb Calman, and you, Reb Ezekiel," the hostess replied. "What a hot day! Do sit down."

"Have some wine," Temerel said, half inquiring, half commanding. With long, dainty fingers she reached for the carafe, lace dangling from her sleeve, and out of a drawer took three honey cakes.

"*L'hayim!*" Reb Ezekiel raised his glass.

"*L'hayim!*" Calman repeated.

"To your health, and peace! May salvation come to us and all our brethren. May our wanderings cease; may we be found worthy of welcoming the Messiah! We have waited long enough."

Calman murmured a benediction over the wine. He had never heard a woman use such phrases and so many Hebrew words. An aroma of almonds and spices emanated from her. The wine was sweet but strong. The hostess sipped hers, while Reb Ezekiel drank half a glass and set it aside. Calman drank his down.

"Have some more, Reb Calman. It comes directly from Hungary. Let me have your glass."

"Thank you kindly, rebbetzin."

"Good wine won't affect you."

"What are you reading?" asked Calman, and could have bitten his tongue.

"A *B'nai Issacher*. No doubt you are amazed to find a woman reading the sacred writings. Of course there's the old saying that a man who teaches the Torah to his daughter spreads heresy. But in our family all the girls are educated. My aunt, the wife of the Rabbi of Tzozmir, is very learned."

"You don't say!"

"Even my grandmother, may she rest in peace, was versed in the Talmud." Temerel blew her nose emphatically into her fine handkerchief. "But the real scholar of our family is Jochanan. A genius without an equal! The elders wanted to ordain him, but he declined the honor. Such a treasure is rare these days, a gift from heaven. There is only one thing I ask of God: that my son may live long and enjoy good health. Father in heaven, if I may only live to rejoice in his virtues!" Raising her glass to her lips, Temerel sniffed at it and then put it down again.

"And where did you say Jampol was?" she asked.

6

Though Calman had planned to leave for Jampol immediately after Pentecost, he decided at the last moment to remain in Marshinov until after the Sabbath. It was agreed that Temerel and Jochanan were to attend Shaindel's wedding on the Sabbath following the Fast of the Ninth of Ab, and the betrothal, God willing, would take place then. Calman had promised to send his coach for the honored guests. Despite Reb Ezekiel Wiener's insistence that the betrothal be formalized at Marshinov, Calman was determined to wait for Miriam Lieba's consent. Times had changed; people no longer forced their daughters into marriage.

At the end of an hour's session with the Rabbi of Marshinov, Calman had given his host two hundred rubles to pray for his, Calman's, soul. Reb Shimmon then took Calman to his rooms. The rabbi's wife soon joined them and both addressed Calman as though he were already a relative. Calman had also received from Reb Moshe, the Rabbi of Chmielev, a piece of amber which had been blessed by his grandfather and was said to have the power to stop bleeding.

Once the Sabbath was over, Getz hastened to harness the coach, and Calman hurried him along. He was already worrying about his affairs back in Jampol, about all the things he had left unfinished. Moreover, any day now, Jochebed was due to give birth.

On the way back Mayer Joel and Reb Menachem Mendel discussed the Hassidic movement. Reb Mendel insisted that despite its virtues, Marshinov and its rabbi could scarcely be compared with Turisk and the holiness of its rabbi. All the holy men were different, he remarked. Reb Mendeleh Riman-over, for example, accepted substantial donations from his followers, and carried a golden snuffbox, but other Hassidic rabbis lived in poverty. To one spiritual leader it was the study of the Torah that mattered most; to another it was prayer; to a third, charity; each according to his preference. Mayer Joel nodded assent, but at the same time he was annoyed by this praise of Turisk. How could Turisk possibly be compared with Marshinov? He had heard that in Turisk the spiritual leader was given to homiletic interpretations. And what did they amount to?

Actually it was Ezriel who irritated Mayer Joel most. Such irreverence! He had scarcely shown his face at the rabbi's, and at the study house had retreated to the anteroom among the loafers and young scamps. He had even boasted of not having listened to the rabbi. Mayer Joel had spoken to his father-in-law of Ezriel's disrespect, but Calman had replied, "What if he isn't a genuine Hassid? He can still be a Jew," implying some pettiness in Mayer Joel. It was clear Calman had no intention of breaking off the match.

Mayer Joel sulked. What was the old proverb? You can't make a silk purse out of a sow's ear. His father-in-law was not a bad sort, he was simply common. Eager to have Jocha-nan as a brother-in-law, Mayer Joel felt that Calman was the one who did not quite belong. The situation was demean-ing. When Jochebed gave birth, he would ask for the dowry still due him, and they would leave the estate, even if they got no farther than Jampol. He would persuade his father-in-law to make a cash settlement for the years of maintenance still owing. Mayer Joel longed to be on his own; a certain watermill interested him. He did not intend to lose his father-in-law's legacy, but neither did he plan to spend his life among such rustics.

As the night wore on, the carriage grew silent. Calman dozed, thinking of his fields of grain, of the railroad ties, of the lime quarries and the spur line he had ordered laid. His financial obligations were enormous; even the government was impatiently waiting for the rail connection. Now one of his daughters was about to be married to none other than the grandson of the Rabbi of Marshinov. A few years ago he would have laughed scornfully at anyone who had either prophesied his present position or suggested he would ever incur such liabilities. He was most certainly in need of divine guidance to keep him from stumbling now.

Reb Menachem Mendel was engrossed in his concern for Ezriel, his only son. The young man had behaved irresponsibly in Marshinov. What if Calman were to break off the match? The young man would be humiliated. He might even be conscripted—God forbid! Why couldn't he at least control his evil inclinations until after the marriage? For the honored memory of his holy ancestors, rather than for the sake of his son, Reb Menachem Mendel implored the Lord's indulgence.

Ezriel, who in Marshinov on the first day of Pentecost had met a young man named Aaron Asher Lipman, also had much to think about. He and his new friend had both been standing in the anteroom, prayer books in hand but not praying. After eyeing each other a while, they had begun to talk. Aaron Asher was undersized, with a huge head and meager body, a few hairs on his chin, bushy sidelocks, dark eyes. Ezriel, noting his narrow sash, highly polished boots, buttoned shirt collar, and above all the look in his eyes, had assumed him to be enlightened.

"Why must God have new angels every day?" Aaron Asher had asked flippantly, approaching Ezriel and referring to the special verses for Shabuoth recited by the reader from a passage in the *Akdamoth*.

"Perhaps the old ones turn sour," Ezriel had answered jestingly.

By the time the services had ended, Aaron Asher had told Ezriel all about himself. He had a wife and three children; his father-in-law, who had a dry-goods store, still supported him, but he occasionally helped out by traveling to Warsaw to buy merchandise for the store. In the big city he came in contact with enlightened people. He would have liked to go to Vilna or Königsberg to study secular subjects, but his wife was a religious zealot, and his mother-in-law dominated the household. If he had been able to scrape together the fare, he would have run off long ago, but then too he hated to leave his children. He talked on and on: the Rabbi of Marshinov was senile; the self-seeking Reb Shimmon was jockeying for leadership; Jochanan was a fool; Reb Moshe, a hypocrite. In Poland, the life of the Jews had become precarious. The storekeepers outnumbered the customers. The Jews had reached a dead end. Self-righteous Jews had dissuaded Czar Nicholas from allotting land to them at the time he had been inclined to do so, and now it was too late. There was no true language in use, simply jargon. Dressing like Asiatics, the Jews here belonged to the period of King Sobjeski. Such a state of affairs could not continue.

"Do you have a solution?" Ezriel had asked.

"We must extricate ourselves."

"But how?"

The congregation had at that point stood up for the Eighteen Benedictions and the conversation had ceased.

Later the two young men had strolled along the road lined with oaks that lead out of Marshinov. Aaron Asher, seven years older than Ezriel, had read extensively in forbidden books and periodicals. He spoke in a singsong, and with his forefinger wound in the fringe of his sash poked Ezriel's ribs for emphasis. "Our educational methods must be reformed. The Jews must master German as well as Russian and Polish. The children must be taught trades, the long caftans abol-

ished, and the beards shaved off or trimmed. Perhaps somewhere—Palestine or the Crimea—land can be obtained for
colonies. The world moves ahead, not backward. Even Joshua
halted the sun for only a few hours," he had concluded, winking mischievously.

11

A week before Shaindel's wedding, Calman sent Getz with the
coach to Marshinov, and it returned bringing Temerel, Jochanan, and a servant girl named Kaila. Over the summer, Calman had added eight rooms to his house and was now able to
put up his guests more comfortably. Miriam Lieba, when he
had spoken with her about Jochanan, had protested that she
was not the type to be a rabbi's daughter-in-law, but she did
consent to look at the young man. If she liked him, well and
good; if not, her father was to drop the matter entirely. Calman found this plan a good one, although others might have
thought it ill-advised.

Miriam Lieba, from behind the curtains of her garret window, peeped out as the visitors dismounted from the coach.
Calman, Mayer Joel, Zelda, Shaindel, and Faigel the maid
were on hand to welcome them. First to alight, bundle in
hand, was Kaila, a tall woman with masculine features. Then
came Temerel, whom the maid almost had to lift down from
the seat, which seemed to be holding her fast. Prayer book in
one hand and handkerchief in the other, wearing a black bonnet, a long-fringed silk scarf, and a black silk dress with a
train, she looked about her and made a wry face; the odor of
cow dung brought on an attack of sneezing. Last to dismount
was Jochanan, stoop-shouldered, pasty-faced, puny, with
overlong sidelocks, wearing a velvet hat and a ground-length
gaberdine tied with a broad sash. Like his mother, he carried
a handkerchief and some sort of sacred book. Miriam Lieba
wanted to laugh and cry at once.

"Miriam Lieba, where are you?" Zelda called.

Miriam Lieba, without knowing why, had taken an immediate dislike to Temerel and pretended not to hear her mother for a while. Her cheeks were burning and she wanted to remain hidden. Even her own sister made her feel embarrassed. She seemed to take the entire visit as a joke. Shaindel's eyes were so merry . . .

Miriam Lieba threw a scarf over her shoulders, only to tear it off the next moment. I don't have to put on airs for those idiots, I'll spit at them! She was ashamed of her timidity and at the same time annoyed by her own irascibility. After all, these people had not wronged her. Her father would not marry her off at gun point. She started down the stairs carrying a Polish book: let them see that she did as she pleased. But seconds later she reconsidered: why vex her parents? Yet some inner force was compelling her to spite these people who had come to size her up as if she were some kind of livestock. Only when she had almost crossed the threshold did she become aware of the stupidity of her action. Turning back, she hastily shoved the volume into the larder, upset a pot of sour cream, and had to jump aside to avoid being splashed.

"Yes, Mother." Miriam Lieba finally appeared.

"Where have you been hiding?" Zelda introduced her daughter. "This is the rabbi's daughter—my younger daughter, Miriam Lieba."

Miriam Lieba knew that she was expected to greet the guests or at least nod on being introduced, but she simply stood still, looking at the shrewd-eyed Temerel.

"A beautiful girl!"

"Thank you."

"And tall. May she escape the Evil Eye."

Jochanan, deep in thought, frowned and suddenly averted his eyes: he had almost looked at a female! Shaindel, noting his embarrassment, began to laugh.

"Let me show you the house," Calman suggested to Temerel. "We have no drawing room, just a roof over our heads."

"Who needs drawing rooms? I have—may you be spared the same—a headache."

"A glass of milk, perhaps?"

"Not before prayers."

Zelda led Temerel to the room prepared for her, where she immediately washed her hands while her own maid held a towel in readiness. Then she surveyed the room: it looked spotless, and the wooden floor, freshly painted, smelled of pine. Three pillows were piled one on top of the other at the head of the bed, with a bolster of the kind popular among wealthy peasants.

"Which is the east wall?"

"That one," Zelda pointed.

Jochanan, shown to his room by Calman, asked the same question: "Which is the east wall?"

"That one."

"Is there really no quorum for prayer?"

"How could there be? We're outside the town."

"In that case, one is allowed to pray alone."

Jochanan washed his hands and began to murmur his prayers, facing the southeast corner rather than east. After finishing the preliminary morning prayers, he put on his phylacteries. He felt strained after the journey; his thoughts had been disrupted. Rumors had reached him that he was to be married to one of Calman's daughters. But why had it been necessary for him to come here? He had endured the journey by concentrating on the sacred book he carried and by reciting the Psalms from memory, while imploring the Lord to protect him from evil thoughts. But he had been unable to avoid glimpses of meadows, fields, peasants, cattle, extraneous objects that he did not care to observe, lest they deter him from proper service to the Creator. One must surmount all obstacles with fortitude. He recalled the precept that one should recite one's prayer as slowly as one counts gold pieces. And weren't the sacred words more precious than any number of coins? "The Lord is righteous in all His ways, and gracious in all His works. The Lord is with all those who call upon Him, with all who call upon Him in truth. He will fulfill the desire of those that fear Him; He will also hear their cry and save them." What words! God is near all who call him. One only need implore, and He responds. How pale are the follies of the world before truth! Jochanan was conscious of calling upon the Almighty with his mind, heart, and every part of him: "Help me, O Lord! I wish only to serve Thee, devoutly, and to my last breath. I ask nothing more!"

Mayer Joel, coming to look for Jochanan and assuming that he must have completed his prayers, opened the door. But the young worshipper took no notice of him as he continued murmuring the Eighteen Benedictions.

III

The day of Shaindel's wedding, Calman had a serious talk with Miriam Lieba. Fifteen minutes later she left him, her pale cheeks stinging red, her nostrils quivering. She went into the kitchen to tell her mother that Calman wished to see her. The aroma of honey cake and fresh loaves baked with saffron filled the kitchen. The fowl and beef had already been made kosher. Wiping her hands on her apron, Zelda left the room. Soon she returned, smiling but with tear-stained cheeks. Little Tsipele came in; though not quite eleven, she was almost as tall as Shaindel, and her hair hung in long braids: yet she still acted like a child. The cook had baked a special patty for her, marked with a T, and had wrapped it in gold paper. Snatching up the hot cookie, she tossed it from hand to hand, complaining that it was too hot.

Zelda, pulling the child to her, hugged and kissed her, tears streaming from her eyes, while she blurted out, "Ah, my poor child!"

"But, mistress, this is a wedding!" one of the kitchen help remarked.

"Go to your father, dear; he wants to talk to you," Zelda said.

"To me?"

"Yes, little chick."

"Look, Papa," Tsipele greeted her father, showing him the cake. "It has my initial on it."

"I'm sure it's delicious, too. Come here, darling."

Sitting at the head of the table, Calman asked his daughter to sit down. She could hardly believe it; he had never before asked her to sit down. She must be growing up.

"Tsipele, have you seen Jochanan?" Calman asked, taking her hand.

"The son of the rebbetzin? I saw him."

"How does he strike you?"

"He has such lovely sidelocks!"

"Would you like him as a bridegroom?"

Tsipele grew serious. "Isn't he going to be betrothed to Miriam Lieba?"

"Miriam Lieba doesn't want him."

"Why not?"

"I don't think she knows herself. Tsipele, I would like you to be betrothed to Jochanan."

Blushing, the girl replied, "I'm too young!"

"Not really. In earlier times, eight-year-old girls were given in marriage. And the actual marriage will not take place for several years. You'll receive fine gifts as a bride. The young man is a prodigy; his grandfather is the Sage of Marshinov. It will be a great honor."

"And what about Miriam Lieba?"

"She won't be a spinster, God willing. She'll find a mate. What do you say, Tsipele?"

"As you wish."

"Remember, Tsipele, this isn't child's play. Jochanan is a great scholar, and an orphan too. He must not be humiliated. You'll marry him, God willing. You won't remain a calf forever."

"I know."

"So—you want him?"

"Why not?"

"Well, I don't want to act without your consent. You agree, so it's all right. With God's help, fortune will favor you. You'll be my pride and joy."

"May I go now?"

"What's the rush? Your cookie won't run away. A betrothed girl must be calm. You'll get a watch and chain as a present, and a dowry and a trousseau. Jochanan is older than you, but not so much."

"How old?"

"Sixteen."

"Oh!"

"That's not so old."

"He's a young man already."

"Naturally. So what? You're a young girl."

"I know that."

"Before you realize it, with God's help you'll be grown up. Time doesn't stand still, darling. How long ago do you think I was your age? It seems like yesterday."

"But you already have such a long beard!" Tsipele laughed.

"What of it? Jochanan's beard will grow, too. When, God willing, you're a married woman, you'll wear a bonnet. With God's help, you'll have children."

"I—a mother?"

"Your mother was a little girl too at one time. I remember her at your age. Your grandfather—may his soul rest in peace —was a scribe of sacred writings, a poor but saintly Jew. Every time, before he sat down to write, he would perform ablutions; your grandmother was a virtuous woman. They have both already joined their ancestors."

"Why?"

"Nobody lives forever. Without making due provision in this world, one enters the next one empty-handed. By marrying a sage, you'll find delight in both worlds."

"Do you think he'll want me?"

"Jochanan? He doesn't look at girls; he'll obey his mother. You are—may the Evil Eye spare you—a beautiful girl. Your hair is black and your face is fair. He'll be pleased. You'll be a virtuous Jewish daughter. And faithful. Isn't that true?"

"Yes."

"Wait. I have something for you."

Fumbling in his pocket, Calman found a silver ruble. "Here, take this."

"Really?"

"Of course."

"Oh, thank you."

"Buy something for yourself. But now, come here."

Tsipele ran to her father; they embraced and kissed. She combed his beard with her fingers. Calman would have liked to lift her up and give her a ride on his knee as he had done only a year ago, but he restrained his impulse.

"Well, that's all," he remarked.

"May I tell everyone?"

"No. At the moment, it's a secret."

"All right."

Picking up her cake, Tsipele walked out, but turned around to look back. Her mother was waiting with open arms.

"I've heard everything, dear. I have only one wish before the Lord, to live to see your wedding—first Miriam Lieba's, then yours."

"Mother . . ."

Mother and daughter kissed fervently, the former weeping. Calman went to Temerel's room, and his wife followed soon afterward. When they left, Temerel sent her maid for Jochanan. Tsipele remained indoors for a while and then went to the barn, where she crawled into a shed with a little sloping roof which was her hiding place. Nearby was a willow tree and a warped block used for wood-chopping. Tsipele sat there contemplating the silver coin while she consumed her cake.

When the maid came to call Jochanan, he was engrossed in

Holy Writ. From all the whispering, he judged that something was going on. Once or twice, while standing at the window, he had seen some girls passing, one of whom, he assumed, was his bride-to-be. Laughter and conversation had reached him from adjacent rooms. Although all was predestined, he implored the Lord that his wife be quiet and virtuous, not a giggler. What was there to laugh about? If man realized how many demons lurked around him, how easily he could stumble and forfeit the world to come, his fears would keep him from laughing.

Marking the place he had reached in the annotation to the Talmud, Jochanan apologized silently to the authors for having interrupted his communion with them. His heart was beating faster than usual. He halted in the anteroom to adjust his sidelocks. Perhaps his future in-laws might want to look him over. . . .

7 🏰

Count Jampolski and his family attended Shaindel's wedding,
and it was there that Miriam Lieba met the young Countess
Helena. Miriam Lieba, who spoke Polish more fluently than
her sisters, was liked by the Gentiles. The two girls were only
a few months apart in age. As soon as the marriage ceremony
was over, the Count and Countess, accompanied by Felicia,
returned to the castle, but Helena insisted on remaining. Taking a seat next to Miriam Lieba at the girls' table, she took a sip
of the festive chicken broth, a bite of carp, a white roll. Various women too shy to approach her mother came to Helena
and made conversation in a mixture of Polish and Yiddish.
When the band struck up and the girls paired off with each
other for dancing, Helena, requesting a mazurka from the musicians, threw a coin onto the drum as was the custom, bowed
like a gallant before Miriam Lieba, and asked her to dance.
The company watched, with a good deal of laughter, chatter,
and clapping, the unusual spectacle of a Polish countess dancing with a Jewess. The two girls had similar figures, though
Helena's bosom was higher. Helena wore silver slippers with
high slender heels and a white gown cut low in front and in
back, with puffed sleeves. A medallion hung around her
throat, and her hair was combed high in the French fashion. A
crowd from Jampol stood in the doorway, watching and jos-

tling each other. "If you live long enough, you see everything," one woman remarked to another.

Before the evening was over, Miriam Lieba received an invitation to visit Helena. But it was not until the day of Tsipele's betrothal—when the Hassidim were celebrating noisily on the grounds of the manor, even urinating on the trees, trampling the grass, and tearing off leaves to use as toilet paper—that Miriam Lieba finally put on her new dress, and carrying the bouquet of flowers she had picked in the fields, started off for the manor house.

Helena, turning the bouquet over to a maid to put into water, took Miriam Lieba to greet her family. The Countess assured her young visitor that she did not look at all Jewish and, having said this, retired to her room. Felicia was annoyed that a daughter of Calman's had to be received at all, but at the same time chided herself for breaking her vow to live humbly and without false pride. Only the day before, she had written in her diary: "If I can't do as Jesus demanded, I prefer to die." So she smiled at Miriam Lieba and complimented her on her dress, one that Nissen the tailor had made—a compliment that was promptly returned.

The Count, wearing riding breeches and an English plaid jacket, both purchased recently, received Miriam Lieba with democratic affability. Sitting down opposite the girls on a bench in the arbor, he chatted about the terrible winters in northern Russia, about the government officials with whom the prisoners fraternized, about the considerable freedom he had enjoyed in exile, having been permitted to ride, hunt, skate. The Siberian peasants went out on bear hunts armed only with clubs. And the natives were tormented by bedbugs. When the Count began to describe how the bugs nested in the moss between the roofbeams of the dwellings and hurled themselves down from the ceiling in the dark to suck blood from their victims, Helena let out a peal of laughter and Miriam Lieba smiled. But Felicia, who stood at a distance and

seemed to be scarcely listening, spat into her lace handkerchief.

"How can you talk like that, Father?"

"If the bedbugs don't care, why should I? We're all made
of the same protoplasm."

Felicia walked off in disgust. Her father talked of nothing
but lice, bedbugs, garbage, rags, anything that was revolting.
Even when he ate, his mind was occupied with filth. It was
enough to turn anyone's stomach, and Felicia knew that he
did it to spite her. During his exile the Russians had infected
him with nihilistic notions and their Godless materialism. In
his pipe he smoked coarse peasant tobacco, which stank up
the house. And that Russian woman—everyone knew about the
woman he had brought back, who occupied a cottage in The
Sands, where the Jews had once lived. Everything had happened as Felicia had foreseen. Her father drank, used coarse
language, and dishonored an ancient and noble family by living openly with a slut. If she had not recognized it as her
Christian duty to accept suffering with humility, and if she
had not loved her unhappy mother so much, she would have
fled the house or killed herself.

Felicia's departure did not annoy the Count, who merely
shrugged his shoulders. Presently the conversation turned to
the Jews.

"We Poles should learn from you people," the Count said.
"We turn gold into mud; you turn mud into gold."

Miriam Lieba reddened.

"There are plenty of poor Jews, too."

"I know, I know, but all of you spend your time plotting
how to get rich."

Helena took Miriam Lieba on a tour of the manor, covering
her mouth with her fan when a yawn interrupted her talk,
pointing out the blue room, the gold room, her own boudoir,
the library. Miriam Lieba had been in the manor only once,
many years before, when as a child she had accompanied Cal-

man on one of his visits. Since then, the building had undergone great changes. Leaks in the roof had damaged the interior. Windows had become crooked, walls had sunk. In the
damp library the books, mostly biographies of saints and gene-
alogical histories, were covered with mildew. Helena, motion-
ing Miriam Lieba to a high-backed chair, seated herself on a
bench.

"It's so lonely here—sometimes I think I might as well be
dead. I don't meet a decent-looking man from one end of the
year to the next," she confided. "But what will become of
you? Will you marry a Jew?"

"Only if he's attractive to me."

"You're right. I could never marry a man I didn't love. Just
recently, in Zamosc, my aunt introduced me to the son of one
of her friends. He and I went for a stroll and right away he
started to prattle about love. As we were crossing a bridge, he
remarked, 'There are a vast number of small fish down there,
extremely small ones.' The moment he said 'small fish,' he became loathsome to me. I thought, you're nothing but a small
fish yourself. Isn't that odd?"

"I understand you perfectly."

11

That evening it snowed and continued snowing throughout
the night, the flakes heavy, dense, and dry as salt. In the morning the temperature dropped and a frost set in. The manor
regained its former glory: the roof lost its patches; the balconies and carved moldings became opulent once more. Crystal
spears hung from the window frames and patterns of frost
blossoms coated the panes. Even the smoke that drifted from
the chimney to the clear sky spiraled elegantly. The dogs,
Wilk and Piorun, barked constantly; the cow in the barn
scraped at the door with her horns; roosters crowed; crows
cawed. The fields, sown with winter grain which had already
begun to sprout, were enveloped in a whiteness without be-

ginning or end. When a young rabbit scurried from some bushes and gazed at the rejuvenated manor house, the Count seized his gun and fired. The rabbit vanished, leaving behind only the barest trace of footprints.

The Count had risen while it was still dark. Though he had lost everything—his wealth, his son Lucian—his appetite for life had not abated. Thrusting his feet immediately into boots, rather than slippers, he strode through the household, slamming doors and waking everyone. Hungry and thirsty, he went outdoors to the well to wash. He would have loved to go hunting if only he had had some pointers or retrievers.

In the kitchen Barbara the nurse ground coffee beans in the hand mill. She prided herself on having inherited from her grandmothers and great-grandmothers the art of brewing coffee. The Count ate voraciously, black bread and butter, and swallowed the dark unsweetened brew. Although he knew it was bad manners, after every gulp he emitted an "ah" like a famished peasant. When a crumb clung to his mustache, he licked it off with his tongue. During his exile, Jampolski had come to the conclusion that etiquette wasn't worth a groschen. He had reread Rousseau. Poland was the victim of too much foppery.

After eating, the Count went to his wife's bedroom. The Countess, who slept so lightly that the faintest rustle woke her, had lit the candle which stood on the night table.

"Mother, get up and take a look at the snow. It's two feet deep."

"Jan, I've asked you repeatedly not to call me Mother."

"Don't you want any breakfast? Something hot to drink?"

"Thank you, nothing."

"You're all bones. Nothing produces nothing. I'll be going into town."

"Why must you always be going to town?"

"To talk to the Jews."

"Why the Jews?"

"Who else is there? All the Poles know how to do well is

weep. They bore me. A Jew will cheat you out of your last
ruble, but he's not dead on his feet, or forever bragging about
some stupid pedigree."

"May God forgive you for such blasphemy."

"What would you like from town? I'll bring you an orange."

"I don't want an orange."

Wojciech tried to help the Count hitch up the small sleigh
—the large one was too heavy and took four horses—but the
Count would not let him. The Countess, hearing her husband
drive off, took the Bible from the night table. She knew to
whom he was running. Opening to the Book of Psalms, she
began to murmur the sacred words. When she came to the
verses about the God-fearing poor man on whom the wicked
sharpen their teeth, surrounding him like a bevy of dogs ready
to swallow him, she paused. Wasn't her situation like that
man's? Wasn't she, Maria, beset by evil? Of her two sons, Lucian was dead and Josef in exile in distant England; her oldest
daughter, Felicia, was a spinster; the estate was confiscated;
and her husband betrayed her. When she reached the passage,
"My mother and father have forsaken me, and God will take
me to himself," she began to sob. Her breast ached. Yes, God
Almighty remained after everything was lost. After weeping,
the Countess usually felt better, but this time she did not. Closing the Holy Book, she kissed the cross engraved on its bind-
ing, and rang a little silver bell until Barbara entered.

"Send in Felicia."

"Yes, your Excellency."

When her daughter came, the Countess asked her to sit in a
chair next to the bed.

"Felicia, I must talk to you plainly," the Countess began.
"You're not a child any more. Your mother won't live forever.
And you know you can't rely on your father. I had hoped the
ordeal of Siberia would purify him, but if anything his soul
has become even blacker. What will happen after my death?
I'm afraid he'll bring shame on himself and on you."

"Mother, you'll get better."

"Perhaps. . . . Open my handbag. There's a key in it. That's it."

"Why?"

"Do as you're told. Now, open the bottom drawer of my bureau. At the very bottom, to the right, you'll find a jewel case. Take it out. Yes, that's it. Now bring it to me."

Felicia, carefully lifting the ebony box decorated with ivory, carried it to the Countess, who opened it. Inside lay strands of pearls, pins, bracelets, earrings, and all sorts of rings, most of them set with diamonds.

"These belong to me alone, Felicia. They're all I possess— my own, brought from my father's house. I don't want them to fall into your father's hands. He'll only waste what they bring. I want you to have them all, with the exception of the smaller strand of pearls. Give that to Helena at her wedding, but not before. She's more like your father and not so helpless as you are. You're more like me. I pray God you will still find a suitable husband. But in case of need, you'll have these. I want you to take them now."

"Mother, it's not necessary."

"I've thought it over. I don't know how much these are worth, forty thousand gulden at least, perhaps much more. If, God forbid, you should be forced to sell, don't go to a cheap jeweler. Go to Warsaw: on Krakow Boulevard is a jeweler named Adam Nosek. You can trust him."

"Mother, you still have years . . ."

"I make one last request to you."

"What is it, Mother?"

"I know Lucian is not alive. If he were, he would have found some way of communicating with us. He is in heaven among the angels, and I shall soon meet him there. After my death, on my tombstone, I want his name engraved as well as mine."

"Mother, you're tearing my heart."

"I want you to be prepared. It's better. The earth is a vale of misery. What did your father give me? A lot of sorrow, a little joy. My soul no longer wants to stay in my body. Look how thin I am, wasted away. I no longer recognize myself. If I could only see you happy! Find a husband, Felicia, and don't be so choosy. He doesn't have to be rich. As long as he's noble and a man of faith. What happened to our fortune? Well, enough. Take the box and hide it with your things. Where will you put it?"

"In my vanity table."

"You keep it locked, don't you? Good. I want to die without any possessions. God loves the poor. Well, you may go."

Felicia hesitated. "You want me to take it now?"

"Yes. How many times do you have to be told?"

"But, Mama . . ." Felicia, bending over her mother, began to kiss her hands, her forehead. She was weeping in a thin mewling voice like a kitten.

The Countess became impatient. "Please go now," she said sharply.

Felicia, sniffling, took the jewel box and left the room, walking with a swaying gait. Of what use were all these diamonds to her? She locked the box in the vanity table in her boudoir. After a while, her tears dried. She stood at the window and looked out. The upper panes were covered with frost, the lower ones had cleared. Outside, the sun was shining. She could see the tracks made by her father's sleigh and the horses' hooves. Two crows picked at the oats in the horse dung, airing their wings. Suddenly, Felicia noticed Helena with Calman's daughter Miriam Lieba, who wore a knitted jacket and a heavy gray wool skirt, while Helena had on a dark green costume, its lapels decorated with laurel leaves. Both carried skates and were on their way to the lake. Felicia turned her eyes away. Her father was the friend of a Muscovite, and her sister the friend of a rich Jewess. All they cared about was pleasure. Mother was ill and Helena went off skating. She had no heart at all.

At that moment, Felicia knew what she would do when her

mother died. She would enter a convent, bring the jewelry as her dowry, and have it made into a crown for the Blessed Virgin. She, Felicia, needed no worldly treasure. Once and for all she would tear from her breast all earthly hopes, all dreams of material happiness. Bread and water and a hard bench were all she needed.

8 ♜

In Wola, a Warsaw suburb, there was a furniture factory that employed about forty men. It was located in a loft which was filled with sawdust and shavings. There Wacek Pracz worked at cutting out holes in a thick board with a hammer and chisel. Nearby, another man sawed lumber, a second planed, a third hammered nails, a fourth drilled with a gimlet. The air was filled with the pungent odors of varnish and glue. Since it was winter, the windows were shut, but some air came in through an occasional broken pane. The building reverberated with the noises of lathes, hammers, and saws. From the yard below came the shouts of teamsters loading furniture and unloading lumber. At one o'clock precisely, the factory stopped work, and the wives, mothers, and sisters of the laborers, their heads covered with shawls, entered the courtyard, bringing hot food, pots of soup, loaves of bread. Seating themselves on logs and boards in the yard, the men spooned up groats, chewed bread and sausage, or tilted bottles of vodka. The air smelled of fried onions and domesticity.

Wacek Pracz sat on a crate near the fence, with his mistress Stachowa. He was above medium height, with a pale, youthful face, light blue eyes, and a blond beard but no mustache. His nose was turned up, his lips narrow, his forehead high. Like the other workmen, he was dressed in a cotton-padded jacket, a shirt open at the neck, patched pants, and heavy shoes. Though Pracz was a peasant name and this man claimed a village near Wloclawek as his home, there were those who whispered that he belonged to the aristocracy. His speech was unlike that of his fellow workers; his curses and vulgarities seemed out of place. After work, he did not accompany the others to the taverns, but went his own way. It was thought that he had probably participated in the 1863 Insurrection, but this was never discussed openly. Everyone knew that "walls had ears and the Russkis had spies planted everywhere." Wacek Pracz was nicknamed the "Squire."

Stachowa came from the people. Before her marriage, she had been a domestic. Her husband, Stach, had died shortly after their wedding, and her daughter Kasia, now eleven, had been born out of wedlock. Stachowa and Wacek lived together without benefit of clergy. The women were curious about Wacek and often questioned her about his habits, his behavior, whether or not he associated with aristocrats, whether he had a family, read books . . . But Stachowa only smiled fatuously. "Do I know? He leaves for work early, and when he comes home, he's dead tired. Sometimes he comes late, but he won't say where he's been. What can a mere woman know of a man? Maybe he has a dozen other women . . ."

"Does he ever beat you?"

"When he's drunk."

Stachowa, a sickly woman whom some claimed was consumptive, had sunken, red-splotched cheeks. She wore her sparse, faded blond hair in a bun, and her pale blue eyes were always tearing, though she constantly smiled. The women did not understand what the "Squire" saw in such a wreck, though it might be simply that she had taken him in when he had been ill and starving, and he had stayed on, becoming attached to Kasia also. "A man is like a dog"—they commented. "Feed him, give him a place to sleep, and he won't leave his kennel."

Stachowa, in apron and shawl, sat beside Wacek, eyes on his mouth as he ate. She had brought him a pound of bread, but he hadn't eaten half of it, or finished the soup. She knew the truth, that his name wasn't Wacek Pracz, and that he was not from a village near Wloclawek. He was Lucian, Count Jampolski, of the Jampol manor. But she would never betray his identity—not even if her flesh were cut open and acid poured into the wounds. He might be a nobleman, but what difference did that make when he had no money and carried a false passport? He acted like anyone else: if he was angry, he cursed her or beat her; often too, after drawing his pay on Saturday, he returned drunk and with empty pockets. If she, Stachowa, hadn't washed laundry for the Jews, the three of them would have perished. But one thing she could say in his favor: he was good to her daughter Kasia, bought marmalade for her and was teaching her to read from a primer. They would have gotten by if so much money had not gone for medicines and leeches.

He handed Stachowa the half-full dish.

"Is that all you're going to eat? I'll be taking half of it home again."

"That's all. My stomach is bloated."

"A few more spoonfuls—please!"

"I said no. Do you want me to have cramps?"

"All right. All right."

"What's Kasia doing?"

"Playing in bed with the kitten."

"Well . . . so . . . you can go now."

"Wacek—come home early today. Look how pale you are —paler than anyone else. You know how tired you were this morning—you could hardly wake up."

Wacek stood up. "Go—for heaven's sake, go."

Stachowa tucked the pot under her shawl. That's how men were—they didn't want your love.

11

Stachowa's room was small. The bed she and Lucian shared was on a gallery reached by a ladder. Below, Kasia sat on the straw mattress of her narrow bench-bed. Her face was small, her hair flaxen, her eyes gray, her skin porcelain white, like that of a doll. She read aloud from her primer:

> *"Tell me, Darling,*
> *Where is the apple,*
> *The coffee-grinder?*
> *And where is the parrot,*
> *Or the cage where*
> *The bird sings?"*

Stachowa paused to listen. What odd things were printed in books! She herself could neither read nor write and signed her name with three X's. But it was fortunate that Kasia was getting an education. The Russians had forbidden the use of Polish—the scum, carrion, boors, accursed Muscovites!

"*He* was here," Kasia said.

"*He?*"

"You know, the other father."

Stachowa grimaced. Her eyes blazed. "I've warned him plenty of times not to set foot in here. The tramp! The beggar! The no-good drunk! What did he want?"

"He said he'd come back later."

"And I'll have the broom ready to greet him with."

She went to the corner and got out the broom. Kasia closed her book.

"Don't do it, Mama."

"You feel sorry for him? After he ruined my life? He left me with a child in my belly and ran off to his whores. Who knocked out four of my teeth? He's a leech, a thief, a leper, a murderer. I don't want him in the house . . ."

"Mama!"

Stachowa stood leaning on the broom. She heard a mouse scratching and, after a while, steps approaching. She cocked her ears. Could it be Wacek? No, Wacek walked like a man, but this was like the creeping of a skunk about to strangle a chicken. She knew it was her first lover, coming to persuade her to give herself to him. Pushing him away a thousand times was not enough. He probably couldn't even get a whore, the wretch; probably had the clap too.

Antek, Kasia's father, opened the door. Seeing Stachowa armed with the broom, he stayed where he was. Short, large-boned, cross-eyed, with a broad nose sprinkled with warts, he wore a cap with a broken visor and a sleeveless sheepskin jacket.

Stachowa glared. "You here again? Haven't I warned you to stay away? Why do you hang on like the plague? Get out! Out! I'll scream for help! I'll call the police."

"Shut up! I'm not trying to kill you. I have a right to see my daughter."

"You haven't. A man who deserts his baby is no father. She's not your daughter."

"Yes, she is—mine and not that escaped convict's you sleep with: that nobody of a bearded young lord."

"Pig! Dog! Hyena! What are you raving about? May God in heaven punish you! May you drop dead on the spot!"

"Be still. Why is she in bed?"

"Because she has no shoes. Now crawl back where you came from!"

"There's something I have to tell you."

"Well, if you must—say it."

"No, it's a secret. Come into the hall."

"No! Sausage is not for dogs, ah no."

"So you won't come?"

"Never."

"And yet you loved me once."

"What used to be, used to be. Now get out!"

"Jadzia, don't be so mean."

"What should I do, kiss you? My enemy! You sucked my last drop of blood. What more do you want? I've nothing left for you. No love. No respect . . ."

Suddenly she burst into tears, her mouth twisting strangely. The kitten came forward from behind a box, staring with its green eyes, and began to mewl.

"Antek, go!"

He went, quietly closing the door behind him.

III

That night, Lucian did not return home after work, but stopped at a tavern on Kercelak Place. Having earned several additional groschen from an extra chore, he ordered a glass of vodka, a pork sausage, and a beer chaser. A single groschen remained, and tossing it in his palm, he sought answers to his fate in the way it fell. Would he, Lucian, die a natural or an unnatural death? The indication was unnatural. Would he be shot or hanged? The groschen seemed to deliberate for a moment, then landed on the side which he had designated "hanged." "Well, let them hang me," he laughed, and again spun the groschen on the table. He belched from the garlic in the sausage, and the beer and vodka began to seep through his head. He was not drunk but his brain seemed to be whirling. "I'll do it! I'll do it!" he mumbled to himself. "Every night I dream about it. It has to happen. What's the difference when?"

At Lucian's feet lay a bundle of wood, tied with rope, which he had brought from the factory. He now picked it up and walked out, carrying it on his shoulders. It would keep their room warm tonight. There was more smoke than light from the street lamps. Other laborers were also returning from their workshops and factories, with bundles of kindling wood, bags of potatoes. Woodchoppers were trudging along with axes and saws; peddlers with baskets of frozen apples, onions, radishes, pans of roasted beans. Streetwalkers loitered at gates and fences. A drunk stood near an unhitched wagon and vomited. A forsaken dog walked slowly along, sniffing at the mud. Madmen and beggars sat around the store stoops, unable to find lodgings in the poorhouses. The frost had let up, but the cold was penetrating. An icy wind blew in from the Vistula.

Stachowa lived on Leshno Street, on the other side of Iron Street, in a building set back behind a fence. Refuse littered the banks of snow. Lucian pushed open the gate and walked into the courtyard, passed the stable with horses and, kicking open the door of a dark hallway, stepped in.

He smelled kindling, rags, washing soda, and had to avoid falling over a washtub. Nothing disgusted him more than the filthy Jewish linen. He pulled open another door and saw Stachowa and Kasia by the light of a wick flickering in a container of oil. Stachowa stood in the middle of the room, her shawl over her head, apparently ready to go out. Kasia sat on her bench-bed.

"Late again," Stachowa said.

"Yes, late again," Lucian replied.

"Well, put down the wood."

He dropped it. "You going out?"

"I have to deliver some laundry. The groats are on the stove."

"Yes . . ."

"The liver is probably overdone."

"You have liver? That's good."

"I bought it because you like it."

"Well, thanks."

Stachowa wrapped the shawl closer about her. At the door she said loudly: "I'll be gone a couple of hours." Then Lucian heard her fumbling in the hall. What is she doing there? he asked himself, though he knew she wasn't doing anything but was only waiting to see if he would call her back. There was silence in the hall. She must be holding her breath. Finally he heard the door slam. Maybe she's still there? he thought.

Lately she had been behaving as if she read his mind. He walked over to the stove and lifted the lid of the pot. Ordinarily, he was fond of liver, but the sausage he had eaten at the tavern had spoiled his appetite.

"Well, Kasia, what are you doing?"

"Nothing."

"Did you memorize the poem?"

"Yes, I did."

"I'll listen to it soon."

Lucian ladled some groats and liver into a tin plate, walked past the table, and sat down near Kasia, balancing the plate on his lap. His appetite revived as soon as he began to eat.

"Want some, Kasia?"

"No."

"Why not?"

"Because it's all for you. I've eaten my share already."

"Have some more."

"No. It's all for you. You work and I lie in bed all day."

"Was anyone here today?"

"*He* was here, the other father."

"Ha."

"Mama chased him away."

"What did he want?"

"To tell a secret."

"Oh? Who else was here?"

"Only that old hag from across the yard, Lisakowa."

"What did she want?"

"Well, she has something bad to say about everybody. This one is stingy, that one is dirty. It's the women she talks about. She thinks I don't know what's going on but I do. When she leaves our house, she goes to someone else's and gossips about us. She comes, sniffs around, and says: 'It smells like liver.' Oh, how I hate her!"

"And whom do you love?"

"Only two people in the whole world. Mama and you. Sometimes I love her more and sometimes I love you more. A hundred times a day she'll say to me: 'You're worse off than an orphan.' Lisakowa comes in and Mama blurts out that I have no shoes, no this and that. Lisakowa says: 'Didn't you just buy her shoes for Christmas? She runs around too much and wears out the soles.' And she always says: 'Why don't you send her out to service? She'll be fed and clothed.'"

"One day I'll break every bone in her body."

"I wish you would."

"What will you give me if I do—a kiss?"

"A thousand kisses. But the police will get you."

"I wouldn't wait for the police. How about a game of tick-tack-toe?"

"Yes."

"First let me hear the poem. You must become an educated lady."

Kasia began to recite. Lucian stopped eating. He listened, holding his spoon in mid-air. How beautiful she was! How gloriously her hair cascaded over her shoulders! How round her brow, how bright her eyes, and what a fair skin! Marble. No—a thousand times more delicate than marble. What an odd shape her lips were. If only she were two or three years older—he thought—I would happily kill that Lisakowa for just one smile from Kasia.

"Well, do I know the poem?"

"Yes, you know it. And I love you. I love you terribly."

"I love you too."

"Remember when you were small how you used to say you would marry me?"

"I remember everything."

Lucian and Kasia began to play tick-tack-toe, writing on a board with a piece of chalk. Kasia grimaced and pouted because she lost every game. Lucian kept looking at her and asking himself if this could really be Antek's daughter. What a great stew the world was! God, the chef, stirred and out came wars, revolutions, migrations. Someday He would strain the whole mess through a sieve. What crazy ideas I get, thought Lucian. Well, it's now or never. He rose to his feet.

"Kasia, I want to tell you something."

"What?"

"I'm going away, Kasia."

"Where?"

"If it hadn't been for you, I would have gone long before. I'm talking to you now as if you were a grownup. I want you to understand."

"Yes . . ."

"I love you. You understand what that means, don't you?"

"I understand."

"I love you, even though you are still a child. But I've wasted too many years here already. Your mother is a good woman and she saved my life. But it's a debt that I can't repay. Since I've been here, I've been neither dead nor alive. Do you understand what I'm saying?"

"Yes."

"I can't tell your mother these things. I hate tears. I'm leaving tonight."

"Where are you going?"

"Abroad."

"Where's that?"

"To another country on the other side of the border."

"Do you have money?"

"Exactly one groschen—but this cross that I wear around my neck is valuable. Tell your mother that I will always think of her with affection. I'll write, and if I get any money, I'll send some. In two or three years I'll come back to marry you."

"Ah."

"Will you wait for me?"

"Yes."

"How long?"

"A hundred years."

"You won't have to wait that long. You're still just a child. What if you forget me?"

"I'll never forget you."

"Tell your mother I've gone but you don't know where. Wait three days, then tell her the truth. Now, do you know what to do?"

"Yes. Today is Tuesday. I'll tell her Friday."

"Yes, that's right. But don't mention my marrying you."

"I won't."

"Kasia, in a few years you'll be grown up—and I won't be so old then either. If they try to make you marry someone else, say no. Pray to God for me. That's all. Each night when you say your prayers, mention my name. Say: 'Father Who art in Heaven, have mercy on Thy son Lucian and his wandering soul.' If my letters should be delayed, don't lose heart. Have patience and faith. I wanted to buy you a present but I had no money. Here is my last groschen. Keep it to remember me by. Don't lose it."

"I'll always keep it."

"Hold on to your printer and study hard every day. If you get the opportunity to go to school, go. . . . Well, I'd better collect my rags now."

Lucian climbed the ladder to the gallery. From under the bed he drew a satchel with a copper lock and side pocket. This bag had been his constant companion all through his months of fighting during the Polish rebellion. For years it had lain under Stachowa's bed. He knelt and dusted it off with a rag, then opened it and took out a bronze-handled pistol and a cartridge case containing six bullets. Inanimate objects are so still, Lucian murmured, holding one of the bullets in his hand. A little thing like this lies around for a hundred years and finishes off someone whose grandfather wasn't even born when it was made. From a basket near the bed, Lucian collected a shirt, a suit of underwear, a woolen scarf, and a vest that his mother had knitted for him. The sum of my earthly possessions, as they say in books. The ceiling was too low for him to stand upright. Still on his knees, he backed his way to the ladder.

"Kasia, what are you doing?"

"Nothing. Just watching."

"Will you miss me?"

"Yes."

Lucian climbed down from the gallery. He surveyed the room sternly, as if suspicious that someone lay in ambush in one of the corners.

"What did I forget? No, nothing. Wait. I want another look at you under the light."

He picked up the improvised oil lamp and brought it close to Kasia's face. She was smiling in a frightened way. Seeing the plate of groats still on the blanket, Lucian removed it with his left hand and placed it on the floor.

"Your hand is shaking," Kasia said.

"Yes, a little."

Lucian gazed at the smoking flame. He thought a moment, then extinguished the lamp.

9 🏰

Helena and Miriam Lieba were skating on the manor pond one afternoon when suddenly a man emerged from among the trees. Young, with a round beard, he wore a sheepskin jacket, his cap was covered with snow, and he carried a satchel in one hand. Helena gripped Miriam Lieba's arm.

"Look!"

"Don't be afraid, girls," the intruder called, coming toward them. "Stand still and let me have a look at you. Obviously, you're Helena. But who is she?" And he nodded toward Miriam Lieba.

"The question is—who are you?" said Helena. But suddenly she knew. In the manor there was a portrait of her father as a young man—looking like this young man.

"You're Lucian. Is it possible?"

"You haven't yet told me who she is," Lucian said.

"My friend, Miriam Lieba—the daughter of the man who leases the manor."

"I'm sorry I startled you." Lucian turned to Miriam Lieba. "Helena was only a child when I left. Now she's a grown-up young woman. Beautiful, too. Don't either of you say a thing about my being here." His tone changed, and he ran his fingers around his neck. "If I'm found, I'll hang."

"Good God, it is you!" Helena exclaimed. "Yes, I remember you . . ." Helena, in her excitement, took hold of Miriam Lieba, and both girls lost their balance and sat down on the ice. Lucian, attempting to assist them, almost lost his own footing. But finally they were on their feet again. Lucian brushed off Miriam Lieba's jacket and dress, and she thanked him. Helena made a move as if to embrace Lucian, but then stopped.

"Yes, I remember you," she said again, in a solemn voice.

"Our mother?" Lucian asked.

"She's sick. Very sick."

"Yes, I know. There was an item in the newspaper about Father coming home. What's the matter with her?"

"Oh, weakness . . . her nerves . . . her heart . . ."

"And Felicia?"

"She's home."

"Well, thank God. But no one must suspect that I'm here. I came halfway on foot, not by the main road, but through the villages. An old peasant gave me a lift in his sled. What shall I do?"

"Come to the house."

"Won't I be seen going in?"

"No. It's safe. Father's in Jampol—he spends most of his time there. Wojciech sleeps all day—besides, he's drunk. Barbara is half blind. Magda keeps to the kitchen. Go straight to the third floor. No one ever goes up there. It's not heated, but . . ."

"When does Father come?"

"At night . . . sometimes, not even then."

"May I go in now? I must get some sleep."

"There's a bed up there. Wait, I'll go and see."

Helena started off without remembering that she still had her skates on, then sat down to take them off. Miriam Lieba hobbled to the edge of the pond, where she leaned on a mound of frozen snow. Her fingers were numb inside her gloves and she could hardly turn the skate screw. Lucian picked up his satchel.

"I was already written off as dead, eh?"

"Why didn't you let us know? Mother is sick because of you."

"I couldn't . . . couldn't. I still can't believe I'm here. I used to skate on this pond myself once. God, how far back all that is. It seems like a hundred years."

He turned to Miriam Lieba. "Who is your father?"

"His name is Calman Jacoby."

"Jacoby, eh? That means Jacob—Jacob's grandchildren. The Jacob who cheated Esau out of his birthright."

Miriam Lieba was silent.

"I studied once . . . studied. But I haven't opened a Bible for a long time. I don't know how long it is since I've been in a church. For men like me, life is finished. We've become isolated from everything. We live amidst gloom and despair."

"The Count will find his way."

"How? I am hounded like a beast. The police have posters out with my name on them. The Czar wants to exterminate us all, the last pockets of Polish resistance. I didn't want to leave Polish soil. But now I must go into exile."

Helena had taken her skates off. "I'll have a look. You wait here."

Going toward the house, she scanned the fields carefully on both sides, cocking her head like a huntress stalking her quarry.

"Have you known each other long?" Lucian asked Miriam Lieba.

"Only since summer. Countess Helena came to my sister's wedding."

"Did she? Things are changing then. Not so long ago, that would have been impossible. My father always felt sympathy for the Jews, but other landowners ridiculed them, even set their dogs on them. At balls, the court Jew was forced to disguise himself as a bear to entertain the guests. Now we're the victims. Where did you learn Polish?"

"From a teacher. From reading."

"You don't look like a Jewess."

"But I am one."

"Of course, but . . . I stand here and think that I'm dreaming. I tell myself I must be dead. I actually was dead, not in body but in spirit. Seeing familiar places revived me somewhat. Yet I know the sun will never shine again—not on us, not for me."

"The Count should not talk that way. The Count will still enjoy much happiness."

"Happiness? I? Well, thank you, it's been some time since I've heard the word. Where will this happiness come from?"

Miriam Lieba was unable to reply. Her throat had tightened and she was shuddering with cold. Looking toward the manor house, she saw Helena signaling to them and told Lucian. Lucian quickly extended his hand to Miriam Lieba and tipped his cap, revealing brown hair and a high forehead. "I hope we meet again," he said.

Confused, Miriam Lieba mumbled: "Yes, thank you."

11

In the evening Calman, home for supper, sat at the head of the table in a chair with a caned back. He dipped meat in horseradish, and crumbs from the bread he was eating scattered over his beard. To his right sat Mayer Joel, Zelda, Jochebed, and Miriam Lieba; to his left, Ezriel, Shaindel, and Tsipele. Jochebed's baby slept in its cradle. Calman had brought a naphtha lamp with a bronze base from Warsaw, and Miriam Lieba did not lift her gaze from it. She stared at the lamp, the burner, the chimney, the glass. A whitish light surrounded the flame and every corner of the room was illuminated. It was difficult to understand how they could ever have managed with tallow candles. Everyone else was already on the meat course, but Miriam Lieba still toyed with her noodles. She put a spoonful of them into her mouth and forgot to swallow them. She squinted at the lamp and it seemed to cast off golden rays. Mayer Joel and Ezriel were, as usual, embroiled in an argument. Mayer Joel was insisting that Egypt was in Asia, and Ezriel that it was in Africa. "How can it be in Africa," Mayer Joel pointed out, "when it's so near Palestine?" Ezriel jumped up to get the map, but Shaindel stopped him.

"What's the rush? Egypt won't get cold."

"I'm afraid that this time Mayer Joel is right," Calman interjected after some hesitation. "The black people live in Africa. Egypt is near the land of the Philistines—"

"Does Father-in-law want to see it in black and white?"

"Don't run. Finish your supper. You're always rushing, Ezriel. The night is long."

"Three continents meet at the land of Palestine: Asia, Africa, and Europe. The Sinai Peninsula—"

"Do you mean Mount Sinai, where the Torah was given?"

"The entire peninsula is called Sinai. The mountain is actually in the Sinai Desert."

"What's that you're saying, Mayer Joel?" Calman asked.

"Who cares about the lies of heretics? Everything is described in the Pentateuch."

"Not everything is in the Pentateuch," Ezriel contradicted. "Where is America mentioned in the Pentateuch? America was only discovered by Columbus."

"Everything is in the Torah! It mentions lands whose locations even the greatest scholars don't know. Where is Hodu or Cush? One sage claims that they are far off; another that they are near. Have you studied the *Gemara Megillah*?"

"Yes, I have. Hodu is India and Cush is Ethiopia. They're far enough away."

"Then, according to you, the Talmudist who claimed they are near was wrong?"

"The Talmudists did not know geography. In those days they had no knowledge of America or Australia. Those countries were discovered afterward. . . ."

"That means the heretics are wiser than the Torah!"

Mayer Joel slammed his fist on the table. The dishes rattled. The flame in the lamp leaped. Zelda had kept quiet but she sided with Mayer Joel. From beneath her bonnet trimmed with pearl beads, she gazed askance at Ezriel. Zelda was unable to eat the same cut of beef as the rest of the family. She was toothless. Faigel had baked a meatloaf for her mistress and Zelda swallowed small bits of it.

"Are you bickering again? I have asked you over and over to eat your meals in peace. Who ever heard of two young men quarreling so much? One says summer, the other winter. It's day for one, and night for the other. The children of some people kiss each other; here we have nothing but arguments. What's the difference where Egypt is? Just be decent Jews. People who write books try to turn everything upside down to make us forget God Almighty and listen to the Devil."

"Mother-in-law, this has nothing to do with God," Ezriel said.

"I don't know. I didn't go to school. But no good comes of such wrangling. Believe me, I know what I'm saying. Asia here, Asia there. Meanwhile you forget to be Jews. As long as I live, I want my sons-in-law—"

"Mama, you always stand up for him!" Shaindel interrupted, indicating Mayer Joel. "If he told you he'd seen a cow fly over the roof and lay brass eggs, you'd believe him!"

"Children, enough! No more battling at the table. Shaindel, don't be so insolent." Calman's voice became stern. "Mother is speaking to all of you. What she says also happens to be the truth. Today one book is popular, tomorrow another. What made Wallenberg become a convert? His father was a decent Jew, a teacher. It was worldly knowledge that started everything. Don't be angry, Ezriel. I don't want to embarrass you, God forbid. You are as dear to me as my own son. But I want you to follow in the footsteps of your father. What does he lack?"

"What does he have?"

"He will have salvation. He will come to the other world—may he live to be a hundred and twenty—with a sackful of Torah. He isn't, God forbid, starving in this world either. Nor are all heretics wallowing in gold. If I need a bookkeeper or clerk, there are ten for every job. There used to be too few. Now we have too many."

There was a sudden silence. They could hear the wick sucking up naphtha. Zelda glanced at Miriam Lieba, who sat with eyes closed, her head bent over her plate, her lips moving. She appeared pale and drawn.

"Miriam Lieba!"

The girl started and the spoon fell from her hand.

"Why do you sit like a dummy? Are you asleep? Why don't you eat?" said Zelda. "Just look at her! Thin as a straw. Have you got a pain, God forbid? Does something hurt?"

"No, Mama. Nothing hurts."

"She's dreaming of a knight on a white charger," Shaindel joked.

"What knight? What charger? Calman, look at your daughter's face. She looks like an invalid. Her mother-in-law-to-be is due any day: she'll take one look and run off to where the black pepper grows. I, myself, would fear such an apparition if I had a son to marry off."

Calman raised his brows. "Why are you so quiet, Miriam Lieba? Why don't you eat?"

"I'm eating, but I'm not hungry."

"You know your future mother-in-law is coming soon from Lublin to meet you. You'll have to fatten up a bit. I won't have Tsipele marry before you."

Everyone grew silent. Faigel brought in the applesauce and tea. Miriam Lieba stirred the food in her dish. Beneath her hair, her ears burned, although her face was white. A strange warmth overcame her. She was not consciously thinking, but her mind seemed full of thoughts. They pressed against her skull. Within her, words were being uttered, scenes enacted. She dared not even meet Tsipele's eyes. Miriam Lieba was generally shy with strangers, but this time she felt bashful in her own family. What's wrong with me? Am I getting sick? she wondered. She rose, went into the hall, and climbed the

stairs to her attic room. For a while she remained standing
in the dark; everything that had happened that afternoon re-
enacted itself vividly. Lucian appeared as if stepping out of
the frame of a painting. He looked at her, smiled, and said
something she did not hear. He was bathed in an ethereal light,
like the visions of saints described in books by Christian mys-
tics.

Why am I so happy? Miriam Lieba wondered. Only a moment ago I was in torment. Suddenly she knew: what she had
been awaiting for so many years was happening. Why hadn't
she realized it before? She wanted to laugh, to cry. God in
heaven, what would come of it? Miriam Lieba locked and
chained her door. She felt the same as she had on Passover
night after the Seder, when she had gone to bed after drinking
four cups of wine. Walking unsteadily to her bed, she lay
down, feeling as though an illness were coming on. Miriam
Lieba lay there for a long time, fully clothed, half asleep, in a
state of intoxication such as she had never known before. The
cold woke her. A midnight moon was shining upon the snow.
The trees facing her window seemed to her to be covered
with blossoms.

III

Miriam Lieba took the path to the lime quarries rather than
the one that led to the manor house. The sky was overcast.
Even the smoke from the lime kilns seemed heavy as clouds.
Snowflakes slowly began to fall. Miriam Lieba idled along,
stopping, looking around her. Yesterday she had made her
way without lingering. But today, as in her childhood, the
huge house with its balconies and cornices seemed enchanted.
In it there lived counts and countesses, proud as ever, despite
the recent changes. Surrounded by gold, silver, books, paintings, carriages, servants, they spoke French and played their
pianofortes. And behind one of those cornices, a warrior was
hiding from his enemies, disguised as a peasant, armed like a

knight—a living hero of Polish history. What was he doing at this moment? Was he still asleep? Or standing at the window, gazing out over the snow? Could he see her? Was he thinking of her? What foolishness! Why would he think of a Jewish girl? He could have any woman he wanted. No, it was madness! She mustn't think such things. She would probably marry some storekeeper from Lublin. . . . Miriam Lieba stopped to rub her hands with snow. The fields, sown with winter wheat, extended on both sides. How strange! She felt that what she was experiencing was something familiar that she had known for years, or been through in another existence— yet it was only yesterday that she had met Lucian. Even the name sounded as if she had always known it. Was it possible? She recalled that she used to etch "Lucian" on the frosted windowpanes with her fingernail. Had she once read about a Lucian, or dreamed of him? Or did she actually remember Lucian from her childhood? Could a child fall in love with an adult?

The snowfall thickened. It chilled Miriam Lieba's face, melting in the part of her hair, settling like an ornamental trim on her shoulders, sleeves, buttons, and the edges of her fur collar. She could no longer see the manor. Across the plowed fields, swirling snowdrifts seemed to jump like imps. From somewhere she heard a shot. Was there a hunter out in such a snowstorm, or had war begun? Miriam Lieba imagined that she heard the blaring of a trumpet. Someone was blowing the New Year ram's horn in the middle of winter. Miriam Lieba turned back. She was afraid the path home would be blocked by snow. There were wolves in the nearby forest. Perhaps it would be simpler if they tore her to bits. Then Lucian would remember forever the girl he had met one day, and who had been devoured by wolves the following morning.

As Miriam Lieba walked she hummed to herself:

> *"Fall, snow, fall*
> *Cover all,*

*My soul is lost
In ice and frost.*"

The verses in Polish described a soul's wish to be hidden in
snow, like a bear in its den, or a seed in the earth. Sleepless the
night before, she had been full of happy fantasies; but with
dawn her melancholy had returned. Perhaps she should remain
where she was. She would be covered by the snow, which
would form a mound over her icy grave. Summer? Perhaps
spring would never come again. Hadn't Ezriel said that one
day the entire globe would freeze over, all creatures die, the
oceans vanish, and winter never end? Perhaps the time had
come. Miriam Lieba stood for a long while. The whirling
wind spun the snow into sheets. Twin snowflakes chased each
other. One seemed to change its mind in mid-course and flew
away. How beautiful the world was, how vast, mysterious!

Miriam Lieba turned her face up and opened her mouth. A
snowflake fell on her tongue and melted against her palate.
She shivered. "It's a dream, a dream," she murmured. "Nothing will come of it. . . ." How odd that Shaindel was already
married, and even Tsipele was betrothed, while she, Miriam
Lieba, daydreamed.

IV

Calman had been gone since daybreak. Zelda had an attack of
stomach cramps. Getz, quickly hitching up the sleigh, drove
to Skarshew and returned with Dr. Lipinski, who relieved
Zelda's pain and prescribed some new medicine. Since he was
in the neighborhood, though the sun was already setting, he
drove on to the manor. After the snowfall, the temperature
had fallen and everything had frozen. The branches of the
trees resembled crystal menorahs. Candles were ignited in
them by the setting sun and then extinguished. The blue snow
sparkled with diamonds. Early stars twinkled in the sky. Somewhere, a dog bayed.

Miriam Lieba stepped outdoors to look toward the manor house. There, downstairs, the rooms would be lit, but upstairs everything would remain in darkness. Between there and here lay a secret known only to God and herself. Breaking the crust of the snow, she rolled a snowball and flung it as far as she could in the direction of the enchanted manor house. A crow, waking, began to caw.

Zelda stayed in bed. Calman and Mayer Joel did not return for supper. Ezriel was the only male present. Shaindel poured gravy over his groats, adding pieces of meat. In the household it was rumored that she was pregnant. Ezriel began telling the girls about the North Pole, where the aurora borealis shone in the sky. For six months of the year it was night; the temperature fell to ninety degrees below; alcohol and quicksilver froze; ice extended over hundreds of miles. At night explorers crawled into sleeping bags made of pelts. Tsipele was dumfounded. Ezriel knew everything!

"I would like to snuggle into one of those sleeping bags myself," Miriam Lieba remarked.

"All by yourself?" Ezriel joked.

Shaindel blushed. "Shame on you for saying such things!"

Miriam Lieba flushed also and her eyes seemed bluer. Uncomprehendingly, Tsipele laughed. Jochebed waddled in from the kitchen.

"What's all the commotion about? Mother is sick."

As soon as Ezriel had washed his hands and said the concluding grace, Miriam Lieba went up to her room. Everything was a vast mystery: the world, mankind, the North Pole, she herself. She seemed to be seething inside, elated one moment, depressed the next, burning hot and cold like the sinners in Gehenna. Ezriel's joke had aroused her. She was eighteen, an age at which her mother not only had been married but had already had children. Standing at her window in the pale evening, she examined the exotic plants that the frost had traced on her windowpanes: palms, cedars, desert shrubs that grew only in Israel—a mirage that must come from the Holy Land, she thought.

Having lit a candle, she threw herself down on her bed and opened a novel that Helena had lent her. The scene was Paris at dusk, and the Marquise, getting into her carriage, directed her coachman to drive to the park. The sunset shed a violet radiance on the Marquise's face and was reflected in the pearls that hung at her throat. The carriage halted. The Marquise stepped out and sauntered down a path. Suddenly her lover was there, rushing toward her and clasping her in his arms. Miriam Lieba's pupils grew large. That was love, that was life! Her lids closed and she imagined what Paris must be like: museums, theaters, towers, castles, brightly lit windows, boulevards jammed with carriages, the odor of flowers everywhere, music, dancing ladies, and champagne corks popping. "Your health, chérie." "Darling, I cannot live without you. Swear that you'll be mine!" "Later, later! Oh, my poor Jean." "Rest in my arms. Kiss me!"

Suddenly she herself was in Paris. She sat in a carriage and Lucian embraced her—simultaneously she was in a carriage, a boudoir, a salon. She was wearing an evening gown, and carried a fan. He wanted to kiss her, but she averted her face. "No, Lucian, I am promised to a storekeeper in Lublin."

Miriam Lieba opened her eyes. The flickering candle had burned low. She blew it out and returned to her dreams. She dozed, awoke, dozed again. She slept fitfully as if she had a fever. Lucian kept appearing before her in different guises, as a civilian, as a soldier in helmet and cape riding horseback, as a traveler on shipboard. They were eloping but there was an obstacle. The sea had been blockaded. An enemy armada approached. A courier had been dispatched. All conspired against her: her father, her mother, Jochebed, Shaindel. Ezriel had cut off his sidelocks and wore German clothes. He whispered in her ear, "Convert!"

She awoke, trembling. She was cold, and the moon was

shining on her. She shifted out of danger, as it was believed that moonlight on a sleeper caused seizures. She sat up, hugging her knees. Outside, it was as light as day. She was hungry, thirsty. She wanted Lucian. What if I went to him right now? she thought. I will run through the fields, tiptoe quietly up the stairs, open his door, and say, "Do with me as you will . . ."

It was daybreak before Miriam Lieba fell asleep. It had begun to snow heavily again. Toward midmorning, voices on the stairs woke her; someone began knocking on her door. She opened her eyes sleepily. The sun was shining and the snow glittered outside. The door opened and in walked Helena. Miriam Lieba stared at her in astonishment.

"Weren't you awake? I'm sorry, but I had to talk to someone . . . and you're the only one who knows . . . outside of Felicia, that is. My father didn't come home last night or the night before either. Mother is too ill to tell. Felicia is no use at all. And Lucian's very nervous. Why didn't you come yesterday? We thought you would. He's been asking about you . . . I thought you were an early riser."

Gradually, Miriam Lieba returned to her senses and began to stammer apologies. "It's a great honor to have you visit . . . but to find me in bed . . . and my clothes are strewn all over . . ."

"Who cares? Yesterday afternoon Lucian was in such a strange mood. Demanded vodka. Suddenly he wanted to rush back to Warsaw. Felicia gave him a necklace and some brooches, part of Mother's jewelry, but he must have money. He has to get across the border. The necklace can only be sold to one jeweler, Mr. Nosek, in Warsaw. But the trip is dangerous. Lucian is afraid to stay here. Someone is sure to find out. And Mother still doesn't know. It's all so strange. Do you suppose we could pawn the jewels with your father?"

"My father is in Warsaw."

"Oh. Perhaps your brother-in-law has money?"

"Ezriel? No."

"I thought Jews always had money on hand. But come, Lucian wants to talk to you. You must convince him to stay for a while. Maybe we can hide him somewhere else. He's afraid of a police search."

"God forbid!"

"Why don't you get up, get dressed—oh, you're bashful? All right, I'll wait downstairs. Don't take long."

"A minute. Thank you. Thank you a thousand times . . ."

Helena shut the door and went downstairs. Miriam Lieba sprang out of bed, poured water from the pitcher into the washbasin, then, after bolting her door, began to wash herself with the cold water. She was trembling with excitement. Wasn't this her fate: to be constantly enmeshed in difficulties and complications? Helena had come to get her. He had asked about her! He loved her!

v

On the way to the manor house, Helena explained the situation to Miriam Lieba. Lucian could not stay at home for long: he risked his life every moment he remained. The Count must be informed; but how could anyone at the manor be sent to the house of that Russian woman, Yevdotya? Besides, the Count had taken the small sleigh and there were no horses to pull the large one. Perhaps Miriam Lieba had someone she trusted who could be sent? Everything must be kept secret.

"Could we borrow a sleigh from the peasants?" asked Helena. "Or what about getting horses from the lime quarry?"

Miriam Lieba did not know what to reply. The quarry would be hard to get to in this storm; but even if they could get there, how could she command the men to lend them horses? The girls pushed slowly on. Helena had boots on, but Miriam Lieba had put on her high-heeled shoes. She had even neglected to wear warm stockings. The path had only been partially cleared. The snow came slanting down, its crystals stinging the girls' cheeks, covering their eyelashes, and encrusting their brows and foreheads. "I'll catch pneumonia," Miriam Lieba thought with a kind of reckless satisfaction. The storm half blinded her. Helena mumbled that the snow was getting into her boots. The girls had intended to take a path that circled around to the back of the manor house so that they could enter from the rear and go straight up a back staircase, but the path was impassable. When they reached the front door, the dogs rushed at Miriam Lieba, jumping and barking, and Helena barely managed to drive them away.

In the front entry, Helena jigged and stamped her feet, dislodging the snow, but Miriam Lieba was too cold. She felt half frozen as, moving stiffly, she trailed Helena up to the attic. She knew she was white as chalk. All the fussing and primping before the mirror had been wasted. The thistles had snagged her stockings and the bottom of her dress. Helena knocked and opened a door. Through a mist, Miriam Lieba saw a different Lucian. He appeared much handsomer and more graceful than he had the other day. He had shaved off his beard and was wearing a green jacket, riding breeches, and German-style leather boots with flexible tops. His hair was parted in the center. Books, a corked bottle, and a glass were on a table. The bed was unmade. Lucian stepped forward. He had been standing in the middle of the room, as if impatiently awaiting them.

"Come in, come in! You probably don't recognize me. I don't recognize myself."

"We nearly froze," Helena said. "Just look at us—half dead!"

"You'll warm up in here. I couldn't imagine where you were. Won't you ladies take your jackets off." He moved toward Miriam Lieba. "If the young lady will permit me? So! Perhaps you'd care for a drink? It's cherry wine, a ladies' drink. That's all I could get . . . But the young lady is completely frozen."

"The wind . . ."

"Perhaps you'd like something to eat?"

"Is she allowed to eat? We don't have anything kosher," Helena interrupted.

"What? Oh . . . kosher, yes. Warsaw is full of Jews. But the lieutenant in our company ate pork, even though he was Jewish. Won't the young lady have a seat? Here, on this chair. May I remove your gloves?"

"Yes—be a cavalier," Helena said. "Where is Felicia? I'll go get something. You are allowed to drink milk, aren't you?"

Miriam Lieba made no reply. Helena went out, shutting the door behind her. Lucian leaned over Miriam Lieba and pulled off her gloves.

"The young lady is frozen. But completely. What cold little hands! Jesus and Mary!"

He held Miriam Lieba's hands in his own for a time, stroked and warmed them. Looming over her, he smelled of cherry wine and of something else—masculine and foreign. Miriam Lieba sat there, knowing that if she had not been so cold, she would have died of shame. Her dress was sodden, her stockings wet through. A puddle was forming beneath her on the floor.

"The young lady should really have a drink. Cherry wine is not forbidden." Lucian poured half a glassful for her and handed it to her. She accepted it, and lifting it with stiff fingers, took a sip, not knowing whether it was kosher or not. She wanted to say something but was unable to speak.

"The young lady should take off her shoes!"

"No, no." Miriam Lieba drew in her feet.

"Ah, bashful! Campaigning in the forests, we had to forget about shame. In the beginning it wasn't pleasant, but one grew accustomed to it . . ."

"Perhaps we should put something on the floor . . . I'm dripping . . ."

"That doesn't matter. What is snow? Water. I expected you to come yesterday. I am in a strange predicament here: I can't stay and I can't leave. I need money. And I want at least to show myself to my parents. I've decided to cross the border—I don't know exactly where, though I've been told one can steal across the frontier in the village of Ojcow. But where is Ojcow? There isn't a map in the whole house."

"My brother-in-law has maps."

"Local maps? I'll have to walk from village to village. It's too dangerous to go directly to the border, or to travel by stagecoach. The drivers themselves inform for the police. Drink some more: you're terribly pale."

"Thank you."

"My mother saved all my clothes. Only the shoes pinch a little. I've shaved off my beard and I'm a country bumpkin again. It's odd how a beard gives one's face a more spiritual expression. Do you know what a beauty you are?"

Miriam Lieba lowered her eyes.

"I do hope the young lady will forgive me. I've lost my manners, grown completely coarse. My father, I hear, has let himself go too. All of us who went through that terrible campaign are disoriented. Some of us have taken to the bottle, others to mysticism. I drink, but I don't get drunk. Everyone knew we were doomed. We were led like sheep to the slaughter, offered up as a sacrifice. Some races enjoy bleeding, and with the Poles it is a sort of passion. We were beaten and we begged for more . . . Our leaders simply led us into ambushes. My one desire is to forget it all. In Warsaw I had already forgotten, but here it all comes back again. Why do you look so sad? You must have a noble soul . . ."

"The Count must not laugh at me."

"I'm not laughing at you. I mean it seriously. I've hit bottom and now it seems to me as if I'm in the clouds. I drank a little to give me courage. . . . Do you have a young man yet?"

"No."

"What will become of you here in Jampol? May I tell you something?"

"Yes."

"I prayed to God—and when I saw you, I knew that He'd heard my prayers. Do you understand?"

"Yes."

"I can scarcely believe it myself. . . ."

Lucian made a move as if to come closer. Helena opened the door, carrying a pitcher, and looked at them laughingly. But then her face changed.

"Felicia's sick too."

10 🏛

1

On Purim, the Book of Esther was read aloud. Tsipele, although already betrothed, rattled a noisemaker, cursing Haman, the villain. Shaindel helped Faigel bake poppy-seed cakes, butter cookies, and a saffron loaf braided top and bottom, which was then sliced lengthwise. Faigel also cooked sweet and sour fish. Zelda, convalescent but still weak, was watched over carefully by Jochebed. Ezriel busied himself making spears, swords, helmets, and masks out of cardboard and colored paper; for the beards, he used flax. Before dinner, the young people dressed themselves in their costumes. Mayer Joel played Ahasuerus, Ezriel was Vajezatha, Getz was Haman, Shaindel was Vashti, and Tsipele was Queen Esther, a role originally assigned to Miriam Lieba. But Miriam Lieba refused to participate, and stood apart. Her gaze fell on the two thick candles burning in the twin silver candlesticks, passed in turn to the naphtha lamp shining in the corner, then to the many Purim presents Calman had received from his employees—oranges, holiday loaves, poppy-seed cakes, gingerbread, bottles of wine and mead—and finally reached the window. Outside, a fiery band of color glowed in the sky, the last vestige of the sunset and the first herald of spring.

This Purim the weather was exceptionally mild. A warm, fragrant breeze blew in through the open window. The fields were soggy, the streams already brimming with the melting snows. Miriam Lieba knew that Ezriel was annoyed because she wasn't watching the play. But even if she did look, she wouldn't understand a thing. Her mind was in a turmoil. Had only six weeks passed? Everything was incredible, and there was no one she could talk to. A month ago Helena, without a word, had gone off to her aunt's house in Zamosc. In the week that Lucian had been in hiding at the manor, Miriam Lieba had seen him only twice more. Then he had gone, leaving her with a kiss on her lips and a promise to write. God, how wildly he had behaved, and what fantastic things he had said. How quickly his plans and moods had changed. When he left, he had intended to cross the Prussian border, but Helena had received a message that he had gone back to Warsaw. And he had behaved very strangely to his parents. Two days before his departure, in the evening, he had gone into Jampol on foot, broken into the house of that Russian Yevdotya, quarreled with his father, and even drawn a pistol. The following evening he had walked into his mother's bedroom without warning. The Countess had managed to stay calm, but the old nurse Barbara had screamed and wailed until Helena and Felicia had dragged her out. Lucian had spent the night in his mother's room, and had left the manor at dawn. Two weeks later, Helena had left for Zamosc. He had not written to Miriam Lieba.

Lucian and Helena had departed, but Mrs. Daiches of Lublin, Miriam Lieba's prospective mother-in-law, had arrived. She had taken one look at Miriam Lieba and sung out: "Yes, you will be my daughter-in-law."

How swiftly the sky was changing now: the reds and purples turned to violet, then the violet faded to a soft gray. The moon floated from behind a group of clouds that resembled a flock of goats. The stars burned like lanterns in mid-air. Mayer Joel had taken off his crown and false beard and laid his golden scepter on the sideboard. Ezriel wanted to continue the performance, but Zelda complained that this nonsense had been going on long enough. Miriam Lieba closed her eyes—not until shards were laid on them would she forget this winter, or this particular Purim feast. Would life bring her any happiness? Would she ever love anyone but Lucian? Was it possible that some day she would be a wife, a mother, even a grandmother? God forbid. She didn't want to live that long. Her sort of person died young. This might be her last Purim. She thought of Lucian's words: "If all else fails, one can always put a bullet through one's brain."

"Miriam Lieba!"

She started. Her mother was calling her. All the others had gone in to the supper table.

"What are you thinking about? Horses have big heads—let them do the thinking."

"Miriam Lieba is afraid the moon will fall," Mayer Joel said banteringly.

"Dreaming of her husband-to-be," Shaindel guessed.

Suddenly, Tsipele burst out laughing.

"What is it, Tsipele?" Calman asked.

"Papa, is it true Lekish the Fool has a gold watch?"

The table shook from the laughter and stamping of feet at Tsipele's odd question. Even Miriam Lieba smiled.

"What made you think of that?"

"Ezriel said so."

"Why do you fill her head with such nonsense?" Calman asked. "She's already betrothed."

"I don't know what she is prattling about. She must have dreamed it."

"He did say it."

"Well, enough," said Calman. "Just because it's Purim we needn't make fools of ourselves. In Shebreshin there was once a tailor who believed that on Purim everyone was so busy feasting that no one remembered King David's psalms. And so each year he went to the synagogue alone and mournfully recited the whole Book of Psalms. There was a time when Jews remembered God."

"Jews always remember God," said Ezriel, "but God forgets the Jews."

"Fie, don't say such things!" Calman said, placing his fist on the table. "If God hadn't watched over the Jews, the Hamans would have annihilated us long ago."

Zelda grumbled under her breath against this young man who had trimmed his sidelocks and was corrupting the children. She wanted to chastise him but restrained herself in view of the holiday. Also Shaindel—luck be with her—was pregnant, and if anyone dared say anything against the apple of her eye she would flare up immediately.

Miriam Lieba got up to get a glass of water.

"Are we ready for the grace?" asked Calman.

"Yes, Father-in-law," responded Mayer Joel.

"Then suppose you begin."

"My lords, let us say grace. Blessed be the name of God henceforth and forever . . ."

Calman narrowed his eyes, nodding his agreement. God had been good to him. He had married off two of his daughters. Tsipele was betrothed. Miriam Lieba's prospective in-laws were coming next month for the betrothal ceremony. Ah, he had had his troubles, but he had prospered and with God's help would continue to do so. Calman lifted his hands, and rolled his eyes heavenward. Mayer Joel intoned the words: "Lord our God, oh, make us not dependent on gifts and loans of men but rather on Thy full, open, holy and generous hand."

Mayer Joel's thoughts strayed as he recited the prayer. He had decided to buy the mill in Jampol. Soon he would build a house for himself there. The one drawback in becoming a businessman was that he would have less time for study and for Hassidism. He was already anticipating Pentecost, when he would go to Marshinov. Now that Jochanan was Tsipele's intended groom, he, Mayer Joel, would be received as a member of the rabbi's family. . . .

Ezriel was thinking about Miriam Lieba and kept stealing

glances at her. Something had happened to the girl, she was
going through some sort of crisis. She seemed to hear nothing
that was said to her, constantly gazed into the distance, and
was growing thinner, paler, more distracted every day. Had
she fallen in love? But with whom? What could be bothering
her? Ezriel had tried to find out, but she wouldn't be questioned. Sometimes she herself came to the room he had taken
for himself in the attic—knocking before she entered, in the
big-city manner. But as soon as she began to talk, she turned
red, lost her tongue; her lips trembled, her eyes filled with
tears, and she was unable to finish a sentence. If he questioned
her, she would run out—embarrassed or insulted, he never
knew which. Had she fallen in love with him? From reading
Slowacki and other poets, Ezriel knew that love obeys no
laws. The writers of the Torah completely ignored human
emotion, man's nervous system. He himself had already deceived Shaindel in his thoughts. Shaindel was always interrupting him in his studies, coming to show him what she was embroidering, or to ask his advice on household matters. She just
wanted to be near him. Calman demanded that he supervise
the account books. And Mayer Joel came to discuss Hassidism, even though he reproached him at every opportunity
with being anti-Hassid. Ezriel was making some progress in his
studies, but not enough. He had set up a timetable, using the
books Wallenberg had given him, to teach himself algebra,
Latin, Greek, history, physics. But he never quite managed to
keep to his schedule. He was attacked by such passions and
fantasies that if he had told anyone about them, he surely
would have been considered a criminal or a madman. It
seemed that the brain could be both sane and insane at the
same time. Ezriel shook his head and murmured:

"*O Fear the Lord, ye His holy ones.*
For there is no want to them that fear Him.
Young lions do lack and suffer hunger:
But they that seek the Lord shall not want any good."

11

An hour after the celebration was over, Miriam Lieba went outside. She stood beside the house, staring up at the moon. Ezriel had remarked that in exactly four weeks it would be the first night of Passover. The wind blowing from the fields was both acrid and balmy. Aimlessly, Miriam Lieba strolled down a path widened by the comings and goings of the family.

Suddenly a figure stood beside her as if risen from the ground. She recoiled and then recognized Lucian. He seemed tall and unfamiliar, dressed in a fur jacket, plush cap, and high fitted boots. His bony fingers caught her by the wrist. She was so taken aback that she forgot she might be seen from the house.

"Miriam," he said, calmly and firmly. "You must come away with me."

"Where?" Miriam Lieba felt her whole body trembling.

"Out of this God-forsaken country. I have money and a passport too."

"But . . . Lucian . . ." She could not control her jaw and her teeth began chattering. "Mother . . ."

"Yes or no. You have to answer me."

"Where have you been?" Miriam Lieba raised her eyes. Fear and pleading were in her voice. He had accosted her like a highwayman.

"I've been in Warsaw. I sold the jewelry. We'll go to Lemberg, and then on to Paris. That's where we'll be married."

Miriam Lieba looked around, fearful that someone might have come out of the house.

"Have you told your parents?"

"I've told no one."

"I must change my clothes," she said, without quite knowing what she meant. Lucian let go of her wrist. He was taller than she and was standing on higher ground. Her throat tightened; her scalp prickled. Only once before had she felt such a sensation when, as a child, she'd been playing hide-and-seek with her shadow on the wall and the shadow had come down and boxed her ears. Lucian took a few steps backward and she realized that he must have been waiting, concealed by the willow near the barn. She moved toward the gate, scarcely able to keep from screaming. She entered the dark hall and began to climb the stairs, halting after each step. Fiery specks appeared before her eyes. Her ears rang. She was sure she was going to faint. She heard Jochebed's baby crying, and Jochebed soothing him. Shaindel and Ezriel were in their bedroom, apparently having an argument but keeping their voices muffled. It wasn't possible that she could leave home and all of them. It will certainly kill Mother, she thought, and Father, too. She reached the door to her room and stood before it. No, I won't go, she said to herself. A rebelliousness seized her and a kind of hatred for Lucian, for whom only an hour before she had been longing.

In the dark she could not find the doorknob, and groped for it blindly. Her room was bathed in moonlight. In the middle of the bed lay a sheet of paper on which, that afternoon, she had written a love poem for Lucian, inspired by what had seemed to her unbearable yearning. How could that be? she wondered. I was almost dying of love. Suddenly she remembered the woman from Lublin who had said, "You will be my daughter-in-law." "No, I will not," Miriam Lieba announced defiantly. "They won't haul me off to market and sell me like a cow!"

For a moment she ceased thinking and stood by the window staring out at the night, the snow, and the moon. "He won't drag me off by force. Oh, I'm such a coward." The life that she would lead if she stayed flashed before her eyes. She saw her future the way a person who is drowning is said to see the past. She would marry the young man who had bribed his way out of military service. The stocky woman with the crease in her brow would be her mother-in-law. They'd shave her head, fit her with a wig, insist that she attend the ritual bath. She'd bear children, wrangle with her mother-in-law, grow old before her time. The life of the Jews was narrow and stagnant. Her mother had had nothing. Jochebed had nothing. The world outside was huge, brilliant. If she went, she would become a countess and have Lucian; she would reside in Paris among its rich boulevards and amorous women. Her mother would die in any case. The doctor no longer held out any hope for her recovery. If she did not go with Lucian now, Miriam Lieba knew that she would always regret it.

But what should she do? Why hadn't he written her even a line in six weeks? How could she trust him? Perhaps it wasn't Lucian at all, but a demon in his shape. She glanced toward her door. Should she bolt it? Should she scream for help? No, she would go down and talk to him. Not now, but when everyone had gone to sleep. Gazing out of the window, Miriam Lieba was overcome with astonishment at her strange destiny, at how swiftly she had fallen in love with Lucian, and Lucian with her. Why must it be me? I'll have to convert. . . . Suddenly she thought of the night of Yom Kippur and remembered a story she had heard of a Jewish girl who had eloped with a Christian youth on the eve of the Day of Atonement. Now on Purim she was about to do the same. . . . The fear that had temporarily receded seized her again. She would lose everything: father, mother, Shaindel, Ezriel, Tsipele . . . she would have to bow down to idols. She, Miriam Lieba?

"No, no. I would rather die," she murmured. She went to her door and chained it, then moved a bench against it. She opened her closet and leaned into its musty darkness. Perhaps it was all a hallucination. Maybe I'm going mad, like Uncle Chaim Yoneh, who hanged himself with his belt. Miriam Lieba stretched out her hand and touched a dress. Then she went to her bed and sat down. Her heart was pounding. She felt nauseous. "I'm going to faint," she mumbled. She fell across the bed, awake, yet as if in a dream. Thoughts came to her; her lips opened and whispered strange words; she saw faces, figures, eyes. Through it all, she knew that Lucian was waiting for her below and that she must come to a decision.

She dozed and dreamed. In her dream, the family was still living in The Sands and it was the Sabbath. Her father was snoring after the holiday meal, her mother was catnapping, Jochebed and Shaindel had gone for a walk, Tsipele was asleep in her cradle. She, Miriam Lieba, had been left with no one to play with.

"Mama, I want to play."

"What do you want to play?"

"I want to play with the shards."

"No, that's not allowed on the Sabbath."

"Well, what can I do?"

"Rock the baby."

"She's already asleep."

"She's apt to wake up. Rock her some more."

"May I write with my chalk?"

"Write with chalk? You shikse!"

"I want to play school."

"Not on the Sabbath."

"I want to go out."

"The door is locked."

"Mama."

"I'll tear your hair out if you don't let me sleep, you little devil. I'll teach you." As her mother leaped from bed, her wig slipped off, revealing her small head with its unevenly shorn scalp. "Calman, where's the cat-o'-nine-tails? I'll teach her. I'll whip her."

Miriam Lieba broke out of her dream. He's freezing out there in the cold, she thought. It seemed to her that she had been sleeping for hours. There was a midnight quiet in the house. Her body felt stiff. She limped to the closet, took out a woolen dress and her fur jacket. Shoes too, she thought, taking off her slippers. And I had better take my shawl. She searched in the dresser for warm underclothes. What else? A kerchief for her head. Her mother had given her a bracelet for Shaindel's wedding. There it was. She had on her earrings.

Could she really be doing what she was doing? Wasn't it all an illusion? Her fear had evaporated, and she had begun to feel almost reckless. "Yes, I'll go away with him. I'll convert—": the mocking voice seemed to come from deep within her, as if it had been lying in wait in some demonic spiderweb. She moved the bench, opened her door carefully to keep it from squeaking, and started downstairs on tiptoe. "They're asleep, they're asleep"—laughter choked in her throat—"I'm as quiet as a burglar. Anyway, he's gone by now . . ." Someone had chained the front door. Miriam Lieba undid the chain, lowering it slowly to avoid making a sound. She opened the door and was slapped by a cold night wind. She was fully awake now, wild, joyous. Suddenly she saw him. He began to run toward her and she placed her finger to her lips.

III

At daybreak someone opened the door of Calman's bedroom. Can it be the wind, he wondered, only half waking. Zelda slept on, undisturbed.

"Papa, papa . . ." He recognized Shaindel's voice. She approached, saying, "Papa, come out. Don't wake Mother."

He got out of bed quietly, put on a bathrobe and slippers, and went into the hall. Shaindel stood shivering in the darkness.

"Papa, Miriam Lieba isn't here," she whispered.

Calman tasted a bitterness in his mouth.

"Where is she?"

"I don't know. The front door is open. She isn't in her bed."

Calman was momentarily silent.

"Did you look in the outhouse?"

"No."

He promptly headed for the privy, located behind the house near the pit where the refuse was dumped. He slipped in the mud, bumped against the shaft of a wagon. Miriam Lieba was not in either of the compartments. Calman turned back. He was wearing only his skullcap, bathrobe, and wet slippers, and the cold cut through him. The wind fluttered his beard. He walked with the measured step of one who knows that he won't find what he is searching for. Shaindel was waiting at the threshold.

"She isn't there?"

"No."

"Papa, God forbid, you'll catch a cold."

"Come, let's take another look upstairs."

Calman and Shaindel ascended the stairs. Miriam Lieba's door stood ajar. Night still clung to the room, but the sunrise had already begun to touch it. The closet stood open, the drawers were pulled out. On the floor lay a jacket and a pair of slippers. As Calman and Shaindel searched, their faces acquired a purple tint; Calman's beard seemed bloodied; a red stain appeared on Shaindel's head-kerchief. On the table lay a sheet of paper. Shaindel tried to read it, but in the twilight the letters were indistinguishable. One could not even say whether they were Yiddish or Polish. Calman closed the door.

"She has run away," he said.

"I'm afraid so."

A verse from the Scriptures came to his mind, but he could not recall the exact words. He had the quotation on the tip of his tongue. His legs almost buckled under him and he sat down on Miriam Lieba's bed. Suddenly he remembered: "The Lord hath given, and the Lord hath taken away."

TWO

II 🏛

I

Two years passed. Jochanan married Tsipele at a sumptuous wedding that cost Calman a fortune. After the seven nuptial days, the couple went to live at the court of the Marshinov rabbi. Temerel could not exist without her son. Besides, Calman's house was soon left without a mistress, for three weeks after Tsipele's wedding, Zelda died. She was buried in the Jampol cemetery, and the engraver was ordered to inscribe a tombstone for her. Jochebed and Mayer Joel moved to a house of their own. Now that Mayer Joel had become the proprietor of the Jampol flour mill, he maintained two residences, one in town and one at the mill.

Only one daughter, Shaindel, lived at home with Calman. Shaindel had borne a son, named Uri Joseph after his great-grandfather the scribe. The baby had already cut his teeth and begun to talk. But even Shaindel did not bring Calman contentment. Ezriel refused to accept the board that had been offered him and had gone off to Warsaw to study. Calman's reproofs and pleas were in vain, and only after much insistence on his father-in-law's part did Ezriel promise that he would not shave his beard, would conduct himself as a proper Jew, and spend all the holidays and his summer vacation in Jampol. In return, Calman sent him eight rubles a week.

After the completion of the railroad, Calman's lumber business declined. He was forced to discharge many of his employees, and they became his enemies. A competitor opened a new shop near Calman's general store, and a price war followed. Since Calman could not be everywhere at once, he had to hire a manager. This raised his overhead, and his competitor, who worked alone, could undersell him. Calman had long since abandoned the tavern. Only the manor and the lime quarries remained. With each passing year, the liberated peasants demanded higher wages for their labor in the fields, regardless of the two years' drought that had caused Calman heavy losses. Nor was there any safeguard against theft. Each day incidents occurred; the peasants drove their cattle over Calman's pasture and felled the best trees in the manor's forest. The same peasants who only a few years before had felt the lash and hastened to kiss the hands of every squire, bailiff, and overseer were now bloated with arrogance and ranted against the Jews. In addition, the renewal time for Calman's lease was near and he knew that the rent the duke would ask would be so exorbitant that he would be unable to pay it. Those who envied Calman had maligned him to the duke and spread rumors that Calman had embezzled amounts ten times the value of the entire manor.

The lime quarries, thank God, were still profitable, but what good would the quarries be if Calman no longer had the use of the strip of land on which the railway spur lay? When he had built the private line, Calman had leased the strip from the duke for the same period as the estate. Now the duke was threatening to deprive Calman of his right of way, thus isolating the quarries.

In the past, Calman had enjoyed untroubled sleep; only Zelda, may she rest in peace, had kept him awake. Now Zelda's bed was always made and Calman, alone in the room, longed for the days when she had nagged him. He would fall asleep and waken, his thoughts giving him no rest. Miriam Lieba, may her memory be blotted out, was an apostate. All the facts had reached Calman: she had yoked herself to that

Lucian, the Count's rascal, who was thought to have perished in the insurrection (if only he had!). She not only wandered about with him but already had a child. How Calman had endured this blow he would never understand. Each time he thought of the disgrace, his eyes flooded with tears. What good was his wealth if every lout could sneer at him as "Lucian's father-in-law!"

Calman no longer led the noon services at the synagogue on the Day of Atonement. He had withdrawn voluntarily, and the Jampol Jews had not protested. However, since Calman still controlled the manor, his enemies' wrath fell upon the Rabbi of Jampol, Reb Menachem Mendel, Shaindel's father-in-law. Influential citizens complained that the rabbi was responsible for his son Ezriel's straying from the path of righteousness— that this young man exerted a bad influence on the common people, that he came home for the holidays with forbidden books and poisoned the children's minds. They also claimed that the rabbi's daughter, Mirale, had not conducted herself properly. Engaged to marry a yeshiva student from Skarshew, a man named Jonah, she had returned the engagement contract. Jonah's relatives in Jampol had broken the rabbi's windowpanes. They had hammered nails into his seat in the house of prayer so that his clothes would be torn. Even the almshouse paupers whom Calman supplied with firewood, beets, and potatoes agitated against the rabbi and against Calman himself.

In Marshinov, the old rabbi was ill again. Reb Shimmon, his first-born, harangued Jochanan and urged him either to divorce Tsipele, the sister of a convert, or to leave the court altogether. Temerel, Tsipele's mother-in-law, sent Calman lengthy messages written in a shaky hand and stained with tears, bewailing the situation.

Calman tossed in his bed. What justice was there? Jews, who wouldn't for all the money in the world pluck a blade of grass on the Sabbath or eat an egg with a bloodspot, heaped shame upon a rabbi, a devout Jew, a saint. Calman's competitors stopped at nothing, they dampened his sacks of flour and denounced him to the tax collector and the commissary of police. Besides, a new form of fraud had cropped up among the merchants. They would declare bankruptcy, then make a settlement. To safeguard themselves, the Lodz manufacturers raised their prices in order to be assured of a profit regardless of such bankruptcies.

Calman sighed. He heard his grandson, Shaindel's Uri-Joseph-Yosele, awake and cry. Burek, the dog, barked. The cows in the stall rubbed their horns against the door. The spring was a warm one, and after two years of drought there were signs that the coming harvest would be fruitful. The winter crops had sprouted early, rain and sunshine had been plentiful: the life of the soil was as unpredictable as the life of man. Scarcity followed plenty. When the earth seemed to have grown barren, the juices of life flowed through her again and she blossomed once more. Who could tell? Perhaps God would still grant Calman some comfort. He knew that he could not remain without a wife for very long. Sooner or later he would have to remarry. He had had only daughters with Zelda, but now that Miriam Lieba had committed such a deed, Calman more than ever longed for a son to perpetuate his name.

11

It was decided in St. Petersburg to station several infantry regiments in Jampol, and barracks had to be built to quarter the troops. It was taken for granted that Calman would not only supply the lumber for the buildings but undertake their construction. Yet, when the bids were opened, Calman's bid, for the first time in his career, was not the lowest. The contract was awarded to a builder from Polish Lithuania by the name of Daniel Kaminer. The soldiers also had to be supplied with flour, beef, and groats, cloth for their greatcoats, and leather for their boots. The enterprise was vast, and even after the payment of various bribes and pay-offs, it meant doubling one's investment. Nevertheless, Calman was not too distressed that this contract had slipped through his fingers. He was not anxious to have further dealings with the authorities. Daniel Kaminer had moved to Jampol from Lomza; he lived in The Sands among the Gentiles. He was a short, thin man, with a pock-marked face and a trimmed beard the color of pepper. His teeth were blackish, his nose red and covered with pimples. Kaminer was fond of vodka and spoke Russian like a native. Apparently he had once studied the Torah, for he was constantly citing quotations from the Scriptures and the Talmud to add point to his crude jokes. He wore a frock coat, a stiff collar, and a velvet waistcoat across which dangled a chain of five-ruble gold pieces. On his head he wore a cap with a leather visor.

Kaminer was a widower and had brought with him to Jampol his twenty-seven-year-old daughter, Clara, a widow, whose husband had died of consumption. Clara had studied at a Russian school, spoke Russian and Polish fluently, and hardly ever spoke Yiddish. She was of medium build, dark, with black burning eyes, sensuous lips, a high bosom, and a small waist. There was a beauty mark on her left cheek; she walked boldly, her head uncovered. Clara played the piano, was clever at cards, rode in a phaeton like a Russian landowner, and promptly became friends with David Sorkess and Morris Shalit, who came fron Vilna. Both men had worked for Calman. Her circle also included Sorkess's and Shalit's wives, Sonya and Tamara respectively; Ignace Herman, a bachelor; Grain, the apothecary; and Itka, Grain's wife, who had been nicknamed Grainicha. Evenings, Clara liked to entertain, serving tea from a samovar while she and her guests played poker or whist. Itka and the other women reciprocated by inviting Clara and her father to their homes, and for a while the gossip was that Ignace Herman had fallen in love with her and that they would get married. Clara herself scotched that rumor by declaring that she would not think of marrying a man who had remained a bachelor until he was well over thirty and barely made a living as a bookkeeper.

Although the two men were competitors, Kaminer depended on Calman, since he could obtain lumber, grain, potatoes, cabbage, beets, cattle, and lime at rock-bottom prices only from Calman. Furthermore, Mayer Joel owned the watermill. Kaminer invited Calman to dinner, but Calman was reluctant to go. He knew that Kaminer employed a Jewess in the kitchen, but one couldn't be sure that such people observed the dietary laws. Instead, Calman said he would come after dinner. Kaminer talked like a heretic, though he did have a mezuzah nailed to the doorpost. He lived like a lord: tapestries on the walls of his house; lamps, divans, and paintings everywhere. The maid had been late with her preparations and dinner hadn't yet been served when Calman arrived. The maid, a Jampol divorcee, was summoned and swore solemnly that she had not deviated in the slightest from the dietary laws. She had personally seen to it that the stove and utensils had been made kosher. Though Calman had already eaten, the odors of borscht and roasting meat that came from the kitchen made him hungry again. Clara did not come in until after Calman had arrived. Passover had ended; it was a rainy day. Clara burst in wearing a silk cape, elbow-length gloves, and a flowered hat. She carried a bouquet of flowers that she had picked. She smelled of perfume. Removing her glove, she extended a pale hand to the guest. Though Calman was not used to shaking a woman's hand, particularly that of a Jewess, he forgot himself. Clara smiled, flashing her teeth, and poured him a glass of brandy. As she chatted with Calman, her pet dog nipped at her ankles. Daniel Kaminer gulped down his drink, grimaced, and wiped his mustache. A few minutes later he left the room. The two were alone together.

"Do make yourself at home," Clara said. "I expect you'll be a frequent visitor here."

"I'm a busy man."

"Nevertheless, you'll find time to come." Clara winked and

laughed. She mentioned how clever and attractive Shaindel was; in St. Petersburg, a woman like that would be the toast of the town. Calman asked her if she'd ever been to St. Petersburg and she replied that she had a cousin there with whom she had roomed at boarding school and who was now the wife of a doctor. Clara introduced Russian expressions into her Yiddish, let out peals of laughter, leaned close to Calman, and even took the lapels of his coat in her hands.

Dinner was a banquet. Clara herself ladled out soup for Calman from the tureen. She helped him to all sorts of vegetables. It irked her to see him eat so little. "That's not enough food for a man," she complained.

When dinner was over, Calman, who had never seen a Jewish woman smoke before, was amazed to see her light a cigarette. She offered him one, and forced him to light it with hers. As he did so, she warned: "Be careful that your beard doesn't catch fire."

Finally the men retired to the study to discuss business. Kaminer did not bargain over prices. He insisted instead that Calman falsify the accounts he presented to the quartermaster.

"That's absolutely out of the question," Calman said.

"It's true, then, you really are simple-minded. There's no one who doesn't steal from the Russians, the Czar included. Russia is based on thievery, the whole world . . ."

"I just don't believe that."

"Don't be an idiot and you'll get along better. The colonel gets his share, and the general too. I send gifts not only to their wives but to their mistresses . . ."

"I give too, but I won't engage in false accounts."

"They wouldn't recognize a true one. When working with pigs, act like one."

After they had argued for some time, Kaminer suggested a compromise. He personally would keep the accounts and append his signature to them. If any questions were asked, Calman would be in the clear. Clara knocked on the door and brought in tea.

"Well, gentlemen, have you reached an agreement?"

"Calman's a trifle squeamish. Nowadays one doesn't come across many such saints."

"A saint? How odd! I always thought that saints slept away their lives next to the stove. My aunt used to say, 'An honest man feeds on grass.' "

"God be praised. I've cheated no man yet and I've made a living."

"Oh, come now, whom do you think you're fooling? One doesn't make a fortune praying. If it's the future world you're after, donate a scroll to the synagogue as my Aunt Sprintza did. In business, one can't afford a tender conscience."

III

Calman was aware that not only he but the Count too considered himself disgraced by Miriam Lieba's marriage to Lucian. As for the Countess, she had died without ever having been told what her son had done. After his wife's death, Jampolski went to visit Helena in Zamosc. It was rumored that he would not return to Jampol, but he was away only briefly. Felicia, now that her mother was dead, was thinking of entering a convent, and had even begun correspondence with the mother superior of a cloister. In the end, nothing came of it. Felicia wasn't really prepared to take the veil. She had not entirely given up hope of marrying and having children. In addition, she realized that in a nunnery she would be constantly surrounded by other women. If her life was to be lived in isolation, she wanted to have her thoughts as her sole companions, and in the manor she had both a chapel and a library that were completely her own. Furthermore, it would be a sin to desert her father, and though he most certainly did not conduct himself like a Christian, she knew it was not the place of his daughter to pass judgment on him.

So both she and the Count stayed where they were. His conduct continued to be the talk of the neighborhood. He openly consorted with his Siberian mistress, Yevdotya, announced that he was planning to go into the fur business, that all he needed was a partner with a little capital; while in exile, he had come to know a host of trappers. The Jampol Jews shrugged their shoulders. They had neither sufficient money nor the confidence in the Count that was needed to back such a commercial undertaking. At length Yevdotya deserted her house in The Sands and left town. Barbara, the old nurse, died. The cook Magda found a more lucrative job at another manor, and only the coachman, Wojciech, stayed on. He was of no value. As soon as he'd saved up a few groschen, he spent them on drink. Cataracts formed on both his eyes and he became half blind. Felicia would have willingly kept house for her father, but the Count managed to find himself a servant, none other than Antosia, the soldier's wife who had taken care of Calman when he had lived alone in the forest. Felicia did not want to allow Antosia, who had a bad reputation, into the house, but the Count insisted that he needed her and that if Felicia didn't like it she was old enough to pack up and leave. Once again he insulted his daughter, calling her an old maid who had sour milk in her veins instead of blood. Felicia, as always, suffered in silence.

Both the neighboring gentry and the Jews of Jampol and Skarshew insisted that the reason the Count stayed locked up in his house all day was that he was ashamed to meet Calman. An attic room whose windows faced to the rear became the Count's sanctum; he almost never opened the shutters. He spent his time drinking and reading, and for months on end was seen by no one. Even Felicia saw him only rarely. The only one for whom he would unlock the door was Antosia. Although the Countess's jewelry had been divided among her children (the largest share had been given to Lucian by Felicia), other assets were still controlled by the Count. He sold a valuable harness for next to nothing. Whenever he needed money, he sent Antosia off to Jampol to pawn various articles. He poured himself whisky by the glass but didn't get drunk.

Fully clothed, in bed, he browsed through old books or worked out various gambits on a chessboard. Three times a day Antosia brought him his meals, but he ate little. If he did go out during the day, he walked through the woods, avoiding the path that led into town. For the most part he left the house only at night, and then he practiced calisthenics in the dark, raised and lowered his arms, breathed in deeply, letting out the air with a roar. When Calman saw him one summer evening astride an old mare, both horse and rider seemed to be half asleep.

But though the Count did not seek the world, the world sought him. Josef, his oldest son, wrote him regularly from London. Jampolski never answered the letters. Josef got news of his father from Felicia, who also corresponded with Helena in Zamosc and even exchanged letters with Lucian and Miriam Lieba in Paris. Whenever Felicia knocked on her father's door, the Count would shout, "Leave me alone. Go away." Once, becoming worried, she demanded that Antosia open the door for her.

"Father," she said, "you mustn't neglect yourself like this."

"How am I neglecting myself? I'm healthier than you are."

For once Felicia lost her temper. "You must see that you're making us both look ridiculous."

"You're ashamed of me? A skeleton like you?"

He made no secret of the fact that he was cohabiting with Antosia, and Felicia heard the maid on her way to him each night. In his old age her father had turned into an animal. He did not go to church on Sundays, observed no Christian holidays, seldom changed his clothes, slept in his jacket and boots. Antosia, rather than the barber, trimmed his beard. His mustache became ragged. His language grew as coarse as a dog-catcher's. He never went near a religious book, but read the works of Voltaire, Diderot, Byron, Heine, and George Sand, as well as a huge history of Freemasonry and books about the French Revolution and the Italian Mafia.

Gradually Felicia realized that the longer she lived with this

uncouth man, the more she would deteriorate physically and
spiritually. She no longer slept at night. Though she ate, she
kept growing thinner. The mother she grieved for had been
exchanged by her father for a slovenly, almost idiotic peasant.
He blasphemed against God, ranted against the Pope. The
news that Helena had married a cousin in Zamosc left her father indifferent, and when she gave birth to a son, the grandfather did not even congratulate her.

One Sunday in April, as Felicia left church (Wojciech was
waiting outside in the britska), someone overtook her, bowed
to her, and introduced himself. He was a man of about forty,
small, thin, with a sallow face, sharp eyes, and a pointed mustache. He wore a scanty summer coat and a derby. A colored
scarf covered his throat. For some reason, Felicia assumed he
was a foreigner. He removed his hat, revealing curly, chestnut
hair already graying at the temples. His tone was familiar, as if
he knew her. He said that his name was Dr. Marian Zawacki
and that he had come from Paris. Lucian had asked him to
convey regards to his sister. Zawacki also mentioned that Lucian was in need of financial help, that he was in danger of
being deported as a public charge. Felicia, unaccustomed to
standing in the street with a strange man, was afraid people
would laugh at her. After some hesitation, she invited Zawacki
to join her in the britska and accompany her to the manor. It
was the first time the Countess Felicia had ever been seen in
the company of a man. Everyone looked and snickered, even
the Jews.

I V

Although the old Count did not generally come downstairs
for dinner, he informed his daughter through Antosia that this
time he would dine with their guest. Felicia was apprehensive,
for her father had forgotten his manners completely. Not
only was he liable to come to the table in a housecoat and
slippers, but he might appear simply for the purpose of insult-

ing Zawacki. Felicia therefore warned the doctor beforehand that her father was not entirely well. "I know, I know," Zawacki replied. "Lucian takes after him. Your mother was the normal member of the family."

Felicia had never heard a total stranger speak this way before. But who knew what the world was coming to? Zawacki had admitted without embarrassment that his father was a Warsaw cobbler and that his maternal grandfather had been a blacksmith in Pultusk. While finishing medical school in Paris, Marian had supported himself as a tourist guide and for a short time had managed a soup kitchen for Polish refugees. It was at the soup kitchen that he had met Lucian and Marisia, as he called Miriam Lieba. Felicia shuddered at every word he spoke. He related how the people of Paris had eaten mice at the time of the Prussian siege of 1870 and how he himself had caught a cat and skinned and roasted it.

It made Felicia feel sick and she said, "I would rather die than eat anything so disgusting."

"What's disgusting about it? We're all made of the same stuff."

"You don't believe that man's soul is divine?"

"Absolutely not," Zawacki replied.

The Count, though generally impatient with people, took to Zawacki immediately. Felicia, who had helped prepare the Sunday dinner, had covered the table with an elegant cloth and the finest china and silverware. But the conversation during the meal revolted her. The men began with a discussion of shoemaking and tanning, the Count wanting to know how leather was tanned, why oak bark was needed, which hides were used for soft leather and which for hard. When they had finished with the manufacture of shoes, the Count's curiosity turned to autopsy. Zawacki described the methods used in opening abdomens and skulls. Anatomy, he explained, had always been his specialty. Moreover, he had a steady hand and wasn't in the least sentimental. When Zawacki described in detail how, after having first removed the fetus from her womb, he had cut open a pregnant woman who had drowned herself in the Seine, Felicia turned white and had to be excused. Zawacki didn't bother to apologize. "After a while you get used to such things," he said. "Why, I sometimes had to boil human heads on my own stove."

He brought regards from Lucian—if Lucian's bitter message could be considered a greeting. Lucian, he said, was a drunken idler and a psychopath to boot. His wife and the child were starving. Lucian's latest plan was either to enlist in the Foreign Legion or to go off to America. When dinner was finished, the Count brought out his chessboard and lost three games in a row to the doctor. As they played, the men rocked back and forth in their chairs, smoking pipes and cursing. Every third word they uttered was *"psiakrew"*—dog's blood. Felicia could scarcely endure being in the presence of this coarse little man in whom all the defects of her father were duplicated. She wanted to get rid of him as soon as possible, but the Count had other ideas and invited Zawacki to stay on for a day or two.

After the Count had gone to bed, Felicia walked out into the night; suddenly she found herself confronted by Zawacki. The doctor was carrying a crooked cane.

"Oh, it's you." Without further ado, he joined her as if they were the oldest of friends. He had gone to school in Krakow, he told her, but had found himself at odds with the other students. Unlike them, he had been opposed to the 1863 uprisings, which he had regarded as nothing less than lunacy. He had known even then that General Mieroslawski was the worst of charlatans and Prince Lubomirski nothing but a pickpocket. As for Mickiewicz's son, what could one say of him other than that a great man had sired a midget? According to Zawacki, not even Prince Czartoryski was worth much, the truth being that the whole bloody business had been nothing but a filthy adventure led by a group of sentimental idiots, irresponsible parasites, and barbaric women. Felicia was appalled. The Count himself was not so disrespectful. Finally

Zawacki left the subject of politics and began to discuss his own affairs. His medical career had started late because he had had to move from university to university. Then, too, Napoleon III's insane war with Prussia and the crazy antics of the Paris Commune had intervened. Thank God, he was at last a certified physician. As he spoke, he constantly shifted from Polish to French and back to Polish again.

"What's going to happen to you, living here among these ruins?" he asked. "A person could easily lose his mind in such an atmosphere."

Felicia defended herself, although she scarcely knew why. "I can't leave my father."

"Let's face it, your father's senile and slightly degenerate besides."

Although it was not her nature to be rude, Felicia found it difficult to control her temper. "You're speaking about my father."

"What's a father? I hadn't seen my father in years; I went home on a visit, kissed him, and then I didn't have three words to say to him."

"Is there anyone who doesn't bore you?"

"Frankly no. Some people are absolutely mad about dogs, but I hate the animals. A dog is nothing but a flatterer, a sycophant. I prefer canaries or parrots. Monkeys are interesting, too."

"All animals are interesting."

"Well, at any rate, they don't talk nonsense, And they die more gracefully than men. People cling to life as if it were all marzipan and rose water."

"What an odd comparison."

"How is it that you've never married?" Zawacki asked suddenly.

The blood rushed to Felicia's face. "No one wants me."

"I'd want you."

Felicia paled. "I'm afraid you're making fun of me."

"Not at all. It's true you're not young, but neither are you old. Besides, you're a good-looking woman. Lucian showed me the photograph you sent him. He also told me about your eccentricities."

"What eccentricities?"

"Oh, your piety and all that. I can't stand women who are too clever—the cunning ones, I mean. Now don't be offended. It's just my way of speaking."

"I see."

"I want to open an office and I need a wife."

Felicia lowered her head. She realized that the man was in earnest. She had received her first proposal.

v

Although Count Wladislaw Jampolski constantly stressed the bankruptcy of the Polish nobility, proclaiming their inferiority to the merchant class and even to the Jewish storekeepers, he was unwilling to have the wedding of his daughter Felicia to Dr. Marian Zawacki take place at the castle. The Count stated it plainly: it was no concern of his that Felicia was marrying the son of a shoemaker—he even regarded it as an honor —but it was impossible for him to meet the shoemaker and his family at the manor or to dine or spend time with them. To Felicia he said: "I'll give you my blessing; go with him where you wish. But I'm not in the mood for any shoemaker parties!"

There was nothing for Felicia to do but weep. Her tears soaked the earth at her mother's grave. She had already knelt for a long time in the chapel before the picture of the Holy Mother, prayed, crossed herself, murmured her supplications. Felicia had no illusions about her coming marriage: Zawacki was a despot, kneaded from the same dough as her father; he would insult her and deride her in the true manner of a plebeian, and he would bring her and his boorish family together. Yet though she would suffer in this milieu, it was preferable to remaining alone with a half-demented father on a manor that belonged to a Jew. If she must submit to a tyrant, why not one of her own age? Who could tell? He might even be good to her, perhaps she could still have children. Her father maintained that sour milk ran in her veins, but it was far from the truth. More than once, at night, Felicia had felt that the blood within her was his.

Lying in bed until dawn, Felicia took stock of herself. She could not become a nun, even if she forced herself to enter a convent. She would be in danger of breaking her vows, and instead of pleasing God she would anger Him. But she could not remain at home. Clearly heaven had destined her to marry. If she was meant to suffer, this marriage would be her cross. During sleepless nights, Felicia vowed to be faithful to Marian Zawacki, to love him like a wife and sister, to try to soften his bitterness, and to show him and his relatives an example of Christian devotion. Why run away from temptation?

But it was not entirely convenient to marry without a mother, a sister or brother. Felicia certainly must have a trousseau, but she had no idea what she needed or how to prepare it. Her father's refusal to attend the wedding was an insult both to Felicia and to Marian's family. Marian wanted to get it all over with quickly, his impatience and contempt for ceremony were similar to her father's. Nevertheless, Felicia could not allow her wedding to turn into a farce. Meditating long and uncertainly, she decided to ask help from others. She wrote a long letter to her sister Helena, asked advice of the Jampol priest and his housekeeper, made inquiries of her Aunt Eugenia and her cousin Stephanie. Felicia could not go to her husband like a pauper without a wardrobe.

The anxiety, nocturnal weeping spells, and lack of sleep undermined her health. She lost her appetite. Instead of gaining weight, she grew thinner, was perpetually constipated. Her periods became irregular. Every few minutes she washed her hands. At night she was tormented by feelings of doubt, turned in her bed, tossed, sighed: would she be able to satisfy a man? Would Marian be disappointed with her the very first night? Would his relatives conspire against her, ridicule her, would she have to return in shame to her father? There were moments when Felicia wanted to scream and tear her hair. But her belief in God, in His Providence and His absolute goodness, kept her from acting desperately.

Felicia discovered that when one seeks help, there are always those who will respond. Old noblewomen, former friends of the Countess, began to show up at the manor, bringing daughters and daughters-in-law. These friends from the past recommended tailors, seamstresses. Nissen, the Jampol tailor, again came to the manor, took Felicia's measurements, fitted her, wished her luck. At every opportunity he mentioned the goodness and generosity of the late Countess. Felicia's decision to marry Dr. Zawacki had in some mysterious way brought her closer to people, even to those who had never known her before.

VI

Her fiancé's father, the shoemaker, Antony Zawacki, had an old house on Bugay Street in Warsaw. It wasn't easy for Felicia to enter a shoemaker's shop and see her future father-in-law, the cobbler, sitting at his bench in a leather apron, sewing a shoe with a swine-bristle needle, surrounded by his five helpers. One bored holes with an awl, one pounded in tacks with a hammer; another rubbed a heel with a piece of glass, and a fourth trimmed a sole with a curved shoemaker's knife. Antony Zawacki, in his sixties, seemed younger than his years. His thick black mustaches coiled up at the ends, and though the comparison embarrassed Felicia, his eyes had the gleam of polished shoes. His hands were hairy, his fingers short, the square nails ringed with dirt. He did not even rise when Felicia entered. Measuring her with an experienced gaze, he called to his wife in the kitchen, "Hey, Katarzyna, we've got a visitor!"

Katarzyna was a small, thin woman with sharp limbs and angry eyes who resembled her son. Seeing Felicia, she quickly wiped her fingers on her apron, executed something like a curtsy, and extended a dirty hand. Felicia had come alone. Marian had not wanted to be present when Felicia met his parents.

"The gracious Countess!"

Felicia walked past a kitchen where large pots boiled on the stove. The helpers received food in addition to their wages. On the table there was a loaf of black bread larger than any Felicia had ever seen. In the living room there was a dresser with a mirror and a vase full of artificial flowers. A roll of flypaper dangled from the lamp. Two framed photographs of husband and wife together and a photograph of Marian in the uniform of a high-school student hung on the wall. Although it was midsummer, the windows were nailed shut, and for a moment the smell of dust and leather nauseated Felicia. She sat on the sofa upholstered in some shiny material, and green wheels spun before her eyes.

"Would it inconvenience you terribly to open the window?" Felicia asked.

"Window? What for? It's still nailed up for the winter."

"My wife is afraid of fresh air," Antony Zawacki said, accusingly. "Excuse my language, Countess, but it stinks here!"

He leaped to the window and, tearing it open, pulled out the length of straw that had sealed it against the wind. A mild breeze smelling of refuse and pitch blew in from the courtyard.

"Well, why are you so quiet?" Antony asked his wife. "Offer the Countess something!"

"I don't need you to teach me manners, Antony! I wasn't brought up in the gutter."

"The Countess must be thirsty."

"Oh, no, thank you."

Husband and wife both went into the kitchen. Felicia heard them wrangling. When Antony Zawacki returned, Felicia saw that he had replaced his apron with a skimpy jacket. It made him look clumsy. A tin stud was buttoned into his shirt collar.

There was an air of plebeian uncouthness in his gaze, his mustaches, his unshaven jaw, and thick neck with its swollen veins. He carried in a wooden tray with a carafe of wine, glasses, and cookies. Katarzyna had by this time also changed her clothes. She wore a yellow dress with a pleated bodice. Felicia regretted that she had allowed Marian to persuade her to visit his parents unexpectedly.

Although in no mood to drink wine, Felicia sipped it and remarked that it was good. The cookies were hard as pebbles. Katarzyna kept returning to the kitchen and her pots.

"The esteemed Countess sees us for what we are: common folk," Antony Zawacki said. "We've earned everything with our own hands—the house, the workshop. Marian had a good head for books. I wanted to make a shoemaker out of him, but he said: 'Papa, I haven't the patience for heels and soles.' 'What do you want?' I asked him. 'To become a priest and have maidservants confess to you?' In short, he wanted an education. 'Well, go ahead and study,' I said. He filled the whole house with books. I gave him everything he needed, but he got hold of a boy, some lame-brain who needed help with his lessons and whose parents could pay. Well, let him be a student, I thought. In this way he got through high school and earned a gold medal. He could have studied at the university here, but he insisted on going to Krakow. His mother began to carry on: 'So far away!—my only son.' I had another son too but no more. Well, to make a long story short, I sent him to Krakow and he studied there. Afterward, he went to France. A war started there and I read in the papers that a rabbit cost fifty francs. There the currency is francs, not guilders. A cat was fifteen francs, and one egg five francs. They have a park where they keep animals, and all the bears and peacocks and the others were eaten. My wife began to wail: 'Our Marian will starve to death!' But, somehow, he came back healthy, if emaciated. He said: 'Papa, I want to marry Countess Jampolska.' 'Where did you meet a Countess?' I asked. 'You may be a doctor, but your father is a shoemaker.' 'Well,' he said, 'times have changed.' What do they call it? De-mo-cracy. He said, 'Naked, we all stem from apes.' 'Well,' I said, 'if it's all right with her parents, it's all right with me. Your wife,' I said, 'will be like a daughter to me—' "

Katarzyna returned from the kitchen. "What's the difference what you said? If our boy loves someone, we like her too."

12 🏠

Many letters arrived for Calman proposing a second marriage, and matchmakers visited the manor frequently. Although his reputation was now blemished because of Miriam Lieba's apostasy, Calman on the other hand was the father-in-law of the Marshinov rabbi's son, and related to the Jampol rabbi and to Reb Ezekiel Wiener. He was also a man of wealth and not quite fifty years old. Girls, young widows, and divorcees were offered to him. A letter came from Binneleh, the Chmielev rabbi's wife in Marshinov and Temerel's sister-in-law. Binneleh wrote that she had been lying awake in bed one night and it had suddenly occurred to her that Calman should marry her sister-in-law, Temerel, Jochanan's mother. What could be finer? Binneleh had not as yet discussed her idea with Temerel, but was certain that Temerel would consent. Temerel had been a widow for too long. As long as she had had to arrange suitable marriages for her children, she had been unable to think of herself. Now that she had married off both her daughters and Jochanan was married to Tsipele, it was a different matter. Binneleh's letter was full of insinuations that the rabbi, her father-in-law, was gravely ill. His days were numbered and her brother-in-law Reb Shimmon planned to succeed his father by force. Binneleh compared Reb Shimmon to Absalom, who had wanted to rob his father, King David, of his kingdom. Calman nodded. He read between the lines. An undeclared war was being waged by the two brothers, Reb Shimmon and the Chmielev rabbi. It was the two sisters-in-law, Menucheleh and Binneleh, who kept the feud going. Binneleh probably reasoned that a match between Calman and Temerel would be a blow against Reb Shimmon. Reb Moshe, the Chmielev rabbi, apparently had no desire to take his father's following, but he begrudged it to his brother and wanted to effect a compromise with Jochanan, the nephew.

Although Binneleh claimed that she had not yet discussed the matter with Temerel, Calman suspected that she had, in her clever way, gathered that Temerel would not be adverse to the match. But the proposal did not attract Calman. It was a great honor, of course, that the daughter of the Marshinov rabbi wanted to marry him, but Temerel would be no wife for him. She was very pious, a scholar, whereas he was almost ignorant. Moreover, she was already in her late forties, perhaps even fifty. For half a lifetime Calman had been married to a wife who had been devout and sickly; in her final years, he had almost never approached her. Lust boiled within him as in his youth. Not even hard work could subdue it. He needed more than a pious female.

Binneleh's letter arrived a week before Pentecost. It had been Calman's intention to go to Marshinov to spend the holiday with the rabbi, and also to visit Tsipele and Jochanan. But the letter confused him. Now he was ashamed to go.

Acting on Calman's indecision, Shaindel was able to dissuade him from spending Pentecost in Marshinov. Ezriel had returned from Warsaw for the holiday, and Shaindel wanted the two men to be together. As a result, Mayer Joel traveled to Marshinov alone and Calman remained at the manor. Cooped up in the house, Calman had nothing to do during the long days. He argued with Ezriel, and Ezriel spouted heresy. "Who," he asked, "saw God give Moses the Torah on Mount Sinai? The Jews have their Torah, and the Christians have something else. If their religion can be false, so can ours.

Hasn't each generation added new laws and new miracles? Is there any mention in the Scriptures of the hereafter or resurrection? No, there isn't. Ecclesiastes states categorically that everything ends with death. All the legends of another world, of a final reckoning, the talk of a Messiah, and a wild ox, and the leviathan are later developments. If there is such a thing as immortality and the soul is rewarded in paradise and punished in Gehenna, why don't the Prophets mention it?"

A great bitterness overcame Calman. He could not answer any of Ezriel's questions and so he rebuked him and then regretted it. Upset, Calman went out for a walk in the fields, occasionally touching an ear of wheat, and counting the grains. If everything went well and there was neither too much rain nor hail, the harvest would bring him thousands. Fruit hung heavy on the trees, cows calved, hens laid. Lime now brought a half groschen more per forty pounds, so that even if the duke didn't renew his lease, Calman would be left with plenty.

Suddenly he saw someone approaching. He recognized the porter from the railway depot, who as he drew nearer stopped and removed his hat. "A telegram for you, sir."

Calman did not know whether it was proper to accept the message on a holiday, but took it, promising the man a tip when the festival was over. When the porter had thanked him and left, Calman tried to decipher the scrawled handwriting of the telegram, but was unable to do so. He noticed two women approaching him, but from a distance he could not make out who they were. It was evident from their attire that they weren't peasants. On the other hand, Jewish young ladies would not venture outside the limits of the settlement on a holiday.

It occurred to Calman that it must be Clara and one of her friends. Smoothing his beard and buttoning his gaberdine, he walked toward them, Yes, the taller of the two was Clara, and with her was Tamara Shalit. Clara had on a wide-brimmed straw hat with a green band, and a light-colored dress, and she carried a parasol. She was fanning herself with a handkerchief. Both women were laughing, and then Clara called out, "Think of it, Reb Calman, I won a ruble because of you!"

"Because of me?"

"Yes, I had a bet. I said it was you approaching, and Tamara said that—"

"Be quiet! I said nothing—" Tamara slapped her arm.

"Happy holiday! I was out for a walk and the porter met me with a telegram. Now you cross my path. Everything at once."

"What did the telegram say?" Clara asked curiously.

"I can't make it out."

"Let me try."

Calman handed the sheet of paper to Clara, who snatched it from his hand. Scanning it rapidly, her eyes lit up.

"You're a lucky man!"

"What is it?"

"It may be a secret. I'd better whisper it."

"No, I'll walk away," Tamara said, turning back.

Clara came closer to Calman and her hand touched his ear. A strange warmth coursed through him.

"Wallenberg is planning to build another railroad. He wants you to come to Warsaw," Clara whispered, "as quickly as possible!"

As she spoke, her hat slid back on her head and remained suspended by a pin. With her hat askew, she appeared younger and more graceful. She was so close to him that his beard rested on her shoulder. She winked and said, "Lots of luck."

11

By chance, Clara accompanied Calman to Warsaw. Though he had already purchased a third-class ticket, when she saw him standing on the platform, she asked him to join her in her second-class compartment. Clara had with her a valise, a hat box, a bouquet of flowers, and a small satchel. She wore a checked suit and a straw hat with cherries on it. The train remained standing for a long time, and some Jampol Jews saw Calman join her. Daniel Kaminer stood on the platform and spoke to his daughter in Russian through the open window of her compartment. Clara's presence did not deter Daniel Kaminer from making coarse jokes. "Watch her closely, Calman. Don't let them abduct her in the big city . . . She's worth money!"

"Papa, you should be ashamed, the way you talk," Clara said reprovingly.

"I lost whatever shame I had a long time ago."

In the car, Clara told Calman the purpose of her trip. She had broken the catch on her pearls and there was only one jeweler in Warsaw who could fix it. She also needed a new dress, and Jampol's Nissen was incompetent. And she wanted several hats, and her aunt in Warsaw, a Mrs. Frankel, was a milliner. Whenever she visited the city, Clara stayed at her aunt's house. She smiled and chattered, bent down and took refreshments for herself and Calman out of her small satchel —chocolates, marmalade, cookies, even an orange. When the train stopped at a station, she sent him out for tea. Beneath her jacket, which she removed, Clara wore a white blouse, so transparent that her bodice and part of her breasts were visible. She removed a flower from her bouquet and fixed it in Calman's lapel. Speaking confidently, she gave him all kinds of advice. First, he must not permit Wallenberg to get the best of the bargain. Wallenberg was a multimillionaire, and labor was more expensive than ever. Calman must not sign any contract in a hurry, because in furnishing railroad ties, a fortune could be lost as easily as it could be made.

Second, Clara reminded Calman that he must come to an agreement with the duke. She had heard that attempts were being made to outbid Calman for the manor. Losing the manor would be the same as losing a hand. If he wanted to maintain the lime quarries and supply the ties, he had to keep the manor, for without it, he would be unable to furnish food for his laborers. It would be impossible if he had to buy every sack of meal and every quart of milk. Calman could not stop marveling at Clara's business sense. She spoke more like an experienced merchant than a woman. He was unable, Calman confessed, to locate the duke, who was on a world tour and hadn't answered his letters. There was a way of solving this, Clara said. She knew a Warsaw lawyer, a drinking companion of the Governor-General and a frequent visitor to his castle. She also had military contacts. Her father was a bosom friend of both Colonel Smirnoff and General Rittermayer, who moved in the highest circles of the Russian aristocracy. They could be counted on to further Calman's cause.

Calman could not help comparing Clara to Zelda, who had done nothing but torment his soul and make him demean himself, live parsimoniously, and surrender everything to his enemies. Clara was young, attractive, clever, and she had a masculine mind. She was honest with him because she wanted to become his wife. She was feathering her own nest, in a way, but that's how things were. Calman moved away from her a little, as the scent of flowers and perfume made him dizzy. After a while, Clara again moved closer to him and, joking, tugged good-naturedly at his beard. Once she placed her shoe over his boot. Her knee moved close to his. Calman literally went pale with desire. He began to pray that the Lord deliver him from temptation. If Clara was destined to be his future wife, he would lead her to the wedding canopy. Lying back on the plush-covered seat, Clara tried to nap. Calman gazed out the window at the parting fields which made a path for the train. Forests danced by, flocks of birds careened overhead, frightened by the scarecrows with their torn clothes and ragged hats. Over everything there was a blue sky with little silver clouds, floating, curling to become pillows, sheep, brooms, and curtains. God's sunlight fell on every leaf, every blade of grass, every flower. Peasants could be seen between the seed beds, pulling up weeds. Peasant women worked over the potato patches. Cattle-filled pastures flitted by, cows with black and yellow patches, their udders milk-laden. A cowherd played on his fife, young men built campfires, horses grazed or simply stood, neck to neck, mutely exchanging secrets. What could be pleasanter than sitting next to Clara and looking out at God's summery day? Everything was beautiful: each windmill, each straw-laden roof, each marsh and pond where geese and ducks splashed.

"If she were my wife," Calman thought, "I could ride like this with her for days, weeks, months! She's young, and might still bear children, a son. I can still have the pleasure of watching my heir study the Torah." Calman hung his head. "Well, but does she really want me? Perhaps she's making fun of me? Enlightened people have a habit of mocking others. And how can I be sure that someone like her would observe the dietary laws, ablutions, and keep promises? What if her word means nothing?"

Clara opened one eye. "Why are you thinking so hard, Calman?"

Calman cleared his throat. "I was thinking of how good it is to enjoy the world without forsaking God. Because if, perish the thought, one forsakes God, both worlds are lost."

"Who forsakes God," Clara countered, "if everything one sees was created by Him?"

"It certainly was."

"On the other hand, one need not be a fanatic."

"Who's a fanatic? A Jew must observe the dietary laws, and a Jewish daughter the laws of purification."

"Do you mean the ritual bath?"

"Yes, the ritual bath." And Calman's face turned red.

"After all, what is the ritual bath? Since one must be clean, why not bathe in a bathtub or the river in summertime? Isn't that more hygienic than a ritual bath, where all sorts of filthy women dip themselves?"

"Cleanliness isn't the only purpose of a ritual bath."

"What then?"

"The soul!"

"What does the soul get out of a ritual bath? And besides, the match won't be canceled because of it." Clara winked, laughing.

Pausing for a moment, she said, "If I had my own manor and lived with a religious husband, I'd build a ritual bath of my own. That way, God would be satisfied and I'd stay clean."

III

Clara's aunt, the milliner, lived on Mead Street. It was her daughter's birthday and there was a party in progress at the apartment. Miss Celina was twenty, according to her mother, but the girls who worked for Mrs. Frankel figured her age as twenty-three. Normally one would have expected a woman of that age to have a husband and children, but everything happened late in Mrs. Frankel's home. One returned at two in the morning and didn't get up till noon; at Mrs. Frankel's a girl was still young at twenty-three. Mrs. Frankel, who had buried three husbands, had Celina by her second, the Commissioner. Somewhere or other there was also a son, who had apostasized and become a Russian army officer. Mrs. Frankel's Jewish neighbors avoided her; she was said to eat forbidden foods and did not cook the Sabbath meal in advance. Although nearly sixty, Mrs. Frankel did not wear a wig. She was dark as a crow, had a beaked nose and black pouchy eyes ringed with webs of wrinkles. Her left eye smiled, while the other blinked. She had a saucy way of talking; she called a hat a pancake, its feather a tail, and a female customer a bargain-hunter. But her crooked fingers were famous and throughout Warsaw her hats were the vogue.

It was known that countesses and princesses were among her customers. The demand for her work was so great that she employed half a dozen girls, who lived with her and were regarded as members of the family. At ten-thirty at night, everyone stopped work and helped prepare dinner. One girl fetched the samovar, another lit the stove, a third made potato pancakes or dumplings. Because of this, dinner at Mrs. Frankel's was a hit-and-miss affair. When the girls got lazy, they bought cold cuts and frankfurters. The bakery boy would bring a basketful of fresh rolls and hot bagels, and as the girls ate, the rolls would crackle between their teeth. There wasn't another workshop in town which had such lively girls. Mrs. Frankel went out of her way to find girls who had spirit; it was known in the trade that any apprentice of hers would become an expert. She even acted as a matchmaker for them. One often saw the coach from the wedding hall draw up before her house. The one thing she could not bear was faulty workmanship. If a girl was awkward, Mrs. Frankel would shriek, "All right, Miss Five Thumbs, hurry home and bake a pudding." More than one girl was known to work on a single hat for half a week.

Oddly enough, Celina had not followed in her mother's footsteps. Mrs. Frankel had done her best to teach her daughter millinery, but the girl couldn't even thread a needle. In fact, the only things she could do well were eat and sleep. Rainy days she didn't get out of bed at all, but just sat drinking tea and cocoa, eating buttered rolls, and rice with milk in her room. Celina had a narrow, swarthy face, a small mouth, a pair of eyes like plums. Her neck was long and her head was covered with black ringlets. She was forever grimacing and spoke capriciously in the manner of an only daughter who can ask for anything. Her monthly period kept her in bed for days. The chamber pot was carried out by her mother, who would complain, "Rots in bed and stinks. She'll rot like that until her hair turns gray."

But when Celina thought of getting up and going out, her mother would thrust her crooked nose out the window, sniff, and say, "Stay where you are, it's sweltering."

Clara called Mrs. Frankel "aunt," although the milliner was related to Clara's first husband. Whenever Clara came to Warsaw, she stayed at her aunt's and arrived with presents for

everyone. This time Celina received a pair of gold earrings as a
birthday gift. Celina had small ears; she owned a trunkful of
trinkets; even while she lay in bed, she primped. But in honor
of her birthday she had risen and put on a yellow dress and
high-heeled shoes. Tall, with a long, thin waist, she could appear elegant when she wished. After dinner, the girls clasped
each other by the hips and danced. The music was provided
by one of the girls, who hummed through a comb. Clara
danced with Celina, whose feet glided gracefully across the
floor. Mrs. Frankel watched with tears in her eyes. Three husbands and six children and all she had left was this creature.
Would the day ever come when Celina would bring her some
happiness?

In the midst of the festivities there was a knock on the door.
Mrs. Frankel answered it. A large, black-bearded man in a
high-crowned hat entered.

"You must be the aunt," Calman said.

"Whose aunt—yours?"

"Isn't she here? Clara?"

"Oh, Clara. Yes, she's here. Take off your coat."

"Who's here? Musicians?"

"Don't worry. No one will bite you."

Calman took off his coat and suddenly felt sorry he had
come. He followed Mrs. Frankel into the apartment, realizing
how big and broad he was in comparison to her. The girl playing the comb stopped. Clara, seeing him, clapped her hands.
"For heaven's sake, he's here. Welcome, welcome!"

The girls giggled, embarrassing Calman, who was forced to
remind himself that he was one of the richest Jews in Poland
and had just signed a contract to supply ties for the railroad
Wallenberg was building for the Czar. "Good evening," he
said. "I told you I would come, and you see, I have kept my
word. I'm going home tomorrow."

"Tomorrow? What's the rush? He flies in like the prophet
Elijah. Come here, sit down. Auntie, this is Mr. Jacoby. I've
told my aunt about you. It's her daughter's birthday."

"Very nice having you here. Would you like something to eat? Our rule is that no visitor leaves with an empty stomach."

"I would have brought a present if I'd known."

"She doesn't need presents. I only wish God would bless her with a suitable marriage."

"Are you starting again, Mama?"

"What's wrong? A daughter may be a blessing, but a mother wants some return on her investment. There are no labor pains in having a grandson. Really, Clara, it's time I had some pleasure out of you, too. I would like to dance at both your weddings. Believe me, Mister Jacoby, there's no other woman like her in the world! Pretty and clever and educated, with a dowry too. I should make every month what she'll bring to a husband!"

Calman's face grew red. The girls exchanged glances. Clara pushed a chair toward Calman.

"Were you at Wallenberg's?"

"I signed the contract today."

"Congratulations! Auntie, Mister Jacoby signed the contract. I tell my aunt everything. We have no secrets."

"*Mazel tov*! Good luck to you! Clara's friends are mine. That's the way we are: one family. Body and soul. Girls, what are you gaping at? Set up the samovar! Don't stand around looking like lumps of clay."

"Thank you kindly. I've already eaten."

"And what if you did eat? The intestine is bottomless. This is my daughter. It's her birthday that we're celebrating."

"In the old times, celebrating birthdays was a Gentile custom."

"There's a saying, 'Where the Gentile goes, the Jew follows!' "

13 ⛫

I

In the Marshinov House of Prayer, the students read quietly. The old rabbi was sick. The Warsaw specialist admitted that his remedies could no longer be effective. "It's a miracle the rabbi is still alive."

Although his sons wanted to transfer the rabbi to the big house, where it was quieter and the air fresher, the rabbi preferred to remain in his study, near the house of prayer. Reb Mendel, the beadle, had that morning propped up the rabbi in bed, dressed in prayer shawl and phylacteries. He had prayed along with the quorum. The rabbi's intimates tried to enter the room to shake his hand, but Reb Shimmon, his eldest son, had told the attendant to admit no one. Since the rabbi had lost his sight, he recited the Psalms from memory, and mumbled parts of the Mishnah. Most of the time, he dozed. Swollen, with a distended stomach and a face that changed each hour, he lay there, his eyes sunken behind his cheekbones. Even his beard seemed to have shrunk. The rabbi could no longer urinate; it was necessary to catheterize him. The catheter emptied into a pot partially hidden under the bed. Several times a day, his nose bled. All the ailments had merged: a blockage of the bladder, an inflammation of the lungs. The body could no longer contain the soul. At any moment the end would come.

Throughout Poland the news spread that the rabbi was

dying. The train from Warsaw kept bringing new loads of Hassidim to Marshinov. The rich arrived in britskas and coaches. From the small villages, people came in wagons, and even on foot. Barren women, in search of a blessing to make them fertile, squatted with their bundles on benches, on the stoops of houses, or simply on the logs and boards that lay in the Marshinov courtyard. The slow process of repairing the complex of rabbinical buildings had been in progress for several years.

Comparing rabbis' miracles, the women shook their bonnets, wiped their noses on their aprons, and dried the tears on their wan cheeks. There was much to discuss, for each rabbi's way was different and each woman had her own trouble. From time to time, Reb Moshe the Chmielev rabbi or Reb Shimmon walked by. Reb Moshe reputedly did not want his father's following. Reb Shimmon, on the other hand, wished to replace his father, but the women insisted that the true saint was Temerel's son, Jochanan, Calman Jacoby's son-in-law. As Reb Shimmon walked by, he overheard a woman declaring: "Is he a human being? He's an angel. There is no saint like him in the whole world!"

Reb Shimmon slowed down. "Do they mean me?" he wondered. He stopped for a moment and the woman continued: "That Tsipele is a saint, too."

Reb Shimmon grumbled. His black beard leaped as if it had a life of its own. He looked angrily at the crowd and barely kept himself from spitting. "Cows, sluts!" he growled. "Who needs them here, the scum? They come to excrete, to pick the bones clean. And Tsipele is a saint to them too now!"

Reb Shimmon stopped at the threshold of the house of prayer. Candles burned in the menorahs. He could hear Jews intoning Psalms, praying for the rabbi's recovery, a group of children praying with their teacher. Reb Shimmon was looking for the men of wealth, the important men, the rabbi's intimates, but they were all, apparently, at the inns. He tugged his beard, bit his lips. "Why do they babble so much? No one lives forever. Even Moses died." Reb Shimmon paced back and forth. For years he had prepared for this day. He had written thousands of letters, entertained every Hassid, committed every face to memory, every name, everyone's needs and requirements. His wife, Menuche, had entertained the women. Reb Shimmon was well aware that in all Poland there was no rabbi's son who had a memory to match his. Actually, he had sacrificed himself for the court. It was he, Reb Shimmon, who had rebuilt the ritual bath, had the corner walls of the house of prayer supported by piles of stones, fixed the roof. He himself had taken care of all debts, all duties, each attendant, each full-time student, each servant girl. Reb Moshe, the Chmielev rabbi, had spent his years in Chmielev. His mother was concerned only with her own ailments. His sister Temerel kept her nose in her prayer books. He, Reb Shimmon, ran the court. Why did they chatter about Jochanan? If Jochanan could be the Marshinov rabbi, then Reb Shimmon could be a priest.

II

Jochanan had been reading in his attic room instead of at the house of study ever since the rabbi had become sick. People crowded about him too much, Hassidim dropped all sorts of hints.

His mother looked at him with misty eyes. He heard others say that after the death of the old man he would be made rabbi, but Jochanan had decided not to accept the office. In the first place, who was he to become the Rabbi of Marshinov? Evil thoughts filled him. He was steeped in lust, wrath, pride, melancholy, and other evils. Second, even if he were worthy, he would not encroach upon his uncle Reb Shimmon, who had served all these years. He would not only be infringing on his uncle's rights but would be insulting Reb Shimmon. No, God forbid. Jochanan remembered the words of the Talmud: it is better to throw oneself into a lime kiln than to shame someone before others. All these things—his grandfather's illness, Reb Shimmon's annoyance, all the whispering behind his back—upset him. A while ago, he had been a half-decent Jew. He had studied in peace and prayed with fervor. He had distinctly felt that he was becoming purified. Now he had grown base again. As he prayed, his mind filled with foolish notions. He studied, but barely understood the words of the sages. Suddenly in the midst of the Eighteen Benedictions, his thoughts grew oppressive, forcing him into a net of temptation. He caught himself by his sidelocks, pulling at them with all his strength, to make physical pain obliterate his desires. He had placed chick peas into his boots to sting his soles. He got up and stood at the lectern to study. He read a section of the Mishnah and recited a chapter of the Psalms, turning his eyes away from the sun, the window, the garden, and the chirping birds on branches. The birds did as God willed, they did not wish to rule one another. A crumb of food, a drop of water were all they needed to sing to God from dawn to sunset, but he, Jochanan, wanted to rule his brethren; to place himself above the crowd. Grandfather is happy, Jochanan thought, he will soon leave his body entirely. He is already more in the world beyond than here. Jochanan began to nod and shake: "Lord Almighty, save me! Heavenly Father, help me, because I am in an abject condition." He went over to the bookcase, removed a book, closed his eyes, and opened it at random. It was a book of his grandfather's. He looked and read: ". . . And know ye that there exists another sort of sadness, the sorrow of those who talk it into themselves that they must rise to the highest mansion, and as soon as they meet with obstacles, they fall all the way down as it is written about Elisha the son of Abujah. He gazed behind the curtain, and was hurt. Because he saw how far the road was and how insignificant man, he grew afraid, and because of this fear became a heretic. For the root of heresy is fear, not the exalted fear but the fear of a slave who likes to transcend responsibility and loses faith in his Master. A rabbi has said: 'Serve the Lord, but don't try to outdo others in serving Him.' "

Jochanan's eyes grew moist. Woe! Heavens! Grandfather actually had spoken to him through the book he had just opened at random! No, he would stop worrying about rank. He would simply be a Jew. Evil thoughts? Let them come, let them assault him. He would pay no attention to them. He would only study and pray . . .

The door opened and Tsipele came in. Jochanan raised his eyes momentarily. A woman, yes, but she was his wife, the mother of his child. Besides, she was not menstruating now. In a long full dress, a head-kerchief, with a silken shawl across her shoulders, she stood at the door.

Jochanan pulled his beard. "Well—"

"Jochanan, my father may come."

"Father-in-law? So—"

"A letter arrived."

"Well, that's fine."

"I brought you a pear."

Jochanan looked directly at her. Almost a child when he'd married her, she was now (may the Evil Eye spare her!) grown up. His mother (may she live long!) said Tsipele was a beauty. She smiled at him. She had a narrow face, large black eyes, an upturned upper lip. Her face exuded the modesty and amiability of those who are not tempted. In one hand she held a pear on a plate; in the other, a knife. "How can she not be tormented?" Jochanan wondered. "It isn't possible that she can control herself so well. Apparently, the evil passions are weaker in women. Or perhaps she is the reincarnation of a sainted soul who came down to earth to correct some small errors committed in a former existence." Jochanan remembered about the pear.

"Thanks, but I'm not hungry. Why should I be? I just ate breakfast."

"You don't look well. Mother-in-law says so, too."

"No one is as one looks."

"I don't mean that. You're thin—" Tsipele half laughed.

"Thin? So what? Must one be stout? It says in the Treatise of Abbot, to increase the flesh is to increase the worms."

"You're not old yet—"

"Does one know when the Day of Death will come? Well, put it down."

"Where?"

"Here, on the table. I'll wash my hands later."

Tsipele came closer. Because her dress was long and wide, one could not see exactly how she walked. She seemed to float. Although Jochanan had lived with her for a year and a half, she continued to amaze him. For all her youth, she was intelligent. The other women quarreled among themselves, but Tsipele got along with everyone. She took care of him. She brought him delicacies. She was modest in bed. She was a light sleeper. When he came to her, he spoke about the Torah, related stories of saints, and she heard him out patiently. He had been favored with a virtuous female.

"Jochanan, I want to ask you something."

"Ask."

"I hear that when your grandfather—one must not say it— you'll become the rabbi."

Jochanan grew paler than before.

"No, Tsipele."

"Why not? Don't you want it?"

"I am not worthy."

For a while were both silent. Then Jochanan asked: "And would you want to be a rabbi's wife?"

Tsipele smiled. "Why should that bother me?"

Jochanan laughed. "And does it bother you that you are not the rabbi's wife?"

"No."

"Well, well, it's all nonsense. These honors aren't worth a pinch of snuff."

"When will you eat the pear?"

"Later."

Tsipele turned to go. Jochanan's eyes followed her. A child in a bonnet and dress, and a mother too. It was all the same to her, and that's the way it should be. Since these things were of no importance, why think about them? Jochanan was lost in meditation. Yes, she had the soul of a saint, a pure body. Satan had no power over such creatures. It was said of them, they were conceived and born in holiness. Jochanan experienced a powerful feeling of love for Tsipele, who although she lived in the lower world reached those heights that were beyond all material laws. He had no such rights. He must struggle with evil spirits, or they would tear him apart. "I'm sorry I didn't say something nice to her," Jochanan thought to himself. "Perhaps give her a coin?" He promised himself that he would praise her after the evening services when she served him his groats with chicken broth.

III

Reb Shimmon paced back and forth in his attic room. Dusk was falling. He glanced out of the window at the ripening fields of grain and potatoes. Cows grazed in the meadows along the river. The woods and clouds had begun to turn from blue to rose. One cloud shaped like a fish opened its huge mouth and with red teeth seemed to be snapping at a curly round cloudlet resembling a hedgehog. Suddenly the fishlike jaws dissolved, the teeth crumbled, and the hedgehog cloud, inflating itself, floated off. Reb Shimmon's eyes grew bright with anger. It went on up there too—they swallowed each other. These days Reb Shimmon was in agony, and at night he could not sleep. Wrath, he knew, was a sin, but he rose in the mornings as angry as when he went to bed. Did they really believe that they could dismiss him like a schoolboy? He had served them faithfully, and now a mere boy was to be made rabbi because it was rumored that he was a saint. In his rage Reb Shimmon cursed Jochanan, calling him fool, idiot, hypocrite. "I won't remain silent," Reb Shimmon mumbled. "I'll see that he's disgraced; I'll tear him up by the roots; when I get finished, there'll be nothing left of this court." Terrible thoughts came to him. Perhaps he should reject his faith altogether? "God forbid, am I out of my mind?" he asked himself. He imagined himself banging on the lectern in the prayer house on Yom Kippur eve and shouting, "Listen to me, there is no God. All is chaos."

Where did such blasphemy come from? He shuddered and begged God to forgive him. The sun went down, and the river became fiery. Crows cawed; the first stars appeared. "Well, I must say my evening prayers," Reb Shimmon mumbled. But he didn't go down to the house of prayer. For the first time in years, he felt no affection for people. They were all false and his enemies. He decided to pray alone, washed his hands, and started the psalm, "Happy is he," Then, stationing himself at the eastern wall, he recited the Eighteen Benedictions, but the words had become meaningless to him. He walked to the middle of the room and announced in a firm voice, "I don't care. I must do it, no matter what the consequences." He walked to his bureau, opened a drawer, and took out a sheet of paper, and after glancing at it, shoved it into his pocket.

"He's secluding himself also," Reb Shimmon thought as he walked into the corridor. "I'll talk frankly to him. There's been enough of this hide-and-seek." He pushed open a door and found Jochanan seated at a table, studying the "Two Tablets of the Covenant."

"Good evening, Jochanan."

"Good evening, Uncle."

"Aren't you going to the house of prayer? Are you already imitating the saints?"

"Saints? God forbid."

"How is it then that you pray alone?"

Jochanan didn't reply.

"All right, Jochanan." Reb Shimmon's tone of voice changed. "I'm putting my cards on the table."

"Sit down, Uncle."

"Why should I sit? I shouldn't speak perhaps, but why all the secrecy? I'm told you want to be rabbi." As he spoke, Reb Shimmon was astonished at his own words.

Jochanan raised his head. "No, that's untrue, Uncle."

"You want to be asked," Reb Shimmon shouted.

"No, Uncle. It will make no difference if I am asked. May Grandfather's health be good, but should he die, God forbid, you will succeed him."

"That's what I thought. But I hear that you're following in the footsteps of Absalom."

"No, Uncle."

"If you want the rabbinate, I'll not oppose you, but I hate intrigue. Absalom at least announced his intentions."

"There isn't a word of truth in it, Uncle."

"Will you swear to that?"

"Is it necessary?"

"Sign a statement."

"What kind of a statement?"

"Here." Reb Shimmon pulled out the sheet he had thrust into his pocket, and read. "I, Jochanan, the son of Reb Zadock, give my word that I will not consent to be rabbi after my sacred grandfather's death. Moreover, I will not hold court either in Marshinov or in any other city. My uncle, Reb Shimmon, promises to arrange for the support of myself and my family."

Reb Shimmon paused. "Sign!" he ordered.

"So be it."

"Here is a pen."

Jochanan dipped the pen, then seeing that it had picked up too much ink, wiped it on his skullcap. Standing, he wrote,

"These are the words of the lowly Jochanan, the son of the saint Rabbi Zadock, blessed be his name."

IV

The rabbi lingered for days, bloated, altered, exhausted. Waking, he recalled that he was Reb Shmaryah Gad of Marshinov, critically ill, close to death. "Have I at least been saying my prayers?" the rabbi wondered. "Are they putting my phylacteries on me?" His hands must be washed; he must tell the beadle. The rabbi attempted to speak but found no words. He wished to write a will designating Jochanan as his successor, but the thought slipped from his mind. There had formed within him a network of thoughts full of Torah, wisdom, and ultimate knowledge such as man never attained in this life. As it is written of the Almighty, "He is both the One who knows and the object of His knowledge," so it was with the rabbi. His thoughts did not come from the rabbi's brain but arose with the spontaneity and ease of spiritual things. The rabbi saw and heard angels and seraphim. He met his father, his grandfather, the sacred Jacob Jospeh, the Baal Shem. He ascended with them to the Palace of the Bird Nest in the Mansion of the Messiah, saw the heavenly Temple, heard the Levites singing and playing musical instruments. He conceived the meaning of many things at once: Jacob's ladder upon which the ministering angels climbed, the Throne of Glory, the Celestial Court of Judgment, the Original Man. The rabbi skirted Gehenna and discovered that Rabbi Nachman was right; Gehenna was shame. Renegade souls despised themselves because they had not served God. Some transmigrated; others were thrown into the sling, to be whirled continuously around the earth. Adam returned to Eden, where he again met Eve and partook of the fruit of the Tree of Knowledge. The snake no longer crawled on its belly. Since everything came from eternity, how could the devil exist? Time was a hallucination;

darkness, merely the border of light; Satan, the tool of God. Pain? There was no such thing as pain. One and many were the same. So were also determination and free will. Does the stomach hurt? An old garment tears. The soul needs new clothing. Does the body suffer? Is there such a thing as a body? All bodies are one. All worlds, one world. How could Cain kill Abel if good and evil were indistinguishable?

The rabbi opened his eyes. "Is it still today?" he inquired. No one answered his question and his eyelids closed. He laughed to himself. "What kind of a question is that? Is it still today? I'm talking like a child. Am I hungry? Thirsty? Am I getting better? Am I dying?" Black draperies closed before his eyes; snakes wriggled. "What do the demons want? I am already beyond their power. Am I in the realm of Nogah, good and evil mixed? No, it's Satan's band. They are coming at me disguised as frogs, lizards, skunks, vipers, with horns and snouts, with claws and tails, with elephant trunks and boar tusks. Mother, I'm afraid! Help me! Father, they want to destroy me! What sort of eye is this? Red as fire. Shabriri and Briri, leave me alone! God, rebuke Satan! Who are you? Namah? Machlath? Marry you? We are not fated for one another. Force? I'll scream for help! I have Hassidim! They'll stand up for me! Mendel, robbers have attacked me, murderers, demons! Father, it's good you are here! I'm in terrible danger! Drive them away! Dogs? They are not just dogs. They're the hounds of Egypt. It's evil, evil! They want to dethrone the Creator. Like the generation who built the Tower of Babel. Who created them? There was darkness before light. Sammael is primeval. The First of the Firsts. How is this possible? It's right. Here is Mother? A good Sabbath, Mother. Yes, Mother, I'm studying. I'm beginning the Mishnah. A bride? You be my bride. The Messiah has come already. All souls are one.

"Mother, something hurts me. My head? No, my heart. Let me go, Mother! I want to return—return!"

Mendel the beadle had left the room for a few minutes.

When he entered again, he found the rabbi dead. Mendel had kept a feather ready, and put it to the rabbi's nostrils. It no longer moved.

"Blessed be the true Judge . . . !"

v

There was commotion in the court. Everyone rushed to the rabbi's chamber: Reb Shimmon, Reb Moshe, Temerel, the rabbi's daughters-in-law. The windows were opened and the prayer of the Justification of God's will was said. Members of the Burial Society lifted the body of the rabbi and lit candles near his head. The curtain of the Holy Ark draped the body. Little clusters of mourners formed here and there. But Reb Shimmon paced restlessly through the court. He had already prepared telegrams to be sent to Warsaw, Lodz, Lublin, and Pietrkow. A number of the Hassidim demanded that the funeral be held the following day, but Reb Shimmon scheduled it twenty-four hours later, so as to permit a number of his closest friends to get to Marshinov. There was no sleep that night; the court remained noisy; lights burned in all the rooms. Mourners wailed, women threw their arms about each other and lamented. Reb Shimmon saw that someone was at the station to meet every train, for people were arriving by the trainload: rabbis, rich men, distinguished members of the community. The terminal was crammed with admirers coming to attend the rabbi's funeral.

The next day there was no merchandise left to buy in the stores. Every oven in every bakery was in use, wagonloads of flour kept coming from the mill, messenger boys could be seen running back and forth through the streets. Rumors spread: a light had hovered above the rabbi's head all night; watchers had observed wings fluttering over the corpse; it was noted that the rabbi's lips trembled as if he were still reciting the Torah. The barren women wailed with piercing voices. Some fainted. The Burial Society had already prepared the shroud.

Reb Shimmon and Reb Moshe were arguing: should the rabbi
be buried in his old prayer shawl with the gold ornaments or
should he wear the new prayer shawl with the silver ornaments? In the midst of all this confusion, Reb Shimmon had
found time to rummage among the rabbi's documents. If the
rabbi had left a will, he wanted to be the first to see it. It had
been the rabbi's habit to store his papers in quilts. There were
many of them, filled with notes that he had written to himself.
No paper of his had been thrown away. Looking for a will in
this mess was like searching for a needle in a haystack. If the
rabbi had left a last testament, Reb Shimmon was unable to
find it.

Though Reb Shimmon was unquestionably right in maintaining that the longer the funeral was postponed, the larger
would be the crowd, pious Jews began to object. A corpse
must not be left unburied too long, particularly in summer.
To do so was sacrilege. Early on the second morning after the
rabbi's death, purification began. The body was washed with
an ablution ladle and rubbed with egg yolk. Once again the
Hassidim argued. Who was to give the funeral oration? Who
deliver the first eulogy? Each one of the rabbis was proposed
by his adherents. Particularly fortunate were those who carried the bier. Thousands of Jews followed the body to the
graveyard. Marshinov's streets were black with people. The
air was filled with the lamentation of women. The crowd
jammed into the cemetery. Some stood on tombstones, others
climbed trees or sat on the branches. The schoolboys climbed
the highest of all. The sacred body had been dressed in
shrouds and a cowl and wrapped in a prayer shawl; a twig of
myrtle had been placed between the corpse's fingers; there
were shards on his eyelids. A body was nothing but a body.

The sons said Kaddish, Reb Moshe's sidelocks shook with
his sobbing, and Reb Shimmon, raising his voice, choked back
his tears. Temerel cried out, "Father," and leaned forward as
if about to faint. Her daughters had to support her.

"Where is Jochanan? We want Jochanan," Hassidim

shouted as they drank brandy. "*Mazel tov*, Rabbi." Jochanan was as white as chalk; he shook his head from side to side. "No, no!" He pointed to Reb Shimmon. "My uncle is the rabbi."

Reb Shimmon's retinue gathered about him. One of his followers held a bottle of brandy; another, a bag with egg cookies and a tray with glasses. "To your health, Rabbi, to your health, Rabbi!" they shouted to Reb Shimmon.

"Jochanan! Jochanan!" The voices grew louder. "*Mazel tov*, Jochanan, *mazel tov*, Rabbi!"

Reb Shimmon turned pale and because of this his beard seemed blacker than ever. "It's insolence! Insolence and impudence!" he muttered. "Gentiles! Libertines! Heathens!"

"Jochanan! Jochanan!" they shouted. All were shouting, even those who had called for Reb Shimmon. Jochanan struggled. He did not wish to drink the toasts. He hid his face in his hands. They wrangled with him as if he were a schoolboy. They tore at him, pulled him. Boys and young men fell upon him: "Rabbi, Rabbi!" they cried. "The Rabbi of Marshinov!" This time Temerel actually fainted. The Chmielev rabbi, Reb Moshe, pushed his way to Jochanan. A path was cleared through the congestion. His voice broke with sobs. "Jochanan, the people want you!"

"No, no."

"Jochanan, you can't defy the whole world!"

"No, no, I don't wish it," Jochanan cried.

"Jochanan! Jochanan!"

Reb Shimmon lurched forward. He clenched his fists. "Murderers! You're drawing my blood!"

Mendel, the beadle, suddenly emitted a wild screech like the bellow of a bull. "Jews, I bear witness before God that the rabbi, may he rest in peace, wanted Jochanan as his successor. May I not live to hear the ram's horn of the Messiah if I'm lying."

"Liar! Fraud! Disgrace to your religion!" Reb Shimmon whined.

"If I lie, Reb Shimmon, may my children lie here!" said Reb Mendel, pointing to the freshly dug grave.

Everyone grew quiet. A thin wail spread among the women. Suddenly, a crow cawed. Reb Shimmon advanced to Jochanan. "Jochanan, *mazel tov!* You are the rabbi!"

And he handed him the document that he had signed.

Jochanan wanted to answer, but he could not. He bent over. He almost fell and had to be supported. His face had changed; it was red and bathed in tears. His wet sidelocks clung to his beard.

"Uncle Shimmon!" he gasped.

"Jochanan, you are the rabbi!" Reb Shimmon shouted. "Good luck to you!"

He turned and walked away. His retinue followed.

VI

In Jampol and the surrounding areas, two items of gossip were constantly being repeated. The first was that Calman would marry Clara, Daniel Kaminer's daughter; the second, that the duke had renewed the lease on the manor for a period of ten years, not to Calman alone, but to Calman in partnership with Clara. Jampol now had something to talk about, laugh at, and mock. Clara had been seen walking, arm-in-arm, with the duke. There were witnesses who claimed that they had seen them kissing under a tree.

Reb Menachem Mendel had been thinking of leaving the rabbinate of Jampol. But when he heard this story about Clara, he decided that he could not remain in Jampol another day. Calman, his in-law, was his only protector. But if Calman became Daniel Kaminer's son-in-law and married a hussy who went about with her head uncovered, he, Reb Menachem Mendel, could no longer accept his protection. Reb Menachem Mendel, usually calm, became unmanageable. Tirza Perl, his wife, and Mirale, his daughter, had never seen him like this before. Snatching up his prayer shawl and phylacteries, he started toward the door, ready to go to the railroad station on foot. Tirza Perl began to wring her hands.

"What kind of madness is this?" she asked.

"I am going to Warsaw! It's the end of the world! It must mean that the Messiah is coming."

"What will you do in Warsaw? We don't even have an apartment!"

"The Almighty will not forsake me."

Wiping a tear with her apron, Tirza Perl agreed. Jampol meant only heartbreak and shame. Besides, here Mirale was already considered a spinster at twenty-two. Tirza Perl could not show her face on the street. Warsaw, at least, was a large city. Ezriel was in Warsaw. Brother and sister might find an apartment together. Mirale went to the manor to see her sister-in-law Shaindel. Shaindel, whose eyes were red from weeping, fell upon Mirale, kissed her, and began to whimper.

"You know everything already?" Mirale asked.

"I can't understand it, I can't understand it!" Shaindel said. "Father is killing himself—without a knife!"

After Shaindel had wept and dried her tears, Mirale told her that her father was leaving Jampol and that she would go with him.

I4 🏛

Calman wanted the wedding to be a quiet one, in the home of a Warsaw rabbi. He was a widower and she a widow; why make a fuss? But Clara had already decided to have the wedding at her aunt's apartment. Clara wished to show off her expensive gown and valuable jewelry. She had a wedding dress stored away that was practically new. Since she'd had no children, she decided she could wear white. She engaged musicians and a wedding jester who knew enough of the language to slip in some Polish jokes. Clara wanted many guests, but she had no relatives in Warsaw besides her aunt, and few acquaintances. Calman, certainly, had no one to invite. Grain the pharmacist and his wife, David Sorkess and his wife Sonya, Morris Shalit, and Tamara would, of course, come from Jampol. Mrs. Frankel's distant relatives, the girls who worked in her shop, the women who had once worked for her as milliners, their husbands, their friends and acquaintances would have to make up the rest of the list. People whom Calman had never heard of would eat, drink, and be merry at his wedding.

It wasn't easy for Calman to leave the manor for the trip to Warsaw. The Sabbath following the Fast of the Ninth of Ab fell at threshing time. Advance plans had to be made for planting the winter wheat. In Calman's forest, trees were being chopped down from early morning until sunset. No matter how diligent the guards were, lumber was always disappearing. Calman had not wanted to re-hire employees who had slandered him after he had discharged them, when he gave up his lumber business. He therefore imported help from other cities. The result was agitation and disputes. Half of Jampol owed its living to Calman, but all of Jampol cursed him. The tailor-journeymen had even composed a jingle about him that the seamstresses and shoemakers sang. The lyrics began:

Calman, the man of money,
Found a girl as sweet as honey.
Fool he was to marry her,
For off she ran with an officer . . .

Yes, Calman had already learned that envy was the people's worst trait. Even in the midst of wedding plans, plans for building a house of prayer, a ritual bath on the estate, and moving into the manor itself, he often longed to drop his responsibilities, his property, his enemies, his false friends, and settle somewhere in some village, some forest, or in a strange city where nobody knew him and he knew no one. Who could tell? Clara might even go with him. However much the people of Jampol slandered him, they literally pelted Clara with slime from head to toe.

Both Jews and Gentiles resented the fact that the Count was being forced to move out of his own house at Clara's insistence. Every day, every hour, there were new insults. In his store in Jampol, anonymous letters were left by individuals who allegedly had seen Clara with every officer, every sergeant major, every soldier in the barracks. Calman knew that it was unwise to show Clara such trash, but he couldn't keep the letters to himself. Her eyes grew fierce. "Their gall is spilling over, is it? It's eating them up, is it? I hope they all have epileptic fits!"

On the very day that Calman left for Warsaw to be married, he received a letter from his son-in-law, Jochanan, the

Marshinov rabbi. It was written in Yiddish, not Hebrew, and read as follows:

> To My Honorable Father-in-law, the Famous Philanthropist, Reb Calman,
> First, I want to inform you that we are all in good health. Praised be the name of God, I hope to hear the same from you and yours. And let us pray that we are saved in this world and the world to come. Second, I would like to inform you that your daughter, my wife, has heard some rumors that have caused me great anguish, and although I do not know if they are true, I would like to remind you that such matters should be considered carefully. The Talmud says that a man's second marriage is ordained in heaven according to his merits. I don't wish to insult you. I am interested only in your welfare. It is a great sin to give a Jewish daughter a bad name and everything should be investigated thoroughly. We have other troubles here, too. I never wanted to take my grandfather's place. I would have left Marshinov altogether if my mother had not prevailed upon me to stay. The Almighty should take pity upon us all. Best regards to everybody and greetings from your daughter, who longs to see you soon.
> Your son-in-law, who is young and poor, a threshold to be stepped upon by the feet of the sages,
> > The Lowly Jochanan, the Son of the Saintly Rabbi Zadock of Blessed Memory.

Calman read on and his eyes grew wet, but he said to himself: "It is too late!"

11

Usually, when Calman went to Warsaw, he stayed at Reb Ezekiel Wiener's, Mayer Joel's father's house, but Reb Ezekiel

Wiener was angry at Calman. Who wasn't angry at him? Even Shaindel, his favorite daughter, was furious at him. Calman stayed at a hotel. Since the groom must not come alone to the wedding, he arranged that David Sorkess and Morris Shalit accompany him to Mrs. Frankel's apartment. They were to call for him at about nine in the evening (the days had again begun to grow shorter), but Calman's watch said a quarter of ten and his attendants had not yet appeared. Calman sat in his room. Even though he disliked the taste of tobacco, he lit one of the cigars he had brought to give away as presents. He was startled by every footstep that passed, but no one came. Doors opened and closed. Men and women conversed in the corridors, murmured, giggled. Everyone in the hotel knew who he was and for whom he was waiting. Had he given them the wrong address? Or had Clara changed her mind at the last moment? Had something happened, some tragedy? The minute hand was already nearing ten, and still no one appeared. Calman could no longer remain seated. He began to pace back and forth. His boots squeaked. "Changed her mind, changed her mind!" he thought or mumbled. "Simply wanted to disgrace me! Who can tell? Perhaps it was all a joke? Everything is possible, everything is possible! They've made a fool of me. They've swindled me out of my property. They'll all have fun at my expense." Calman knew that it wasn't so, that it couldn't be so. Clara wouldn't go to such extremes. Daniel Kaminer was no longer a youngster. But new suspicions sprang up every minute. Maybe she wasn't a widow at all, and her husband still lived. Perhaps he would appear and break up the wedding. Perhaps Clara suddenly decided to become converted. If Miriam Lieba could commit such a sin, why shouldn't Clara be capable of it? "I knew all along that things wouldn't go smoothly!" Calman said to himself. A spark fell from his cigar and he imagined that a fire had broken out at Mrs. Frankel's. It had consumed the entire apartment. Everyone had been burned to a crisp. "I shouldn't have defied the whole world! Jochanan is a saint, and when a saint is annoyed, it's not good. God Almighty, help me, help me!" Calman began to pray. "Not for my sake, but for the sake of—"

Calman heard footsteps. The door opened. There stood David Sorkess and Morris Shalit in top hats, canes in their hands—two little "Germans"—smelling of perfume.

"Here's the bridegroom!" David Sorkess cried out, hoarse with drink.

"Pridegroom, I mean bridegroom!" Morris Shalit shouted arrogantly.

Usually these men spoke to Calman with respect, for they both owed him their living. But now that he was about to become Clara's husband, he had fallen even in their eyes. From their frivolity, Calman guessed that they looked on the whole thing as a Purim prank.

"What took you so long?"

"The bride is adorning herself!" And both of them burst out laughing.

Calman went down with them. There was a slight opening of doors, revealing half faces of women. A droshky with two horses and an ornate harness waited outside. Children flocked around it. When Calman appeared, they began to shout: "Hurrah! Hurrah!" In the street, everyone seemed to know where he was going. Calman, his head bowed, sat between his two attendants on the upholstered seat. "Why are they so perfumed?" he asked himself. He was about to marry a modern woman, a Russian, but at the same time he felt contemptuous of worldly conduct. Why did they fuss so much? Why were they so gay? They wouldn't live forever.

At the gate of Mrs. Frankel's house, Calman saw droshkies, people in party clothes, obviously wedding guests. Climbing the steps, Calman felt like an ox about to be slaughtered. "Maybe it is not too late to escape?" he thought. He heard music, shouting, women giggling. The door to Mrs. Frankel's apartment stood ajar. Heat emanated from within, an odor of flesh. The orchestra had begun to play, the jester was performing, couples danced. They led him inside as if to a ball. All faces were laughing, all eyes shone. Perfume assailed Calman. His head began to whirl. It was crowded here, terribly warm. The naphtha lamps were dazzling. Some of the guests openly mocked Calman, others congratulated him, pressed his hand. The rabbi and the beadle from the Warsaw rabbinate were already there. The rabbi sat down to inscribe the marriage contract with a steel pen. He asked: "What's the bride's name?"

"Clara," said Daniel Kaminer.

"Clara is not a Jewish name. What was the name given her when you were called before the Holy Scroll?"

"She's named after her grandmother, Keila Rebecca."

"Then why didn't you say so?"

Despite the confusion, everything went according to the law. Calman was helped into a white robe, to remind him of the day of death. Four men raised the poles that supported the marriage canopy. The others carried twisted candles in their hands. Calman was led under the canopy and Clara was brought in, dressed in white silk with a tulle net over her hair. Her face was uncovered; she smiled at Calman. Saying the benediction over a cup of wine, the rabbi gave it to Calman and Clara. Clara extended her index finger and Calman placed the wedding ring on it, saying "Behold, thou art consecrated." The rabbi read the marriage contract in Aramaic, which Calman did not understand. Here and there he caught a word that was similar in Hebrew.

Oddly enough, when the rabbi began to recite the second benediction, the same girls and women who had been laughing impudently grew silent. Here and there, a woman wiped away a tear. It is not child's play to be born, to marry, to bring forth generations, to grow old, to die. These are matters no jester's witticisms can belittle. Calman's eyes misted over. Did Zelda, may she rest in peace, know what he was doing? Was her soul hovering nearby? Was he really committing a sin, or would something good come of this?

The canopy was removed. A tumult followed—congratulations and kissing. Clara and her aunt hugged one another, shaking back and forth. The men had already started drinking brandy and eating ginger cakes. Cherry brandy and liqueur were served to the women. The rabbi congratulated Calman. Afterward, Daniel Kaminer took the groom by the arm and, in his Lithuanian accent, half seriously, half jokingly, advised Calman as a father-in-law and as a friend. Calman too was served a drink. Clara, having embraced her aunt, kissed Celina, Tamara Shalit, Sonya Sorkess, Itka Grain, and then approached Calman.

"Well, don't you have anything to say? My husband!"

Calman could not speak. His eyes brimmed with tears and he could not quite see her. Finally he regained his voice. "Let us not forget God!" he said.

III

Business had taught Calman how easy it was to make a mistake. One figured and figured and then forgot that two and two make four. In accounting for the very smallest expenses, one sometimes forgot the largest. This was exactly what happened to Calman. He had been living at such a pace, had been involved in so many transactions, that he had forgotten the most important thing. Clara had promised to go to the ritual bath before the wedding, but Calman had not asked her whether she had kept her word. Sitting at the wedding banquet, he was reminded of other things that he could not understand, having missed them in the first place. Mrs. Frankel had told him that she bought meat at a kosher butcher's. But what about the salting and soaking of the meat? And what about her kitchen? Had she been careful not to mix the dairy dishes with the meat dishes? Did she consult an authority when in doubt? Dared he, Calman, eat here? Could one expect a woman with an uncovered head to keep a kosher home? He saw no evidence of respect for God here. If that were so, he,

Calman, might be eating forbidden food at his own wedding. And if that weren't enough, he would be lying this very night, God forbid, with a woman who had not made her ablutions. Calman's stomach felt hollow.

"Can it be that I am mad?" he thought. "Yes, I am in their power, in the company of Satan!" Calman choked on every bite. "What have I done? How is it possible? The Evil one must have been deceiving me! This means that all the accusations against me are true!"

The musicians played on; the jester in mixed Yiddish-Polish entertained the guests with Polish theater and cabaret jokes. The rooms were filled with noise and laughter. But Calman sat there, depressed. "Is there any way out? What must I do, according to the law?" Calman knew the answer: he must stand up and run as if a fire were chasing him. He must fast, repent, and torture himself for the sins he had committed. He recalled the words of the Rod of Punishment: How hot are the fires of the seven hells and how many metamorphoses must one bear until one can come even to Gehenna! For a moment he rose, as if to leave the table and escape. But he sat down again. Ezriel's words came to mind: "The Jews have their Torah, the Christians have their own laws. Did anyone see Moses receive the Torah on Mount Sinai? It is all legend."

"Well, well, I'm doing fine and becoming a heretic to boot," Calman thought to himself, astonished that the Evil Spirit had so swiftly steered him to the abyss.

"I must escape," he told himself, but he could not compel himself to move. He remained sitting, sipping his chicken soup, chewing the meat, listening to the peppery jokes of the jester, looking at the women with their bare arms, naked throats, powdered faces, hearing their wanton shrieks. Clara did not remain in her seat next to Calman. She was constantly being summoned elsewhere. New guests kept arriving with wedding presents as if this were a marriage between a bachelor and a young girl. Calman stared at them from beneath lowered brows. Who were they? How did Mrs. Frankel know so many people? Why were they so excited? And why had Clara wanted such a crowd? When Clara returned to him, Calman thought he had never seen her look so handsome. Her skin glowed. She wore as much jewelry as a queen. Pouring some wine for him, she said, "Drink, this is a wedding!"

And in worldly fashion she clinked his glass with hers.

"Is it kosher wine, at least?" Calman asked, ashamed of his own words. No longer confident, they sounded apprehensive and insincere.

"Kosher, kosher! Everything is kosher!" Clara scolded good-naturedly, winking as she did so. Calman understood what she meant: "*You* aren't such a saint."

Calman drained the glass and she poured him another. He recalled a verse from the Scriptures: "And wine that maketh glad the heart of man." His head reeled, his knees felt heavy. "Well, what of it? Gehenna was for people too, not dogs," he told himself. "According to the holy book, everyone ends up on a bed of nails, anyhow . . ." He began to feel a kind of resentment against the Creator. Zelda had been a pious woman, and how had she been rewarded? Work, sickness, a short life. And the schoolchildren that Chmielnicki had buried alive? They hadn't even known the taste of sin . . . Even according to Ecclesiastes, human beings and animals are the same. The dead know nothing.

By the time the crowd began to disperse, it was daybreak. Clara had rented rooms in a nearby hotel. A droshky waited outside to take them the short distance. People were rising to start the day, but Calman was going to a Gentile hotel with an unpious woman. Rows of keys hung on the wall behind the dozing desk clerk. Jerking awake, he gave the key to a servant. The marble stairway was carpeted. Clara's arm was on Calman's as they walked up. Skillfully, the servant carried the two valises, unlocked the door, and let the couple into the dusky suite. He lit a lamp and Clara tipped him. The room was large, the ceiling high. It was strangely cold. Clara opened the door to the other room. Calman thought she seemed very much at home. Before closing the door behind her, she said, "The toilet is in the hall, to the left."

When Calman returned, he found Clara in a lacy silk nightgown, her hair down, her feet in slippers. She had apparently put on fresh perfume. She reminded Calman of the queens and princesses that were engraved on banknotes and medallions. Suddenly she said in Polish: "Well, get undressed."

"Yes, certainly."

Calman was ashamed to undress before so grand a lady. Putting out the light, he began removing his new boots, which burned his soles, even though they cost fifteen rubles and were made of kid. He remembered not having said his nightly prayers, but he couldn't see where to wash his hands in the dark. He closed his eyes. Lust for Clara had faded away, and only fear remained.

15

I

The attic apartment of 19 Krochmalna Street, consisting of two rooms and a kitchen, was inhabited by Todros Bendiner, a sexton's son, who had returned to Poland after having spent several years wandering around Berlin, jobless and hungry. Bendiner's vagabond life had ended in illness; finally he had settled down in Warsaw as a baker. He had ruptured himself kneading the heavy dough and now only did such light work as stoking the ovens, sweeping the bakery floor, and running errands. Even though Todros Bendiner had six children, he partitioned off an alcove in his small apartment and rented it out.

Ezriel knew a Hebrew teacher who recommended the room to him, and he decided to take it. Rytza Leah, Todros's wife, served Ezriel his meals, and he paid ten gulden a week for room and board. The tiny room had a window which looked out on a courtyard. Ezriel's furniture consisted of a bed, a table, one chair, and a bookcase.

As he sat at his table studying, his eyes would stray from his book now and then to stare out into the courtyard. The building was inhabited by the very poor. The people disposed of their slops out of the windows; there was no drainage in the court, and deep puddles formed. Garbage was heaped high around the refuse box and the stench was so strong that it rose to Ezriel on the third floor.

The courtyard served both as workshop and marketplace. A dyer used it to carry on his trade; an upholsterer could be seen busily stuffing chairs and sofas. There was even a stall with cows, and women carried empty jugs and pans into the courtyard and took them away filled with milk still warm from the udder. Periodically the janitor appeared to feed potato peelings to his goat. Women hung out their wash to dry and aired clothing and bedding, beating out the dust with heavy sticks. Often the sound of animals and chattering girls would mingle with voices chanting the Torah, for there was also a Hassidic study house located in the building.

It was Monday, customarily the day for beggars to collect alms, and a tattered host swarmed through the courtyard gates and into the building. The beggars trudged up and down stairs, knocked on apartment doors, and exhibited crippled limbs. In a cheder located in the tenement, some of the children recited the Pentateuch. Most of the youngsters, however, were outdoors playing with sticks and strings and bits of broken dishes. A group of them were amusing themselves by tormenting a boy with rickety limbs, trying to knock his hat off.

Ezriel sat with Malinin's *Book of Problems* open before him. The problem he was considering involved a cattle dealer who had sold half of his oxen, a third of his sheep, and a quarter of his calves. "Well, if you want to get ahead, you've got to sweat," Ezriel remarked to himself, imitating the tone of his tutor Belkin. The small table at which he sat was covered with textbooks and dictionaries. Ezriel read, listening with one ear to what was going on outside. A candle burned in one of the windows, apparently at the head of a corpse. In these flats there lived the paralyzed, the blind, the mute, the insane, those for whom there was no room in institutions. Occasionally a woman in labor could be heard screaming in pain. People wandered about in the dark cellars, where mice scurried around even at midday. Work went on from early morning until late at night. Ezriel had long since learned that the harder people worked, the less they earned.

"How can it be otherwise," Ezriel mumbled to himself, "when it's all a play of blind forces? Matter and energy . . . the survival of the fittest. Justice? No, justice is impossible in such a universe. If there is no God, there is no sin. It's all a jungle."

Rytza Leah entered.

"Three letters for you."

"Three? Thank you very much."

Two were from Jampol—one from Shaindel and one from his parents. The third letter came from someone called Justina Malewska and was postmarked Warsaw. The envelope was blue and the address was written in an ornate hand. Inside the envelope was a sheet of matching paper. It read as follows, in Polish:

> Esteemed Mister E. Babad,
>
> I have just returned from Paris, where I made the acquaintance of your sister-in-law, the Countess Maria Jampolska. Knowing that my father has business dealings with your father-in-law, she asked me to convey her regards to you. I have just learned your address. I am generally at home until noon, and can also be reached evenings. I am a Wallenberg. I hope that we will meet soon. Best regards.

Ezriel read the letter over many times, but it did not occur to him at first that the Countess Maria Jampolska was Miriam Lieba. He now tore open the other envelopes and learned from Shaindel that a letter had come from Wallenberg's daughter which she was sending on to him. Shaindel also wrote that Yosele—Uri Joseph—was well and a smart boy, asked a great many questions and missed his daddy, and she, Shaindel, also wished it were time for him to come home on vacation. She had many other things to say; in fact, she covered several sheets, writing on both sides and along the margins for good measure. The third was a joint letter from his father, mother, and Mirale. In Hebrew, his father wrote that he could no longer take the insinuations of the Jampol elders and wanted to move to Warsaw. He had been told that many rabbis not officially employed by the community were able to earn a livelihood in the big city. Perhaps Ezriel could find a flat for him in a Jewish neighborhood? Was a rabbi by chance needed on Krochmalna Street?

His mother's postscript was full of anger: "I can no longer live among these ruffians. They make our lives miserable. Jampol is another Sodom . . ." Mirale had added two lines: "Ezriel, save us from this slime. Your sister, Mirale."

Ezriel shoved his books aside. Such fanatics! He could no longer remain cooped up in this narrow little room. He had to go out into the street. The Countess Maria Jampolska of Paris was his sister-in-law. Wallenberg's daughter invited him to her home. His father was coming to settle in Warsaw for good. Time did not stand still. Ezriel began to look over the sheet-draped garments hanging on the wall and decided to put on his navy-blue jacket. He would buy himself a new collar, and he would trim his beard as well. Luckily, the laundress had brought back his wash. He wondered if he should visit Madame Malewska that evening. No, tomorrow would be better. Picking up his copy of Euclid, Ezriel went outdoors and found the June day was sunny and warm. He walked down the refuse-strewn stairs and out into Krochmalna Street. It too was filled with noise and bustle. Slops were being thrown from open doors and filth ran down the gutters; a window opened and garbage flew out. There were many bakeries on the street and the chimneys belched smoke. The stables attracted flies. The street was alive with a thousand activities. Cobblers sat outside on their benches, mending shoes. Women seated on stools and doorsteps nursed their babies. A gang of urchins followed a mute, chanting: "Dumbbell!" Couples quarreled, and neighbors sought to make peace between them. Ezriel made his way to the ruins of the Mirowska barracks. The barracks, which should have been torn down completely as relics of the old Polish rule, instead formed the center of a mass of peasants' carts, dray wagons, and droshkies, for this neighborhood was one great market dealing in fruit, vegetables, and meat. Leaving Ziabia Street, Ezriel entered the Saxony Gardens. Because of the warm spring weather, the park was almost as crowded as the rest of the city. A charitable society was holding a lottery opposite the stand where mineral water was sold. Benches had been set up and tents erected. A poster announced that among the items to be raffled off was a milch cow. Children rolled hoops, played ball. Adults played a game called "extra," in which a ball was thrown from one player to the other, while a third, the "runner," tried to intercept it. The Russians had banned *palant* and other games that were specifically Polish.

Ezriel tried to read Euclid, but his desire to study suddenly left him. He began to stroll back and forth. For a while he remained standing at the pond. Boys in sailor suits and girls dressed up like little ladies threw crumbs to the swans. The nurses and governesses addressed them in Polish and French. Here there were no Jews in long capotes or women with bonnets and wigs. The men wore straw hats or an occasional top hat or derby. Unlike the unkempt beards of the Jews, theirs were trimmed into points, spades, wedges, their mustaches curled up like springs or jutted straight out stiff as wire. The young wore their soft shirt collars open over their jackets—Slowacki fashion—in the manner of the famous poet. But the older people, although it was summer, had on stiff collars and broad neckties. Everyone seemed stylish. Light trousers went with dark jackets, overcoats were worn or carried, shoes were polished to a high gloss, and canes were silver- or bone-handled. The gymnasium and university students walked about in gilt-buttoned uniforms. Ladies' hats looked like plates laden with flowers and fruits, and most of them had veils as well. Dresses were tight-waisted, beribboned, and pleated; gloves were almost elbow-length; parasols and fans blazed with colors. Lovers walked arm in arm, smiled into each other's eyes, hid in shaded paths. Everything here had a worldly glow: the fountain, the greenhouses, the flower beds. Bearded, white-aproned Russians carried ice-cream casks on their heads. There was a confectionery in the park, and a dairy, where young people drank sour milk. Ezriel again sat down on a bench and enmeshed himself in Euclidean theorems, but he could not concentrate.

How should he behave tomorrow at Justina Malewska's? Should he kiss her hand? Pay her a compliment? Should he address her as Madame or Gracious Lady, or Honorable Lady? What should he do if he were offered food? Should he accept it? Or refuse? How long should he stay? Should he extend his hand first? Or wait until she offered hers? Did he need a calling-card? What if he had to meet her husband, relatives, friends? How should he address them? Ezriel shook his head. He had changed! A few years before, he had been a real man and never had to demean himself. Now suddenly he was dependent, inferior. It would mean years of study for him to master Russian, Latin, Greek. So many languages and subjects were needed in order to finish the seven grades and earn a diploma. He must learn worldly manners, choose the right profession, and after all that he would still be nothing but a persecuted Jew . . . How odd, that the future world was easier by far than this one. In it, there was one reckoning, God. Here one was forced to consider countless directors, inspectors, laws, regulations, rules of etiquette, forms—a code far more complex than the Shulhan Aruk, the book containing the Jewish laws.

Ezriel sat there, absorbed in thought. Someone tapped him on the shoulder. He trembled, recognizing Mr. Wallenberg, whose office he had once visited.

"Pardon me, aren't you Mr. Jacoby's son-in-law?"

Ezriel stood up. "Mr. Wallenberg!"

"Yes. I was strolling through the park when I saw you, sitting deep in thought . . . I recognized you at once—"

"Oh, it is an honor for me! Only today I received a letter from your daughter—"

"I know, I know. We were speaking of you the other day.

Your sister-in-law, the Countess, met my daughter. A small town, this world, eh? How is your father-in-law?"

"All right, thank you."

"I believe you already have a child?"

"Yes, a little boy."

"Well, that's fine. It's been a while since I've seen your father-in-law, but I think I'll soon be doing business with him again. That is—if conditions permit. Negotiations are in progress to build another railroad, rather a large project, but so far no final decisions have been made. Don't say anything to him yet. An honest man, a responsible man, but old-fashioned. . . . My daughter tells me that the Countess is a beauty, though in terrible straits. You'll find out about it from her. I see that you've given up wearing a caftan."

"Yes, I'm studying."

"You're doing the right thing. The first time I saw you I knew you were a sensible young man. Where have you been hiding all this time? I told you once that I was prepared to help you."

"Oh, thank you, I know that you have no time."

"True, but one doesn't live for oneself alone. Come to see me. I've made it a habit to walk three-quarters of an hour each day. One feels confined in an office. This summer I intend to visit Carlsbad. I have a villa and some property on the Vistula. My family is moving there soon. I hear your mother-in-law died."

"Yes, quite some time ago."

"I know. I sent your father-in-law my condolences. What are your plans?"

"I hope to get my degree and study medicine."

"Why medicine?"

"I don't know myself."

"Well, doctors are needed too. Jews like doctors. A Jew will skip a meal but buy medicine. They *are* sick, as a matter of fact. Diabetes is especially prevalent among them, and consumption as well. Where are you studying?"

"Privately, with tutors."

"I can help you. The chief inspector of all intermediate schools in Russian Poland is a friend of mine. Generally, I don't approve of using influence—I believe in the honest way. But every rule has its exceptions. Are you on bad terms with your father-in-law?"

"No, we're not on bad terms."

"He isn't angry that you've removed your caftan?"

"He's happy I haven't shaved off my beard."

"A compromise, eh? I understand. What are you doing this evening?"

"Nothing special."

"Then why not come along with me? I'll only stay in the office about half an hour. Have supper with us. My daughter will be there too, and she'll tell you about your sister-in-law, and you can tell me all about your studies. I'd like to help someone. Why shouldn't it be you—for your father-in-law's sake, and for yours too, of course."

"I don't know how to thank you, but—"

"Why 'but'?"

"I'm not properly dressed."

"You are decently dressed. Clean—that's the main thing. What does one expect of a student? Come! You won't have to eat pork. You aren't religious, after all, are you? God doesn't care what you eat. All He asks is that you love your fellow man, isn't that so?" And Mr. Wallenberg, to show off, chanted in a Polish-accented Hebrew: "Thou shalt love thy neighbor as thyself . . ."

I I

Who could have foretold that Ezriel would be riding in a carriage that very day! From the window he looked out at Warsaw. To his left were the Saxony Gardens. In the park, an obelisk like a huge finger pointed at the sky. Soon the carriage turned into Krakow Avenue. King Zygmunt's monument and

the castle where a Russian governor-general ruled instead of a
Polish king loomed in the distance. They passed Berg Street,
named for the regent who had helped suppress Poland. Polish
history permeated every cobblestone, every brick, but Russian
was the language on all store and street signs. The sidewalks
were crowded. In the gutter, among the carriages, wagons,
and droshkies, a horse-drawn omnibus pressed forward—on
its way from the Vienna depot to Praga. The carriage reached
the wealthier section of the city. The farther they went, the
lower the houses became and the greater the spaces between
them. After Jerusalem Avenue there were villas, gardens, and
even orchards with fruit trees. Many Lithuanian nobles, exiled
to Poland after the Insurrection of 1863, lived in this neighborhood. Mr. Wallenberg's villa, located near Hozia Street,
was surrounded by a garden. A watchman opened the gate, a
stableboy in livery came out to tend to the horses. A servant
opened the front door, bowed, and took Ezriel's hat. Ezriel
was dazzled by the splendor. The parquet floors shone; paintings in carved and gilded frames hung on the walls; the lamps
were decorated with crystal prisms which reflected the colors
of the rainbow; earthen urns contained palms, fig trees, and all
sorts of exotic plants. The rugs were thick. Mr. Wallenberg
led Ezriel into a salon and introduced him to a gray-haired
lady and several young men and women. Ezriel kissed the elderly lady's hand and bowed to the others. Mr. Wallenberg
spoke in a deep, resonant voice. "This is Calman Jacoby's son-
in-law. Just imagine—I recognized him at the Saxony Gardens
. . . Here is my daughter, Justina, who wrote to you . . ."

Justina Malewska was small and dark, somewhat resembling
the women in Japanese prints. Her upswept coiffure looked
like a wig. Her eyes shone, keen and merry. Pearls glowed at
her throat, diamonds sparkled in her earlobes. She extended a
soft hand with pointed fingers covered with rings. She looked
at Ezriel with mocking familiarity.

"Isn't that a strange coincidence? I write you a letter, and
my father meets you in the park. My meeting with your sister-

in-law, the Countess, was also a coincidence. I'll discuss the details with you later. One thing I can tell you now—she is very unhappy."

"Why?"

"A thousand reasons. The Count is completely mad. The Polish colony received him as a hero, but he has antagonized everyone. He associates with all sorts of charlatans and adventurers. All doors are closed to him now."

Madame Malewska hesitated, fanning herself.

"I'll be frank with you: he drinks. Perpetually."

"Oh."

"Everyone adores the Countess, but because of her husband, they've stopped inviting her to their homes. She's not well, either. She had a difficult delivery; she was close to death. I am concerned for her health."

"How is the child?"

"A little angel!"

The door opened and the maid announced dinner. Ezriel saw how the men offered their arms to the ladies. He did not know what to do. Madame Malewska smiled, and took his arm.

"The gentleman has no objection?"

"I am deeply honored," Ezriel replied.

The meal lasted a long time. Meat, vegetables, and compotes were served. Madame Malewska discreetly showed Ezriel how to conduct himself. He sat with a napkin tucked between his lapels, ate foods he had never tasted (the plates were decorated with pictures of Napoleon), and drank dry wine. Everything was guided by rules, each gesture was deliberate. Ashamed of his ignorance of etiquette, Ezriel determined to remember everything. His shyness seemed to have disappeared. The wine put him in a gay mood. He bantered with Madame Malewska and she laughed with her small mouth.

"The Countess spoke very highly of you. Could she be in love with you?" teased Madame Malewska.

"Why me, of all people?"

"Who can tell what goes on in a woman's heart? We'll discuss it later, but it would be better if she returned to Poland."

"With him?"

"How can he come? They would arrest him."

"What would she do here alone?"

"I don't know. Is there a chance of her making up with her father?"

"Out of the question."

"I was at her house. She is the most destitute countess I have ever met. I needn't tell you there is no lack of impoverished aristocrats in France—Polish and even French. Here in Poland, a Potocki works on the Vienna train. He's a cashier or a conductor. This world is no ivory tower. One cannot hide from reality, no matter how much one might want to."

Ezriel had thought that apostates would avoid all talk of Jews, but Mr. Wallenberg discussed Jews at the table and later in the salon. He was, apparently, well informed on Jewish affairs. Western European Jews, he said, had adapted themselves to the customs of the countries in which they lived, but Polish Jews had remained a tribe of Asiatics. When a Western European Jew died, he made provision in his will for community needs—the Auerbach Orphans' Home in Berlin, Frankel's Israelite Seminary in Wroclaw, Oppenheimer's and Magnus Levy's legacies—the huge sums given by Jews in England and in the United States, the institutions built for orphans, for poor children, to teach them trades, the funds put into schools, hospitals, rabbinical seminaries! What did the Warsaw Jews have? A filthy hospital and a wretched soup kitchen. As for Hassidism, there was no need to talk about them at all. They were savage Bedouins. And what about the conduct of the progressive Jew in Poland? He lived for himself. He felt no responsibility whatsoever for the community. His daughters were taught to mouth some French and dabble on the pianoforte. The Jewish woman in Poland bathed in luxury, even if her husband was on the verge of bankruptcy. In contrast, Wallenberg mentioned Adolf Kremier, and a Sephardic Jew from America who had taken the post of consul-general to Rumania in order to help the Rumanian Jews; he spoke of the Jewish financiers who had boycotted Rumania because of its persecution of Jews, the Parisian Rothschild who had loaned the French government two hundred million francs to help pay reparations to Prussia, and of the two daughters of the London Rothschild, Anna and Flora, who had collaborated on a history of the Jewish people. Was there anything comparable to these examples among the Jews of Poland?

Ezriel noticed that when Wallenberg discussed the Jewish question he grew as excited as if he were still a Jew himself. His voice became loud. Pounding his fist on the end table next to his chair, he almost shattered a vase. His sideburns were already completely gray. His face was red. His belly seemed about to escape his waistcoat, and his throat was encased in a high, stiff collar. His black eyes blazed with anger, then filled with that Jewish concern about humanity that no holy water could wash away. Silent and maternal, Madame Wallenberg gazed at her husband, nodding her gray coiffure as if in acceptance of age-old truths that defied all challenge. The Gentile sons-in-law listened and said nothing. The son and daughters held discussions of their own at the other end of the salon. Ezriel heard them speaking of shoes. After a while, Wallenberg was left alone with Ezriel. Wallenberg did not speak for a moment. Quickly he drank the coffee that he had allowed to grow cold.

"So you want to become a doctor—" he said finally.

"Yes."

"May I ask you something?"

"Of course, please do."

"Are you a believer?"

Ezriel did not know what to answer.

"Not in the usual sense."

"In what sense, then?"

"Some higher power must exist."

"Do you believe that this higher power revealed itself to

Moses on Mount Sinai and gave Jews the Torah and the Talmud and all the commentaries that the rabbis will continue explicating until the end of creation?"

"No, I am not that much of a believer."

"If that is so, then why are you still a Jew? I'm speaking to you frankly: no matter what you want to become, a doctor, an engineer, or a banker—you won't get there easily, being a Jew. I mentioned the Western European Jews. They are devoted patriots. Many Jewish young men died for Prussia and for France as well. A good number received decorations. During the war it came to the point where the Prussian Jews had to step out of the Alliance Israelite. One could not be at war and belong to the same organization. Recently there was a trial in France involving a crooked Jewish firm, and the rightist press immediately began agitating that Jews again put on yellow caps and return to the ghetto. During the war the Jews of Metz were nearly driven out of town. You probably don't read the newspapers, but I do. I read everything. For every Jew who gets a medal, hundreds get beatings. Our Polish press has been quite decent until now, but recently there was an angry article in *Gazeta Polska* protesting against the Jews in long caftans who attend concerts in Swiss Valley, screech jargon at each other, and don't bother to use handkerchiefs. The difference between Jews and Gentiles is that the Gentile who wipes his nose with his fingers doesn't attend concerts. A Jew does both. Can you foresee how this will end?"

"You can't expect all the Jews in Poland to have perfect manners."

"That's true, but a minority is always picked on, especially a minority with social aspirations. There was a time when I believed that if the Jews were to remove their caftans and learn to speak the native language, everything would be fine. Now I see that it's not so. To the rest of the world, the modern Jew is a ruthless competitor. In two thousand years, the Jews have accumulated a reservoir of skills that no other people possesses."

"What should the Jews do with their skills? Cast them aside?"

"No, but—"

Justina Malewska joined them.

"Father, I don't want to interrrupt you, but I must speak with Mr. Babad about his sister-in-law. You're talking, as I can hear, about all sorts of things, but this concerns a living person."

"Yes, Daughter, speak to him. He is an intelligent young man."

"Come, we'll go into another room."

Ezriel excused himself. Justina led him into a smaller salon or drawing room. Ezriel did not know what to call it. There was a clock supported by a satyr, and many mirrors hung on the walls, which were covered with yellow silk. Justina began to recount the circumstances that had brought her together with the Countess, as she called Miriam Lieba. Justina spoke of a dozen things at once: of her ties to the Polish colony, of her meetings with Polish leaders, writers, artistocrats, of how she had been received in Paris salons. Soon she spoke of the desperate need that dominated the Polish colony: their begging had reached the depths of degradation. The Poles had "borrowed" her last franc, and she had barely enough money to return home. Lucian was a drunkard, an adventurer, a beggar, all rolled into one. He ate in cheap soup kitchens. He constantly threatened to join the Foreign Legion, which most probably would not even accept him. The Countess went hungry. Justina paused for a moment. Her throat moved as if she had swallowed something.

"What I have to tell you will shock you, I know, but you are now the person closest to her."

"What is it?"

"She's become a laundress to keep from starving."

16 🏠

In Paris the Jampolskis lived in one room on a dead-end street
of the Belleville quarter. It was a street of stables, bakeries, and
laundries. Winding steps led up to the attic on the fourth
floor. They occupied a room with a slanting ceiling and a tiny
kitchen in which the big washtub was a permanent fixture. It
was fortunate that they lived in the attic, for there was always
room in the hall to hang laundry. Factory workers, an old
cavalier, a rentier, and a streetwalker lived on the floors beneath them. On the roof, boys who kept pigeon coops guided
the birds with long poles. In the more affluent streets, water
could be drawn from taps, but here the concierge still brought
up cans of water from the pump. At night, barrels of refuse
were taken to the garbage wagon, and one had to hold one's
nose because of the stench. Slatterns gossiped through windows, and the streets and courtyards swarmed with dogs, children, and beggars. During the siege of Paris, not only had all
the cats in the neighborhood been eaten, but the mice as well.
In the days of the Communes, the quarter had been the scene
of mass meetings and demonstrations. Rebellious women carrying torches had come out of these streets to burn down
Paris. The street boasted a number of war widows, and several of its residents had been sent to Devil's Island. Because

there were few Poles in the neighborhood, Miriam Lieba had learned to speak French.

Her life with Lucian had been bitter from the start. Lucian had quickly squandered the two thousand rubles he had obtained in Warsaw for his mother's jewelry. He would come home raving each evening about how traitorous the leaders of the Polish colony were, how they had driven Poland into a hopeless uprising, how corrupt and scandalous was the Polish Military Academy in Genoa, the thievery that went on in the distribution of goods to emigrants, and how the wrangling between different factions was being used to foster personal ambitions. He had expressed his hostility so openly and for so long that he had cut himself off completely from the Polish colony. He got a job in a furniture factory, but soon quarreled with his employer. He tried other jobs, but never held one for more than a few weeks. Frenchmen were not drunkards, but Lucian came home intoxicated every night. More than once, Miriam Lieba went hungry during her pregnancy. After quarreling with her, Lucian would disappear for days at a time and return ragged and filthy. Her situation became so bad that Miriam Lieba ate in a cheap kosher soup kitchen that the Alliance Israelite had opened after the war for poor Jews. A neighbor, a laundress, advised Miriam Lieba to take in bachelors' laundry and gave her several addresses. The streetwalker on the second floor suggested a more lucrative profession.

After leaving home with Lucian that Purim evening, Miriam Lieba had enjoyed only a few happy weeks: the journey to Prussia, and later the trip across Germany. They stopped in Dresden, Leipzig, and Frankfurt and spent some time in Breslau. The Poles greeted Lucian as a hero, invited him and his young wife to their homes, banqueted them in cafés, sang patriotic songs. Miriam Lieba met Polish aristocrats, political leaders, officers, and even writers. In Paris, they lived for a while in a hotel. They took a trip to Deauville. In the warm forenoon, what a pleasure it had been to stand on the sand and watch the waves, foamy and wrinkled; to gaze at white sailboats out at sea; to hear the cry of the seagulls; to meet the rich Frenchmen, Englishmen, Germans, and even Turks and Indians who came there to bathe in the sea and gamble at the casino.

In those days, Lucian had been content. To Miriam Lieba it all seemed a busy holiday, one that would never end. Paris was full of music, everyone was singing. The war of 1870 had passed like a bad dream and Parisians mourned and celebrated. They showed Miriam Lieba where the barricades had been, the buildings that the Communards had burned, the remnants of the Bastille, the streets where artists, prostitutes, anarchists, and apaches lived. It seemed to Miriam Lieba as if France were constantly celebrating Purim. There were always people in costumes, singing and amusing themselves; tables were set out on the sidewalks, paupers played instruments, danced, sipped wine from bottles, and ate long loaves of bread. Magicians with parrots and monkeys wandered through the courtyards. Even the officers, with their braid-trimmed hats, the soldiers in red pantaloons, and the gendarmes wearing capes, all seemed part of the masquerade. There were outdoor cafés everywhere, theaters, bazaars, parades, exhibitions of books, paintings, sculpture, antiques. Here one saw a Negro, there someone in a turban, here a giant, there a dwarf. One could sit on the upper deck of a horse-drawn omnibus for a few centimes and see the carriages, the ladies, the famous palaces, boulevards, bridges, churches, monuments. Miriam Lieba remembered the names of certain streets from novels.

But Lucian's money and his good nature ran out simultaneously. For days at a time, he said nothing. When he left the house, Miriam Lieba never knew where he went. She cooked, but he did not come home to eat; the meals spoiled. He quarreled with her and cursed her; later he begged her forgiveness on his knees. First, he smothered her with kisses, then he struck her. In bed, boasting of past conquests, he made perverted demands. Miriam Lieba suffered a difficult pregnancy. She had to work until the day of her delivery. They were so much in need that Miriam Lieba took a neighbor's advice and bought horse meat. She had headaches, stomach cramps, dizzy spells. She was convinced she would die in childbirth. Although she went to church every Sunday and passionately read the story of the Christian martyrs, she slipped away quietly to a synagogue and gave the beadle half a franc to say prayers for her and light a candle for her soul.

11

Of all that Miriam Lieba endured in Paris, two torments were the most trying. First, she just couldn't manage to keep her apartment clean. She had been accustomed to a neat room since childhood, a properly made bed, things always in place, and life with Lucian had turned her into a slattern. Cockroaches swarmed in the kitchen. There was a hole in the roof, and the rain came through. The stove smoked. Mice nested beneath the floor. No amount of sweeping kept the place tidy. Lucian habitually dropped paper, trash on the floor, stuffed dirty socks and handkerchiefs into corners, scattered about newspapers, magazines, and notebooks, which he did not permit her to throw away. He acquired the habit of lying fully dressed on his bed, smoking one cigarette after another, and spitting at the ceiling. The privy in the courtyard was filthy, there was always a chamber pot in the flat. The neighbors' children urinated on the stairway. When Miriam Lieba gave up and decided to take in washing, tubs of dirty laundry littered the kitchen. A kettle of shirts and underwear boiled on the stove. There was a stench of soap, lye, washing soda, and bluing. At night, after Miriam Lieba extinguished the lamp, there was so much noise that she could not sleep. Later when the child, Wladzio, was born, the little apartment overflowed with diapers, swaddling clothes, bottles, nipples. They lived in a section of Paris infested with mice, bedbugs, fleas, flies, and beetles that resisted extermination. Cats, mouse traps, flypaper, and refuse exuded foul odors. Every Saturday night Miriam Lieba would heat a tub of water and bathe and wash her hair, but Lucian merely dipped his finger in the basin each morning and ran it across his face.

Miriam Lieba was disturbed as much by Lucian's lies as by his lack of cleanliness. He was either as silent as a recluse, or he lied. He could not even be truthful about where he bought a loaf of bread. Whenever he had a job, he deceived Miriam Lieba about his salary. He would tell her he had met a neighbor on the street—when the neighbor was actually sick in bed. He would boast of a bargain when he had overpaid at the market. Coming home, he would brag that he had helped to capture a thief or put out a fire, or had saved a girl from suicide. Although the Poles in Paris had long since severed all relations with him, Lucian would babble about his meetings with political figures, his connections with exiled leaders in Austria, Silesia, and Russo-Poland, or relate some conspiratorial plan to liberate Poland. There were only traitors in France's Polish colony, but Lucian had found patriots elsewhere who would readily sacrifice themselves for the liberation of their motherland. Promises of help had come from Garibaldi, the Sultan, President Hayes, and Bakunin, a Russian revolutionist whose wife was a Pole. In the ranks of the patriots were Mickiewicz's friend, the poet Odyniec; the writer Ujejski; a Madame Kuchokowska; the former Countess Skarbek, who had influence in Rome, especially in the Vatican; a Countess Walewska; an old officer, General Kolaczkowski . . . Miriam Lieba eventually realized that Lucian had collected the names of dead people. He even insinuated that Dr. Zawacki, who had married his sister Felicia, was a delegate of the secret organization and that he had sent Zawacki to Poland on a political mission.

Instead of finding a steady job and earning bread for his family, Lucian spent his time reading magazines, clipping ads from newspapers, and writing letters, to which he seldom received answers. Miriam Lieba sold her bracelet so that Lucian could go to London to see his brother Josef. In the Channel, a storm broke out and the ship nearly sank. Lucian lingered in London for over a month. He returned emaciated, complaining that Josef had become a bourgeois, a flat positivist, and an admirer of the Jew Disraeli. Lucian was forever contradicting himself. He claimed both that Poland was lost and that liberation was near; that he was a republican and a royalist; he preached that Russia was Poland's worst enemy and then proposed a Slavophile plan for a union of all Slavic peoples to stand against West European decadence. Constantly sick, he had had an attack of bronchitis and an abscess in his ear. For a while he was convinced that he had contracted syphilis, although he solemnly swore that he hadn't been near another woman. The child Wladzio fussed at night and Miriam Lieba carried him about on a pillow and sang lullabies to him until he fell asleep. The moment she put him back in his cradle, he began to toss about again. "Throw the bastard out once and for all!" Lucian would say.

Miriam Lieba would burst into tears. "What else do you want me to do?"

She learned to scream and curse. When men visited the prostitute, she no longer ran from the window. She became adept at haggling with the market women over the price of tomatoes, a head of cabbage, a cauliflower. Although Lucian and Miriam Lieba tried to conceal the fact that they belonged to the aristocracy, the street soon found out. The postman read the title on their letters. The neighbors, the shopkeepers, the venders who sat behind the fruit and vegetable stands began half contemptuously to address Miriam Lieba as "Madame la Comtesse." What kind of countess was she? She spoke the French of the rabble. She took in washing. They discovered that she stemmed from Polish Jewry. Her husband, the Count, argued with street loafers, with school children. Dirty himself, he demanded cleanliness and quiet in this narrow street.

Now Lucian, for the hundredth time, had left home. When he was out of the house for a few days. Miriam Lieba slowly managed to clean up. Even Wladzio grew calmer. Wringing out some customer's blue shirt, Miriam Lieba bent over the washtub and glanced through the attic window. She could glimpse a great deal of Paris—chimneys, pigeon coops, attic windows, birds, church steeples. The sun's reflection flashed gold or silver in the windowpanes. In flight, the pigeons' wings grew red as fire. From the city there arose a roaring, a clucking, a singing, a sound of music, a whistling. A golden mist hovered over the eternal carnival. Miriam Lieba had lost everything, but she did not yearn to return to Jampol. Her mother was dead. Everything else was as far away and as insubstantial as a dream.

A mirror hung over the sofa. Miriam Lieba gazed into it. No, trouble hadn't aged her. A young face looked out at her, with tired eyes, pale lips, and blond hair that the sun had turned golden. She was toil-worn but still pretty. For a moment Miriam Lieba thought that if worse came to worse she could always follow the same course as Mademoiselle Meyar on the second floor.

III

Wallenberg knew quite well that one does not discuss an apostate daughter with a pious Jew and so he did not mention Maria Jampolska to Calman. Nevertheless, he had decided to help her return to Poland. Madame Malewska, his favorite daughter, was constantly reminding her father of the unfortunate Countess.

He finally obtained an audience with the Governor-General and somehow wangled an amnesty for Count Lucian Jampolski. The offense was an old one, and moreover it had been committed by a young man who had barely been able to distinguish between right and wrong. Besides, Poland was now calm; hundreds of nobles had returned from exile to settle on the land. Polish literature and the Polish press were dominated by positivism. After Napoleon III's downfall, the

Poles had lost all hope, and even the Polish exiles in France had been silenced. What harm could a Lucian Jampolski do the mighty Russian Empire?

The announcement of Lucian's pardon was officially dispatched to the Russian ambassador in Paris. A few days later, Lucian received notice of it from the consul. Madame Malewska wrote about it separately to Miriam Lieba, enclosing a few hundred francs for their fare home in the letter.

17

In Warsaw, winter came early that year. The very first day after the Feast of Tabernacles, a heavy snow fell. The court-yard apartment on Obozna Street in which Miriam Lieba now lived was in perpetual darkness. Wladzio was sick; the barber had come and painted the child's throat. Now Wladzio, a stocking full of hot salt around his neck, sat in bed playing with his toy soldiers, among them a lead Napoleon mounted on his horse. Wladzio was three years and four months old and prattled in a mixture of French and Polish. He was as fair as Miriam Lieba and had golden hair and Lucian's turned-up nose. At the moment his blue eyes were alive with anger. He didn't want to stay in bed and didn't want a hot stocking around his neck. Too young to remember winter, he recalled days filled with light, a blue sky, pigeons, puppies, kittens, an open door through which children came and went. That place had been called Paris. Here in this new place called Warsaw, snowflakes fell, the sky was gray, the door was always shut, the wind blew, and the panes rattled. Wladzio kept lining up the soldiers and knocking them down with his foot. He began to cry.

"What's wrong, angel? Does your throat hurt?" Miriam Lieba asked.

No, it wasn't that. Wladzio wanted to go back to Paris.

"Why Paris? You're home now. This is Poland, your own country."

Wladzio screamed in rage.

"Soon, dear, soon. We'll go. Be quiet and I'll play the harmonica for you."

But though Miriam Lieba played, the child remained restless. She took some French coins from a tea container and gave them to him. He continued to cry until, tired out, he fell asleep. Miriam Lieba couldn't get back to her work and sat watching him sadly. As he slept, his lips moved as if he were suckling. Occasionally his forehead twitched as though unhappy thoughts were passing through his mind, and he would rub his nose with his little fist. He had already suffered so much. He'd had scarlet fever, measles, and a difficult time cutting his teeth. Wasn't it enough that she was forced to struggle? Why had she brought another being into this world of torment? Apparently it had been God's will. She often read the silk-bound Bible, containing both the Old and the New Testaments, sent her by Lucian's Aunt Eugenia. Her favorite story was the one about Job and his sufferings, and how he had accused the Almighty. It was too bad, she thought, that she had not studied religious books sooner. If she had, she would have chosen Jesus rather than the abusive Lucian. But it was too late for her even to think about entering a cloister now.

It was time for her to begin cooking and she went into the kitchen to make a fire. Bending down, she picked up a few pieces of kindling and poured naphtha over them. Not until the fire was blazing did she shovel on a mixture of coke and coal; coal was too expensive to use by itself. Almost immediately the stove began to smoke because of the faulty flue. Whenever there was a wind, the smoke backed into the room. Miriam Lieba had several times reported this to the landlord and he had promised to have it repaired, but landlords never keep promises. The janitor had assured her that the chimney sweep would come and clean out the chimney, but no sweep appeared. Miriam Lieba closed the door to the living room to keep the smoke away from Wladzio. She began to cough. How could she stay healthy if she inhaled so much smoke and soot? And it was always so cold. She opened the cupboard and looked for something to cook. In it were only a few potatoes, a bag of rice, and half an ounce of dried mushrooms. Some lard, wrapped in paper, lay on the windowsill, but there was neither butter nor milk. Before she started dinner, she must clean up from yesterday. The night before, she had been too exhausted to stand over the sink scouring pots. Having fashioned a brush out of straw from the mattress, Miriam Lieba began to scrub the pans with ashes.

"No, I should never have left France," Miriam Lieba thought. "Wladzio was right. It's not so bad to be poor there."

No doubt about it, she had been foolish. She should have known that Lucian would be unable to keep a job. The Wallenbergs had treated them as if they were family, had given her books and dresses, rented the apartment for them, furnished it, and paid three months' rent in advance. Surely Lucian's job had been easy enough; he had been given decent clothing and a job in the office of the railroad at sixteen rubles a week. Without exerting himself, he could have advanced to inspector or even higher. But the moment he'd gone to work he quarreled with one of his associates, and before the first week was over, he'd got drunk and called Wallenberg a dirty Jew. Wallenberg had been very gracious and had asked for nothing more than an apology and a promise from Lucian that hereafter he would conduct himself properly and remain sober. But though Wallenberg had behaved like a true Christian, Lucian had continued to insult everyone and that was the end of the job. If Mrs. Malewska had not come and given Miriam Lieba fifty rubles, there would not have been a crust of bread in the house.

"Idiot! Madman!" Miriam Lieba mumbled.

Suddenly, for some obscure reason, she felt better and began to sing a Parisian street song. Wladzio was growing up and the worst was over when a child reached school age. She would become a governess or learn to be a hairdresser like Mirale. After all, she wasn't very old, not quite twenty-two. Miriam Lieba became tense. What day of the month was it? She hadn't had her period. No, she couldn't be pregnant!

II

On his return to Warsaw, Lucian had immediately gone to see Kasia. But Stachowa had died, and the neighbors told him that Kasia's father had claimed the girl. They were unsure whether Antek lived in Wola or Ochota. Lucian began working for Wallenberg and hadn't the time to search further. He had brooded about the girl for so many years, it seemed strange to be in Warsaw without her. Was he still in love with her? No, what he felt transcended ordinary love. Kasia, now barely fifteen, had been only a child when he had lived with her mother. The girl's slavish docility had fascinated him. She had made him think of the days when the Slavs worshipped idols, brought sacrifices to Baba Yaga, and kept slaves and concubines. Often in fantasies he had seen himself as a pasha or a maharaja, both the symbolic and the actual father of his subjects. During the insurrection, when the Polish press had praised Lincoln's struggle to free the Negroes, Lucian had secretly sympathized with the Confederates. The decree liberating the Polish peasantry had seemed a bad one to him. Meeting Polish emigrants, he had often insisted that freedom poisoned the multitude. The mob must serve. Also, women were only happy when they had masters; the suffragette movement, which came to Poland along with the positivist ideas, had been a sign of national corruption to Lucian.

Having fallen out with the Jew Wallenberg, he now had the time to renew old friendships. He went to see Lisakowa, Stachowa's former neighbor, who told him that she had heard that Kasia had gone into domestic service, although she didn't know where. Lisakowa also told Lucian the location and number of Stachowa's grave, and the address of a brewery at which Antek's brother worked. The brewery was on Iron Street and Lucian easily located him. Antek, Lucian discovered, was living with a woman on Freta Street. Lucian walked slowly over to Freta Street and found the woman at home.

At first mistaking him for a police agent, she denied any connection with Antek. However, when Lucian assured her that he was a former friend of Stachowa's and had just returned from France, she became more tractable. She wiped off a bench with a rag, invited him to sit down, and told him all that poor Kasia had been forced to endure during the time he had been away. The girl had been employed in many households and had already run away from several of them. Because of these delinquencies, their former neighbor Lisakowa had on her own initiative gone to the police and petitioned them to place Kasia in a home for wayward girls. At this moment Kasia was working for an old couple, the Wrobels, who lived on Furmanska Street. Antek's mistress was telling all this to Lucian in confidence, she explained, because Antek didn't want anyone to know where his daughter was.

Having at last obtained the information he needed, Lucian walked over to Furmanska Street. Pan Wrobel's house was pointed out to him, a crooked, tile-covered building; Pan Wrobel lived just behind the gate, on the ground floor. Lucian knocked and heard Kasia's voice.

"Who's there?" she inquired.

"Is Pan Wrobel in?"

"No, he's not."

"Your mistress?"

"No one's here."

"Open up, Kasia. It's me, Lucian."

Lucian heard her muffled outcry. Though she did not unchain the door, she pulled it open and he saw her face. It was the same Kasia, but older, prettier, pigtailed, her gray eyes filled with fear and astonishment. She drew back her upper lip, exposing broad teeth.

"Well, why don't you let me in, Kasia?"

"The old woman doesn't permit it."

"Do you think I'm going to steal something?"

"I'll be punished."

"Aren't you happy to see me?"

The door opened and Lucian crossed the threshold. Kasia stood there, grownup, in a calico dress, with scuffed house slippers on her bare feet. She had a woman's bosom.

"No, you're not happy to see me."

"I'm frightened." Kasia began to tremble.

"Of what?"

"I was told not to open the door. The old woman will kill me."

"Do you remember me?"

"I remember."

"I've been looking for you everywhere. I wrote to you, but I never got an answer. You're sure you haven't forgotten?"

"No."

"Do you still have the book I gave you?"

"Yes, the book and the groschen."

"Why are you so frightened of people?"

"I'm not. *They* are. The old man has a safe full of money. He counts it every night. The old woman's trunk is packed with gold and pearls. They keep the door chained and bolted."

"Do you ever go out?"

"I have a day off every other Sunday. I must be back by four o'clock. If I'm five minutes late, the old woman starts shouting at me. She beats me, too. She's sick, but when she hits me, my cheeks swell."

"Now I'm here, the beatings will stop."

"No."

"Now kiss me."

"I can't. It's not proper."

"You little fool, who told you that?" Lucian pulled Kasia to him and kissed her, but she did not return his kiss.

"You remember everything?" he asked.

"Everything."

III

"I wrote to you," Lucian said. "Didn't you get any of my letters?"

"Not a single one."

"They were sent to your mother's address."

"I know nothing about them. They probably tore them up."

"Can you read?"

"Only the primer."

"Yes, I understand. Well, it's not too late to educate you. Does your father help you?"

Kasia shrugged her shoulders.

"How can he help? All he does is take my money. If I need a dress or shoes, he buys them for me. The rest he pockets."

"You don't love him?"

"Sometimes a little."

"But you love me more?"

"More than anyone!"

"And I thought you'd forgotten me, Kasia. I wrote, though I knew it was useless. Look what they've made of you. As for me, I'm married and have a son, but my love for you hasn't changed. I kept longing for you the whole time I was away. I knew you were thinking of me."

"Yes, I did think of you."

"Did you believe I would come back?"

"Some day."

"Now I'm no longer wanted by the authorities. I've been pardoned. My sister Felicia lives here in Warsaw. She's married to a doctor. My wife was Jewish but she turned Christian.

I had a job but I couldn't stand the man I was working for. Anyway, I don't want a job. I want my freedom. Kasia, I had to find you. When I love, it's for good."

"I, too."

"I love my wife as well, but one love doesn't interfere with the other. Do you understand?"

"Yes."

"She's my wife and you are my daughter. No, more than a daughter! If it weren't forbidden, both of you would be my wives. I'd marry you, too."

Kasia looked troubled. "Is that possible?"

"Yes, it's possible, but forbidden. In our times there's so much that is forbidden. Don't do this, don't do that. It's our legacy from the Jews. Do you remember the night I left?"

"Yes."

"What did I tell you?"

"Many things."

"Kasia, I don't want you to stay in this house another minute. Come away with me."

"Where am I to go?"

"To my house or to my sister's. We'll see."

"I'm only paid once a quarter. I get two rubles. I've received nothing for this quarter."

"What's two rubles? Let them keep the money. Hurry up, get your things."

"But they might be robbed."

"What's that to you? They've worried a lot about you, haven't they?"

"The door will lock behind me. No one will be able to get in."

"They'll manage."

"No," Kasia said, drawing back. "I'm responsible for the house. I can't do it."

"What nonsense! They whip you and you're loyal to them. Do you have shoes?"

"Yes."

"Get dressed."

"But isn't this a sin?"

"Suppose it is? You belong to me and I can dispose of you as I see fit. I am both your father and your husband—your God also. I'll take you to my sister. Her husband is a doctor. She's a good woman. She's not satisfied with the maid she has. If she doesn't want you, you'll come to my house. That way we'll be near each other. You won't have to work hard and you'll be free to go out whenever you like. Here you're like an animal in a cage."

"When I go out to buy something, the old woman tells me not to talk to anyone. If she thinks I've been away too long, she beats me with the broom."

"And you want to be loyal to such bloodsuckers? Come along."

"They may return at any moment."

"If they do, I'll handle them. I'm a Polish count and they're vermin. You'll see, they won't dare open their mouths."

IV

To help start her husband in his medical practice—Dr. Marian Zawacki had opened an office on Kreditowa Street—Felicia had obtained a thousand rubles from her Aunt Eugenia, whose will included small bequests to Josef, Lucian, Helena, and herself. The understanding was that the thousand rubles were an advance against Felicia's share of the inheritance. Felicia had also sold half of her jewelry, and Zawacki's father had supplied the remainder of the necessary money. Dr. Zawacki, because he spoke French and had taken his medical degree in France, and was also married to a countess, attracted a rich clientele. Elegant ladies and gentlemen crowded his waiting room from morning to night. Felicia had brought furniture and paintings from the manor house and had hired a maid and a cook. The doctor traveled in a coach drawn by two horses and driven by a coachman. To Felicia it seemed that God was at last repaying her for all the suffering she had endured. The four hours that Marian devoted to office calls brought in between fifty and eighty rubles a week, and he was constantly being summoned to the bedside of aristocratic Poles, wealthy Jews, and high Russian officials. He found time for everything, for his office and home calls, for his study of foreign medical journals. He had even been invited to read several papers at the university and so had become acquainted with the faculty. At night he took Felicia to the theater or opera, or played cards with his colleagues. One look at a patient was sufficient for him to make a diagnosis. He criticized books and plays with the skill of a professional reviewer.

Whenever Felicia remembered how Zawacki had entered her life, she thanked Providence. Prepared for the worst, she had received the best. Marian seldom spoke harshly to her. Every groschen he earned was turned over to her. Although short, he was of a passionate nature. Every night with him in the wide French bed seemed like a dream to Felicia. To be lying with a man! At the time of her wedding she'd been so thin her ribs had protruded. Zawacki had given her drops to stimulate her appetite and had prescribed injections. She had already gained ten pounds and looked younger and prettier. The wrinkles around her eyes disappeared. Her fatigue, her constipation, her headaches, and the spinal pain she had had since girlhood vanished. Felicia was ashamed to admit it, but a little temporal good fortune had radically altered both body and soul.

Nevertheless, she worried. Years had passed and she was still not pregnant. How dreadful if she was no longer able to conceive! She wanted a child and so did her husband; on several occasions he had remarked that the basic purpose of marriage was reproduction. Another disturbing factor was her husband's lack of interest in religion; each Sunday he found another excuse to avoid going to church. Jokingly, he blasphemed against God, Jesus, the Apostles. Felicia couldn't understand how a grown man could preach such materialism. All truths, Zawacki claimed, could be discovered in the laboratory with the help of telescope and microscope. He agreed with Darwin that man was descended from the ape, and he contended that humans were the only intelligent beings in the cosmos. There were no truths beyond man's comprehension.

Her brother Lucian also annoyed Felicia. Now that he had lost his position with Wallenberg, he was forever coming around asking for small loans. He didn't behave responsibly toward his family. Lucian, Felicia was aware, could have found a more appropriate wife than the girl he had married, but since Miriam Lieba had abandoned her family and borne him a child, the least he could do was to take care of her. Every time she visited her brother's home, she was shocked by the disorder she found there. Lucian drank; Miriam Lieba spoke despairingly. There was a frivolity in her manner that ill suited Calman Jacoby's daughter. But even that was not the sum total of Felicia's worries. Clara, Calman's wife, had forced the old man out of the manor house. Count Jampolski was living in a broken-down shack which had once been occupied by a steward. Antosia had moved in with him and behaved as if she were his wife. Felicia had invited her father to live with her in Warsaw, but he had replied that he wished to die on the manor and he needed no one's help or advice.

On that cold December afternoon Felicia was alone, as Marian had already left for the hospital. There was snow on the ground outside. If she had been in her room in the manor house, she would have looked out on wide fields reaching to the horizon. Here on Kreditowa Street, all she could see was a mass of houses and a thin sliver of sky. Felicia sat in her boudoir in an upholstered chair, near the warm tiled stove, her feet propped on a footstool. She was attempting to read a novel by Balzac that Marian had told her was excellent. Felicia had never liked any of Balzac's works. Not only were they licentious, but they had that curious attitude toward man, a mixture of contempt and adoration, that Felicia found in all

modern books. Man had become god to them, and they both
worshipped and blasphemed Man-God. Felicia would read a
line and then look up. Had the flowers been watered? Had
the maid dusted the furniture? Was the cook burning the soup
again? Someone had just entered the house and was speaking.
The maid knocked on the door.

"Madame, your brother, Count Jampolski is here."

"Well, show him up."

"He's not alone. There's a girl with him."

"What kind of a girl?"

"A servant."

Felicia became tense. "All right, show them both up. See
that they wipe the mud off their feet."

v

Felicia lectured Lucian reprovingly in French in the manner
of an older sister; she gave him ten rubles but refused to take
Kasia in. It was twilight. In the streets passersby stopped to
stare at the odd-looking couple. What was this aristocratic
young man doing with such a girl? Why was he carrying her
bundle? Snow began to fall and Kasia wrapped herself in her
mother's shawl. The shawl was too large for her; its fringes
dragged on the ground.

Halting momentarily, Lucian puckered his lips as if about to
whistle. Should he really take her home with him? No, Miriam Lieba would make a scene. He thought of Ezriel and
Shaindel, who now lived in Warsaw and had an apartment on
Leshno Street. Shaindel refused to visit Miriam Lieba because
she was an apostate, but Ezriel came to the house often. Lucian didn't think that Shaindel had a maid. Perhaps Shaindel
and Ezriel would be happy to get Kasia. Miriam Lieba, having
just learned that she was pregnant, was in no mood to grant
Lucian any favors. "She is more vicious than ever, the bitch.
She's bursting with hatred. Felicia is right. I am mad, mad. I
am destroying myself slowly but surely."

The snow continued to fall; it became colder. Lucian walked in the direction of Marshalkowsky Boulevard, searching for a droshky or a sleigh. A passing policeman looked the couple up and down and shrugged his shoulders. At Marshalkowsky Boulevard, Lucian found a droshky. He helped Kasia in and gave the driver Ezriel's address.

"Don't worry, Kasia dear," Lucian said reassuringly. "It may seem hard now, but we'll find a place for you. You've lost nothing. Remember, I'm responsible for you. You have a protector in me."

"I know that."

The droshky pulled up at Ezriel's house, which was across the street from a church. Lucian paid the fare and got out. Night had fallen. The street lamps had already been lit. Smoke fell like sheets from the chimneys. A man selling roasted potatoes warmed himself at his brazier. Only after he had walked through the gateway of the house followed by Kasia did it occur to Lucian that he should not have come here. Ezriel might be enlightened, but Shaindel had inherited the natural stubbornness of the Jew. How could he be sure that Ezriel was at home? What should he tell them? Whatever he said was bound to compromise him. Lucian searched through the list of tenants. The light was so dim and the writing so poor that he could not decipher the names. The janitor came out of his cubicle and told Lucian where Ezriel lived. The building was new and had three stories.

"Who's the girl?" the janitor inquired.

Lucian mounted the stairs without answering. How insolent these peasants had become! Lucian had a desire to punch the man in the nose, or kick him in the belly. If this was what democracy meant, to hell with it! It was all a result of that cursed French Revolution. It had destroyed the last vestige of human decency. When he stood in front of Ezriel's door, he gave Kasia her bundle and then knocked. Shaindel opened the door. Having seen her only once since his return, Lucian had difficulty recognizing her. She had put on weight and was obviously several months pregnant. Her dress was hitched up in front and was not particularly clean. Evidently she had been washing the dishes, for she held a straw brush in her hand.

"I'm Lucian Jampolski," Lucian said. "Very likely you don't remember me."

"The Count!" Shaindel took a step backward.

"I've brought this little girl along with me. Isn't that odd?"

"Come in, please. You also. Wipe your feet."

"Is your husband at home?"

"No, but I'm expecting him back any minute."

Seated on a bench in the kitchen was a young woman in her early twenties. She wore a cheap gray skirt and a blouse with a high collar. Her hair was twisted into a braid and wound around her head. Lucian stole a quick glance at her and thought that he had met her before. Though not homely, she had a bony nose and the sad expression of the Jew. Her gaze had a keenness often also found among the French and Italians. Her lips were thin and severe; her eyebrows grew together. Her forehead was higher than most women's and had something masculine about it. Lucian felt embarrassed before this stranger and began to speak without knowing exactly what he was saying.

"Do you know how long I've known this child? Ten years, and she's only fifteen now. Her mother hid me from the Russians. A fine woman, God rest her soul. She saved my life. That was just after the uprising. I regard Kasia as my own child. A sister, or a daughter! Can you imagine what her father's done to her? Put her into service with the vilest people, absolute exploiters! I just couldn't permit her to remain in such slavery. 'Get your things and come,' I told her. They tried to stop me, but I paid no attention to them. So, now she's here. I thought I'd take her home with me, but that would be inconvenient. Your sister's too edgy these days for a surprise such as this. I thought that since you don't have a maid, Kasia might be just what you need. That is for the time being. Later I intend to send her off to school."

Shaindel's dark eyes grew large and round. "First of all, we don't need a maid. That is, we do need one, but it's beyond our means. Second, there's no place for her to sleep."

"What about the kitchen?"

"My sister-in-law is staying the night with us. I forgot to introduce you. This is my husband's sister, Mirale."

"Oh, so you're Ezriel's sister. Your brother told me all about you. Your father, I believe, is the Rabbi of Jampol."

"He was the rabbi. My parents are in Warsaw now."

"Is that so? How did that happen? Well, that's very interesting. Anyway, I find myself burdened with this girl and I absolutely must find a place for her. It's already night . . ."

"Won't the Count come into the parlor? There's no need for us to stay in the kitchen. Wait, I'll make a light," Shaindel said.

"Forgive me, but I don't have the time. If she can't sleep here, I must look elsewhere. Perhaps I can get her a room in a hotel. A child her age can't be left on the streets, particularly in winter."

"God forbid! She'd freeze to death. But the Count can see for himself that we have no room here. We have a sofa in the other room, but that's where my sister-in-law will sleep. We have nothing to cover the girl with. If we had bedding, she could sleep in the kitchen. But without a blanket, it would be too cold there."

"Yes, yes, I see. Thank you anyway. Come along, Kasia."

"Perhaps she'd like something to eat. Would the Count care for a glass of tea?"

"Are you hungry, Kasia?" Lucian asked. Kasia shook her head.

"It's such an unfortunate accident," Shaindel said, "to have such an esteemed visitor and be unable to be of assistance."

Shaindel, attempting to speak elegant Polish, was constantly making mistakes. She knew she should inquire about Miriam Lieba, but she could not bring herself to mention her sister's name. To the family, Miriam Lieba was as good as dead.

Shaindel often quarreled with Ezriel about the visits he made to Lucian's house. Decent Jews were not friendly with apostates. Moreover, Shaindel feared that the wanton Miriam Lieba would lead Ezriel astray. Shaindel had been told that Lucian had even lived in sin with some woman despite the fact that he was married to Miriam Lieba. Now he came barging into her house like a thoughtless boor.

"Well, good night. Forgive me for dropping in so unexpectedly."

"My husband will be here soon. If the Count should care to wait."

"No, I'm sorry. I don't have the time. Every minute counts now. Remember me to your husband." Lucian turned to Mirale. "It was a pleasure to meet you. You do resemble your brother, but only slightly. Good night."

"A good night to the Count," Shaindel said, interrupting. "If the worst comes to the worst, bring the girl back here and we'll fix up some kind of a bed for her on the floor."

"No, we're not as bad off as that. But thanks just the same."

VI

The frost, more severe than ever, nipped at Lucian's ears; his nose grew as hard as wood. Pausing in front of the gate to Ezriel's house, Lucian peered from left to right. Next to him, Kasia, shivering in her mother's shawl, breathed submissively like an animal. Sleighs drove by, their bells ringing. The windowpanes of the houses across the street were white. Though it was not late, it was so still that it seemed to be midnight. An occasional snowflake fell, an icy dew, shining needlelike against the gaslights. Lucian placed his hand on Kasia's shoulder. In the milder Parisian climate, one could almost live outdoors. He had been able to drift along with little effort. He had longed for the bitter Polish winter, for intrigue, for the humility of the common people, whom he loved with his own kind of aristocratic passion. Now again, as after the uprising, when he constantly had had to evade the Russians, he was in difficulty. "What do I do now?" he asked himself. "Perhaps I should just kill her." He toyed with the idea. "I'll take her down to the Vistula and throw her in. She won't resist." He was thirsty but he couldn't make up his mind whether it was water or vodka that he wanted. Actually it was a thirst for adventure. He needed to do something terrible, beat someone or find himself in some grand predicament. He was ready to fight the Russians, or even the Poles, who had submitted to Russian rule. He muttered curses, not knowing whom he was cursing. He wasn't really angry, just strangely irritated. "Well, something is going to happen tonight. She is again in my power," he thought. He shivered and bit his lower lip. A sleigh drove past. Lucian raised his hand and signaled it to stop.

"Driver, take me to a hotel."

"What hotel?"

"A cheap one. This child has nowhere to sleep. All I need is the simplest of rooms."

The driver shoved his sheepskin cap to the back of his head, and said, "I know a place on Mylna Street."

"What number?"

"We'll drive up there and I'll show you. But I don't know if they'll let her in."

"That's my worry."

Lucian and Kasia got into the sleigh. The ride was a short one. They drove down Karmelicka Street to Nowolipie Street, and then turned into Mylna Street. The hotel was old and decrepit. Lucian paid the driver and escorted Kasia into the building. In the lobby behind the desk stood a small kinky-haired man in a corduroy jacket. He had a round face, a broad nose, small shiny eyes, and skin yellow and pock-marked as swiss cheese.

"This girl's an orphan," Lucian explained. "Her mother was a servant on our manor. She needs a place to sleep for the night."

"Does she have a birth certificate?"

Lucian turned to Kasia. "Do you have a birth certificate?"

Kasia didn't answer.

"She must have some sort of papers. We'll look for them later. They're probably in her bundle. Anyway, it's only for the night. Tomorrow I'll find her a situation."

"How old is she?"

"Sixteen."

"She doesn't look it. Does the gentleman intend to stay with her?"

"What's the difference to you?"

"It's a difference in price."

"Suppose I do decide to stay?"

"Then the room will be two rubles."

Lucian noticed a peculiar glint in the clerk's eyes.

"All right, let it be two rubles."

Lucian took out the ten-ruble note that Felicia had given him, and threw it on the counter.

"Ten kopecks for key money," the clerk said, as he carefully examined the bill in the lamplight.

"What sort of fee is that? Oh, never mind."

"And two rubles ninety kopecks for security."

"What kind of security?"

"Security."

The two men looked at each other and the clerk's eye seemed to wink.

"Too bad I haven't my pistol with me," Lucian thought. "The next time he opens his mouth, I could let him have it." The clerk handed Lucian five rubles' change.

"When do I get it back?"

"When you leave, if everything's in order."

A barefooted woman, her apron half tucked up, appeared carrying a bucket of slops. She had piglike eyes and the clumsiest feet Lucian had ever seen. After some hesitation, the clerk selected a key.

"Is the bed in 23 made up?"

"Who for?"

"This little girl. She's an orphan."

"An orphan, eh? I'm an orphan myself. Is this your bundle?"

The woman put down the bucket and lit a candle. Lucian and Kasia followed her up stairs so steep and narrow they could barely be climbed. At the top of the stairs, the woman stopped to catch her breath. The corridor was narrow and the doors of the rooms looked like those of prison cells. In the hall was a basket filled with dirty laundry and a broom propped against the wall. Lucian smelled a strange odor, a blend of something musty and oily. He heard a mutter of voices; a woman laughed. She seemed to be alone in the room. It was mad laughter. The key to Room 23 didn't fit properly. The woman twisted and pushed but the lock remained shut. She handed Lucian the candlestick and grasped the key with both hands, turning sharply. The door swung open. Lucian smelled the stench of rotting straw. He looked into the room and by the light of the candle saw an iron bed, a broken-down chest of drawers, a rush mat lying on the floor. The mattress of the bed was a straw sack, and a coarse cloth covering served as a sheet. The pillow was stuffed with feathers, not down.

"Well, here it is," the woman said.

Lucian handed her ten kopecks. The woman looked at the money scornfully. "I never get less than a gulden."

Lucian would have liked to spit in her face. "Here's your gulden."

"You can't keep the candle burning. We've got to watch out for fire."

"Look, it's freezing in here."

"Well, the room was heated only this morning. The flue's no good; the heat escapes up the chimney."

After the woman left, Lucian attempted to lock the door but found that the hook for the chain was missing. He said, "All right, take off your shawl, Kasia. Are you hungry?"

"No."

"Then I guess it's time for us to turn in."

"Aren't you going home?"

"No, I'm staying here."

"Where will you sleep?"

"With you."

VII

Lucian awoke in the middle of the night. He'd dreamed he'd been wrestling with an ape and the creature had grasped his throat with its paws. He heard voices, men speaking Russian, and he listened intently. The police! His ribs felt icy. If only he'd had enough sense to bring along his pistol. He groped in the dark and found his pants, shoes, and socks. Any minute, he knew, the men would start climbing the stairs. But, no, there wasn't a sound now. Should he wake Kasia? He slipped out into the corridor and listened. From where he was, he could see the night lamp burning downstairs. Suddenly he heard footsteps and he started to back away. Was there another exit? His hand touched doors and latches. At the end of the hall, to the right, was a closet. He tiptoed in and found himself surrounded by crates and baskets. His coat caught on a nail; he pulled himself free. His heart seemed to stop; he stood listening with his entire body. A light glimmered in the corridor, apparently a candle. He held his breath, silent, fearful, his brain no longer functioning. Men were chattering in Russian: someone replied in Polish, but what had been said eluded Lucian. That almost forgotten terror that he'd known when he'd been on the run, hiding in woods and ditches, returned to him. The light was coming closer, the figures also. Then, inexplicably, the hall was plunged into darkness and there was silence. "Could I have been imagining it all?" Lucian wondered. Yet he dared not leave his hiding place. "Not so fast," he decided. He didn't know how long he remained standing there. He dozed, awoke, forgot what had happened and where he was. The image of the ape he had dreamed of returned to him, hairy, its teeth flashing. He shook himself and the hallucination disappeared. The corridor remained dark and silent. Slowly and with great deliberation, Lucian raised his hand and scratched his ear with one finger. Then he fell asleep and seemed to be in Paris.

He shuddered and something fell, a board or a box. He tip-toed out of the closet and advanced down the hall, trying each door as he passed. Had Kasia been arrested? Or was she still here? He did not remember which room was theirs. He had no matches. All the doors were chained and bolted. How could that be? The door to his room hadn't been locked. When he came to the stairs, he began to descend, one step at a time. Coming to a landing, he rested. It seemed to him that the stairway went on forever. The light below had been extinguished. Had they locked the front door? Was all of this merely a trick to lure him from his hiding place? Well, if it were, they wouldn't take him without a fight; he'd never surrender. At any rate, the girl belonged to him and that couldn't be changed.

Yes, the light was out in the lobby. He felt the edge of the desk and stumbled against a bench. Apparently there was a small step down at that spot. He had nearly fallen. Reaching the door, he opened it, and was almost driven back by a blast of wind. Now he remembered that he had not taken his tie and scarf. He paused momentarily at the threshold. He was free! They couldn't do anything to Kasia.

He walked out and turned to the left. As he lunged down a narrow crooked street, the cold cut into him. "Go back," he warned himself; the street looked like a dead end. He ran in the opposite direction and came to some public building in front of which a soldier stood guard near a sentry box. Lucian slowed his pace to a walk; the soldier eyed him suspiciously but said nothing. Lucian found himself on a broad avenue lit by gas lamps. He passed a watering trough and a well. Although he was thoroughly familiar with Warsaw, he didn't know where he was. This was not Karmelicka Street, toward which he had thought he was heading. Well, it didn't matter. He pulled up the collar of his coat and continued walking. At last he came to a street sign which read *Tlomacka* and he knew where he was.

He broke into a run and then stopped suddenly. Kasia had probably given the police his name. Did she know that he was a Jampolski? If she did, the authorities would certainly seek him out at his apartment. They might already be waiting at the gate on Obozna Street. Where should he go? If he wandered about on a night like this, he would freeze to death. What about Ezriel's? He was ashamed to go there. Felicia's? Her apartment would be dangerous, too. "Now there is no door left open to me," Lucian mumbled to himself, as if he were quoting a line from a poem. The evil spirit that dogged his footsteps had amused itself by pretending to release him from peril and then entangling him again. A very clever spirit, very clever indeed. An interesting and perverse idea occurred to him. Why shouldn't he return to Freta Street and spend the night at Antek's? His being hunted again exhilarated Lucian. He had accomplished what he had been planning to do for years. There was, he remembered, a Jewish hotel on Grzybow Place, not far from Bagno Street. He could spend the night there.

VIII

In the commissariat of police, the sergeant sat in a railed-in cubicle separated from the rest of the room. His jacket unbuttoned, the sergeant, a fat man, was half asleep, snoring slightly. On the table before him was a newspaper and half a glass of cold tea in which floated a wedge of lemon. The sergeant stirred and scratched his slightly exposed belly. A few minutes later, in walked Kasia, still wrapped in her oversized shawl and led by a Polish policeman. Her face was impassive

and her manner docile. The policeman coughed and the sergeant opened his eyes a crack and smiled that typical smile of
porcine complacency and disdain.

"And who's this one?"

"I picked her up in the Hotel Gwiazda on Mylna Street."

"Ah, a young whore."

"No, she's been seduced. It happened tonight. Some count
did it."

The sergeant was now completely awake. He smiled, exposing the few massive teeth he had left in his mouth.

"How long did it take to think that one up?"

"No, it's a fact. We received the information from the
coachman who drove them to the hotel. He's one of our people. The man's name, according to her, is Count Lucian Jampolski. She was in service on Furmanska Street."

The sergeant arranged himself more comfortably in his
leather-cushioned chair, and then buttoned his jacket and
tightened his belt. He did not believe the story he was being
told but was nevertheless amused by it. Usually on a winter's
night only drunks and old prostitutes, anxious to have a place
to sleep, were brought in. The sergeant would have liked to
question Kasia, but, having just arrived from Russia, knew no
Polish. As he measured the girl up and down, his almond eyes
lit up with destructive joy. To his left lay a protocol book.
The sergeant picked up a pen, tested it on his thumbnail, and
dipped it into a half-empty inkwell.

"What do they call you?"

"Kasia."

"Kasia, eh? Your surname?"

"He wants to know your last name," the policeman said,
translating into Polish.

Kasia said nothing.

"Now see here, you're being spoken to. Answer!"

Kasia's face remained impassive.

"Is she deaf or something?"

"Tell him your name, you little trollop."

"Kasia."

"Your last name. Kasia what? Kasia is only your given name. Look, I'm called Stefan Krol. What do they call you?"

Kasia stirred slightly.

"I forgot."

"You've forgotten your own name? What's your father's name?"

"Antek."

"Antek what?"

Kasia did not answer.

"So you're a tough little nut," the sergeant said through clenched teeth. "Where does her father live?"

"He wants to know where your father lives," the Polish policeman said, translating.

"On Freta Street."

"What number?"

Kasia did not move an eyelash.

"He asked you what number."

"I don't know."

"What does your father do? How is he employed?"

"What's that?"

"Is he a shoemaker, a tailor, a blacksmith, a crook?"

"He goes to work."

"Where?"

Kasia did not know what to answer.

The sergeant winked at the policeman. They began to whisper to each other. The sergeant emitted a throaty laugh.

"What did you say the Count's name was?"

"Lucian Jampolski," Kasia replied.

"Where does he live?"

Kasia didn't know where Lucian lived.

"Where do your employers live?"

"On Furmanska Street. Number 3."

"What is their name?"

"Wrobel."

"Well, there, now listen to that. She does know something,"

the sergeant remarked to the policeman and to the world in general.

"We'll have to walk over to the Wrobels' and see what they have to say. How old are you?"

"I'm almost fifteen."

"Almost fifteen. You're beginning your career early. What did this Count do to you?"

The sergeant continued to question her intensively, the policeman acting as interpreter. Other offenders were brought in to the commissariat, but they were kept waiting. Kasia remembered everything clearly—that is, except for last names and addresses. The sergeant pinched her cheek.

"Are you hungry, little sweetheart?"

"No. Yes."

"Wait, I'll take care of you."

The sergeant wrote something on a slip of paper.

"All right, she's yours now."

"Come with me."

The policeman took Kasia gently by the arm and led her through a number of rooms and then down a staircase into a cellar. A door was thrown open and Kasia was pushed into a room. She was aware that she was in prison but wasn't afraid. The cell stank. Even before her eyes became accustomed to the darkness, she knew from the snores and sighs that she heard that she was surrounded by women. Finally, as in a dream, faces, eyes, hair emerged from the shadows. A hoarse voice called out to her, "Hey, you, what are you doing standing at the door? Won't you please step in and be friendly?" And the speaker laughed shrilly.

"Look, she's nothing but a kid," another woman remarked.

The snores accelerated as if the sleepers were trying to cram as much rest as possible into the time allotted them. There were yawns, growls, and a mixture of curses. Some of the women were lying down; others were sitting. Bodies were strewn all over the floor. A bluish-white light, dawn reflected by the snow, seeped in through the barred window.

"Hey, do you see, she has a shawl!"

"Give it to me."

"Girls, she's only a baby."

Someone made an obscene remark, making everyone laugh. A heavy-set woman lit a match.

"That's right; she's only a kitten. Come here, darling. Let me have the shawl."

I X

Twenty-four hours later, Kasia was released and taken by the policeman who had arrested her to her father's house on Freta Street. Antek was not at home, but the woman he lived with was there, busy at the tub, washing linen. Her face fell when she saw that Kasia was accompanied by a policeman.

"Is this the woman your father lives with?" the policeman asked Kasia.

"Yes."

"Are you two married?"

"No, officer. What would I do? The lazy bum wouldn't go to a priest."

"Do you know that living like that is a criminal offense?"

"I know, but, sir, what could I do? What happened to you, darling? Just look at her! What did she do? Steal?"

"No, worse."

The policeman related the whole story. They were looking for Lucian Jampolski. The woman wiped her hands on her apron.

"What a disgrace! It will kill her father. The Count was here the day before yesterday, wanting to know where she worked. Like a fool I told him."

"Oh, so you told him. Why? You'll be called as a witness."

"I'll testify. I'll swear on the cross and tell everything. In he walks, looking as handsome and stylish as you please, honey dripping from his tongue. He lived at her mother's once; the girl was just the same as a daughter to him. What did I know about it? I come from humble people. I can't read or write. I said to him, 'She's working for the Wrobels on Furmanska Street. But you leave her alone, sir; her father doesn't want anything to happen to her.' He thanked me and left. I thought he had a present for her. Everything comes in handy these days. But he just went and seduced her, the fox. I call it a shame and a disgrace. She's not even fifteen. What will she grow up to be now? Antek's going to take this hard. It's his only daughter. And where were your eyes, miss? What did she go off with him for? You've made us a laughing stock."

"Don't worry, we'll catch this bird."

"Well, he should get what's coming to him. Such a smooth liar. He sat on this very bench. I didn't tell Antek because I was afraid he'd worry. He's got an awful temper. What did the Count tell you, the usual stuff? Don't you have any brains? Now, listen here, answer when you're spoken to."

Kasia remained silent.

"Well, the damage is done. She's ruined. A poor child, an orphan. Let's hope she doesn't get pregnant. It'll be awful when the neighbors hear of this. Antek will be wild. Is it my fault, officer? How could I know that the man was such scum? I was taught to answer politely when a person speaks to me. We don't live in a wilderness. I may be a sinner, but I go to church every Sunday, rain or shine. I never fail to light a candle. The day before Easter, when the priest comes to bless the bread, he doesn't leave here empty-handed. I wanted to be a mother to her. I didn't want her to leave home. Her dead mother, Stachowa, was like a sister to me. But Antek said, 'She'd better get used to working.' "

Suddenly Kasia interrupted, "You're lying. It was you who drove me out of the house."

There was a moment of silence and the woman retreated a step.

"It's you who are the liar."

"I'm telling the truth. You hardly let me have a crust of bread. You locked the breadbox."

"Officer, it's a lie. She's made up everything. She ought to be flailed. Antek wanted to beat her. He tried, but I burned the stick. He'd soaked it in slops. She may be your daughter, I said, but don't forget she's an orphan. Let God punish her. So it was me that he hit, my body. You ungrateful creature, you little bitch. Don't count on me any more. I don't care if your father breaks every bone in your body."

"Whipping is against the law," the policeman observed more to himself than to anyone else.

"Yes, I know, but sometimes a man just has to hit out. There was a fellow on this street who beat his own child to death. He's still in prison. He got five years; he's been in three and a half already. His wife brings him food packages every Friday."

"Beating is against the law."

"Well, God's will be done."

"You'll all be called as witnesses. And don't let her out of the house. She has to show up in court too."

"Absolutely, officer. We'll keep an eye on her."

A number of women had gathered at the door of Antek's house. When the policeman left, they moved aside to make a path for him. Then they entered the house.

"What's happened?"

"Can't you guess?"

They gathered in a corner and began whispering to each other. As the story was related to them, they glanced over their shoulders at Kasia. She stood in the center of the room, wearing a ragged shawl instead of the fine, broad one she had inherited from her mother. When Antek came in, the women grew silent. He stood at the threshold in a torn sheepskin jacket and a cap with a broken visor. His clothes were spotted with paint and mud, although he hadn't worked for a long time. Even his face was speckled with paint. Out of the corners of his close-set eyes he glanced at his daughter, and then fixed his gaze on a shelf full of pots and bottles at the other side of the room.

"What's this mob doing here?"

"A dreadful thing has happened to Kasia," the woman who lived with him announced. "It's a real misfortune."

"I've heard. But what do they want?" Antek pointed at the still silent women.

He took a step toward them and the women began to push in the direction of the door. The apartment emptied quickly. Antek looked at Kasia but said nothing. He knew what happened to girls who had no mother to care for them.

"All right, take off your shawl."

18

I

Calman never mentioned Miriam Lieba's name, and no one dared speak of her in his presence. He had mourned seven days for her after her flight, and she had ceased being one of his daughters. Mentally he compared her to a fingernail disposed of, to hair trimmed off forever. Nevertheless, he could not help hearing reports of her. He knew she had returned from France and was living somewhere in Warsaw with that vicious goy, and that she had given birth to a child. His enemies sent him "poison pen" letters through the mail; he'd start reading these letters and then rip them to pieces. Well, he had more than earned whatever was said. Although he avoided thinking about Miriam Lieba during the day, he could not control his thoughts at night. He had brought forth an apostate; through her, wicked men and Jew-baiters might descend from his loins. What could be worse? Yet was he any better than the offspring he had spawned? Like Esau, had he not sold his birthright for a mess of porridge?

Calman lived in the manor house, occupying the Count's bedroom and sleeping in his bed. Clara had not only taken over the house, but had purchased its furnishings. All that remained for the Count was what Clara had let him have: a mare, a cow, a few books, and a britska. Calman continued as always to provide the old Count with oats, flour, barley, and groats, and he was also permitted to hunt in Calman's forests and fish in his pond. However, Jampolski's needs were decreasing. Antosia now cooked for him only once a day, and never anything but rye dumplings with milk. Yes, Count Jampolski in his old age had divorced himself from all luxuries while Calman, the Jew, had taken up residence in a palace, amid gold, silver, porcelains, lackeys, and servants. He slept in a velvet-canopied bed, on a horsehair mattress. Next to him in a twin bed lay Clara, partner to his estate and his lime quarries. She called herself Madam Clara Jacobowa, and she was pregnant. She might even be carrying a male child. Yet even the hope that she would produce a son who would say Kaddish for him after his death did not keep Calman from realizing that he had committed a grave error.

From the very beginning of their marriage, they had argued bitterly and she had spoken like a wanton woman. She did as she pleased, without advice from him. She dismissed his help and hired her own, wrangled with the neighboring landowners, and invited guests Calman did not want in his house. Calman had always spoken kindly to the peasants and had overlooked their minor delinquencies, but Clara was extremely strict with them. Any peasant whose cow strayed into Calman's pasture had to pay a five-ruble fine. Everyone had to account to her. When she entered their office, the cashier and bookkeeper had to rise. She had quickly squandered her few-thousand-ruble dowry, buying her dresses in Paris. She was now talking of remodeling the manor house. Until she became pregnant, she had continued to go to the ritual bath for Calman's sake, performing this virtuous act with resentment and insisting that no other woman be present when she entered the water. A bathtub with a lid that could be locked had been ordered for her private use. In the opinion of the women of Jampol, the ritual bath was defiled by her licentious conduct. Her spidery stockings reached her hips and were attached to a corset, the attendants reported; her slips, chemises, and underpants were made of silk and were lavishly trimmed with lace. She rode to the ritual bath in a carriage!

Although Calman worked hard (the expenses had increased exorbitantly), he slept fitfully. Who would have imagined they could spend so much? Clara lived like an empress, flinging money about, ordering people around. Before the marriage, she had bought a queenly trousseau, and her closets were filled with clothes and accessories, but as soon as the wedding was over, she complained she had nothing to wear. She screamed at the maids and constantly criticized the kosher cook Calman had brought from Warsaw. When she wanted the smallest thing, she yanked the bellpull. All her whims and her passion for luxury were indulged, yet she never stopped complaining. The meat was either too tough or too tender, the soup too fat or too watery, the compote too sweet or too sour. Although the floors shone so brightly that Calman thanked God each day that he didn't slip, Clara insisted they were dirty. She lied so much and made so many accusations that Calman could hardly believe his ears. He knew wicked people existed; where else did wars come from, or the calamities that had befallen the Jews? But for a Jewish daughter to know so much about sin! Her words of endearment were mixed with derision. She mocked Calman's beard, his long capote, his prayer shawl, his praying, and his habitual "God willing." She would speak to him affectionately and then address him as a stranger. Although the peasants had no love for the Polish gentry, they resented the fact that a Jew was living like a count in a count's own manor house. The priests, now forbidden to complain about the Russians, vented their anger against the Jews. In Jampol and Skarshew, Calman's enemies spread all sorts of slander about him. It was rumored that in his household there was cooking on the Sabbath, that the utensils were not kept kosher, that Calman had relations with his wife on her impure days. Mayer Joel hardly spoke to his father-in-law. Jochebed avoided him. An occasional postcard came from Tsipele, but Jochanan did not add his greetings in his own handwriting. Shaindel had an apartment in Warsaw. Calman wanted her to stay at the manor with Ezriel and the child Yosele, but Shaindel kept making excuses. Calman knew the truth; she hated her stepmother Clara.

Hate, hate, hate! He found it everywhere. Plots of one kind or another were constantly brewing among his lumbermen and clerks. The peasants were always quarreling. The Rabbi of Gur's Hassidim wrangled with those from Alexandrow. Tamara Shalit denounced Sonya Sorkess. Sonya Sorkess made fun of Mrs. Grain, the apothecary's wife. Everyone, Clara said, was a thief. When Calman suggested that if Clara bought fewer ornaments there would be less chance of her being robbed, she replied scornfully, "Don't think you're talking to your Zelda! I am Clara, and I love pretty things, not Jampol rags!"

11

Twice each month Clara gave a party or *wetcherinka,* as she liked to refer to it in Russian. The same people were always invited: Colonel Smirnoff, Lieutenant Papricki, the druggist Grain and his wife, David Sorkess and Sonya, Morris Shalit and Tamara, and sometimes Dr. Lipinski from Skarshew, and such officials and minor clerks as are only to be found in a small town. A military band was hired to play. For Calman the *wetcherinkas* meant only trouble: they cost too much; Clara, preparing for them as if for a wedding, required new clothes; the floors were waxed and the house was cleaned and dusted, even though it already shone. For the few days preceding the *wetcherinka* Clara cried, scolded the servants, and threatened to run away or kill herself. Calman appreciated the words of the sages who claimed that all sinners were either partly or totally insane.

Calman found himself eating with Gentiles. The food was kosher, but what about the wine? It was strictly forbidden to drink wine with Gentiles. Although Calman himself did not taste the wine, he suffered agonies sitting beside these modern Jews and Gentiles, listening to their blasphemy, flattery, and mockery. Each time Clara wore a new dress, they praised it extravagantly. Every delicacy tasted like something out of paradise. But their praise was edged with ridicule. There was venom in their politeness. While eating their host's bread, they made fun of him. Their conversation, usually in Russian, was spiked with double meanings; their eyes winked and their tongues hissed. When the men told jokes, the women laughed wildly. Cruelty and lechery were the substance of their humor. They knew all the best spas, all the most chic hotels. They knew everybody. Calman ate in silence. He was afraid to think of the many sins resulting from such a banquet.

The *wetcherinka* did not reach its height until the musicians began to play and the dancing started. Clara passed from hand to hand. Her gowns were extremely low cut, back and front. As she danced, her skirt flew up, exposing her legs. She danced with all the men. With Colonel Smirnoff, she put her hand on his epaulette and he clasped her waist; as they danced, the spurs on his polished boots jangled. In the hallway hung the swords of the officers. Calman, more astonished at his lack of foresight than shocked at the behavior of the others, could only blame himself. What had he thought she would devote herself to—studying the Bible? Didn't he have eyes in his head? Or had Satan pulled the wool over them? How could a Jew, the son of pious parents, witness such goings on? Did the mezuzahs on the doorposts approve? And God? "I am mad, mad!" Calman said to himself. "I deserve to be torn to pieces and drenched in acid!" Licentiousness was everywhere, in every glance and smile. The ladies were bareheaded; the pianoforte tinkled, the trumpet blared, the drum pounded. A company of adulterers and harlots had gathered in his house. Could these women be anything but whores when they let strangers touch their hands, their shoulders, their hips?

Calman stood against the wall, his hand on a chair. Opposite him, in a mirror, he saw himself, in a knee-length frock coat and a silken skullcap. His beard seemed shorter, even though he hadn't touched it. Had Clara trimmed it while he slept? Despite the heat of the stove, Calman felt an icy chill in his ribs. Colonel Smirnoff's face was flushed from drinking; his short blond hair bristled like a hog's, his eyes watered, his coarse laugh seemed to imply: what's mine is mine, and what's yours in mine, too. Winking at the lieutenant, he clicked his heels, calling out to the music: "Da-da! Hop! Hop!" The lieutenant's wife, on the other hand, danced with David Sorkess. That's what happened at a *wetcherinka:* they exchanged wives.

"Is it real? How did it happen? Have I forgotten God?" Calman asked himself.

The music stopped. Colonel Smirnoff bowed to Clara, Lieutenant Papricki to Tamara, David Sorkess to Nadia Ivanovna. Clara approached Calman. Half naked, adorned with rings, earrings, and brooches, she faced him, her diamonds quivering. Her cheeks were rouged; her eyes flashed as she smiled.

"Why are you standing around staring like that? Do you expect us to cry?"

"No."

"If you don't enjoy these evenings, I won't have them any more."

Calman said nothing. It was not her fault, but his. "May my name be blotted out." For the first time in his life, he cursed himself.

19 ⌂

Reb Menachem Mendel Babad sat in his study on Krochmalna Street with a Talmudic commentary open before him. The book was *The Face of Joshua.* On the table, amid a confusion of manuscripts, lay a steel pen; next to it stood an inkwell. Reb Menachem Mendel had already brewed tea for himself in the samovar. As the morning progressed, he smoked his pipe, made notes, and studied. He had little time for himself here in Warsaw. Women were constantly coming to consult him on religious matters; occasionally a lawsuit had to be decided; everyone wanted the rabbi's advice, and this included thieves and fallen women, who were forever asking him to work out the proper dates on which to celebrate the anniversaries of their relatives' deaths. Observing such anniversaries was their only pious act. Near the reading stand in Reb Menachem Mendel's study was a six-branched candelabra where long candles burned in commemoration of the departed. Though Krochmalna Street required the services of a rabbi, it was not easy for the rabbi to make a living. Donations were collected weekly, but Tirza Perl suspected that the beadle who made the rounds pocketed more than the twenty-five percent due him. The rabbi's income decreased every week, and expenses were high in the city. Rent had to be paid each month, not yearly. Butter was sold by the ounce, milk by the quart, wood by the

bundle, potatoes by the pound. It was embarrassing for Tirza
Perl to shop at the market or deal with the butcher. Her
neighbors did not buy in the small quantities she was used to.
They cooked in big pots, for Russian trade had brought prosperity to Poland. Apartment houses were being built everywhere and new stores were being opened. Facing the same
courtyard as the building in which Reb Menachem Mendel
lived was a stocking factory and a shop for manufacturing silk
thread; there were also cobblers, tailors, and joiners in the
buildings. Yes, the Jews, God be praised, were doing a prosperous business. But an unofficial rabbi received no salary.

Reb Menachem Mendel pulled at his red beard. Some latter-
day commentator had attempted to analyze difficult passages
in the text of *Maimonides,* but his explanations were casuistic
and ambiguous. His interpretation contradicted Rabbi Samuel
Edels's commentary. Was it conceivable that Rabbi Samuel
Edels could have been in error? The new era was almost unable to understand the ancient way of thinking. Yet one had
to try, and now and again heaven assisted the scholar. Reb
Menachem Mendel drew on his pipe, picked up a glass and
took a sip of watery tea, put the glass down and rubbed his
high forehead. Trying to solve these problems was like banging one's head against a stone wall.

He began to chant as he read. Who would have thought
that things would turn out as they had? He was in Warsaw.
His son Ezriel had separated himself from everything Jewish.
Despite his responsibilities as a father, he had discarded the capote and was studying to be a doctor. Mirale had moved out
of the house, was not interested in marriage, and was training
to be a hairdresser. She spent her time combing the hair of rich
ladies. Suddenly Reb Manachem Mendel had found himself
childless. What had he done, he wondered, to deserve this?
Somehow the guilt had to be his. Ezriel might have married
the daughter of the Skarshew rabbi, but Reb Menachem Mendel had preferred a match with one of Calman's daughters.
And how that had turned out! One of the other Jacoby girls

had become an apostate; Calman himself had married a wanton. How did the saying go? One sick sheep was sufficient to infect an entire flock. Now it was hard to know whether anyone would recite Kaddish for him after his death. If he didn't keep on studying the Torah and storing up good deeds, he would arrive in the next world empty-handed.

"Well, let's see what *The Face of Joshua* has to say for itself."

There was a knock on the door. Tirza Perl was still asleep in the bedroom, and Reb Menachem Mendel opened the outer door himself. A woman stood at the threshold, and so he averted his face.

"Papa, it's me, Mirale."

"Oh you. Well, come in."

His face flushed. Since his daughter had left home, she seemed like a stranger to him; he was embarrassed in her presence. He looked at her. She had a hat on her head, not a shawl. The upper part of her body was covered by some fashionable-looking garment. Did she bathe herself with scented soap? Reb Menachem Mendel sucked on his pipe.

"Well, Daughter, what do you have to say for yourself?"

"I've come for some linen that I forgot to take."

"So!"

"Mother is asleep?"

"It seems so."

"Father, there's no need for you to be angry with me," Mirale said.

"No need, eh? Your brother has become completely irreligious. I'm told that he even visits that apostate, Miriam Lieba. You've left home. You've both brought us nothing but shame and disgrace."

"What have I done wrong? All I'm doing is learning a trade."

"The first thing a Jewish girl must do is marry."

"Marry whom? That good-for-nothing Jonah? You yourself said he was a fool."

"I? God forbid."

"I'd rather die an old maid than marry such a simpleton."

"Well, how old are you now? You're twenty-four, may you avoid the Evil Eye. Other women your age have children."

"What have I missed? Someone from Skarshew told me that Jonah has become an assistant teacher in a cheder. He has a sick wife and a houseful of children. I've lost a lot, haven't I? Look at me, Papa. You may look; I'm not a stranger. Do you see how I'm dressed? I work and I earn money. I don't have to depend on anyone. Is that such a sin?"

"A Jewish girl marries."

"I'll marry. I'm not seventy years old. I'll have a husband I like and not some schlemiel that Yankle the Matchmaker has chosen. How can that hurt God?"

"No one can hurt the Almighty. 'Is it any pleasure to the Almighty that thou art righteous?' The commandments were only given to assist men. When you marry, you settle down. If you associate with loose women, it's easy for you to go astray. The Talmud says that if we go into a spice shop, pleasant odors cling to us, but if we go into a tannery, we come out stinking. One is easily trapped by the words of heretics. Who are these contemporary philosophers? A pack of murderers and lechers!"

"Many of them are decent people."

"The body is everything to them. If, as they say, there is no God, then it doesn't matter what one does. At first we are tempted by some minor sin, but as soon as that is committed, the will lures us into more serious evil. Without law and a judge to administer the law, there is no reason why one should restrain oneself. Why not give in to evil completely?"

"Because one is a human being."

"A human being! If one does not serve the Almighty, one is even less than an animal. Animals kill only for food; murderers enjoy killing."

"Papa, exactly who are all these murderers? The peasants?
Don't they work hard enough to feed the world?"

Reb Menachem Mendel looked at his daughter in astonishment.

"Why bring in the peasants all of a sudden? Some are decent and some are wicked."

"Where does the bread you eat come from? Someone has to plow and sow so that you'll have your Sabbath loaf. The peasant works for everyone and goes hungry himself. Do you call that justice?"

"It was destined that the peasant remain poor."

"No, Papa, it isn't destiny; it's robbery. Everyone fleeces the peasant: businessmen, aristocrats, even your pious Jews."

"Only swindlers rob people."

The bedroom door opened and Tirza Perl entered the room. Her shoes were unlaced. There was a red kerchief on her head. Her dress was baggy and she looked sallow and drawn. Warsaw had made her old.

"Well, look who's here. The debates are beginning again!"

"I ask him a simple question but I don't get an answer."

II

How unfathomable are the ways of Providence! Temerel, instead of marrying Calman, Jochanan's father-in-law, became the wife of the Komarover rabbi, a recent widower, who in addition was her daughter Yentel's father-in-law. The match was arranged by Hassidim of both courts. Although Jochanan did not approve of the match, he made no attempt to influence his mother. The Komarover rabbi did not stem from an illustrious line. His grandfather had been a dairyman. His father, Reb Abraham Komarover, had established himself by performing a number of exorcisms. Claims had been made that his touch had cured a paralytic, that a cripple had thrown away his crutches at the sound of the rabbi's voice, and that a barren woman blessed by the holy man had become fertile. His had been a lifelong war against the powers of evil; he had beaten them with his cane and driven them off to remote places. His earnings had been kept in earthen jars and had consisted of gold, silver, and copper; he had refused to accept paper money. He had left everything to his son, Shraga Mayer. Shraga Mayer had named his youngest son after Reb Abraham, and it was this youngest son who was now married to Yentel.

Although Shraga Mayer had inherited his father's mannerisms and his following, not even the most ardent Komarover Hassid was under the illusion that Shraga Mayer was the old man's equal. Reb Shraga Mayer shouted and stamped his feet, but the demons paid no attention to him. Neither barren women nor the spiritually ill, neither those afflicted with hiccups nor those possessed by demons came to him for help. His beard was a fiery red, his eyebrows disheveled. More than once Temerel burst out laughing, watching him. He made such strange gestures, prayed so noisily, and the religious commentaries he attempted to write were illiterate. But Temerel wanted to get married. Who likes to live alone?

Her mother agreed to the match. Reb Shimmon was opposed, but the negative attitude of her brother only convinced Temerel that she was acting wisely. So the marriage took place and Temerel settled in Komarov. A few weeks after the wedding, she took a trip to Marshinov to visit her son.

"How are you, Mama?" Jochanan asked.

"Praised be the name of God," Temerel answered.

"How are things with the Komarov rabbi?" Jochanan knew that he should have called his stepfather "uncle," but could not bear to say the word.

"What do you expect? He manages. When benedictions have to be said, he says them. He ushers in the Sabbath and he sees it out." As she spoke, a mischievous glint came into Temerel's eyes. Suddenly she pulled out a handkerchief and blew her

nose loudly. "Jochanan, I've signed my own death warrant."
Tears flowed down Temerel's withered cheeks.

Jochanan trembled. He pitied his mother but dreaded hearing about the many grievances she had against her husband,
since the Law prohibits listening to gossip. Yet, how could he
prevent her from complaining?

"Don't worry, Jochanan, I'm not going to talk about forbidden matters," she said teasingly.

"Maybe things will get better."

"How? You can't make a silk purse from a sow's ear."

What had she expected, Jochanan wondered. A man from
such a family! He changed the subject. "Is Yentel all right?"

"I guess so. But what use is she? That husband of hers is
another barbarian. In all my life I've never met such vulgar
people."

"Well, well . . ."

"What am I going to do, Jochanan? They're unendurable.
They constantly grate on my nerves."

"You can't expect all people to be the same."

"Your poor father was a true saint. May the qualities that he
had not die out! You take after him, Jochanan, may you live
to a ripe old age. Your uncle Reb Shimmon is a hard man, but
nevertheless wise. The rest of them! Do you know what they
do after they eat? They—forgive the expression—belch.
Come one o'clock in the afternoon, they're all snoring like
bears. At three, they're famished again. They can only think
of one thing: food."

"Mama, the rabbi's a scholar."

"Jochanan, you speak like a child. Even I, a mere woman,
catch him in errors. If his scribe Reb Israel didn't correct
everything, people would laugh themselves sick. Whatever
has to be written is written by Reb Israel. And what does he
get out of it? He's starving to death. My husband pays him in
promises. The man's not a rabbi; he's nothing but a crooked
peddler."

"Mama!"

"Why are you shocked? Because a man is called a rabbi, does that make him one! A water carrier can have the soul of a rabbi and a rabbi be nothing but a swindler."

"You're right, Mama."

III

Usually great throngs of Hassidim descended upon Marshinov during Pentecost, but not many people came in the weeks immediately preceding the holiday. Though Jochanan was devoted to his followers, he welcomed this lax period. Nothing suited him better than seclusion. He opened the book known as *The Two Tablets of the Covenant* and began to study the treatise dealing with the rituals and customs of Pentecost. He had been in a melancholy mood that morning, but his spirits improved after prayers. Why was he worrying? He did not have to be a saint. Supposing he did burn in Gehenna? Since there was a Creator, what did man have to fear? Jochanan listened to the birds twittering. A rooster crowed, perhaps one of the fowl which would be slaughtered for the holiday. Well, what difference did it make? Slaughterer, knife, rooster were identical. There was no death. Life existed in every tree and every blade of grass. Jochanan listened more intently, heard crickets chirping, frogs croaking. In the study house, men were chanting the Torah. Somewhere close by, children were reciting a passage from the Pentateuch—or was it the Mishnah? Suddenly a butterfly flew into the room and alighted on the page of the book Jochanan was reading. Love for this creature which had no knowledge of evil and served the Creator in its own way welled up in him. He wondered if it were capable of thought. Did it somehow sense the sanctity of the holy book on which it was resting? Its speckled wings were as delicate as silk. Was it trying to read something? Was it thirsty or hungry? On the table before him was a glass of tea he had been sipping as he studied. He poured out a few drops of the liquid and dissolved some sugar in it. "Drink," he said, addressing the insect.

The butterfly did not move. But the sugar did attract a fly. It stood on the table bending its tiny head, somehow getting itself entangled in its hind legs. Another fly dropped down, landed on top of the first. Jochanan saw what the creatures were doing. All living things united, the small as well as the large. Everything was either male or female. Suddenly the meaning of the passage, "And rejoice with trembling," became clear to him. He himself was trembling in a kind of ecstasy. Who could help but exult when God's greatness was to be seen everywhere? When winter came, this poor fly would die of the cold. He himself would probably live somewhat longer, but no one was immortal. Only the soul mattered. Then what was the sense of worrying? One must serve as one could. One must be joyous. Jochanan rose and began to pace up and down. God was present, watching him and listening to his thoughts. Sinners were to be pitied; they were God's children also, but having forgotten their father, they suffered torment even while indulging in their sensual pleasures. Yet the suffering that they inflicted upon themselves served some purpose. God had created Satan so that man should have free choice, although the path chosen by sinners was the more painful one. Transgression! Ruin! Jochanan rubbed his forehead. His thoughts were too dangerous. He must dismiss them from his mind.

The Hassidim had told him of a Russian organization whose members were committed to overthrowing the Czar. They wanted to help the peasants, taught them to read newspapers. Some of these people had assassinated a governor or a prince, and had been exiled to Siberia. Jochanan grasped his beard. How could the Czar be overthrown? And what if he were? Another Czar would come along. Meanwhile, the revolutionaries suffered. In Siberia, the winters were very cold. But was a soldier who killed on orders guilty? He only did as he was told. As for the Czar, he had been born Czar. Jochanan had learned that some of the revolutionaries were Jews. He groaned. Small wonder! Those who abandon the Torah and associate with the wicked and speak their language become ensnared.

The door opened and Mendel the beadle entered.

"Rabbi, there's a stranger outside, a Hassid, who would like to see you. He wants to get your opinion on something."

Jochanan raised his hand. He constantly prayed that his following would decrease, but nevertheless the Hassidim continued to come. His opinion? What advice did he have to give? Yet how could he refuse to see the man?

"Well, tell him to come in."

As Jochanan spoke, a small, yellow-haired man entered. His beard was also yellow. Everything about the man was yellow: his freckled face, his hat, his patched coat, even his eyes. An odor of axle grease and far-off places came into the room with him.

"Peace be with you, Rabbi."

"Peace be with you. Good day. Be seated."

The man remained standing.

"Where do you come from?"

"I'm from Wysoky. Actually I'm a Turisk Hassid. Where I come from, you go to the court either at Turisk or at Beltz. In our town there are a few Hassidim of other courts as well, but they don't have houses of worship. One of them is an old Kotsker Hassid. He likes to tease the community by smearing cheese on his mustache on the ninth day of Ab to make people think he's eating on a fast day. May it never happen to you, Rabbi, but my daughter began to suffer from terrible stomach pains. The doctor in Zamosc told her to go to Lublin and have an operation. By the time she arrived in Lublin, the pains were gone, but the doctor said that didn't matter, that she must have it anyway—how do you say it?—surgery. We went back to Wysoky and the rabbi said, 'Well, if it's better, it's better. Anyway, I don't believe in the knife.' But when she got home the pains started all over again. She almost climbed up the walls. I was told to take her to Warsaw. In Warsaw one specialist says cut it out—I forget what he called it. Another specialist says, wait. The rabbi, may his life be long, has a reputation as a saintly Jew, and although I'm a Turisk Hassid, I've run up expenses coming here. Whatever the rabbi thinks best, I'll do. Forgive me, Rabbi, I forgot to give you . . ." And the Turisk Hassid pulled a piece of paper and a silver coin out of his pocket.

"Thank you, I don't accept money," Jochanan said. "How can I advise you? God is the adviser."

"You don't take money?"

"No. But thank you just the same."

"In Turisk, even paupers give. It's said that nobody is helped by a rabbi who refuses money."

"Obviously the Turisk rabbi needs it. My father-in-law is a wealthy man."

"Rabbi, what should I do about my daughter?"

"How can I tell you that? I'm not a doctor. You pray and I'll pray. One never knows whose prayers will be answered."

"But I need your advice, Rabbi. I'm an uneducated man. How can I come to a decision when the specialists don't agree? The Turisk rabbi doesn't believe in the knife, but there are times when it's needed. The daughter-in-law of the rabbi had an operation herself. She went to Vienna for it."

"So? It was probably necessary."

"The rabbi was against it, but she didn't listen to him. The doctors say the operation saved her life. Her father is a rabbi, too, and he insisted that she have it."

"Honoring your father is most important of all."

"Rabbi, what should I do?"

"Ask another doctor."

"I don't have a gulden left. I spent my last one to come here. You must tell me something, Rabbi."

Jochanan looked down and saw something that startled him. There was a gold watch in his satin waistcoat, a wedding present from Calman. Jochanan was overcome with shame.

He had been searching in his drawer in an attempt to find a few groschen to give to a poor man and here in his vest pocket was a scrap of that gold from which the ancient calf had been carved. Woe unto him. How easily one forgot and was ensnared by Satan. He lifted the watch as if it were unclean.

"Reb Shloime—that's your name, isn't it?—take this watch and sell it. Don't tell anyone I gave it to you. It's gold, pure gold."

"The rabbi's watch? No, I couldn't."

"Please, Reb Shloime. I am forbidden to have anything like this in the house. The longer I keep it here, the graver my sin. Believe me, you will be helping me. Perhaps because of you I will be forgiven. I should not have worn it even for one day. See a specialist, and if you have any money left over, use it for traveling expenses."

"I just can't take the rabbi's watch. One must give to a rabbi, not take from him."

"Reb Shloime, please. The Almighty will assist you because you have helped me."

"I refuse to take it."

"I command you to."

Jochanan knew that he should not have used the word "command." A word such as that was only uttered by a saint. But there was no other way to overcome Reb Shloime's obstinacy. Silently Jochanan prayed for the Hassid's agreement. The Wysoky Jew's yellow hands began to tremble.

"Rabbi, you're a saint, a great saint."

"Please, you mustn't say such things. I am only doing what the Law commands. You wouldn't have found a groschen on the persons of the ancient rabbis, but in my house there's gold. This trinket can save a life. What good is it to me? Take it. God will certainly help you."

"The rabbi swears to that?"

"With the Almighty's help."

"I won't leave until the rabbi promises me my daughter will get better."

Jochanan was disturbed. What did the man expect of him? How could he give such assurances? He himself was a transgressor. For all he knew, he had committed a host of such sins as he had discovered today. How many other things had he forgotten? Now the Evil Spirit was forcing him into the ways of pride. The only solution was to flee, go into exile. Yet should he promise? If he did not, the man might consider his unwillingness a bad omen.

"Yes, I promise you."

"She'll get well?"

"With God's help, she'll bring you joy."

"Rabbi, my business is bad."

"He who giveth life also giveth food."

"Rabbi, my wife's knee hurts. They say it's hermetic."

Jochanan found it difficult to keep from smiling; Reb Shloime meant rheumatic. He bit his lip and reminded himself of the Diaspora, of the destruction of the temple and of the sufferings of the Jews. Removing his hands from his face, he said, "Your wife will recover completely."

20

When a son, Alexander Jacob—or Sasha, as Clara called him
—was born, Calman was ecstatic. God had granted him an
heir. Clara had had a difficult pregnancy, had grown unusually
large. In the middle of winter, she had a craving for cherries
and Calman had managed to obtain them from a rich landowner who had his own hothouse. Sasha entered the world
large and husky. The Warsaw accoucheur said it was a miracle that the child was delivered without tearing his mother's
womb. He bellowed like a six-months-old baby and had a
head of black hair. The circumcision was like a wedding and
included a banquet for the poor. Both the Skarshew rabbi and
the new Rabbi of Jampol came to the ceremony. The child's
grandfather, Daniel Kaminer, recited the benediction. Although Clara's breasts were heavy with milk, she engaged a
wet nurse. The nursery was decorated sumptuously. Clara
bought a scale in which to weigh the infant, imported a baby
carriage from Berlin, read books and articles on child care.
The child grew and began to walk and talk in his tenth month.
Calman bought the boy an amulet to ward off the Evil Eye.

Before Sasha was even three, he started to climb trees.
Wildly mischievous, he mistreated the pets the peasant
woman brought him as gifts, stepped on the puppies, at-

tempted to strangle the kittens. He threw a baby chick into the water. He dismembered his toys. Finding a knife somewhere, he cut off a doll's head. At first Calman consoled himself saying that it was all because the boy was, may the Evil Eye spare him, so amazingly strong. But as time went on and the child remained incorrigible, Calman's fears increased. He complained to Clara that the boy ate too much. He forbade the child toy whips, swords, and guns. But Clara warned Calman not to interfere.

Jampol found the boy a subject for gossip. They laughed at him and cursed him. Clara bought him a pony and a small britska with a fancy harness. She forbade him to speak Yiddish and hired a French governess. He was taught not to answer when he was addressed as Senderel, to respond only to Sergei and Sasha, his Russian names. Eventually Clara herself began to have trouble with him. He grew fat from overeating, hit his governess and the maid. He laughed wildly. The townspeople nicknamed him Ishmael. Calman was furious, but the name was appropriate—Sasha was a savage.

Finally, after much discussion, Calman convinced Clara that a tutor should be engaged to teach the boy religion. Sasha pulled at his teacher's beard and laughed at the man's fringed garment. It was said by Calman's enemies that his son's black eyes concealed a devil. The boy made fun of everyone, stuck out his tongue, spat, ridiculed Yiddish. Suddenly he acquired a passion for lighting fires. It was impossible to hide matches from him. Whatever fell into his hands burst into flame. The servants predicted he'd burn down the manor house. Clara finally slapped him herself. He broke into laughter and hit back. He began to howl and retch. One afternoon he set fire to a haystack. That day Calman spanked him. The boy shrieked, "You dirty Jew," and kicked his father.

Calman lost control of himself and hit Sasha with all his might, then locked himself in his office and wept. It was the first time since Zelda's funeral that Calman had cried out loud.

Sasha's nose was bloody; he had a swollen cheek. Clara pounded on the office door and, when Calman opened it slightly, shouted, "If you ever touch my son again, I'll kill you."

Calman threw the door wide open.

"Go ahead and kill me, you slut. Your filthy blood flows in his veins."

"Be careful, Calman; I'm not going to warn you again."

Calman fasted the next day and recited the whole Book of Psalms. He swore that this was the end, that he would never make peace with his wife, but she came to him that night, kissed him, tickled him, playfully counted the hairs of his beard, and promised to stop her private war against the Hebrew teacher. But several days later she decided that the manor absolutely had to be renovated. She had waited long enough. The building was impossibly old-fashioned, the roof an incredible patchwork.

"It was good enough for the Count. Why not for you?" Calman protested.

"The Count! You know he's an old idiot."

The reconciliation scarcely over, another quarrel began. It would take many thousands, Calman said, to rebuild the manor. His money was tied up in the business and he was short of capital. Besides, God's needs preceded everything and he had promised to build a prayer house on the estate. Clara laughed, wept, threatened, called him names and warned him that she would run away with the child, or commit suicide. She even announced that she would take a lover and make Calman a cuckold. He sat on the bed in his long nightshirt, skullcap on his head, his beard in disarray, dangling his feet. Clara disliked arguing in the dark and had lit a candle. Calman saw his reflection in a mirror; there were gray hairs in his beard. The world beyond was already calling to him and he was spending his time wrangling with this bitch who had borne him a monstrous child. She paced up and down the room in her bare feet, her hair hanging down over her shoulders, her naked breasts visible through her nightgown. As always when they argued, she addressed him by the formal "you."

"You're wasting your breath arguing, Calmanke. The house will be renovated. All this talk will do as much good as bleeding a corpse."

"I'll build a prayer house and a ritual bath first."

"A ritual bath? Who are you going to soak in it, the Queen of Sheba?"

"You foul-mouthed woman!"

"You feeble old lecher."

Calman could no longer listen to such wickedness. During her pregnancy, when she had feared for her life, she had prayed to God. Now that she was well again, she blasphemed. He picked up his pillow and a blanket, and went into another room to sleep.

II

Clara wrangled with her father as well as with Calman. In his old age Daniel Kaminer had grown foolish and wanted to marry Celina, Mrs. Frankel's daughter. Clara was anxious to prevent the marriage. She was his only heir, and if he married he might spawn a half-dozen more children. Father and daughter spoke to each other sarcastically, argued and bickered. Clara informed him that his contract with the government might easily be cancelled. General Rittermayer would prefer to do business with her. Since she controlled the manor, she could underbid Kaminer. Moreover—as she pointed out in a guarded manner—she was in a position to expose him. The old man became so furious that he burst out laughing. They didn't come any smarter than his daughter. He suggested a compromise; he'd give her half his fortune now. Why should she wish him dead? But maybe she'd poison him anyway. Clara laughed. "If you weren't my father, I'd marry you myself."

"Yes. And if your grandmother had wheels, she'd roll."

"Honestly, what do you want with Celina?" Clara asked, crossing her legs. "You're much better off living as you always have. You know what I mean."

"Ah, it's different when you get old."

"Does she really appeal to you? She's such a mess. Some day she and her room will float off together. Till now she's spent her life sleeping at her mother's house; she'll finish it sleeping at yours."

"I'll wake her when I need her."

"What a man!" Clara said, laughing. She adored her father. The two of them understood each other perfectly.

"How do you know she'll have you?" Clara asked.

"We'll have to talk it over with Auntie."

"Who'll do the talking?"

"You," Daniel Kaminer said.

The conversation continued, each trying to be wittier and more salacious than the other. Daniel Kaminer denied that his fortune was as large as his daughter claimed it to be. But she knew where every ruble was invested. Pencil in hand, she worked out an exact division. The two of them haggled like tradesmen. Then they started teasing each other all over again. Suddenly Daniel Kaminer grew sad. "If only your mother were alive." His eyes moistened. Clara wanted to cry, too. She went to the credenza and took out a bottle of brandy and a carafe of liqueur, poured a drink of brandy for him, liqueur for herself. It annoyed her that in his old age her father wanted a woman to replace her mother. But having been appointed matchmaker somewhat mollified her. Nevertheless, she anticipated having difficulties with Celina; the silly girl would be unable to make up her mind. It would have to be made up for her. On the other hand, it was pleasant to have an excuse to visit Warsaw. And then, of course, best of all was the money she was to receive from her father. Why wait for an inheritance? She hoped that he would live to be a hundred, or even longer. Who was there in the world closer to her than he?

She had been wanting to go to Warsaw for some time, and for a number of reasons. Her plans to renovate the manor required the services of an architect. She was also anxious to consult her lawyer. Moreover, there were a number of people she wanted to see, among them Miriam Lieba and her mulish husband Lucian; Ezriel, too. Until her pregnancy, Clara had been busy courting the Wallenbergs, but the difficult time she had had bearing her child had interrupted her social activities. After the delivery, there had been a procession of wet nurses, maids, and governesses to add to the confusion. Since Sasha's birth she had visited Warsaw only a few times and then always to see doctors. It was now more than three years since the baby's birth and Clara looked younger and prettier than ever. However, the trip was not as easy as it might seem to arrange. Sasha was so wild that Clara did not like to trust him to the servants. Leaving her possessions behind worried her, too; she dreaded the possibility of thieves breaking into the manor house. On the other hand, she couldn't stand guard over her property forever, like a dog chained to its kennel. What sort of a life would that be for a rich, intelligent woman? She must hire servants she could trust. She'd have to find the right tutor for Sasha. Boys respected men more than women.

So as not to leave an angry husband behind her, she made up with Calman. Let him build both his ritual bath and his synagogue! In Warsaw she would get estimates on how much the construction of the buildings would cost. Clara went even further. She told Calman about her agreement with her father, and offered to lend Calman money to assist him in his plans. After all, she was his wife, the mother of his son. "Calmanke," she said, stroking his beard and peering into his eyes, "you don't realize it, but I'm the best friend you have."

"If you could only be like this all the time," Calman replied gruffly. "All I want is that we live like human beings and remember God."

"And what do you think I want? If only half of what I wish for you would come true . . . Your good fortune, Calmanke, is mine."

Calman, after having satisfied his lust, was soon snoring, but Clara lay awake for a long time. The clock seemed to her to be ticking at a feverish pace. Her pulse was beating just as quickly. She couldn't stop planning, wanting, and hoping. It was as if her blood were boiling within her. "What's happening to me? Why am I so driven? And what am I so afraid of?" she asked herself. She knew the answer; obstacles always littered the path to her happiness.

III

In Warsaw, before going to Mead Street, Clara drove to Marshalkovsky Boulevard to buy gifts for her aunt and Celina. What madness, Celina was to be her stepmother! Men were so stupid . . . Clara bought a pair of large gold earrings for Mrs. Frankel and a fur stole for Celina. She saw her own attractiveness mirrored in the knowing glance the sales clerk gave her. "I'm a pretty woman," she thought. "It's worth having a guilty conscience because of me." She imagined herself a man in love with such a woman. When she got into the droshky, she put the packages on her lap. There was no one, experience had taught her, who could not be bribed. You could even buy off God with a ritual bath or a prayer house. The summer day was warm, not hot, and a breeze blew from the Vistula. The odors of fresh fruit and new potatoes permeated the air. Street cleaners splashed the gutters with a white fluid resembling diluted builders' lime. Despite the din created by droshkies, omnibuses, coaches, and pedestrians, the chirping of birds could be heard. It was already noon. Clara had had nothing to eat since an early breakfast but she did not want to arrive at her aunt's with a full stomach. No insult was greater to Mrs. Frankel than a guest who had just eaten. Mrs. Frankel loved to serve and be served food, to give and be given presents. A variety of aromas floated down the stairway; the odors of borscht, cutlets, tomatoes, parsley. Clara inhaled deeply; the smells titillated her appetite. When she knocked, two girls ran to open the door and began to clap and shriek as soon as they saw who it was; Clara never arrived empty-handed. Shears in hand, Mrs. Frankel hurried toward them. In her haste, she had neglected to remove the scissors from her fingers. She kissed Clara first on the lips, and then on both cheeks, and topped it all by screaming with joy. Clara kissed the girls, too.

"Where's Celina?" she asked.

Although it was afternoon, Celina was still in her bathrobe and slippers. "Well, if she appeals to him, it's all right with me," Clara thought, kissing the girl.

"She has an ache in her shoulder," Mrs. Frankel explained apologetically. "Last night we rubbed her down with turpentine, but it hasn't helped. So I told her to sleep as long as she wanted to. Anyway, there's no reason for her to get up."

"You never can tell; she might hatch a few eggs . . . Auntie, I've brought you both a little something."

"A little something! What a spendthrift you are, Clara."

"What do you want me to do, take my money to the grave with me? These earrings are for you. Pure gold!"

"Oh, it's too much, Clara. I can imagine what they must have cost."

"And this little neckpiece is for you, Celina. Feel the nice furry animals."

"Look, Mother. Isn't it gorgeous? Oh, Clara, it's just exquisite."

"Shush, don't make such a fuss. You're a good-looking girl and you should wear nice things. All right, the rest of you, don't stare. I haven't forgotten a single one of you. You'll all get something. Honestly, Auntie, I'm as hungry as a bear."

"Hungry, are you?" And Mrs. Frankel skipped girlishly into the kitchen. There was a pot roast simmering on the stove; peas were boiling. Whatever the peddlers had hawked that day in the courtyard, Mrs. Frankel had bought: raspberries, gooseberries, cherries, and currants. There was bread left over from breakfast, but Mrs. Frankel sent a girl to the bakery to buy a fresh loaf and some warm Kaiser buns. Clara removed the jacket of her suit and her ostrich-plumed hat, one of her aunt's creations. With only a blouse and skirt on, the thickness of her waist and the fullness of her bosom became apparent. Childbirth had filled out her figure. Now she no longer needed to pad her hips and her buttocks. "Oh, Clara, you have such wonderful taste. Isn't that brooch new?" The girls looked at her with admiration. Everyone had to examine and touch her. One girl, an expert on fabrics, lifted Clara's skirt to inspect the material on the left side. Clara began to answer questions. Having read the Parisian magazines, she could describe the very latest fashions. In the midst of the commotion, Mrs. Frankel entered, bringing hors d'oeuvres. As if addressing a yard full of hens, she called out: "Scat . . . Shoo." Laughing, the girls hurried back to their wires and feathers. They were busy preparing for the winter season.

Clara refused to eat alone, insisted that Mrs. Frankel and Celina have something with her. Mrs. Frankel pointed to her throat and swore that she was full up to there, but as soon as she took a bite of food her appetite returned miraculously. Celina scarcely touched anything. Her mother grimaced scornfully. "Just look at the girl, Clara. This is her breakfast."

"I've already had a pretzel with milk."

"That's food? What's going to become of her?" Mrs. Frankel's tone changed. "Clara, darling, she'll kill me. I don't sleep at night. There's scarcely a trollop in the world who doesn't find a husband. But Celina's still an old maid. It hurts me here," she said, placing her hand on her chest. "A girl who refuses to leave the house."

"I suppose you'd let me?"

"Be quiet, or I'll slap that saucy face of yours. A young man used to come to see her, handsome as a picture, a ladies' tailor; he had a tiny little mustache. When the girls saw him, they almost fainted. He worked at Silvermintz's, earned twenty rubles a week, and he was exempt from the draft. No wonder the girls buzzed around him. Who gets such a prince these days? Originally he'd come because of a customer, but when he saw Celina I thought he'd been striken with an epileptic fit. It made me feel good. Who knows? Perhaps they were destined for each other. My fine friends were envious already. But did that girl make an effort? About as much as a wall. He talked and she yawned. Pretty soon he lost interest. Did you ever hear of anything so awful?"

"What's so awful about it? I didn't like him."

"Whom do you like, you idiot?"

Clara smiled. "What's he like, Celina?"

"Oh, he's just a fop. Tries to give you the impression that he's Mr. Somebody."

"And just who are you? It happens that you're my daughter and I've got to love you. But if you weren't—"

Mrs. Frankel didn't finish the sentence. Tears fell from her eyes. She took out a handkerchief and blew her crooked nose.

When Clara announced that afternoon that her father was not getting any younger and was looking for a wife, someone he could trust, Mrs. Frankel's left eye snapped open. It had occurred to her that if Daniel Kaminer were not so avaricious and lewd, he would be a perfect husband for her. A man who lived by himself was worse off than a dog. And how long could she struggle with her shop? Her strength was ebbing.

"You understand, Clara, I'd have to talk it over with Celina."

"With whom else?" Clara asked. "It's Celina we have in mind."

Mrs. Frankel puffed herself up like a brood hen hatching an egg. Her eyes looked bloodshot. A piercing note entered her voice.

"I thought you were a smart woman, Clara," she exclaimed shrilly. "But you're talking like a fool."

"Auntie, let's not kid ourselves, Celina's no child. Before you know it, she'll be thirty. It's time she got married. And my father's no octogenarian; he's not even seventy."

"I don't want to talk about it any more, Clara. I'd rather see her in the Gęsia Street cemetery."

"Well, no is no, but you don't get such an opportunity every day."

"Clara, you've hurt me. All right, he's your father I know, but what else can be said for him? He's nasty, a Litvak, and he talks like a lecher. Can't you find something better for Celina? You should be ashamed of yourself."

"All right, I'm ashamed. But I'm not speaking for myself; my father sent me. Don't think I'm going to get a match-maker's fee. Let's forget that Celina's your spoiled darling and look at the facts. She's not young, can't do anything, certainly not keep house! Of what use is she? My father knows all that. Suppose she did get a young man! As soon as she started to act the way she does with you, he'd serve her with divorce papers."

"What are you talking about? She's a charming, sweet girl, and good-looking, too. I'll admit she's a trifle spoiled, but she'll make someone a good wife. She doesn't run around like the sluts of today."

"Who's she going to get? The ladies' tailor? Well, he hasn't asked her yet. From flirting to behold-you-are-consecrated is quite a jump. And even if he does stand under the canopy with her, what's twenty rubles a week? You'll have to give her a dowry. A young man doesn't want to work for somebody else forever. He's probably younger than she and she'll have to mother him. The first time he swears at her, she'll come running home. Auntie, I only want the best for Celina. I love her like my own sister. But we must be practical."

"Oh, so you want to be practical? Your father's an old man and a drunkard to boot."

"How old is he? Let me tell you, he's a lot stronger than

most of the young ones. Have you ever felt his grip? He's thin, but powerful. He does take a drink now and then, but never too much. And I've never met a smarter man. You should have the money he makes. He's educated too, a Hebrew scholar. I know that I sound like a matchmaker, but after all we're family. He'll sign over one of his houses to her, or something comparable. What's more, there'll be a money settlement written into the marriage contract. She can be sure of one thing: she won't be in want. Look at me! Didn't I marry a man twenty years older than myself? I was not much older than Celina when I went to live with Calman."

Mrs. Frankel shook her head from side to side. "Clara, you're such a schemer. You have a man's head on your shoulders. Calman's not like your father; he's a respectable man. He lost his wife and he remarried. Your father's been a widower for thirty years. You can't do anything with a man who's a profligate."

"Well, no is no. But you can't turn me against my father. If I weren't related to him, and didn't have a husband, I'd take him myself. He knows the world. You can talk to him. Every word he says is worth listening to."

"He should have a wife his own age."

"Why, when he can get whomever he wants? Don't be offended, Auntie: there's an old saying that one has the right to proposition even the rabbi's wife."

"I'm not offended."

Both women lapsed into silence. Mrs. Frankel sat, her nose wrinkled, her lower lip protruding, trying to contain her anger. Her legs felt heavy. She knew full well that Celina couldn't be dragged to the wedding canopy, but the fact that someone had had the audacity to suggest an old widower for Celina was insulting. It was now clear to her why Clara had been so generous with her gifts. "The sly witch," Mrs. Frankel thought. "Insinuates herself into my confidence and then spatters me with mud. It would be better for Celina to die a spin-ter." Clara's eyes glistened as she thought to herself, "A lot of difference it makes to me. That's some bargain he's losing. Anyway, she hasn't given her final answer."

Clara rose to her feet. "Auntie, let's not be enemies."

"Why should we be? Have I lost anything? Sit down and I'll bring you your applesauce."

"No, Auntie, I've got to run along."

Clara took a quick look at herself in the mirror, and then left. Mrs. Frankel's knees were trembling. Even her own workshop seemed unfamiliar to her. She stood at the threshold of the workroom and watched the hustle and bustle. One of the girls was ironing, another was pulling felt, a third was sprinkling water on some material. The room was infernally hot and clouded with steam. There was the odor of something burning. "Devils in Gehenna. What are they doing? What do I need all this for? I don't have the strength to go on any longer." She rushed off in search of Celina, found her in the bedroom, taking off her nightgown.

"Mama?"

"Just look at you!"

Mrs. Frankel slammed the door shut. She had a bitter taste in her mouth. All of her life she had worked hard, and what had she got for it? Other mothers could take satisfaction in their children. She had given birth to something rotten. A girl who spent her life in bed, who wouldn't even dip her hands in water! Did she deserve anything better than an old man? What would happen to her when she didn't have a mother to depend on? There wasn't any money for her to inherit. Mrs. Frankel imagined herself dead. Who would dress her in her shroud? Suddenly she remembered God. "Why am I living?" she asked herself. "What will become of my soul?" One thing she could do while she was still alive: buy a plot in the Gęsia Street cemetery and order a tombstone. Otherwise, when she was buried, she would be completely obliterated.

IV

When Miriam Lieba and Lucian had returned from France, Clara had tried without Calman's knowledge to find a job for Lucian. She was impressed by the fact that her stepdaughter was a countess. There was also the fact that Clara had taken over the Jampolski estate and wanted to make some amends. Lucian, however, had ignored her halfhearted attempts, and Miriam Lieba had not been interested in her favors. Every now and again Clara would hear something about Lucian. He had come to terms with Antek and had taken Kasia in as his maid. For a while he'd worked for the Warsaw Benevolent Society, but then something dreadful had happened. A number of the charitable ladies who supported the Society had formed a group which staged dramatizations of stories and poems by various Polish writers. Only a very select audience attended these performances, which were held in the drawing room of a member of the group. Occasionally some highly placed Russian official would be invited, sometimes even the Governor-General himself. The ladies and their daughters made the costumes. The dialogue was written by an amateur writer. Lucian didn't care much for his work at the office, and managed to get himself sent out on loan to the ladies. After he'd taken part in several of the plays, the women agreed that he was a born actor. His name was even mentioned in the *Kurjer Warszawski*. But the older ladies, having heard rumors about him, began to insist that he no longer be invited to participate in the plays. They didn't think it safe for their unmarried daughters to meet him. The younger generation argued that a hero of the uprising should be treated with charity.

Then suddenly scandal broke. Clara, who at that time was still tied down to the baby and was not coming to Warsaw, had never been able to learn the details. She did know that there had been an antique music box involved. Apparently the box had disappeared from a house after a visit by Lucian. He had come through the front door to see the lady of the house and later the same night had returned through the back door to visit the maid. The lady of the house had found him in bed with the maid and had chased him into the street, clad only in his underwear. He had been arrested and sent to jail for two weeks. Later it was discovered that he had embezzled money from the Society and had been planning to elope with a young woman student. Oddly enough, the Wallenbergs had stood bail for him. They had also made good the sum he had stolen from the Society. The music box had turned up later in an antique shop on Holy Cross Street.

For a time, Clara lost track of Lucian. Then she was told that he had become the protégé of the widow of an actor, a certain Elzbieta Bobrowska, a seamstress, and was doing walk-ons at the Rozmaitosci Theater. Kasia had given birth to a child, who had immediately been deposited in a home for foundlings. She was now acting as housekeeper for a widower on Chmielna Street. It was said Lucian had sold her to the man. These stories fascinated Clara. She remembered how little interested Lucian had been in her when they had first known each other. He had promised to write to her but hadn't kept his word. Clara forgave him. All right, he had acted foolishly. The one thing she couldn't forget was that he had never once tried to kiss her. Nor had he been the only man with whom she had failed. Her good looks and her aggressive manner did not assure success with everyone. Grisha, her first husband, had left her before he'd got consumption. Men would start off hot in pursuit of her and then suddenly lose interest. Colonel Smirnoff's ardor, for example, had cooled off considerably. Finally he'd been transferred to another garrison. The same thing had happened with General Rittermayer. Curiously enough, the only man who couldn't stop wanting her was Calman.

Often on sleepless nights Clara would meditate on this. When she'd attended the gymnasium she'd had crushes on her teachers and on a number of boys, but had always been re-

jected. It was these failures that accounted for her marriage to
so crude a man as Calman. Not being able to get love, she had
settled for money. She remembered the evenings she'd spent at
Grain's, playing cards with the Sorkesses and the Shallits.
Good cards had always flown her way. They'd all joked
about her good fortune at cards which meant failure in love.
Every so often David Sorkess would kiss her, and Morris Shal-
lit liked to pinch her bottom. But they never took her seriously. Even the inscriptions that officers and students had
written in her school album had been more ironic than romantic. Whenever Grisha got angry, may he rest in peace, he
would curse her for being so vulgar. But in just what way was
she vulgar? She certainly dressed with chic. She knew how to
play the piano, could speak Polish well and Russian perfectly.
Her French wasn't too bad either. What did other women
have that she did not?

That afternoon, having left Mrs. Frankel's, Clara paused in
the courtyard at the gate and looked about her. She'd been so
anxious to get to Warsaw, but now that she was there she
didn't know what to do with herself. Should she go to see the
unfortunate Miriam Lieba, or pay a visit to Shaindel? Perhaps
she might look in at her tailor's. She had been given the address of an architect but wanted to find out more about him
before seeking him out. There was her lawyer, of course, but
he was always so busy. From the newspaper Clara had learned
that a famous Italian composer was that day conducting one
of his own works at the Dolina Szwajacarska. But she couldn't
attend a concert by herself. Alas, a woman could not go anywhere unescorted. Men were lucky. Theaters, cabarets, clubs,
and even the hangouts of thieves were open to them. A man
could buy a woman for a few rubles if he wanted to. He could
indulge all of his desires, no matter how perverse, and his
reputation didn't suffer. If only she had been born a man, she
would have shown the world a thing or two. Clara finally decided to visit Miriam Lieba on Obozna Street.

The droshky that she hailed took her down Hozia Street

and out into Krakow Boulevard. Clara had the coachman
draw up at various shops, where she bought toys for the children and some flowers for the Countess. She made clear to the
shopkeepers that the gifts were to be wrapped attractively because they were intended for members of the aristocracy. The
sales people smirked and bowed politely. Now that it was
summer, Obozna Street didn't look as desolate as it had when
Clara had last been there. The acacia and fruit trees were in
bloom. Birds were singing; dogs were chasing each other.
Small girls sang as they rolled hoops in the middle of the
street. Their song was about a haughty lady who refused to
become an empress and later disdained saving her life by
marrying the executioner. Clara listened. Young though the
children were, they were already singing of love. She was
overcome with desire. Her father was planning to take a girl as
his wife, and she, his daughter, had shut herself up with an old
man, a religious fanatic. "A ritual bath, of all things," she
mumbled. "It's high time I found myself somebody else." She
paid the driver and entered the courtyard of the house where
Miriam Lieba lived. She knocked at the janitor's door and gave
the man a gulden to go upstairs and announce her. Clara stood
watching the janitress pump water. A crippled old woman
hobbled across the narrow yard, tapping with her cane and
grumbling to herself.

The janitor returned, cap in hand. "Forgive me, madam,"
he said, "but they refuse to open the door. They've locked
themselves in."

"Maybe they've gone out."

"No, the Countess is there. I heard her. She shouted at me."

"Where are the children?"

"The children? A lady took them away. Dr. Zawacki's wife
. . . to the country . . . to Wilanow."

"Well, thank you," Clara said, and she tipped the man
again.

He bowed deeply. "God bless you, madam. Perhaps I can
be of further assistance to you?"

"No, never mind. I'll go up there myself."

"Something may be going on there. The Countess is in a bad mood."

"It doesn't matter."

Clara mounted the stairs, holding the packages in one hand and her pocketbook in the other. When she reached the door of Miriam Lieba's apartment, she gave it a kick. She didn't know quite why, but she was determined to beat on the door until she received an answer. There was the sound of footsteps within.

The door was flung open. Clara saw a woman dressed in a cotton skirt that was too short, and wearing scuffed slippers on her bare feet. The woman's half-faded golden-blond hair had been hastily combed and was held in place at the top of her head with a single hairpin. Yes, it was Miriam Lieba. But she was so changed that Clara had difficulty recognizing her. In a few years she had become old and emaciated. Her cheeks were pale and hollow; her eyes, sunk deep in their sockets, were underlined with heavy shadows. Lusterless, they were the eyes of a person who has grown tired of life.

"Well, what do you want?" Miriam Lieba spoke angrily. On her breath was the odor of vodka.

"Forgive me, Countess. I am your father's wife—Clara. We met several years ago."

The two women studied each other. Miriam Lieba's lip curled as if she were about to say something cutting.

"Clara?"

"Yes, your father's wife."

"What are the flowers for? We haven't had a death here yet."

"God forbid. They're for you, Countess."

"Well, come in."

Clara was surprised to see what sort of a place the Jampolskis lived in. The plaster on the kitchen walls was crumbling; the stove was littered with dirty pots and pans. Onionskins, potato peels, the remainder of a bag of chicory were scattered on the floor. The window was shut. There was a cloying, sweetish odor that suggested the apartment had been neither aired nor swept in weeks. Miriam Lieba took Clara into the living room, which was in the same disorder as the kitchen. The drawers of the dresser were open and clothes and laundry were scattered everywhere. On the table was an empty liquor bottle. Here, too, the windows were closed. Miriam Lieba shuffled to the center of the room and remained standing there.

"It's a mess, isn't it?"

"It doesn't matter."

"Some very generous people have consented to keep my children. I'm here by myself. There's no sense in doing any housework. What shall I do with the flowers? There's no water in the barrel. I stopped tipping the janitor and so I don't get any water. Just put the flowers on the table. Let them wither. Everything around here withers anyway."

"I'll have the janitor bring you a bucket of water."

"No, don't bother."

Clara laid the bouquet on the table and put the packages on the windowsill. She looked for a chair to sit on, but all of them were piled with clothing and other objects. Miriam Lieba took hold of a chair, tilting it to clear it of clothing.

"Won't you sit down? No one comes to see me, that's why . . . Did you send the janitor up? He knocked on the door."

"Yes, I asked him to announce me."

"Why did you do that? I never let him in. We're at war with each other. He's a spy, too. Gives information about me to the comissariat. They've already registered my furniture. The marshal came in with a policeman to attach my possessions. I owed eighteen rubles and fifty kopecks. What brings you here? Now no one comes to see me."

"But you are my stepdaughter."

"What? I'm still someone's daughter? I'd forgotten. Sometimes I feel I've never had anyone. I just exist, like a stone on the riverbank. Well, how is he, my father? I call him Father although he's disowned me. When I left, he told everyone I was dead. He observed shivah."

"Countess, you can be sure that he thinks of you."

"He thinks of me? What does he think? I can't even remember what he looks like. Is his beard gray?"

"A little, not entirely."

"You have a child now, don't you?"

"Yes, a son. Sasha. He always asks about his sister the Countess. When he was born, I wrote you a letter, but I never received an answer."

"You wrote? When? The letter probably came when Lucian was at home. He steals my letters. He steals everything. He must have taken that, too. Well, now that I'm a grown woman, I'm blessed with a brother! That's really funny. When I was a child, I always wanted a brother. I envied girls who had little brothers to play with. But now it's a trifle too late for something like that." The tone of Miriam Lieba's voice changed. "This seems to be the final act of my little tragedy, or perhaps it's a comedy after all. What difference does it make? Unfortunately I don't have a thing to offer you, not even a glass of water." Miriam Lieba rose, ready to show her guest out.

21 ♟

At last Ezriel had enrolled at the Szkola Glowna, which the Russians had transformed into a royal university, and was studying medicine. Wallenberg had kept his word and had helped. He knew most of the faculty and was friendly enough with the dean to have him to dinner. Ezriel found studying for a degree difficult. The Russian language still confused him, although he did well in mathematics, physics, chemistry, and botany. He had heard that students in foreign universities led a gay life, drank endless tankards of beer, and played all kinds of pranks on the rector and the university administrators. Nothing of the sort went on in Warsaw. One had to work hard to get into the university. Political activity on the part of the students was discouraged by the Russians. The Polish press was constantly preaching the same sermon: industrialization and culture was its theme. Polish youth was becoming increasingly preoccupied with education. It was almost considered a patriotic duty to become a doctor or an engineer.

Ezriel was now the father of two children; the older one, Uri Joseph, or Joziek in Polish, already attended school. The younger child, Zelda or Zina, went to kindergarten. But Ezriel still walked about in a student's uniform. Evenings, while Joziek did his homework, Ezriel looked over his own lecture notes. He was taking courses in the history of medicine, ana-

lytical chemistry, surgery, and ophthalmology. Anticipating
the curriculum, he was always ahead of the assignments and
frequently read additional books on the subject, not required in
the course of study. He rummaged about, frowned, hummed
to himself. The habits of the study house stayed with him. The
Polish and Russian students were not as serious as he. They
joked in the morgue. For him, medicine was no laughing matter. First of all, it was a science and an art. Second, it bordered
on mysterious realms. How little was known about the functions of the brain! No one had as yet discovered how traits
were inherited. Wherever one looked, one was presented with
riddles. The study of medicine was a great responsibility. Ezriel's throat constricted and his mouth became dry each time
he entered the morgue. The corpses lay on the metal tables,
covered by sacks. The smell of formaldehyde made Ezriel's
head reel. He couldn't grow accustomed to the rigid cheeks,
glazed eyes, deformed noses, and sagging chins of the dead.
These bodies had only recently been living creatures, hoping
and planning. Ezriel could almost hear them whispering to
him, "Too late, too late." It seemed to him that in death they
had discovered a truth that would have altered their lives radically if they had learned it in time.

Once Ezriel saw a student put a cigarette into the mouth of
a girl who had died of poisoning. The other students winked
at each other and laughed. They found life and death equally
funny.

That year Calman had again invited Ezriel and Shaindel to
visit the manor with their children. Clara thought well of university students. Besides, Zina, Ezriel's daughter, was about
the same age as Sasha. In any case, whom else could Calman
invite? The apostate Miriam Lieba? Tsipele, the wife of a
rabbi? Jochebed and Mayer Joel, who remained aloof? Ezriel
and his children were the only ones who could possibly stay at
the manor. However, Ezriel and Shaindel were in no hurry to
accept the invitation. Shaindel still found it difficult to pass
even a day with Clara. One look at her father's new wife,

Shaindel said, gave her a spasm. Ezriel liked the manor's fields, forests, and meadows, its rural calm, but if Shaindel wasn't happy there, what sort of vacation would it be?

In the summer evening Ezriel sat at the table reading a biology text by the light of a lamp suspended from a chain. As he read about centrosomes, chromosomes, protoplasm, and cytoplasm, he listened with one ear to the activities going on in the apartment. Ezriel liked quiet, but Shaindel was noisy. Or maybe it just seemed that way to Ezriel. He still loved Shaindel, but her increasing corpulence disturbed him. After the birth of each child, her waist broadened several inches. Her bosom had grown pronounced, her hips too round. Only her face and legs remained maidenly. Constantly warning her to eat less chocolate, jam, and halvah, he had shown her published proof in a medical journal that sweets ruined the teeth, accumulated fat around the heart, and even led to diabetes. Shaindel ought to be especially careful, he told her, since her mother had been diabetic. Shaindel insisted that it was Ezriel's fault she overate. She longed for him constantly and it made her yearn for food.

Actually, Shaindel had remained provincial. She could not give up her small-town habits, and bore a grudge against Ezriel for studying so much and reading so many books. She still spoke the Polish of a peasant and could not even write an address properly. Her own son, Joziek, caught her in errors. Shaindel no longer wore a wig—but she had remained a pious Jewess. She attended the ritual bath, asked advice of rabbis, threw coins into the alms box for the holy rabbi Mayer, the Miracle Worker. For two and a half weeks out of the month, Ezriel was not permitted to go near her. When a child sneezed, she tugged at its ear. On the eve of a new moon she gave the children a potion to prevent worms. Behind Ezriel's back, she consulted wonder rabbis and even gypsies. At times it seemed to Ezriel that Shaindel played a perverse game with him, regressing as he advanced. How had he harmed her, that she should wish to oppose him?

Her jealousy of Miriam Lieba had developed into a mania. He had to promise solemnly not to visit her sister, or even speak to her. Shaindel swore on her mother's memory that if she found he had visited Miriam Lieba or had even spoken to her on the street, she would take the children and run away, or commit suicide.

"I'll leave and you won't know where I am!" Shaindel would scream. "My blood will run down the gutter!"

And although time and time again he swore to avoid Miriam Lieba and not answer her letters, Shaindel continued to harangue him: "You fiend!" she wailed. "You filthy liar. Hurry up, rush off to her. When you come back, I'll be lying with my feet toward the door . . ."

In her rage she would pound her head against the wall.

II

Ezriel did not have to look far to see the workings of heredity. Joziek took after his mother. The boy was small and dark-skinned, had black eyes and hair, red cheeks, and a small nose. He was as good-natured as Shaindel had been when Ezriel first met her. In his cap and brass-buttoned black jacket with its military collar, he looked like a toy lieutenant. Joziek got the very highest marks, nothing but four pluses and fives. He spoke Russian like a native, and had acquired fluent Polish from his playmates. Ezriel had engaged a French mademoiselle to teach the boy, and he had learned French quickly. No subject proved too difficult for him. He was a favorite of both children and teachers. Shaindel often said that she had grown stout merely from looking at her Joziek.

Zina, nearly three years old, was blond and blue-eyed and tall for her age. Shaindel had to discipline her constantly. When Zina was denied anything, she had a tantrum. She had started to talk early, but in a language of her own. She put everything that she found into her mouth, and had once swallowed a button. At times expressions appeared on her face that reminded Ezriel of his grandfather Reb Abraham Hamburg. Whenever Zina threw her toys about, stamped her feet, or cried, Shaindel remarked, "Look at that temper. There's no doubt about who her father is."

Yes, the drop of semen, barely visible through a microscope, had somehow carried from one generation to another thousands of physical and spiritual characteristics. How were the mannerisms of Zina's Turbin grandfather hidden in the chromosomes? Was it the work of a few molecules? Or did some kind of tiny soul dwell in the semen? Anything was possible. Was not matter itself a secret? No one had seen an atom or a molecule. Nor was the true character of gravity, magnetism, electricity, or sunlight understood as yet. What then *was* known? Indeed, was knowledge possible for man when all his experience had to be filtered through the prism of space and time and the purely subjective categories of quality, quantity, and causality? Ezriel knew that he should devote all his time to his medical studies, but he found himself drawn to the works of Spinoza, Kant, Fichte, and Schopenhauer. How could one go on living in the midst of such mystery?

"Ezriel, come to bed."

"Yes, dear. In a moment."

"You'll ruin your eyes, Ezriel. You don't let me sleep either."

"I'm coming. I'm coming."

Ezriel was still not making his own living, and Shaindel's dowry had already been consumed. Nevertheless, they had hired a maid. Her name was Tekla. Ezriel heard her rearranging the straw in her mattress. Evidently she was about to retire for the night. She had her own little world. She ate and slept in the kitchen. It was there that her friends and suitors visited her. Sundays she went to church. Once a month she received a letter from her native village, written by the county clerk. Ezriel would read it to her: "First of all, we are happy to report that we are all in good health. God grant that you are healthy also. Second, we would like you to know that our cow

Kwiatula has calved . . ." Under her pillow, Tekla kept an Egyptian dream book. She dreamed nightly of gold pieces, broken eggs, black tomcats, and dreadful men who chased her with sticks and swords. Ezriel turned off his lamp and went into the bedroom.

"Shaindel, are you asleep?"

"How can I sleep when you have the light on and keep on rustling pages? And Zina will have me up at six."

"I must study. I can't accept your father's generosity forever."

"If you'd listened to me, you wouldn't need my father's help. Look at Mayer Joel. He's a rich man."

Ezriel undressed and got into bed. He wanted to take Shaindel in his arms, but she was still in an "impure" condition.

Ezriel said good night, tried to fall asleep, but sleep wouldn't come. In the dark he visualized the morgue, the tables, the sacks, the dead faces. Why had the tall young man hanged himself? Why had the redheaded girl jumped into the Vistula? How much did a person have to endure before he was driven to do such a thing? Were they now at peace? Was their sleep actually eternal?

Ezriel tossed, doubt-ridden, in bed after the work-filled day. Was it worthwhile to struggle so to become a doctor? Did he really have an aptitude for the profession he had chosen? He was permitted to practice a little now under the supervision of a doctor, but it seemed to him that his diagnoses were rarely correct. And why bother to cure people when hundreds of thousands perished to advance the political ambitions of Queen Victoria or to indulge the caprices of Abdul-Hamid? Here in Warsaw, people lived in dark cellars, three families to a hole. They were devoured by lice, hunger, consumption. What good was medicine if people were driven to death?

Ezriel had had great hopes that progress could be achieved through education. Yet knowledge itself turned out to be extremely precarious. The entities which were said to constitute matter seemed to have almost magical properties. Moreover, the various materialistic theories, and Darwinism in particular, had put almost all values in jeopardy: the soul, ethics, the family. Might was right everywhere. Man's ancient beliefs had been bartered for the telegraph. But what could Ezriel do about it? For him the old traditions were already destroyed. He was left with nothing but examinations and dread. He had forsaken God but he was dependent upon all kinds of bureaucrats. He had made a mistake, Ezriel felt. But what exactly had been his error? How could it be rectified? As he lay in the darkness, it occurred to him that the young man who had been found hanging in an attic room in the Old City and whose dissection Ezriel had witnessed must have had much the same thoughts as he was having now.

III

Mirale had rented a room on Dzielno Street. She had been lucky. She was gifted at the trade she had decided to learn. Six weeks after beginning her apprenticeship, she knew how to set a coiffure. She was sent to the houses of wealthy ladies and given a percentage of the fee by her employer. The women on Marshalowsky Boulevard and Senator Street were delighted with the way Mirale curled locks or braided chignons. When spoken to, she listened respectfully. None of her clients were scratched by combs or hairpins. She pulled gray hair out by the roots so that it would not grow back. She was skillful with scissors, tweezers, and curlers. Would anyone have thought that this quiet girl had so many ideas of her own? When Mirale returned to her room in the evening, she became another person. She put a pot of water for tea or potatoes on the stove and took some bread and herring from the table drawer where she stored food. While preparing supper, she did the lessons that Ezriel's friend, Aaron Lipman, had mapped out for her. She was studying Russian, Polish, and geography. Aaron read to her from Buckle's *History of Civilization in England* and Mill's *Principles of Political Economy*. He analyzed for her Czernishewski's novel, *What Must Be Done?* Mirale, however, learned even more from Aaron's conversations with her than from the books he read to her. Things were happening in the world. The Parisian communards had been hanged, but their ideas could not be destroyed. Aaron told her about the nihilists, the Narodniki, the European socialists. The serfs, though they had been freed by Czar Alexander, remained uneducated and in peonage. Europe was moving forward, but Russia refused to budge. In England, Parliament had more power than the Queen. France was a republic. Lincoln had freed the American slaves. But Russia was still governed by an autocrat. The Jews of Western Europe spoke civilized languages and sent their children to modern schools. Here the Jews spoke a barbaric jargon, dressed like Asiatics, and believed in dibbuks.

How long could they exist in such ignorance? There was only one remedy, Aaron said—education. When people were conversant with the laws of nature and informed about what had happened in the past, they could no longer remain docile. Aaron's program for the future was not always consistent. One day he insisted that the Jews learn Polish, and the next that they study Russian. He had periods when he believed that Poland's salvation lay in forgetting her national aspirations and getting down to the real business of industrializing herself and educating her citizens. At other times he regarded the ousting of her oppressors as her most important task. Whatever his program, he was certain of one thing: the Jews must assimilate. Whenever Ezriel dropped in, he backed up his friend. After all this time, it wasn't very likely that the Messiah was going to come. The Jews would remain in Poland. Since that was so, they'd better reform their synagogues and schools and start dressing like everyone else. This was the second half of the nineteenth century, not the Middle Ages. Ezriel and Aaron did not agree about everything. Aaron was a partisan of the Narodniki. Ezriel did not think that the Jews should get involved in Russian politics. Their first job was to stop being religious fanatics. Anyway, their allegiance was to Poland; let Russia worry about itself. The men would argue and bicker angrily, using terms that Mirale did not understand, referring to people of whom she had never heard. Aaron made fun of the leaders of the world: priests, generals, aristocrats. He considered the Russian peasantry superior to everyone. Ezriel was always so negative in his attitude that Aaron nicknamed him "the pessimist." Finally they would stop debating and sit down to a game of chess. Ezriel would start out boldly and seem the better player, but he soon became bored with the game. Aaron would tug at his remnant of a beard and meditate about each move interminably.

"Where do you think I should put my bishop?"

"That's no bishop. That's your queen."

"Oh, it's my queen, is it? Well, yours isn't worth a pinch of snuff." Suddenly Aaron would begin to chant from the Book of Esther: "Will he force the queen also before me in the house?"

Mirale would break into laughter. Although they spoke constantly of assimilating, they couldn't stop quoting the Scriptures. Aaron was small and dark, and had a high forehead. He was a student of law at the university and supported himself by teaching at an orphan asylum. He was also the founder of a group dedicated to self-education. The group met three times a week in Mirale's room. Ezriel, too, sometimes came to the meetings. The group studied economics, sociology, biology. They were constantly arguing about the important issues of the day: the plight of the peasants, women's rights, the new books. Aaron had a way of attracting people to himself. Among those who came were Alexander Zipkin, a student whose father had once managed the Lithuanian estate of a Polish landowner; Sonya Rabinowitch, a midwife; and Esther Eisner, who had come to Warsaw from Bialystok after having been divorced from her husband, a manufacturer.

Esther was now a seamstress and conducted her own business. Vera Charlap, another member of the group, was the daughter of a rabbi. Vera had run away from home to study at the conservatory. She had developed consumption and had been forced to spend three years in the resort town of Otwock. Now she supported herself by giving piano lessons to the children of wealthy Hassidim. The language spoken at the meetings was a mixture of Russian and Polish. Vera also knew Hebrew. The oldest member of the group was Sonya, who was an inveterate cigarette smoker. Esther Eisner amused everyone by mimicking the gossipy shrews who patronized her shop. Mirale loved to listen to the lectures and the debates that followed them. What was the difference between absolutism and democracy? Did a woman have the right to do as she pleased with her body? What road should today's youth take? The names of well-known writers, critics, and revolutionaries were mentioned. There was talk of the French Revolution, and the young Russian intelligentsia, men and women who "went out among the people." Karl Marx had founded the Internationale; Bakunin had created the Alliance; a student by the name of Karakozoff had attempted to assassinate the Czar. In foreign countries, Russian socialists were publishing revolutionary books and magazines that were being smuggled into Russia. Yes, both in Russia and in Free Europe history was on the move. The arguments went on so long that the floor became littered with cigarette butts. Although what they were doing was not forbidden, Mirale kept the curtains drawn. The Warsaw police became suspicious any time young people gathered in a group. Any stranger seen entering an apartment was reported to the comissariat by the janitor of the building.

IV

After leaving Miriam Lieba's, Clara went to Ezriel's apartment, but he was not at home. She chatted with Shaindel and for the hundredth time invited her to visit the manor. Shaindel explained that Ezriel was at his sister's and suggested that if Clara wanted to see him she would find him there. By the time Clara arrived at Mirale's, Ezriel had gone. Alexander Zipkin offered to escort her down the stairway, which, he warned her, was so dark one could easily slip. Zipkin was a tall, bushy-haired man. Under his jacket he was dressed Russian style in a satin blouse, striped trousers, and a tasseled belt. A cigarette dangled from the corner of his mouth. He had dark eyes and heavy eyebrows, a lean face with side whiskers, and a thin, straggly mustache. As Clara descended the stairs, he took her arm casually and spoke to her in the confident tone of a so-phisticate. When they reached the street, he made no motion to return to Mirale's. Clara asked where he was from and what he was studying. Zipkin explained that his father had originally been Prince Radziwill's bailiff. Berish Zipkin had been so highly thought of by the Radziwills that he, Alexan-der, had been taught by the same tutors as the Prince's chil-dren. Consequently he had become a good horseman and an excellent swimmer. But after the uprising a large portion of the Radziwills' land had been divided among the peasants. Al-though the Prince had escaped complete ruin, he had no longer required the services of a bailiff. So Berish Zipkin had moved into town. Alexander had begun studying medicine in Kiev but had transferred to the University of Warsaw, where he had met Ezriel, who had introduced him to Aaron Lipman and the other members of the self-education group.

"The truth is, it's a complete waste of time," Alexander told Clara.

"How can you say that? Education is very important."

"For the people perhaps, but not for a bunch of old maids."

Clara suggested that he visit the manor during his vacation, mentioning Sasha's need for a tutor. She hailed a droshky and they drove to a confectionary on Theater Place. They sat talking over a cup of coffee about love, literature, money, and the situation in Russia. Zipkin, it turned out, had spent some time in Lomza and had patronized the same apothecary as Clara. Alexander had had some experience in teaching and as a tutor had gained entry into the homes of a number of wealthy families. As a matter of fact, he was living for the summer in the house of a rich merchant who was vacationing in Carlsbad with his family. A maid had been left in charge of the house, but Zipkin had let her go off on a visit to her parents in the country. "If you doubt my word, madam," he said casually, "you're welcome to come and see for yourself."

"You know very well that a respectable woman doesn't visit a bachelor's apartment."

Zipkin laughed. "I haven't raped anyone yet."

"There's always a first time."

"My victims would have to absolutely implore me."

"Well, believe me, I'm not the imploring type."

The apartment was only a few blocks away, on Leshno Street. Despite the lateness of the hour, they decided to walk and sauntered down Tlomacka Street past the newly erected synagogue. No lights were on in the building. Piles of lumber and bricks still littered the yard. Zipkin stopped and looked at the Star of David on top of the cupola.

"Now what's the sense of all that?"

"Jews still believe in God."

"Not the ones who built this synagogue."

The conversation turned to religion. Zipkin said straight out that he was an atheist. People spoke of God, but where was He? Had anyone seen Him? Each race worshipped a different idol. Man, as Darwin had proved, was descended from the apes. He was just another animal: *homo sapiens*. Zipkin began discussing the doctrines of Marx, Lassalle, and Lavrov. The Polish Jew, he said, had once had a real place in society. Before the liberation of the serfs, he had acted as an intermediary between the landowners and the peasantry. He had outlived his role and become little more than a parasite. He wasn't productive, didn't speak the language of the country in which he lived, and sent his children to cheders. How long was the Jew going to wash himself in ritual baths and walk around in tzizis?

Clara burst out laughing.

"What's so funny about that?"

"You don't know why I'm in Warsaw. I'm looking for someone who can build a ritual bath."

"You're joking."

"No, I'm not."

And Clara, with a smile on her lips, told Zipkin about Calman's plans. When Zipkin asked her why she had married such a man, she replied, "I can't explain it even to myself."

Clara knew that it was unseemly for her to go upstairs with Zipkin, but she had no desire to go back to her aunt's and listen to her complaints. And Zipkin was interesting. She liked the way he spoke Polish. He quoted the modern writers, had seen the fashionable plays, visited the latest exhibitions of both the Polish and foreign painters, and knew many of them personally.

When they approached the house and Zipkin rang the bell, Clara glanced quickly over her shoulder as if she suspected that she was being followed. Someone was waiting for her, she mumbled; she must go home. Zipkin paid no attention to what she was saying. The gate opened and the janitor appeared. Zipkin tipped the man and taking Clara firmly by the arm guided her through the doorway. She climbed the stairs with him, her face burning as if from a slap. Her heels were too high; the stairs were too long.

"Just where are you taking me?" she asked. Her mouth had become dry.

"I've already told you."

When they reached the third floor, Zipkin opened a door which led into a hallway. As soon as they were in the hallway, he pulled her to him. His presumption repelled Clara.

"Please," she said, pushing him away. "I want you to light a lamp."

He did as she asked, and led her into a drawing room. The place was dusty. Two brass candlesticks stood on the sheet-draped piano as if at the head of a corpse. As she moved around the unfamiliar room, inspecting the pictures and knickknacks, Clara felt both fear and desire. Zipkin had wandered off somewhere. The air was heavy with the odor of camphor. The dry furniture squeaked, and she felt warm and sticky. A moth began to flutter about the candle Zipkin had lit. Clara looked into a mirror and studied her reflection. She tried to smile at her image, but it gazed back at her with grave aloofness. How many more years of youth did she have? She'd had husbands, but no lovers. If she waited much longer, she might be denied that experience. The candle was smoking. A bit of dust dropped from a stove with a gilded cornice. For a moment Clara thought she heard a key in the door that led to the hallway. Were the owners of the house returning? Her heart began to pound. "I mustn't die here," she thought.

Zipkin returned. He had taken off his jacket and looked taller in his belted blouse. He was carrying two glasses of wine. He handed Clara one and touched his glass to hers.

"To your health."

"My, it's strong."

"Unfortunately there's not a thing to eat in the house."

Clara was aware of the passion in his look. His face was pale. His dark eyes seemed insolent, yet humble too. He spoke in incomplete sentences and breathed heavily. As a rule, Clara was overcome with laughter when men tried to approach her, but this time she remained serious. An unfamiliar sadness took hold of her. "Let's not do anything silly," she protested.

"It's even sillier to do nothing and wait for the grave."

He went into the corridor and bolted the front door, remaining there for a time as if listening for footsteps. He was tense when he returned.

"The neighbors are all at the spas. The whole building is like a cemetery," he said.

"Sometimes I think the whole world is a cemetery," Clara

answered, astonished at her own words. Zipkin moved a bit closer to her.

"True, but one can have fun even in a cemetery."

v

Late that night Zipkin escorted Clara to her aunt's house. No droshkies were available after midnight and so they had to walk. They stood at the gate to the courtyard exchanging the weary kisses of those who are only half awake. When the janitor opened the door, Clara tipped him twenty groschen. Zipkin gave her a final quick pat on the shoulders. She climbed the dark stairway, then paused for a moment to lean on the banister. "Am I happy?" she asked herself, and listened as if waiting for an answer. No, she was not. But why shouldn't she be? She had wanted a lover. Was it weariness or was she ashamed of appearing at her aunt's at such a late hour? No, those were not the reasons. What did men really think of women such as she? How did they talk about them? Zipkin had sworn not to say a word to Ezriel, but he would surely boast to someone. They were to meet the following evening at Semodeny's Confectionery and would discuss Zipkin's visiting Jampol during his vacation. "Well, what's done is done," Clara said, yawning. It was bound to happen sooner or later. She knocked on the door of her aunt's apartment and waited. Her high heels made her feet ache. Her corset cut into her flesh. Her temple was throbbing. Mrs. Frankel appeared, wearing a long nightgown and holding a candle in a brass candlestick. She seemed extraordinarily old and wrinkled; her hair was disheveled and witchlike.

"Oh, it's you. What a scare you've given me. How can a person just run off and not return until dawn? If I'd been sure you were out having a good time, I wouldn't have cared. Let your husband worry about you. But who knows what can happen. The droshkies fly by so fast, you've got to have wings to escape them."

"No, I wasn't run over, Auntie. I was just out somewhere and I lost track of the time."

"Oh, you lost track of it, did you? Well, come on in. I lay down but I couldn't shut my eyes. That's how foolish I am. If everyone isn't in the house, I toss and turn like a worm. Well, now that you're here, tell me, are you hungry?"

"Hungry? No, I'm just so tired I can't stand."

"Well, your bed's made. How about a glass of milk?"

"No, Auntie, thanks just the same."

"You remember our little talk. Well, I've had one with Celina, too. One tries to keep things to oneself, but out they come. I told her everything, the whole painful truth."

"Why did you do that?"

"I don't know why she should be so choosy. Well, we'll talk about it in the morning. A mother can fool herself, but never completely."

"So, she's reconsidered already," Clara thought, but without any feeling of triumph.

She walked into the bedroom and began to undress. Though the room was warm and stuffy, Clara felt cold. She was accustomed to having things happen as she willed them. That night a man had done with her as he had willed, a strange madman who seemed to have dropped from the sky. Clara took off one shoe and then sat still on the edge of the bed, her head bowed. What was his name? Oh yes, Zipkin. What did he look like? She couldn't remember clearly. She was content that her longing to have a lover had at last come to fruition. Yet behind her satisfaction there was a threat of failure. Too easily, too easily, she murmured to herself. He will never take me seriously. Well, and Calman? Certainly he did not deserve it . . . Clara had told her aunt she was not hungry, but her stomach felt hollow and she was thirsty too. It was an effort to stretch herself out on the bed, as if during the night she had become twice as heavy. She heard a dog barking and a neighbor's child crying. My God, I may be pregnant. She was amazed the thought had not occurred to her sooner.

She closed her eyes but couldn't fall asleep. Again she entered the confectionery, and heard the orchestra playing. Once more she strolled down the street with Zipkin. She heard him say, "Where is God? Has anyone seen Him? Man is just another animal." Dozing at last, she dreamed that she was mortally ill and lay in a wide bed, propped up by pillows. On her bedside table were medicine bottles and glasses, as well as half an orange, not yellowish gold as oranges usually are, but red. "Probably to give me blood," Clara said to herself in her dream. "But why do I need blood if I'm going to die?" Calman was there also, wearing a white beard and long sidelocks like a rabbi's. A young man who looked like Zipkin came in, but it was her son Sasha. Clara said to him in Polish, "Now you'll have to get along without me."

"No, Mother."

"It's not my decision."

Clara awoke shivering. Her foot seemed to jerk of its own accord. He heart beat rapidly just as it had in that unfamiliar drawing room when she had thought that she was about to be discovered by strangers. She sighed. It was already morning but the light seeping through the draperies was dusky and reddish. She knew she had had a bad dream but could not remember it. Someone had been sick. A rabbi with long sidelocks had come in. Only the image of the half orange returned to her clearly. Suddenly she recalled what had happened the previous night and sat up in bed. She wanted to look at herself in the mirror. "I'm to meet him at Semodeny's," she said to herself. "God in heaven, who would have thought that it would have happened so quickly! As if it had been fated." There was the sound of birds chirping. Turning her face to the wall, Clara went back to sleep. Again she saw the half orange, the medicine bottles, and the old man who was supposed to be Calman. And she was ill, about to die.

22

I

The crops were not abundant in Poland that year. On Calman's estate, the wheat was sparse, and the grain fell out before it was threshed. Calman's losses were heavy. The wages he paid out to the farmhands were greater than his income. There were duties to be paid, and the duke always demanded his rent on time. The potatoes were small and coarse. There had been no rain for weeks and the grass was scorched. Since there was insufficient hay to last the winter, the peasants sold their cattle cheaply. Normally in August wagons lined up in great numbers before Mayer Joel's water mill, and the peasants waited for days to have their grain ground into flour. But this year there was little to grind. The peasants stopped buying not only luxury items like dry-goods, shoe leather, female trinkets, and herring, but even staples like naphtha and salt. At night they sat in the dark or burned kindling wood, discussing all manner of things. Old peasants said that a flaming witch had been seen in the sky; she rode a broom and was followed by three fiery rams. In the forest, near the village of Maciejow, an old crone was said to have met the Antichrist complete with tail and horns. Frogs and worms had rained down on the village of Lipsk.

The peasants blamed the drought on the Jews. How could there be plenty, when the Jews dried up the earth's juices, drew turpentine from the trees, chopped down the forests, and fouled the air with smoke from lime kilns? Calman had imported threshing machines from Germany. He lived in the Count's manor house with his haughty young wife and their rebellious child. The boy now had a tutor called Zipkin, a man with black eyes and curly hair. Calman himself they could tolerate, but his wife was hostile to the peasants. In the harvest heat Clara went riding each day with the tutor from Warsaw. An amazon in riding clothes, she waved her crop and went off with the stranger into the thick forest among the bogs and caves. What was there to prevent such a trollop from sinning with that spoiled young dandy? Some peasants had even surprised the couple bathing in a forest stream, he in his underpants, and she in her chemise. The peasants chewed turnips, spat up saliva out of starved bellies, and their women remarked: "Oh, well, a young stallion is better than an old nag."

The talk of the peasants and the gossip of the Jews reached Calman's ears. Calman himself was suspicious. He warned Clara that no good would come of her loose behavior. Clara laughed at him. What was he thinking of? One man was enough for her. She didn't give a hoot for Zipkin. Horseback riding—why not? It improved her health. Bathing—what should she do in a heat wave, sit huddled by the stove? She was no frump; she was a sophisticated woman. Let God have His due and man his. She had lent Calman money to build a house of prayer and a ritual bath. What more did he want? Zipkin had done wonders with Sasha, had practically made the boy over. In a few weeks Sasha had learned more from him than from all the previous teachers put together. Hadn't Calman noticed how much calmer the child was? He kissed his parents' hands, no longer set fires, stopped hitting his governess. Zipkin was a born teacher—if only he could be prevailed upon to remain. Unfortunately, when the holiday recess was over, he would have to return to the university. Why, then, was Calman so annoyed? People always had big eyes and long tongues. They even slandered the rabbi.

To prove to Calman how much she loved him, Clara came to his bed at night and kissed and fondled him. She said amusing things and behaved so comically that Calman was forced to laugh and forgive her. Suspicion had stimulated his lust. He could not get enough of her. Laughingly Clara complained that he was breaking every bone in her body. He fell asleep exhausted, satisfied that she had told him the truth. But like Noah before the flood, he both believed and did not believe. He knew that it was a sin to hate—"Thou shalt not hate thy brother in thy heart"—but he could no longer look Zipkin in the eye. He refused to eat at the same table with him. Even Zipkin's effect on Sasha's manners did not please Calman. The boy was not being trained according to the *Ethics of the Fathers*, but was learning stunts like a dancing bear. Now he bowed and scraped and said thank you like the officers and dandies. He walked with a mincing step and had a false smile on his lips. Calman actually preferred the earlier period when Sasha behaved like a savage.

At night Calman sighed in his sleep. When he awoke in the morning, he was ashamed to put on his prayer shawl and phylacteries. As he recited the Eighteen Benedictions, tears ran down his beard. At night Clara's words confused him, but his judgment returned with dawn. "What could the son do except sin?" Was Zipkin a Joseph the Saint? And where would Clara have learned the fear of God—at the Russian school she had attended, or from mixing with officers? Certainly not from the cheap novels she bought or the plays she saw in Warsaw that taught women how to be adulteresses? Clara herself had told him what took place in those farces. The husband always turned out to be a simpleton and the lover a brilliant fellow. Calman recited a saying from the Proverbs: "She eateth and wipeth her mouth and saith: 'I have done no wickedness.'" Yes, Clara had sinned and was still sinning. He had signed over his property to her, and now she was making a fool of him. People stared, pointed, and laughed at him. A man with horns! But what should he do—drive her away? The law was on her side. The judges, lawyers, courts of law had been created to protect the wicked. They would take everything away from him and give it to the adulteress who had never once soiled her hands in dishwater. This was what the Gentiles termed justice.

"Father in heaven, what kind of filth am I walking in?" Calman cried out, clutching his head. "How can this have happened? I am after all the son of God-fearing people." Did he dare recite his prayers, or put on his phylacteries? He was unclean. His home was a bawdy house. No, he was not worthy to utter holy words. Calman put his phylacteries away.

11

Calman did not sleep that night, he lay in his bed still and tense. He could hear Clara snoring and talking in her sleep. She cried out, "Alexander." A man nearing sixty, Calman lay curled up in bed, combatting Satan. From the netherworld of passions a voice rose bidding him grab an ax and first hack Clara to death and then her lover. God forbid that he should yield to such an impulse. Yet it showed to what depths a man had sunk when the Evil Spirit made such suggestions to him, and in the month of Elul, just before the High Holidays. God knew what he, Calman, son of Sender Jacob, was thinking. How could so many catastrophes have befallen him? His daughter was an apostate. He, himself, was only one step away from the abyss. Was it his wealth that had led to such disasters? He had always had a bad temper. Once Zelda (may she rest in peace) had so provoked him that he slapped her. He had forced himself to forget this wickedness, but the Almighty remembered.

Though he found it painful to remain lying on his side, he did not change his position. He should be tortured. But what should he do about Clara? Good and evil warred within him. The Evil Spirit assured Calman that he was already lost. "Rise up and avenge yourself," Satan screamed. "What sort of a man are you? Show the lechers that Calman is no fool. Beat them! Kill them. The peasants will testify in your behalf. It is the mighty who rule; let them know who is most powerful. Remember that even the Talmud says: 'Whoever is the strongest is the victor.' Did not Phineas, the son of Eleazar, with a spear kill Zimri, the son of Salu, and Cozbi, the daughter of Zur? She is a married woman; she deserves death. But you don't have to kill her. Cripple her so that no man will ever want to look at her again. Don't wait, Calman. She'll have respect for you then, and when she grovels at your feet, you'll spit on her."

Calman clenched his fists. He felt if he rose now he would be so strong that he would not need an ax and could smash her skull with his bare fist. He was a giant. He would not allow himself to be shorn of his locks like Samson.

Though Calman's anger increased, the voice of reason continued to whisper. "How much longer do you have to live, Calman?" it asked. "Your beard is already gray. Run away from them, Calman. They have sinned, not you. You're still a decent Jew. Remember your father and mother and your saintly ancestors."

Calman could lie still no longer. He sat up in bed, waking Clara.

"What is it, Calman?" Clara asked.

Calman didn't answer.

"Calman, what's wrong?"

"Shut up, you whore!"

His spirit no longer thirsted for revenge. He bent over and made his ablutions with water from the pitcher that stood on the floor. Then, having put on his slippers and his dressing gown, he groped his way toward the door, bumping against a candelabrum. In this vast building, Calman never knew where he was. He walked out of the house and down the stone steps into the cool night. The sky above him was dense with stars. Staring into the darkness, Calman realized that only a single step separated life from death, piety from evil, truth from

falsehood. How careful one had to be! He breathed deeply.
The sweat dried on his body. His wrath subsided. He sat
down on a stone. The sky seemed close enough to be touched.
No, he was not a man of violence. There was a God. Calman
knew that his first concern must be for his soul.

The front door of the house opened and Clara came out
into the night, dressed in a long white nightgown.

"Calman, what's troubling you?"

"I don't have to tell you, Clara."

"It's all false, Calman. I swear on my mother's grave."

"You did not lie with him?"

"He's never even touched me. I swear to you before God."

Calman sat there, trembling with fear. "Do you know what
an oath is?"

"I know, Calman. Believe me, I do."

III

In the morning Calman entered the dining room. Clara was
breakfasting with Zipkin. Calman was not dressed in his capote and vest but had on a quilted jacket and skullcap. He
walked over to Zipkin. "We have no need for a tutor here,"
he announced. "Please be good enough to leave my house."
Zipkin stopped eating. For a moment Clara was speechless, but
then she said: "Calman, have you gone mad?"

"Clara, I'm still master here. I don't want him around."

Zipkin half rose from the table. Clara leaped to her feet.
"Don't listen to him, Alexander. He's out of his mind. He
can't give orders around here. Everything in this house is
mine."

"Pack your bag. Your train leaves at eleven."

"Calmanke, you'll pay for this." Clara picked up a knife
from the table as Zipkin walked out. Calman took hold of her
wrist and twisted it until the knife fell from her hand. She
began to scream.

"Help me, someone! He's broken my arm."

The servants paid no attention to her. They were on Calman's side. The night before, Calman had planned exactly what he would do. Now he moved calmly about, putting his plan into action. He ordered Antoni, the coachman, to drive Zipkin to the train in the britska. He himself led the horses from the stable and harnessed them to the coach. Then he packed his books and clothing and loaded them into the vehicle. Apparently in anticipation of spending the winter on the road, he took along his fur coat.

Clara at once sent a messenger on horseback to her father. She stood at one of the attic windows, pale and frightened. Her husband had set upon her like a brigand, had driven Sasha's tutor away, and injured her hand. Calman was leaving the manor at a time of economic crisis. Zipkin had fled like a coward, hadn't even said goodbye. Clara considered going downstairs and throwing herself at Calman's feet, but she was ashamed to humble herself before the servants. Nor was it likely that the gesture would help her. Calman's eyes were ablaze with anger as he greased the carriage wheels and skillfully arranged the harness. Clara began to calculate just where she stood at the moment. She was co-holder of the lease on the manor, but the lime quarries would not be hers until Calman's death. The demand for railway ties was only half what it had been. The mill belonged to Mayer Joel. Clara was familiar with court procedure but she had had no experience with a divorce action. Perhaps Calman would bring witnesses into court to testify against her. Clara went into the nursery, where Sasha's governess was giving him his French lesson.

Taking the boy by the hand, she led him downstairs.

"Go and say goodbye to your father," she told him, and then returned to the attic window.

Sasha approached his father hesitantly. "Papa, are you going somewhere?"

"Yes, I'm going away."

"Where to, Papa?"

"Back to the Jews."

Sasha felt an impulse to laugh. His father was so comical. He looked more like an old beggar than anything else. He had a long beard, wore strange clothes, and was always walking around with a prayer book in his hand. All he talked about was God and the Jews and what you could and couldn't do. Clara once more descended the stairs and walked out into the courtyard.

"At any rate, kiss the child goodbye," Clara said.

Calman remained silent.

"The coach doesn't belong to you. You have no right to take it."

"Everything here is mine," Calman said.

"That remains to be seen."

"Stay away from me or you'll be sorry."

"Do you want a divorce?" Clara asked.

"I want to be rid of you."

Clara was silent for a moment and then said, "There's one thing I think you ought to know. I'm pregnant."

Calman had a desire to seize her by the hair and drag her along the ground as had been done to adulteresses in the old days. He spat.

"There is a God."

"Come, Sasha darling. If you want war, Calman, you'll get more than you've bargained for."

Why did I keep quiet so long? Calman wondered, after Clara and the child had gone back into the house. Now that he had discarded his worldly pride, his courage had returned. She had committed adultery, not he. Let the wicked feel shame, not the righteous. He had visited Marshinov just once since he had been married to Clara. During his marriage he had been unable to face Jochanan and Tsipele. Now Calman had decided to spend the Days of Awe in that holy place. Let everything at the manor fall apart; he had been working for the devil anyway. Antoni returned, having taken Zipkin to the station, but Calman planned to do his own driving.

IV

Calman, to the amazement of the town's inhabitants, drove into Jampol without a coachman. He went first to his office, located next to a granary. At the back of the building there was a tool shed in which were stored the implements needed for lumbering as well as various odds and ends he had accumulated from the tavern he had once owned.

"Well, you're busy, eh?" Calman said as he walked into the office.

The surprised bookkeeper and clerks had their account books and ledgers open before them. No one said anything. Calman was sure they had been gossiping about him a moment before.

"I'm leaving to visit my son-in-law the rabbi," Calman announced. "I'll be in Marshinov for the holidays, perhaps longer."

Morris Shalit reached for the pencil he carried behind his ear.

"You're going to become a Hassid."

"No, only a Jew. Mayer Joel will take care of things in my absence. He'll sign whatever papers are necessary."

"Mayer Joel? He'll need a power of attorney."

"Yes, we'll have to go to the mill. Take along pen and ink and the sealing wax."

"Do as the boss tells you," David Sorkess said, quoting the proverb.

Calman did not usually issue orders without first hearing the opinion of his employees. Now he stood in the office, silent and determined, whip in hand. The clerks quickly finished the tea they had been drinking. When they tried to pile into the coach, they found that it was so loaded with Calman's possessions that no more than two of them could get in. Ignace Herman climbed up on the box beside Calman. The Jampol merchants came out of their shops to stare. The women, too, left their duties to observe this strange phenomenon. The disheveled heads of girls appeared at the windows. It was obvious to everyone what had happened: Clara had driven Calman from the manor. It was known that a mounted messenger had brought a letter for Daniel Kaminer and, not finding him at home, had trotted off to the barracks in search of him. The Jampol Jews shrugged their shoulders: Calman had made his bed, let him sleep in it.

The carriage trundled along the dirt road that led to the mill. The few wagons waiting their turn there made way for Calman. The peasants doffed their caps and bowed. Mayer Joel came out. He was covered with flour—even his black beard was powdered gray by it. Calman dismounted, and took Mayer Joel aside to speak to him. Mayer Joel was to superintend operations at the lime quarries for a couple of weeks and also take care of Calman's interests at the manor. Calman could no longer endure living with a depraved woman. Mayer Joel listened and stroked his beard. This was the beginning. He had always known that eventually he would take over the property for good. Who else? Ezriel was no business man, and Jochanan was a rabbi. Mayer Joel stood with his father-in-law near the dam. As they spoke, they watched the foaming water spill over the wheel. It was a mild, sunny September day. *"Babie Lato"*—woman's summer—was the way the peasants described this time of year, when the air is full of gossamer. The odor of hay, manure, the scent of pine were everywhere. Chickens and roosters clucked and crowed. Some peasants were transporting logs and boards for a barn which they were building. A ladybug landed on the lapel of Calman's coat.

"Do come into the house, Father-in-law," Mayer Joel said. "You know that you're always welcome here."

"You must ask the clerks in too."

"Never mind them. Let them stay outside."

Jochebed had been busy baking bread and had not seen the coach drive up. She stood with a spatula in her hands, a kerchief on her head, and a broad apron tied around her waist. There were flat cakes in the oven, and on the stove chicken soup was boiling in a pot held by a tripod. Teibela, Jochebed's oldest daughter, was peeling onions. The boys were off at the cheder in Jampol. Jochebed's youngest child was in its standing stool, busily banging with a ladle. Calman stopped in amazement. Jochebed was almost the image of Zelda. He shuddered. She had the same narrow chin as her mother and a similar wart with three hairs growing from it. Seeing her father, Jochebed put down the spatula and clapped her hands in exactly the same way as Zelda would have done. In her eyes was that look of melancholy that no amount of prosperity could banish. A smile brightened her face for a moment and then disappeared.

"Father."

"Jochebed."

She spoke to him just as Zelda would have, love and reproof mingling in her tone. Why did he visit them so seldom? The children were constantly asking for their grandfather. He had become almost a stranger to them. Then, reaching into the pocket of her apron, she pulled out a soiled handkerchief and blew her nose. Calman noticed a prayer book lying open on the table.

"You bake and pray?"

"I was reciting a few chapters from the Psalms."

"How's your stomach? Do you still get that burning feeling?"

"When I eat sharp food."

"Why don't you see the doctor?"

Jochebed's lips puckered in disgust. "What do doctors know? As long as you keep breathing, you're all right."

"A woman your age should be in good health."

"I'm not so young any more. Teibela has already had a proposal."

Teibela's lips tightened. "Oh, Mama, are you starting that again?"

"Have I said anything false? It's true, isn't it? I just want to live long enough to dance at your wedding."

Calman listened awe-struck. Those were the very words Zelda had once uttered. It was as if his dead wife had miraculously risen from the grave.

Mayer Joel interrupted, "Wouldn't you like something to eat, Father-in-law? Let's go into the living room."

They sat talking for a long time. Finally they called in the clerks. Mayer Joel knew all about Calman's lime quarries and the lumber business. The questions he asked showed that he was a clever businessman, even shrewder than Calman. "How does he know so much?" Calman wondered. "Has he been spying on me all these years? Has someone been revealing my business to him?" Mayer Joel could take over the running of Calman's various enterprises at once; he revealed that he even had a lawyer who could handle any litigation that might come up.

"I can die," Calman thought. "I am no longer needed." It was not death that he wanted, however, but the life of a Jew.

THREE

23 🏛

After giving orders that she did not wish to be disturbed, Clara locked herself in her room, sat down at the desk, and wept. Her good fortune had lasted not seven years but seven weeks. It was hard for her to believe that it was all over. Both her lover and her husband had deserted her.

Now she had just had an unpleasant visit from her father. Daniel Kaminer had spoken sharply. One either behaved properly or stayed unmarried; at least one did not go around in broad daylight with a university student. Kaminer already knew that Calman had for the time being signed over his business to Mayer Joel, and he suspected that the son-in-law would be a tough nut to crack. For one thing, Mayer Joel visited the gentry, and for another, he was on good terms with most of the officials. Rittermayer was now in St. Petersburg; Smirnoff had been transferred. It was said that the new colonel was vicious, but Daniel Kaminer had not as yet even met him. As things were, Kaminer could do little to rectify his daughter's mistakes. Moreover, he was about to be married and was going to Warsaw to visit Mrs. Frankel and Celina.

As her father spoke, the tears ran down Clara's cheeks. "If I should die," she said, "please take care of Sasha."

"You're not dying yet, Daughter. You'll outlive me."

And Daniel left, slamming the door behind him.

When Mayer Joel came to the manor to talk things over with Clara, she refused to see him. Her message to him was, Do as you please. Two days later she departed for Warsaw, leaving Sasha behind with the governess.

On this visit to the capital, Clara did not stay with Mrs. Frankel, but went to the Hotel Krakowski. As soon as she entered the hotel room, she threw herself on the bed and wept. Later, having made herself presentable, she took a droshky to a small restaurant which was located near the university and was frequented by students. She looked around for Zipkin, but the first person she noticed as she entered was Ezriel. If he had not caught sight of her as well, she would have left immediately. He was drinking tea with another student.

"Good heavens, this is a strange coincidence," he said, rising and hurrying toward her.

Clara had difficulty in restraining her tears.

"Why didn't you visit us during the summer? What do you have against me?"

"I told you we couldn't, Clara."

"Why does Shaindel dislike me?"

Ezriel had no doubt as to whom Clara was looking for. Zipkin himself had not only told Ezriel what a jealous old fool Calman was, but he had not spared Clara. He had called her a parvenue, citing as proof a ridiculous error she had made in quoting a Latin epigram. Having made his excuses to his friend, Ezriel escorted Clara to another table. He was nervous and sat on the edge of his chair, which was turned at an angle away from the table. Clara ordered a cup of black coffee. For a moment there was a strained silence, neither knowing quite what to say. Finally Ezriel remarked that Zipkin had not attended classes that day.

"Why not?" Clara asked. "Is he ill?"

"I don't know."

"Let me tell you, your father-in-law is a fool. A big fool!"

And Clara began to relate in short, abrupt sentences how Calman had chased Zipkin from the house for no reason at all. God was her witness that she had done nothing to be ashamed of. "If there had been the slightest truth in his suspicions, it wouldn't hurt so much. I don't care what people think of me." Clara began to sniffle and sob. Everything about her was overdone: the hat she was wearing had too many plumes; her cheeks were too heavily rouged; she had on too much perfume. The students looked at each other and smiled. A woman dressed so extravagantly was a rarity there. Ezriel lowered his head and blushed.

"Don't take it so hard," he said hesitantly.

"But it's all been so humiliating and painful."

Clara seemed on the point of crying again. Finally she managed to get control of herself. "I must tell him how sorry I am. It was a misunderstanding. Do you know where he lives?"

"No, I don't. It's somewhere on Leshno Street in some businessman's apartment. The owner is away taking the baths at some spa."

"Doesn't he have his own rooms?"

"I really don't know."

"I'm not staying at my aunt's this time. I'm at the Hotel Krakowski," Clara said, as if to herself. Ezriel understood that he was to pass this information along to Zipkin. Both of them were silent for a long time. Clara did not even wait for her coffee. Aware of Ezriel's embarrassment, she got up. Ezriel rose with her.

"I must go. I have a great deal of shopping to do. The coffee? Well, don't inconvenience yourself . . ."

"It doesn't matter. I'll drink it."

"Come to my hotel, I'll take you to the theater. Bring Shaindel along."

"Will you be in Warsaw long?"

"I don't know. My father has decided to marry in his old age. My aunt's daughter, as a matter of fact." And Clara dabbed her eyes again.

Ezriel said goodbye to her. They were now being looked at with open mockery. The students grimaced and whispered. As soon as Clara left, they surrounded Ezriel. "Who was that bit of fluff? Why was she sobbing? Have you gone and got her with child?" Half guiltily, Ezriel swore that it was his stepmother-in-law, but the students shook their heads: "Tell that to your grandmother!"

Clara strolled along New World Boulevard. What a stupid coincidence—of all people, she had to run into Ezriel and cry right in front of him. That was how a pregnant chambermaid conducted herself. Clara shuddered; *she* was pregnant. For the second month she had missed her period. "Well, I'll do as the chambermaids do: throw myself into the Vistula." Pausing in front of a shop window, she glanced at the manikins dressed in autumn coats with fur collars and muffs. "What's wrong with being a doll like that?" Clara mused. "They don't even know they exist. Death is the only consolation. It cancels all errors, all sins, all failures."

Clara walked on. Whenever she had fallen in love, bad luck had always followed, bringing vexations, complications, and misunderstandings. What should she do now? She did not know Zipkin's address. She could not compromise herself further. The students' leering had been apparent to her.

11

Dinner was being served in the home of Jacob Danzinger on Leshno Street. Danzinger, who sat at the head of the table in an armchair, was a small, ruddy-cheeked, bright-eyed man. He wore a gray goatee and was dressed in a black suit, a high stiff collar, and a ribbed vest. Jacob had a huge napkin tucked under his collar. As he ate, he joked with his two daughters and his son, Zdzislaw. The family had only recently returned from Carlsbad, where they had gone to drink the waters. Because of the tariff war between Russia and Germany, the price of woolens had climbed, and Jacob looked forward to making a large profit on the goods stored in his warehouse. Although not a worldly Jew, he owned a pew in the reformed German synagogue. He spoke Polish fluently, but with an accent, read the Hebrew daily *Morning Star*, was a follower of Reb Abraham Stern, may he rest in peace, and knew Reb Chaim Selig Slonimski, both leaders of the Enlightenment in Poland. His wife, Rosa, the daughter of a wealthy merchant from Kalish, had a large red birthmark covering one side of her face. This birthmark had brought Jacob Danzinger a dowry of eight thousand rubles. Mrs. Danzinger spoke French and played the piano. When she argued with her husband, she called him "Zydek"—old-fashioned Jew.

Sabina, the oldest of the girls, was in her twenties. She was short and stout and had a head too large for her body. But, on the other hand, she had been fortunate enough to inherit her mother's blond hair, and had blue eyes and a snub nose. Sabina had attended a fashionable boarding school to which only a very few Jewish girls were admitted. She had studied French, English, and Italian literature and wrote poems in Polish which she never showed to anyone. For years she had been working on a translation of some sort. Her father had put aside a considerable amount of money for her dowry, and each year the accrued interest made the sum larger. Sabina had refused to have a marriage arranged for her. She was so fastidious that if a dish were not cooked to her satisfaction she would not touch it. Garlic, radishes, onions, and herring she considered taboo. Most of her classmates were already married and had children, but Sabina was not even officially engaged. She spent her days and evenings in her "Blue Room," reading difficult books, and was perpetually warring with her family. Her sister Anna was still in high school; her brother Zdzislaw worked for his father and was about to be made a partner in the firm.

In the middle of dinner, the family heard the doorbell ring. A few minutes later the maid entered to announce that a messenger was outside with a letter for Mr. Zipkin.

"What do you want me to do about it?" Jacob asked. "Take the letter."

"He won't give it to anyone but Mr. Zipkin himself."

"You know that Mr. Zipkin has moved."

"He wants his new address."

"We're not an address bureau," Mrs. Danzinger announced, raising her eyebrows.

"Let me speak to him," Zdzislaw said, and went to the door. A moment later he returned carrying a blue sheet of paper in one hand and an envelope in the other. Zdzislaw, the family clown, was short and stout; his neck was thick and bullish and his hair was curly as a sheep's. He had dropped out of the gymnasium without graduating, but had been taken into his father's firm. Zdzislaw had assured the messenger that he was Zipkin. Now he planted himself ceremoniously in the center of the room and, having raised one of his hands dramatically, began to declaim:

> My dearest Alexander,
>   I arrived in Warsaw yesterday, and went immediately to the restaurant near the university, but couldn't find you. I am staying at the Hotel Krakowski, Room 8. I have been enduring the tortures of hell; I cry constantly. Come quickly or I will die. Please give this messenger your answer.
>
> > Forever,
> > Clara

When Anna burst out laughing, Mrs. Danzinger banged on the table with her hand. "Anna, be quiet. Let me see that letter, Zdzislaw."

"Mother, don't make so much noise," Sabina said crossly. She glared at her sister Anna, a tall, slim girl who already went to balls and won prizes for dancing. Numerous young men pursued her. Sabina pushed her plate away. She had just received a blow from which she would never recover. Nevertheless, decorum must be maintained. Sabina had always known in her heart that Zipkin was a liar and a charlatan. She had never believed any of his sweet words. The man was an egotist who acted as if what happened to the world concerned him deeply. He had written her passionate love letters while carrying on an affair with this woman who awaited him breathlessly in a hotel room. Sabina could no longer remain seated. The tears that she was seeking to restrain threatened to spill forth at any moment. Her cheeks became flushed; her forehead perspired. She folded her napkin and walked from the room, her head bowed. Her feet could be heard in the hall, and then the sound of her door being locked. Mrs. Danzinger put on her gold-rimmed glasses and having picked up the sheet of paper held it at arm's length.

"How disgraceful," she said, and then she turned to her son. "You shouldn't have done that."

"We had to find out the truth sometime, Mother. I told you he was a fake."

"All men are beasts."

Jacob Danzinger continued chewing a chicken leg. "He's coming here this evening. I'll have a talk with him."

"And what will you talk about?" Mrs. Danzinger asked, taking off her glasses.

"I'll tell him to fish or cut bait. Either marry or go to hell."

"Jacob, what language. Remember this is Warsaw and not Lodz. How do you know she still wants him?"

"As soon as you marry, you forget such nonsense."

"Students are forbidden to marry."

"He'll quit the university. He'll never become a doctor anyway. He doesn't have the patience. I'll take him into the business."

"Into the business? After such behavior? A fine father you are." Mrs. Danzinger rose from the table. "I've lost my appetite." And she walked out of the room.

The others finished dinner in silence. Now that his wife had left the table, Jacob no longer used his fork. As he sucked loudly on a chicken bone, he plucked a crumb from his beard and tossed it into his mouth. He kept shaking his head and sighing.

Zdzislaw seemed pensive. He already regretted his prank. He pitied his sister. Anna's face had become serious, too. She realized that she should not have laughed. Sabina would never forgive her. What had happened was not funny. There were no limits to the treachery of the male species. Anna thought of all the men who had sworn their eternal love for her; they were probably just as false.

III

At precisely eight that evening Zipkin arrived at the Danzingers' carrying a small bouquet and rang the bell. The new room he had moved into on Dluga Avenue had turned out to be far from satisfactory. As Zipkin saw it, his entire summer had been wasted; he had become so involved with a woman older than himself that her husband had ordered him out of the house. He was behind in his studies, and for that matter in everything else. On his way to the Danzingers', Zipkin had reviewed the situation for the hundredth time. He had behaved foolishly at Kiev University and had almost lost his life in a useless demonstration. It was a miracle that he was once again at school and not in exile in Siberia. But had he abandoned his ideals? Perhaps he lacked the necessary strength for revolutionary action, although he still believed that the masses must be educated and given their freedom. Zipkin considered himself an atheist. He had no intention of being married by a rabbi. Marriage was a barbaric rite, and absolutely out of tune with the times. But that had not prevented him from telling Sabina that he looked forward to the day when they would stand together under the wedding canopy. He had made promises he could not keep, had borrowed money he could not repay. He forgot to write to his parents and to his sister Sonya, who had made herself sick worrying about him.

"What's happened to me?" Zipkin asked himself. "I used to

be such an earnest fellow. I told everyone the truth, even Radziwill himself. Everything's gone wrong because I have been too cowardly to leave this country. I am too egotistical, too much in love with comfort." A revolutionary had once said to him: "Anyone who likes white shirts becomes a reactionary sooner or later."

"Yes, I do have too much dislike for dirty shirts and I despise vermin."

The maid opened the door. "Ah, flowers," she said, looking at him mockingly. "I'd better put them in water." And she gave him a spare smile. When Zipkin entered the dining room, he found only Jacob Danzinger at supper, not the entire family as he had expected. There was one other setting on the table, apparently for him. "What's going on here?" he wondered, and asked out loud, "Where's everyone?"

There was the hint of a smile on Jacob's lips. "My wife has a headache. Anna's off somewhere. Sabina's locked herself in her room. Zdzislaw's seeing to his own business. I'm here all by myself."

"Is it all right for me to see Sabina?"

"If she'll let you in."

"Something's happened," Zipkin thought. On his way over, he'd had an odd premonition that he was heading for trouble.

Jacob Danzinger stroked his beard. "Sit down. I'd like to have a little talk with you."

"Certainly. Thank you."

"Just a minute."

The maid brought in two plates of rice with milk and cinnamon, a dish that was only served at the Danzingers' when no one special was expected. Zipkin took a spoonful of the concoction but found himself unable to swallow it. Jacob Danzinger picked a grain of rice out of his mustache.

"Alexander, it's difficult for me to talk about this. You understand I'm only speaking for myself. I have no idea what is going on in Sabina's mind. After all, I'm not God."

"What's happened?"

"We've reached a point," Jacob Danzinger said, with an amused twinkle in his eyes, "where we have to know where we stand. Either your intentions are honorable or they are not. If they are, you must cut out the nonsense and get married."

The last word was spoken with great speed.

"Get married? The Ministry of Education doesn't permit it. There was supposed to be a new decree, but . . ."

"Tell me, who is Clara?"

Zipkin turned pale.

"Are you spying on me?"

"Not at all. But you can't keep such things hidden. A letter came for you today. It was opened accidentally."

"When? What kind of a letter?"

"I have no idea. Zdzislaw read it. I know boys will be boys, but there is a limit. Tell me, who is she? Does she live at the place where you were working—on that estate?"

"This is sheer madness."

"If you're in love with her, then you can't have my daughter. On the other hand, if you have some feeling for Sabina, you and she must settle the matter between you."

"I would have to leave school."

"I am speaking as a father. A man of my age can forgive a lot. What Sabina will say is something else again. Well, go ahead and eat your rice; it's not poison."

Zipkin lowered his head. How could she have done such a thing? He had specifically told her not to write him at the Danzingers'. She had done it purposely to compromise him. He pushed his spoon into the rice but forgot to remove it. His face had become flushed. His ears burned as if they had been slapped. Lifting his eyes from the table, he stared at the lamp above him with its bronze chains and its porcelain lampshade. Zipkin became conscious of the wall clock ticking. He noticed how the silver shone on the credenza. Outside, it was cool and still and dark, already September. Should he give up the university, he asked himself, should he become an employee of a capitalist? Jacob Danzinger seemed to have read his mind, for he said, "If you don't want to go into the business, you and Sabina can go abroad. In France, even a grandfather can be a student."

"Yes, that is true."

The maid brought coffee. Jacob Danzinger began to talk shop. Because of the tariff war between Russia and Germany, trade was prospering. Lodz was growing with the speed of yeast and was already known as the Russian Manchester. Why did Russia have to import so much? There was nothing that could not be produced in her factories. If only the Jews would be given a free hand, as in the rest of the world. Jacob Danzinger subscribed to the Polish newspapers and to the one Jewish magazine published in Polish. He remarked to Zipkin that old Montefiore was again planning to go to the Land of Israel. In Kesheniev, money was being collected to resettle Jews on farms. A Hungarian Jew had become an Egyptian pasha. Who would have believed such things possible a few years ago? And was it true that the fires in the villages around the Volga had been set by people called nihilists?

"Anything is possible."

"What's the value of such fires? It's the poor who are left homeless, not the rich."

Zipkin did not answer.

"Such people will destroy the world," Jacob Danzinger said, dipping his hand into a finger bowl.

IV

In Sabina's room, blue was the predominant color. There was a blue rug on the floor, the wallpaper was blue, there was a chair of blue; even the lamp had a blue shade. The gilt cornice of the tile stove and the gilt-framed pictures on the walls were all the more conspicuous in contrast to the prevailing color. Sabina sat reading a book bound in velvet at a round table that was covered with a blue tablecloth. A white blouse and a dark skirt clothed her plump body. The light of the lamp fell on her blond hair. When Zipkin entered, Sabina continued reading, to show that she was much more interested in poetry than she was in him. Finally, she raised her large head and stared at him with her blue eyes.

"Ah, it's the Don Juan of Nalewki Street."

Zipkin bit his lip. "Sabina, I didn't come here to listen to your humor."

"No, of course not. You expected me to give you a medal. Come closer. Sit down. Here on the chaise."

"Thank you."

"Don't think your behavior surprised me," Sabina said in the tone of one who has considered a matter carefully and now understands it thoroughly. "I never trusted you. That's the plain unvarnished truth."

"I hope that this does not affect our friendship."

"Why should I be friends with a fraud?"

Zipkin paled. "I guess I'd better go."

"Wait. You'll leave when I permit it, not before. Your kind doesn't have the right to leave when he pleases." Sabina laughed, exposing wide yellowish teeth. Despite her outward gloominess, Sabina's sense of humor was famous in the family.

Zipkin crossed his legs. "What are you reading?"

"What difference is that to you? Just who is this Clara? The wife of that landowner you wrote me about in Carlsbad?"

"Possibly."

"Why don't you go to her? Poor thing, she can't stop crying. She's at the point of death."

"Is that what the letter said?"

"More or less. Perhaps she'll divorce her rich husband and marry you. According to your letter, her son must be a dear little boy."

"Stop being sarcastic."

"You described him yourself. I never took you seriously. That consoles me now. Just how many women do you have on the string?"

"Sabina, I didn't come to confess to you, but to say good-bye. I want to thank you for the happy hours we spent together."

"You needn't thank me. They weren't so happy. You had better times with Clara. Have you had supper?"

"Yes, thank you."

"Who else was in the dining room?"

"Only your father."

"Oh. What did he say to you?"

"He's angry, too. Nevertheless, he would like us to get married." Zipkin blushed when he said the word "married," which seemed to have slipped from his mouth against his will.

Sabina seemed on the verge of laughter, but her face became stern. "Get married, to a charlatan?"

"Darling, no one's going to force you."

"I should think not. If my dear father could, believe me he would. How did you meet her? You've never wanted to take a job before."

"We met here in Warsaw."

"And you fell madly in love?"

"If that's what you want to call it."

"What else? She never stops crying. I have one question I'd like to ask you. Please give me an honest answer for once."

"What's your question?"

"No, I want you to swear first. Give me your hand."

Zipkin rose hesitantly and took Sabina's hand, which was warm and moist.

"On your word of honor."

"On my word of honor."

"Go back and sit where you were. I don't like a big hulk like you hovering over me."

Zipkin seated himself again.

"Did you bring her here? I mean, to this house?"

Zipkin swallowed hard.

"I did."

"And she sat on this bed?"

"I don't want you to faint if I tell you."

"Do you think I'm the swooning type?"

"Yes, she did. Is there anything else that you want to know?"

Sabina's face had grown white. But, as with her father, a trace of laughter remained in her eyes. "Tell me, do you think there's anyone lower than you are?"

"I have no idea."

"Well, I have. Get out of here and never come back. I don't want to hear from you ever again. Is that clear?"

"Clear enough."

And Zipkin rose to leave.

"Not so fast. I told you I'd throw you out when I've finished. When did all of this happen?"

"I didn't write the date down. One evening."

"Did the janitor see you?"

"No, I don't think so. The gate was still open when we got here," Zipkin lied.

"And when did she leave? The next morning?"

"No, the same night."

"I'm getting rid of this mattress. And the bed, too. Incredible as it may seem, it felt strange to me. Why did you do it?"

"Because you wanted to stay a virgin."

"Did you expect me to become a streetwalker like her?"

"She's not a streetwalker."

"What did my father say?"

"That we should get married at once."

"Oh, at once. Don't worry, I'll let you go in a minute. Remember, it was you who swore eternal love for me. I didn't even like you at first. I thought you were a poseur. You told me how heroically you behaved in Kiev and how deeply concerned you were with humanity. I never lied to you. You knew that I didn't believe in free love. I thought that somewhere, underneath everything, there was a spark of decency in you. Well, tell me what are you going to do now?"

"Leave the country."

"With her?"

"Don't be foolish. As far as I'm concerned, she doesn't exist."

"Who does exist for you? What will you do when you go abroad?"

"I don't know. Throw myself into my work."

"What sort of work? Making bombs? Agitating?"

"Not agitating, enlightening."

"*You* enlighten *others?* That is funny. Well, all right, get out. Now I mean it."

"Good night, Sabina. Forgive me."

"Good night. Don't ever come to see me again. Don't try to write to me. Whatever I felt for you is gone. When you cross that threshold, you cease to exist for me."

"Well, stay in good health."

Sabina did not answer. She had already picked up her book and had resumed reading. Zipkin closed the door quietly. For a moment he stood in the hallway as if he expected to be called back.

"Well, that's done with," he said to himself. This was the second time he had been thrown out of a house.

v

It was early as yet, not even ten o'clock. Zipkin walked out of the unbolted gate and lit a cigarette. He was not angry with Sabina; she had acted as a correct young woman should. But Clara he did not understand at all. What did she want? She knew quite well that the Danzingers had returned. She was a shrew and must be avoided like the plague. Zipkin did not want to return to his room. He needed company. Having crossed Karmelicka Street, he turned into Dzielna Street, looked up and saw that there was a light in Mirale's window. Shadows moved across the curtain, signifying that Mirale was entertaining guests. Zipkin entered the building. "Well, it seems that I'm destined to sacrifice my life for humanity," he muttered as he mounted the stairs, and immediately wondered what a materialist such as he could mean by destiny. Who had destined it? Such mad thoughts passed through one's head. "Well, now I'm finished with lies. I'm free at last. That's the end of just living for myself." He experienced the kind of momentary relief one feels when one has lost everything. He even felt physically light and buoyant. It didn't matter that he lacked even the price of a meal. From now on, he would have to support himself by tutoring. He rapped three times on the wall, a sign that it was not the police, and the door opened.

"Look who's here," Mirale said, extending her hand.

"What's all the noise about?" Zipkin inquired.

"Oh, there's a big discussion going on. Come in. Ezriel and Aaron are battling to the death."

She entwined her arm in his and led him into the apartment. The room was warm and smoky. There was a babble of voices, everyone talking in Polish. It was the usual crowd—Ezriel, Aaron, Esther Eisner, Vera Charlap, and Sonya Rabinowitch. Some were drinking their tea from glasses, and others from their saucers, Russian style. Zipkin heard Ezriel say, "If you take that position, anything is justifiable. You say that Nechayev had the right to kill Ivanov. In effect, you are deifying the murderer. He becomes the defender of the people. That's what your *Catechism of a Revolutionary* says. Its idol is Bakunin, a common murderer."

"Oh, so Bakunin's a murderer. Those who go about hanging working-class women are as innocent as lambs, I suppose. You know what would have happened if the Jacobins hadn't used the guillotine: the revolution would have failed and the Bourbons would have kept their stranglehold on France and Europe as well."

"Was Napoleon an improvement over Louis? Besides, the guillotine did a lot more than cut off the heads of the Bourbons. What about Danton and Robespierre?"

"There are always some errors. You know the saying, 'When you chop wood, you must expect shavings.' The French Revolution had to happen. Europe had to enter the new era. Russia hasn't had a revolution, and where are we? Lost in darkness. Whatever we have now, we owe to the French: the Internationale, the strikes in England, the fact that we're talking together the way we are now. Would the serfs have been freed if there had been no French Revolution? And let me tell you, we wouldn't be students at the university, either. You and I would still be packed away in the ghetto."

"Bravo, Aaron," Sonya Rabinowitch exclaimed, clapping her hands. Then suddenly seeing Zipkin, she called out, "Well, here's a latecomer." Everyone became silent.

"Just what is the point at issue?" Zipkin asked.

"Oh, it's just the usual babble," Ezriel replied. "Although England has had no revolution, she does have a parliament. Your friends take a contradictory position: they are both for and against the use of violence. In fact, they want to be constitutional nihilists . . . They're forever trying to reach the masses, who don't want to have anything to do with them. What do the muzhiks do to the young women sent out to teach them? They rape them. The men are handed over to the police. The whole theory of *Obshchyna*, going out to the people, is ridiculous. Who are the avengers of the people? Nothing but bandits. It was the peasant Komisarov who captured Karkov, wasn't it? Isn't that typical of the entire movement?"

"All right, let's hear your program."

"Do nothing unless you know what should be done. I say that we should follow the injunction of the Hippocratic oath: never harm, only heal. Of what value were the last two Polish uprisings? Did the Paris Commune help anyone? Or the Dolgoshunzes? Whom did the Fifty benefit? What good will come from the execution of those political prisoners who have been condemned? I understand that out of 193 prisoners, twelve have already committed suicide and thirty have gone mad. These terrorists simply don't have what it takes to be revolutionaries. It's as if when a surgeon is needed a butcher is sent for. The government is definitely sick, but terror can't make it well."

Zipkin drew himself up to his full height. "Just what butchers are you referring to? Czernishewski? Herzen? Lavrov? Exactly what do you suggest, Ezriel? Whom would you choose to sponsor the revolution, a group of old ladies? And what of those who are in power? Have they taken the Hippocratic oath? Do they think twice about destroying hundreds of thouhands of people? Have you read the recent revelations about the Turkish War and the machinations of the Great Powers? Why don't you write to the aristocracy and suggest that they all take the Hippocratic oath?"

"Because I'm not entirely mad."

"No, that's not the reason. You want to be safe and stay out of prison. You have your career as a doctor to think of, but there are others who are willing to lay down their lives for the people."

"Don't you want to be a doctor? Anyway, sacrificing your life doesn't feed the hungry. No one eats because cities are razed. Moreover, what people are you referring to? You consider yourself a Russian, Zipkin, but this is Poland. And, as a matter of fact, the people in this room aren't even Poles. They're Jews."

"Jews? Why bring up the Jewish question?"

"Well, what will happen to the Jews? Are we to be destroyed because we don't have a peasantry?"

"Who's talking about destroying? In the new society, Jews won't be storekeepers and usurers. Today the Jew is still on the side of the exploiters. He's owned by the gentry."

"Does this include your own father?"

"You should be ashamed of yourself, Ezriel. Yes, my father, along with the rest. True, I am his son, but I can see the role that he plays in society. He's been nothing but Radziwill's

tool. In the morning he prayed; the rest of the day he stole
from the peasants. Why should the peasants love him?"

"And why should you be on the side of the peasants? If the
peasants could, they'd kill both you and your father."

Mirale began to shout, "Ezriel, you're getting too personal.
Leave our parents and the Jews out of it. Sit down, Zipkin. I
agree with you. A parasite is a parasite, even if he's your father. You'll have some tea, won't you?"

VI

They continued to drink tea, eat bread and cheese, and argue. Zipkin, Ezriel saw, had suddenly become the most violent
of extremists. He spoke with enthusiasm of Vera Zasulich's
assassination of Trepov. There were times, he said, when it was
necessary to burn one's bridges behind one. He had a higher
ideal than just getting a diploma. He even ridiculed those revolutionaries who put all their hopes in the establishment of a
parliament. "What's come over him?" Ezriel wondered. Ever
since he'd come to Warsaw, he'd been one of the moderates.
Moreover, he'd been squiring a wealthy young lady, and had
begun to talk like a Polish positivist. Did this sudden change
have something to do with Clara? But how? The question
under discussion was whether, in the process of liquidating the
aristocracy, one had the right to risk the lives of innocent by-
standers. Ezriel argued that this was a crime, but all the others
were against him. "One can't consider individuals when the
world's future is at stake," Aaron declared. Sonya Rabinowitch commented that this was not a war to be waged with
powder puffs.

"Just tell me this," Mirale said to her brother, "when they
fight, do the aristocrats consider the people?"

"Do we have to follow their example?"

"Your brother would like to have freedom brought in on a
silver tray with a lace doilie on it." Zipkin was joking, but

there was an angry smile on his lips. He poured some tea into a saucer and sucked on a lump of sugar. All of the women agreed with him. "Why are they all so bloodthirsty?" Ezriel wondered. They were Jewish women, members of the race which had sworn to uphold the Ten Commandments. Mirale was only one generation removed from their father and mother. Only a short time before, she had been reading their mother's prayer book. How old was she? Ezriel began to calculate. He recalled the winter day in Jampol when Mirale had entered the study house to tell him that Calman Jacoby had come to meet him. Now he spent his time cutting the dead apart, and Mirale plotted to kill the living.

"When one talks about sacrifice," he said, "one must think of oneself as the offering. Let us assume, Zipkin, that Utopia has been achieved, but to win it you have had to forfeit your life. There is singing and laughing in the streets, but you lie in your grave. There is no life after death. After all, we don't believe in the immortality of the soul. When you die, you're dead forever."

"Stop scaring the chickens. Do you think life is such a bargain? What about the soldiers who are dying in this war? Who's going to lead them to paradise?"

"I didn't kill them."

"You killed them with your so-called positivist ideas and your acceptance of tyranny. You shiver over the suffering of one poor innocent, but what of the millions who die of consumption, rot in prison, and swing on the gallows? Do you know what the death rate is among the muzhiks? Every year, tens of thousands of peasants starve to death."

"He knows that, but he'd like to forget it," Mirale cried out.

"How does that give me the right to sacrifice another?"

"Who's speaking of anyone else? Those who are fighting sacrifice themselves."

"You speak of all this fighting as if it were something new. People have been fighting for thousands of years. What have all those battles produced?"

"Civilization. Our modern world, with all its virtues and faults. Mankind has moved forward, not backward."

Sonya Rabinowitch clapped her hands. "Bravo, Zipkin, bravo."

Finally, Ezriel and Aaron began a game of chess. Zipkin talked with Sonya Rabinowitch. Esther Eisner paced back and forth on high-heeled high-buttoned shoes, chewing on a piece of bread. Esther, the divorcee, was small and dark-complexioned and looked much younger than she was. She wore her hair in a bun with a comb in it, not upswept in the current fashion. Esther was considered illiterate, even though she associated with intellectuals and spoke their jargon. She spoke Polish fluently but swallowed the last syllables, so that one couldn't make out the case endings. Sonya Rabinowitch, who had completed gymnasium and was a serious reader, didn't care for Esther and enjoyed catching her in errors.

Vera Charlap sat down and watched Ezriel and Aaron play. The doctors had assured Vera that her lungs had healed, but she still occasionally coughed blood and became feverish. She predicted that she would die some rainy day and that none of her friends would attend her funeral. A rabbi's daughter, she knew Hebrew well and liked to draw Ezriel into religious discussions so that she could exhibit her knowledge of Jewish lore. Whenever Vera felt sick, she sent her maid to fetch Ezriel. She had thick red hair and a porcelain white face. There was always a string of artificial pearls around her long neck, and heavy earrings dangled from her ears. Vera suffered from homesickness, especially on the Sabbath and during the holidays. She would sit at Mirale's enveloped in a beaded silk shawl and wail, "Now Father is praying. Now they are singing the Sabbath hymns in my house."

Mirale, who despised religion, would say angrily, "If that kind of fanaticism appeals to you, why did you leave home? Go back and marry a Talmudic scholar."

"That's easy enough for you to say, Mirale."

VII

Zipkin stood at the bookcase, browsing among Mirale's books. He opened a volume without looking down at the page. What a fiasco. He had lost everything—both Sabina and Clara. Why had Clara written that letter? Just to embarrass him. There could be no other reason. Zipkin suddenly remembered that he owed Jacob Danzinger hundreds of rubles—he had no idea what the exact amount was. Sabina was right when she had called him a fraud. He had once read that a man only blushed in public. But as he stood there in the shadows, with his back to his friends, he felt the blood mount to his face. He had to return the money. Now! At once! But how? He had nothing. It was true—he was both a seducer and a thief. "I should never have taken money from them." It occurred to him that in a similar situation Radziwill's son Ludwig would have killed himself. Had he not tried to commit suicide when he had lost five thousand rubles in a card game? Zipkin shook his head from side to side as if to rid himself of such nasty thoughts. "Yes, I have fallen low." Zipkin tried to read so as to forget his disgrace momentarily, but the words danced before his eyes. "Well, I will kill myself. At least I'll prove that I'm no embezzler." He took a step in the direction of Ezriel and Aaron.

"Whose move is it?"

"No kibitzers, no kibitzers," Aaron mumbled, his body swaying.

Ezriel lifted his head and looked at Zipkin out of the corner of his eyes. He had never liked the man but was unwilling to indulge in petty spite. Clara wanted Zipkin to know where she was, and Ezriel would deliver the message. But Zipkin wasn't leaving yet . . . Ezriel moved his rook and bit his lip. He knew the move was wrong, but he had already lost the ambition to win.

"So that's your move," Zipkin interjected.

"Yes, that's it. Why haven't you been to school?"

"To hell with the university."

"So soon? Are you through studying?"

"I'm through with everything."

"What's happened? Did you win the lottery?"

"I've either won it all or lost it all," Zipkin said, his words spilling out at random. It occurred to him that Ezriel was to blame for his misfortunes. If Ezriel hadn't taken him to Mirale's and introduced him to that ridiculous self-education circle, he would never have met Clara. No, it had not been Ezriel but Aaron who had first brought him to the group. "Well, what's the difference? They're all a bunch of Polish idlers."

"Well, I think it's time for me to go."

"Just a moment, Zipkin. I have a message for you."

"What is it, Ezriel?" Zipkin felt a knot in his throat.

"It's confidential."

Zipkin was sure that Ezriel was the bearer of more bad news. He was about to receive another slap in the face. Hatred for Ezriel, Clara's step son-in-law, welled up in him. His hands grew moist. They'd probably been talking about him all evening, and he, idiot that he was, had stumbled in like a blind horse into a ditch. Out loud he said, "Well, let's hear the big secret."

"Come outside."

"What secret do you two have?" Aaron asked in astonishment.

"Whenever there's a secret, look for a thief," Vera Charlap announced, translating a Yiddish saying into Polish.

Zipkin said goodbye to everyone. Usually he shook hands when he left, but this time he merely said, "Well, ladies, don't slander me too much."

Mirale smiled. "My, he is in an odd mood today."

"Why are you so flushed?" Sonya Rabinowitch asked.

Zipkin left, followed by Ezriel. The conversation in the room ceased. As soon as Ezriel had closed the door, Zipkin said, "All right, Ezriel, let's have it. I have bared my breast. Plunge the dagger in."

"It's nothing like that. Clara's been looking for you. She's in Warsaw."

"She is. Where?"

"At the Hotel Krakowski."

"Where did you meet her?"

"At the restaurant—near the university."

"Well, that's strange. Thank you, Ezriel. I want to apologize. I thought that . . ."

But Zipkin did not finish. "Good night. See you soon."

Ezriel returned to the chess game.

Zipkin remained standing in the dark. So that's how it was. She was in Warsaw. She had come to look for him. His heart felt lighter. Tears came to his eyes. It wasn't because he loved Clara. But someone still wanted him, and Ezriel, whom he had regarded as an enemy, had been decent enough to give him the message. Not everyone in the world, it would seem, was corrupt. "I am a deplorable egoist," Zipkin confessed to himself. "I don't think enough about other people. That's why things have turned out as they have." He considered not going to see Clara, and thus ending the affair. All the same, he knew that he would go. He hoped that she had not yet checked out of the hotel. The janitor opened the gate for him; Zipkin tipped him ten groschen. He walked quickly, every now and again looking around for a droshky. "Well, what shall I do? She's young and her husband is old. She's never loved him . . . The whole institution of marriage is nothing but a mire." He began to walk faster. "What was that nonsense about burning my bridges behind me? What should I do, really? Partition land that does not belong to me? Become a lumberjack in the summer and sleep with my boots beneath my head? Everyone is so mixed up."

Suddenly Zipkin looked up and saw that he was standing in front of the Hotel Krakowski.

VIII

The lobby was empty. The clerk who usually stood behind the desk was not there. Zipkin looked around. "If I only knew which room she was in." He caught sight of the guest register and started to scan the pages. Yes, there was her signature—Clara Jacobowa. But what was her room number? The clerk appeared, a small, chunky, flaxen-haired man with the pink eyes of an albino. He was in his shirt sleeves.

"Who are you looking for?"

"Mrs. Clara Jacobowa."

"She's probably asleep. Who are you?"

"Her brother," Zipkin said quickly, astounded at his own lie.

"What do you want with her? I can't allow you to go upstairs at this hour."

"It's very important. Her child's ill. I've just come from Jampol."

Zipkin took out a coin and gave it to the clerk, who eyed it suspiciously, hefting it in his hand.

"She's in room 8. That's on the first floor. But she can't be disturbed."

Zipkin ran up the stairs. Arriving at room 8, he knocked on the door. When there was no answer, he began to beat on it.

At last he heard a voice, "Who's there?"

"It's Alexander."

He stood holding his breath, his eyes lowered, listening. He could hear her striking a match and then moving about in her slippers. When she opened the door and he saw her, she seemed like a stranger to him, older, as if in the last few days she had suddenly become middle-aged. Her hair was tucked beneath a net and she was wearing a dressing gown.

"I thought you'd get here much earlier," she said, looking at him sadly.

"How could I? I didn't know you were here."

"Didn't the messenger tell you?"

"What messenger?"

"I sent you a note. Didn't you receive it? Well, you'd better come in."

In the room, a candle was burning in a bronze candleholder. The bed was rumpled. A magazine, a bagel, and a garter lay on the table. For a moment there was a strained silence and then Zipkin said, "I told you I wasn't living there any longer."

"But you didn't say where you were living."

"I didn't get your note."

"Who got it, then?"

"The Danzingers."

"They opened it?"

"Yes."

"The man who delivered it said he handed it to you personally."

"It wasn't me. It was Zdzislaw. That's the son."

"He sent the reply?"

"He must have."

"Well, then, how did you know I was here?"

"Ezriel told me."

"When? Where? Well, it doesn't matter. That I survived the last few days proves to me I must be immortal."

When Zipkin took her in his arms, she leaned her head on his chest and sobbed softly. There were deep circles under her eyes.

"I thought you were finished with me," she said, once more addressing him with the familiar "thou." "I kept waiting and waiting. I almost went out of my mind. Calman's left. He's run off to his son-in-law, the rabbi. He deserted me."

"Is that what he said?"

"He took his winter coat with him. Mayer Joel is taking care of his business interests."

"Well, I understand."

"What right do they have to open your letters?" Clara asked. "Are you engaged to that girl?"

"That's finished."

"I asked you whether you were and you denied it. Why is it over? Because they opened my letter?"

"I don't love her."

"But you were engaged?"

"Not really."

"What then? Well, it's clear enough to me. A woman becomes fond of a man, and immediately she's in trouble. What do I do now?"

"That's simple enough. Give me a kiss."

"Alexander, I'm pregnant."

Zipkin's hands fell from his hips. He took a step backward.

"Whose child is it?" he asked, the tone of his voice suddenly altered.

"You know whose child it is."

"How can you be sure? You told me that you slept with him, too."

A bewildered look came into Clara's eyes. She didn't know what to answer.

"I'll get rid of it if I can. It's a very dangerous business for me."

"No more than for anybody else."

"If you want me to die, I will die."

Where is the other garter? Zipkin asked himself, staring at the table. All this talk of pregnancy and abortion had cooled his ardor. He had a desire to flee. Zipkin looked toward the door.

"Don't run away," Clara said. "Sit down."

As Zipkin seated himself, he noticed the other garter lying on the rug, and touched it with the tip of his shoe. How complicated everything had become. The affair reminded him of one of those illnesses which start with the sniffles, a cough, or a headache, and before you know it, the patient lies dying.

IX

Zipkin stayed with Clara that night. He left early the next morning, before the servants awoke. As they kissed and fondled each other, he made all sorts of promises to her that he had no intention of keeping. This coarse woman who slept with two men would never become his wife, nor would her child receive his name. It was one thing to have an affair with Clara and quite another to marry her. It seemed to him that this distinction should be obvious to her, as well.

Zipkin was to meet Clara at Semodeny's at one o'clock. He hadn't had much sleep and was on his way back to his room on Dluga Avenue. He stopped off at a coffee shop on Bielanska Street to have breakfast. He was more sleepy than hungry. The waitress brought him a newspaper along with his eggs and rolls. Zipkin ate, alternately scanned the paper and dozed. Clara had promised to pay him two hundred rubles for tutoring Sasha, and he was determined to send this money to Jacob Danzinger as partial settlement of his debt. On the other hand, was it proper for him to take so large a sum for a few weeks of tutoring? Wasn't it really nothing but a bribe?

In the newspaper Zipkin read an article about the summer horse show. It criticized the Poles for considering horseback riding vulgar. In London, the paper pointed out, ladies rode in the public parks and even hunted on horseback. Almost every article and news item in the paper contained allusions to Western Europe and the United States. In other countries, the houses had plumbing, the cities wide streets, sidewalks, and clean gutters. Here in Warsaw, a woman was criticized for being a pediatrician. Abroad, that sort of thing was no longer even news. In foreign cities policemen helped school children across the street; circuses and exhibitions were lit by electricity; the universities lent students books; one did not have to inform the authorities when one moved to a new apartment, or constantly show one's papers. Zipkin turned the pages of the paper and yawned. Yes, it was a large world, a free and enlightened one, and he was buried in Poland. "I must get out of here before it's too late," Zipkin thought. "I've had enough of the provinces."

Zipkin had forgotten his key and was forced to knock on the apartment door.

"Oh, it's the master," the Gentile maid said, throwing the door open. "You've been away all night."

"I stayed with a friend."

"Shall I bring you breakfast?"

"I've already eaten."

"There's a letter for you."

Zipkin entered his room and found the letter lying on a chair. It was from his father. Berish Zipkin wrote that business was bad and that his wife had had an attack of gallstones. Sonya was tutoring. There was a postscript in her handwriting, written in Russian: "Is life as tedious in Warsaw as it is here? There's just nothing in this town. The young men have only one ambition—to make their boots squeak." Zipkin lay down on his bed in his clothes. "Yes, Sonya dear, it's boring here, too," he mumbled. "More boring than you can imagine."

He fell asleep and dreamed that he was wandering through a series of rooms all constructed of petrified wood. Petrified mushrooms grew from the walls and ceilings. In front of him was a pit and to the rear a body of water. There was a bridge over the water and a passageway that led into the pit. He didn't know which way to go. He was hiding from someone —an informer, or an *agent provocateur*. "No, they won't take me alive," Zipkin said in his sleep. "I'd rather drown myself." Thirty years of life were enough.

He awoke with a start. It was raining outside. Streams of water ran down the windowpanes. From far off came the rumble of thunder; to Zipkin it sounded as if furniture were being moved in a room upstairs. A moment later there was a knock on the door and the maid entered, carrying a pink envelope. "This came by messenger," she said, and she stood there in her shabby slippers, staring at the sleepy-eyed Zipkin.

"Thank you," he said, taking the letter.

"The man's waiting for your answer." There was a look of wonder in the woman's eyes, the rustic's astonishment at the complexity and deviousness of city life.

Zipkin recognized the stationery. The letter came from Sabina. He opened it and saw her ornate, curlicued handwriting:

> Dear Pan Zipkin:
> Circumstances beyond my control force me to write to you. I have no particular passion for ownership, but you did borrow my volume of Musset's poetry. The book was a present from a friend who is no longer alive. Please return it to me at once. There are also several small matters that I would like to discuss with you. Would it be possible for you to meet me at Spivak's Confectionery at four o'clock? I have purposely chosen a confectionery on Nalewki Street, so that you will be in the kind of surroundings that suit you best. Don't forget the book.
> Your devoted
> Sabina

24 ♙

I

It was predicted in Marshinov that this year the town would be half empty at Rosh Hashana. Reb Shimmon had left Marshinov and had moved to Stiktin, taking with him the richest supporters of the court. Most people thought that the remaining Hassidim would also defect. The proprietors of the town's inns and rooming houses held a meeting to discuss the situation. Jochanan was called a procrastinator, a schlemiel. Also present were Marshinov's butchers and fishmongers; in fact, all whose living was dependent on the court. Everyone agreed that Jochanan had wrecked the town's economy. Reb Shimmon would not have abandoned Marshinov if Jochanan had paid more attention to the business of the court instead of soaking himself in the ritual bath day and night. Many suggestions were offered, among them that the rabbi be warned that unless he made peace with Reb Shimmon, the town would take action against him. A butcher demanded that Jochanan be driven out of Marshinov with sticks. Some recalled the story of a rabbi who one hundred years before had been expelled from the town in a wagon drawn by oxen, and on a Friday, so that he had been forced to spend the Sabbath on the road. As was usual at such assemblies, after a great deal of angry debate and shouting, the only decision that was reached was to hold another meeting. What was there to be done with a rabbi who was determined to destroy himself? Marshinov had enjoyed many years of prosperity. Those years were over; from now on, Stiktin would have all the luck. Yet, while all the talk was going on, Marshinov was filling up with people. Several hundred Jews had already arrived by the time of the first penitential prayers. Many of them were Hassidim who had come to the court for the first time. Those who had predicted that the prayer house would be empty were embarrassed. Every train brought hosts of worshippers. The teamsters did not have enough space at the station to pull up their wagons. Many visitors walked from the train, carrying their bundles. The innkeepers brought down straw mattresses from the garrets, and cooked in huge pots and kettles. High rates were demanded in advance for a night's lodging. The butchers went out into the villages to buy up cattle. The fishmongers sent Gentiles to set up nets in the Vistula. Suddenly Marshinov seemed too small to hold all of Jochanan's following. Not since Marshinov had become Marshinov had anything like this happened. People wracked their brains for an explanation.

Jochanan himself was apprehensive. He had been indifferent to the attack of his mother and advisers when they upbraided him for permitting Reb Shimmon to leave. He had never wanted to be rabbi and still could not understand why he had been appointed a leader of Jews. Now that a following of thousands had assembled, with more expected, Jochanan was terrified. What did heaven want? He remembered what the Scriptures said about vanity: "Pride goeth before destruction and a haughty spirit before a fall."

Was this another form of temptation? Or was he one of those who never earn Paradise but get their just due in this world? As he prayed and studied, his tears wet the pages of *The Two Tablets of the Covenant*. Oh, how simple it would have been for him if his grandfather had been there to guide him. But his grandfather had gone to heaven and dwelt among the celestial sages, leaving the burden to be borne by him.

Thousands of Jews longed for him to pray for them. But with what good deeds could he approach the Lord of the Universe, he who possessed only evil thoughts and worldly ambitions? Shouldn't he leave Marshinov? Jochanan asked himself. Shouldn't he go into exile and fast and castigate himself—in summer prick himself with thorns, in winter roll in the snow? If he were a mere wanderer, no one would pay him homage. Tsipele, long may she live, would not serve him soup or milk or preserves and indulge him in luxuries.

But dare he run away? Did he have the right to abandon his congregation because he longed for martyrdom? No, he did not, particularly not now on the eve of the Holy Days. Jochanan probed himself daily. He was a mass of faults, but he did have one virtue: he loved the Jews. The sight of beards and sidelocks filled him with joy. Only embarrassment kept him from kissing every Jew he met. His love for his people was apparently a gift from heaven. Jochanan clutched his beard. "God Almighty, help me. Father in heaven, we are only weak humans. What thou dost not bestow upon us, we do not possess."

11

Calman Jacoby was among those who came to Marshinov for the holidays. He drove his carriage himself, one of the first of the faithful to arrive. Tsipele ran out to meet him, followed by two of her children, Zadok and Zeldele. Gadele, the baby, was in its cradle. Tsipele, now grown tall, wore a bonnet on her shaven head. Although she was only twenty-four, she had a son old enough to be studying the Talmud. Zadok was fair, light-eyed, yellow-haired, and wore breeches, a velvet hat, a long gaberdine, and knee-length stockings. As he walked, he played with the fringes of his sash, winding them around his finger. Zeldele, a graceful child, resembled her grandmother Temerel. Tsipele could barely keep herself from hugging her father unrestrainedly. She had disapproved of his marrying

Clara, but she had heard how much his wife had made him suffer. Relief and sadness mingled in her gaze as she noticed the baggage he had brought with him: the prayer books, the clothing, his fur coat. He had changed so much since she had last seen him. Now his beard was almost entirely gray and his body was shrunken and bent.

"Oh, Papa, Papa," she cried out and could say no more.

"This is Zadok, eh? Almost ready to get married!"

"Grandpa."

Zadok kissed Calman's hand. Zeldele hung back shyly. A moment later Mendel the beadle and Kaila the maid came out of the house followed by a host of yeshiva students and hangers-on. And then finally Jochanan appeared.

"Sholem aleichem, Father-in-law."

"Aleichem sholem, Rabbi."

"Welcome to Marshinov. You've been away from us too long. We all missed you. I trust that you are in good health."

"Praised be God, yes."

Jochanan checked his natural inclination to ask after the rest of Calman's family, so as not to have to mention the names of women. He did not even glance at Tsipele. When others were present, the rabbi and his wife did not address each other.

"How was your trip?" Jochanan inquired.

"Thank God, good."

"The children are thrilled. They missed their grandfather."

"I have some gifts for them in the carriage."

"Gifts? It is written that he who hateth gifts shall live," Jochanan said.

"Oh, but they are children."

"They must be taught correctly from the beginning. 'Train a child in the way he must go.' "

Finally Jochanan returned to his study, having invited Calman to join him there later in the day. Tsipele herself helped carry in her father's baggage. His room in the attic had a brass latch on the door and a mezuzah enclosed in an engraved sheath on the doorpost. Calman unpacked the presents which he had purchased in Warsaw, where he had stopped on his way to Marshinov. For Tsipele he had brought a pair of diamond earrings; for Zadok, a prayer book bound in cedarwood and decorated with pictures of the Wailing Wall and Rachel's tomb; for Zeldele, candies and an assortment of small presents. Calman had even brought presents for the rabbi and Temerel, who had come to spend the holidays with her son. To show her respect for her father, Tsipele herself brought him a pitcher of water, a towel, and a basin. Though he assured her that he was not hungry, she insisted that he wash his hands and sit down to eat. At dinner, Calman found that his appetite had returned. A circle of people formed around his table. Tsipele and the children were there, as well as a number of students. Calman was embarrassed. Why were they honoring him? There was nothing extraordinary about him. At the manor, he had been treated with contempt. He dipped his bread in the gravy, and his eyes became moist.

"Why did I wait so long?" he asked himself. "This is heaven and that was hell."

"Grandpa, is there really a salamander at your place?" Zadok suddenly asked.

"A salamander? No, I've never seen one."

"Why not? The fire in the lime kilns has been burning for seven years."

"Not continuously. Besides, the heretics deny the existence of salamanders. No animal can live in fire."

Tsipele bristled.

"Why must you repeat what the heretics say?"

"They say, God forbid, that this year there'll be a shortage of citrus fruit for the Feast of Tabernacles," one of the onlookers said, removing his pipe from his mouth.

"Why?"

"Because of the Turks."

"But citrus fruits come from Greece, not from Turkey."

"Aren't the Greeks Turks?"

"No. The Turks are the sons of Ishmael, and the Greeks the

sons of Javan," Calman replied. The students listened in silence. Here in Marshinov, Calman was a man of the world. After grace, he retired to another room with his daughter and seated himself in an easy chair. Tsipele sat opposite him. The beaded bonnet that she wore gave her youthful face a sedate appearance. Her dress was so long that the tips of her shoes were barely visible. This was no longer the playful Tsipele who had once ridden on Calman's shoulders, but the wife of the Marshinov rabbi, the mother of three children.

"Oh, Papa," she said, "you can't imagine how much it means to me to see you again."

"I missed you, Daughter."

"I used to wake up at night, worrying about you."

Tsipele asked after Jochebed, Mayer Joel, Shaindel, Ezriel, and all of the children, including Senderel. She did not mention Clara. Suddenly Calman thought of Miriam Lieba. This daughter of his, the wife of a scoundrel and the mother of Gentile children, was still alive somewhere. She was a branch that had been torn from the tree. Calman would go for months on end without recollecting her once and suddenly, as now, the memory of her would come without warning. Calman's eyes became moist. Tsipele lowered her head, sensing of whom her father was thinking.

III

Although the countries where Jews lived in exile continued to war against each other, killing and plundering, for the Jews, thank God, this holiday season was the beginning of a period of devotion and prayer. Rich men and paupers prayed in the same words; all attended the Rosh Hashana banquet, and ate the traditional dishes, challah with honey, carrot stew, carp, the head of a sheep. A benediction was made over a fruit tasted for the first time that season. It was usually pineapples or grapes. None of the Jews in Marshinov went hungry, God forbid. True, Mendel, ignoring the rabbi's instructions, made certain that all the rich men whom Reb Shimmon had not taken with him were seated at the table, while the poor were left standing. But what was so bad about standing? When one came to a rabbi's, one expected to be jostled and pushed; sweating there dissolved one's sins. As long as one was in Marshinov, there was no need to worry. A prayer shawl was a prayer shawl, whether brocaded or not. Though Rosh Hashana was a judgment day, Marshinov was delirious with joy. The rabbi prayed. He wept. His tears made the congregation exult, for it was known that the angels collect the tears of a saint in a wineskin to intercede for the children of Israel when Satan the accuser brings indictments against them. The praying continued both days until four o'clock. Because the study house was overcrowded, the younger men strolled in the orchard wearing their prayer shawls and their skullcaps.

Yellow leaves drifted down; occasionally an apple, a pear, or a chestnut dropped from a tree. The sun shone. Cool breezes blew in from the fields. The rabbi missed no part of the liturgy, but the Hassidim managed to find time to discuss the intricate matters that they were studying, and Reb Shimmon's defection from Marshinov. Women were to be seen everywhere, strolling down paths and across the grass. The older women wore old-fashioned dresses with trains, bonnets ornamented with bows and satin ribbons, and fur-trimmed velvet capes. Long earrings dangled from their ears; tarnished necklaces, long out of style, hung about their necks, their finest jewelry having already been given to their daughters and daughters-in-law. They walked haltingly, their bodies stooped, holy books and large handkerchiefs in their hands, their lips moving in prayer. All of them requested the same things from heaven: a year more of life, enough to live on, the company of their children and grandchildren, the coming of the Messiah. For when the Messiah came and the dead arose, there would be no more death. The old people noted that three men and one woman had died that very day in Marshinov, so that their deaths must have been decreed in heaven the previous Rosh Hashana.

The young matrons wore silk capes and fashionable bonnets and walked proudly with a light step. Small earrings sparkled in their ears and thin chains glistened at their throats. Their prayer books had copper or silver clasps and gold-trimmed covers. Their shoes had high heels and pointed toes. It was hard to believe that these frivolous-looking creatures bathed in the ritual bath and had husbands with beards and sidelocks. Temerel, who had come to Marshinov to observe the holidays, and her sister-in-law, Binneleh, the Chmielev rabbi's wife, set the style for the women. Temerel wore a white satin dress embroidered with flat beads and edged with lace at the sleeves. She had on a kerchief embroidered with diamonds. Binneleh, daughter of a rich man, a woman whose face was still unlined and rosy-cheeked, promenaded in a silver bonnet and a dress styled according to the latest Paris fashion. When she moved, her silver slippers showed from the hem of her dress. Concealed in her handkerchief was a tiny vial of perfume which she sniffed constantly when she sat in the women's synagogue with its odors of wax, dust, and perspiration.

The day after Rosh Hashana, most of the faithful left to go about their business. Jochanan's prestige had now been fully restored. His words were repeated everywhere and he was compared not only to the Pzhyscher rabbi but even to the famous Kozhenitzer preacher. There was also a good deal of talk about Calman. Everyone had seen him praying at the Eastern wall in his shawl and white linen robe. It was noticed that he remained standing during the reading of the scroll. He had paid for the lodging of ten poor Jews and had been called to the lectern the second day of the holiday. He had, however, not left when Rosh Hashana was over. From this it was deduced that relations between him and Clara were strained.

A few days later, a new horde descended on Marshinov for

Yom Kippur. There was a run on roosters, sacrificed before the holiday for the redemption of sins. Temerel reserved a white rooster for Jochanan. The prayer house was again filled to capacity for the night prayers. Early on the morning before Yom Kippur, the rabbi and his family gathered to offer the sacrifice. Gadele was also there. Tsipele held the baby in her arms. The men held the roosters by the feet and swung them overhead; the women did the same with hens. This sacrifice, which ended with the eating of the chickens, always caused Jochanan anguish, even though the Torah stated explicitly that animals had been placed on earth to feed men. Did one have a right to be more pious than the Pentateuch? It was known that when an animal was slaughtered according to the laws of kashruth and the benediction was devoutly said, the spirit of the creature was purified. Migrant souls, the souls of saints, were imprisoned in animals. Nevertheless, it disturbed Jochanan to take a fowl by its claws and feel its body trembling. Although birds committed no acts of piety, neither did they sin. Who could say that he, Jochanan, was more worthy to live than the creature sacrificed for him? The ritual slaughterer, who had arrived at the court at dawn, slaughtered the birds with a short-bladed knife. Jochanan stood nearby, his head lowered, his face pale, remembering the story of Cain and Abel as well as the words, "And the preeminence of man over the beast is naught." He began to rub his forehead. Thousands of Jews had assembled to draw new faith from him, but he doubted.

In fact, Jochanan had been disgusted with bodily existence for a long time. He never stopped envying his father and grandfather, who had already cast off the burdens of material life and now existed in supernal regions.

25 🏛

During the holiday season, Calman had no desire to leave
Marshinov. What awaited him at home? An adulteress and an
ungovernable child. He was no longer young. He had had his
fill of business. At the feast of Succoth, Calman prayed in the
Tabernacle and spent the night there with Jochanan and his
inner circle. It was good to lie under a feather comforter and
look up at the stars through the branches which made up the
roof. On the seventh day of the feast, he stayed up all night
praying with the Hassidim. On the eighth day, he recited the
prayer for rain. On Simhath Torah, he participated in the first
procession celebrating the Torah. It was a long time since he
had been so happy. He danced with the other worshippers and
treated them to wine and mead. Although no one got drunk,
everybody was slightly tipsy. Calman contrasted his pleasure
now with the misery he had known at Clara's parties. He
calculated that he had enough money with him to enable him
to remain in Marshinov for five years. After that, it would be
up to God.

But as soon as the holidays were over, the Hassidim departed and snow fell on Marshinov. The House of Prayer was
empty. The courtyard grew so still one could hear the last
leaves tearing away from the branches. Only a few yeshiva
students and hangers-on remained. The old men, having been

in each other's company for so long, grew irritable. They dozed by the stove, or sat over their books sucking their pipes. Calman busied himself studying a volume of the Mishnah. But how much study could he stand?

He paced nervously back and forth through the rooms of his daughter's house. Gadele, the youngest child, had the measles and Tsipele would not leave his bedside. The window of the room was draped with a red curtain. When Calman entered the room, Tsipele would put a finger to her lips to indicate that the child was sleeping. Calman went to his own room and lay down on the bed, but how could he sleep when he had been doing nothing for weeks? That evening rain drenched the windowpanes. A dry warmth rose from the stove, and there was a rustling sound as if a friendly house demon was burrowing among the rags and feather dusters. Calman knew that with the coming of Hanukkah Marshinov would again be as pleasant as it had been. But this was only the beginning of the month of Heshvan, and there were almost sixty days to Hanukkah. After the evening services, the maid brought him a plate of soup and some beef stew, but he had no appetite. He put on his overcoat and walked out into the night. Tsipele called after him that it was foolish to go strolling about in such weather. Calman walked, not knowing where he was going. His fur coat became wet. The darkness was almost impenetrable, and he tapped with his cane like a blind man. Finally he reached the station. There was a tiny lamp burning, but the ticket agent's cage was closed. No train was due in for hours. Calman sat on a bench, staring off into the darkness. Was there no place in the world for him?

He rose and started back to Tsipele's. The rain had turned to snow. It fell at an angle, dry as hail. As he trudged along, he felt his face swelling and his eyelids congealing. He'd been through many blizzards, had spent nights by himself in the forest, but never before had he experienced such darkness. It seemed to him that he had been walking for hours. At the rabbi's house, the only light visible was in Jochanan's room.

Everyone else had retired. Calman was about to knock on his son-in-law's door, but changed his mind. There would be nothing to say. He must not take Jochanan, who was a godly man, away from the Torah.

He returned to his room and lit a candle. Its reflection flickered beyond the windowpanes, where a second Calman fidgeted, imitating his movements. Calman seated himself on his bed. The chimney whistled. The shingles on the roof rattled. A cold wind blew through the room from corner to corner. Calman recited the prayer spoken before retiring. He was afraid that he would not be able to sleep, but as soon as he closed his eyes he dozed off. Clara came to him; she was naked and she coiled her hair around his body, laughing like Lilith. Calman awoke, burning with lust. Not even in his youth had he known such desire. He threw off his blanket. Sitting up, he listened. A mouse was gnawing at the floorboards like a creature with a saw in its jaws. Calman reached down, picked up one of his boots, and with it pounded on the foot of his bed.

"Be still, devil."

11

The snow fell. The flakes whirled in the wind. Every gust was laden with white. Snowdrifts formed. The wind scurried over the earth, tearing up straw roofs in the hamlets, knotting braids in horses' manes, exposing furrowed fields and sweeping paths and highways. Occasionally Calman was struck in the eyes as if by a handful of salt. At times it seemed as if cold fingers pressed on his lids. He kept shaking off the snow. Had he been in a sleigh, the trip would have been difficult enough. But the coach skidded constantly, and when it did, the horses stopped dead. Calman was reminded of the story of Balaam's ass. Nevertheless, if one says alpha, beta must follow. If one sets out, one must continue on one's way. Calman, dressed in his fur coat, a bashlyk on his head and straw overshoes covering his boots, sat on the box, arguing with himself. He should have remained in Marshinov. Why was he going to Jampol? Whom did he want to see? His wife, who had slept with another man? It was true that Reb Alter, the assistant rabbi of Marshinov, had ruled that the Law permitted Calman to live with his wife. As long as there was no witness to prove her adultery, she was presumed innocent. On the other hand, Reb Alter had warned that in a case where there was the slightest suspicion it would be best for a man of faith not to go near her, especially if she could not be trusted to practice the prescribed ablutions.

"Gee-up! To the right! Brrr! . . ."

The snowfall grew even denser. Jampol was not far away, not more than fifteen verst, but Calman was afraid, God forbid, of losing his way. He drove into a tempest. Swirls of snow fell across the plain like whirling sprites. From time to time, an entire pillar rose like a white column of locusts ready to drag him and his coach and team off to the Treasure of Snow, to the Congealed Ocean. The chestnut-colored horses turned white as if they had suddenly aged. Their hindquarters seemed to be moving on the same spot. The snow piling up on Calman's shoulders and fur cap transformed his head into a sugar cone. Who could tell? Perhaps he was destined to perish in the storm. He had thoroughly earned his punishment. A man of his age who could not control his lust deserved death. Calman pulled a flask of brandy from his breast pocket and took a swallow. It wouldn't do to get drunk, but it would be worse to catch cold. The frost penetrated his fur coat, his jacket. His feet were numb. Where should he go? To the manor or to the mill? Calman stopped directing the horses, no longer signaled them with his whip. He concentrated on searching for signs of the road. Here and there he made out traces of the highway. As long as it remained light, he realized that he was in no real danger. Behind the clouds, the sun shone. Shadows raced across the plain. Occasionally a flash of red glowed on the snow like a glimpse of a sunset.

Thanks be to God, the coach rolled onto a forest road

on which one could no longer lose one's way. Firs lined the road on either side, the snow lying like white cats on their branches. It was already twilight. God forbid lest a highwayman emerge from behind the thickets. Calman was too weary to defend himself. He prayed to God, although he was ashamed to do so. The good who travel with an innocent purpose suffer no harm; but the goal of his journey was evil. What help could he expect?

The snow continued to fall but not as heavily as before. Occasionally Calman heard the cawing of a crow. How could these creatures stand the cold, Calman wondered. It seemed to him that he had been riding through snow and winter for weeks, months, years. Night came and the darkness descended in an instant, as if suddenly the lights in the sky had been turned off. One moment the snow was still blue and gleaming with diamonds, and the next, everything had turned black. The coach had lanterns, but the panes were frosted over and Calman's fingers were so stiff he couldn't strike a match. He would have to rely upon the horses. Animal's eyes were keener than man's. The horses were moving so slowly that Calman had to call out to them, "Gee-up. Gee-up." He felt like laughing. Here he was, a sixty-year-old man, imperiling himself for a woman who had betrayed him. He thought of Zelda, God rest her soul. If she wanted him to be punished because he had married a loose woman, the sight of him in such a predicament was all the revenge she needed.

As Calman drove into the manor, the dogs tore at their chains and barked at him. Apparently they had forgotten their master. At last, Antoni the coachman appeared and took the horses. The half-frozen animals were led into the stable and covered with blankets. Calman could barely climb from the box. He restrained himself from inquiring about Clara, and walked into the kitchen, where a fire was burning. When he removed his coat, which was stiff and round as a barrel, it remained standing on the floor. He pulled the icicles from his beard, stepped out of his overshoes and boots, and began to warm his feet. Suddenly Clara appeared. She had on slippers, and a sleeveless coat over her nightgown. A net was thrown over her hair. "You certainly picked a fine time to come," she said.

"Well, I'm here," Calman replied, "and I'm alive. I have God to thank for that."

Calman was hungry, but it seemed that in his absence Clara had discharged the Jewish cook. He was afraid to drink even a glass of tea. He sat near the open stove, chewing on a dry crust of bread like a beggar. He added a few pieces of kindling to the fire. His face was flushed. Clara kept pacing back and forth in front of him.

"How's Sasha?" Calman asked.

"He's in Warsaw."

"In Warsaw? By himself?"

"No, he's at school there."

"I don't understand what you're saying, Clara."

"Well, it's not very difficult."

"But who's taking care of him?"

"His governess, of course. I rented an apartment for him, and hired a maid."

"What kind of a school is it?"

"A private school."

A Gentile school, of course. I deserve what I get, Calman thought. Who else would return to such a shrew? For no reason at all he threw a piece of bread into the fire. A childish thought occurred to him. It was like a sacrificial offering. He moved away from the stove to avoid singeing his beard.

"Don't you miss him?" he asked. "I have other children. He's your only child."

"He won't be for long."

Calman became pensive again. "When did you see him last?"

"I go to Warsaw constantly."

Now it was all clear to Calman. She was carrying a bastard. She had rented an apartment for herself and her lover and had so managed that she had an excuse to go to him whenever she wished. Though Calman was in anguish, he marveled at her cunning. His running away had fitted conveniently into her plans. He knew that he should not share her room, but all the other rooms were unheated. He walked into the room, lay down on the bed, and covered himself with a feather comforter. Tired though he was, he could not sleep. Clara, who was also wakeful, coughed continuously. It was the cough of an enemy. Still, he did not regret his difficult journey back to her. In Marshinov he had nourished the illusion that a reconciliation between them was possible. But now her adultery was revealed. She had sent his child away, his only son, his heir. The boy was almost certainly eating non-kosher food. There was no longer the possibility of arranging a truce. He could not even eat a spoonful of food in his own house. Everything was unclean. She might even try to poison him. Once started down the road of evil, there was no end to what a person could do.

"Well, why are you so quiet?" Clara suddenly asked. "Usually when a husband returns from a trip, he tells his wife about it."

"What is there to tell you?"

"You didn't even bring me a gift."

"What kind of a gift? There's nothing to buy in Marshinov."

"You might have sent me a postcard."

Calman was disgusted with her falseness.

"I didn't have anything to write. There was nothing to say."

"What did I do to you? Drown your ducks in the lake?"

"My worst enemy couldn't have hurt me more."

"Is it my fault that you're crazy, and obsessed with Zipkin?"

"I'm not crazy."

"Calmanke, you are. You should go to a doctor. You've nothing to be angry about. The child must be educated. We can't let him grow up to be a peasant. If you want him to have a Hebrew tutor, they're not hard to find in Warsaw. As far as I'm concerned, he can study the Torah with the greatest rabbi."

"He's eating non-kosher food."

"Why non-kosher? The maid is Jewish."

"Why did you discharge the cook?"

"Because of you, Calman. What point was there in keeping her when you weren't here? If you stay home and behave like a normal person, we'll start obeying the laws again. Your Mayer Joel treated me as if I were a thief. What a boor he is."

Calman knew that everything she said was untrue. Nothing but lies. Yet his anger began to disappear. Her voice soothed and caressed him. He wanted both to beat and to hug her. If he made up with her now, he told himself, he was lost. She would demean him. It would be as if he himself were delivering his soul to Asmodeus.

"Calmanke, come to me."

"I swear before God that I'll never touch you again. If I do, may all the punishments recorded in the Book of Curses fall upon me."

The next morning, Calman moved out of the manor house and into the house where he had once lived with Zelda, may she rest in peace. He hired a woman from Jampol to be his housekeeper and began to live alone.

26

Just as the Simhath Torah dances and the prayers for rain ended, winter began in Warsaw. On the Sabbath on which the first section of Genesis is read, snow and hail fell. It was unnecessary to tear down the Tabernacles after the holiday. The wind had already scattered the branches in all directions. The wealthy freeholders lit their ovens and went about wearing felt boots, plush hats, and fur coats. They ordered their wives and servants to prepare hot soup with barley, dried mushrooms, and beans cooked in fat. The early frost took the poor by surprise. According to the newspapers, sickness and starvation were rampant in Poland. There was a shortage of coal in Warsaw because the locomotives were unable to haul enough freight cars, and flooding rivers disrupted transportation. The news from Galicia and Upper Silesia was also bad. In Warsaw, because of a shortage of glaziers, a broken windowpane often could not be replaced and many windows were boarded up. Without shoes, underwear, and warm clothes, the children sickened. The Children's Hospital on Alexander Street was filled to capacity. Convalescent patients could not be discharged because they had nothing to wear, and they moved about in the wards among the sick. At night, long lines of homeless people gathered before the police commissariats. These indigents were permitted to sleep on the commissariat floors, but in the morning they were driven out into the cold.

The Polish press appealed to the public. The Warsaw Chamber of Commerce began preparations for a ball, the proceeds of which were to be used to assist the poor. A number of philanthropic organizations proposed holding a bazaar. Famous actresses, singers, and society ladies promised their services as salesclerks in the booths. Wallenberg pledged a large donation. But the number of those who were to receive help far exceeded the number who could give it. It was difficult to know whose need was the most urgent. The peasants had eaten their seed and were now starving. Even some of the wealthy Warsaw freeholders were unable to obtain fuel with which to heat their homes. Most of the coal that reached the city went to the factories.

The situation was even worse among the Jews. Mobs of paupers convened outside the community house, but the beadles refused to let them in. The angry crowd wept, scolded, cursed the Hassidim, whom they accused of allying themselves with the assimilationists, thus delivering Warsaw into the hands of semi-converts. A feud had raged between the Hassidim and the non-Hassidim, ever since the Russians had issued a modern dress decree. The non-Hassidim had wanted all Jews to adopt European-style clothes: hats, long trousers, shoes with laces or buttons. It was said that the Rabbi of Kotsk had been in favor of European dress, but the Rabbi of Gur and his followers had insisted on the Russian capote, trousers tucked into the boots, a kerchief around the neck, and the Russian cap adapted to the native style. In addition, Hassidim had for some time been agitating against Reb Yukele the Chief Rabbi of Warsaw. But on his death, no new chief rabbi had been appointed. Instead, a rabbinate was placed in charge of religious matters. Among those who came for assistance to the community houses were mourners with corpses at home. They had been unable to secure burial plots, shrouds, hearses.

Lucian and Miriam Lieba were also homeless. Lucian could

spend the nights at the house of Bobrowska, the seamstress and actor's widow, who was his mistress. An old friend of hers, Cybulski, a director of a small theater, from time to time gave Lucian parts as a walk-on. Miriam Lieba's sister-in-law, Felicia, had practically adopted Lucian's children, Wladzio and Marisia. But she would not take in the children's mother because Miriam Lieba drank. Miriam Lieba herself did not want to become a burden. Ezriel helped her out. He rented an attic room for her on Leshno Street, opposite Kercelak Place, which contained an iron stove with a tall smoke-stack. Ezriel bought her a bed (Lucian's furniture had been sold at public auction), a kitchen cabinet, and two chairs. It was a narrow room with a slanting ceiling and a window perched high on the wall like a small head on a hunchback. In order to look outside, one had to stand on a bench. The place did have one advantage: a private entrance.

Since there was no coal available, the room was nearly as cold as the street. The window was caked with ice. The water that Miriam Lieba brought up from the pump froze in the pail. The crumbling, unpainted walls became brown with mold. Although Miriam Lieba wrapped her jacket around her feet, she couldn't get warm. Ezriel brought her bread, cheese, herring, sausage, knowing that she would spend whatever money he gave her on whisky. She ate hardly anything and complained that Ezriel's gifts only served to attract mice. When he didn't visit her, she missed him; when he did, she spoke harshly to him.

"What do you want of me? Let me die in peace."

"Miriam Lieba, you must get a grip on yourself."

"Why should I?"

Ezriel went about dressed in his student uniform, his collar turned up, and his hands drawn into the sleeves of his jacket. He himself was susceptible to colds. His children had been ill the entire winter. Shaindel had been forced to have the doctor in to prescribe for them. Evenings, Ezriel sat beside Miriam

Lieba's bed, listening to her complaints. "Who can understand the ways of nature?" Ezriel would ask.

II

There was a soup kitchen on Iron Street where a meal cost only six groschen. The menu never varied: it was always barley soup with a dumpling or a tiny piece of meat in it. Lard was used for cooking. The kettles boiled from early morning until late evening, and the place was patronized by poor laborers and the unemployed. As soon as one batch of patrons was finished eating, they were hurried out to make room for another. The intellectuals sat by themselves at the "Gentlemen's Table." Lucian had lunch there every day. One of the habitués was Zbigniew Chwalski, a former landowner who blamed his ruin on the liberation of the serfs, but who actually had gambled away his fortune. Chwalski, who was tall and heavy, always brought along his small, thin wife, Katarzyna. Katarzyna's face was as dry as a fig, and her snub nose was perpetually red. As she ate, she berated the Russian tyrants, the perfidious French, the Polish *nouveaux riches*. She was forever talking about that convert Wallenberg who helped the Jews, was an intimate of the Russians, and lived in a palace while Polish aristocrats were forced to eat in soup kitchens. The Chwalskis were not the only anti-Semites at the "Gentlemen's Table." Zhulkowski, who wore a beard and still dressed in a caftan, was even more vehement on the subject than Chwalski. He always brought along a tin pan for his ration. He would place it on the table reserved for the gentry, add enormous amounts of salt and pepper, and begin his diatribe. According to him, the Freemasons and the Jews were responsible for every conceivable evil. They had plotted the partition of Poland, to undermine the Catholic faith. In fact, it was impossible to differentiate between Masons, Protestants, and Jews. They were all the same. Disraeli, Bismark, the Rothschilds, and Wallenberg all took orders from the same masonic high priest. Alexander II was a secret member of the conspiracy and had abolished serfdom for that reason. He had made a Russian Jew by the name of Ginsburg a baron. Sarah Bernhardt was not only an actress but one of the secret couriers of this organization composed of nihilists, liberals, and communards. To what depths Poland had sunk was exemplified by the fact that two Jews, Leventhal and Orgelbrand, headed the country's principal publishing concern. Another Jew, Ungar, was the custodian of Polish art.

Whenever Zhulkowski began to speak, a group gathered about him. Sooner or later, his conversation would get around to the Old Testament. Had not Abraham saved his life by deluding Abimelech into thinking that Sarah was Abraham's sister? Hadn't Isaac followed his father's example? Hadn't Jacob cheated Esau out of his birthright? Hadn't his brothers sold Joseph into slavery? By nature the Jew was a coward and a usurer, a worshipper of the golden calf, physically dirty, haughty, obstinate, and dishonorable. His aim was to monopolize the wealth of the world. Zhulkowski quoted a German writer to the effect that Cain was the prototype of all Jews. At first Lucian had argued with Zhulkowski. Were all Catholics as innocent as lambs? Didn't Christians consider the Old Testament sacred? But Zhulkowski had a dozen answers for each question, and gradually the two men became friends. Lucian told Zhulkowski about Miriam Lieba. Over a glass of beer, he outlined a plan to rob Wallenberg. Zhulkowski shook his head in criticism. Robbery? Theft? That was the way the Jews behaved, not Polish aristocrats. Zhulkowski had a much better plan. They must found an anti-Semitic party and publish books and periodicals to inform the people of how they were being betrayed. Zhulkowski referred to similar movements in Prussia, Hungary, Rumania, and Russia. Had Lucian read the articles of Lutoslawski? Did he know about the "Black Hundreds"? Was he familiar with Renan's essays on religious history? Had he read about the proposal Victor de Istochy had made in the Hungarian parliament, the gist of which was to deport all Jews to Palestine? Did he know that in Prussia everyone was saying: "The Jew is our misfortune"? Even the *Gazeta Polska* had recently run an article attacking Yiddish, a jargon closely associated with the nefarious Talmud that taught Jews how to cheat Christians and defile the Host. Was Lucian aware that the modern Jew, the so-called "assimilationist," was even more dangerous than his old-fashioned brother with his long capote and sidelocks? For the latter at least stayed in the ghetto, while the former had pushed his way into every strata of Polish society and was carrying on his destructive work.

Oddly enough, Zhulkowski toured the Jewish-owned book and antique shops on Świętokrzyska Street every day after lunch and continued his discussions with fellow customers in the stores' back rooms. He was forever mounting the ladders placed against the bookshelves, and fetching down musty volumes to browse through. Although he never bought anything, the Jewish proprietors always addressed him respectfully. He carried on high-flown discussions with the Jewish salesgirls. He even borrowed books from the shops. For years, Adam Zhulkowski had been gathering material for some vast work. His hatred of the Jews had begun when a manuscript of his had been rejected by the publisher Leventhal. Catholic publishers had also rejected his essays, but it was Zhulkowski's theory that they had been influenced by the opinions of the Jews.

III

It had reached the point where Lucian could not stop talking about murder. When he visited Miriam Lieba on Saturday nights, he always spoke of his plans to do away with Bobrowska. Lucian never failed to bring with him a bottle of vodka, some food, a small pail of coals, and a bundle of wood. He would light the iron stove, lie down under the blanket with

Miriam Lieba, put out the lamp, and babble for hours. He would rob Wallenberg, kill Bobrowska, and then run off to Sicily or Corsica with Miriam Lieba and Kasia. Though his words were only the ravings of a drunk, Miriam Lieba noticed how much they excited him. He could no longer make love without such talk. As he spoke, he would flourish his pistol, place the muzzle against Miriam Lieba's forehead and say: "Darling, shall I shoot?"

"Go ahead, shoot."

"You'd be killed immediately."

"The sooner the better."

When he was with Bobrowska, Lucian spoke about killing Miriam Lieba. Miriam Lieba paid no attention to his antics, but Bobrowska begrudged him the murder of his wife. She wanted to do it herself with a knife, not a gun. Bobrowska would then suck the blood from Miriam Lieba's throat like a vampire. Later, while Miriam Lieba was in her death agonies, Bobrowska would lie with Lucian. Although only a seamstress, she was descended from the nobility. She boasted of how her grandfather had lashed a score of peasants to death. She related how during the uprising of 1863 Cossack officers had used flagellation to arouse aristocratic women sexually. In the morning, Lucian and Bobrowska would tell each other their dreams.

Lucian was not able to see Kasia as much as he wished. He could only visit her when her employer, Pan Chodzinski, was at the steam bath. He began to think about murdering Chodzinski too, and asked Kasia where the old man kept his money. "Why talk about it?" Kasia replied. "You won't kill him."

"How can you be so sure of that?"

"You're just not a killer."

"Yes, I am. I'll put an end to that old dog."

"Why? He's going to die anyway."

"I want his money."

"You'd be killing him for nothing. You wouldn't find it. No one knows where he's hidden it."

Though Kasia was too much of a peasant to appreciate Lucian's perversities, he kept asking her if she were not jealous of his wife and Bobrowska. Wouldn't she like to revenge herself on Bobrowska? How would she do it? He kept putting words into her mouth and forced her to comply to his perversions. He wheedled and begged until she gave him money. Lucian had arrived at a new low and he was aware of it. He was without a job. His children had been taken from him by his sister. He ate in a cheap soup kitchen, lived off Bobrowska, and hung around waiting for a walk-on at the theater. The only thing that kept him from being a complete derelict was his appearance. But even keeping himself looking presentable became more and more difficult. Bobrowska's apartment was infested with vermin. Though hot water was poured into the cracks of the woodwork and poison scattered about everywhere, the bugs always returned. Miriam Lieba managed to keep herself moderately clean but slept on a torn pillow, the feathers of which blew all over the apartment. Bobrowska washed Lucian's clothes and occasionally pressed his suit, but all his clothing was worn out and needed to be replaced.

Lucian's rage had grown so intense that he could not repress it. Whether awake or asleep, he dreamed perpetually. In the morning, he always awoke tired and with the urge to lie down again. He was constantly yawning and stretching. Formerly, he had enjoyed cold weather, but now he could not bear it. His fantasies were always of South Sea Islands or South American plantations where natives toiled while he sat drinking wine on shady porches. Thoughts of love and murder never left him. He became incapable of dealing with everyday matters It was almost as if he had been swallowed up by his grandiose dreams.

IV

Pan Chodzinski, the man for whom Kasia worked, left for Grodzisk to spend Christmas with his sister. He was to be away for several days and possibly over New Year's. Kasia remained to take care of the house, but Chodzinski had arranged for her to eat her holiday meals with a neighbor, a shoemaker, because it was not right for a girl to be entirely alone during this happy season. Although Chodzinski had bought a Christmas tree, he would not have it decorated with candles, for fear that his apartment would catch fire. Nor would he allow Kasia to go to church, because there were so many thieves around during the holidays. He particularly did not want her to attend Midnight Mass. Kasia was glad that her master had left. Despite his impotence, he continued to harass her. Kasia's young son, Bolek, was being brought up by a woman who lived almost at the very end of Dzika Avenue, near the Catholic cemetery. Kasia paid a ruble a week for the child's board, thirteen rubles a quarter. All that she earned in that period was five rubles. The rest she managed to scrape together by selling bones, potato peels, the presents that Chodzinski gave her, and the occasional coins she got from Lucian. Kasia, though barely twenty-one, already had a handsome five-year-old boy who resembled Lucian. If it had not been for her father's assistance, Kasia would never have been able to raise the child. Chodzinski must never learn that she was the mother of a bastard. It was only on rare occasions that she could visit the boy. Even on Sunday, her day off, Chodzinski insisted that she go to church with him. Now that Chodzinski was not around, Kasia could behave like a mother for a few days, and Lucian could again visit her freely. Recently it had become more difficult to see him because Chodzinski had given up going to the steam bath on the same day each week. Sometimes he skipped a week, and there was no predicting on what day he would go. The young men on Chmielna Street did not know that Kasia had a lover and a child and pursued her as dogs do a bitch. But Kasia was only interested in Lucian. Though Lucian came to her drunk from the arms of another woman, a visit from him was still a holiday for her. She served him cookies and jam from Chodzinski's larder. Lucian hid nothing from her, told her all his sins, and revealed to her his most private thoughts. Although she did not understand much of what he said, it was good to listen to him. She often caught him in lies, but that didn't matter. Men liked to boast. Although he was so much older than she, Kasia thought of him as a child. He chattered like Bolek, laughed and grimaced exactly as the boy did. At times he would threaten to murder Chodzinski, strangle Bobrowska, do away with his wife, the Jewess, or merely commit suicide himself after killing Kasia first. What did all such babbling mean? Thus far, the only one he had harmed was himself. Kasia dreaded only one thing—becoming pregnant again. But Lucian had learned a trick that prevented conception. Thank God, her period came regularly. Despite her poverty, she dropped a groschen in the church box each month and had a candle lit at the altar of her patron saint.

While Pan Chodzinski was away, Kasia would be able to spend some of her nights with Lucian. Lucian had promised to buy the boy some presents and take Kasia in a droshky to Pawązek to visit him. Lucian hadn't seen Antek in years, but had even agreed that they meet and visit Bolek together. How strange it was that his former enemy should now be his father-in-law, Bolek's grandfather. Antek now had his own woman, and plenty of work to do. A great many homes were being constructed in Warsaw, and he had become a mason. He earned seven rubles a week, sometimes as much as ten.

Lucian had meant every word when he made these promises to Kasia. Unfortunately, that Christian soul Felicia had prevailed upon her husband to invite Lucian and his wife to Christmas dinner. At first Zawacki had been stubbornly opposed to the idea. He was determined not to have his charlatan brother-in-law or his psychopathic wife around. But Felicia's eyes had grown red from weeping. After all, Lucian was her brother. Besides, the children were asking to see their mother and father. Felicia could not rob her angels of their parents. After much discussion, Zawacki gave in. Felicia sent clothing

and fifteen rubles in cash to her sister-in-law so that Miriam
Lieba could make herself presentable. Felicia also wrote Lucian a letter begging him to accompany his wife and to conduct himself like a gentleman, at least during Christmas.

Miriam Lieba gave Lucian the letter that Felicia had sent to
him, and also three of the fifteen rubles. He must have some
money in his pocket. Then Miriam Lieba made Lucian swear
on the crucifix that he would accompany her to his sister's, no
matter how low his opinion was of Felicia. As if this were not
enough, Bobrowska announced that she was planning to give a
dinner to celebrate God's birthday, and that if Lucian disappointed her on this occasion she would have nothing more to
do with him. She knew that Chodzinski was going away and
suggested that Lucian bring Kasia along. Why should the girl
be left alone on such a holy day? Bobrowska was too old and
clever to be jealous. Actually, she had wanted for a long time
to have that fresh young thing around, to talk to and drink
whisky with. Later all three of them could carry on in the
manner Lucian had suggested to her.

How was Lucian going to convince Kasia to visit Bobrowska when Pan Chodzinski had forbidden her even to attend
Midnight Mass and had arranged for her to eat her holiday
meal at the shoemaker's? And how was he to celebrate Christmas Eve with his sweetheart when he had to accompany his
wife to his sister Felicia's? How, too, would it be possible to
make Kasia feel friendly toward Bobrowska when Kasia hated
her, called her crazy, bitch, and the like? Lucian had still another plan in mind, but the obstacles to its fulfillment were
many. Yes, he had ensnared himself in a web that even the
devil could not escape. Usually, Lucian's lies got him out of
his predicaments, but this time it looked as if the stew he had
cooked would choke him. However, Lucian had often observed that if one kept one's head, one always found a way
out, or else chance offered a solution. And that is exactly what
happened. Despite his helplessness, Lucian felt lucky. The

angel that watched over him would extricate him from all entanglements.

As it turned out, the shoemaker's wife at whose house Kasia
was to eat came to tell the girl that she could not have her to
dinner after all. On Christmas Eve, if there were an odd number of guests, there was a superstition that one of those present
would die before the year was out. The shoemaker's family
consisted of eight people and she could only include Kasia,
who was a paying guest, if Pan Chodzinski were willing to pay
for two instead of one. But Chodzinski was known in the
courtyard as a miser and the shoemaker's wife doubted that
the old man would even pay for Kasia. The janitor proposed
that she eat at his house, but Kasia hated the janitor and his
household. A large family was cramped into one tiny room,
where the laundry was washed as well. With a Christmas tree
in it, not even another pin could fit into the room. Besides, the
janitor owned a dog, blind in one eye, who barked and bit.
Eating at the janitor's was out of the question. Pan Chodzinski had left on the stagecoach at three o'clock on the day of
Christmas Eve. Lucian arrived at Kasia's around three-thirty,
carrying a bottle of sweet brandy and a bag full of cakes.
Kasia told him what had happened and Lucian consoled her. It
seemed to him that Providence itself was working for him.
Sitting with the girl in the kitchen, he poured a drink for her
and for himself. Kasia made a face. The liquor was too strong,
and Lucian ridiculed her. "You call this liquor? It's water!"
After the third glassful, Kasia stopped grimacing. Her gray
eyes twinkled. Her upturned nose became red. She began to
mutter that she would get drunk and forget her troubles. Lucian embraced her, kissed and flattered her. He was not drunk,
but seemed to be. He played their old game, calling himself
her husband, lord, and master. Whatever he told her, she must
do, even if he ordered her to jump into the Vistula. Suddenly
he said: "Get dressed quickly. Come with me!"

"Where? I must not leave the apartment."

"Let the apartment go to hell!"

"Where are you taking me? The old man will kill me!"

"If the old rascal lays a hand on you, I'll chop it off!"

Kasia mumbled something about her duty, thieves, the janitor, but Lucian assured her that he would take full responsibility for her going. Kasia put on her high-buttoned shoes, her Sunday dress, and threw a shawl over her shoulders. Lucian seldom went out with Kasia. The few occasions on which he had taken her for a walk or to visit their child, he had waited for her at the end of Iron Street. This time he made no attempt to hide. All the neighbors in the courtyard were already drunk. For the girl, his walking out with her was a sign of his devotion. He was no longer ashamed of her. Kasia fumbled with the lock, and Lucian helped her hang it on the door. He dropped the key into his own pocket. To avert her suspicions he told her that he had bought Bolek a toy sword. They strolled along arm in arm like lady and gentleman. He led her to Iron Street. Kasia asked: "Where are you taking me?"

"To Baba Yaga, into her caldron."

"Oh, do be serious!"

"I'm taking you to a brothel and turning you over to a pimp."

When Kasia realized that he was taking her to Bobrowska's, she objected violently. She even tried to run away. But Lucian held her fast. "Don't be an idiot. She is a goodhearted woman, a motherly soul. If you're not happy there, you can always leave. She doesn't eat people alive . . ."

He reminded her that she had promised to obey him blindly. He muttered something about her sainted mother, Stachowa. He even poked Kasia lightly in the shoulder, a sign that he was displeased and that it would be dangerous to thwart him. Before entering Bobrowska's house, he took the bottle of liquor from his pocket and gave Kasia a drink.

"Take a deep one . . ."

Bobrowska's room was half swept when Lucian brought Kasia inside. Sawdust was sprinkled on the floor. In the window stood three candles of different colors, in memory of the Trinity. The Christmas tree was already decorated with ornaments and tinsel. Odors of carp, cake, vegetables, and ginger permeated the apartment. Bobrowska was still in her petticoat. She was doing many things at once—cooking, baking, hemming a dress. On the table stood a pressing iron filled with glowing coals. The apartment was warm and steamy. The parrot shrieked like a human being. Bobrowska's red and perspiring face lit up with a smile. Although Lucian had promised to bring Kasia, Bobrowska had learned by now that his word could not be depended on. Suddenly there he was with the girl. Bobrowska had already had a few drinks. She ran to Kasia, embraced her, kissed both her cheeks, and sang out: "Don't say a thing. I know all there is to know. Take off your shawl!"

Lucian hesitated for a moment and then said: "I must go out again."

"Go out where?" Bobrowska asked suspiciously. "It will be dark soon."

"I'm afraid I'll be somewhat late for dinner."

"Where are you going? What's wrong with you? I was planning to call in my neighbor so that we wouldn't be an odd number."

"You needn't do that. I won't be here for dinner."

Bobrowska's green eyes lit up. "You were fooling me, eh? Why did I prepare everything? Why did you bring this girl here if you're running off to your wife?"

"Elzbieta, I'll come later. I can't tear myself to bits. Meanwhile, you two get acquainted."

Lucian whistled in relief and slammed the door. She heard him running down the stairs. For a moment Bobrowska was transfixed. Then she screamed in a voice unlike her own: "Madman! Maniac! Parasite! Dog!" She opened the door as if to run after him, but instead she turned to Kasia and commanded: "Take off your shawl. You're staying here . . ."

V

From Iron Street, Lucian ran back to Leshno Street, in the direction of Kercelak Place. It wasn't snowing, but some invisible, prickly substance was falling from the sky. Even at this late hour, Christmas trees were still being peddled. Pine needles covered the sidewalks and the air was permeated with the odor of pine and wintry forests. The stores were selling starch cakes shaped like stars, crosses, pictures of holy figures with wings and halos above their heads. Colored candles, glass balls, and tinsel for decorating trees were displayed in the shop windows. Hay for placing under the tablecloth and stalks of wheat for standing in the corners of rooms were also on sale. Drunken revelers staggered down the street, hoarsely bellowing their songs. Choirboys passed by in their surplices and cowls. Lucian sprinted along. Having eaten little in the last few days, he had grown light, as though he were hollow. He would go to bed irritated and arise with the same feeling. Within him something fluttered constantly, as if his heart hung on a thread. He had had his hair cut for Christmas. Bobrowska had removed the stains from his clothes. His dress shoes had been half-soled. With his derby hat perched sideways on his head, in his fresh collar, wool shawl, and polished shoes, he still looked the dandy. He had not wished to disgrace Felicia by his shabby appearance. When he reached his wife's attic room, he opened the door and saw a transformed Miriam Lieba. Combed and dressed almost to perfection, in a skirt a trifle too short—Felicia was an inch shorter then she—Miriam Lieba stood there, a hat on her head and a fur neckpiece over her shoulders. She wore earrings given to her as a wedding present by Lucian's Aunt Eugenia, may her soul rest in paradise. Miriam Lieba had apparently powdered and rouged her face, because she was not as wan as usual. Lucian stared at her, astonished. All winter, he had never seen her out of her nightclothes. She had always been huddled in a thick shawl. She was still pretty. God, what had he made of this woman!

He said: "Truly, you look marvelous!"

"Go on, laugh at me—"

"No, dear, it's the truth."

"Oh, my cough is choking me," said Miriam Lieba, and she began to cough into a handkerchief. She put on a worn plush jacket. On the bed was an old muff and numerous little boxes and bags.

"What are those?"

"Stars for the children. I bought something for the adults, too. You forget, Lucian, that you are a father."

"No, I don't forget. Come, it's getting late."

"I can't walk in these shoes. We'll have to hire a sleigh."

"Do you have any money?"

They added up their small change. Miriam Lieba hung a lock on the door, and they walked down the stairs, which were covered with mud. The odor of cooking carp came from all the doors. Miriam Lieba suddenly remembered Passover evenings in Jampol. How different it had all been, and how long ago! . . . Someone, carrying up a Christmas tree, blocked the passageway. They had to wait a long time for a sleigh. Miriam Lieba seated herself, and Lucian, playing the cavalier, covered her with the sheepskin lap robe. The sleigh skidded right and left, almost spilling Miriam Lieba out, and she clutched at Lucian's arm. How long was it since she had seen her children! Not since the end of the summer. Actually, she had not gone outdoors all winter. She had sat at home, just as cold as those Polish patriots who still languished freezing somewhere in the Siberian tundras. If not for Ezriel, she would have been completely isolated from the world. Choking as she coughed, she sucked on some rock candy. Yes, Felicia was a Christian soul, but it wasn't easy for Miriam Lieba to visit her own children as if she were an outcast. The driver drove to Kreditowa Street through Iron Street. They passed by the gate that led to Bobrowska's apartment. Afterward they turned into Grzybowska Street, and from there to Krolewska. Miriam Lieba could not believe that the world was still full of people who dressed up, primped. The short section of Marshalkowsky Boulevard that they crossed was filled with sleighs, crowds, and pre-holiday excitement. Luxury goods jammed the shop windows. The newspapers spoke of shortage and starvation. Yet, in spite of all the poverty, new fashions still appeared. On this street there were women dressed in fox furs, sables, and magnificent hats, and elegant gentlemen with racing dogs.

When Lucian and Miriam Lieba walked into the Zawackis' apartment, the household was already prepared for the holiday ceremonies. Presents for the servants were piled on a table in the drawing room. Balls, bells, pine cones, and silver tinsel hung on the Christmas tree, which had a star on top. At the foot of the tree stood a miniature manger inherited from Felicia's parents and grandparents. In it were displayed figurines of sheep, cattle, shepherds, angels, the Child Jesus, the Blessed Mother, the three Wise Men from the East, their slaves, donkeys, and camels—everything painted gold or silver and covered with artificial snow. Felicia embraced Miriam Lieba, kissing her on both cheeks. She also kissed Lucian. A governess brought in the children. Miriam Lieba's eyes filled with tears. She glimpsed Wladzio and Marisia as if through a mist. Both had grown in the few months they'd been away from her. Wladzio had on a velvet suit with knee-length trousers, and his blond hair was parted in the middle. It was the same Wladzio, but a patrician affluence emanated from his face. Marisia's dress was trimmed with lace, her braids tied in red ribbons. Wladzio blushed, bowed, hesitated a moment before leaping into his mother's arms. The little one began to move backward, her face wrinkling to cry . . .

Kissing the children, Lucian was filled with resentment. "I'll take them away from here! I'm still alive. After today, everything will change. They will forget this period of their lives

. . ." He decided he would settle in Sicily or Corsica and take along Kasia and Bolek. All he needed was the fare and a sum of money to purchase a house or a bit of land. He would begin anew and wed his Slavic strength to the southern sunshine . . . The democratic refuse that the French Revolution had spread throughout Europe would sooner or later in turn be swept away with a fiery broom . . .

Dr. Zawacki spent the entire time in his office, reading a medical journal. He despised sentiment, tears, impassioned conversation, and waited for the family, in his own words, "to soak itself out." What the devil was the sense of all these holidays? he wondered. How much longer would people cling to these empty myths? Would mankind remain ignorant forever? The following day he would have to visit his father, the shoemaker, in the Old City; listen to his and to his mother's reverent observations, eat all the cooking and baking that lay so heavily on the stomach. What came of all these festivities? The priests, those wastrels, went around sprinkling holy water, robbing the poor of their last few groschen. The rabble glutted itself, and appendicitis attacks, stomach poisonings, heart failures, and apoplexies followed. Coffinmakers and undertakers would have a busy season.

Hearing Felicia's step, he put the journal aside. She had come to summon him to their guests. To please her, he even planned to attend Midnight Mass. "Well, what is love?" he reflected. "Another irrational thing . . ."

VI

Even before the meal had ended, Lucian rose and announced that he had to leave, promising to return later. Although Miriam Lieba had become reconciled to his insulting treatment of her, she had never imagined that he would run off and leave her and the children on Christmas Eve. She gazed at Lucian in bewilderment. Felicia pleaded with her brother to remain and attend Midnight Mass with the family. "A little prayer won't hurt you," she argued. Marian Zawacki was in the midst of presenting historical evidence that Christmas had never been a Christian holiday and that, even from the theological viewpoint, there was no indication that Jesus had been born on the twenty-fifth of December. The fasting and celebration on that date were relics of pagan times when the populace feared the angry spirits of the winter solstice. Wiping her tears away, Felicia begged her husband to stop blaspheming.

In the midst of it all, Lucian said goodbye.

Zawacki called after him: "Come back, little brother-in-law. There is a present here for you, too."

"Yes, thank you. I'll be back."

Lucian hurried out. His watch indicated a quarter to nine. The frost that night had become drier and more piercing. Lucian walked down Marshalkowsky Boulevard and turned into Chmielna Street. Sleighs glided by, their bells ringing. Through half-frosted widowpanes there gleamed the light of candles and Christmas trees. Drunks staggered by, croaking songs, rushing forward to kiss people. The streetwalkers loitered as usual at the end of Chmielna Street. Lucian's plan was simple. He would get into Chodzinski's apartment, locate the money that the miser had hidden somewhere, and before the gate was closed, steal out into the street and go on to Bobrowska's. Kasia had often told him that her employer kept money in the house. The only problem was where. The old idiot wasn't due back until the day after next, or perhaps not even until after the New Year. There would be plenty of time to cover up the traces. Racing over the icy sidewalks, breath coming from his nostrils, Lucian considered the situation. He had hoped for a long time that Chodzinski would go on a trip. He had frequently urged Kasia to get to know Bobrowska better. Bobrowska had even promised to teach Kasia how to sew. But Kasia had obstinately refused to hear of it. All at once, both his wishes had been granted. Now he could manage everything without interference. Weren't these omens that the beginning year would be a lucky one for him? Despite his having just finished a large meal, he felt light. In the street, the flames of the gas lamps cast trembling shadows. The sky was filled with stars. Lucian glided rather than walked. The wind, blowing from somewhere on the North Sea, thrust him forward. "Oh, it's a good frost. It's good to be alive," Lucian exulted. "A sin? The old man's money would be squandered any way, or he would leave it to some church . . ." Lucian daydreamed about Corsica, where there was hardly any winter. One walked among palm trees by the shores of the Mediterranean. Laws were not taken too seriously. As in Napoleonic times, bandits still operated there.

A streetwalker accosted Lucian. "Not now, girlie," he said. "Maybe on my way back . . ."

Everything seemed to be working in his favor. He met no one going through the gate. Unobserved, he walked úp the stairs. A lock hung on the door, but Lucian had taken both the big and the little keys. Although no light illuminated the stairway, he quickly found both keyholes. Removing the lock, he replaced it so that it only appeared to be locked. If the janitor decided to check, he would find everything in order. Entering, Lucian closed the door, bolting it from the inside. In the breast pocket of his overcoat lay a loaded pistol, but Lucian knew that he would not have to use it. The janitor had more alcohol in his head than in his glass. Only one thing would be dangerous—lighting a candle. Lucian decided to work in the dark. At the threshold of the living room, he let his eyes grow accustomed to the dimness. A street lamp and the lights from the neighboring apartments broke the darkness. The reflection of the snow on the roof across the street cast a luminous light of its own. It was now about a quarter after nine. A good hour and a half remained before the gate was locked. Lucian decided to begin with the bedroom. Misers habitually secreted money in mattresses. Lucian pulled apart the bed linen, searched beneath the pillow, felt the mattress. Should he slash it open with his knife? The mattress was old, its stuffing almost gone. There was nothing to be found in it. A commode stood at the left of the bed. Lucian tried to open it, but all the drawers were locked. Should he force it—but how? He needed some sort of tool, a file or crowbar. How could he have forgotten to bring such a thing along? He walked into the kitchen. The darkness seemed to grow less from one minute to the next. He could see everything, the pantry, the pots on the stove, as if it were midday. A cleaver hung on the wall. He removed it and hefted its weight in his hand. This was not the proper tool, but if he lingered until the gate was closed, he would be left in a trap.

Cleaver in hand, Lucian turned back to the bedroom. He was calm, but warm. He wanted to remove his coat, but finally decided against it. In this kind of situation, one could easily forget something. There were letters and papers in his coat. Just as Lucian had felt confident he would have no trouble in entering the apartment, he now sensed that there was no money in the commode. He would force the drawers and lose time for nothing. Nevertheless, he broke open a drawer and began to tap around inside. There were collars, magazines, cuffs, all sorts of knickknacks. He tore open the second drawer, which creaked and squealed. The brittle old wood smelled of starch. He dumped out shirts, handkerchiefs, neckties, scarves, and socks, to reach the drawer bottom more quickly. It was unnecessary to force the third drawer, which he struck from the inside with his fist, loosening it immediately. Again he found all manner of foppish accessories. "How he indulges himself, the devil!" Lucian snarled. He began to grow angry, his armpits perspired. His throat grew dry and he had to cough—two deep coughs and one light one that brought up the phlegm. He wiped his mouth with a handkerchief.

"Have I missed anything?" he asked himself, resting for a moment. Apparently he had grown unaccustomed to physical exertion. His arms ached, his heart pounded. He was not jittery but tense. He had just eaten, but something like hunger began to gnaw at him. Perhaps the old codger kept some whisky or liqueur on the premises? As he stood there, sparks drifted before Lucian's eyes. A dreamlike design formed—spots, stripes, flowers—of green, blue, and violet. They changed shape, assuming all kinds of geometric patterns, both tangible and ethereal. What was this? As a child, when his nurse had tucked him into bed, he had had similar visions. Oddly enough, he even recalled the colors, the combinations, the whole dreamlike design.

Lucian shuddered. There was no time for fantasies. He had to search through everything and leave before the gate was closed. Every second was precious. Everything hung on a scale between life and death . . .

Going into the living room, he went to the window, tucked up the curtain, and consulted his watch. It was later than he had imagined. The small hand pointed to ten and the large to five. Only half an hour remained.

VII

The church bells rang. Everywhere, from all the streets, all the houses, from palaces and cellars, from luxurious apartments and attics, people were on their way to Midnight Mass. The churches filled rapidly. At every altar stood a stable with a crib representing the birth of Jesus in Bethlehem.

The Russian New Year fell thirteen days later, but Poland always was, and remained, a Catholic country. Even the Czar could not uproot the faith of the people. The Russians continued to build new Greek Orthodox churches. In Praga, they had constructed a *sobor*, its crooked Greek Orthodox cross of solid gold gleaming on high. It was said that similar *sobors* were to be built in Warsaw and in other large Polish cities. But what was the use of spacious structures, copper cupolas, the rich holy decorations, when inside, the churches remained empty and the priests preached to the walls?

Bobrowska ate Christmas dinner with Kasia. By candlelight, surrounded by the scent of the Christmas tree, Bobrowska spoke frankly to the girl. "What a savage that Lucian is! What a deceiver, numbskull, hothead! How little one can depend on him! He has a talent for ruining himself and everyone who has anything to do with him!" Drinking and talking, Bobrowska refilled Kasia's glass. Kasia made a face with each mouthful, but Bobrowska urged her on: "Drink, darling, drink down your sorrow! Life would be unbearable without lots of brandy."

Bobrowska stuffed Kasia with delicacies until the girl's stomach ached. Kasia drank until her eyes became glassy. She began to mumble words in the peasant jargon she had picked up from her parents in her infancy. She used such comical expressions that Bobrowska was forced to laugh: "Hey, girl, you're a peasant, all right! You drank it in with your mother's milk . . ." Bobrowska asked how often Lucian visited her, where he slept with her, when, how—but Kasia only smiled drunkenly, revealing her widely spaced teeth. Suddenly, as if severed, her head fell on the table. Bobrowska laughed: "You're drunk, girl, completely soused . . ." Bobrowska's knees were shaky too, but she managed to stand up, and led, almost carried Kasia to a windowless alcove which contained her spare bed. There she lay the girl on the bed where Lucian usually slept. Kasia gasped once and lay as if in a faint. Bobrowska smiled to herself: "What a scoundrel! What a fool, swine, rogue! Left two sweethearts and went off to his own wife, that Jew bitch. Or who knows? Maybe not to his wife, either. He must have found himself another whore. Did it mean anything to such a rake, such a pimp? Did he have anything to worry about?" He gorged himself at her house, snored in her bed, loafed the days away in soup kitchens among the derelicts. Even the few gulden he got in the theater he earned because she, Bobrowska, had recommended him. And how did he repay her? Of all times, on a holiday, he runs off and makes a fool of her.

Bobrowska was angry, but inwardly she laughed. "Just let him come here! Don't worry, he'll come."

She'd greet him with a broom and a slap. She'd land one on his jaw, one on his lousy undershirt. Let him just step across the threshold . . . Bobrowska wobbled back to the table. There could no longer be any question of going to church. She was too tired, too drunk. As they rang, the bells lulled her. Each chime stirred her deeply. She had once been young, handsome, had had desires, dreams. She had had a father, a mother, brothers, sisters. Where had they all gone? All had become dust and ashes . . . She had loved Bobrowski and Cybulski, who was now an important theater director and had no time for her, the son-of-a-dog . . . He was busy, terribly busy . . . But he had plenty of time for the whores. "Well, let them have their way. I earn my bread! What's already happened, even the devil can't take away from me . . ." Bobrowska tried to pour herself some vodka, but only a single drop remained. She placed the glass to her nose, inhaling. Suddenly the door opened and Lucian walked in. Bobrowska laughed joyfully. She wanted to make a cutting remark, but could not get the words out. He looked pale, disheveled. "Here comes the squire!" she crooned.

And she pointed at him with an index finger.

Lucian bristled.

"Where's Kasia?"

"I ate her. Hee, hee . . ."

"Where is she?"

"In the alcove. Dead drunk."

Lucian waited a moment, then moved a step closer to her.

"Elzbieta, I've killed a man!"

Bobrowska's smile froze on her lips. "Killed?"

"Yes, killed."

"And may I ask whom?"

"The janitor in Chodzinski's courtyard. He didn't want to open the gate for me, so I shot him in the stomach."

"The janitor? What were you doing in Chodzinski's yard, with her here?"

"I was . . ."

"So you're a murderer, too—" And Bobrowska, half sobered but feeling unusually heavy, remained seated. Her legs seemed paralyzed. She hiccuped and belched at once.

"Are you joking?"

"No, it's the truth."

"Well, that's just fine. Fine and dandy!"

Bobrowska, still smiling, stared at him, startled not so much at what he had done as at her own indifference and sluggishness. Fatigue had overpowered her. She seemed to have become rooted to the bench. Her tongue was stiff and she knew that whatever she said would sound foolish.

"Well, did it pay, at least?" she asked.

Lucian looked at her with the bewildered expression of someone who didn't quite understand what was being said to him.

"I found nothing. He had papers there, but they were junk as far as I'm concerned."

"Yes, I understand."

"He must have taken everything with him."

"Uh-huh."

"I must go away at once. The *glinas* may come here looking for me any minute." Lucian used the underworld nickname for the police. He stood there lopsided, pale, his clothes unbuttoned, his hat shoved back on his head, his hands in his pockets. Taking out a cigarette, he thrust it into his mouth and then spat it out. Bobrowska remained seated. Her stomach was as inflated as a drum, but she was completely sober now.

"Why did you do it? We could have had such a happy holiday."

"—I did it. I needed money."

"What will happen now?"

"I don't know, I don't know."

"How will they know that you did it?" Bobrowska asked after a while.

Lucian was silent, lost in thought. Then he said: "Kasia will run home tomorrow and they'll learn everything from her. She's a fool and a peasant—"

"You're just finding that out? We won't let her go home."

"What do you mean?"

Bobrowska did not reply. Lucian removed his overcoat and laid it over the cover of the sewing machine. He doubled up like someone with cramps.

"Are you hungry?" Bobrowska asked. "I left everything for you."

Lucian raised his brows questioningly, as if he did not understand what she was saying.

"Hungry? No. But do you have something to drink?"

"No."

"Slopped up everything, did you? Well, I'm dead tired."

Noting a chair in the middle of the room, Lucian sat down. He did not remove his hat. His eyes remained shut for a while as if he were about to doze off. Then he opened them again. They expressed no regret, no fear, only a weariness and the perplexity of someone awakened out of a dead sleep. Bobrowska slowly turned in her chair to face him.

"I put her down in your bed."

"Well, let her rest."

"You shouldn't have done it, Lucian. If at least you'd killed the old man. How was it the janitor's fault?"

"A clod, I wanted to get out and he wouldn't let me. He tried to hit me with the key."

"Did he recognize you?"

"I doubt it."

"Oh, it's a sin, a sin. He was surely a father of children. And on this holy night besides."

"Shut up!"

"You shouldn't have done it, dear, you shouldn't have done it. What will you do now? Unless throw yourself in the Vistula."

"The Vistula is frozen over—"

"What will you do?"

"I'll go away and that will be that."

"Away where? And what will become of me? I'm not even thinking about your children—"

"What happens will happen."

"Now I understand why you brought the girl here."

"You understand nothing. It was a coincidence. It was because the shoemaker didn't want to have an odd number of guests."

"What shoemaker? What are you talking about?"

"I know what I'm saying. Tomorrow, keep her here as long as you can. I'll leave first thing in the morning. I'm too tired now. Or should I kill her too, to keep her from going home?"

Bobrowska shivered.

"What are you saying? Not in my house. They'll question me as it is."

"No one will question you."

"Yes, they will. They'll ask the girl where she spent the night and she'll lead them to me. You'll make off and they'll drag me to the police station."

"So what do you want me to do? Give myself up?"

"You shouldn't have done it, Lucian. What good did it do you? You got nothing anyhow."

"He hid it, the scurvy dog. Under the floor, or somewhere. I should have stayed until morning. I simply didn't have the time to search."

"Certainly. You should have stayed until daybreak. In the morning, you could have come out and no one would have been the wiser. You would have spared yourself committing this sin—"

"I wanted to come to you. I knew you were waiting."

"I would have waited a while longer."

"It's all your nagging. Well, now it's too late. You all brought me to this. You gnawed at me like a worm. And Miriam Lieba, that Jew bitch, kept berating me. I wanted to take another look in the daytime, but Kasia would have raised a fuss. Everyone hindered me, that's the truth."

"I didn't hinder you. I prepared a meal for you. For you and your sweetheart. You went away and left us like two fools."

"I went away because my sister, that lunatic, wanted to do a good deed . . . A gang of women have climbed on my back, each one pulling in her own direction . . . Well, I'm tired."

"I'll make the bed right away."

Bobrowska wanted to rise but was unable to do so. Lucian stood up and went to the alcove. Kasia snored. It was ink-black there, hot and stuffy, smelling of food. For a while Lucian stood over Kasia's bed, listening to her breathing. Perhaps he should strangle her? He felt no animosity toward her, but human life no longer had any value for him. He knew that in the courtyard there were cellars for storing limestone. He could carry her down, throw her into some cellar, and it would be weeks before she was found. By that time he would long since have escaped to America, or to Africa . . . Everyone was in church. There would be no witnesses . . . Lucian had even begun to extend his hands toward Kasia's throat when he suddenly changed his mind. No, not now . . . It would be better at daybreak . . . Let Elzbieta get to sleep first . . . He stretched out on the wide bed, placing his hat on the floor beneath it. He lay there still, hollow. "I don't even have pangs of conscience," he mused. He was somewhat concerned about wrinkling his suit, but he didn't have the strength to undress. On that evening years ago when the police had searched the hotel on Mylna Street, he had nearly died of fright. Now, all fear had left him. He had even buried his pistol in a snowpile, leaving himself unarmed. Lucian closed his eyes. He neither slept nor remained awake. A black stillness enveloped him. He had a strange sensation as if for the first time in his life he was really resting. Death must be like this. After a while, he began to dream. Wool was being wound around a huge ball by dwarfs. "Who needs so much yarn?" he wondered. "And could it all have come from one spinning? No, I'm dreaming . . ." He heard footsteps. Elzbieta came in. She was barefoot and in a bathrobe. She bent over him, kissed his forehead. "Well, don't be so despondent!"

"I'm not despondent."

"Pray to God, poor man, pray to God!"

"I'll pray to no one."

"Wait, I'll undress you."

Elzbieta knelt, unbuttoned his shoes, drew off his socks. Afterward, she began to take off his trousers, jacket, shirt. She fussed over him as if he were sick. She had difficulty in taking off his collar and he helped her remove the collar pin. Finally she lay down beside him.

27 ♜

Events moved swiftly. Catastrophes, coming one on top of the other, recalled the passage from the Book of Job about the messengers with evil tidings. It started with the bomb thrown at Alexander II, followed by the pogroms in Warsaw! The beatings, the lootings, the smashing of windowpanes and furniture, the tearing of bed linen, lasted three days. Twenty-two Jews lay wounded in the hospital. Oddly enough, many Warsaw Jews had fought back, and twenty-four Poles were wounded. The Jewish community protested. The Polish press published a condemnation of the incident and declared that Ignatiev's agents had suffered a defeat. The Polish nation would not permit itself to be incited against the Jews by the Russian conquerors. Warsaw was not Elisavetgrad or Kiev or Odessa, where large numbers of peasants had taken part in the pogroms. But the shame, the disappointment, and the sobering effect the massacres in Russia had on the modern Jews in that country were felt just as strongly by the enlightened Jews in Poland. A proclamation issued to the Ukranian peasants by the "Ispolnitelny Committee" was reprinted in the sixth issue of the clandestine newspaper, *Narodnaya Wola*, and had found its way to Poland. The proclamation called for further pogroms. The pogroms were also welcomed by the followers of the *Czorny Peredel*. It was known that a Jewish revolutionary was one of the authors of the proclamation. Jochanan, the Marshinov rabbi, was not surprised. Why shouldn't evildoers make pogroms? And what was the difference between Gentile evildoers and Jewish ones? As long as Jews were associated with the wicked, how could they rise above them? Jochanan felt that the last throes preceding the arrival of the Messiah had begun. In the Zohar he had found an allusion to the war between Gog and Magog and the beginning of the End of Days, which indicated they were about due. Reb Menachem Mendel, Ezriel's father, the Rabbi of Krochmalna Street, was attacked by a hooligan. While Tirza Perl, his wife, put a cold compress on Reb Menachem Mendel's hand, he sat down to study a page of the Talmud. Was it something new for Jews to be beaten?

It was the shaven ones, who emulated the Gentiles and spoke their language, who cried out in protest. In Kiev, as the Jews in the synagogue were mourning the victims of the pogrom, a group of Jewish university students entered. One of them, Alenikov, ran up to the reading desk and called out: "We are your brothers! We are Jews like you! We regret we tried to be Russians. The events of the past weeks—the pogroms in Elisavetgrad, in Balta, and here in Kiev—have opened our eyes. We've made a tragic mistake. We are still Jews!"

The Jewish-Russian newspapers, *Russki Yevrey*, *Razsviet*, and *Voschod*, published a series of articles discussing the events. It was obvious that many Jews would have to leave Russia. But where would they go? Factions formed: one in favor of emigration to America; the other, to Palestine. Both sides planned to organize socialist colonies. Both preached that the Jew must stop being a middleman, must settle on the land and be productive. Aaron Lipman and Mirale had a falling out. Aaron had become an adherent of the Palestinian faction. "What could be crazier," he argued, "than sacrificing oneself for the muzhiks who kill Jews? How can Jews be connected with a party that incited massacres in the name of social justice?" In his room, Aaron had a secret library, several scores of volumes of brochures, as well as bound editions of clandestine newspapers. He tore them up and burned them in the stove, spitting into the fire. Stomping his feet, he shouted: "May their names be blotted out! Thou shalt utterly detest it and thou shalt utterly abhor it, for it is a cursed thing."

When he came to Mirale and told her what he had done, she said: "You're no better than a rioter yourself!"

And she pointed the way out of her house.

Aaron's eyes seemed to turn inward.

"What do you want to do? Lubricate the revolutionary machine with Jewish blood?"

He went out, and Mirale slammed the door behind him, bolting and chaining it as if fearing he might change his mind and return. But this had not come as a surprise. For weeks they had been wrangling over the same question. Many other young Jews in Russia had reacted like Aaron, had become frightened by reality, infected by a contagious nationalism. Did they think a revolution could be made with silk gloves? Did they imagine that in the struggle against exploiters Jewish shopkeepers would be spared? Didn't they understand, the cowards, that the pogroms against the Jews were simply the beginning of the general rebellion that was sweeping the peasantry and even the working classes? How did they think absolutism would be smashed? With ringing phrases? How strange! It had been Aaron who had taught her to understand all this. He had brought her books, brochures, had read to her Lassalle's *The Essence of the Constitution*, had explained Jan Mlot's brochure, *From What Does One Live?*, and had familiarized her with the works of Belinski, Pisarev, Herzen, Lavrov. Aaron had guided her as if she had been a child. But now that she had grown spiritually and could stand alone, he had become a renegade. Palestine had become the only salvation of the world for him, a desolate country where some baron or other, an exploiter, was trying to establish colonies for a few confused students. What madness!

"Jews! Jews! Jews! Everything was measured against the Jewish yardstick! But didn't chauvinistic Russians, Poles, and Germans do the same? Didn't all misfortunes stem from the efforts of ethnic groups to pull only for themselves, prepared to sacrifice mankind to their own insignificant interests?" Ezriel had told Mirale that their father had been beaten. She was upset. But how could one acquire a world view from such incidents? And who was he, this father of hers? A zealot, a parasite who produced nothing, ate the peasants' bread, lived off the workers' labor, while he disseminated false ideas and superstitions. "Certainly, it wasn't his fault. He had been raised that way. But how long would the people continue to sleep?"

It was not easy for Mirale to break off with Aaron. How long was it since they had planned to live together? Now it was all over . . . Mirale began to pace back and forth. She glanced out the window at the Pawiak Prison. The windows were not only barred, but wire netting had been placed over them so that neither air nor sunlight could enter. The prisoners confined within were fated to perish from hunger, in damp and darkness. Mirale had not yet actually done anything to help redeem mankind. Aaron had prevented her from becoming involved. He had postponed the final step with words, theories, yeshiva-student philosophies. Now that he was gone, she would act.

11

All the windows in Wallenberg's villa had been smashed by hoodlums. There had been no mention of the incident in the newspapers, the censor having specifically forbidden it. The shutters remained closed for a long time because it had become difficult to obtain glass. Surely it was a disgrace that so distinguished a family (it was connected by marriage with the best families of Poland) should suffer the same indignities as the poor Jews. Wallenberg wasn't very distressed about it. On the contrary, this action against him by a handful of rowdies had finally convinced him to do something about a project that he had had in mind for a long time. For years he had been dreaming of giving Poland a truly liberal newspaper. He had also thought of founding a publishing house, and a magazine dealing with popular science. Wallenberg feared that positivism was beginning to lose its attraction for the Polish people. Instead, many of the radical intellectuals were accepting the Russian theory of social revolution. Polish nationalists, on the other hand, still indulged in hopes of a new patriotic uprising against the Czar. Ideas such as these could only result in further unrest and repression. The Polish press, ostensibly loyal to Russia, was badly edited and ran pedantic articles that were utterly incomprehensible to the ordinary person. Now that there had been a pogrom in Warsaw itself, Wallenberg felt it was high time for the masses to be educated. He purchased *Czas*, a newspaper that had recently gone bankrupt.

Wallenberg decided to call his newspaper *The Courier*. There were enough enlightened persons in the cities of Poland to provide a readership for a paper whose mission it was to combat that new monster known as anti-Semitism. Conservative Poles, too, might in time be numbered among its readers and would learn how their religious fanaticism and isolation endangered them. The paper would also try to stem the growing interest of Jewish intellectuals in anarchism and nihilism. Such a paper would have to be staffed not only by experienced journalists and writers but by those who in addition were thoroughly familiar with the Jewish way of life. Suddenly Wallenberg thought of Calman Jacoby's son-in-law, Dr. Ezriel Babad. Wallenberg had helped liberate that young man from the study house. He had seen Ezriel grow from little more than a dreamer into a practicing physician whose specialty was nervous diseases and mental ailments. Wallenberg knew that Ezriel's office was on Nowolipie Street and that he was on the staff of the Bonifraten Mental Hospital. Ezriel had already published several articles dealing with medicine in the Jewish-Polish magazine *Jutrzenko*. Wallenberg was one of those people who read everything, even articles in medical journals. Ezriel Babad's style was light and his articles had evinced a healthy skepticism rare among Jews. The Jewish writer in Poland, it seemed to Wallenberg, was either a committed atheist or fanatically religious. Neither type was right for *The Courier*.

Wallenberg was celebrating his sixtieth birthday at a party in May, and he sent an invitation to Dr. Ezriel Babad. The Polish Benevolent Society, the Society for the Development of Art, and a number of orphanages and homes for the aged, jointly announced plans for a testimonial dinner in his honor. The Polish newspapers published his photograph, and he received a handsome medal from St. Petersburg. The Governor-General and the Police Commissioner sent him their congratulations. Wallenberg, however, accepted only those honors he dared not refuse. These people praised him to his face, but conspired against him behind his back. The Ministry of Communications often received anonymous letters containing accusations against him. The very same newspapers that now praised him so highly had in the past carried articles in which he had been called a Shylock and a bloodsucker. His life consisted of one crisis after another, all of them the fabrications of envious people. He sometimes thought of himself as a circus performer constantly forced to walk a tightrope over a mass of hissing adders. And now a testimonial dinner. For what reason? No, he did not need the congratulations of his enemies and competitors. His birthday party would be for his family and close friends only.

Wallenberg's invitation to Ezriel included Shaindel, and caused quite a stir in the Babad household. Shaindel said she had no intention of visiting a convert. For many years now, Ezriel had been begging her for his sake to improve her Polish. It wasn't right for a doctor's wife to speak Yiddish or the illiterate Polish of the peasants. Ezriel himself had begun giving her lessons. Somehow or other, she couldn't learn. He realized that it was not inability but obstinacy that made her such a poor student. Other women learned from their children, but Shaindel spoke to hers in Yiddish. As if this were not bad enough, she had begun to neglect her appearance, although she did keep the house clean, if not tidy. It finally got to the point that Ezriel considered her too dowdy to take visiting. At first, she had not been interested in going, but now she accused him of being ashamed of her. It was true. Other doctors' wives had graduated from the gymnasium. Shaindel, when she was in the company of such women, was afraid to open her mouth. Taking her to the Wallenbergs' was out of the question. Actually, Ezriel was somewhat apprehensive about attending the affair himself. He had not learned to dance and, though a physician, was as ignorant of the great world as a yeshiva student. Each time he attended a party, he envied those young men who since childhood had spoken the Gentile tongue, worn modern clothes, and mixed freely with girls. How confidently they strutted about in their stiff shirts and tailcoats. How gracefully they kissed the women's hands. Ezriel could not get used to this way of life. The cheder and the Talmud had made him unworldly.

Whether he wanted to or not, he felt he had to put in an appearance at Wallenberg's party. Dressed in his doctor's smock, Ezriel wandered around his office. He was no longer surprised by anything his patients, both men and women suffering from nervous maladies, told him. He even felt an affinity with the inmates of the asylum where he was a staff doctor. His brain was a little insane asylum of its own. There weren't many patients that morning. His clientele usually came in the afternoon. Ezriel paced the freshly waxed floor with nothing to do for the moment. He had not chosen to be a "giver of enemas" but had entered a branch of medicine that was still almost totally unexplored. What went on there in that piece of white matter whose parts were designated the cerebrum, the cerebellum, and the medulla oblongata? Was free will also one of its constituents? If not, how was it possible to talk about responsibility and duty? When he listened to the voice of his own spirit, it seemed to him that he heard the cry of all the generations. He recognized the voices of his parents and grandparents within himself. At times it seemed to him that he heard even more ancient voices, the idolatrous ones of pagan ancestors. Existence had always meant the same chaos; the ego had always wanted everything for itself—money, fame, sex, knowledge, power, immortality. But this savage was constantly coming up against the resistance of the world with its restrictions and taboos. Was it any wonder that people went mad? How much strain could the mental mechanism stand? Ezriel heard the doorbell and buttoned his smock.

The patient, ushered in by the maid, was a young man who had been married for three months. As he spoke, his eyeglasses became foggy with tears. His wife wanted to leave him, he told Ezriel. The neighbors knew all about it. His mother-in-law and father-in-law kept tormenting him. What was he going to do? He needed a woman, but as soon as he drew close to one he became impotent. Ezriel suggested hydropathy. Oddly enough, the young man's words made Ezriel nervous. Words, he knew, had a strange magnetic power. Once a woman had told him that whenever she sat down to eat, her plate would suddenly fill up with lice. A short time afterward Ezriel was seated at dinner and had the illusion that the same thing was happening to him. Was it any wonder that mental doctors were more susceptible to insanity than other physicians? The fact was that there was a touch of madness in everyone.

The young man paid his forty kopecks and departed. His office hours over, Ezriel sought out Shaindel, whom he found in the kitchen ironing a shirt for him to wear to the party. Shaindel was again pregnant, already in her fifth month. Ezriel's suggestion that she have an abortion had infuriated her. Seeing him enter, Shaindel turned over the ironing to the maid. In her view it was improper for a doctor to enter the kitchen. She and Ezriel went into the living room.

"What was the matter with that young man?"

"The same old story. Nerves."

"My nerves are killing me, too. I'm forever wanting to cry."

"I still think that you ought to go to the Wallenbergs' with me."

"Let's not talk about that again. I don't intend to eat pork in the house of some convert."

"The Wallenbergs don't serve pork."

"I wouldn't go there even if my life depended on it."

For a while, husband and wife remained silent. There was a sadness in her eyes that Ezriel had never noticed before. She seemed terribly afraid of something and at the same time ashamed of her fear and anxious to conceal it. Ezriel shook his head.

"Remember that Simhath Torah when you balanced a melon on your head and said that you were the Empress of Jampol?"

Tears came to Shaindel's eyes. "It's hard for me to believe that it ever happened. It seems like a hundred years ago."

III

Wallenberg had written that the party would be for an intimate group, but that evening, as Ezriel's droshky pulled up before Wallenberg's mansion on New World Boulevard, not far from Hozia Street, a long row of coaches lined the driveway. They were occupied by distinguished couples. A number of the men were in uniform. The horses, their necks drawn up, could barely stand still. The liveried coachmen helped the gentry from the carriages. Over everyone the purple luster of a large sun shone, as it rolled over the orchards, gardens, and streets that trailed off toward Wola. For a moment Ezriel felt that he had seen and experienced all this before. He seemed to recognize the pale blue sky, the formations of the clouds, the odor of horse dung. There was even a dusky familiarity about the strange faces. Ezriel himself did not know why, but the city of Turbin came to his mind, his grandfather, the eve before a holiday. In a specially made dress coat, a top hat, and white gloves, Ezriel now felt shy, as he had in his childhood when on the first night of Passover he went to prayer wearing his new boots, new velvet hat, and new capote, with a fistful of nuts in its pocket. Wasn't he overdressed? Was his tie crooked? Did his clothes seem too new? Everyone spoke French. Although Ezriel had studied French, he had never learned to speak it. There was a hymn sung during Pentecost the words of which stated that if all people were writers, all skies parchment, and all forests pens, it would still be impossible to write out all the secrets contained in the Torah. In a way, this was also true of worldliness. Ezriel was sure that he was committing some blunder, even though he tried his best to conform to all the rules of etiquette that the secular Shulhan Aruk prescribed, and which could never be fathomed by those who were not brought up on it.

In the foyer, Ezriel gave his top hat and cane to the Swiss servant, and the gravity with which the man accepted these articles assured Ezriel that he did not appear inferior to the other guests. At least not yet. He walked into the drawing room with the humility of one who has done everything possible and, because of this, must feel confident . . . Wallenberg and his wife stood at the entrance. Wallenberg looked inquiringly at him as if not recognizing him at first, then suddenly pumped his hand and remarked that he had planned an affair for a handful of people but that it had turned into a ball. Ezriel had not seen him for years. He had grown stout and his sideburns were completely white. Madame Wallenberg looked like an old woman. Her white coiffure shook in sympathy as she told Ezriel how sorry she was that Shaindel had not been able to come. After a while, Madame Malewska approached. She too had grown round and heavy.

Everything happened too quickly and smoothly, as when one is in a state of semi-intoxication. Ezriel was introduced to bemedaled men and to women with deep décolletages. He heard the announcements of high titles, famous names—he

discussed the weather with total strangers. In the huge dining
hall, tables were set for about one hundred and fifty guests.
Silver, porcelain, crystal, flowers, and candles glittered. Ezriel
did not know where to look first: at the amazingly beautiful
ladies smiling down from gold-framed portraits or at the living women who swarmed about—somewhat less comely than
their counterparts on canvas, but each with her upswept hair,
her jewelry, her special expression. This was not a house
party, but a première at the opera, an exhibition at the
Zachęta. Here, at a converted Jew's mansion, the elite of Warsaw society had assembled. The Governor-General had suddenly come down with the grippe, but the Chief of Police was
there, the dean of the Warsaw University, and numerous
other dignitaries, each with his epaulets, stripes, and decorations. Russian was heard, as well as Polish, French, and even
English, which had lately become the fashion. Lackeys sped
about noiselessly, showing the guests to their seats. Ezriel sat
at the foot of a long table, where apparently the younger
guests had been placed. He was joined by a boyish-looking
young man whose pointed mustache seemed pasted on, and by
two girls who appeared to be twins. Madame Malewska came
over and introduced Ezriel to his neighbors, announcing
names that he forgot as soon as he heard them. He realized
that he was the only Jew at his table. A young woman with a
sharp nose said to him: "Isn't the dining room divine?"

"Yes, magnificent."

"Everything has been rebuilt, enlarged. Have you noticed
the new painting by Matejko?"

"Matejko? Where?"

"There."

And she pointed her finger toward the other end of the
room.

"I prefer Brandt to Matejko—" a young man remarked.

"I'd give them both up for Zmurka . . ."

A discussion on painting began. For a while Ezriel thought
he would be left sitting there, excluded from the conversation.

From his limited experience, he knew how painful this could be and how long such a meal could seem. He began to search for a subject that could, at least for a while, link him to these people. Should he ask the young man a question? Should he attempt to discuss art? Should he wait until someone spoke to him? He had arrived in a more or less confident mood, but now he was one step from despair. The others apparently noticed what he was enduring, and their eyes seemed to avoid him. There ensued the kind of mysterious anathema, cast by those who are speaking, upon someone who had not joined in at the beginning. Well, I'd better be quiet. I won't burden anyone, Ezriel decided. As if his decision had been secretly revealed to the others, two of them addressed him simultaneously. One of the twin sisters asked him to pass the salt shaker. At the same time, a young man remarked casually: "We were introduced, but I did not get your name. My name is Gewalewicz. Julian Gewalewicz."

"I'm honored, my name is Babad."

Ezriel quickly realized that it wasn't polite to give only his surname, but he could not, in this place, utter two such Jewish names as Ezriel Babad. Numerous times he had spoken, half in jest, of changing his first name to make it sound more Polish, but the name Ezriel did not readily lend itself to alteration. It was a stubborn name that would not allow itself to be assimilated. The young man inquired whether Ezriel was a visitor to Warsaw.

Ezriel realized that he could not conceal the truth.

"I was born in Turbin, in the province of Lublin. My father was the rabbi there. I am in medical practice here on Nowolipie Street."

For a moment there was silence. Ezriel's simple words had ended all tension. Ease replaced it, and the kind of intimacy that only truth can produce.

"Where is Turbin? Near what city?"

A conversation began about the Lublin region, about its peasantry, gentry, Jewry. It seemed that the twins had an aunt

near Tomashow and that the mustached young man also had
relatives in that section. A squire sitting nearby, who had been
listening, also joined the conversation. He had some knowledge of Jewish affairs and asked Ezriel if he had studied in a
yeshiva.

"Not actually in a yeshiva, but I did study the Talmud."

"The Talmud?"

Everyone grew curious. In what language is the Talmud
written? Hebrew? Chaldean? What is Chaldean? Does anyone speak it? Is it written from the right to the left? And
what, for example, is written in the Talmud? Ezriel answered
everyone. He became so deeply involved in conversation that
he was not quite aware of having finished his meal. The toasts
began. Prelates, generals, editors, the Russian chief of police,
the president of a scientific society—all joined in toasting the
great intelligence and benevolence of their host. The company
shouted "Hurrah!" and "Vivat!" and drank his health. Here
and there at the table someone made a sarcastic remark. It was
clear to everyone that all the praise and devotion proffered
this converted Jew had one basis—money.

IV

When the dancing started in the drawing room, Ezriel's shyness returned. But the rich feast, the wine, and the entertaining experience at the table had left him cheerful and somewhat
made up for the fact that he wasn't dancing. He wasn't the
only one. There were other guests who stood near the wall
watching the couples. Some gathered in side rooms. Men conversed and smoked cigars. In a corner, an elderly woman fixed
a young girl's gown that had apparently come loose at the
waist. As the older woman fussed, the young one tapped her
foot in pique. Her face was remarkably red. Ezriel understood
the cause of her annoyance. She was missing a dance she had
anticipated. Just as he was, everyone was taking this affair
much more seriously than was reasonable. Despite the music,

the drumming, the polkas and mazurkas, the fashionable clothes, the costly jewelry—there was still the tedium that is always present when strangers without common purpose assemble, each with his own pride, ambition, and humility. There really wasn't anyone to appreciate all the elaborate coiffures, all the toil that the tailors, hairdressers, and corsetières had put into these toilettes. People kept introducing one another, and the men never stopped touching feminine hands with their beards and mustaches. Ezriel remained standing for a while before a painting: hunters, pointers, snow-covered fields, a distant forest. A deer had been shot and a trickle of blood stained the snow. All had been painted with expert knowledge of the subject, yet the picture did not hold Ezriel's attention.

"Why am I so impatient?" Ezriel wondered. "I used to stare for hours on end at the awkward illustrations in my mother's *Haggada* . . ." Suddenly someone poked him in the side with a familiarity that startled him for a second. He turned and saw Wallenberg, and a lady of about thirty, a brunette, whose hair was combed simply into a chignon. She was dressed differently from the others. Her gown, barely ornamented, seemed to have been made by an ordinary seamstress. She was smiling the smile of a Jewess who encounters a compatriot among Gentiles. She had heavy eyebrows and black eyes, and the kind of attractive down often seen on the upper lip of a dark-complexioned woman.

Wallenberg said: "I thought you were dancing, and I find you admiring my pictures. Madame Bielikov, this is the young man I've been telling you about, Dr. Babad, a neurologist. Madame Bielikov comes from your home town. You're from Vilna, aren't you?"

"I from Vilna? God forbid! I come from the Lublin province."

"Oh, yes, what am I taking about? You are, of course, Calman Jacoby's son-in-law. Madame Bielikov comes from Lithuania. Her husband was a neighbor of mine. That is, we were neighbors for a while in Druskenik, near the Nieman River. I owned a villa there. Ah, how time flies! There is something I'd like to talk to you about, but I don't know when. Could you come to my office perhaps? What do you do on Saturdays?"

"The same as the rest of the week."

"And you are a rabbi's son! How about this Saturday at two?"

"Certainly."

"Well, that's settled. I'll be expecting you on Saturday. I must go now. Talk to each other. Madame Bielikov understands Yiddish."

After Wallenberg left, they both stood there for a while, not knowing what to say. Finally Ezriel remarked: "His hair has turned completely white."

"Yes, one grows older, not younger," Madame Bielikov observed in Polish, but with a Russian accent. "When we lived in Druskenik, he still had black hair. Do you practice in Warsaw?"

"Yes."

"My husband was a doctor, an army doctor." And the woman grew silent.

"I'd never want that kind of career," Ezriel said, after an overlong pause.

"Why not?"

"I'm not fond of barracks."

"Oh, my husband had nothing to do with the barracks. He was connected with a military hospital. Sometimes that is more convenient than a private practice."

"Do you live here in Warsaw?"

"Yes, on Zielna Street, not far from Prozna Street."

"Is that near Kreditowa Street?"

"Kreditowa Street is on the other side of Marshalkowsky Boulevard."

"Yes, of course. I know a Dr. Zawacki who lives there."

"I know Dr. Zawacki."

"I come from the village of Jampol. Dr. Zawacki is married to the daughter of the local squire."

"Yes, I know. Madame Malewska told me about you and about the Countess—how is she related to you, is she a cousin?"

"My sister-in-law. She and Madame Zawacki are sisters-in-law."

"Madame Malewska told me all about it. Now I understand. So you're the one! Madame Malewska is a friend of mine. We used to see each other more often. Lately she's been busy, and I've been occupied with my children. My husband is dead."

"I see."

"Well, Warsaw is a small town. What's become of your sister-in-law?"

"She is sick and miserable."

"Unhappily, one hears of such things. People lose themselves and go to pieces. Where is she?"

"Some place in Otwock. For a while she was in a sanatorium. Now she's found a place of her own."

"Consumption?"

"Yes."

"And her husband—what's his name? Is he still in prison?"

"Lucian? Yes, but he'll soon be out."

"I've heard of all sorts of crazy things that seemed to be sheer madness. Apparently the Wallenbergs did everything they could for him."

"Yes, they did."

"There are people who must hurt themselves. It's hard to understand why they do it. Would you care to sit down?"

v

They sat on a chaise longue and talked. Her parents were Jewish. Her father had taught school and as a sideline had written petitions to the Russian authorities. She, Leah, or Olga, had been orphaned early and had gone to live with a wealthy aunt in Vilna. There she met her late husband, Andrey, who had been studying in St. Petersburg. His father had been a ladies' tailor, a pious Jew, but he had adopted the Greek Orthodox faith. When Olga married him, she had also "converted a little." Madame Bielikov had been speaking Polish, but the last words were said in Lithuanian Yiddish. She smiled sadly as she said them. Well, what was the difference? There was no God anyhow. If there were a God, so many tragedies would not occur. She and Andrey had been happy. One day he had gone to bathe in a tiny stream where one could scarcely wet one's knees, and had been found drowned. How had it happened? Perhaps he'd suffered a heart attack. But he had never complained about his heart. Suicide? Why should he have committed suicide? He had led a happy life. Only one thing was peculiar. He had been discussing death the day before. What had he said? That if he were to die, he was not to be wept over, for a dead person was like one who had never been born. He had said this half jokingly.

When had it happened? Almost two years ago. How was she getting along? They had saved up a little money and she received a small pension from the government. It was, to be truthful, difficult. Wallenberg had offered help, but she had refused. Andrey would not have wanted it. He had been a proud person. The Petersburg University had published his dissertations. He had left an extensive library in four languages. Andrey had not only been interested in medicine. He had been an amateur astronomer. She still had a small telescope somewhere about. In Druskenik he would sit up nights at a time, observing the stars.

At first, Ezriel asked the questions. Then her turn came. She had still not quite figured out his connection with Dr. Zawacki. His sister-in-law was also Felicia's sister-in-law. Lucian was his brother-in-law. "How in the world does a person make such a mess of himself?" Madame Bielikov asked.

"The human brain is the greatest enigma of the cosmos—"

Madame Bielikov looked at him with surprise.

"Odd, those were Andrey's very words."

They rose and walked into the salon. She said: "Of course you do not know how to dance."

"No."

"There could be no doubt about that with a yeshiva student."

"Do you dance, madame?"

"Not any more."

Madame Bielikov had to leave early. She had a maid, but the girl was inexperienced, having just come from the village. Madame Bielikov's boy, Kolia, was only four years old. He woke up at night and cried and only his mother could calm him. Ezriel offered to escort her home.

"You needn't ruin your evening because of me."

"I have no reason to stay."

They left without saying goodbye, according to the English custom. It was difficult to find a droshky in this neighborhood. They strolled diagonally across New World Boulevard. The night was warm, somewhat humid, and filled with vernal odors. There were gardens and orchards nearby. Crickets chirped as if in the country. Birds awoke, twittering. The flickering gas lights made the darkness seem denser. Every now and again, a coach or wagon passed by. Lightning, flashing at the edge of the sky, foretold hot weather. Between the trees and bushes, villas could be glimpsed, mansions with pillars, garrets, carvings, fountains. Shadows moved behind the draperies. Occasionally, a dog barked. The sidewalk was uneven, and Madame Bielikov nearly fell. Ezriel took her arm.

"A strange night," Madame Bielikov remarked.

"All nights are strange."

"Yes, you are right. And all life is incomprehensible."

After a while, they got a droshky. It was not yet midnight, but Warsaw was already asleep. The streets were empty except for a few late pedestrians and streetwalkers. The droshky turned into Berg Street and passed Kreditowa Street. At the intersection of Marshalkowsky Boulevard and Prozna Street the driver went into Zielna Street. Madame Bielikov pointed out a two-storied building with balconies, and reached for her pocketbook.

"No, madame, God forbid!"

"Why should you pay for me?"

"Just because."

"How can I thank you? Well, it was really very pleasant. In my situation it's burdensome to attend a ball. How nice that we met!"

"I wouldn't have known what to do with myself either."

"Someone would have taken pity on you . . ."

Ezriel helped Madame Bielikov out of the droshky. He stood with her at the gate, waiting for the janitor to open it. She smiled at him, inquisitively, as if to say: "Is this all?" She exuded a secretive familiarity. The janitor's footsteps could be heard. Madame Bielikov extended her hand to Ezriel. Her glove was warm. She squeezed his hand slightly.

"Good night. My thanks again."

"Good night."

The gate closed. He did not hear her steps immediately, as if she too were lingering on the other side. Only then did it occur to him that he might have asked to see her husband's medical library . . .

VI

The doctors who worked at the Free Clinic for the Poor generally dropped in at their lounge before leaving for home. Most of the young ones were involved in social-service activities and had founded an association of their own called "Health," which issued pamphlets in both Polish and Yiddish. The subject they talked about was always the same—the filthiness in which the poor Polish Jews were forced to live. A doctor who was on the staff of the Jewish Hospital on Pokorna Street described the terrible conditions there. Mice ran through the corridors; there were no decent toilet facilities for the patients; the Jewish Society for the Sick brought preposterous foods for the invalids, heavy Sabbath puddings, onions fried in chicken fat. Another doctor spoke of the new Jewish hospital that was to be built and of the great need for Jewish nurses. Ezriel thought of the women who had brought their lice-infested undergarments to his father, the rabbi, in cases of irregular menstruation, to avoid the sin of cohabiting while unclean. An elderly doctor who specialized in diseases of the lungs said, "We're still knee deep in the Asian mire."

"But look what advances have been made by the Jews of Western Europe."

"They don't have the Hassidim to contend with."

Ezriel was about to leave. Suddenly the porter who made tea and swept up handed him a letter in a blue envelope. Ezriel's heart skipped a beat. The letter was from Madame Bielikov.

> Honorable Dr. Babad:
> Perhaps you remember me? We met at the ball at Pan Wallenberg's. I told you then that my boy, Kolia, awakes at night in fear. I have been told that he suffers from Pavor nocturnus. Since neurology is your speciality, I would consider it a privilege if you would consent to examine the child. Kolia and I are almost always home and we will be happy to see you at your convenience. You must certainly not go to any special trouble. Although we only met briefly, I feel as if I have known you for a long time. I hope you have not forgotten me entirely. If I am too bold, do not take offense.
> With my esteem and my best wishes,
> Olga Bielikov

Ezriel read the letter again and again. It emanated warmth —in the address on the envelope (E.P., E.P.—Esteemed *Pan*, repeated twice, the most formal salutation), in the penmanship, the uneven margins, even in the blot on the paper. It seemed to Ezriel that between the lines he could detect the woman's proud hesitation before she had sent it. Only the day before, he had been reading about telepathy. Wasn't this an example of telepathy? He had thought about her and his thoughts had forced her to write to him. He was not the only neurologist in Warsaw. Ezriel still had a little time and he decided to read up in the medical encyclopedia on the subject of Pavor nocturnus. "Should I bring flowers?" he asked himself. He read, without really knowing what he was reading. "Is it possible that I have fallen in love with this woman? It would kill Shaindel . . ." His heart pounded and the letters danced before his eyes. "Should I go there today? Should I wait? What suit should I wear?" Suddenly his weariness left him and he was filled with anticipation. Everything had changed— the desk, the bookshelf, the courtyard, the formations of the clouds. What innumerable combinations of vapor and light there were! How inadequately words described it! What, for example, was now going on in his brain? If only one could see all the physical and chemical changes! Nerves trembled, cells moved, substances blended. The few words that Madame Bielikov had written had started a turmoil in his marrow, blood, stomach, sex organs. Not only the brain, but every part of the human body reacted to symbols.

He started toward his house. He had already missed lunch and had more patients to see in the afternoon. Ezriel had often envied the doctors with more tangible specialties than his—the internists, venereologists, dermatologists, gynecologists. They more or less knew what they were about. He had entered a domain where almost nothing was known.

VII

Ezriel had brought flowers for the mother and a box of chocolates for the children. Natasha, the older girl, curtsied gracefully. Kolia aped her in childish fashion. Jadzia, the maid, hurried off to place the bouquet in a vase. The country girl with

her flaxen hair and plump cheeks flushed with delight at the
sight of a male visitor. It was a warm evening outside, but
indoors there was a springlike coolness. A mild breeze blew in
through windows that opened on densely leaved trees. Ezriel
compared this apartment with his own. Here the parquet floor
gleamed. Everything was in its place. Each article had been
polished, scrubbed. He could not get Shaindel to keep their
rooms tidy. There was always some disorder.

Ezriel examined Kolia. Seating him on a bench, he tapped
him below the knee, looked into the boy's eyes, listened to his
heart, his lungs. Organically, the boy was sound. The eight-
year-old Natasha was already studying the piano, and her
mother asked her to play for the doctor. Then Jadzia led the
two children off to bed. The brother and sister bowed, said
good night, and thanked him for the chocolates. Ezriel sat on a
chair, Madame Bielikov on a sofa. The floor lamp with its
green shade cast a diffused light. How erect she held herself!
How cleverly and tactfully she spoke! How discreet was her
smile! In this room, European culture was not a phrase but an
actuality. Ezriel explained to Madame Bielikov that Pavor nocturnus was a form of nervousness, one of those functional disturbances the origin of which is not known. Nevertheless, he
asked whether there was any insanity, epilepsy, or other nervous disorders in the family.

"Andrey was a nervous person," Madame Bielikov said
thoughtfully.

"Oh."

"I myself have my moods."

"Who doesn't?"

"There are some people for whom everything goes
smoothly—both internally and externally."

The maid brought tea, cookies, fruit. Afterward, she asked
her mistress for permission to take a walk. "For as long as you
like," Madame Bielikov replied.

"Good night, Doctor sir."

They drank tea and conversed with the ease of old acquaintances. She inquired about his practice. He told her about the insane at the Bonifraten Hospital: the quiet ones who dreamed while awake, and the maniacs who had to be confined to strait jackets; the melancholics steeped in perpetual gloom; the paranoics who convinced themselves that they had inherited great wealth, had buried treasure hoards, and were connected with the royal court. There were a fantastic number of Messiahs among the Jewish patients. Women were more susceptible to erotic insanity than men. Insanity was really a disease of the brain, but more than any other affliction it was linked to social factors, culture, and religion. Ezriel remarked that, in the broad sense, knowledge of the brain included all the sciences, all the arts, all thoughts and feelings. We study the psyche even when we are studying Latin or tailoring.

Madame Bielikov smiled. "Would you call a tailor a psychologist?"

"There is a philosopher who believes that all things are ideas. As pure logic, this premise is more consistent than all the other philosophic theories."

"Andrey used to toy with such thoughts. For a while he attended courses of the philosophy faculty, in Russia and in Germany."

"Have you been abroad?"

"No. When we met, he had already completed his studies. We always planned a trip to Switzerland, to France, to England, but we never went. The children—"

"I, too, would like to see what's going on on the other side of the border."

"You are still young. You'll see it. Andrey always used to speak of the Alps."

"I've never seen a mountain of any sort. Neither a mountain nor the sea."

"Nor I . . ."

There was a balcony in the apartment. Madame Bielikov suggested that they go out on it. There were two chairs. Ezriel and Olga Bielikov sat in the darkness, conversing. The sky was filled with stars. Stillness reigned in the street. Ezriel could not quite make out Olga's face. He only heard her voice. She discussed her home, her parents, the gymnasium. She had always been a serious person. Other girls liked sunny days, but she had enjoyed the rain. She had preferred to bury herself in books and above all to daydream. Especially after her parents had died. She used to argue with her mother as if she were still alive. She had literally seen her a few times. How was this possible? She spoke of her relatives. Somewhere in Bialystok she still had an uncle, her father's brother. There were some cousins, too. She remarked: "When I became converted, I naturally estranged myself from everyone. They must have cursed me."

"Do the children know about their Jewish ancestry?"

"Yes, they know. You can't keep anything from them."

"Do you have friends here in Warsaw?"

"Friends? Not really. I still don't know what I'm doing in this city. I came here by chance after Andrey's death, and somehow I remained. Actually, Warsaw is alien to me. Yes, the Wallenbergs—they're really my only connection."

"They're very important here."

"I know. But I wouldn't exploit a friendship. Actually, I hesitated to write to you concerning Kolia—"

And Madame Bielikov suddenly stopped speaking. Ezriel summoned up courage. "If you hadn't written, madame, *I* might have written—"

"Why do you say that?"

"Oh, I don't know. I've been thinking about you. Sometimes a casual acquaintance makes an impression—"

"Yes, of course. I am not naturally bold, but I think that you still retain a touch of the yeshiva student."

"I'm afraid so."

"Actually it's appealing. Andrey was a worldly man. But a modest one as well. An odd mixture of boldness and shyness. He could tell a general the truth without blinking. He said things that could get one banished to Siberia. But at the same time he was as timid as a schoolboy. Natasha is exactly like him. Kolia is more like me—"

"Both are unusually handsome children."

"Thank you."

"And the stars in the heavens perform their own function. They sparkle and blink."

"Yes, the stars. I believe I've told you that Andrey was an amateur astronomer."

"Yes."

"He would spend entire nights at it. I sometimes looked through the telescope, too, at the Milky Way and other things up there. What is the meaning of it all?"

"We know nothing."

"If you come again, I'll take out the telescope. It's packed away somewhere. It's a small one, but one can see a great deal through it. The moon is particularly interesting . . . What's your wife like?"

"A good woman. A devoted mother."

"Well, how much more can you ask? Most men are satisfied with that. Besides being husband and wife, Andrey and I were like two comrades. We always had something to talk about. But so much happiness is not allowed by the powers on high."

VIII

Was it on his third or fourth visit? He took her in his arms and kissed her. She started but did not pull away. They were standing on the balcony. He had been thinking about it constantly, but it seemed to happen of itself. In the dusk, she clasped his wrists.

"No, don't!" she whispered.

"Why not?" he asked.

"It's too soon. I take these things seriously . . . The time hasn't come yet."

And her voice seemed to break.

Had he offended her? Other young men had had love affairs, but he was a novice in such matters. Looking at the sky he wondered: "What place do all these petty complications occupy in the universe?" He listened to the beating of his own heart. It was as quiet here, on Zielna Street, as in a country meadow. There was an incessant rustling which might have come from crickets, the wind, or a ringing in the depths of the ears. It seemed to Ezriel that the summer night, so full of things, was waiting too, absorbed in its own kind of cosmic tension. He was about to apologize to Olga, but within the shadows of her face he saw her black eyes gleaming with a mixture of timidity and joy. She came closer to him.

"Funny—before my husband's tragedy," she said, "I thought I would be the one to die first. I don't know why. I was young and healthy. I just had a premonition. Ever since I was a child I've always been uneasy when things went smoothly. I would be overcome by an expectation of disaster. But that anything should happen to him never occurred to me. You surely don't believe in superstitions."

"I no longer know what to believe in."

"Andrey was a rational man. Perfectly so. Still, sometimes he'd say things that astonished me. I myself am somewhat superstitious. I have always been a fatalist. 'Simple luck,' as they say in Yiddish, guides a man. A mysterious hand. But why should God devote himself to each person individually?"

"If there is a God, He is capable of that, too."

"What do you think of spiritualism? There's a big stir about it in Warsaw right now."

"I don't believe in it."

"Neither do I, but—a woman talked me into it. She said she could put me in contact with him. The very thought of it struck me as a desecration. If he were able to reach me, he would have found a way to give me some sign. How many nights I have lain awake and prayed. Ah, I can't explain it to you. At first he was always absent from my dreams. Lately I've begun to dream about him."

"What do you dream?"

"I don't know. I can't remember. I don't feel that he is dead —still, somehow I do. It seems rather that he is gravely ill. Like a person who has suffered a stroke. He is in great peril, and because of that, he's especially dear to me. What are dreams?"

"No one knows."

"What is known? What is the purpose of all this? I lost my father very early and I used to dream of him every night. Afterward, when Mother died, Father was thrust into the background and Mother replaced him, as if there were not room for both of them in my dreams. Isn't that odd? Now Andrey comes every night. He is so pale, listless, sad. It is indescribable. As if he's ashamed of what happened to him."

"What does he say?"

"I can't remember. Nothing important. When I wake up, I wonder why he has such trivial things on his mind. Later, I forget it all. Why are dreams so quickly forgotten?"

Suddenly there was a childish screaming and weeping from the bedroom. Madame Bielikov caught hold of Ezriel's hand. Kolia had awakened and was crying loudly. He was having an attack of Pavor nocturnus. Olga began to pull Ezriel after her and he followed her to the children's room. Standing beside the bed, he listened as she calmed Kolia. "What is it? Darling, sweetheart, my little angel! Oh, he is completely drenched in sweat!" She pressed her lips to Kolia's face, hugging him and comforting him in the words of a mother. Natasha's breathing could be heard from the other bed. Finally, Kolia fell asleep again. After his mother had straightened his pillow and blanket, she tiptoed out of the room, followed by Ezriel, who took her arm. They stood on the threshold between the bedroom and the dimly lit living room. Ezriel felt the warmth of her trembling body.

"Is it really Pavor nocturnus?"

"Yes, a mild form."

"There can't be anything between us—" she said in a

muffled voice. "You have a wife . . . It just doesn't make sense . . . What would become of us?"

"Logically, you're right."

"How can one not be logical?"

They walked into the living room. The clock pointed to half past eleven.

"Well, I'd better be going."

She led him into the hall. She closed the door to the living room and once more they were in darkness. They stood silently, tense, with a sense of anticipation, an inner tautness. They seemed to be listening to forces that were about to decide their fate. He started to reach for his hat but did not take it. As if with a light of their own, Olga's eyes glittered in the dark.

"Can't we just be friends?" she asked.

"Yes, of course."

"I scarcely dare say this, but you're so much like him—the same sort of temperament . . . his kind of pride . . . It seems unbelievable . . ."

He embraced her and they kissed—long, silently, with the desperation of those who can no longer resist their passion.

I X

Ezriel sat in a droshky on his way home. He was not so much happy as astounded at what had happened. For years he had read about love. Now he was having an affair of his own, a real affair, full of secrecy, and danger. After all, his marriage to Shaindel had been a prearranged match. She had grown prematurely stout and frigid. Warsaw was asleep. Ezriel leaned against the side of the droshky, inhaling the cool air. His childlike pleasure in being pulled along by a horse was mixed with the adult satisfaction of having succeeded with the opposite sex. Fortune had been good to him. He had finally involved himself in a risk-laden game with secret encounters, hidden pleasures. Mundane boredom suddenly gave way to a life full of expectation, as in a novel, a play . . . But what should he tell Shaindel? Where had he been? How long would he be able to deceive her? She was pregnant, in her late months. Divorce her? He could never do that. He had Shaindel to thank for everything. Even his having been invited to Wallenberg's was due to his being Calman Jacoby's son-in-law. Foolish ideas ran through his mind. "I am a doctor, I am carrying on an affair. What could be more European than that? I've gone pretty far since Jampol." He fell into a blissful little reverie. Startled, he awoke from his daydream. He had imagined that Shaindel had died in childbirth and that he had married Olga. They had left the country and settled in St. Petersburg on Nevski Prospect . . . He shook himself, mumbling, "God forbid! May she live to be one hundred and twenty!" Involuntarily, he began to pray to God: "Lord of the Universe, protect her, make sure that she be delivered safely! I vow to contribute eighteen rubles . . ." Again he caught himself, realizing that he was praying. "What's wrong with me? I have all the symptoms of a neurasthenic!" The horse stopped. "How wonderful animals are, compared to humans! They have everything—humility, serenity, faith, inner detachment . . ."

For a long time he tugged at the gate bell. The night was warm, but he felt cool. He was a non-sleeper in a city sunk in slumber—a debaucher returning after a night's revelry . . . "What shall I tell her?" He could not think of an explanation. If the world were truly nothing but atoms and combinations of atoms, how could there be anything like sin? The same molecules of water into which a ship once sank might today rescue a child dying of thirst. How could the endless transmigrations of matter be kept track of unless there existed a universal ledger of accounts . . . A dog began to bark. The janitor came to open the gate. He was in his underwear. Ezriel gave him twenty groschen and he took the tip without saying thanks.

Ezriel climbed the stairs. How dark it was! His childish fear of the dark had never quite been uprooted. "What would I do if a demon grasped me?" He visualized a dark being, tall as if on stilts, soft as cobwebs, with elf locks, goose legs. Ezriel smiled to himself. "How difficult it is to rid oneself of superstition. It possessed an atavistic power; though, according to Weismann, acquired characteristics could not be inherited. Well, that hadn't been definitely established. And why couldn't they both be correct, Lamarck and Darwin?" Ezriel ran up the last few steps, as when a boy in Lublin he had returned from some night errand. He knocked hastily and soon heard Shaindel's footsteps. Evidently she had not yet been asleep. She had on a nightgown and her abdomen protruded. Her hair was disheveled, her face sallow.

"Where were you? Woe is me! What I feared should not even befall my enemies!"

"I was with a patient."

"What sort of patient?"

Ezriel entered the apartment.

"A child. He's suffering from Pavor nocturnus. He wakes up in the middle of the night in fear. It's a disease."

"Did you sit there waiting for him to wake up?"

"That's the only way one can make a diagnosis."

"And what would you have done if he had awakened two hours later?"

"I am a doctor, not a shoemaker," Ezriel said, amazed at how easy it was for him to lie. Nor was it actually a lie. Shaindel stood looking at him in astonishment.

"Why didn't you tell me that you would be so late? You know how I worry."

"I decided to go there at the last minute. This is the first time I've had such a case."

"Who is it? Where does the family live?"

"On Zielna Street."

"Don't they have other doctors there?"

"Wallenberg referred them to me."

"Are they young people?"

"They have two children, a girl of eight and a boy of four. Converts."

"Converts? A person goes off and disappears—" Shaindel began to speak forgivingly. She realized that Ezriel was telling the truth and she was overcome with remorse. She had doubted him and without reason, poor man. She was much too jealous, always filled with the worst suspicions. He worked hard, days and even nights. "Oh, I couldn't live without him. If, God forbid, he ever deceives me, I'd kill myself!"

She said: "You must be hungry."

"Hungry? No."

"Did they at least give you a glass of tea?"

"They are fine people."

"What does the husband do?"

"He is an army doctor."

"A doctor himself? If that's so, you don't even get paid."

"It's an extremely interesting case. When you need an accoucheur, it'll be free too."

"Well, it's your business. Most doctors rake in money, and you only deal with madness and nonsense. Waking up like that is sometimes caused by the child holding its hand over its heart . . . Is the woman good-looking?"

"A devoted mother."

"Is there another kind? I thought you'd become disgusted with me and run off with someone else," Shaindel said, despite herself.

"You silly woman!"

"I get such crazy ideas! On the other hand, what am *I?* A frump. I cause you nothing but trouble. Often you seem like a saint to me. You are a doctor and I am a drudge. You can't even show me off to your friends."

"Don't talk such nonsense. You are my wife and I love you. You're the mother of my children. If not for you, I wouldn't be a doctor."

"Well, that's enough flattery for tonight."

28 ⛪

I

During vacation, Clara's children, Sasha and Felusia, went to Jampol to visit their grandfather Daniel Kaminer, who now had three children by Celina. Clara was still annoyed with her father for not having kept his promise to turn over half of his property to her before marrying Celina. But Daniel Kaminer was anxious to see his grandchildren, who in any case could not stay in the city during the summer. Then, too, Calman had insisted before divorcing Clara that their son be permitted to spend a few weeks each year with him. Calman paid fifty rubles a month for Sasha's support. It had also been agreed that Clara would engage a Hebrew teacher for Sasha, keep the boy out of school on Saturday, and maintain a kosher kitchen. Although Clara neglected to fulfill the other terms of this agreement, she feared that if Sasha did not visit his father, Calman would stop sending her money. Clara gave Sasha a prayer book that he had received for his bar mitzvah to take along on the trip, as well as a fringed garment, which he was to put on before meeting his father. Since the divorce, Calman and Daniel Kaminer no longer spoke to each other. It was now Mayer Joel who managed Calman's property and discussed whatever business was necessary with Kaminer.

Clara was distressed to see the children leave. On his summer visits, Sasha was showered with presents by his father.

Calman attempted to study the Pentateuch and Mishnah with him, let the boy ride horseback, and indulged all his whims. There was a constant struggle between Calman and Daniel Kaminer for Sasha's favor. Calman would not even look at Felusia, although allegedly she was his daughter. The girl sensed that there was something wrong and was jealous of her brother. She often announced that she had two fathers, Papa Jocoby and Papa Zipkin. At times she insisted that she was not her mother's child but had been left in a sack by a gypsy. Clara was unable to calm the child's fears. To quiet her own feelings, Clara bought her daughter expensive dolls, and dresses, and pampered her with sweets. Sending Sasha and Felusia to Jampol was no simple matter for Clara.

Nevertheless, the children needed fresh air, and Clara time for herself. Their governess Louisa accompanied her charges. Clara was determined that this summer she would at last do something she had been planning to do for a long time. Zipkin's in-laws were summering in Carlsbad. Sabina was suffering from a stomach ailment that had been diagnosed by some doctors as gallstones, and her parents wanted her to go along with them. Sabina had refused to go without Alexander. She pointed out that while she was taking the cure in Carlsbad, Alexander would be spending his time with Clara. Rosa, who was forever urging her daughter to get a divorce, argued that here was the opportunity to get rid of that charlatan. Rosa assured her daughter that in Carlsbad she would meet really interesting men. Sabina was still young. She would fall in love with someone worthy of her. Her dowry had remained in her name and was still on deposit at the bank. A divorce would free her from her suffering.

Sabina, however, did not want a divorce, and her father too was opposed to ending the marriage. The couple had a child, a darling boy, Kubuś, and Zipkin was in charge of the firm's bookkeeping and accounting. Though he wasn't much of a businessman, at least he was honest. Zdzislaw, now married to a girl from Lodz, wanted everything for himself, and Alexander sided with his father-in-law. Jacob Danzinger didn't dare go off to Carlsbad and leave everything in Zdzislaw's hands. Zdzislaw was unstable, a speculator; his wife, avaricious; and his father-in-law, a bankrupt ne'er-do-well. Alexander, although he did have faults, was dependable.

Finally, Jacob Danzinger had his way. What was there to worry about? To begin with, Jacob didn't believe that there was anything between Alexander and Clara. Anyway, if a man occasionally made a fool of himself, it was no tragedy. What did all the salesmen and business agents do to amuse themselves on the long trips they took into the heart of Russia? One couldn't keep too close a watch on a man these days. Alexander was Sabina's husband. They had been married according to the laws of Israel as laid down by Moses. Alexander was the father of Sabina's child. Why suffer because of a lot of nonsense?

This family dispute had been going on since Pentecost, with Sabina constantly changing her mind as to what she should do. One moment she was ready to accompany her family to Carlsbad, the next moment she was not. She agreed to a divorce and then accused her mother of trying to break up her marriage. Alexander pretended that he didn't know what was going on but privately hoped that he would be free of Sabina for a few months. She had grown progressively surlier and more disagreeable, was cold, and imagined she had all kinds of outlandish diseases. Of late, for example, she had become worried about her breathing and was constantly visiting doctors to have her lungs examined. Whenever Zipkin was with Clara, he assured her that Sabina would be away for the summer, and Clara and he would be free to enjoy themselves.

At the last moment (she already had her passport) Sabina changed her mind. Instead of going to Carlsbad with her parents, she leased a villa in Polanka, one station away from Warsaw. Her reason was obvious to Clara. The village was so close to Warsaw that Zipkin need not stay overnight when he went to the city. There were frequent trains to the suburb all year, and in summertime their number was even increased. Clara felt that Sabina had played a trick on her and decided to pay back in kind.

She sent a messenger to Zipkin's office with a letter in which she wrote that after a sleepless night she had decided that the time had come for Alexander to make up his mind. It was either Clara or his wife, but not both. She was tired of deceit. She'd suffered enough insults. Actually, she didn't even have the status of a mistress. If Zipkin decided to remain with his wife, Clara's heart and her door would be closed to him for good. She had signed her name in blood, an act which even she recognized as vulgar.

II

Clara had instructed the messenger to deliver the letter and not wait for a reply. Zipkin opened it immediately, although when he received it there were some customers in his office. He paled, recovering quickly. "It was bound to happen sooner or later," he thought. "Perhaps it's better this way." As long as he was occupied with business matters, it was easy for Zipkin to accept his dismissal. "Affairs are not meant to go on forever. Such a bargain isn't hard to replace." That day the books were being closed for the month. Zipkin sat in a rear office with the assistant bookkeeper, Rubinstein, a young man with a large shock of curly hair. The abacus clattered continuously. Both men were smoking cigars. One moment they would be discussing debits and cash accounts, and the next, actresses and opera singers. Zdzislaw kept coming into the room, playing the boss. The firm's letterhead actually read *Jacob Danzinger & Son*, but in fact, Zdzislaw had little power.

Jacob Danzinger had made sure that he would not become another King Lear, to use his own expression. He had, however, let Zipkin know that Sabina was being left the larger portion of his estate. "Well, one can't have everything," Zipkin said to himself. Clara was an excellent mistress, but not suitable as a wife. Sabina, Zipkin assured himself, would become a different person as soon as Clara was out of the picture. The whole business with Clara had been nothing more than a bubble that had to burst.

Nevertheless, as the day wore on, Zipkin became lonesome. He read Clara's note over and over again. By twilight her signature in blood had begun to look ominous. He had intended to stay in town that night, to have dinner at Clara's and then take her to a concert, or a play. They would have been as free as birds. Suddenly to present him with such an ultimatum! Zipkin picked up the letter once again and read each word carefully. There wasn't a sentence, not even a phrase, that didn't exude passion. "You know how much I long for you. Each time we met was an adventure for me." What would he do with himself now? Sit in Semodeny's Confectionery with no one to keep him company? The thought of his sister Sonya came to him. She had recently come to live in Warsaw. She had a dark room on Dzika Avenue and did some tutoring. Although Zipkin loved her, he had avoided her because Sonya had friends who were active in the political underground. Sonya was one of those women who become beautiful and arouse admiration at a very young age. By the time they reach their early twenties, their charm has already begun to fade, and they become a disappointment to their parents, friends, and to themselves. At sixteen Sonya had received marriage proposals from the wealthiest and best-educated young men in the town where she lived. Now at twenty-six she was considered an old maid who had missed her opportunities. She had dark hair, dark eyes, a fair skin. Her figure was good, but her eyes had become sad and her personality reflected her state of resentment. Her rare meetings with her brother in Warsaw always ended in a quarrel. She quoted mediocre writers, and used phrases which, to Zipkin, seemed utterly banal and silly. She kept a diary and would announce that she had gone to sleep at two o'clock the night before because she had written ten pages in it. When Zipkin asked her what she wrote about, she would answer: "Oh, about many things," and she would smile secretively. Zipkin could not help insulting her whenever she was with him. She would cry softly, and then smile and say: "It won't help you, Alexander. I love you anyway."

It was odd that after living in Warsaw for years Zipkin now found himself isolated. He no longer maintained any ties with his classmates at the university. The group of self-educators had disappeared. Some of its members had been arrested; others had fled. Still others, provincial boys and girls, had committed suicide, although no one knew exactly why. A handful had emigrated to Palestine, where, in settlements founded by some baron, Hebrew was being spoken. Although the *Israelite* was critical of this newly created Jewish nationalism, its opposition did not prevent the movement from spreading. Meetings were held and were well attended, particularly by the Lithuanian rabbis and the opponents of Hassidism. The revolutionaries, too, were again agitating silently. Zipkin was no longer interested in such activities. Only at Clara's did he meet liberals and radicals with whom he could converse about what was going on. As for business friends, there were Zdzislaw and his crowd, who thought of nothing but money.

After leaving the office, Zipkin proceeded to a restaurant where he read the newspaper while he ate. Without Clara, life seemed gray and uninteresting. The scandals in Bulgaria, the economic rivalries between German and British companies in East Africa, the fuss about gold in the Transvaal, all seemed trivial to him. Here in Warsaw everyone was excited about the horse races and the lottery being held in the Saxony Gardens. These activities were of little interest to a man who had been thrown out by the woman he wanted to make love to. Zipkin started for home. As he walked down New Senator Street, he asked himself, "Are all these strolling couples really happy?" If they were, perhaps it was because they'd never known real love. "Take that old fellow barely able to drag his feet along. What is the purpose of his life? What does he hope for? Why is he pulling at his beard? No doubt he has a small hoard hidden away somewhere." Zipkin climbed the stairs to his apartment, unlocked the door, and lit the kerosene lamps. All the furniture, the ottoman, the armchairs, the piano, were covered by sheets to protect them from the dust. The place smelled of naphthaline. He opened a window. Should he go to a cabaret? Or drop in at the chess club? The last train to Polanka might not have left yet. But the thought of traveling to the station, buying a ticket, getting on the train, and then getting off and walking in sand through the dark repelled Zipkin. Yes, the air was fine in Polanka, and Kubuś was a splendid boy, but Sabina would begin lamenting and complaining about her ailments as soon as Zipkin arrived. For all he knew, she might even treat him worse than before when she discovered that Clara had broken with him.

"I'll read a book," Zipkin announced to himself. He glanced at the volumes in the bookcase and immediately lost interest in them. He reminded himself that he owed his parents a letter, but lost the desire to write as soon as he looked at the inkwell. He began to rummage about, pulling out drawers in the writing table and chest in search of he scarcely knew what. How could one endure the sort of life he was leading? "If only I had a bottle of whisky." He sat there staring at the wallpaper. Suddenly he was overcome by the urge to abuse himself like an adolescent. He started to tremble. "I'd better go out and look for a whore." He closed his eyes. "No, I wouldn't enjoy it. I might even not be able to do anything. I'll go see Clara. She won't throw me out. There's no reason why we can't discuss this matter."

He arose quickly. For all he knew, she might not be home. Probably she'd already started going out with other men. He had a bitter taste in his mouth and felt nauseous. He closed the window, thinking it might rain. Sabina dreaded the smallest drop of water, the tiniest ray of sunlight. He must not get to Clara's too late. When he put out the light, he stumbled in the darkness, unable to locate the door, like someone just awakened from a deep sleep.

Finally, after banging his knees against a chair, he found himself outside the apartment, racing down the stairs. He didn't hail a droshky because Berg Street was so close it was faster to walk. At last he caught sight of Clara's house. Yes, there was a light on in the parlor. Was she alone? "She's not above bringing a man to her place," he thought, and stopped to catch his breath. He was ashamed to be so dependent on a woman. But what else was there to be addicted to? To heaven? He had not yet decided what he planned to do, but he knew that it would be something extreme that would alter his entire life. It occurred to him that this must be the way a man felt when he entered the casino at Monte Carlo determined to wager all that he possessed.

III

He rang the bell and, as he waited, listened. Apparently there were no guests inside. Finally he heard footsteps and then Clara's voice.

"Who is it?"

"It's me, Alexander," he said hoarsely.

There was silence. She was probably deliberating. Zipkin held his breath. He knew that everything hung in the balance. If she ordered him away, he would never see her again. Perhaps Clara realized this also. She drew the bolt, unfastened the chain, and swung open the door. She wore a dressing gown and slippers. She had changed her hair style and seemed thinner than when he had seen her last. There were dark rings under her eyes, yet somehow to Zipkin she seemed more alluring than before. They stood gazing at each other.

"Apparently you don't recognize me," she said in Polish.

"Oh, I recognize you."

"Well, come in."

Zipkin walked into the hallway and then into the living room. He took off his straw hat but kept it in his hand. Although his cigarette had gone out, he did not remove it from his lips. He noticed a change in the living room, but couldn't figure out what it was. The curtains? Were they different? No, she had removed the chair in which he usually sat. Clara glanced at him, and he paled. An expression of girlish obstinacy came into her eyes.

"I hope you've come to a decision," Clara said. "If not, you're just wasting your time."

"I can't understand what's got into you."

"You know well enough. You're not a simpleton. I don't care for the position that you've assigned to me."

"What exactly do you want?"

"I told you in my letter. You must choose between us."

"I just can't divorce her like that."

"It's either her or me. This two-woman arrangement has to end."

"If I leave her, I'll lose my job," Zipkin said, and regretted his words immediately. He began to blush.

"Are you telling me that you get paid for your love? All right. But I've had my fill. I'm not the fool you take me for. Why I put up with it for so long is beyond me. I don't intend to haggle with you. I've told you already: it's either here or there."

Clara smiled. It was the same smile that appeared on her lips before she jumped all his pieces when they played checkers. In that smile were mingled victory and feminine compassion. Zipkin said nothing. He removed the cigarette butt from his mouth. The tone of her voice annoyed him. He didn't like the way she stood with her hands on her hips. He moved over to the stove and reached out his hand as if to warm himself. If he deserted Sabina, he would be left without a kopeck. Her dowry had been kept in her name. Anyway, he wouldn't think of taking money from a woman whom he was abandoning. What should he do? Should he marry Clara? Was he to give his name to a woman who had already had two husbands and had gone to his room the very first night they met? Could he become the stepfather of that barbarian Sasha? And for how long would Clara interest him? She was certainly already forty, if not more. "Well," he said, "you can't expect me to come to such a decision immediately."

Clara hesitated for a moment. "Forgive me for saying so, Alexander, but the place for you to think such a matter over is in your own home."

"You're telling me to go?"

"No. But I'm ready to free you from all your responsibilities, even from your obligations to your own daughter. I can't stand this sort of life any longer."

"It's hard for me, too."

"Exactly how hard? We just can't go on talking forever. Words, my dear, are no longer of any use. Don't think this decision has been easy for me. You'll never know how much I've suffered."

Zipkin began to pace up and down the room. What should he do? He glanced at the window and then walked over and pulled back the curtain. Then he turned slowly back toward Clara.

"All right," he said. "I've made up my mind."

"Yes?"

"I don't want her. I want you. But we can't remain in Warsaw. We must leave."

"Where will we go?"

"Out of the country."

"So . . ."

"If not, there'd be too much for us to contend with."

"Yes, that's true."

"Are you willing to go with me?"

"Yes, I'm willing."

They looked at each other in amazement, surprised at the turn their conversation had taken.

"Where do you think we should go?" he asked.

"I have no idea."

"Perhaps America? At least one can earn a living there."

"What will you do—sew pants?"

"Possibly."

"All right. I wanted Sasha to graduate from the gymnasium, but if he can't, it's just too bad."

"One can go to school there, too."

"He'll have to start all over again. But I don't care. If my father wants to keep him for a few years, I won't oppose it. The boy is still young. He's just starting life. I'd like to make the most of the few years that I have left."

"Why do you say the few years?"

"I don't know. Just because. One can't be sure. If I can't be your wife, I don't want anything."

"Come, let's go to bed."

"I'll go anywhere you want to go, but you must swear that it will be as we've agreed. I want it in writing."

IV

In the middle of the night, Clara awoke, terrified. Someone was ringing the doorbell and pounding on the front door. Through the cracks of the shutters came the first blue light of dawn. Zipkin and Clara had not been asleep for long. Clara shook Zipkin awake.

"Alexander, someone's knocking on the door. Don't you hear?"

"Do you have any idea who it can be?" he asked.

"None whatsoever."

Clara put on a dressing gown, and Zipkin a robe and slippers. Finally, after some discussion, it was decided that Clara should go to the door while Zipkin waited in the parlor. The foyer was dark.

"Who's there?" Clara asked. She had the feeling that the person on the other side of the door was coming to destroy her happiness.

"It's me. Sonya."

"It's your sister," Clara shouted to Zipkin. She opened the door and Sonya slipped in, seeming almost more shadow than girl.

"Forgive me, madame. The circumstances that have brought me here are quite unusual. I've been wandering the streets since eleven o'clock. The police were going to arrest me."

"What for? Alexander, come out here." Zipkin hurried into the foyer.

"What's happened, Sonya?"

"Oh, so you're here. They've searched my house."

"When?"

"At about eleven. I had been to the theater with Mirale, Ezriel's sister. On Przejazd Street. She was with a young man. He's not Jewish. When I got to Dzika Street, Notke, the landlord's son, said to me, 'Go somewhere else. Your place has just been searched.' I went to your house, but the janitor wouldn't let me in."

"What were they looking for? Have you done anything?"

"Here in Warsaw? Nothing. You know—I've moved to the place Mirale used to have. I told you—they have a printing press now. They're living together. Oh, I shouldn't have said that. It's a secret. They ran away too, even before I did. As soon as they heard the word 'search,' they just rushed off."

"Well, come on in," Clara said, at last recovering herself. "What are we standing out here for? Mirale was supposed to do my hair, but she never showed up. I thought she was sick. Who is the young man?"

"Oh, he's nice. One of them. Their leader. They met me yesterday and took me along."

"How did you know that I was here?" Zipkin asked embarrassedly.

"I had no idea that you were. I thought you were at home or out of town. I don't even have my birth certificate with me. I came here because I thought Madame Clara would be sympathetic. It's all so strange to me somehow. I really don't know what to say in apology. There was someone following me. I don't know who it was."

"A police agent, perhaps?" Clara asked, half in anger. "He followed you here."

"No, not an agent. He left when I arrived at your house, Alexander. As soon as I rang the gate bell, he walked on."

"Let's get out of the hall," Clara said sharply. "What a night it's been. It's dawn already. Forgive the way the place looks. We have our own problems. Alexander, may I tell her?"

They walked into the parlor. The curtains were still drawn, and the room lay in a twilight that made their faces appear pale, blurred, like images on a dimly lit stage.

"Tell her what, Clara?"

"We're to be married, Sonya. Alexander's leaving his wife."

"Alexander, is it true?"

"It is, Sonya. I never loved Sabina. My marrying her was a mistake."

"But what will become of Kubuś?" When no one answered the girl's question, she continued in a different tone of voice. "I never cared for Sabina either, and she doesn't like me. Well, congratulations. Your happiness is mine. Now Felusia will have a father."

Clara, choked with emotion, coughed to clear her throat. "Well, both Alexander and I have made our mistakes, Sonya, but that's over with now. We're leaving the country."

Zipkin interrupted, "We'll take you with us, Sonya. It's best that you leave at once, perhaps even before we do. Don't you think so, Clara?"

"Unquestionably. What does she have here that's worth staying for? Sonya, our plan is to go to Paris, and later, if possible, to America."

"To America? Oh, my God."

"Alexander, you go back to sleep. I'll make a bed for her on the sofa. If you're hungry, Sonya, I can give you a glass of milk and a roll. A stale one, I'm afraid. I was in such a state yesterday that I ate nothing. Suddenly your brother appeared and everything was all right again. What sort of printing press do they have? Does she live with the Gentile?"

"Not like man and wife, if that's what you mean. They wanted me to join the organization, but I gave them no definite answer."

"Don't get mixed up in all these conspiracies, Sonya," Zipkin said. "The time isn't ripe for that sort of action. Here and in Russia the reactionaries have taken over. There are *agents provacateurs* everywhere. It'll end with you being packed off to jail. Who'll get you out then? You see my situation. I can't stay in Poland any longer."

"Yes, Alexander, I understand perfectly."

v

The clock in the living room struck ten. Zipkin opened his eyes. Clara was still asleep beside him, snoring as if it were midnight. Zipkin ran his hand across his brow. Had he been dreaming? No, Sonya had in fact arrived in the middle of the night. There had been a police search. He had given Clara his word that he would divorce Sabina, had even signed a paper to that effect. So, that was how things were! He lay there and looked at Clara, amazed at where his passions had led him. Yes, she dyed her hair. He could see some gray growing in at the roots. As she slept, Clara's face looked fat and middle-aged. There were wrinkles on her cheeks and her skin was pitted. Had she had smallpox? Last night, consumed by desire, nothing but lying next to her had mattered. Now, seeing her in the morning light, he wondered, "Where will I go with her? How will we live?" He got out of bed and put on a robe and slippers. When he opened the door, he saw Sonya seated on the sofa which she had used as a bed, reading a book.

"So you're up already," he said.

"I didn't sleep a wink."

"Why not? You said you were so tired."

"All this has unnerved me, Alexander."

"To what are you referring?"

"Oh, various things. No, I'd better keep my mouth shut."

"You can be frank with me. But there are many things over which we have no control."

Zipkin went into the kitchen and washed. "Exactly what kind of an animal is man?" he asked himself, and then yawned. "I'm so weak, and yet I take such a burden upon myself. I'll collapse under the load." The night before, he had thought of himself as a giant. Now he rose with his temples throbbing, his legs aching, and a pain in his back. "Am I arthritic? Perhaps I have a bad heart." He put his index finger into his mouth and poked at a molar he knew was loose, meanwhile looking at himself in a mirror that hung above the sink. His hair was already getting thin. "Will I never again be at peace with myself?" he mumbled. "If my parents knew what I've become, they'd die."

Clara entered, dressed in an expensive negligee. With cosmetics on, she once more appeared young and animated. She looked at him searchingly.

"I didn't hear you get up."

"I didn't want to wake you."

Clara became tense. "Alexander, I know that she's your sister and will soon, if you keep your promise, be my sister-in-law. I wish her only good. But now is not the time for us to have a chaperon. The next few weeks we must live alone."

"She doesn't have to travel with us."

"I don't care what she says. I know where her sympathies lie, even though your wife wouldn't even let her into the house."

"Sonya is not my main consideration here."

"Alexander, I don't want to nag you, but it's important that everything be done quickly. You don't have to wait for a divorce. You can send Sabina a bill of divorcement from America."

"No, I can't leave without saying something."

"Why not? You'll only be saving yourself some breath and Sabina unnecessary tears. You consider yourself a Don Juan, but you don't know anything about women. She'll move heaven and earth to keep you. You don't have—if you'll forgive my saying it—the strongest of characters. How much money do you have?"

"Not a groschen."

"Aren't you the cashier?"

"It's my father-in-law's money."

"What about the dowry?"

"I've already told you about that."

"Well, if you want to be a fool, go ahead. You know how impoverished I am. How can a man permit himself to be without a kopeck? Don't get angry, but that's stupidity, not idealism. For whom were you working? The devil? Well, I'll just have to sell the furniture, but I must be certain that you won't have a change of heart. Our decisions must be definite. Neither of us is a child."

"I must have a day or two to think it over."

"What's there to think about? If you intend to back out, let me know now. You either do something like this immediately or not at all. We don't need passports; we'll just slip across the border. Our only baggage will be two suitcases. Once we're out of the country, we have the whole world to choose from."

"Yes, Clara, that's true."

"I have certain matters to put in order before we leave. Unlike you, I can't sit around and brood. First of all, I must go to Jampol and have a good talk with my father. I just can't push the children off on him. I have a few things to say to Celina, too. Besides, her mother is there, and I'd like to see her before I leave. Don't think all of this is such an easy matter for me."

"When do you plan to go?"

"The exact time doesn't matter much. But I must be sure

that when I speak to them I won't be making a fool of myself. I've done too much of that in my life already."

Zipkin swallowed hard. "Go and talk to your father."

"You've made up your mind then? You have no doubts? Remember, I can't trifle with my own father. When I go there, I must be able to give him all the facts."

"You may tell him everything."

"Well, that's what I wanted to hear from you."

29

I

Calman Jacoby was sixty-five. There had been a time when he had thought he would be dead by that age. According to the Talmud, a man who reaches the age when his parents died should begin to think about his own demise. Besides, he had worked hard and suffered much. But thank God, he was healthy. Behind his white beard, his face remained ruddy and his eyes clear. His back was still as straight as it had ever been. God had blessed Calman with strength.

Mayer Joel was now in full charge of the estate, and the lime quarries, which were now almost exhausted. Calman had turned everything over to his son-in-law, who had enlarged the mill and installed rollers to grind sifted flour. Calman himself still performed heavy labor, not out of necessity but because he was accustomed to it. He rose, as always, at sunrise, ate black bread and cottage cheese for breakfast, and drank a large glass of water. He handled sacks, helped to load the lime, harnessed horses, even chopped wood. He could not spend all his time studying the Mishnah or the Talmud. He had lived for years without a wife; lust seethed in his veins. Without anything to do, he would lose his mind.

No, Calman had not reckoned with old age. He had once believed that as the beard grayed, one's thoughts became pure. But it was not so. Even being a great-grandfather had not been able to quiet his passion. Yes, he was already a great-grandfather because Jochebed's daughter, Teibela, was a mother. Jochebed, who was eighteen years younger than her father, behaved like an old woman. In a bonnet, with glasses on her nose, she sat most of the day reading *The Lamp of Light* and *The Inheritance of the Deer*. Her father, however, lacked the patience to read for very long.

Even at prayertime, evil thoughts assailed him. At night his imagination seethed with the nonsense he had known in boyhood or when, as a widower, he had coveted Clara. The Jampol matchmakers continued to swarm around him with potential brides; they were even proposing that he marry an eighteen-year-old orphan girl. Calman knew that, according to the Law, he should marry. As it is written in the Scriptures: "In the morning sow thy seed and in the evening withhold not thine hand." Nevertheless, Calman had been unable to come to a decision. When, each year, Daniel Kaminer celebrated a circumcision or had a family feast, Calman was disgusted. Why sire children in one's old age? Why leave orphans?

He now lived alone in one room of the house he had once occupied with Zelda. He had set aside another room for prayer. He had procured a Holy Ark, a Scroll of the Law, a menorah, the volumes of the Mishnah, the Talmud, and other holy books, as well as a lectern, a cantor's pulpit with a candelabrum, and even a copper basin in which to wash one's hands. An eternal light in memory of Zelda's soul burned at the door. He had also provided a guest room for the use of traveling Jews who from time to time visited the estate to solicit subscriptions for books, or to collect money for the support of poor brides. A Jampol woman took care of Calman's house. Calman himself looked after every visitor. He had a bed for everyone. He gave each visitor food, a night's lodging, a few coins, and sometimes even a measure of corn, a pot of groats, millet, or whatever was left over. At times, though infrequently, so many visitors came that a quorum could be formed for prayer. Usually Calman had to pray alone. He walked back and forth in his prayer shawl and phylacteries. He had won and lost a world here. A daughter had been converted. Thank God he had good children as well. Jochebed was an honorable woman, Tsipele a saint.

Calman prayed, reflecting. He kissed the phylacteries worn on the head and on the arm by touching them and then bringing his fingers to his lips. He also kissed the fringes of his prayer shawl. He stationed himself at the Eastern wall for the Eighteen Benedictions. This house of prayer had been his salvation. Here he retired with all his worries and anxieties. He knew well that one must not open the Holy Ark without reason. But occasionally he had a desperate desire to slide back the curtain that protected it, and open the door. The wood within was reddish, wine-colored; wrapped in satin, crowned with bells, and decorated with a tassel and fescue, the Scroll of the Law leaned against the wall of the Ark. It seemed to him that the smells of the spices of the Garden of Eden emanated from it. The Law that Moses had given on Mount Sinai was inscribed on the parchment.

Calman bowed his head and kissed the Scroll. He would die, but this Holy Scroll which he had had inscribed would be passed on from generation to generation. Jews would be called up to it, would kiss it, walk with it, hold it aloft, and dance with it at the Rejoicing of the Law. On the satin mantle, within the Star of David, embroidered in gold was the statement that Calman, son of Sender Jacob, had donated the Torah in memory of his wife Zelda, daughter of Uri Joseph. God willing, when he arrived in the other world, this Torah would count among his good deeds. But who would there be to recite Kaddish for him—Clara's little jewel, Sasha?

11

During the winter Calman could, more or less, forget that he had once had a wife like Clara. But in summertime, when Sasha came to stay with his grandfather Daniel Kaminer and visited Calman, the boy was a constant reminder of his life with Clara. Calman saw before him a son who—may the Evil Eye spare him—grew like yeast. At each of his sudden appearances, Sasha's stature and clothes were so altered that Calman hardly recognized him.

One summer day a grown youth, wearing a jacket with gold buttons, a cap with an emblem, riding breeches and boots almost knee-high, and looking like a Gentile, came to see Calman. More broad-shouldered than tall, healthy, with a shock of shining black hair, he had already begun to use a razor. Speaking a broken Yiddish and laughing with gypsylike eyes, he bewildered Calman for a moment.

"Papa, it's me, Sasha, Senderel!" And Sasha smiled with strong white teeth such as the Jewish boys in Poland did not have.

"How did you get here?"

"By train. Felusia is here too."

Calman pretended not to have heard the name.

"How are you? How is your mother?" Calman asked, and instantly regretted having referred to Clara.

"Everything's fine. I'm giving my teachers a hard time. Mama screams at me."

"Why does she scream?"

"Oh, she screams all the time. I don't learn enough. My marks aren't good. She thinks I should only get five pluses. I don't give a damn. I'd rather have a good time."

"What is having a good time?"

"Everything. Swimming in the Vistula, exercising. Across from our school there is a girls' school and we have fun with the girls. We play tricks on them. Here is my ritual garment!" Sasha suddenly began to search beneath his blouse. "I brought my phylacteries to Jampol, too. I am a Jew."

"Well, thank God."

"Papa, do you still have the gray mare?"

"Does the Hebrew tutor still come to give you lessons?"

Sasha hesitated a moment.

"The rabbi with the goatee is gone. A Hebrew teacher was supposed to come, but because of the exams I didn't have time. After vacation, I'll begin again. I have the Pentateuch, and the prayer book and all the rest."

"You can have the mare, but while you're here you'll have to learn a chapter of the Pentateuch, and pray as well."

"I left my phylacteries at Grandfather's."

Sasha was impatient with praying. He would tap his feet and laugh, then grow serious and snatch at a butterfly that flew in through the open window. If it were possible to do so, he would have done everything at once: ride, swim in the pond, eat. He had walked all the way from Jampol. Calman brought in his phylacteries and a prayer book, but Sasha had forgotten everything. He did not remember that phylacteries had leather straps. Calman wrapped them first around the boy's strong arm, and then to form the prescribed letter "Shin" continued them around Sasha's hand and between his fingers. He recited the benediction for him and made him repeat it. Meanwhile, the housekeeper prepared delicacies for the guest. Sasha adored Passover egg cakes and cookies all year round. Pacing back and forth across the prayer room, he gaped at the walls. He stopped for the Eighteen Benedictions but did not beat his breast, or bow to "give thanks." Calman was ashamed and alarmed. Nevertheless, he was fond of the boy. Although he resembled Clara, certain of Sasha's mannerisms reminded Calman of his own father, Sender Jacob, may he rest in Paradise.

Calman made excuses for Sasha. "How was it the poor boy's fault? He was raised among idolaters." In the midst of prayers —he hadn't even removed his phylacteries—the boy approached Calman and, taking him by the shoulders, kissed his forehead. Calman was astonished. That was how Clara used to act. In the midst of anything, she would start kissing.

"Papa, I love you."

"I'd rather you were a Jew."

"What am I—a Gentile? When the priest comes to our

school, the Jewish pupils leave. The Gentiles call us names and we crack their jaws for them. Papa, I'm proud to be a Jew."

"Proud? Why proud?"

"I'm proud . . . They are anti-Semites, but we don't give a damn about them. We can punch, too. The teachers make all sorts of remarks. I answer back. I'm afraid of no one. Once, because I talked back, I got a zero. That's the worst mark. But I didn't care."

"It's best for a Jew to be among Jews," Calman said. "Then he's spared such battles."

"How can I be among Jews? There is no Jewish high school. I want to be an engineer, but the machinery and everything else belongs to the Gentiles. Why don't Jews own land? Why don't they live in Palestine?"

"In the Land of Israel? Because they sinned, and God drove them out."

"The Gentiles sin, too, and they have everything."

"The Jews are God's children, and with his own child a father is strict."

"Some say there is no God."

Calman trembled.

"Who says that? Remove the phylacteries! The phylacteries are God's sign and you speak such nonsense."

Calman helped Sasha remove the phylacteries. In the kitchen he drew a dipperful of water from the barrel for the boy to wash before eating. Sitting at the table, he waited for Sasha to finish and say the benediction. Sasha disposed of one butter-fried pancake after another, washing them down with milk and simultaneously glancing toward the manor house, which was now an officers' club. He had met the officers' wives and daughters the previous year. He had ridden their horses; the officers had taught him to shoot. This year he looked like a full-grown man.

After the benediction, Calman accompanied Sasha to the stable. The gray mare was still fit for riding, though she had aged. The saddle had been mislaid and had to be searched for.

Meanwhile, Sasha went to the river for a swim. Apparently, his mother had not infused him with any sense of modesty. He began to disrobe, exhibiting no bashfulness before his father. Mentally, Calman compared him to Ham, Noah's son.

In addition to disgracing Calman, Sasha reminded him of Clara. He had her face, her eyes, and occasionally even her voice.

III

At night, when Calman was unable to sleep, he would rise and go into his makeshift synagogue. First he would knock, to alert the corpses who pray there after midnight. Lighting the naphtha lamp that hung from a wire above the table, he would open a volume of the Mishnah and study. Sasha, whom he had been seeing every other day, had not appeared for a week. Outside, a mild breeze was blowing. The fields and forests stretched for miles around. Who could estimate how many devils, imps, and hobgoblins congregated there?

Two gilded lions on either side of the Ten Commandments formed the cornice of the Ark. A mezuzah hung on the doorpost; only a real synagogue was exempt from a doorpost amulet. Calman chanted the first Mishnah: "Seven days before the Day of Atonement, the High Priest was taken away from his own house unto the Councillor Chamber and another priest was made ready in his stead, lest aught should befall him to render him ineligible. Rabbi Judah says, 'Also another wife was made ready for him lest his own wife should die, for it is written: He shall make atonement for himself and his house; that is, his wife.' They said to him: 'If so, there would be no end to the matter.'"

Calman chanted the words, tugging at a tangle in his beard. He glanced at the commentary of Rabbi Yom Tov Heller and saw before his eyes the ancient Temple, where in the innermost chamber of the sanctuary, the Holy Ark, the cherubim were all made of gold. Into this Holy of Holies once a year the

High Priest would come, dressed in a breastplate and vestment, with a cowl on his head, carrying a pan in which to burn incense. Surrounding the inner sanctum were the various buildings of the Temple. Priests would bring sacrificial animals to the altar, and burn fats and fried meal offerings. Farthest away was the temple court, where all Jews could enter. It was so full that there was no room left for a pin, but when the High Priest intoned the name of Jehovah, the courtyard expanded so that all might bow and kneel.

Calman was filled with longing for the ancient times, when Jews lived in the Land of Israel. Thrice yearly they made a pilgrimage to Jerusalem. They owned their own fields, forests, vineyards, fig trees. A king ruled over the Jews, and men prophesied. All the same, Calman thought, there was sinning, too. Jeroboam placed two golden calves in Bethel and Dan and the Jews worshipped them. How could this have been possible? It was beyond comprehension.

Calman did not even remember when he had learned the chant in which he prayed and studied. It had come down to him through generations of ancestors. The words of the Mishnah were very clear; they dealt with an ox, a jackass, a thief, a murderer, a wedding, a divorce. Yet each word had an indescribable flavor. The Hebrew letters were steeped in holiness, in eternity. They seemed to unite him with the patriarchs, with Joshua, Gamaliel, Eliezer, and with Hillel the Ancient. The tannaim spoke to him like grandfathers. They argued with him as to what was right and what was wrong, what was pure and impure. They made him a kind of partner in sharing the Torah's treasures. Among these shelves of sacred books, Calman felt protected. Over each volume hovered the soul of its author. In this place, God watched over him.

THE ESTATE

ONE

I 🏛

Daniel Kaminer was suddenly taken ill. He grew feverish and began to cough. Celina gave him tea with raspberry juice and rubbed his neck and back with turpentine, but it did not help. When morning came, he could not get up. He asked for a mirror. Overnight his face had become sunken, and his goatee seemed to have shriveled up. "Celina, I'm dying!" he said.

Celina began to weep. She immediately sent to Skarshew for a doctor; Daniel Kaminer had pneumonia. He was cupped, and leeches were applied to him, but he grew worse hourly.

His daughter, Clara, was abroad. She had written from Paris that she had quarreled with Zipkin and that he had left her. She had lost money in Monte Carlo. She had made the acquaintance of a Russian Jew, a merchant of the First Guild, who was permitted to live outside the Pale. She wrote short, insinuating letters whose sentences usually ended with rows of dots. One thing was clear to Daniel Kaminer: his daughter was traveling a slippery path. Felusia, whom Clara had left with him, was now a part of his own family. But when you were dying, nothing mattered. Daniel Kaminer had mixed feelings about the next world. There had to be a God, but the immortality of the soul was hard for him to accept. What happened to the souls of dead people? Where did they go? How long could a soul hover over a cemetery or remain in a cold synagogue?

Daniel Kaminer had not lost his sense of humor. He groaned and joked. To Celina, who was already mourning him, he said: "Shush! Don't wail! You'll awaken the Angel of Death . . ."

"What will become of us?"

"There are so many widows, there'll be one more."

"What will I, may it never happen, do with my children?"

"Marinate them in vinegar . . ."

Although Daniel Kaminer jested, he worried about his brood. He had accumulated no capital and had had a few bad years. The Russians owed him money, but the dead can claim no debts. Celina had the brain of a mite. She would not be able to collect a cent. His mother-in-law was paralyzed. She could no longer work and had to be supported. What would Celina do with the children? If Clara were at home, he could at least discuss the situation with her. But she was abroad. For hours at a time Daniel Kaminer did not think at all. He lay struggling with the phlegm that filled his throat and lungs. He imagined that if he could get rid of it with one mighty cough, he would get well instantly. But when he tried to cough, he felt a stabbing pain in his side. His head burned, his feet had fallen asleep, his fingers felt numb.

Celina walked around in a soiled housedress, worn-out slippers, and a dirty kerchief on her head. She wept and continuously munched on something. Every now and then she would stop at Daniel's bedside and shake her head in a gesture of grief as old as womankind. It occurred to Daniel that within a year she would probably be remarried. There's always someone to take your place. He hadn't lived right, he thought. He had often heard old people say that if they could live their lives over again, they would know what to do. But what actually would he do differently if he were now forty? Would he become a Hassid and spend his days in the study house? Would he drink more, eat better, have more women? No. One cannot be wiser than fate.

Daniel Kaminer fell asleep. He dreamed that Russia was at

war and that he had been ordered by the Czar to provision the army. The regiments paraded before him, Cossacks, Circassians, Tartars, carrying guns, spears, and swords. They sang a monotonous song, utterly sad and as if from another world. Could they be dead? Do corpses wage war? Daniel awoke with a coughing fit—and a plan. He would send a telegram to Warsaw ordering Sasha to come at once. He was convinced that his grandson was not nearly as wild as he appeared to be. It was true that he had been behaving badly since his mother had left. There had been complaints from the director of his school. But if a boy were left at the mercy of God in a large city, why shouldn't he indulge himself? Daniel Kaminer had long sensed that the boy understood people and that he had a smooth tongue. Perhaps he had a talent for business as well. Sasha took after the Kaminer side of the family. Daniel Kaminer sent for Colonel Shachowsky, an elderly Russian with whom he was doing business. Although the colonel had often disagreed with Kaminer, he was upset to see him so ill and insisted on sending for the regimental doctor.

Daniel Kaminer said: "Your Excellency, I am already as good as gone. My grandson Sasha is my heir."

"Yes, I know him, the handsome one."

"He will take care of my orphans."

Colonel Shachowsky burst into tears. Celina brought him a glass of whisky. He promised Kaminer that he would help Sasha in every way possible. When the regimental doctor came, he again prescribed cupping, but the patient grew worse. His breathing sounded like a saw, his nose bled. A sexton from the Burial Society suggested that the patient make his confession, but Kaminer refused. "One doesn't grow fat from confessing," he quipped.

By morning he was dead. Colonel Shachowsky ordered the military band to play at the funeral. Although the Jampol rabbi declared that it was forbidden to play music at a Jewish funeral, the pharmacist, Grain, objected and called the rabbi an ignoramus. There were by now many enlightened Jews in

Jampol and they sided with t' druggist. Sick as she was, Mrs. Frankel came from Warsaw, bringing Celina a hat with a black veil. The Burial Society demanded an exorbitant fee for the plot, but Colonel Shachowsky warned them that he would have them sent to Siberia if they overcharged the widow. The Russians and heretics took over the burial. Mrs. Grain, Tamara Shalit, and Sonya Sorkess sewed a shroud for the corpse. The military band and a company of soldiers followed the hearse, playing military marches. At the cemetery, Grain, David Sorkess, and Colonel Shachowsky eulogized the deceased. The wives of the officers sobbed when they saw Celina and her many orphans, one smaller than the other—like a row of steps. . . . Everyone already knew Sasha. The men patted him on the back. The women comforted him. They all said the same thing: it certainly would have been better had he been able to graduate from the gymnasium and enter the university. But since he had to take over his grandfather's business, they would teach him, help him, and God would protect him.

The officers of the Jampol garrison kept their word. Colonel Shachowsky, who was always late with his payments, covered all his debts promptly. Mayer Joel, Calman's son-in-law, had also become a contractor and had been a competitor of Kaminer's, but now all orders were given to Sasha. It turned out that the boy had the Jewish instinct for trade. He learned so quickly that people were astounded. He even knew whom to bribe. He made sure that both the colonel and General Horne, who had replaced General Rittermayer, received their customary due.

At first Mayer Joel tried to fight back. He held the lease on the estate and was the proprietor of the mill. He could supply products more cheaply than Sasha. He planned to go to Warsaw, pay the necessary bribes, and get the contracts away from Sasha. But Calman intervened. He still had something to say. The lime quarries and the railroad had remained in his name. First of all, he told Mayer Joel, Sasha was not a stranger. He was Calman's son, and Mayer Joel's brother-in-law. It would be a disgrace before the Gentiles for a sister and brother to go into competition. Second, Mayer Joel was a rich man. How much did one need? One didn't take one's money to the grave. Third, Sasha had to support a widow and orphans. Fourth, the authorities were on Sasha's side. Calman saw clearly which way the wind was blowing. The boy spent his days and nights at the officers' club, rode in their sleighs, associated with their wives and daughters. As long as Sasha had studied at Warsaw, he had caused Calman no shame. Now he had come to Jampol to disgrace him. But no good could come from an open rift. If one pushed a boy like Sasha too hard, he might decide to become a convert out of spite.

11

Sonya received a letter from her brother. It was postmarked Paris, and Zipkin had filled four closely written pages:

Dear Sonya:

I have wanted to write to you for a long time, but I didn't have your address. When I left Warsaw, you didn't know what you were going to do, not even where you would be staying. I hear from Mother and Father that you keep changing your address, and in this respect we seem to be alike. In the past few months I have moved in and out of so many hotels and furnished rooms that I'm dizzy. I must tell you immediately that our parents still do not know the circumstances of my trip abroad, despite the fact that Clara demanded that I tell them. Instinct told me that the adventure wouldn't last long. I see from their letters that you have kept your promise and have also not told them the truth. I am grateful to you with all my heart. I was afraid that Sabina might give everything away, but she too has kept quiet. It's good they weren't dragged into the mud with us.

Yes, Sonya dear, you were right, a thousand times right. I

did act like a suicidal fool. I always thought I was the practical one and you a romantic young girl who lived in a dream world. Now I must admit that you understand people much better than I do. I can't tell you, little sister, how much I have suffered. It seems to me that it is years, not months, since I left Warsaw. Kubuś is like a fantasy to me, although I long for him day and night. I see him in my dreams. I know I shouldn't burden you with my mess, but I must tell someone or I will choke. I am shattered both psychologically and physically. Believe me, if it were not for our parents, I would kill myself.

To relate all my experiences and tell you what I had to put up with would take a book, but I'll try to be as brief as possible. No sooner had we left Poland than Clara changed. It was as if the devil had suddenly possessed her. She became dreadfully nervous, complained that she missed her children, that she was ill, that she had done a foolish thing, and so on. In Berlin she insulted the chambermaid. Her behavior was so coarse I couldn't believe my ears. She began to count every penny, argued with waiters, suspected everyone. She reminded me constantly that I had no money of my own. Suddenly she announced that she wanted to go to Monte Carlo before visiting Paris. It was because of a man called Mirkin, a Jew from Russia who lived at our hotel, that she changed her plans. It would take a Turgenev or a Boleslaw Prus to describe him. He'd get up in the middle of the night and order roast duck. He traveled with a male secretary, who was his procurer as well. Forgive my mentioning it, but it's the truth. He had money to burn. He exported Siberian furs to Western Europe and had branch offices everywhere. He also dealt in rugs from Bukhara, and the devil-knows-what-else. He was at least sixty-five years old, blind in one eye, and had a wife and married children somewhere. You should have seen how these two charlatans, he and Clara, were immediately attracted to each other. As soon as they met, I ceased to exist for her. She had once sold herself to Calman Jacoby. Mirkin was even older and uglier, and Calman at least was an honest man.

Sonya, you must be smiling as you read these lines. You warned me. If only I had listened to you. I should have spat on her, but I was so beaten and drained that I simply didn't have the strength to make a decision. Like an idiot I dragged along after her to Monte Carlo and suffered the punishment I deserved, even much worse than I deserved. At Monte Carlo the old buzzard played roulette and lost many thousands. Clara tried her luck as well and lost over a thousand rubles. I'm sure she thought she'd take Mirkin away from his wife and become a millionairess again, but he was too cunning a dog. As long as it suited him, he played along with her and plied her with caviar and champagne. Then one day he received a telegram—or pretended to—and off he went. He said he would return to Monte Carlo and even left his secretary, or whatever you want to call him, behind. In the end the secretary too disappeared. What his real intentions were, the devil knows, but he was to have joined Clara somewhere later on. All this, you understand, put an end to our relationship. I saw her at her vulgar worst. You won't believe it, Sonya, but there were days when I actually starved because my few-hundred rubles had been spent on fare. To make a long story short: we said goodbye, or rather we separated without saying goodbye. She tried to ingratiate herself with me all over again. But no matter how worthless I am, I didn't stoop that low. I left cursing not her (scum will be scum) but myself and my disgusting frivolity.

For a long time I dared not write to Sabina. When at last I did, I received no reply, and I couldn't blame her. I had betrayed everything and everybody: Sabina, myself, the child, and all that is decent. I have completely lost all self-respect, and that is the worst of my tortures. It causes me anguish such as I hope you will never experience.

Why do I trouble you, dear Sonya? How can you help me? This is my situation: actually I don't have a franc. I have sold my gold watch and everything else for which I could get money. I want either to come home or to go to America, but I don't have the fare. I owe rent at the hotel. I envy every dog in the street, every cat, every worm. Sonya, you must get hold of a hundred and fifty rubles—although I can't imagine where you can get such a sum—and send the money to me. You once spoke of a dowry that our parents were holding for you. I will, of course, repay you and be forever grateful. I have no one but you. If you too turn away, there will be only one way out for me.

Sonya, don't be angry. I suffer constantly. I never imagined that a person could suffer such hell. There is no heater in my room and it is bitterly cold. My soul feels even colder. I'd like to ask one other favor: Would you see Sabina and talk the situation over with her? I don't want to force myself on Sabina, but I did her a terrible wrong and I'd like to try to straighten matters out. Speak to her, and from what she says you'll know whether she can ever forgive me.

Europe is beautiful, elegant, free. But for me the whole world has become miserable. The Jews here have one good thing: a soup kitchen run by the Alliance Israelite. I eat lunch there, to keep from starving. Yes, your brother has become a beggar. The types one meets there are beyond description. I never knew such freaks existed.

Dear, enough bitterness for one letter! I kiss you a thousand times. If you can't help me, at least write. It will be a comfort.

Your broken ALEXANDER

My dear Alexander, sweet brother of mine, dearest!

Do you remember what I said to you that morning in Clara's house? Whatever happens, I'll always love you.

When I said them, I did not mean my words to be prophetic. Yet I must have had a premonition. I want to tell you that from childhood on I've loved you with a terrible love. It may be a sin to admit it, but I loved you more than I loved our parents. I don't know why. Perhaps because you are so hot-blooded and wild. I remember once when you hit me (how long ago that was!) I forgave you immediately. Well, enough sentimentality!

I didn't reply at once because I tried to find some way of helping you. I did all I could, but here in Warsaw I couldn't raise one hundred and fifty kopecks, let alone rubles. I too have suffered a misfortune. But there is no point in writing about that now. I only want to tell you that Mirale is still gravely ill in the hospital and rumors persist that the person responsible for her illness is her best friend. It makes one shudder to think that such a thing is possible. He denied it vehemently, but nevertheless he found it necessary to disappear. How I have survived all this baffles me. You are an atheist, but I still believe in God, and perhaps that is what has saved me. I'm disappointed, terribly disappointed, not in humankind but in certain people. I still believe that a better tomorrow is coming and that the sun will shine again. If I did not believe that, I could not breathe.

I have a job as a clerk in a store here in Warsaw. Yes, I stand behind a counter in a haberdashery and sell ties, cuff-links, socks, and other such items. I work hard, and I must be there early to open the store in the morning. It closes at seven, but I stay to straighten up. By the time I come home and finish supper it is eleven o'clock. I fall into bed and sleep like the dead.

It's sheer luck that your letter arrived on a Friday, because the store is closed on Saturday. Dearest, I want to tell you everything in proper sequence. On Saturday morning I went to see Sabina. Kubuś is more charming than ever, but Sabina was sour as acid. She didn't want to let me in. She vented all her anger on me, then looked at me with an expression of sarcasm and laughed in my face. If she is to be believed, her only wish is that you send her a Jewish divorce. Obviously her mother is egging her on.

Now would you believe this. I left her apartment and walked aimlessly up Krakow Boulevard. Suddenly someone called me—a woman dressed completely in mourning. I was terribly startled. Who did it turn out to be—Clara! I wanted to avoid her, but she caught me and gripped me so hard that my wrist still hurts. It seems that her father has died. I insisted that I had nothing to say to her, but she begged me not to leave her. She began to cry in the middle of the street, and I was embarrassed. I went with her to a café and there she sobbed and talked continuously for three hours. Fortunately the place was empty. I cried too. The glasses of coffee the waiter brought us filled with our tears. Dearest, what can I tell you? I know all her faults, but she's still not as heartless as Sabina. A vulgar person can also have a soul. I can't tell you everything she said. Essentially, she's sorry. The Russian merchant visited her in Warsaw but she sent him away. She spoke about you as if you were an angel. How strange it all is! She swore to me that she longs for you day and night, and that she is prepared to wash your feet and drink the water (her words). . . . She wanted me to give her your address, but this I categorically refused to do. She wanted to send you money but I knew this would have humiliated you. Instead, I forwarded your letter express to our parents and today (Tuesday) I received a telegram from them saying that they are sending you money. Forgive me, dear brother, for letting our parents know. I couldn't let you die alone in Paris.

Yes, I forgot to add that Clara's son, Sasha, has left the gymnasium and has taken over his grandfather's business. Clara reports miracles of him. Felusia is back in Warsaw with Louisa. Now, Alexander, I want you to know that there is nothing to keep me here in Poland. I can't go home. I'm afraid I'll catch Mirale's sickness. . . . It's going around. Everyone is getting sick. . . .

I needn't tell you that my job gives me little pleasure. I'm also depressed, because I've suffered a great disappointment. I now have only one desire, to go to America. Somehow or other I'll manage to scrape together fare money. But I don't want to go alone. Wait for me, Alexander, and I'll join you. You want to go to America and it's better for us to go together. Answer immediately. I kiss you and hug you to my heart.

Your devoted SONYA

P.S. Answer quickly, for every day counts.

Dearest Alexander!

I wrote you yesterday and today I am writing again. Clara came to see me at the store and begged and insisted that I give her your address. She would not let me work. I was afraid the "Old Man" (that's what they call the boss) would fire me. I did not give her your address, but I promised to send you her letter. I'm enclosing it. Do as you think best. She seems to love you, but as God is my witness, I don't understand her kind of love. I guess I'm just a provincial girl, a "simple miss from Kuniev" as you once called me. . . . Whatever happens, answer immediately. Have you received the money from our parents? Is it enough?

Kisses.

Your SONYA

P.S. If our correspondence should be terminated, you will know that I have fallen sick. . . . But I still hope for the best.

The letter that Sonya enclosed, from Clara to Zipkin, read as follows:

My dear Alexander:

I write and cannot stop crying. Perhaps my tears will be proof that what I say is true. Within a short time I have lost the two people closest to my heart, my father and you, and truly I don't know why God has seen fit to punish me in this way. I have just spent a few hours with your sister and gather from her that you consider yourself completely in the right and blame me for everything. But what you don't seem to realize is that the moment we left Warsaw you changed. It was as if an evil spirit possessed you. I was so happy that we were at last together after so much effort and strain, but you sat in the train silent and brooding and would not even answer when I spoke to you. I thought that for some reason or other you were in a bad mood, and decided to leave you alone (I have some pride too). But your "mood" continued throughout the entire trip. I am afraid that you've forgotten how you behaved, or you've made yourself forget. Your every look cut right through me. You clamped your thin lips together and nothing would pry them apart. You glared at me as if I were your worst enemy. I knew that it hadn't been easy for you to leave your family, but I left children too and, what's more, I divorced a wealthy husband because of you.

I made more sacrifices for you than I have ever made for anyone. And how did you repay me? With scorn and insult. When I struck up a conversation with the lady in the yellow hat, you made remarks that embarrassed me. You didn't even have the courtesy to pick up my handbag when I dropped it, and at every opportunity demonstrated to the other passengers your lack of respect for me. I left our compartment and went out into the passageway to cry—on the first night of our "honeymoon." When we arrived in Berlin, you went off for the day, leaving me in the hotel. On your return I asked you where you had been and you refused to tell me. How a person could have changed so overnight is something I will never understand. The only explanation I can think of is my wicked luck. It has plagued me ever since I was old enough to reason, although I've always tried to be nice to everyone. I know that you disliked my suit and hat, but why wouldn't you go to the tailor with me when I asked you to? You wouldn't even take a look at the fashion book. It was only after I had spent so much money and effort that you expressed your opinion in one word, "vulgar." It was like pronouncing a death sentence. What was so "vulgar" about my costume? Silk, velvet, and ostrich plumes are stylish. Everyone else showered me with compliments. I repeatedly tried to straighten matters out with you, but you have the most "refined" way of ignoring those who are close to you. You literally prevented me from speaking, and whenever I did manage to say something, you made fun of me. You brought things to such a pass that we spent our nights apart instead of being together every moment. You know that what I write is the truth, and if I'm lying, may I not live to lead my Sasha to the wedding canopy. Yes, I'm swearing like a fishwife, as you would put it, but believe me, a fishwife has more heart than you. You were in a rotten mood and you took your anger out on me, knowing that I was dependent on you. Your sarcasm concerning my German was misplaced. How else could I have communicated with Germans? Everyone, knowing we were Russians, complimented me on the way I managed to make myself understood. In a strange city you made me go everywhere alone, and although I took it with a smile, believe me, if you had tasted my heart at that time you would have been poisoned.

Now regarding that old man, Mirkin, around whom you've built a whole nest of accusations. His only sin was that he acted humanly and kindly. He was an old man, old enough to be my father, and he was too worldly and experienced not to sense what was going on between us. To whom else could I have turned when you were so inconsiderate? I have been alone too often in my life. Why should you have objected when an elderly person, and a cripple at that, displayed some fatherly feeling toward me and showed me around a city that he knew well? Even a dog can't always be alone. Apparently you were only waiting for an opportunity to play the jealous lover, although one would have to be mad to have suspected my conduct. Would I abandon my dear children for someone who already had one foot in the grave? And as far as Monte Carlo is concerned, it was your idea to go there, not mine. I wanted to go directly to Paris. But *you* suddenly became enamored of Mirkin. I foresaw that Monte Carlo would be the end of me. You spun such a devilish web around me that even now, no matter how I try, I cannot make head or tail of the whole thing. You seemed to want to drive me into Mirkin's arms. It was quite obvious that he was amorously inclined. You egged him on, and I noticed more than once that you did everything possible to compromise me. I still have not been able to decide whether you planned all this, or whether it just happened. If it was a preconceived trick, then it was the most contemptible thing a person could do. And even if you did act on the spur of the moment, it's bad enough, for it shows that deep in your heart your intentions were far from noble. I swear before God that it was you alone who drove me to play roulette, possibly in the hope that if I lost everything I would commit suicide. God in heaven, is this what you call love? You wanted to destroy me—that's the plain truth. Your eyes reflected such malevolence that the memory of them still makes me shudder. I had even begun to be afraid that you were going to poison me or kill me in some other way. I couldn't stand it any more and I told Mirkin about it. Had he been a stone, I would have confided in it.

It's true that Mirkin attached himself to me and proposed marriage—that is, as soon as he could divorce his wife, from whom he was already separated. Is it my fault that I'm still attractive to men, and especially to someone like Mirkin, who was always traveling and hadn't enjoyed the taste of a real home for a long time? Believe me, old and crippled as he was, he was fantastically successful with women. I myself saw how beautiful women threw themselves at him. He was fabulously rich and clever besides. Despite his grand talk, I never took him seriously even for a moment. I told him that I loved only you. He was sorry, he said, because my love obviously was not returned. He wanted to give me a string of pearls worth twenty-five thousand rubles. I only laughed at his generosity. And all this happened only because you were hiding some-where and obviously trying to push me off into an abyss. I want to tell you right here and now that Mirkin still hasn't given up. He followed me to Warsaw and I barely managed to get rid of him. He wants to turn over a huge estate to me, and believe me, old and homely as he is, he has more soul than you. If I could only get myself to love him, I would be the luckiest woman in the world. Unfortunately for me, I am not that kind of person. I swear to you by all that is holy that this man has not so much as touched me. It's all the same to me whether you believe me or not. Having survived that tragic journey, I have decided that it is time to stop struggling against fate. My life has been one great disaster, and my father's death has reminded me that I won't last forever. I have put on mourning and I believe that I will never take it off again. I am also not completely well and I have a feeling that it will be—as they say—sooner rather than later.

Your sister positively refused to give me your address, but promised to send you this letter. So be it. I just want to add one thing: Any time you are prepared to admit your mistakes and to come back to me, I will receive you with open arms. Your Felusia is a sweet girl. After my father's death, Sasha took over his business affairs and I can already see that his luck will be better than mine. He is clever, intelligent, and in the short time I was away has grown so much spiritually and physically that I hardly recognize him. He is truly the only comfort of my bitter existence.

Write me before it is too late!

Your CLARA

Dear Clara:

I solemnly swore never to write to you again, but I must reply to your letter. I realize that your words to me were sincere, but I have long since come to the conclusion that sincerity can be partner to the worst kind of falsehood. Your long letter indicates to me that you have no conception of either how you behaved or even who you are. I can only tell you how things looked to me. I may be wrong, but if I can't trust my own eyes, what can I trust? You started on our trip feeling that you were a woman of property and I a pauper whom you were supporting. The tone you adopted toward me from the very beginning was so obvious that I cannot believe it was not deliberate. How much self-deception can a person practice? You immediately began to treat me as if I were your valet. You talk about being conspicuous. No one could have made more of a display of herself than you did. You made it obvious to everyone that you had money, and I had nothing! As far as your clothes were concerned, I can only say that your outfit made you look like a caricature. When I met you at the station, I almost vomited. You wore a hat as large as a washtub, piled high with a whole storeful of feathers. Your suit, with its beaded embroidery, was a model of tastelessness. You had doused yourself with so much perfume that the scent was overpowering. Everyone stared at you. That is the sad truth. How could you be so blind as not to realize how ridiculous you looked? Nor did it end with your lack of taste in clothes. Once on the train, you flirted shamelessly with all the men present, who winked at each other and laughed behind your back. The only explanation I could think of was that you were drunk. The women in the train gave both of us dirty looks. Once we were in Berlin, you insulted the chambermaid, the waiters, even the desk clerk at the hotel. Since we weren't married and were traveling on separate passports, why talk about a honeymoon? Why talk about the children you left behind? Why bare your heart to every stranger? Forgive me for these harsh words, but they are the truth. You developed a shopping mania. You spent seven hundred marks for trinkets and unnecessary things. Your purchases only led to further expenditures, because you had to buy additional luggage to accommodate them. You bothered the help at the hotel to such a degree that they began to whistle under their breath when they saw you coming. When I called your attention to the fact that you were incessantly ringing for the servants, you screamed at me and even tried to hit me. I understand now that the trip must have played havoc with your nerves, but I too was emotionally upset and your behavior drove me to despair.

What you write about Mirkin is a pack of lies, but I'm no longer jealous, and if you two were to marry I'd wish you both happiness. Nevertheless, you behaved wantonly. You write that he never even touched you, yet he kissed and fondled you in my presence. Believe me, I'm not suffering from hallucinations. In Monte Carlo you went completely mad. After the first round you won, you imagined that you could break the bank. Mirkin became so familiar with you that he even visited your room in his bathrobe and slippers. You not only confided in him but insulted me in front of him and that flunky, his secretary. Are these not the facts? Or do you still think I'm making it up? During the day you went promenading with Mirkin; then at night after visiting the casino the three of you played cards until dawn. You drank too. It isn't true that my behavior toward you was hateful and sarcastic. I had paid too dear a price to take our situation lightly. But I was shocked to the core. I have been alone now for many weeks and you'll never know how much I've suffered. I've had time to think, and I still can't find the explanation for what happened to you, or why you shattered our dreams and trampled everything underfoot. When your Don Quixote and his Sancho Panza left to join some other Dulcinea, you returned to Warsaw, where, as you yourself have written me, you later had a rendezvous with Mirkin. You've also been busy arranging a career for your Sasha, while I remained abroad, penniless and hungry. How I was able to go on and not commit suicide is still a mystery to me. These are the hard facts. Because of you, I've lost everything, yet I bear you no resentment. You are what you are, and if I was such a poor judge of character, then the fault was mine. One thing I do beg of you: let me be and let Sonya be. What you and I felt for each other was not love but the basest passion, and such relationships can only end with a hangover.

I won't deny that I still yearn for your body. At the same

time I know that any new encounter would only lead us to catastrophe. Well, enough of that. Forgive me, and kiss Felusia. I will probably be going to America soon and begin what is called "a new life," although I have lost my appetite for everything.

In your letter you invoke God as your witness. I could do the same if I believed in His existence. To my sorrow, I don't —and neither do you. That, I'm afraid, is the reason for all our madness.

ALEXANDER

2

Mirale had been arrested for subversive activities; there was
word from Otwock that Miriam Lieba was in a critical condition; and Ezriel's wife had borne him a boy. Ezriel had to engage
a nurse, arrange for the circumcision, and invite his parents
as well as his father-in-law, Calman. All these events presented
Ezriel with spiritual and practical difficulties. Circumcising an
eight-day-old child seemed to him an act of barbarism. Why
stop at that? Why not offer sacrifices as well? It was true that
most of the assimilated Jews in Warsaw still circumcised their
sons, but where was the logic? Must he, Ezriel, a doctor living
in the second half of the nineteenth century, emulate an act of
black magic that a group of Bedouins had performed in Asia
four thousand years before? But not to have the circumcision
was impossible. Shaindel would die of mortification. Ezriel's
parents had wept and suffered over Mirale's arrest. This new
blow would be too much. And could Ezriel do such a thing to
the other grandfather, Calman, whose money had paid for his
education? He might even lose his position at the hospital and
in the clinic. A Jew who did not have his child circumcised
had to be an atheist, and, therefore, politically suspect. Ezriel
was forced to find a *mohel*, and invite his parents to his house,
although he was ashamed to have his Gentile neighbors see his
father in his rabbinical fur hat and his mother in her ancient

bonnet. He was ashamed of being ashamed, and his feelings grew even more intense. Although Shaindel kept a kosher kitchen, Reb Menachem Mendel and Tirza Perl had no faith in it. They announced in advance that they would eat nothing in Ezriel's house. To top it all, the infant developed dysentery and there was no certainty that he would survive eight days, and if he did, whether the circumcision could take place on time.

Besides, Ezriel had been foolish. He hadn't told Olga Bielikov that he was about to become a father for the third time. Shaindel's confinement, the complications surrounding the circumcision, and the infant's illness robbed him of the evenings when he would normally visit Olga or meet her at the Saxony Gardens. When he did manage to join her, he appeared distracted, pale, exhausted. It wasn't easy to stroll arm-in-arm with one woman when the other was still recuperating from the birth of your child. Ezriel was conscience-stricken, but at the same time he brooded about whether to give up his Judaism. Why did the Jews segregate themselves? What did they hope to gain? Why all the martyrdom? The Messiah was not coming. The faithful believed in a world to come, but what use was Judaism to someone like Ezriel? Why be a member of the Jewish community, pay them taxes? Ezriel daydreamed about going to Russia with Olga, or of settling with her in France, or in America, where one could live freely, without bearing the burden of generations.

In Ezriel's breast pocket lay a letter saying that his sister-in-law, Miriam Lieba, was close to death. Her husband, Lucian, was still in prison. Her father had disowned her. Her sisters, his wife included, wanted nothing to do with her. At least he should be with her in her last days. But with things as they were, how could he leave town?

He listened to his patients, but he was no less distracted than they. Shaindel's delivery had been expensive. He had been forced to borrow a hundred rubles from a usurer at exorbitant interest. He prescribed all sorts of remedies for the sick: hypnotism, baths, medicine to banish pain, to quiet the heart. But these merely stilled the symptoms. Society itself with its antiquated laws, empty privileges, religious fanaticisms, exploitations, was a fertile soil for madness. What should he do? Wage war against it all, the way his sister Mirale did? History had proved her wrong. Ezriel knew that as soon as one madness disappeared, ten others replaced it. Every revolution had its Robespierre, its Napoleon, its Metternich. Millions of young men had already perished in all kinds of righteous campaigns, but the Bismarcks and the Podbiedonoscevs still ruled. Warsaw was seething over the assassination of the provocateur, Minsky, who had betrayed Maria Bohuszewicz and her group. Kawalewski had just been hanged. The revolutionaries in Russia were divided and had broken into factions. They vilified each other. What would become of his sister? For ten years she would sit in jail and come out a broken old woman. Probably disillusioned as well. Each day in the Shlisselburg Fortress, in the Citadel, in every prison, young people hanged themselves, poured kerosene over themselves and set themselves on fire, or wrote letters of repentance to the Czar. A large number of political prisoners in Warsaw went insane and were sent to him as patients at the Bonifraten Hospital.

Ezriel often discussed these things with Olga Bielikov. She had confided to him that she too had belonged to a revolutionary circle during her gymnasium days. Even now she sympathized with the revolutionaries, but she was a mother. Besides, she had noticed a great deal of egoism and hypocrisy in the rebels. Yes, something needed to be done—but what? What would happen to Natasha and Kolia if she were imprisoned? And how would this help the people? . . . Olga continued to speak about one thing and another. She had nothing to do in Warsaw. She did not feel at home with either Jews or Poles. The Russians who came to Poland were of the worst sort. Her children were lonesome. She had no women friends. Finally she blurted out that she was too young to remain single. Sooner or later, she would have to marry. She made it clear that Ezriel would have to make a decision. What sort of life was this—to hide before a maid, before children, neighbors? What was the sense in sitting in the Saxony Gardens or in the theater when they yearned to be together? He walked with her at night on a dark path in the park and lusted for her. The few times that she had surrendered herself to him in the kitchen or in Kolia's bed had only whetted his desire. She was fiery in a way he had never known. What she said upset him. With someone like Olga, one could travel, enter society. He could even discuss his work with her. But how could he desert Shaindel and the children? Would Olga forsake Kolia and Natasha for him? There was no escape from his entanglements.

In the midst of all these problems, the circumcision took place. Reb Menachem Mendel and Tirza Perl arrived in a droshky. Calman came from Jampol. He was the one to hold his grandchild at the circumcision. Reb Menachem Mendel and Tirza Perl were to be the godparents. A mohel who boasted that he had circumcised the infants of all the well-to-do Jews came and charged a fifteen-ruble fee. Tirza Perl demanded that Ezriel name the boy after her father, Reb Abraham Moshe Hamburg, but Ezriel did not want to handicap his son with such old-fashioned names. Officially, the child was registered as Michael—Misha.

Shaindel sobbed in her bed when she heard the cries of her son. Ezriel stood by with lifted eyebrows. He considered it a foolish act to stamp a child's body with the mark of Judaism at a time of anti-Semitism and pogroms. But he was not the master here. In the living room a chair had been set aside for the prophet Elijah, as was the custom. There were little round cakes on a tray. Beakers of wine had been filled. Ezriel wore a skullcap and recited the benediction: "Blessed art Thou, our Lord, our God, King of the universe, who has sanctified us by Thy commandments and has commanded us to make our sons enter into the covenant of Abraham our father." And the quorum of Jews replied: "Even as he has entered into the covenant, so may he enter into the Law, the nuptial canopy, and into good deeds."

II

Justina Malewska, Wallenberg's daughter, invited Olga Bielikov's children, Natasha and Kolia, to her villa in Wilanow for two weeks. Olga was suddenly free. Ezriel felt that he had to go to Otwock to see Miriam Lieba, who had suffered another hemorrhage and he asked Olga to accompany him. But she was not so easily convinced. They might run into people who knew them. Where would they sleep? Ezriel, who knew Otwock, tried to reassure her. The chances of meeting acquaintances in the stagecoach were small. There was a hotel in Otwock, and the journey would only take about six hours. They would leave at eight in the morning and arrive at two in the afternoon. The air in Otwock was good. Neither of them had taken a holiday that summer. Why not spend a few days in the country? Olga continued to hesitate. She felt that their relationship was sinful. Andrey no longer appeared in her dreams, as if, in death, he were aware of her scandalous behavior. She was not only risking her own reputation but was sullying the names of her children. At first, Olga said no. But finally she reconsidered. She was not accustomed to spending the summers in the city. She longed for trees, green grass, cool breezes, for the smell of field and forest. And she wanted some time alone with her lover. The heroines of the French novels that Olga read did not permit obstacles to keep them from rendezvous in cheap hotels or in the Bois de Boulogne. She, at least, was not betraying a husband.

Everything went smoothly. Ezriel took several days' leave from the hospital. Shaindel obviously could not accompany him. At a quarter to eight in the morning, Ezriel sat waiting in the stagecoach on Gnoyna Street. Five minutes later, Olga joined him, wearing a freshly ironed dress, a straw hat with a green band, and carrying a satchel and a small bandbox. There wasn't another Jew in the stagecoach. Olga sat next to Ezriel. The August day was warm. After crossing the Praga bridge, the coach passed by fields and villages. In a marketplace, peasant women sat beside cans of milk and baskets containing chickens, ducks, mushrooms, vegetables. Jewish women in wigs and bonnets bargained and haggled with the peasants. Officers drilled soldiers in the barracks courtyard. In several of the villages it was market day. A carousel whirled around in a meadow. In front of a church, a band played for a wedding. Twigs decorated the horses' harnesses. The peasants of the Warsaw countryside were not as poor as those in Turbin. Ezriel and Olga passed huts covered with shingles and even roofs of tin. From taverns came the sound of concertinas. In the village stores the shelves were laden with leather goods, hardware, haberdashery, dry-goods. Farther on, there were woods, summer cottages. Polish squires had their villas here. Russian officials came out for the summers. The six hours passed quickly. In Otwock, the stagecoach rolled up to the inn where Ezriel and Olga were to stay. The proprietor requested Ezriel's passport, according to which Shaindel *née* Jacoby was his wife. How could anyone know that Olga was not Shaindel? It went so smoothly that Olga was amused.

They were given a room in the attic, with a French window. It was neat and cool. After lunch, Olga went for a walk while Ezriel visited Miriam Lieba. Miriam Lieba had at first stayed in the sanatorium but now lived in rooms not far from the hospital. Many consumptive women lived in private homes, looking after one another. The winters were severe and the houses were often snowed in. But the air in this season was even purer than in summer. There was always a smell of pine in the town. All of Poland praised the wonders of Otwock. A consumptive could even grow new lungs here. . . .

Ezriel got lost each time he visited Otwock. How could one locate a street in the midst of a forest? Potato fields and pastures were scattered all over the city. At last Ezriel found his way to Miriam Lieba's house. When he entered her room, she was lying in bed. Bottles of medicine stood on a chair. A kitten sat at a window licking one of its paws. One look and Ezriel knew that Miriam Lieba was close to death. Her emaciated face was altered beyond recognition. Gray hairs mingled with the gold. Her neck seemed unnaturally long. Her teeth had changed, protruding in a sort of mirthless smile. Her skin was sallow. Only her eyes remained the same. Ezriel stood speechless a moment.

"Miriam Lieba!"

"Ezriel!"

Then for a long while neither spoke. Afterwards, Miriam Lieba said in Polish: "It's good you came. I'm dying."

"Don't be ridiculous!"

"Look here, he's brought flowers. Put them in water, Ezriel."

As soon as she spoke, Miriam Lieba seemed herself again. She began questioning him about Shaindel's delivery, about the newborn child, about Joziek, Zina.

"How does Papa look?" she asked.

"Pretty well, but his hair is white."

"Do you think he'll observe the seven days of mourning for me?"

Ezriel trembled. "Don't talk such foolishness!"

"Oh, men are such cowards. Mother used to say: 'I'm not an ox. I'm not afraid of slaughter. . . .' "

Miriam Lieba grew silent again. She looked at Ezriel, and her eyes twinkled. Soon she dozed off, seeming to forget her visitor. Quietly, Ezriel began to unpack the things he had brought her: sweet cream, sardines, chocolate, a bottle of cognac. The door opened slowly, without a sound, and Miriam Lieba's neighbor, a yellow-haired woman with the overly red cheeks consumptives sometimes have in the early stages of their illness, thrust her head in. She beckoned to Ezriel and whispered to him that the doctor had been there the day before and had said there was little hope for the patient. She also informed Ezriel that Miriam Lieba's sister-in-law, Felicia, had spent the weekend with her. Felicia was making efforts to get Lucian freed before it was too late. Miriam Lieba had signed a petition to the district attorney requesting her husband's release from prison before her death.

III

It was the first night that Ezriel and Olga Bielikov had spent together. The window was open, and moonlight shone in. Cool breezes blew in from the Otwock forests. Ezriel had looked at death, but his lust for life had not diminished because of it. Too happy to fall asleep, they kissed for hours. Even while possessing each other, their desire increased. If this night could only last forever! If they could go to an island somewhere! If they could forget everything and everybody and merely live for this intoxication! Ezriel had had nights of passion with Shaindel, but his affair with Olga had stirred fresh powers in him. He spoke as the mad do, uttering insane fantasies. They fell asleep at dawn. The sun and the birds awakened them. Warsaw weekdays were prosaic; here in Otwock, nature celebrated a holiday, a lengthy Pentecost, all green and light. Flashes of light danced on the walls and the ceiling, as if someone across the way was playing with a mirror. A bird chirped: "Tsif-tsif." Another gave a long whistle; a third crowed angrily as if calling dire warnings into the thicket of needles and pine cones. "Cuckoo!" a cuckoo repeated again and again. Ezriel and Olga listened and kissed. Ezriel jokingly explained to Olga the philosophical meaning of its call: the world was neither matter nor will but "cuckoo." In the beginning there was "cuckoo" and in the end there would be "cuckoo." All had been created by the celestial cuckoo and his plan was: "cuckoo . . ." In Warsaw one forgot that there were such things as birds in the world. How could mankind have survived all the wars, all the plagues, all the famines and deaths if not for such music?

The chambermaid knocked, asking if the guests wanted tea, coffee, cocoa. She brought a jug of water from the pump. The water was cold, fresh, and seemed full of subterranean secrets. Ezriel and Olga were no longer modest before one another. They washed side by side in front of the washstand. Afterwards, they sat down to breakfast. The poppy-seed rolls were crisp between their teeth. The milk smelled of udder. The cottage cheese was sprinkled with caraway. The coffee was somewhat burned and had too much chicory in it. But it was tasty nonetheless. After breakfast, both of them returned to bed. Ezriel embraced Olga and said: "Now we know each other a little better."

"Yes, but what will come of it?"

Ezriel dressed and went to see Miriam Lieba. Olga was to meet him at the stagecoach. Even Miriam Lieba looked fresher and somewhat healthier this morning. There was a maid there who served both Miriam Lieba and the woman with the yellow hair. Miriam Lieba was in a talkative mood. Could Ezriel persuade her father to come to see her? She wanted to see him before she died. Perhaps Ezriel could arrange for Lucian's release. He had suffered enough for his crime. Why wasn't Ezriel going to visit Tsipele in Marshinov? Was it true that Jochebed was already a grandmother? Miriam Lieba told him that her children, Wladzio and Marisia, had come to see her once. Oh, how handsome they were! Gloriously beautiful, but somehow estranged. The boy still had some feelings for her, but the girl seemed entirely cold. The neighbor fussed about. She apparently wanted to say something to Ezriel. Miriam Lieba raised her brows. Finally she indicated that she wanted to be alone with her guest.

"You come so seldom," she said to Ezriel, "surely we'll never see each other again."

"Don't be a fool."

He raised the pillow and helped her to sit up. He noticed

that she was wearing an attractive nightgown, probably a present from Felicia. She had put on cologne and combed her hair. Even on her deathbed, she remained coquettish.

Ezriel said, "You're still lovely."

"Oh, who thinks of such things?"

Suddenly Miriam Lieba said: "Did you know, Ezriel, that I was in love with you, before Lucian appeared?"

Ezriel paled.

"I've loved you too. All these years."

"Shaindel was jealous. How old was I, anyhow? Perhaps seventeen. Afterwards, he bewitched me. Well, I paid dearly for it."

"Did you at least have some joy with him?"

"Now and then, a day or two."

Ezriel bowed his head. Miriam Lieba looked toward the window. "Ezriel, do you believe in God?"

"What do you mean by God? In a God who acts like a person? No."

"I always did believe. Now it seems to me that there's nothing. The priest will come, and all the rest of it. What shall I do?"

"Don't think about it."

"What should I think about? Yes, I *do* believe. But when the pains come and I can't catch my breath, I begin to waver . . . Ezriel!"

"What is it, dear?"

"Don't betray Shaindel!"

Ezriel could not see the connection between the two thoughts, but he had long ago perceived that the law of association was not as consistent as psychologists thought. The human mind jumped freely from one subject to another.

"Why should I betray her?"

"Oh, you may. It doesn't pay to do wrong."

"Yes, that's true."

"Give me your hand."

3 ♜

I

The winter was over. It had been a difficult one. The severe frosts had toppled sparrows from the Warsaw trees. In the fields, the winter wheat froze beneath the snow. Calman Jacoby contracted a stomach typhus but miraculously survived. About to assume partnership in a Lodz factory, Jacob Danziger, Zipkin's father-in-law, had come home at summer's end, jolly and well-fed. Four months later he had a heart attack and in eight days he was dead. He was buried in Gęsia Street cemetery, in the first row. Madame Rosa was a widow. Sabina, Zipkin's deserted wife, enveloped herself in black, her face heavily veiled. The dry-goods business was taken over by her brother, Zdzislaw.

Another who died that winter was Pan Wallenberg's wife, Pani Matilda. She never emerged from the anesthesia after a gallstone operation. She was buried in the Catholic cemetery in Powązek, in the Wallenbergs' family crypt. A famous Polish sculptor made the monument according to Wallenberg's design: an angel with Matilda's face stood on a pedestal. The monument cost ten thousand rubles.

Now it was spring again. Streams splashed into the Vistula. The mud began to dry up. In the synagogues and Houses of Prayer many mourners said Kaddish, for Warsaw had been rampant with typhus, croup, scarlet fever, and all kinds of maladies. In the churches, mothers, wives, and sisters lit candles to the saints in memory of the deceased. Spring had come early. March was warm. Matzoth was being baked in the Jewish bakeries. Jews came to Reb Menachem Mendel to sell the unleavened bread. Reb Menachem Mendel couldn't see to write the bills of sale, and the yeshiva boys helped him. In the Gentile houses, before Easter, a priest came to bless the bread. The janitors and pious women followed behind him.

At the Wallenbergs', Easter was celebrated with great pomp. A bishop blessed the bread that lay on a golden tray. The whole family gathered to celebrate the holiday. But Pan Wallenberg had turned melancholy. As long as Pani Matilda had been alive, no one had been aware that he loved her. He had often been angry with her. She was not as intelligent or alert as he. She had been easy to deceive. When there were no visitors in the house, he used to scold her in the Jewish manner, call her "silly woman," "idiot," and other names. Offended, Pani Matilda would weep. Sometimes he would shout at her using a phrase he had heard from his father and grandfather: "You *beheimah*, you cow!"

Then in apology he would kiss her eyes and promise her jewelry. Now that Pani Matilda was dead, it became clear how fond he had been of this simple woman. When he spoke of her to his children, the tears began to flow. He closed off her bedroom, hired a man to lay fresh flowers on her grave daily. He severed his connections with his beloved *Courier*, though he still put money into the paper. His appetite left him, his stout stomach shrank. Pouches hung beneath his eyes. He even lost his taste for Havana cigars. The doctors felt that a trip abroad would benefit his health, but he refused to go. "Without her," he said, "it would be worse than hell!"

Pan Wallenberg began to write his memoirs, intimating his end was near, but he could scarcely hold a pen. His handwriting was shaky, blotted, and blurred. He wanted to dictate to someone, but his secretary was busy in his office, and, besides, he did not trust her. Intimate things could only be revealed to a person one felt close to. It occurred to Madame Justina Malewska, Wallenberg's eldest daughter, that Olga Bielikov might be just the person. Olga's Polish was adequate and she could spell, had good handwriting, and he would not be embarrassed in her presence. At first the idea did not appeal to Wallenberg, but finally he saw that his daughter was right. He would be more at ease with someone who had suffered a similar loss and could understand his feelings. Olga Bielikov still mourned her husband. She had not remarried.

Wallenberg agreed and Justina arranged the rest. A devoted daughter, she really loved her father, unlike the younger daughter, Pola, for whom pleasure took first place. Justina felt it would be good for her father to have a younger woman around, and it would be a blessing for Olga Bielikov, who badly needed an income. Justina Malewska drove to Olga Bielikov's in her carriage, explained everything, and Olga, as anticipated, gratefully accepted the opportunity. She was somewhat apprehensive about making errors, but Justina assured her that a dictionary would solve most of her problems, and gave her twenty-five rubles in advance. After Madame Malewska's visit, Olga went to Marshalkovsky Boulevard and bought herself a pair of shoes, a hat, and gloves. She could not go to the Wallenbergs' looking like a beggar.

The following day she took a droshky to Pan Wallenberg's villa. He greeted her cordially, treated her like an old friend, even cried in front of her. Then he took her into his office and began dictating the first chapter of his memoirs. He made no secret of his Jewish ancestry. He spoke of his grandfather, who had paid a head tax each time he came to Warsaw, of his grandmother, Beila Brachah, who wore a bonnet and on Fridays brought a pot roast and chicken soup to the poor at the almshouse. Olga was touched by these homely descriptions. It could have been her biography that he was dictating in stentorian tones. Pan Wallenberg paced back and forth in his gaiters, occasionally blowing his nose and wiping away his tears. Olga too felt a tightness in her throat. The recent converts of her acquaintance were ashamed of their Jewish ancestry. Wallenberg called things by their true name. He dictated to her for three hours straight, and although Olga had studied at a Russian school, her command of Polish was such that she was even able to correct a phrase here and there, or suggest the right word. Pan Wallenberg adjusted his gold-rimmed spectacles, read what he had dictated, and nodded his gray head in approval. The chapter had turned out magnificently.

11

The sun was warming everything. In the Saxony Gardens the lilacs were blooming. In the streets, rails were being laid for horse-drawn trolleys. Pavements were torn up. Dray wagons delivered cobblestones and track sections, which were unloaded and neatly stacked, ready for use. Mighty hammers pounded. In Praga, in Wola, in Ochota, even in the center of Warsaw, factories were springing up. From Germany, France, the United States, there came machinery so huge that it was impossible to understand how human minds could have invented it or how human hands could have put it together. On Krakow Boulevard and New World Boulevard the gas street lamps were being converted to arc lights. The banks had more capital: manufacturers and merchants received loans at small interest. The housing authority extended credit and Jews began to build. Land became expensive and buildings soared upward—four and five stories. Rows of houses were erected around two and three connecting courtyards.

The revolutionary circles created by the "Proletariat" party had been dispersed by the police. A new political movement, both patriotic and liberal, a mixture of radicalism and nationalism with a touch of anti-Semitism, had sprung up in Poland. Some Poles, however, still remembered the gallows in the Citadel, the martyrdom of Bandrowski and Kunicki, Osowski and Petruszewicz. Nor had they forgotten the strike in Lodz and the Zyrardow massacre. A second "Proletariat" succeeded the first. In Vilna, Bialystok, Riga, Minsk, the Jewish intelligentsia and workers engaged in socialist activities. There were those who considered themselves "Narodowolces"; others sympathized with Plekhanov, the Marxist; still others were anarchists; and some spoke of forming a Jewish socialist party. Mendelsohn, the son of a Jewish banker in Poland, organized a Polish socialist group in Paris. Farther left than the revolutionaries in Warsaw, he demanded that Polish workers renounce Polish nationalism, stop celebrating national holidays, and become completely merged with the world proletariat. So widespread was socialism among modern Jews that Jewish boys and girls in Vilna, Minsk, and Bialystok sent their Russian comrades money, helped them smuggle banned literature into Poland, obtain hectographs, paper, type, and whatever else was needed to further revolutionary activities. The Russian organizations themselves had a large Jewish membership.

Tragedy struck Ezriel's sister. The women's division of the prison in which Mirale was serving her sentence was called "Serbia." She began to suffer from heartburn, and occasionally vomited. It was not like Mirale to complain or ask for a doctor. Stefan Lamanski, her mentor, had taught her that a revolutionary must suffer proudly and mutely. But the political women prisoners who shared her cell noticed that her waistline was thickening. It was soon obvious that Mirale was pregnant. The prisoners did not know whether to laugh or cry. It was common knowledge that Mirale had worked with Stefan Lamanski and helped him with an underground printing press. There had even been a rumor that they had actually lived together as man and wife. Although Mirale had kept it a secret, the rumor proved to be a fact. Suddenly it was out in the open. Ever since she had dedicated herself to the revolution, Mirale's periods had been irregular. Ezriel had told her it was due to nerves, and prescribed a remedy. It would have been possible to help Mirale if she had recognized her symptoms sooner. Quinine and other abortive aids could have been smuggled into the prison. One of the women was a midwife. But Mirale was now in her fifth month.

In the period of Mirale's imprisonment she felt she had suffered every blow that fate could deliver. She had been beaten, insulted, tortured. She had contracted an inflammation of the intestines and had spinal pains. The district attorney had boasted to her that her organization had been filled with informers. To prove it he had described her apartment in detail and enumerated her visitors. It was clear that there had been traitors among her intimates. But who were they? These *provocateurs* destroyed one's faith in humanity, caused confusion, doubt. As if this were not enough, there was no peace among the comrades in the cell. Women became hysterical, wailed, tried to kill themselves. Some cursed their revolutionary activities. Others fussed about a crust of bread, an article of clothing, a comb, a rag. The discussions and disputes daily grew more bitter. The women argued, formed cliques. Each day Mirale warned herself anew not to be drawn into these conflicts. Outside the prison, reaction ruled. Inside, there were squabbles over words, phrases. One had to be stronger than iron not to become involved. Mirale did her best. She did not speak for hours, read the books that were available in the prison library. She stopped participating in the debates. More than once she stuffed her ears with balls of soft bread to keep from listening to empty words, angry remarks, the absurdities voiced about socialism, the role of the peasant, Polish independence, the place of women in society.

There were moments when Mirale was afraid of breaking down, but she kept reminding herself of Stefan Lamanski. How would he have acted in such a situation? What would he have said? She saw his face, his eyes, heard his deep voice. She imagined him whispering words of comfort to her. Hadn't he suffered even more than she? Hadn't he thrown away a home and a career for the sake of the masses? Hadn't he fought, day after day, against stupidity, ignorance, obstinacy, and even betrayal? Mirale recalled his words: "The revolutionary must be prepared for everything. He must not lose sight of his goal for a single moment. He must rise above mundane pettiness, accidents, weaknesses, errors. He must battle not only the enemies outside, but also the lazy, the incompetents, the windbags, the fools, and the opportunists, within the ranks, who try to exploit the revolution for their own gains. The revolutionary must be capable of compassion and justice, but he must also be able cold-bloodedly to cut away such destructive dissidents as the Tichamirovs, Minskys, Goldbergs—all who, willingly or unwillingly, help the enemy strengthen his position." On another occasion he had said: "If one can't stand the smell of gunpowder, one can't build barricades."

But Mirale was not prepared for what was happening to her now. It was a shame and a disgrace in itself, a slap in the face for the party, a source of comfort to the authorities. When Mirale lay awake at night, her doubts and suspicions bordered on madness.

III

They were doing the wash. In the kitchen there was a tub filled with blueing. A laundry pot boiled on the stove and Tekla, the maid, stirred the linen with a piece of wood. There was a smell of soap, washing soda, and the remnants of supper. Shaindel hung diapers to dry on a makeshift line. Although her hair was already graying, she was forced to occupy herself with an infant, suckle it, rock it, stay awake nights. Ezriel too was constantly fatigued because the child kept them up. He had often said that this was one son he didn't need. But Shaindel wouldn't hear of an abortion. Now she was paying for it. She wore a short petticoat, her bare feet thrust into battered slippers. Her breasts were those of a wet nurse; her eyes expressed irritation. Joziek and Zina sat in the parlor. Joziek had just enrolled in the university as a law student and wore a student's cap and uniform. He smoked openly like an adult. He was not as tall as his father but had inherited his mother's beauty. There was a bluish sheen to his black hair. His face was light, round; the nose straight; the lips full. The dark eyes were serene, preoccupied. This particular evening Ezriel thought that Joziek did not look well. Reading an introduction to jurisprudence, shaking ashes into an ashtray, he kept looking distractedly at his sister, at the window, at the door. Zina, already in her fourth year at the gymnasium, had two golden braids. She resembled Ezriel, but there was also something of Miriam Lieba about her. In her infancy, Zina had been wild, raucous, but now she was dreamy, girlishly capricious, inclined to laugh, to cry, to spite her mother, to nurse secrets. The girls at school often gave parties, sometimes inviting a couple of boy students, but Zina always found excuses for not attending. She seemed to have inherited Ezriel's bashfulness. Joziek was good at mathematics, but Zina could not cope with algebra. Now she wrote out problems, erasing, nostrils quivering.

"Joziek, you must help me!"

"What is it?"

"I'm confused."

"Well, sister, there have been worse tragedies!"

Ezriel came out of his office. He too had been in the midst of reading a book, but now he wanted to take a walk. He did not have an appointment with Olga, but he felt like walking to Zielna Street. There was a good distance between Nowolipki Street and Zielna Street, but he could make it in twenty minutes, perhaps even less. It was 9:30, but Olga never went to sleep before one. He had spent the day among the insane. At night he read about them. He had to clear his head. The nosology of insanity, the etiology, the symptomology, pathology, diagnosis, prognosis, the care—how nicely the textbooks classified everything! How accurately they defined the idiot, the cretin, the imbecile, the epileptic, the hysteric, hypochondriac, and neurasthenic. Instead of admitting that little was known about what went on in the human brain, either healthy or sick, the professors stacked up Latin names. And what was going on in his, Ezriel's own skull? He allegedly cured others, but he himself suffered from all sorts of psychic disturbances. He was obsessed with phobias, worries, superstitions. He wrestled with compulsive ideas. "What would happen if—?" That was his recurring fantasy. If he won seventy-five thousand rubles. . . . If he were to discover a potion for eternal life . . . If he found a way to become omniscient. . . . If he possessed hypnotic power that could control everyone's will—he daydreamed like a schoolboy. Whenever he was alone, he lay on the couch. He wanted only to dream, to ponder. What was time? What was space? What was the atom? What was gravity? Where did the first cell originate? Could life be the result of chemical accidents? What powers were concerned with his deceiving his patients, Shaindel, himself? His parents were both sick, dependent on him, but the moment he decided to go to see them he put them out of his mind. He was haunted by a feeling that his life was nearing a crisis. He would soon have to make an important decision. But why? Why believe in premonition like a servant girl? "I am tired," Ezriel muttered to himself. "I have too many burdens . . . Mirale is still in prison . . . They may still send her to Siberia . . ." Shaindel came in from the kitchen. Zina raised her face from her book.

"Oh, Mother, look at yourself!" And she laughed.

Shaindel grew annoyed. "What is it?"

"You're all smudged."

"Well, what of it? Your fingers are smeared with ink."

"You look so funny."

"When you're busy in the kitchen, you get dirty. Are you going out?" Shaindel said, turning to Ezriel.

"I must take a walk. My head is filled with nonsense."

"Where are you going? You say you're going for a walk and you come back at one in the morning. I haven't been out of the house all day."

"Well, come along."

"You know I don't have the time. You suggest it because you know I won't go."

"Why do you say that?"

"Oh, enough! When will you be back? I'm ashamed to face the janitor. Every night you drag him out of bed."

"You know that's not true."

"It's true. The children know it too. Ask them."

"I won't ask anyone. Good night, children."

Going down the stairs, Ezriel took long strides. He passed the Przejazd, Przechodnia Street, crossed Iron Gate, and soon found himself on Graniczna Street. The scent of trees and grass came from the Saxony Gardens. The streets smelled of horse manure, sewers, rotten fruit. It was a neighborhood of bazaars and inns. In the semi-darkness, carts, covered wagons, and dray wagons were still being loaded. Late stagecoaches drew up, discharging their passengers. On Krolewska Street he suddenly saw the arc lights that lit up Marshalkovsky Boulevard. This section of Warsaw was entirely Europeanized. Open horse-drawn trolley cars skimmed along the tracks, bells ringing, conductors selling tickets. A man wearing a red cap switched a section of rail with a metal rod. Zielna Street was dark and quiet. At the gate of her house, to his surprise, Ezriel saw Olga. She stood there as if waiting for someone.

"Whom are you expecting?"

She smiled. "You, naturally."

"I wasn't supposed to come."

"I know."

"Do you practice black magic?"

"I felt you were coming."

"Are you a mind reader?"

"I always have been."

IV

He looked at her more closely. She was wearing new clothes and appeared youthful, elegant, almost rich.

"What's happened?" he asked. "Did you win the seventy-five-thousand-ruble lottery?"

She smiled mysteriously. "If I wanted to, I could win even more."

"You're speaking in riddles."

"Yes."

For a moment they were both silent. Then he said: "Would you like to walk or go inside?"

"Let's walk for a bit."

She placed her white-gloved hand on his arm, her touch so light that he felt her hand must soon slide away. They strolled along Krolewska Street, passed Prozna Street, and were soon at the Saxony Gardens. Usually they would have had something to discuss immediately, but now they were both silent. "Something has happened," he thought. He felt almost shy. Instead of entering the park, Olga remained standing at the gate, leaning against the stone posts in which the iron railings were imbedded. Here he had a better view of her. She had never seemed so intriguing and mysterious. Her eyes gleamed with joy. He grew alarmed, suspecting he had lost her, although he did not know how.

"What has happened?"

Olga's face became serious. "We must make an important decision today. It concerns you, too."

"What is it?"

"Wallenberg has made me an offer."

"What sort of an offer? Does he want to marry you?"

"Yes."

In the darkness, Ezriel felt himself flush. He felt ashamed, like the betrayed hero in a story.

"How did it happen?"

"Suddenly. I don't understand it myself."

"Oh."

"I must give him an answer."

"When?"

"Tomorrow."

Ezriel did not reply immediately. He moved his arm to free himself from her hand. She held on a moment longer, then let go. He too leaned against the rails, and stared at a house across the street. Now he understood his uneasiness of the past days, his disturbed sleep, and distorted dreams. "Why hadn't this occurred to me immediately?" he wondered. "After all, I knew she was working with him . . ." He stared at a lighted window on the second story, at shadows gliding behind the draperies—male and female. What were they doing? Were they dancing? All at once the woman beside him had become alien as only a person can who has withdrawn all that has been given. He had a sudden urge to run away. He reconsidered quickly and decided to remain calm, proud, and not to make foolish scenes like the patient who had gone to look at his former sweetheart through a keyhole . . . Ezriel had no desire to degrade himself before this woman who simultaneously carried on an affair with him and permitted an elderly millionaire to make overtures to her. All was lost. At least he must retain his human dignity. He even grew lighthearted, as always happens when there is an end to uncertainties.

"Well, why are you silent?" she asked.

"What can I say?"

"Come, let's go. You have a lot to say. You mustn't think that I deceived you from the beginning." She spoke with a tremor in her voice. "I'm not as frivolous as you think."

"I no longer know what you are."

"I'm the same Lithuanian girl." She suddenly said in Yiddish, "Love is no toy for me," and continued in Polish, "I waited for you beside the gate. I hoped you would come. I called you."

"What for? To be best man?"

Olga stopped. "You know how rich he is and the position

he holds. But if you want to marry me, I'll say no to him. He's a decent man and I like him, but I'm yours. Do you understand?"

"Yes."

"For my own sake, as well as my children's, I can't remain someone's sweetheart forever."

"I understand."

"You keep telling me you can't divorce your wife. What's left for me? To live a life of shame?"

"It's not a shame."

"Not for you, but for me. The children are growing up. Natasha understands everything already. How long can I live a hidden life? Even Jadzia guesses the situation. Once she found one of your blond hairs on the bedding. God in heaven, if someone had told me that I was capable of such a thing I'd never have believed it. If someone had told Andrey that I could conduct myself in such a manner, he would have shot that person. It's against my nature, my upbringing, everything I believe in. To share someone with another woman . . ."

"What actually do you want me to do?" Ezriel asked. "My wife won't divorce me. I can't force her to do so."

"I want nothing. Oh, you could manage it! True love finds a way. We could go abroad, to America. One can't hold a husband by force. You even once mentioned converting. In that case, every bond between you and Shaindel would have been broken. I know these are nothing more than words to you, but I say them because I want you to believe that I'm ready for anything. I would go off with you tomorrow."

"I'm listening."

"I'm willing to give up Wallenberg's millions for you, but what are you prepared to do for me?"

"Everything, except murder a human being. As far as that goes, I'm still a Jew."

"Oh, those are empty phrases. You won't kill her. Having survived Andrey's death, I know that one doesn't die of anguish."

"You were young. You're still young. For Shaindel it would be the end. Besides, it would make me a thief too."

"I don't know what you mean."

"I studied on her money. Stealing and killing aren't part of my character."

"Money can be repaid."

"She has a baby as well."

About to laugh, Olga suddenly grew sad.

"A baby?" she asked, astonished. "When did that happen?"

"It happened."

"And you said nothing to me all the while?"

"I had no reason to say anything."

"Well, that's odd. I felt you were keeping something from me. What is it—a boy or a girl?"

"A boy."

"Well, *mazel tov*," she said. For a moment her eyes became merry.

"God willing, the same to you and Wallenberg," he replied also in Yiddish.

"Two children are enough. I once dreamed of having a child of yours, but that's impossible now. What is he called?"

"Misha."

"What else will I discover if I continue to ask questions? Perhaps you have one or two more sweethearts? Well, that's that."

They walked in silence, a bit apart, each lost in thought. They came to Alexander Square and stood there looking at the gas-lit street lamps and the obelisk looming above them against the night sky. The square was empty and quiet as at midnight. Shadows concealed Olga's face.

"When did all this happen?" Ezriel finally said.

Olga shivered. "It was all very sudden. I can't understand it myself. He'd always been so correct. He was dictating. We talked a little. I've known him for such a long time. He was always weeping because of Matilda. I consoled him as well as I could. I really felt sorry for him. We grow wretched in old age. We're wretched when we're young as well. All at once he began talking to me in an entirely different tone. I can't understand it!"

"What about your religion? You'll have to convert again. He'll want you to become a Catholic."

"Yes, he insists on it."

"Well, Jesus won't mind."

"Don't laugh. This is serious."

"What we won't do for a couple of millions!"

"I don't need millions. If I were greedy for money, I wouldn't be pleading with you. All I want is to provide for my children."

"We all say that."

"It's true. What sort of happiness will I have? He's an old man. He has sons, daughters, sons-in-law, daughters-in-law, grandchildren. He's a patriarch, and I'm terrified when I think of it. Justina in particular makes me feel ashamed. All this luxury means nothing to me."

"He'll leave you a fortune."

"Since you don't want me, why be so cruel about it?"

"I do want you. More than you imagine."

"Those words don't mean anything!"

"I can't destroy four people. I can't throw aside my family any more than you can disregard your children."

"Well, then, there's nothing to say."

They stood for a while longer as if searching for something in the gravel at their feet. A breeze blew in from the Vistula. Somewhere a train whistle sounded—drawn-out and sad, as if longing for distances. After a while they started back. Olga clung to his arm as they walked down Mazoviecka Street to Holy Cross Street. In the semi-darkness Ezriel stopped to look at a Buddha crouching behind the windowpane of a store—stout, burnished, naked, with a gem in its forehead. "How can the Hindus reconcile Nirvana with corpulence?" he mused. He tried to read the title of a book, but the erratic light of a street lamp made the Gothic characters illegible. They continued on, crossing Marshalkovsky Boulevard, and were once more on Zielna Street. They spoke in clipped sentences. Just to say something, she commented on a house, a store, a sign. "Warsaw's filthy," she blurted out.

"Well, you'll soon be in Paris," he replied.

"In Paris? What makes you say that?"

"He'll take you on a trip around the world."

"How do you know that? Yes, a trip . . ."

They were now standing on Zielna Street. The branches of closely planted trees on both sides almost met over the roadway. The shadows cast by their dense foliage formed a net on the pavement. Gates were being locked. Window lights went out. A dog bayed. This street, to Ezriel, filled with love, secrets, quiet meetings, late farewells, was like a mysterious garden. It occurred to him that he had never seen it in daylight.

"Well, this is probably our last time together," he said.

"Why? We can remain friends."

"Oh? Well, good night."

"Don't run away. If you want to, come up. Jadzia is not sleeping at home tonight."

"Where is she?"

"Her sister is sick."

"No, Olga, why?"

"I thought that . . . Well, perhaps you're right."

"Good night."

"Don't be in a hurry. After all, you write for Wallenberg's paper and you may be invited to various functions. What I mean is that we won't be able to avoid each other. I don't want to avoid you. We've had happy moments. I'll never forget that night in Otwock."

"What are memories?"

Olga, apparently, was reluctant to let him go, but Ezriel was overcome with impatience. He wanted only to be alone with the blow he had received. Olga made a gesture as if to kiss him goodbye, but he only extended his hand. She squeezed it and he pulled it away, tipped his hat, and walked rapidly down the street without looking back, although he knew she was waiting for him to turn. He had conducted himself with dignity and that somehow eased the pain. At least he hadn't acted like a beggar.

Soon, he knew, the longing would start, the passion, the emptiness, the regret, but of one thing he was certain: he would never cry on anyone's shoulder. As he walked, his face burned. If she put her children first, why shouldn't he? This logic was irrefutable. He was suddenly overcome with a profound love for Joziek, Zina, even for Misha. They were his flesh and blood. He was responsible for them. To Shaindel, on the other hand, he was deeply in debt. He was a psychiatrist, not a madman. There was something else, too. He knew that his firm behavior would hold Olga with a force that no psychology could explain.

4 🏛

I

Everything was as it had been. His mother with her wrinkled face and the satin bonnet covering her shaved head; his father in his velvet capote, with the sash around his waist and the skullcap above his high forehead. His mother had no teeth left; her empty gums showed when she spoke. His father's beard had grown white and seemed shrunken. He was sitting in an armchair at the table. Although his father could see little, a kerosene lamp with a milky white shade stood on the table and some books lay open before him. He spoke to Ezriel: "So, here you are. Well, praised be the Almighty that we can see you. I've missed you, missed you badly. After all, you are my son. My only son. No small matter to have an only son. Your mother talks about you endlessly. Since Mirale's misfortune, your mother's love for you knows no bounds. Well, it all comes from above. Mercy too, but we don't always have the power to receive it. The rigor of the law comes from us, not, God forbid, from Him. If a father gives his child a nut and the child swallows it, shell and all—how is the father guilty?"

"The father should have warned him, or removed the shell. You are referring, of course, to our Father in heaven."

"Naturally. He gave man reason so that he could choose. He gave reason and a law which tells what is allowed and what is forbidden. But we refuse to listen—so how can we blame Him?"

"We might listen if we knew they were the words of God. But how can we be sure? Each people has its own religion."

"If man could actually see the workings of Providence, he would have no doubts and, therefore, no free will. This world is based on free choice. Of what can we be sure? Of life? Of one's livelihood? Man must constantly choose between truth and falsehood. If the heavens opened and we could observe the celestial host, then everybody would be a saint. Do you understand me, or not?"

"Yes, Father, I understand."

"Everything is easy for angels. Therefore they have no reward. Man must fight for his faith. Every day, every minute. Even the holiest man doubts."

"Yes, Father, I see."

"What's new in medicine?"

"Nothing much. One has to find out everything for oneself."

"Well, they do find out things. Once there was no hope if you became blind. Today, your good friend, what's his name, told me that now an operation is possible. I need only wait a little while longer. When I can't see at all, when the—how are they called—cataracts become larger, it will be possible to remove them. As it is said: 'Before the light comes, there must be a deeper darkness.' "

Tirza Perl called Ezriel into the kitchen. She stood near him with her rounded shoulders, her bonnet perched on the back of her head. Her glasses, minus one lens, rested on her beaked nose. A book lay on the kitchen table, *The Lamp of Light*. "What sort of misfortune has befallen Mirale?" she asked sharply. "Woe is me!"

"I don't know, Mother."

"You don't know? There was a girl here, a hunchback, one of *them*. The things she said made my ears ring. I don't want your father to know. He has enough troubles of his own, poor thing. What sort of catastrophe is this? I'm afraid to go out into the street. People will spit on me or stone me. Such a terrible disgrace doesn't even happen to barbers and musicians."

"Mother, it isn't my fault."

"What do these people want? It would have been better if she had converted. I'd known I had lost a daughter. I don't sleep nights, Ezriel. What do they want?"

"To redeem the world."

"Such evildoers! They're crazy. Do they think that God Almighty will remain silent? He destroyed Sodom, didn't he?"

"Let Him do as He pleases!"

"What are you saying? Why aren't you more careful? I couldn't understand what she was saying, the hunchback, I mean. My ears filled up with water. My face burned so much, I couldn't see her. I just sat there."

"Yes, Mother, I understand. But how are you guilty?"

"How am I guilty? People curse the parents of such an evildoer."

"Mother, I must go."

"Well, go. Now you see what happens when one forsakes God."

Ezriel went to say goodbye to his father, whom he found dozing in his chair. The old man awoke with a start. Ezriel shook his hand and then kissed his mother. He walked down the dark steps. He had not realized until now that she knew about Mirale's pregnancy. The hunchback had told her. What joy in her old age! At the gate Ezriel collided with someone, a man. Somehow Ezriel sensed in the darkness that this person had a connection with him. Later he thought about this moment. It was one of those things for which there is no explanation, unless one accepts the existence of a sixth sense. "Excuse me, sir, could you tell me where the rabbi lives?" the man asked in Polish.

"Turn to your right. Perhaps I can help you. I'm his son."

"You're Dr. Babad?"

"Yes."

"Doctor, I must speak to you. The janitor is about to lock the gate. Let's go outside."

"Who are you? What do you want?"

"Don't be frightened, Doctor. I'm not as bad as people say. I want to introduce myself to your worthy parents, but since fate seems to have ordained our meeting, let it remain this way. I beg you, Doctor, be patient a few minutes and don't judge me until you've heard what I have to say. That's all I ask."

"Who are you?"

"My name is Stefan Lamanski. I'm your sister's husband."

Ezriel remained standing where he was. "Her husband? I didn't know that she had a husband."

"Not officially, but—please, come outside. The janitor is waiting. Yes, I'm her husband and wish to remain her husband whenever she is freed, or whenever I succeed in getting her freed. I'm in a terrible position, Doctor. I wanted to speak to your parents but knew that they don't understand Polish. That's why I haven't done so before this. I thought of approaching you, Dr. Babad, but was told that you are—how shall I put it—an impatient man, and I need to speak to someone who is both patient and good."

"What's on your mind? Where were you going?"

"I? It doesn't matter. Wherever you are, Doctor. Generally I am a resolute man, but I've already walked past your parents' house many times without going in. I purposely came late today so as not to meet visitors. I'm sorry but I don't speak Yiddish. And here I bump into you. Isn't that a strange coincidence? I'm in such a nervous state that everything seems odd. I'm not well; I have a fever. I shouldn't have gotten out of bed. But the slanderous rumors that have been spread about me and the unfortunate thing that has happened to Mirale have confused me so much that—don't take offense, Doctor— I know I'm not making sense. I really don't know where to begin. I'm accustomed to all kinds of difficulties, but what has occurred is beyond the powers of one person. There are some blows one can't defend oneself against. I suppose, Dr. Babad, that these disgusting tales have reached you too."

"Yes, I've heard."

"Who told you? Well, it doesn't matter. It's a lie, Dr. Babad, a vicious lie. I would swear to it, but we freethinkers don't even have the privilege of swearing by some higher power. All I can do is give you my word of honor that I am the victim of criminal slander. Do you know that there is a price of five thousand rubles on my head? Even my own comrades, for whom I risked my life, are now anxious to get rid of me. I can't leave the house, because I'm afraid I'll be shot in the back. I've told them I'm ready to stand trial before them and if found guilty to put a bullet through my own skull. But even the right to defend myself has been denied me. I mentioned earlier that I have nothing to swear by, but there is the memory of my mother. It is sacred to me, more sacred than anything in this world, and I swear by her bones that everything I'm saying now, Dr. Babad, is the absolute truth!"

Stefan Lamanski covered his face with one hand. This stranger, who called himself Mirale's husband, was crying in the street.

11

Only now did Ezriel realize that they had reached the corner of Ciepla Street. To the left were the police barracks; to the right, the barracks of the Volhynia regiment. It was dark and quiet. Stefan Lamanski took out his handkerchief and murmured: "Please excuse me, Doctor."

In the past months Ezriel had more than once thought about this man, who was accused of being an *agent provocateur,* who had involved his sister in illegal activities. As a boy in cheder, Ezriel had not taken the side of Simeon and Levi, who had slain the inhabitants of Shechem because of their sister Dinah. He had sympathized with Jacob, who on his death-bed had cursed the brothers: "O my soul, come not thou into their secret; into their assembly, mine honor, be not thou united." But of late he had begun to understand the anguish of these men at seeing their sister treated like a whore. Now his sister's seducer stood before him, wiping the tears from his eyes. Her lover, Ezriel saw, was a poorly dressed man. Un-shaven and pale, as if after an illness, he wore a cap with an oilcloth visor and carried a wooden box. He reminded Ezriel of an army recruit. He called himself Mirale's husband! In that case he was his brother-in-law.

Ezriel said: "What did you want of my parents? You know they're old-fashioned. A rabbi . . ."

"I know. You mustn't think, Dr. Babad, that I made my decision lightly," Stefan Lamanski replied. "My situation is such that I must leave. It's a matter of life and death. I don't want to be sacrificed to satisfy my one-time comrades' malice. I say malice because our movement has split and the resulting struggle can only help the enemy. Some so-called patriots have infiltrated our ranks and, under the guise of socialism, are again trying to delude the people with dreams of an insurrec-tion. I needn't tell you, esteemed Doctor, how hopeless such fantasies are and how harmful to the proletariat. For wherever the fire of nationalism starts burning, the atmosphere is imme-diately poisoned by chauvinism, by the hate of brother for brother. Who then stands to gain? The exploiters, of course, who feed off the people! Those vampires have ruled for gen-erations, stealing bread from the masses and collaborating with the enemies of Poland. I needn't tell you what role our last king played; think of it. First as lover of bloody Catherine and later, after he had enslaved Poland, as a sycophant at her court, like those pimps who in their old age carry the chamber pots in the brothels. What did these noblemen do in 1863? They appealed for help to the peasants and workers. Fortu-nately, the common man understood that a native hangman is no better than a foreign one, and wouldn't have anything to do with their adventures. Understand, the ones who paid for all this were always the workers, for in the final analysis they square all the accounts. Now this nationalistic plague has flared up again. And where? In our own ranks. Oh, I can't begin to explain to you what is going on. These so-called revolutionaries keep speaking about the worker and his situation, but they're really concerned with only one thing—the return of the Polish nobility to power and the taking away from the people of those shreds of rights that Alexander had granted to them. It would mean that Poland would be freed from her foreign yoke, and a native yoke substituted instead. In Western Europe, especially in France, there are groups who understand this danger and continue to warn us against it. Their leader, a young man of superior intelligence, came to Warsaw not long ago—illegally, of course, under another name. Had he been caught, he would have been strung up. He happens to be Jewish, and you would not believe this, Dr. Babad, but the comrades stooped to the lowest form of anti-Semitism. I don't keep my convictions secret, and so much poison has already been generated by my former colleagues against me that they stop at nothing. It is to their advantage to destroy me. In so doing, they overlook the real *provocateurs* within their own ranks. The truth is—they are all *provocateurs*. Because a traitor is a traitor whatever he may be called —but why am I bothering you with all these details? You're certainly not interested in them."

"Why not? I've heard that this division exists among the Russians, but it's news to me that such frictions exist right here in Poland."

"Actually, I shouldn't have told you all this. It's true these are not party secrets and I trust you, Dr. Babad, because you're Mira's brother. Still, they are internal squabbles.

"I've been sick for several weeks, really sick, and my nerves are shattered. I've stopped sleeping and that is killing me. I used to have nerves of steel; now I jump at the squeak of a mouse. I have a feeling that I'm not speaking coherently. You asked me something, but unfortunately I don't remember what it was. This is also due to my nervousness. Oh, yes, about your parents. As I have mentioned, I must go abroad, and I would like at least to have one look at the child. . . . I know how embarrassing it must be for you to hear these words, but still, it is my child, our child, Mirale's and mine, a child of love. I know how the philistine looks upon such babies, but I'm above that, and I am convinced that you, Doctor, are not so fanatical as to be contemptuous of an innocent being just because a formality has been omitted. If Mirale were not in prison and your parents wished us to go through some ceremony, I would do it to spare them unnecessary grief. One has to make a distinction between members of the older generation, who can no longer understand the course of progress, and those hypocrites who wrap their reactionary intentions in revolutionary phrases. . . . In short, I had hoped that they would give me the address."

"They don't know the address. My father, especially, knows nothing at all about it. My mother did hear something but—"

"Well, if that's so, it's a lucky coincidence that I met you, esteemed Doctor. I hope you'll understand how much I'm suffering and what a look at my child would mean to me. This may sound sentimental, provincial, but there are biological processes that—"

Stefan Lamanski stopped talking. They had gone past Mirowski Place and found themselves on Elektralna Street. The windows were dark, the gates locked. Ezriel felt uncomfortable. What if a patrol were to come along and arrest them both? And what if one of Lamanski's fellow revolutionaries was following him? Ezriel had heard frightening stories about the nihilists and their acts of revenge. He had to get away from this person, the sooner the better.

He said: "The child is on Dzika Street, near Powązek. But I warn you, they are affiliated with your enemies. You don't want to walk into a trap, do you?"

"Who are they? I know everyone from that group . . ."

"Their name is Cybula—" Ezriel said. "His name is Jonas Cybula. He is a locksmith."

"A locksmith? Cybula? The name is unfamiliar."

"As far as I know, they're members of the organization. The one caring for the child is a hunchback, but I don't remember her surname. Her name is Edzia."

"A hunchback? I don't know her either. What's the number of the house?"

Ezriel gave him the number.

"Well, I'll go there tomorrow. Does the locksmith work at home?"

"I've never seen him there."

"Thanks, thanks a lot. I don't have to tell you, Dr. Babad, that the whole thing was—how shall I express myself—entirely unplanned, a catastrophe, but it will all come out well."

"What good can come of it? She'll serve in prison for another six years, and afterwards they'll probably exile her to Siberia. What good can come of a child raised without parents?"

"This barbaric order can't endure for long. Something must happen soon."

III

It was already half past twelve when Ezriel said goodbye to Stefan Lamanski and started home. He felt chilled. His head and feet ached. "What's happening to me? Am I getting sick? Despite the past, despite what I owe her, what I have with Shaindel is no life. . . . Everything has become a bore. I don't even have the time to study. Everything is just disgusting routine. I'm an idiot, too. I had a chance to have a career, to have Olga. Actually I sacrificed everything for Calman Jacoby's daughter. Well, those who permit themselves to be destroyed have no right to complain." He had to hurry. He had to be up at seven o'clock, but he walked slowly. "If at least I hadn't brought children into the world!" He was suddenly filled with rage against Shaindel. He had pleaded with her to get an abortion, but she was one of those rabbits that must bear and bear. "Well, I'll be revenged, I'll go away. What would happen if I were to die? She'd live on. She'd probably remarry. Only an imbecile like me kills himself for such parasites!"

He came to the gate and rang the bell. The janitor mumbled something as he opened the gate. Ezriel didn't even have a tip for him. He clattered up the dark stairway. "Demons? If only demons existed! This would indicate that there was something else . . . that creation was not just a Darwinlike charnel house. . . ." Opening the door with his key, he noticed a light in the living room. "He still hasn't gone to bed, the savage!" Ezriel muttered. "Ruining his eyes with all those idiotic books!" The jurisprudence of the jungle. . . . He opened the door and saw Joziek. The boy was sitting in an armchair, without a book, in an unbuttoned jacket, his hands on his knees, hair disarrayed. Joziek, who always seemed calm, with all buttons fastened, now looked disheveled. "What's wrong with him?" Ezriel wondered. "Why aren't you asleep?" he asked. "Why ruin your eyes with this stuff? Get undressed and go to bed."

Joziek did not even stir. "Papa, I must talk to you."

Ezriel bristled. "What about? It's late. Soon I'll have to go to work."

"Papa, sit down."

"What's happened? Speak up."

"I can't continue at the university!"

"What then? Will you sell onions?"

"I'm going away."

"Where are you going? What in hell is wrong with you?"

"I'm going to Palestine."

Ezriel laughed.

"Well go, in happiness and peace. Give my regards to Mother Rachel!"

"Papa, it's no joke."

"What's happened? Did you hear one of the Lovers of Zion make a speech? Did you read Pinsker's brochure?"

"Papa, it's more serious than you suppose."

"What's more serious? What are you babbling about? Either tell me nothing or everything. I haven't the patience to pull the words out of you."

"Why are you so angry?"

"My anger is none of your business. Talk, because I still want to sleep a few hours. Even a horse has to rest sometimes."

"Oh, Papa, I'll tell you tomorrow."

"Not tomorrow, today. But make it short! I'm listening! What's happened? Where do you want to run? What sort of madness is this?"

"Papa, I can't stand it any more."

"What can't you stand?"

"This anti-Semitism. You'll never know, Papa, what I faced in school. I didn't say anything because it wouldn't have helped. Now I must tell the truth. Everyone tormented me: the teachers, the students. A hundred, perhaps a thousand, times a day they threw my Jewishness up to me. You studied alone, at home, but I had to go to school every day. I was beaten too, innumerable times. Now something has happened that I . . ."

"What happened?"

"I went into Lurse's with two other students. We were sitting quietly at a table when two bullies started baiting us. They wanted to insult us. Finally, one of them tore off my cap and threw it on the floor. I challenged him to a duel, but he replied that he wouldn't duel with a Jew. He hit me, too!"

"Why didn't you hit back? You were with two others."

"Oh, he was a head taller than I. The others were frightened. Everyone laughed. Someone poured water into my cap. I came home without it, without my honor too. Papa, I can't stand it any more! I'd rather die."

"Well, we've lived like this for two thousand years."

"That's long enough. A man who can't speak up when his cap is being filled with water is no man."

Ezriel felt his heart pounding. "Yes, that's true. But Palestine won't solve anything."

"What will? I've thought it all over. If I don't go away, I'll have to kill myself. First him, then me. But I wouldn't even recognize him. It's something I'll never forget."

"When did this happen?"

"Yesterday."

"Yesterday? Where were your friends?"

"They sat like little lambs. Jews aren't men. You know that, Papa. We're emasculated."

Ezriel was silent. For a long time he remained standing at the door. Then he entered Joziek's room. He took a book from the shelf, opened it, read a line, and put it back in its place.

IV

"What actually do you expect me to do?" he asked. "The Turks are no better than the Poles or the Russians. Don't be fooled."

"I know, Papa. But it's our country, our earth."

"How is it ours? Because Jews lived there two thousand years ago? Do you know how many nations have perished and assimilated since that time? If we changed the map to what it was two thousand years ago, three-quarters of mankind would have to be moved. And how does it follow that we actually come from these Israelites? Where did I get my blond hair and blue eyes? The ancient Hebrews were all dark."

"How do you know? And then, I'm dark. I can't search through my genealogy."

"What will you do there? Drain the swamps and catch malaria? Is this why you graduated from gymnasium?"

"Papa, I can't stay here any more. I hate this city. I don't want to be pointed at as the one who was slapped."

"A Turk might hit you, or an Arab."

"I'll strike back."

"If you can. We've received blows in our own country too. The Babylonians, the Greeks, the Romans. Poland has been torn as well."

"The Poles are at home here. They lead normal lives."

"You could become a Pole, even a Russian—" Ezriel regretted his words as soon as he said them.

"Is that a solution?"

"No, but—to be free, one needn't begin everything over. You can study in Western Europe. Jews aren't beaten there."

"They are, they are. I read *The Israelite*. 'The Jew is Our Misfortune—' this is the slogan everywhere now, in Prussia, in Austria, in Hungary. I can't take on the beliefs of those who beat me."

"And what do you believe? What do we modern Jews believe? Well, I must go to sleep. I had a hard day myself. It's all a question of names. I'm no radical, but all this nationalism is false. What's the difference between a Prussian and an Austrian, a Dane and a Norwegian? Why did the German states wage war for hundreds of years? It's all madness."

"That madness is the law of life."

"It won't always be like that. What separates them? Not ideas. They all want power. Take America, for example, a thousand nationalities. You can become an American too. All you need is a boat ticket."

"All Jews cannot become Americans."

"Why worry about all Jews? Oh, you're only a boy and you repeat everything you hear. The Jews can return to Palestine as much as the Hungarians can become Tartars. We'll talk again tomorrow. Good night."

"With your opinions, Papa, I'd become a socialist."

"To spite whom? They'd jail you as they did Aunt Mirale. The prison's big enough."

"What can one do?"

"At least not make things worse. How can one fight madness? There's no cure. That is the truth."

"Papa, I want to leave."

"Well, I won't stop you."

5 ⛫

I

My dear Papa and Mama [wrote Sonya to her parents], Forgive me for not writing in Yiddish. I tried, but somehow I've
forgotten too much. I don't remember all the letters, and after
all, you both know Polish. This is our fifth day in New York.
It's only two months since we said goodbye, but it seems to me
as if I've been traveling since I was born. First the trip to Berlin, then on to Paris, to Cherbourg, and later by boat to America. Thirteen days on the ocean. We were in a storm too, and
the religious passengers cried, "Hear O Israel" and said their
confessions, although there was no danger. You know how
frightened our Jews get, especially the women. Almost all of
them were seasick. For three days I was ill and, excuse me,
vomited up everything. I ate only a few biscuits all that time.
Thank God, Alexander was a good sailor. But he was depressed and still is. Don't worry, he'll come out of it. If I had
taken this trip without Alexander, I would have died of loneliness. He is such a devoted brother. He was concerned only
about me and my comfort. It wasn't very comfortable, because we were traveling steerage. We didn't sleep in beds but
in bunks, like soldiers, he with the men and I with the women.
I still shudder when I think of how much dirt and boorishness
I encountered aboard ship. It was a nightmare. But I'd rather
remember the beauty of the ocean, the flying fish and the dol-

phins that leaped over the waves, dipping and diving. The magnificence of the Atlantic is beyond description, especially when the sun goes down. Once after a rain we saw a rainbow stretching from one end of the horizon to the other. One never had enough of the view. I'd stand by the rail half the days and even half the nights, just looking. How vast the ocean is! How endless! It is astonishing to realize it has existed since the world began. Sometimes, in the distance, we saw the silhouettes of ships. One of the passengers let us use his binoculars. Some of the young people put letters in bottles which they sealed and threw into the ocean. It's funny to think that a person drowns immediately, but a bottle can float for thousands of miles and reach a shore. I enclosed a greeting to you, my dears. . . . There was a group from Odessa and Kiev with us. They were former students, intellectuals, and some workers too. Some of them call themselves Am Olam, people of the world. They hope to form colonies in America and live together, sharing everything. Others are opposed to them, and discussions went on all night. They were so noisy that we couldn't get any sleep. The food wasn't too good. Many ate nothing but potatoes in their skins, and herring, because the food was not kosher. They all had their own opinions and wrangled with each other as though still at home and not in the middle of nowhere. Alexander would not participate in these debates and they resented it, but I wouldn't let them criticize him. Finally we arrived in New York. Long before we reached the harbor, the Statue of Liberty came into view and everyone shouted: "Hurrah!" The officials let us off quickly. Immigrants only have to show that they have five dollars or ten rubles.

Oh, I can't tell you how different New York is from all the other cities! Berlin and Paris were marvelous, but still somewhat like Warsaw and Kiev. New York is another world. It's as if one were walking upside down. It's not as pretty as Paris, far from it! Even ugly. Most of the houses aren't plastered, the bricks are visible. There are no courtyards here either, children play in the streets. I studied French in gymnasium, but I don't understand a word of English. On the ship we all spoke Russian. They gave me an English reader, but Americans pronounce words differently. Even their mouths seem different from ours. Only God knows if I'll ever learn this language. We went to the Jewish section and Alexander immediately disapproved of New York. You know he becomes either inspired or dejected. We rented a room from a widow, who also gives us lunch. The Yiddish here is different from what we speak at home. It is mixed with English. The landlady is called the "Missus," and the tenants, "boarders." It is terribly hot here. Food must be kept on ice. People go around half bare and many sleep on rooftops. The roof of our house is flat, a sort of Oriental roof, and at times I imagine myself in Persia or Palestine. Many Germans as well as Jews who speak German live in this neighborhood. With them one can make oneself understood somehow. (They are called "Yekies" here.) The Americans themselves are unusually patient and polite. When you ask them about a street, they lead you there. The colonies that our young people wanted to go to are somewhere far off, many days' journey by train, and, they say, in the wilderness among Indians. Incidentally, one sees in New York Negroes, all black, as well as Chinese, without pigtails. One meets Spaniards, Italians, and even some Poles. There are iron bridges over many streets, and trains run on them. There are also trolley cars. Everything is so ludicrous. In the trolley you throw the ticket into a glass vessel. Aliens here are called "greenhorns." Yes, I am a "green girl." That's what everyone calls me.

My dears, you needn't worry about us, although it doesn't seem as splendid here as the agent claimed. Many people are out of work. On a street that they call the Pigmarket, workers stand, waiting to be hired. One carries a saw, another the head of a sewing machine, or some other tool of his trade. Along come the bosses or their agents, and the whole procedure resembles a slave auction. One seldom sees a ragged or dirty or

barefoot person here. Everyone eats white bread, even paupers, and no one is afraid of saying what he thinks. Women,
too. Sometimes I want to laugh at everything. Work isn't considered demeaning. I'll have to work in a factory, or "shop."
Alexander will surely find something too, although he talks
only about settling in a colony or returning to Europe. He's
been very foolish, but why dwell on that? Sabina was distant
to me from the beginning. I only feel sorry for the child. . . .

My dears, we think and speak of you day and night. I suspect Alexander will write you a letter full of despair, but don't
take it too seriously. Everyone feels that way at first. One is
terribly nervous and wanders around as if in a dream. At
times, I imagine I'm still aboard ship. Everything shakes—the
room, the street, the ground, the sky. But they say one grows
accustomed to it.

How are you, my dear sweet ones? I know how you worry
about us, and you may laugh at me, but I only want to bring
you here, so that we'll all be together. There are many synagogues and religious Jews with beards, although they all wear
short cloaks. This crisis won't last forever, and one day we'll
still be happy. I kiss you a thousand times and press you to my
heart. I hope you will write me a long letter full of details, like
mine, because when I write to you, it seems as if you are near
me . . .

Your devoted daughter,
SONYA

11

Zipkin's letter to Sabina:

Dear Sabina,

I have already written you twice, once from Monte Carlo
and again from Paris, but you didn't find it necessary to reply.
Now I'm writing to you for the third and last time, from New
York. It isn't in my nature to burden anybody and I don't

know how much longer I'll continue to make the effort. Apparently I'm fated to self-destruction. How else can I explain the mad things I've done these past years? I've driven myself into a corner, from which there seems to be no escape. You can probably see the difference in my handwriting. Today from 6 a.m. until evening I stood at a machine making covers for boxes. I've always taken the side of the exploited but never imagined the hell that exists in every workshop or factory—the noise of the machines, the dust, the stink, the insults of the overseer, or, as he is called here, the "foreman." I never understood that a day, an hour, even ten minutes, could last so long. The feet ache, the eyes close, one's head feels as if screws were being bored into it, and all this, six days out of the week, for the miserable wage of five dollars. I step on something called a pedal and this bends a tin sheet. During the morning I think of nothing but the lunch whistle. We eat lunch in a bakery, standing, or sitting on a high stool that only Americans could have invented. Afterwards I begin to dream of the whistle which means the day is done. We live across from an "El." Every time the train passes, our windows and all the furniture in our room tremble. Everyone assures me that one becomes accustomed to it. But it's an insult to humanity just to accept such conditions. Yet it comforts me to know that I am looking at bitter reality.

I could go on forever about New York. This city reflects the chaos in my soul. Everything here opposes our way of thinking. What is beautiful in Europe is considered ugly here. What is comical to us is serious to them. In spite of their democracy and liberty, votes are purchased at election time. Bribes are openly accepted. The butcher, the corrupt policeman, the tavernkeeper rule here. Death has no special significance. Mortuaries stand between barbershops and restaurants. Cemeteries are not fenced in. Beside a stable there's a hospital. Women drink great mugs of beer in taverns. The men speak only of boxers and circus athletes. Negroes shine shoes on the sidewalks. Speakers declaim in the midst of the city. The architecture drives me wild. I try to read the English newspapers. Not one serious word about the world situation—only news about prospective weddings, funerals, amusements. Mister "This" arrived, Mrs. "That" has gone away, Miss "Something-or-Other" has become a bride. The sermons of the priests, ministers (as well as rabbis) are printed as if these people had discovered the North Pole. Everything else is advertisements. Even churches advertise. Spiritualists advertise. The heat too is vulgar. It burns hellishly, and there is a constant clang of fire wagons. I have already visited the famous Coney Island. One takes a long ferry trip to get there. When I arrived, I found the true meaning of the word plebeian. The screaming, the confusion is indescribable. One eats sausages, "hot dogs," gets one's fortune told in cards. In a sideshow one views a woman with two heads, a girl who is half snake, wax figures of kings, presidents, Popes , murderers. Meanwhile one nibbles candy and peanuts. In the midst of this tumult stands a monk, or a sort of missionary, and shouts that Jesus is God and that one must save one's soul. You won't believe it, but Sonya and I, out of sheer boredom, rode a carousel, and I even tried chewing tobacco (yes, the Yankees chew tobacco!).

Well, enough complaints about New York. There are good things here also. There's a socialist paper, printed in German, although its socialism is diluted. Jews play an important role here, especially the German ones. Someone has told me that America must be discovered over again by each person who comes here.

I am writing to you because I've learned the tragic news of your father's death. Sonya told me about it while we were still in Paris, but I withheld my condolences. He was my only friend and protector in the family and it really grieves me to have caused him suffering in his final days. But one need have no regrets for the dead. It's fortunate to be rid of this disgusting world with its useless efforts and empty hopes. What I am going through here I can't explain to you. I'm spiritually paralyzed. The more I think about what I've done and how unhappy I made you, the child, my parents, and myself, the more fantastic it all seems to me, as if someone had bewitched me. At times it seems to me that I've already died, and am in Gehenna. Sonya has told me that you insist I send you a Jewish divorce, and I'll certainly do so, but do me one favor: write to me about Kubuś and send me his most recent photograph. I am his father. When I've received your reply, I'll go to a rabbi (they call themselves "Doctor" and "Reverend" here) and send you the divorce. I hope you'll forgive me for having sinned against you. I want you to know that Clara sent long, apologetic letters to me in Paris and wanted to rejoin me but I never replied. This woman ruined me and has killed my belief in humanity. You may rest assured that I will never marry again. I forgot to add that Sonya is working in a dress factory, learning to sew on a machine (here, she is called an "operator"). Her situation is no better than mine, but she has the humility that makes everything easier. After a day's hard work, she takes classes in English. She also stood in line for half a Saturday waiting to get opera tickets to hear Patti, who, a while back, charmed St. Petersburg. She goes to all kinds of lectures.

I myself have decided nothing. There are days when I'm ready to return to Europe. I only have to save enough for my fare. But sometimes I plan to settle in a colony, deep inland, among forests and prairies, and forever break away from so-called civilization. The Am Olam have founded such colonies here. A few have already failed, but others refuse to surrender. Occasionally I meet young people. In a certain sense, politics is an obsession here too, as it is in Russia. Famous socialists arrive from Germany, even the daughter of Karl Marx came on a visit from England. There's great concern about anarchists, particularly those who have been sentenced to hang. But it seems to me (I don't know why) as if everything here is

imitation. Something is lacking, I don't know what. The loneliness, naturally, makes me moody. I hope you'll answer
promptly, for I may soon be back in Europe, or somewhere in
the state of Oregon, near the Pacific Ocean. I'm sure I won't
remain in New York. Forgive me and kiss Kubuś for me,
often.

Your ALEXANDER

6

I

It was a hot September day. That afternoon, there were only a few patients in Ezriel's office, the usual neurasthenics, each with his or her particular illness and complaints. The man who served tea opened the door to Ezriel's examining room and admitted the last patient. Ezriel stood looking out the window and did not turn immediately. He stared into the courtyard, at the garbage can, at the children playing around it, at the surrounding buildings, whose windows revealed entire apartments, segments of Jewish domesticity. Joziek's trip to Palestine was already a certainty. Shaindel walked around the summer resort with a handkerchief soaked in vinegar around her head, and took sleeping pills. It was a weekday, but it seemed to Ezriel as if it were a Sabbath eve. An inescapable boredom had followed him from Turbin to Lublin, from Lublin to Jampol, from Jampol to Warsaw. Smoke rose from the chimneys. He watched girls sweeping floors with worn-out brooms as they sang old, tired melodies. A golden dust fell over everything. Out of the distance there came a sound that could be either the chanting of children in a cheder or the croaking of frogs in a country swamp. The children in the yard began to play a game of buttons. The janitor's dog sniffed at a stone. "Why do I have to live through all this? How long will it last?" Ezriel asked himself. To go to Falenica would mean to lie next to Shaindel and spend the night explaining that going to Palestine was not the same as dying. To remain in town meant to eat chicken broth and noodles in a dirty restaurant on Karmelicka Street and then to sit at home reading the case histories of more neurasthenics, more melancholics, more paranoics. A phrase in Ecclesiastes occurred to Ezriel: "All things are wearisome." Ezriel, when he turned from the window, was astounded to see Olga standing at the door. She looked pale, though she was smiling. "Is this the way you receive your patients?" she asked.

"Oh, they drive me insane."

There was a pause, then she said: "I have a number like everyone else. Here it is!"

She handed him a blue ticket.

"What's the trouble?" he asked, in a professional tone.

Olga bit her lip. "Oh, everything."

"Nerves?"

"Yes."

Again they were both silent. He saw everything at once: the sadness in her eyes, the trembling of her lips, the new straw hat, the white blouse, the gray pleated dress, the white pocketbook. She had selected the things he liked. Even her earrings were a pair he had admired. She stood before him with an expression at the same time rebellious and humble.

"What has happened?" he asked.

"I've told him the truth."

"Wallenberg?"

"Yes, about you. It's over. I could not love him. I love you."

Ezriel's eyes grew moist. "You're my last patient. Let's go out."

"Don't you have to go home?"

"Yes, but I won't go. They're all in the country."

"Joziek, too?"

"He's spending some time with his mother, before leaving for Palestine."

"Palestine? How odd."

He kissed her on the cheek. She caught his hand in hers and pressed it. He spoke with a tremor in his voice. "It would be better if you waited for me downstairs. I must stop at the administration office on my way out."

"I wanted to write to you, but somehow I couldn't. I'll wait at the Gardens' gate on Ziabia Street."

"I'll be there soon."

He accompanied her to the door, and then went to the office. He passed the door of the dentist, the obstetrician, the surgeon, the pediatrician, and heard a variety of moans. Only the cashier was in the office. He took his hat, gave the girl the patients' tickets, and left, skipping down the stairs. His feet grew light as a boy's. How many times had this happened in his life—resignation, then victory! Everything that had appeared mundane and trivial to him had suddenly grown festive. The sun's rays were no longer too hot. The odor of flowers came from the baskets of women vendors. Racing down the street, he was nearly run over by a droshky. For a moment he could smell the horse's muzzle. At the gate of the Saxony Gardens, near the stand selling hoops, balloons, toy horns, rubber balls, stood Olga. She smiled the shy smile of those who are relieved at having surrendered. They went into the park. He took her white-gloved hand and they walked like a boy and girl on their first date. Though the path was level, they seemed to be walking downhill.

"Why is Joziek going to Palestine?" Olga asked.

"He was insulted in a restaurant, and he doesn't want to serve in the Czar's army, not even for the single year that's required of students."

"Who insulted him?"

"What's the difference? He's become a Lover of Zion. He wants to go back to the land of his ancestors."

"What does his mother say?"

"She's completely broken up."

They looked for a place to sit, but all the benches were occupied. The women's hats were ornamented with flowers and fruit: cherries, grapes, plums. Little boys, mostly in sailor suits, rolled hoops. Girls played ball, danced in a circle, chanted childish doggerel. At the lake, governesses helped children throw crumbs to two floating swans. In the distance an orchestra played and a trumpet blared. It was unseasonably hot. After a while, Ezriel and Olga came out on Niecala Street. They found a café opposite the Brill Palace and sat down at a table. Olga ordered coffee. Ezriel, who had not eaten lunch, ordered new potatoes and sour milk. The late-afternoon sunlight glinted through the separations between the draperies, quivered on the waxed floor, on the tapestried walls, in the prisms of lamp crystals, on the gilded frames of the pictures. Two golden-green flies chased each other around the ceiling lamp. A man with a flowing mustache and a red nose, obviously one of the local landowners, was reading a newspaper and smoking a cigar. The waiter went back to the counter with the order.

"When did all this happen?" Ezriel asked.

"Several days ago. No, it was the day before yesterday. No. Sunday. He asked me and I told him the truth. But I would have told him anyway."

Ezriel lowered his head. "I longed for you all the time."

Olga, who until now had been smiling, suddenly grew serious. "It was more than longing for me."

"What was it?"

"Death. I can't live without you."

Her mouth trembled. She knew that a woman does not admit such things.

11

Everything moved so quickly. Joziek had just been talking about Palestine and now he was leaving, even before the holidays were over. Shaindel returned to the city, fluttering over the boy as if he were mortally ill, pleading and weeping; but he was adamant. With packed valise and no bed linen, he was ready for the land of his ancestors. He was to travel with a group from Lithuania, who had assembled in Warsaw. They sang, rolled cigarettes, and spoke of ships, seaports, the free acreage that Baron Rothschild was granting settlers, and Turkish law. Listening to them, Shaindel cracked her fingers. No matter how often Joziek explained to her how harmful the Jewish Diaspora was, that a people must have a homeland, a language, a worldly culture of its own, Shaindel could not understand. She insisted he was a victim of the Evil Eye. It was madness for a boy to leave his mother, father, and the university for Palestine. There was starvation in the holy cities. The Arabs were still as wild as the ancient Ishmael. The swamps were malaria-ridden, the soil chalky, barren, and rocky. Shaindel knew that one went to the Holy Land to die, not to live. Those for whom the groschens in the almsboxes were collected went there. Shaindel had once studied about Jerusalem, the grave of Rachel, the Cave of Machpelah, but she did not actually believe that Palestine existed. If it did—it was located somewhere at the end of the world, near the River Sambation, or the Tower of Babel. Shaindel cried until she had no tears left and talked until she lost her voice. Ezriel had borrowed three hundred rubles to pay Joziek's fare. Calman had also contributed. But why give him money when the group intended to live communally? Shaindel had met the other boys. They were swarthy, unkempt, with weary eyes and tousled hair. They wore black shirts with sashes, spoke Russian and a mixture of Yiddish and Hebrew. There was a girl going with them who had taken the biblical name of Abigail.

After Joziek's departure, Shaindel became disconsolate. Usually for Rosh Hashana she had prepared challah, carp, apples with honey, and bought grapes to make the benediction, "who hath preserved us in life," as had been the custom in her father's house. And each year she prayed in her mother-in-law's apartment, which was turned into a synagogue on the

Days of Awe. But this year Shaindel spent both days of Rosh Hashana in bed. She did not even go to hear the blowing of the ram's horn. Ezriel urged her to accept the situation. What did one do if a child died? Joziek was alive. They had already received a letter from him, from Constanz. But Shaindel refused to be consoled. Within his own house, Ezriel recognized a classic example of melancholia. Shaindel had all the symptoms: the grief, diminished alertness, lack of appetite, the inability to sleep, the constant repetition of the same words day and night. Ezriel prescribed the usual remedies: bromine and opium. Shaindel slept for a long time but arose empty-headed, as she said. Time stopped for her. Her skin grew parched. She crept from room to room, pale, preoccupied, looking off into space. Although Ezriel knew that Shaindel was sick and not responsible for her actions, he could not control his annoyance. She did not take care of little Misha. Ezriel sensed an element of hostility in Shaindel's melancholia. She wasn't so confused as not to know what she was doing. She had grasped at this misfortune as a drowning man clutches at a straw, blaming Ezriel for Joziek's departure. He had shown his son that home meant nothing. She began to predict that Zina too would come to a bad end. She had no girl friends, spent too much time with books. It was a terrible thing to say, but she was, God forbid, following in the footsteps of Miriam Lieba.

Her words were so full of spite that Ezriel scarcely knew how to answer her. Actually the situation was far worse than she realized. Ezriel was caught in a trap. There was not a day when he did not consider deserting this household that was destroying him both spiritually and physically, even though the ignominy of such an act seemed impossible to him.

The night before Yom Kippur, Shaindel pulled herself together and went out to buy a long, memorial candle. In preparation for the fast, she forced herself to eat a little more. The following evening, in a holiday dress, she took a prayer book and went to the synagogue to pray.

Zina and Tekla, the maid, remained with Misha. Ezriel too left the house. There had been a time when Nowolipki Street had been a Gentile street, but now only Jews lived there. Yom Kippur candles shone from the windows. Jews were on their way to prayer. The men were dressed in white robes and slippers, and wore their prayer shawls under their coats. The women wore beaded capes, silk or satin dresses with trains, and their most precious jewels. In a top hat and frock coat, his beard combed into two silver-white points so sparse that every hair could be counted, an enlightened Jew was on his way to the German synagogue, escorting a woman in a hat trimmed with ostrich plumes. In Wola, the large red sun set among purple clouds, like plowed furrows. All the shops were shuttered and bolted. Even the Gentiles walked by with muted steps. The horse-drawn trolley rode past, half empty. Not far away, on Krochmalna Street, the "Pure Prayer" was being read to Ezriel's father, who had become blind. His mother wept at the lighting of the candles. Millions of Jews in Russia, Germany, Palestine, Yemen, even in America and Argentina, were beating their breasts at confession during the evening services, praying for forgiveness to the Almighty God. In the small towns they were probably still lighting wax candles and allowing themselves to be whipped.

But their God was no longer Ezriel's God, or their prayers his prayers. What meaning did the Declaration of Vows have for him? Nevertheless, he hummed the melody of Kol Nidre to himself. If You are there, God, forgive me. If You are not—what is there? A great pity filled Ezriel for man who must learn everything for himself, must pay dearly for the slightest achievement. Even if God's plan for the world was eventual bliss, man remained His martyr.

III

Shaindel grew worse. She developed a persecution mania and complained that Ezriel wanted to kill her. She refused the medicines he prescribed, because she feared he wanted to poison her. Although Shaindel knew nothing about Olga, she spoke of another woman, whom Ezriel would marry after Shaindel's death. Ezriel was amazed. There was a trace of logic in all her madness. Through what power had she surmised that her rival was a modern, educated woman? "You don't have to poison me," she told Ezriel. "I won't last much longer."

"Shaindel, what's the matter with you?"

"I'm not altogether crazy. I know your tricks."

Ezriel had often discussed hypnotism at home. He had even taken Shaindel to see Feldman, the hypnotist, conduct a séance. Shaindel now accused Ezriel of hypnotizing her. She insisted that Feldman "spoke" to her every night and that was why she could not sleep. She knew that Ezriel sometimes treated his patients with electric massage. He had had a telephone installed in the apartment and Shaindel had actually accused him of electrocuting her with it. Ezriel learned from a Dr. Halpern, a neighbor, that Shaindel had come to him and bared her heart. She had told him that Ezriel had electrocuted her head and left leg and that the poison he put in her food had burned through her heart. He had delayed her period and had contrived a plot against her with their daughter, Zina. The girl laughed at her, mimicked her behind her back. When the doctor asked Shaindel why she thought her own daughter would want to make fun of her, Shaindel had replied: "Because, after they bury me, they want to convert."

"What you should do is eat, drink, and become healthy despite them," Dr. Halpern had advised her.

"No, they are stronger than I. I'll have to give in," she had replied.

What a misfortune to deal all day with the madness of strangers and at night come home to an insane wife! Ezriel wrote a long letter to his father-in-law. Calman came to Warsaw to try talking his daughter out of her delusions, but Shaindel reproved him for conspiring with her enemies. Calman suggested that she come to stay with him at the manor or that he take her with him to visit Tsipele and the Rabbi of Marshinov, but Shaindel had replied: "Father, you want to fool me into leaving the house."

"Daughter, why should I fool you? You're my child. I'm an old man now."

"He has hypnotized you, too."

Joziek wrote often from Palestine. Each letter was more optimistic than the last. It was warm in Palestine. In the morning it rained, but by afternoon the sun shone. The sky was bluer, the stars seemed bigger. Joziek took care of cows and horses, was learning Hebrew, had a dog and a gun, had grown muscular and tanned. He sent photographs of himself—working at a wine press, riding horseback, standing near a tent holding a gun. Although Shaindel's sickness had been brought on by Joziek's departure, she would not read his letters or look at the photographs. She would grimace, as if to say: "I know these tricks."

The news that the doctor's wife had lost her mind spread quickly along Nowolipki Street and the surrounding areas. Although Shaindel had learned to wear a hat when she left the house, she now put a shawl over her head, as she had done in Jampol. She walked about shabbily dressed, in battered shoes with trailing laces. Shaindel's suspicion that Ezriel wanted to poison her affected him strangely. He began to fear that Shaindel might do him bodily harm. Who could say what a person in her condition was capable of? He had heard many gruesome stories in the hospital. Mothers had slaughtered their children, men had set fire to their houses, hacked up their wives. Ezriel slept fitfully at night. He would fall asleep and soon wake up. He began to keep a knife under his pillow to protect himself.

Tekla, the maid, left her job in the middle of the quarter because Shaindel accused her of putting magic herbs into the food. Shaindel now had to take care of Misha. The child became extremely nervous, complained that his mother smelled bad. He was afraid of her and called her a frog. Ezriel realized that Warsaw was a small town. Everyone knew of the tragedy—his patients, the doctors with whom he worked. It was dangerous for him, for the children, even for the neighbors. Olga, who was aware of what was going on, never mentioned it. But she grew more indulgent with him, no longer objected when he was late, or even when he did not come at all. When Ezriel asked the advice of a colleague at the hospital, he was told frankly that Shaindel must not remain at home.

It was easy to say, but where could she be placed? Patients slept in the corridors of the Jewish Hospital. There were private sanatoriums either in Warsaw or its vicinity, but they did not accept Jewish patients. There were also state institutions, but it was questionable whether they would admit her. Shaindel knew little Polish and no Russian. She had grown even more pious, carried her prayer books everywhere, was overzealous in keeping the kitchen kosher, and constantly consulted the rabbi on matters of rabbinical law. In an asylum without kosher food she would die of hunger. Ezriel tried to find a place for Misha, but Warsaw had no nurseries of the kind that were (according to the newspapers) found abroad. There were only the foundling homes where illegitimate children were raised. Despite all the achievements of modern civilization, in a European metropolis like Warsaw there was no refuge for a soul-sick woman and a neglected child.

Olga suggested to Ezriel that she raise Misha with her own children. Ezriel did not know what to say. He was afraid that taking Misha away would throw Shaindel into complete despair. The family would be scandalized. His father-in-law, Mayer Joel, and the Rabbi of Marshinov would discover that he was permitting his child to be raised by a convert. Ezriel explained the situation to Olga. Something climactic was bound to happen. He must wait a little. Events seemed to be drawing him closer to Olga. He longed for her the moment they were separated. She found opportunities to be with him, waited for him at the clinic, left Natasha and Kolia with the maid and joined him at the hospital. She stopped concealing their relationship from the neighbors, the maid, the children. Ezriel knew well that Olga could scarcely wait for the day when Shaindel would enter an asylum. He caught himself too wishing for that day.

7 🏛

I

On the Day of Atonement, Calman was at his son-in-law's in Marshinov. The rabbi paused in his discourse before the taking of the scroll from the Holy Ark to quote from the chapter of the Book of Isaiah which is read on the Day of Atonement: "But the wicked are like the troubled sea when it cannot rest, whose waters cast up mire and dirt." The rabbi was referring to the growing number of enlightened Jews. On that Holy Day the rabbi said things that were entirely out of character. In calling the "moderns" to task, he utilized their own expressions. "A wicked person," the rabbi said, "always wages something—war or love. This may seem to be a contradiction," he continued. "War expresses anger; love, kindness. What connection is there between the two? And how can one wage love? The answer is that man is born to serve. If he does not serve God, he serves man. 'The fool hath said in his heart, there is no God.' Since a wicked man does not believe in the Creator, his brain is only concerned with admiring flesh and blood. He extols one man because he is rich; another because he is comely; a third because he is shrewd; a fourth, powerful. Those who think only of material things are jealous. Jealousy brings anguish, and anguish leads to conflict. It is written: 'Jealousy is cruel as the grave.' There is a kind of love that may be compared to death. The love that arises from envy kills. The love of the wicked is as destructive as war. The wicked man wants to take what another possesses. He looks on a woman as booty. Though at first he may treat her gently, once he has satisfied his lust, he will torture her. The love of the wicked is basically violent."

When Calman heard these words, he thought of Clara. She always talked about love but was actually consumed by rage. Her lover, Zipkin, whom she had brought to the estate to tutor Sasha, envied the rich, though he pretended to side with the poor, and what had been the outcome! Zipkin had deserted his wife and gone off to America; Clara was a divorcee, left with an illegitimate child. She had only what her son Sasha gave her. Calman had heard from Sasha that her health was poor. She suffered from stomach trouble and female ailments. One could justly say that she was like the troubled sea whose "waters cast up mire and dirt." Still, Calman pitied her. She had destroyed herself. Had he still been wealthy, he would have provided an allowance for her. But she was to blame for his being poor. Because of her, he had left his business and let Mayer Joel take over. Calman now lived on his son-in-law's bounty, although he still worked a little on the manor enterprises and at the lime quarries, which were almost exhausted. But he was nearly seventy and his strength was waning. Mayer Joel had asked Calman many times to live with him or to rent a room in Jampol. Why should he live alone? But Calman would not leave the Chamber of Prayer he had set up in his cottage on the estate. He had grown accustomed to the quiet of the surrounding fields, to the singing of the birds, the broad sky that extended to the end of the world. Besides, he was his own master. He had no steady maid and prepared his own food over a tripod. He milked the cow, or a peasant girl milked her for him as he watched. He also had a horse and wagon. On the day of the Sabbath eve on which the prayers for the new month are offered, or before a holiday, he would drive into Jampol to pray in a quorum. He had purchased a burial plot for himself in the Jampol cemetery. He wanted to lie next to Zelda, although he was afraid she would be ashamed of him in the other world and would reprove him for marrying Clara . . .

It was a bad winter. The snow lay high, the frosts were bitter, and the peasants predicted the winter crops would freeze. This would be the second year of famine, God forbid. Calman developed trouble with his teeth. He had always had healthy teeth, now suddenly they had begun to hurt. His daughter, Jochebed, urged him to go to Warsaw to see a dentist. But she herself hadn't a tooth in her head. She had become an old woman. Then why should he make a fool of himself with dentists? It was better to pay for one's sins in this world than to wander off to hell or become transmigrated. He had committed enough transgressions, had raised bad children. Some of his grandchildren were Gentiles. Woe unto him, he had left no Jewish male descendant, for Sasha was a heathen. It was an act of mercy from heaven that Calman was allowed to exist. He now fasted on Mondays and Thursdays. He did not touch meat for the entire week. He no longer had new clothes made, but wore his old capotes. In cold weather he remained at home, seated beside the stove, studying the Mishnah, reciting his prayers, even looking into Zelda's Yiddish Pentateuch. His eyes bothered him too, and Mayer Joel brought him glasses that enlarged the characters. Oddly enough, his lust still hadn't cooled. Man apparently retained desire all his life. Although Calman ate simple foods and slept on a hard straw mattress, he still dreamed of women. In his dreams he cohabited with Clara, and even with Antosia, the maid, who had once served him in his hut in the forest. Years ago Antosia had been drowned in the Vistula, near a village somewhere. But the Lord of Dreams knows nothing of aging or death. At times, even while awake, Calman was shaken with passion. Sitting at the Mishnah, a graybeard, his cheek swollen from toothache, with ruined eyes, heavy of foot, he would suddenly have a shameful thought. Calman could barely shake it off.

"Oh, woe is me, Father in heaven!"

One day Sasha entered the Chamber of Prayer. He had his sleigh and driver waiting outside. He told Calman that Clara was in Jampol. She was going to America and had come to say goodbye.

"To America—well!"

"She wants to see you."

"What for?"

"She wants your forgiveness."

"Tell her I forgive her."

"What are you afraid of? She's not going to make love to you."

"I'm not afraid."

"Maybe you can talk her out of making a fool of herself. Papa, how old is she?"

"I don't know."

"She says she is forty-two. She must be at least forty-six."

Calman did not reply.

"A foolish woman. Stupid."

Sasha glanced at his watch. He had neither the time nor the patience for these errands. Once he had only been ashamed of his father, now his mother embarrassed him as well.

11

Sasha spoke a while longer with his father and was reminded by Calman to wear his phylacteries. "Why wear phylacteries if there is no God?" he asked. Then he left. He got into the sleigh, covered his knees with a fur piece, and drove off. Although it was bitter cold, Sasha wore only a short fur jacket, riding breeches, and high, fitted boots. A hunting hat with a green feather in it was set jauntily on his shock of pitch-black hair. He was so healthy, so full of energy, that he had an impulse to leap from the sleigh and tear up a tree by the roots. People complained of all sorts of illnesses, weaknesses, pains, but Sasha did not know what sickness meant. At night as soon as his head touched the pillow he fell into a deep sleep. He ate the heaviest of foods, drank tumblers of whisky without suffering any discomfort. He could walk miles and ride horseback all day without tiring. The officers' wives whispered among themselves about his sexual prowess. He had a straightforward attitude toward women. No sneaky tricks, no bargaining, sighing, or delay. Yes was yes; no was no. He spoke frankly and coarsely. He hated sentiment, indecision, made no secret of his disdain for the sex that was so comically built, weak of character, full of wiles and dodges, always ready to dominate the male and betray him. Not yet nineteen, Sasha had already had the experiences of a thirty-year-old. He had seen women ruin men: they wove a net about a man, entangled him with duties, ensnared him with parasitic children, and finally destroyed him, jeered at him, buried him, and absorbed his inheritance. True, the poor woman herself did not enjoy her triumph. But the instinct of a spider existed in all females, from the court lady to the washerwoman. Sasha had already determined never to marry. In love, it was always best to deceive. For all their cunning, women were inclined to become attached, to lose their reason. They believed in male promises, even if it were the offer of the moon on a silver platter. It was only a matter of how to present a lie, any lie, and it would be accepted. There was no brutality they would not forgive if it were properly explained away. Sasha had read of this in books and discussed it with companions.

He sat in his sleigh, gazing at the snowy fields, at the chimneys of the lime quarries that belched smoke, at the castle where he, Sasha, had been born and where the officers' club was now located, and at Jampol, which was growing before his eyes. A balconied building several stories high had already been erected. In the distance he could discern the contours of the barracks and his Uncle Mayer Joel's watermill. It seemed strange to him that he was part of all this. He was a guest at the officers' club, and was having affairs with several of the officers' wives. The manor and the lime quarries were practically his property, although on paper the estate still belonged to some duke and the lime quarries were in his father's name. Every merchant in Jampol had to come to him, the contractor, to sell his wares. He dealt with the police, with the county natchalnik, with Colonel Shachowsky, with the colonel's wife, his daughters, even with General Horne in Warsaw and with his family. Sasha Jacoby enjoyed the protection of the governor of Lublin, the governor of Pietrkow, the Governor-General of Poland himself. "How can this be?" Sasha wondered. Most young men had no high-ranking connections whatsoever, but he kept making new ones. If things went on like this, he would be summoned to St. Petersburg to the Synod, perhaps even to the Czar. It was all so simple: everyone, no matter how great, needed money, a good word, pull, advice. And it was easy to do favors, for favors paid off. As for women, they could be bought with a smile, a look, a compliment. The main thing was not to be confined to one group, or to pass up any opportunity. Even a squire's lackey had to be tipped; a dog at court must be petted. Of all methods, bribery remained the best. Sasha had not yet met a functionary who had refused one. There must be some favor that would tempt the Czar himself.

"Hey you, Wladek!"

The driver turned around. "Yes, sir?"

"What's going on between you and Magda?"

Wladek scratched his head. "She's a decent girl. My enemies make trouble between us."

"They envy you, eh? It won't do them any good. You'll get her."

Wladek halted the sleigh. "Her stepmother is mean. She hates me and I don't know why."

"An old dog in the manger," Sasha said. "Can't eat the hay herself and won't let others have it."

"Well said."

"I'll have a talk with her."

"Oh, sir, I'd be so grateful. The master is so kind!"

"Well, we're both men."

Yes, Sasha knew how to exploit everyone to his advantage; nevertheless he had his own troubles. First of all, Celina, his grandfather's widow, and her brood, his little aunts and uncles, had become his responsibility. From the day that Sasha took over his grandfather's contracts, he had paid them a weekly stipend. Celina went about disheveled; the children had runny noses, and Celina's old mother was living with them. Sasha wondered how long he could endure them. But his grandfather had left a will. Colonel Shachowsky was, in a sense, the protector of Celina. It wasn't easy to rid oneself of her. His mother's plan to travel to America also irritated Sasha. Observing the impropriety of strangers was not the same as seeing it in one's own mother. Since childhood, Sasha had borne grudges against this woman who had always vilified his father and run around with dandies. It was she who was the reason for his hostility toward the female sex. The affair with Zipkin, the bastard child she had borne him, the trip abroad with her lover, had humiliated Sasha.

III

After his grandfather's death, Sasha had divided the house. Celina and her brood lived in one part and he in the other. He had taken the divans, and all the best furniture. In Celina's part of the house the mess accumulated. It always stank of smoke, onions, and the lavatory. A Gentile maid, Hanka, took care of Sasha's rooms. She dusted, washed, scrubbed all day long. The master seldom ate lunch at home. He was always invited somewhere, or else ate in the restaurant of the officers' club. Hanka cooked small meals for herself and sang the day through like a bird. The master occasionally came to her bed at night, but he managed it so she shouldn't become pregnant. He brought other women to the house as well, but Hanka knew it was best to keep quiet about it. She swore by the cross that hung around her neck that she would keep her mouth shut. Hanka had one wish: that Sasha should not marry. She had already made up her mind that as soon as he brought a wife to the house she would curtsy politely, congratulate him, and be off. Now his mother had arrived, not a wife, but she also disrupted the household. Clara sent Hanka on errands, gave her advice on how to run things, and ordered her around: "Don't go there, don't stand here." Hanka was at odds with Celina and her children, but Clara invited these brats with their dirty noses, and their shirttails hanging out, into the apartment. She gave them cookies and wine and ordered Hanka to serve them milk or cocoa. It was an insult to Hanka, but she consoled herself that the fine lady would soon be leaving for America. Hanka eavesdropped when the master spoke to his mother. She demanded money from him. She cried, complained that she hadn't had a real life with his father. Hanka heard Sasha say to her: "You won't last long in America either!"

And Clara had replied: "If that's so, I'll throw myself into the ocean!"

The mistress was in a better mood today. She was sitting on the sofa, one leg crossed over the other, and knitting a jacket for her daughter, Felusia, who had remained in Warsaw with her governess. Hanka kept stealing looks at Clara. She wasn't a stranger, she was the master's mother. She had his eyes, his mouth, the same expression, the same shrewd smile. But how could a woman her age carry on love affairs with someone in America? Apparently Clara sensed Hanka's unspoken disapproval, for she suddenly exclaimed: "Hanka, come here!"

"Yes, mistress."

"Sit down. I want to talk to you about something."

"Oh, thank you, I can stand."

"Sit down on the footstool."

"Thank you."

Clara made a few more stitches, then placing the yarn on

her lap, said: "Hanka, you appear to be a clever girl. Tell me, what do you think of my Sasha?"

Hanka turned red. "Who am I to think anything? I am nothing but a servant here."

"What is a servant? Men are all the same. Give them an ugly queen and a pretty gypsy and you know which one they will pick. Hanka, I am his mother and I have the right to know. How does he conduct himself?"

"Oh, so-so."

"Do women come to him?"

"Sometimes."

"And they stay the night?"

"No."

"Does he sleep with them?"

"Oh, mistress, how would I know? I don't peek through the keyhole."

"When does he go to sleep?"

"Depends."

"Late?"

"Not early."

"And when does he get up?"

"Sometimes he sleeps late. But sometimes he has to get up at sunrise."

"Hanka, you are loyal to him, aren't you?"

"Yes."

"Hanka, a young man his age must not live like this."

"What can I do? I am only a maid."

"Sometimes a maid can also be effective, if she thinks."

"Mistress, he does as he pleases. He takes no advice. Everything must be exactly as he commands, to the letter. I listen to everything he says. Like a trained dog."

"A person is not a dog."

"Yes, but—"

A key could be heard in the front door. Sasha had come home. Hanka leaped up from the footstool and ran back to the kitchen. Until then she had never discussed the master's secrets with anyone, and now she had uttered words that she should perhaps have best left unsaid. The mistress would fight with him, quoting her. Hanka remained in the kitchen, tense, with cocked ears. "Oh, she got everything out of me, the black-eyed beast. He will get angry and throw me out. What will I do then? I've become attached to him, attached to him. I love him, for all his wildness . . . " Hanka felt a strong hatred for this sly woman who was running off to her lover in America and was robbing Hanka of everything—her job, her happiness. What was she to do? Take a rope and hang herself? Hanka heard talking, but she could not make out the words. Mother and son were arguing. Sasha raised his voice. "He may come and beat me—" Hanka said to herself. Once, when she had forgotten something, he had slapped her and pulled her braids. He carried a gun, too. Hanka had a holy picture hanging in the kitchen. She threw herself down on her knees, put her palms together, and began to pray. Afterwards, she tiptoed to the door. She walked silently, her head taut as a hunter's. She heard Clara say: "At your age, one does not give all of one's power to the devil. The stallions that are used for racing are not allowed to go near a mare."

"Mama, I don't want to hear such talk!"

"It's better now than later when you will be left without strength."

"I am as strong as a lion."

"A lion can also grow weak. Remember, my son, this is no small thing. We had a relative who lived in Lomza. He was a Kaminer too. A giant of a man. I used to call him uncle, though he was a distant cousin of Father's. He carried on with all the Gentile girls in Lomza. Suddenly he became paralyzed. The man gives away the marrow from his bones, and the woman takes everything into herself. You know the saying: 'A fool gives, a wise man takes!' "

"Mother, enough!"

"It would be better if you were married. It's all the same to me. I wouldn't mind if you made me a grandmother . . . I won't be here anyway."

"I'll never marry!"

"Why not?"

Sasha was silent for a while. "Rather than have someone sleep with my wife, I prefer to sleep with someone else's."

"For shame, how you speak!"

"It's the truth."

Hanka's eyes filled with tears. He'll never marry! I'll be here forever . . . She began to back away like an animal, before she turned and went into the kitchen. She had already eaten twice that day, but the good news made her hungry. On the stove stood a pot of leftover noodles. She had intended to throw them into the garbage, but instead she began to gulp them down, finishing every last one of them. Then she began scouring the pot with straw and ashes. "I won't let them weaken him," Hanka mumbled to herself. "I'll bewitch him, make him part of my body . . . " Hanka had heard at home in her village of such a love potion: the woman washed her breasts and then used the water in preparing the food of the man she wanted. It was disgusting, but if it helped, it was worth it. Hanka stationed herself before a mirror. For a long while she looked at her own reflection: the straw-blond hair, which here and there had golden glints; the red cheeks, short nose, blue eyes: the full lips that revealed wide teeth, as strong as a dog's. Her throat was white and thick and around it hung a string of coral, a gift from Sasha. Her breasts were so firm they seemed as if about to burst her blouse. "Why did he need those old biddies?" Hanka wondered. "I am prettier than all of them. I am more devoted to him too . . . " Hanka showed herself the tip of her tongue. She laughed, saw that her dimples were still there, and then turned her gaze to the wall, on which hung the copper pans and basins. This very night she would wash her breasts in one of these basins and at the first opportunity would pour some of the water into his soup. . . .

Calman sat in his House of Prayer studying the Mishnah. The day was cold but sunny. A lacework of light and shadow fell across the broad, yellow volume. Calman was reading the *Treatise of Sotah:* "When Rabbi Meir died, there were no more diligent students left. When Ben Zoma died, there were no more expounders. When Rabbi Joshua died, goodness departed from the world. When Rabban Simeon ben Gamliel died, the locust came and troubles multiplied. When Rabbi Eliezer ben Azariah died, wealth departed from the Sages. When Rabbi Akiba died, the glory of the Law ceased—"

Suddenly Calman heard footsteps in the other room. It was not the scuffling of Beila, the maid who came once a week. This was another footstep, long-forgotten yet familiar. At the door stood a noblewoman in a long fur coat, a wide-brimmed velvet hat trimmed with ostrich plumes. He was overcome by the odor of perfume. Calman paled. It was Clara, his divorced wife. For a moment he was unable to speak.

"Yes, it's me. Calmanke!"

Calman trembled. "What do you want?" he asked, choking. He could not catch his breath.

"What is the matter? Don't you recognize me?"

"I recognize you. You mustn't come in! We mustn't be under the same roof!" Calman warned her angrily, observing at the same time that she had aged.

Clara took a step forward. "Why are you shouting? I want to speak to you."

"We must not be under one roof!"

"What shall I do, tear the roof down?"

"We must not be alone together."

"Why not?"

"It isn't allowed! This is a holy place."

"Well, come outside then. Yes, still a fanatic."

"You go first!"

Clara shrugged her shoulders but did not move. He had grown entirely white and once again wore long sidelocks.

Clara could hardly believe that she had once been the wife of this ancient Jew. She felt ashamed, wanted to laugh. After a while Calman opened the door, so as not to be closeted in the room with her. He remained standing at a distance.

"What do you want?"

"I must speak to you."

"Speak."

"I can't do it like this. I can't shout at you. Here is a bench. Sit down and listen. May I sit down too?"

"What do you want? Why did you come?"

"I have an aunt here, and half sisters and brothers. I haven't, God forbid, returned to you, but I must talk to you. Or are you a savage?"

Calman looked around, fearing God and observers. Someone might come in. Mayer Joel, the maid, or even a peasant who remembered Clara. Jampol would have a good topic for gossip. Calman felt himself grow hot.

"You sit there, on the bench."

Clara wiped the bench with her glove and sat down on the part she had cleaned off.

Calman leaned against the oven. "I am sorry, but there is a law."

"Yes, a law. That's the kind of law that causes pogroms," Clara said. "We are still Asiatics. The civilized world laughs at us. But I didn't come to talk about that. I won't try to reform you. Have you become a rabbi? Your beard has doubled in length . . . Calmanke, listen to me carefully! I must go abroad and I am planning to leave Felusia with Celina and my aunt. With God's help, I'll send for her later. It's a question of six months, or at most a year. During that time she must be taken care of. Whatever you say, Felusia is officially your child and you have to pay for her upkeep. I am left without money. You're a pious Jew, to be sure, but you took everything away from me."

"I took everything away? You got twelve thousand rubles as a divorce settlement. You've cost me a fortune. You put thousands of rubles into the manor house and into all those other whims of yours."

"We won't settle accounts now. I could have had everything you see here. I didn't have to let myself be bought off for twelve thousand filthy rubles. But I've done so many foolish things. That was one more. You must take care of Felusia."

Calman grew pale. "Of that bastard?"

He glanced toward the door as if afraid that someone might be listening. A cry seemed to tear itself from his throat. For a second he wanted to run to her and hit her. But he restrained himself. He did not want a scene with this contemptible creature, nor did he want to touch her. She was filth.

"Have you stooped so low?" he rasped.

"Yes, I have."

"To whom are you going? To your lover?"

"Yes."

Calman shivered. His eyes bulged as he looked at her. There was something different about her, a blend of insolence and coarseness in her expression that hadn't been there when she had been his wife. She stared back at him with the viciousness and curiosity with which beasts sometimes examine a human being. This was not a woman but a devil. In *The Righteous Measure* Calman had once read of demons who disguised themselves as human females, lived with men, and even married them. The children they produced were half devil, half man. Could Clara be one of these creatures of the netherworld? Calman began to back away, his legs shaky, his face as white as his beard.

"Get out!" Calman shouted in a voice so loud and harsh that he himself was frightened by it.

Clara burst out laughing. "Calmanke, you really are a fool."

"Get out!"

"Calmanke, I don't need your money. I just came to say goodbye. I'm taking Felusia with me. I wouldn't leave her here for any treasure in the world. She has a rich brother and he loves her. He will provide us with everything we need."

"Why did you come here? To mock me?"

"No. Just to take a last look at you. After all, we're not strangers. We have a son. No power in the world can take that away. I'm not completely well and such a long trip is always connected with some danger. I wanted to see you once again. If you can forgive, please forgive me."

"What use is my forgiveness? You deliberately intend to do an evil thing. Don't you believe there is a Creator who can punish you?"

"Yes, Calmanke, I believe, but my love is stronger even than my faith and my fear of hell. A millionaire asked me to marry him. He was ten times as rich as you've ever been, but I could not stand him. He was too much like me."

Calman shook his head. "Is Felusia Zipkin's daughter?"

"Yes, Calmanke, she is Zipkin's daughter and I am taking her to her father. I have a feeling that I will not live too long and I want the girl at least to have a father. Why don't you get married? What kind of life is this, living here in the wilderness? Have you become a hermit?"

Calman stared at her. His eyes filled with tears. "Clara, it's not too late to repent. I pity you. I pity your Jewish soul. The Proverbs say of the sinner: 'Who confesses and forsakes shall obtain mercy.'"

"What good is mercy? I cannot live without him. I yearn for him day and night. Calman, there is one favor I want to ask of you."

"What is it?"

"If I die in America or on the trip there, see to it that Sasha says Kaddish after me. If he refuses, you say the Kaddish. After all, you loved me once. I loved you too in my own way."

"We could have been happy. But it wasn't destined. I have not deserved happiness."

"Will you do what I ask of you?"

"You will outlive me. But if you don't, I will do it."

Calman covered his face with both hands.

8 🏰

When Clara was a child, an older female relative had told her a story about a girl who had jeered at a zaddik. The saintly man had pronounced a curse on the girl: she was to remain young forever. All the women of her generation grew old, wrinkled, bent, but she retained her black hair and rosy cheeks. When her husband, too, grew old, she refused to live with him any longer. Her grandchildren were ashamed of her. The young women made fun of her and called her "grandma." Finally her life became unbearable and she drowned herself in a well.

Clara in a way found herself in a similar situation. She was too well along in her forties (how well along, she would not even admit to herself) to have such a young child and to be going off to America to join her lover. Although Calman Jacoby had been too old for her, Zipkin was too young! He wrote her such passionate letters! Clara was somewhat uneasy about the journey in general and about this distant land where it was night when it was day in Poland. Ships did sink. Passengers did become ill, die at sea, and their corpses were thrown overboard. The newspapers were full of such stories. America might be her undoing! Though Clara knew that her fears were all due to nerves, she could not prevent them from dominating her waking hours and even her dreams. To make matters worse, she began to have the early symptoms of menopause.

She felt hot and cold in turn, had flashes and headaches, and tired for no apparent reason. Her corset became oppressively constricting. Although the doctors assured her that these were all normal symptoms of change of life, she began to fear that there might be a cancerous growth in her stomach. In the past Clara had concerned herself little with the possibility of death, but now she was full of worries concerning her health. Women of her age died. They had heart attacks, neurological disorders, gall-bladder trouble. Her own mother had died young. Who knew whether there were good doctors in America? Alexander was virtually a pauper. She would not have a decent place to live. She might even have to work.

Clara had been having her hair dyed for several years, but now, no matter how frequently she had it done, the gray came through almost overnight. What would it be like aboard ship? An ocean voyage took two or three weeks, sometimes longer. Would there be a hairdresser available to do her hair? She would arrive in New York with a head of white hair! She would look more like Felusia's grandmother than her mother!

Luckily, Sasha did not need anything from her. He was, if anything, too independent. She knew he was involved with some of the wives of the officers and officials and that he owned a revolver. God, all the things that came into one's mind during a long, sleepless winter night. One's whole life flashed by, all one's mistakes, all one's foolishness.

Grisha, her first husband, had been dead for so many years, but she still remembered his insults, the names he had called her. She carried on old quarrels in her mind, easily finding the clever retorts she couldn't think of at the time. She settled accounts with her dead father. He had almost literally driven her into the arms of the Russians, from whom he got his contracts. Smirnoff had actually raped her. And then Calman! What had it all meant—fate? Both her grandfathers had been pious Jews. Her father, on the other hand, had been a *maskil*, an enlightened Jew. He had eaten on Yom Kippur and then smoked his cigar. He had used language a man does not use in front of his daughter. Well, let him rest in paradise. But she could not shake off the confusion of thoughts that crowded in on her night after night. Had she had the right to break up Alexander's home? Had it been right to keep him in ignorance of her affairs with the Russians? But such twinges of conscience were more than counterbalanced by the intensity of her desire. Fantasies tortured her brain. Sleep came in fits and starts, filled with spasmodic dreams: a hospital, a funeral, a morgue; or suddenly she would be lying with Alexander, or even with a total stranger who fondled her and spoke to her with words of madness.

One afternoon, on Clara's return from her lawyer's office, where she had filled out passport applications for herself and Felusia (Louisa was a French citizen), Louisa had met her in the entrance hall to tell her that a Monsieur Mirquin was waiting in the drawing room.

"Monsieur who?"

"Mir*quin*."

Clara burst out laughing at Louisa's pronunciation of the name, with the accent on the last syllable. But when she spoke, she sounded irritated. "Why did you ask him to wait? If I am not at home, then I am simply not at home."

"Oh, madame, he nearly forced his way in. Such a wild Russian!"

"Well, he'll have a long wait."

Clara swept into her boudoir. The ardent wooer! She had developed an aversion to this wealthy man who had courted her in Europe, and was responsible for the break with Alexander. For a time she had heaped deadly curses on him. Still, when he had disappeared with no word at all, it had irked her, and after her return to Warsaw she had been lonely. Often weeks had gone by and the front doorbell hadn't rung. After all this time—Mirkin! What was the saying—sour cabbage doesn't spoil. It had been frosty outdoors. She had had coffee at Lurse's and had done some shopping at Jablokowski Brothers, bringing home a hatbox and a package. Now she stood before the mirror, touching up her hair. Her face was red with cold, and her eyes were shining. She applied a powder puff to her nose and sprayed herself with eau de cologne. Then she took a quick sip from a liqueur flask. What does he want, she wondered. On the way to the drawing room, she noticed the heavy fur coat, plush hat, and silver-knobbed umbrella hanging in the entrance hall.

As she opened the door, Mirkin stood up, a short, thickset man with a tanned face, milky-white hair, and a gray mustache tapering off at the corners. He was wearing a suit tailored in England, a broad cravat embroidered in gold thread, and a high collar. He reeked of wealth, travel, the Riviera. Removing the cigar in its ivory holder from his fleshy lips, he bowed, spread out his arms as if to embrace her, but Clara's look discouraged him. Deftly depositing his cigar on an ashtray, he lifted her hand to his lips. His fat fingers were covered with signet rings. He would have looked distinguished were it not for a grayish film, a cataract, covering his left eye.

"When one waits," he sang out in Russian, "one's patience is rewarded."

"I certainly did not expect you, Gospodin Mirkin."

"Forgotten me already, have you?" he cried hoarsely. "But Mirkin does not forget. If Mirkin likes someone, it's for good!"

"You never even wrote."

"What am I, a writer? I've just arrived on the Berlin Express. Clara Danielovna, you get younger and prettier all the time! Little dove, it's like tasting a delicacy just to look at you." He used the Yiddish word *maachel*, as he smacked his lips and vigorously clapped his hands together. Two links set with large rubies glistened in his cuffs. Clara smiled.

"Compliments so soon."

"Compliments? *Krasavitza!* I speak the truth. Boris Davidovich is no flatterer. With me, everything comes from here." And he thumped his broad chest.

11

Clara decided not to tell Mirkin she was on the point of leaving to join Alexander. He had not stopped talking, and mainly about himself. Yes, he'd been to Carlsbad during the summer: he'd had no choice. You can't fool the liver. If it goes without mineral water even for one season, it lets you know about it. As long as he had been in Carlsbad, why not go to Italy? Nice? Oh, yes. He had only just come from Nice. He was staying at the Hotel Europeiski. His secretary, Yasha? Why, yes, he always traveled with him. Monte Carlo? He had managed to squeeze Monte Carlo in, too. And luck had been with him; he'd won. He chortled noisily. Clara regarded him in open amazement. He spoke like a man who had no idea whatever that there were such things as poverty, sickness, failure, death. "Can he be pretending?" Clara asked herself. He was in his late sixties. Didn't he read newspapers? Didn't he see the obituary columns? He chattered on about an exposition, horse races, some baron or other, a lottery. After a time he began to question Clara. How was her father? Dead? Ah! And that fellow, her friend—what was his name? Oh, yes, Zipkin! Clara was about to invent some story, but instead she blurted out the truth. Alexander, she said, was in New York. She was preparing to go to him. He had been divorced from Sabina. What was he doing? He hadn't as yet fully established himself. He'd been thinking of going into farming. In the meantime he had a modest position and was studying as well. His sister Sonya was with him. She had learned a trade and was working. Mirkin gave a short cough and began to drum on the arm of his chair with his white-bearded fingers. When he spoke again, his voice had the self-confident tone of one who had quickly grasped and assessed a given situation.

"A farm, of all things! Why a farm?"

"His father had been commissar on the Radziwill estates. The farm was part of a collective run by a group that called themselves Am Olam."

"Socialists? Anarchists? I've heard of them. They founded a colony, but nobody wanted to work. They traded wives and went hungry. They ran like mice."

"Really? He's also mentioned private farming. The government offers land to settlers."

"Fantasies!"

"Actually, I'm hoping he will complete his medical studies. He already has five semesters of credit."

"Start now? Well, I suppose it's possible. But it will take an iron will, and money, too."

"I'm afraid he doesn't have much of either."

"Not if I remember him correctly."

Louisa came in and served tea and cookies. Early-evening darkness was filling the room. Clara suggested that she light a lamp, but Mirkin said he loved the winter twilight. It was one of the things that drew him back to Russia. The Riviera was superb, but one tired of it. Nowhere on the Continent was there such snow, such blueness, such stillness as here. True, Warsaw was not Moscow or St. Petersburg, but it was better than Paris. There it just rained and the cold was damp and miserable. One never saw a sleigh. London was simply as dark as Egypt. Mirkin had been to New York too, on business. A cold city, full of drafts. Clusters of houses, without charm, without intimacy. As it grew darker, Mirkin's face was lost in shadow. Clara could no longer distinguish his bad eye from the good one. His voice took on an intimate tone.

"I don't understand you, Clara Danielovna. Truly, *nie ponie-mayu!*"

"Have you never heard of something called love?"

"Yes, yes, but it must make sense! Let's not deceive each other. You're a mature woman, not a miss of eighteen. A woman of your age and in your circumstances needs comforts."

"True."

"Clara Danielovna, we could both be happy!"

"Are you starting that again?"

"I could not forget you. Zipkin is not for you. Absolutely not. A grown man, but with—what do you call it?—the psychology of a—a *maltshishek*, a boy, nothing more. To start studying at his age! He'll come to nothing. He'll ruin himself and, God forbid, he'll ruin you, too. He should never have left his wife."

"I didn't force him into anything, Boris Davidovich. I left a husband too."

"Is he really the father of the girl I saw in the hallway? She's a beauty."

"She is."

"I realize it's not a simple matter; but still—America? Who goes to America? The American rich spend more time in Europe than at home in the United States. Their children are educated in England. What is there to do in New York? Sew aprons?"

"As a matter of fact, he wants to settle in California."

"California. Well, everything is possible. Clara Danielovna, let's have supper together. Let's go for a sleigh ride."

"We can eat here."

"But we cannot go for a sleigh ride here."

"You haven't changed in the least. I must have a look at my Felusia. And get some light in here. It's snowing again."

Clara rose from her chair and in the same instant Mirkin jumped up from his, caught her in a quick embrace, and kissed her squarely on the lips.

"Boris Davidovich!"

"There'll be enough left for him. We could enjoy ourselves, Clara Danielovna, we could burn up the world! Money has no importance for me. All of Europe is open to us, the whole world!"

"You have a wife."

"A wife? A Xanthippe! There was never any genuine relationship between us. It's all a matter of spite with her, pure spite. She lets herself be led by a band of grasping lawyers. She wants only one thing—money. From the first time I saw you,

Clara Danielovna, that night on the Berlin Express, I have always thought: 'This is she. This is my angel.'"

"That's how you talk about all women."

"Don't insult me. I am no longer young, but my heart is full. One gets lonely, Clara Danielovna. One yearns for youth, the old times. We can go abroad, anywhere—everywhere, alone. A woman like you, my dear, deserves luxury. I'm not happy with my triumphs, that's the truth. I'm not understood. I need someone close, to whom I can open my soul. Most of the little ladies are simply—ducks."

Suddenly he gasped as though his breath had failed him. He lurched forward, pulling Clara to him. He held her pressed against his protruding stomach as in a vise. She tried to struggle free, but it was impossible.

"Please, Boris Davidovich!"

"Excuse me, excuse me. I did not realize—meant no harm. I tried to forget, but it's not easy to forget. I always saw you in my mind's eye—on the train, everywhere. I would still like a few good years—seven good years, as they say."

"And what happens then?"

"You will be provided for. Well provided for."

"I was provided for once before."

"I'm a rich man. I won't take my money with me when I go. My children have not behaved well toward me. They have always sided with their mother. They have made absolutely no effort to see my side. I'm a lonely man despite my possessions."

Mirkin's voice cracked. He was seized by a fit of coughing and pulled out a handkerchief. Outdoors, the street lights went on suddenly and filled the room with bright, snow-reflected light. Mirkin's blind eye blinked rapidly, as though it had seen something frightening.

"Well, well—I'm sorry. Please forgive me."

III

Clara seldom really talked with Louisa, Felusia's governess. For one thing, they had no language in common. Clara's French was inadequate and Louisa's Polish consisted mainly of mispronounced words and broken phrases. For another, Clara found it difficult to understand this French old maid living out her years in solitude, attaching herself to the children of strangers. Louisa could sit for hours at the window just staring at nothing, like a cat. Didn't she need a man? Had she no thought for her old age? She had brought with her from France a cookbook and a "dream interpreter." These two books comprised her entire reading. Nevertheless, now and then she let fall a word or phrase indicating that some process of thinking was taking place in her mind, that somewhere she had retained a vestige of French esprit. On a sudden impulse, Clara decided to take Louisa into her confidence. Louisa knew, did she not, that Clara loved Alexander. But now Mirkin had come back into the picture, desperate, offering to lavish his wealth on her, take her abroad in the most luxurious style. In fact, he wanted Felusia and her governess to join them. What should she do? She implored Louisa to be completely candid. What would Louisa have done in a similar situation? Louisa's dark eyes sparkled.

"I, madame, would go with Monsieur Mir*quin*."

"Even though you were in love with another man?"

"The other need not know. Monsieur Sipkin is in America. The trip can remain a secret. Monsieur Mirquin is rich. Monsieur Sipkin is *très charmant,* but poor as a churchmouse. Madame can arrange things so that Sasha can forward Monsieur Sipkin's correspondence to Warsaw. Madame could send her replies to Sasha, who could put Russian postage stamps on her letters and send them to America. Monsieur Sipkin need never know the truth."

Clara had to laugh. She had never expected such cunning from docile Louisa. Her face, normally placid—if not dull—

had become animated. Her words, accompanied by quick gestures, had spilled out so quickly and idiomatically that Clara
had difficulty in following her. There had been a time when
Clara could seek advice from her aunt, but the old lady was
paralyzed. And suddenly Louisa, without hesitating, had
offered a feasible plan. That very day Clara had received a
letter from Zipkin: its tone was depressed and depressing. He
missed Clara, to be sure, but she had better prepare herself for
hardships. He was no longer working at the "shop" where he
had been employed, because of a row with the foreman. He
hoped to find another job, but there was a Depression—rents
were comparatively high, and maids were downright prohibi-
tive. There was no real middle class in America. People were
either rich or poor. On his part there was not one bit of good
news, but something wonderful had happened to Sonya.
Yackiewicz, her friend from Kuniev, had come to New York.
Sonya had no idea at all that he was there. Then, quite by
chance, they had met at the Yiddish Theater and a few days
later had been married. Yackiewicz had a whole circle of
friends from Russia, and one of them had given the couple a
party. There had been many toasts, plenty of drinking, and
much lively discussion. Three days later they were back at
work—Sonya making dresses and he in a shirt factory. Yes,
things were rather prosaic in New York. The news from the
farm in Oregon was not encouraging. There was, it seemed, a
wide disparity between theory and practice. As Clara read on,
she felt a growing emptiness in her heart. She had not quite
finished when the doorbell rang.

Louisa came in and in a conspiratorial tone announced:
"Monsier Mir*quin.*"

Mirkin came right in and began talking at once. He had
tickets to the opera. First loge. *Rigoletto.* Would Clara come?
He wanted to spend the day with her. He had a sleigh waiting
outside. His voice was hoarse but strong. He hadn't even removed his fur coat. Eager for her consent, he stood on the
threshold in a state of ill-concealed impatience, his fur hat in

one hand, a cigar in the other. His face was flushed from the cold. His cataract-filmed eye blinked madly.

Clara raised her eyebrows. "May I change my clothes at least?"

"Every minute is valuable."

"To you—not to me. And if you don't mind, Boris Davidovich, hand your coat to Louisa. You're not a muzhik."

Mirkin was already taking her too much for granted. Still, Alexander's letter had weakened her position—there was no use denying it. She knew she was making a mistake once again to sell herself to an old man. But nevertheless she went off to dress. After all, who was she to be so proud? He could find younger, more attractive women than she. Alexander was totally impractical. She opened her clothes closet and stood there with her hands covering her face. What game was fate playing with her now? Why should this have to happen to her? She summoned Louisa to help lace up her corset. She stood with bared breasts in front of the Frenchwoman while, with deft fingers, she helped her dress, chattering all the while. But only one word registered with Clara: madame, madame, madame. Had the old fox bribed her? First her father had sold her, now she was selling herself. Yes, to be a "madam"—that would be better. Something inside her ached and laughed at the same time. She was aware of her own cheapness. Yes, both Grisha and Calman had been right. She was what Grisha had called her, vulgar. She sprayed herself with perfume and put a chocolate into her mouth. She felt better. What was the saying? If you can't go across, go around.

In front of the house stood a sleigh and two gray horses— not one of the little sleighs one rented for a few guilders to trot around the park, but a baronial equippage, elegantly fitted, with a handsome harness for the horses, brass lanterns on either side, and a bearskin rug to cover the feet. The coachman, too, was grandly uniformed. He cracked the whip, the horses bounded forward, and Clara fell on top of Mirkin. The sleigh went so fast that Clara had trouble orienting herself. The snow had transformed the city. The whiteness was almost blinding. The sky raced past. The houses glided backward. Clods of snow flew from the horses' hoofs. After a while Clara realized that they were on Marshalkovsky Boulevard.

"Where are you taking me?"

"To Wilanow."

"We'll never get back in time for the opera. And I have to change."

"There will be time for everything."

Mirkin was not Zipkin. Zipkin used to pull her into the first half-decent coffeehouse, order a cup of coffee, light a cigarette, and spin out his dreams. Mirkin arranged for everything in advance: the tickets, the sleigh, presumably the restaurant where they were to lunch. He did not need to agonize over every kopeck. Clara laughed to herself. How tightly he held her! And how loud his breathing was! She wondered if he had asthma. It might be better if she turned Louisa over to him. They had left Marshalkovsky Boulevard and were driving along the Mokotow fields—broad and white as far as the horizon's edge. The spirals of blue smoke curling up from the chimneys of the low houses suggested the burning altars of underground temples where idolatrous rites were being performed. The whip cracked, crows cawed, the snow alternately glistened white in the dazzling sunshine and blue in shaded areas that sparkled like closely set diamonds. The entire scene, the snow shapes—dunes, hillocks—awakened in Clara a youthful, half-forgotten lust for adventure. Well, Clara said to herself, I must live. Mirkin held her around the bosom, but she no longer fought him off. He pressed close to her, moved his heavy hand into her muff, breathing like a bellows. Well, he was paying for it. If you eat pork, let the gravy run! She would speak with him openly, have a clear understanding. Alexander? Men demanded chastity from women, but they themselves felt free to do anything they wished.

They did not go as far as Wilanow. A building emerged from the white landscape. It was a restaurant, with a snow-covered emblem over the door. The sleigh glided to a halt, and the coachman helped them out. A heavy door opened, creating a cloud of vapor. The walls inside were decorated with mounted heads of deer, stuffed birds, and a wild boar with long twisting tusks around his snout. It smelled of beer, wine, roasting meats. From another room came a burst of male singing. Clara hesitated on the threshold. It was altogether too Gentile. It was like falling into a robber's den. But the frock-coated headwaiter advanced toward her with an ingratiating smile. Everything was ready—it had all been reserved in advance—the table, luncheon, the wines, the liqueurs. There was a steady flow of plates, platters, glasses, bottles. The caviar was the best. There was lobster. The main course was venison. The rolls were hot from the oven. Mirkin chewed, drank, dabbed at his mouth with his napkin, and held forth about the various dishes. He bent low over his plate, fell on the food like a glutton, and kept refilling Clara's glass. Greed shone out of his good eye—the hunger of those who can never be sated. He perspired, panted, sighed. Clara turned away. She saw herself in him as in a mirror. He wanted to cram everything into the years that remained to him, to savor all he could before it was too late, just as she did.

"Clara Danielovna, I've rented a room upstairs, to rest in after lunch," he said in Russian.

Clara laughed, replying in Yiddish. "Boris Davidovich, you've made your decision without consulting the boss."

Mirkin was about to answer when Yasha Vinaver, his secretary, emerged from somewhere: a small man in a fur coat, a fur hat, a woolen muffler, and ear muffs. His face was round and red like an apple. He smiled joyfully and stretched out his arms and fur-gloved hands as if to embrace Clara. The waiter tried to take his hat and coat from him, but Yasha Vinaver seemed not to notice him.

"What is he, a spy?" Clara said to Mirkin.

"Not a spy, Clara Danielovna, my gracious lady, but your most devoted friend and admirer," Yasha Vinaver said. "You have become younger, madame, and even more beautiful, a splendid picture of feminine charm! Unbelievably beautiful! It makes my heart jump just to look at you!"

"You'd better check your coat and hat," Mirkin said.

"What? Of course! When I saw you, Clara Danielovna, I forgot about everything. I became, as they say, dazzled by your radiance . . ."

And he went to the checkroom.

He's Mirkin's spy. He will tell Alexander, Clara thought to herself. She suddenly knew that the pair had conceived some plot against her. Mirkin's visit and Yasha Vinaver's appearance had been arranged for some evil purpose. She had been trapped. She became both angry and frightened. She looked at Mirkin reproachfully and asked: "What is this comedy all about?"

Mirkin's healthy eye, behind its white brow, became round and gay. The eye of a pig, Clara thought.

"There's no comedy, Clara Danielovna," he said protestingly. "I love you and want you. It's as simple as that."

9 ⛫

I

Years back, after Lucian had been caught by the police and the Warsaw press was regaling its readers with the details of the murder he had committed, how he had tried to rob Chodzinski, taken Kasia to the home of the Bobrowska woman, and abandoned his wife and child in the middle of Christmas dinner, it seemed to Felicia as if the world was ending. Articles about the crime by reporters and feature writers were spread over entire pages. They improvised and wrote deliberate lies. A noble Polish name was being disgraced and there was no one to prevent it. Could this be the behavior of a Christian country, Felicia kept asking herself. It was clear to her that everyone was enjoying her anguish—the police, the judge, the prosecutor, even her own maids, whom she had fed and clothed. Her husband, Marian, had begun to lose his aristocratic patients. Helena wrote from Zamosc that her children were ashamed to go to the gymnasium, because their Uncle Lucian was a murderer. Felicia locked herself in her boudoir, refused to come out, and wept. When she did come out, it was only to go to a church where no one knew her. She sank down in front of the statue of the Holy Mother, where she knelt praying for hours.

She stopped eating and couldn't sleep at night. She began to look drawn and anemic. Marian dosed her with all kinds of medicines, but she grew worse. She felt sorry for her husband. He, too, began to look thin. He had had to advance huge sums to the attorneys, pay for the victim's burial, support his widow and her orphans. Marian's earnings had fallen off and his savings were being depleted. Felicia became convinced that her death would free Marian from an intolerable burden, that she was only an obstacle to him, and she prayed to God to take her without delay. She could no longer satisfy Marian's masculine needs, and she was prepared to step aside for a younger, more attractive woman.

There were days when it seemed to Felicia that the end was imminent. She lay in bed hardly able to move a limb, dozed off, awoke, dozed again, only to awake once more with a start. She had nightmares in which she saw devils and angels. She saw in turn her dead father and mother. She saw colors of such luminescence that they could only be of heavenly origin. She smiled inwardly. How foolish man was to fear that which would deliver him forever. The soul only began to live after the body died. She begged Marian to buy a plot for her in the cemetery, order a coffin, and select a tombstone. Every time she suffered a spell of nausea and her head began to whirl, she would send for the priest to hear her final confession.

"A bit premature, my dear," Marian would remark. "You're getting better every day."

It developed that Marian was right; God was not quite ready to accept her. She began to sleep a lot to make up for all the wakeful nights of the past, and was assailed by hunger so ravenous that it was enough to cancel out all the days she had not eaten. But what had she to live for? What was there still for her to accomplish on this earth? Suddenly she saw her mission—she would be a mother both to Lucian's children and to the murdered janitor's orphans. What would become of them if she were to die? Marian would not for the rest of his life pay for the sins of his miscreant brother-in-law.

The answer was so simple that Felicia could not understand how she had not thought of it during all her months of illness.

Now that she had a purpose, she stifled her shame and visited Wojciech Chodzinski's widow in her cramped hovel. At first the woman drove her away. Wojciechowa's sons threatened to beat Felicia up.

"Get the hell out of here!" they screamed. "You lousy murderer's sister!"

They set the dog on her and threw sawdust and stinking rags at her. The girls insulted her, and her gifts were thrown back in her face. There was a moment when Felicia decided to leave the miserable household to its fate; instead, she mustered every ounce of strength she had. How would the good Lord Jesus have acted in such a case, she asked herself. What would the holy St. Francis have done? Would they have let themselves be driven off by taunts? She fell to her knees before the orphans, showered them with money and clothes. She even tried to help Wojciechowa with her washing, and it was the mother who was the first to be won over. Gradually, one by one, the children made peace with her. Who would have believed that after such rebuffs Felicia would meet with success? Even the dog ended by nuzzling her shoes and wagging its tail.

It took eighteen months for the case to come to trial. During this time Felicia clothed Wojciechowa's children, packed the little ones off to school, got the older boys apprenticed so they could learn trades, and sent the girls to work in decent homes. At first Marian laughed at her, called her a fool and a hypocrite. Like many liberals and radicals, Marian did not believe in philanthropy. Reform was what was needed! It was the government that must be forced to set up democratic institutions and thus bring about equality for the masses. What good was charity? But in time Felicia's goodness had its effect on him. He offered to help. Felicia did not stop at the janitor's family. She was prepared to take on Bolek, Lucian's illegitimate son, and Kasia as well. But Bobrowska had taken Kasia and her little boy under her protection. They moved in with her, and Bobrowska would have nothing to do with Lucian's sister.

As it turned out, Felicia's actions helped not only the murderer's victims but the murderer himself. The ladies of Warsaw began to talk about the Christian mercy Felicia had shown. Word of her deeds reached the prosecutor, the judge himself—a Russified Pole. Priests read sermons about the unhappy Lucian and his ordeal. Articles appeared in the press. Aristocratic ladies who had stopped using Zawacki's services returned to the doctor. And when Felicia was called to testify at the trial, the same reporters who had originally maligned her now described her as a martyr. She began to receive invitations from charitable groups that counted ladies of the highest society among their patrons. Lucian had faced twenty years at hard labor, or even life imprisonment. The judge, however, imposed the minimum sentence under the charge. Privately, he confided that he had been swayed not by the arguments of the counsel for the defense but by the sister of the accused—her words, her manner, her tears.

11

At the time of the Polish uprising against the Russians, Lucian had devised for himself a foolproof method of withstanding suffering—he would tell himself that he was dead. Each time that he was faced with an unendurable situation, he would imagine that he was no longer among the living, he was a ghost, a corpse, free of all hope, all need. He had heard about the living dead, those tormented souls who wander about in limbo unable to find refuge in their graves. He imagined himself to be one of them. He had read about fakirs who, in a state of self-induced catalepsy, let themselves be buried alive. Had not all his life been a futile struggle against the forces of darkness? Had not malevolent fate hung over him right from the start? Could the strange events of his life be explained in any way other than that he had been born under an evil star? Lucian had felt the hand of destiny while still a boy, the spoiled young panicz of the manor. He had been given everything:

clothes, weapons, food; the love of his parents, his sisters, his brother. The servants idolized him; the peasants fondled him; even the animals—dogs, cats, horses—were especially affectionate toward him. Nevertheless, the object of all this adoration suffered so miserably that even as a boy he had thought of shooting himself. He contracted every childhood disease and as an adolescent developed all kinds of phobias. He blasphemed against God and ran to the priest to confess. He stole, spat on sacred pictures, throttled chickens like a polecat, tortured rabbits. He had no inclination whatever for study but was adept at devising stratagems for avoiding it. Lust for women seized him early. He was afraid of contagious diseases, scandals in the family. Having read in an encyclopedia about consumption of the intestines, he promptly convinced himself that he had it. His mother mentioned an instance of insanity in the family, and he was seized by panic, certain that he was becoming mad. As far back as he could remember, he had always had a foreboding of some approaching catastrophe.

Catastrophe came soon enough with the uprising against the Russians. He roamed the forests, suffered hunger, cold, dug graves for friends. His father was exiled to Siberia and he himself was sentenced to death *in absentia*. Then the hiding in Warsaw, working in the furniture factory, moving in with Stachowa. Later his elopement with Miriam Lieba and starvation in Paris, his disillusionment with the Polish colony in France, his subsequent return to Poland, the entanglements with Kasia, Bobrowska, and the rest. The years had run by like a bad dream. But what had been the point of it all? And why had it all ended in the stupid murder of a poor janitor, the father of ten children?

In the long months in prison awaiting his trial, Lucian had groped for some answer, but this riddle had no solution. His life had been a crazy amalgam of bad luck, vicious circumstance, poor nerves, weak character, and lack of will power— one dreary waste. But then, weren't the lives of others—of the entire human species for that matter—just as chaotic? Felicia had sent him a Bible in prison, but, bored as he was, he had not been able to read it. The Jehovah of the Old Testament played cat-and-mouse with the Israelites. They were always being insubordinate and He was always punishing them. The New Testament promised bliss in the Kingdom of Heaven, but what guarantee was there that such a kingdom existed? Had not the Popes themselves carried on murderous wars? Had not the Russians, Prussians, and Austrians—three Christian nations—torn Poland to pieces, hanged men, whipped women, committed countless crimes? Would they have done these things if they truly believed in God and the teachings of Jesus?

Life was so senseless that death, by comparison, made a great deal of sense. Lucian entered into his death fantasy so wholeheartedly that it almost became true. He reached a state very like the Nirvana he had read about many years ago in his father's library. The examining attorney had had no difficulties with him. He had confessed everything, signed every paper placed in front of him. He had even told them about his plans to organize a Polish crime syndicate to rob Wallenberg. The lawyers retained by Felicia later pleaded with him to retract his admissions, but he would not hear of it. The other prisoners in his cell jeered at him and he took their mockery in silence. He was prepared to accept his fate, whatever it might be—to die on the gallows, to rot in Siberia. He lay in his bunk, ate the pasty bread and watery grits, patiently suffered the cold, the heat, the stench of the urinal, the filth all around him. The thieves and murderers who were his fellow prisoners played cards, smoked cheap tobacco, sang maudlin tunes about love and the women who betrayed it, about the convict's sad fate and his hopes for freedom. But Lucian felt no such sentiments. He had lost interest in the world, with its illusory joys and pretensions.

The trial was almost a *cause célèbre*. The newspapers published long accounts of it. Artists came to court to sketch Lucian's portrait. Ladies fought for tickets of admission. But none of it had an effect on Lucian. He barely heard the witnesses' testimony, the arguments of the prosecution, or even those of the defense counsel. Nor would he exercise his prerogative to make a final statement. When asked by the judge if he had anything to say in his own defense, Lucian had replied, "No, thank you. Nothing."

At the trial's end, however, something began to stir in him. The prisoners congratulated him and the guards squeezed his hand. For the first time that he could remember since his childhood, he was enjoying some prestige. A Jewish book dealer on Swiętokrzyska Street had published what purported to be Lucian's life story in a series of weekly brochures that sold for one kopeck an issue. The prison warden had summoned Lucian to his office to show him the brochures, and the warden's wife had come to see the hero of this odyssey in the flesh. The naïve woman had taken for truth the fabrications concocted by the author. When Lucian had tried to tell her he was neither as heroic nor as despicable as the brochure depicted him, the good woman begged him not to destroy her illusions.

Gradually life in prison came more and more to resemble life outside: it was trivial, monotonous, filled with futile hopes and senseless wranglings. Lucian took up cards, smoked Majorca tobacco, and waited for packages. Felicia came to see him and they conversed through the bars. Bobrowska sent him notes that a bribed guard wedged into Lucian's bread ration. From these he learned that Kasia had left Chodzinski and together with Bolek had moved in with Bobrowska. Bobrowska was teaching her to sew. After a time the letters stopped coming. Lucian learned through the grapevine that Bobrowska was again seeing her former lover. He was directing plays in a summer theater called Pod Lipkom. Lucian surmised how Bobrowska had gotten the old rake to come back to her; she had probably offered him Kasia.

III

The convict in the next bunk, Wojciech Kulak, was chewing on the heel of a loaf of bread and from time to time he spat. He was short, broad-boned, snub-nosed, with a long upper lip and the slanted eyes of a Mongol, an impression strengthened by his shaved head and yellow complexion. His nicknames were "Tatar" and "Chink." He was doing time for murder, and he had four more years to serve. He was also a *przydup-nik*, or pimp, and still retained a partnership in two houses, one in Szylce, the other in Tamki. The madams brought him packages. Wojciech never lacked tobacco or the numerous other amenities that money could buy. He was paying monthly retainers to the guards and to the warden himself. He was regularly supplied with vodka, sausages, roast duckling. He received a steady flow of mail but couldn't read, so Lucian became his "interpreter," as Wojciech called him. For this he received Kulak's protection against the toughs and bullies who extorted weekly tribute from the more docile inmates. Everyone knew that Kulak kept a curved Tatar knife in his cell, and he had been heard to boast about a loaded revolver hidden away somewhere. In a fight, Wojciech seldom used his hands. He butted with his head, like a bull, or kicked with his heavy wooden shoes. He was afraid to hit with his fist, he said, because it was like delivering a death blow.

"Hey, you crapulous count!"

Lucian was silent.

"Hey! Lousy squire!"

It was early afternoon of a summer day, but the cell was dark. The bars were covered with wire meshing that cut off most of the light. Only on the cracked plaster of one wall was there a feeble play of sunlight. The ceiling was crisscrossed with massive beams. The outer walls were so thick that the tiny window was little more than a niche. Both Lucian and Kulak wore the regulation gray cotton pants and short jackets. Kulak had taken off his shoes and his enormous toes were as long as a man's fingers. He was reputed to be able to cut bread with them, and even roll a cigarette.

"Hey, you three-groschen aristocrat!"

Lucian had learned that in prison you don't answer the first or second time, not even when addressed by Kulak. The ones who jump at the first peep are the greenhorns, and usually all they get for their pains is an insult or a crude witticism. A seasoned convict pretends not to hear when spoken to, at least not until he feels like talking. Kulak, it appeared, had something to say.

"What is it?" Lucian finally asked.

"What are you thinking about?"

"Nothing. Nothing at all."

"Women, eh?"

Lucian smiled. "Can we help ourselves?"

"Don't get too deep into that mire; you can lose your mind, and then what? A little won't do you any harm, but too much and a screw goes loose or you burst a blood vessel."

"Let it burst."

"What are you gonna do when you get out? Thought about that?"

"No, haven't decided yet."

"What are you gonna do with that bitchy grandma Bobrowska? Let her live?"

"I don't want to end up back here."

"Afraid, eh? Wetting your pants, aren't you? Not me. I'll have somebody's guts. I'm gonna use that knife."

"They'll have you back here in no time."

"Not me. I was too damn hotheaded the last time. I let somebody have it in front of witnesses. This time it'll be a nice quiet job, I'll take him into the Praga woods. We'll eat, drink, chat, real chummy. Then I'll say to him: 'All right, my friend, you sang your little song. Cross yourself, you're going back to God.' Then, right in the guts."

"They'll nab you sooner or later."

"Crap. They don't nab so easily. Even when the cops suspect you, what can they do? I deny the whole thing. You, my noble sir, are afraid of a little persuasion. They slap your rear and you tattle on your own father. I can take a blow. If I keep my mouth shut they can't pry it open with hot pincers."

"In the meantime you're back rotting behind bars."

"How long? They can't just hold you, they gotta let you go. That's the law. We know the goddamned code better than the lawyers. A trial is a trial. And we know what to do when some bastard starts blabbing. We pack him off to the other side, and to make sure he gets there we put him in a trunk. Understand?"

"It doesn't pay. For that moment of revenge the price is too high."

"A preacher, huh? Then what the devil did you go chasing Chodzinski for? Why did you hang around with all that scummy bunch? You're gonna be one of us, all right."

"No, Kulak. I'm not going to spit out my lungs behind bars."

"What are you gonna do?"

"Go away somewhere."

"Where? What are you gonna live on?"

"Find something, some kind of job."

"Like what? What are you good for? You have delicate little hands. Nobody would trust you with a broken shilling. Where would you go, to the caves of Lucifer?"

"To Corsica. Maybe Sicily. Maybe California."

"And do what?"

"Buy a piece of land. A little house."

"And do what with the land? Cultivate it with your snout?"

"Oranges grow by themselves. You don't do any cultivating. You have a few hundred trees and all you do is pick the oranges when they ripen. You sell them and have your livelihood."

"Sure, sure, it's so simple a kid can do it. You're fooling yourself, my friend. They're waiting for you just like that?

There were three hundred Polacks on a boat headed for America—and thirty-one croaked on the way. It was in the papers. The food was all maggoty. They weren't even sent off like Christians, just thrown to the fish."

"Well, once you're dead it doesn't matter too much whether you're fodder for worms or fish."

"Once they get there—the ones that get there—they're sent down to the coal mines. The mine caves in and they're choked by gas. Sure, I'm no scholar, but I know what's going on. They got a Depression there, that's what they got."

"Still better than to rot here."

Kulak thought for a while. "You think I like it here? Every day is like a year. The goddamned honorable judge says: six years, six nice little years. To talk is easy, little father, but to sit in this pen is another thing, especially in this hot weather. You want to get out in the country, find a nice little pond and dive in—I can swim like a fish. You want to go to bed with someone. And what's wrong with dropping into a tavern and siphoning off a few mugs of beer? This is a dog's life. I lie in my hole and get all kinds of crazy thoughts. Hey, you. Nobleman! I want to ask you something."

"What now?"

"You believe in God?"

"Absolutely not."

"Then who made this swinish world?"

10 🏛

I

Lucian was released from prison in mid-May. Felicia, in her husband's carriage, waited for him at the prison's back gate. Although the weather was warm, Lucian appeared in a heavy overcoat, a pair of cracked shoes, and a faded derby. At first, sister and brother did not recognize each other. To Lucian, Felicia looked like his mother. Dressed in black with a veiled hat, Felicia was still mourning for Miriam Lieba. Her blond hair was shot with gray. Lucian had grown thin, jaundice-yellow, and there were threads of gray hair at his temples. Brother and sister embraced. A small crowd of curiosity-seekers had assembled at the prison gate. The coachman brandished his whip and the coach trundled into Iron Street and from there down Grzybowska Street—to Kreditowa Street. Lucian had recognized neither Warsaw nor Felicia's house. On Krolewska Street and Marshalkovsky Boulevard he had noticed horse-drawn trolley cars. He got out of the carriage and walked quickly through the gate of the building where Felicia lived. The maid had already opened the door to the apartment. No one saw the ex-convict as he dismounted and climbed the front stairs. Dr. Zawacki happened to be away from home that day. Wladzio and Marisia, Lucian's children, were at school. Janina, the daughter of the janitor whom Lucian had shot and whom Felicia had adopted without Lucian's knowledge, was also out. Felicia had prepared a room and clothes for Lucian. He went into the bathroom, where the fire already burned in the stove for heating water. On a bench lay underwear, a bathrobe, and a pair of new slippers. The tiled bathroom had a white marble bathtub. Lucian smiled to himself as he scrubbed his body with a sponge and scented soap: "If only Wojciech Kulak could see me now . . ." He dried himself with a Turkish towel and put on the bathrobe and slippers. In his room he found a summer suit, a straw hat, a linen shirt, a stiff collar, a silk tie, and a pair of shiny new shoes. One could apparently get everything ready-made in Warsaw now as in Paris. Felicia had even remembered to supply suspenders, cuff-links, garters. He stood at the window facing the courtyard. The servant girl who had let him in came up with a sack to remove his old clothing. She took it directly to the trash bin.

Everything took place quietly. He dressed and his appearance was completely changed. It was not more than two hours since he had left the prison, yet it seemed as distant as if it had happened years ago, or as if he had read about it in a book. Standing before the mirror, he hardly recognized himself. He felt the cleanliness of his shirt, the fresh underwear and socks. The shoes were so light that he seemed to be barefoot. The straw hat fit.

Felicia opened the door and cried, "My dear!" in a whimpering tone.

Taking his arm, she led him to the dining room. Lunch was usually eaten at four o'clock, but a second breakfast had been prepared for Lucian. A cook in a short apron, with a white cap over her blond hair, came in, and the maid, too, fussed about him. The table was covered with a white cloth. There were fresh rolls in a straw basket, milk, sour milk, white cheese, Swiss cheese, and a vase full of flowers. Was it like this every day or was it a holiday? In the years of his imprisonment he had forgotten that such things as saltcellars and flowers existed. He had almost forgotten how to cope with a napkin and the silver. He smiled at the servants, winked, but they looked embarrassed and did not smile back. Felicia asked if he wanted tea or coffee. When he had indicated his preference, she turned to the cook and said: "The Count will have coffee."

Lucian nearly burst out laughing. "The Count, of all things!" He ate and tried to remember his manners. One must not grab. One must not chew noisily. It was not proper to finish every last bit on one's plate. But he was hungry. The rolls were insubstantial, melted in his mouth. The fried eggs only increased his appetite. "Well, I'll not perish from hunger!" He drank the coffee and his head spun as if from liquor. He became sleepy and began to yawn, covering his mouth as he had been taught as a boy. Felicia nodded her head at him with motherly devotion. At first he had thought she reminded him of his mother; now she seemed to resemble their grandmother, whose picture had once hung in one of the manor living rooms.

"You're tired?"

"Yes, tired. "

"Go to your room and lie down."

"Yes, I'll take a nap—" He spoke in the same plebeian, good-natured tone as Wojciech Kulak.

Felicia escorted him back to the room where he had previously changed. Only then did he notice the bed: two spotless pillows, a red satin blanket in a lace coverlet. A portrait of Lucian as a mischievous boy, painted by a French artist, hung over the bed. It was all too good to last.

"Shall I undress or lie down in my clothes?"

"If you're sleepy, undress. You still have three hours before dinner, and Marian may be late. He has a lecture—"

"Well, thanks."

Felicia threw him something like a kiss. Lucian began to undress. He was no longer accustomed to suspenders, a collar, cuff-links. The collar buckled. A cuff-link fell out of a cuff. When he finally lay down on the bed, he felt an odd sensation: he seemed to be sinking into a downy bottomlessness. He felt as if he were floating. Everything was too clean, too light. He was sleepy, but he could not sleep. "Is it still the same day? How can one day be so long? Am I really free?" In prison when Lucian had dreamed of the day he would be free, he had always imagined a tavern, noise, prostitutes, music. But Felicia had brought him home like a student from a boarding school. Acacia trees faced the window. Across the way, someone tinkled on a pianoforte, the notes blending with the song of a solitary bird. It was quieter here than in prison. "Is this happiness?" Lucian asked himself. "Did it pay to have dreamed of this?" No answer came to him. He closed his eyes and slowly fell asleep.

11

Lucian dreamed he was back in prison. There was a fight between Wojciech Kulak and another inmate. Someone drew a knife. Lucian awoke, frightened and lustful. He had long ago observed that dreams of murder provoked his lust. Was everyone like this? Or only he? Sitting up, he wiped the sweat from his brow. He had spent years in prison, had had innumerable thoughts, but had come to no decision. He had had many plans: to emigrate to America or Corsica, to become a monk, to settle on a couple of acres in Poland, to go to Siberia. But what he really wanted to do still escaped him. There had been fantasies too—to rob Wallenberg, to take revenge on Bobrowska's lover, to join the rebels who wanted to overthrow the Czar and abolish wealth. He had also dreamed of joining the underworld, Wojciech Kulak's gang. . . . What hadn't run through this mind that for years had had eighteen hours out of every twenty-four to brood in. . . . Sitting in bed now, Lucian yawned, stretched. All his emotions became entangled within him: fatigue, lust, embarrassment at the thought of meeting his brother-in-law, his own children. And Felicia had mentioned that she had adopted a girl. What girl? "Why would she adopt a girl if she already had Wladzio and

Marisia?" He had bathed, was clean, but he itched and had to scratch himself. He had an ache in one ear, felt a drawing sensation in a back tooth, a nostril was stuffed as if he had a cold. His hair, cut short across his skull, prickled. "Ah, the devil! This swinish life!" he muttered. "I must go to a brothel this evening!" Suddenly he burst out laughing. He recalled the day a new convict, a boy of seventeen who had slain his own mother, had come into the cell. Wojciech Kulak, the beast, had raped him that very night. . . . "Swine, real swine!" Lucian said to himself, "Life was raw there without hypocritical masks!" A shiver moved down his spine: an icy thread, zigzagging from nape to pelvis.

Someone knocked. Lucian had forgotten what to reply. "Well!" he called out.

Felicia opened the door. "You aren't sleeping? Dinner is ready."

"All right."

"Lucian, dear, I must tell you something." Felicia became grave.

"What is it?"

"I've told you that I adopted a girl. Her name is Janina. I want you to know who she is. I don't want any misunderstanding to arise."

"Who is she?"

"The victim's daughter. I had to do it. She's a fine child."

"What victim?—Never mind, I understand."

"The others I placed in jobs, but Janina is an able, noble girl. She is a good student. Outstanding. It would have been painful for me to place her in domestic service. She has forgiven you. She's a true Christian soul and has become so fond of your children that she's like a blood sister to them. More than once it was she who brought you packages where you were. I wanted to write to you about it, but then I thought it would be better not to."

"Oh?"

"Well, say something. I hope it doesn't bother you."

"Why should it bother me? People like me are used to everything."

"I had to expiate the sin. Perhaps that is why God heeded my prayers. . . ."

"It's all right."

"Don't remind her of anything. Above all, don't indicate that you know who she is. Certain things must not be said here."

"Yes, certainly."

"What's wrong with you? Are you still sleepy?"

"No, I'm not used to white bed linen."

"My poor brother! You've suffered enough! You've paid for your mistakes. May God fill your heart with good thoughts!"

Felicia's face grew blotched. Tears ran down her cheeks. Not having a handkerchief with her, she closed the door and went off to cry in another room. Lucian got out of bed. The soft mattress had made his bones ache. He clenched his fists and breathed deeply. He had an urge to spit but dared not stain the floor here. He wanted to use obscene language, to argue with someone, to curse. It was too refined here, too quiet. "It's not for me!"

He had learned stunts from Wojciech Kulak. He lifted his sock with his toes and brought it to his hand. Once more he had to put on the stiff collar, the tie, fuss with the collar pin, the cuff-links. "Filthy business! Worse than leg irons!" Lucian growled. "I have a scar on my Adam's apple already!" He began to yawn all over again and at the same time poked his finger against his chest. He had accustomed himself to the prison chamber pot, but this convenience under his bed looked too elegant. Was it porcelain? There they would have wanted to eat from out of such a fancy vessel! . . . Lowering his head, he meditated. Miriam Lieba was dead. He hadn't seen the children in years. Felicia had sent him photographs, but it wasn't the same thing. What did she say? The victim's daughter. "Well, who cares?" Lucian went in search of the drawing room or dining room (he had forgotten the arrangement of the apartment). He opened a door and saw everybody. Marian Zawacki did not seem old, but the two ruffs of hair on either side of his bald head were gray. Wladzio had grown half a head taller than Lucian. He resembled his mother, but everything that had appeared delicate, sad, sickly in Miriam Lieba looked masculine, strong, and youthfully brutal in him. He had flaxen hair cut in a brush, steel-gray eyes, and an upturned nose. He wore a school uniform with a high collar. He was to graduate from gymnasium in the summer. He stood up and walked over to his father. There were dimples in his rosy cheeks when he smiled. He kissed Lucian without saying a word. Beside his son, Lucian felt small and old.

"So, this is the way you are!" he said. "All grown up."

"Why not? Time doesn't stand still." The boy laughed.

"Do you remember him?" Marian Zawacki asked the boy.

"Of course. He once took me to the Lazienki Park and we ate at a table outside. He bought me a hoop. Do you remember?" he said, turning to Lucian.

"No, I don't remember. But I have a poor memory. Children always remember."

"I even remember Paris."

"That's impossible. You were three years old when we returned from Poland."

"I remember. The train and everything else. Father doesn't believe me. . . ."

Wladzio grew red. He had become accustomed to calling Marian Zawacki "Father." But now that their real father had returned, Felicia had instructed the children to call Zawacki "Uncle" and her "Auntie."

Marian Zawacki, after kissing Lucian on both cheeks, took hold of his arm and said: "Well, you're looking fine."

Marisia was four years younger than Wladzio and resembled Lucian. She was small, somewhat dark, with brown eyes. Her brunette hair was plaited in two braids. Not yet fourteen, she was already as reserved as an adult. She grew cinder-red, facing her father, smiled timidly and made a sort of curtsy. Lucian was immediately taken with his daughter. He kissed her on the temple, took her by the hand, and did not know what to say. Finally he said, "You're a pretty girl."

"Not so pretty."

"You look like your late grandmother, my mother."

"Yes, so Mother says. I mean Auntie . . . " And Marisia grew even more confused.

Janina, the daughter of the janitor, had also risen from her seat. Although she was dressed genteelly, Lucian recognized the peasant in her. She was a girl of seventeen, broad-boned, with a red face, protruding cheekbones, a round nose. There was a rustic amiability in her watery eyes. She reminded Lucian of the country girls who herded geese or goats. It was hard to believe that she was as adept at her studies as Felicia boasted. Her hair, put up in braids on each side, was straw-colored. Marisia had narrow hands with long fingers (Felicia had mentioned that she excelled on the pianoforte), but Janina had the wide hands of a servant, her arms covered with freckles. Around her throat, above the high bosom, was a string of coral. Felicia introduced her, "This is our Panna Janina."

Lucian extended his hand. The girl blushed furiously.

I am going to sleep with her, Lucian immediately decided.

III

That final morning Wojciech Kulak had reversed himself and given Lucian a lesson in self-control. "Don't go to that Bobrowska woman or to the other one. You'll kill one of them, and then what? You're too hot-blooded. If you've hidden a gun somewhere, forget about it. Men like you can't stop going 'bang, bang!' " He then gave Lucian the address of a friend of his on Marienstat Street, where there was a coffee shop and a brothel. He gave him the password and even recommended a one-time sweetheart of his own. "I'd rather it were you than others—" But Lucian did not go there. Instead, he went to Marshalkovsky Boulevard and from there to Iron Street. He stopped at a train crossing where for a long time he stared at the passing cars, the locomotives, the rails, the switches. Freight trains went by loaded with lumber, coal, naphtha. Whistles blew, grubby workers signaled with flags and lanterns. Chimneys belched smoke, steam. Lucian longed to be on a train going somewhere. But he had neither passport nor money. He turned back toward the city. Bobrowska's house was located between Lucka and Grzybowska Streets. The building had the same fence, older now, sagging, and broken down. It had been snowing the night he had left there. Now through the open gate he saw a pair of barefoot children, playing in the dusk. Suddenly a familiar figure approached. It was her walk, not her face, that he recognized. Kasia. She was dressed city style—without a shawl, in a calico dress, high-heeled shoes, and carried a basket. She had grown taller, broader, and wore a chignon like an older woman. How was this possible? How old was she? He stationed himself at the gate. Still she did not recognize him, but said, "Excuse me," as she was about to pass him.

"You're excused," he replied, not moving.

Kasia looked up at him and froze. "Lucian!"

"Yes."

"God in heaven!"

She could not speak, moved her hand as if to cross herself, but managed only half the gesture before dropping her hand again.

"Yes, it's me," Lucian said at last. After some hesitation he added: "I'm not exactly dead yet."

"When did you get out? You had another year or more."

"There was an amnesty because of the Czar's birthday."

"Oh, yes."

"Well, how are you? How is Bolek?"

"Bolek is a big boy. A real student. Goes to school. Every day but Sunday."

"Every day? What else? You've become a seamstress, have you?"

"Yes."

"Don't tremble. I won't kill you. I'm not even armed," Lucian said, astonished at his own words. Kasia was standing before him, pale, open-mouthed. She kept shaking her head.

"Oh, how you scared me!"

"You must have a bad conscience if you're so nervous."

Kasia didn't seem to understand. "You look so nice. Elegant!" she said.

"But not as elegant as that old goat Cybulski," Lucian blurted out, again surprising himself.

Kasia retreated a step, looking grim. "I must go in."

"Is he waiting for you?"

"I bought something for the house."

"What did you buy?"

"Thread."

"Thread? I won't do anything to you, you needn't be so afraid. I only want the truth."

"Yes, the truth." And Kasia looked as if she had swallowed something.

"Who drove you to all this?" Lucian whispered. "The old fool or you yourself?"

Kasia looked behind her. "We can't talk in the street," she murmured.

"Sure we can. Speak frankly."

"It just happened. You went away and we were left like orphans."

"Who is this 'we'? That slut, Bobrowska?"

"All of us. He was so friendly . . . He is such a good old man . . . He brought presents: sausage, whisky, this, that. We thought you'd never get out of that place alive."

"Oh."

"And there he was, so jolly. Joking about everyone. He promised to help the child and all of us."

"What else?"

"That's all."

"How do you manage this? All three of you in one bed?"

"What? God forbid!"

"How then?"

"Nothing."

"I want the truth!"

"He is so old. Perhaps seventy. He only wants to pat and kiss. Sometimes he pinches or tickles. Bares his soul. His life often is so bitter—"

"What's so bitter about it?"

"All sorts of things. He was driven out of the theater. The big one with the pillars. He started to drink. And he is Bobrowska's old friend. From way back, and—"

"And what?"

"Nothing."

"You love him?"

Kasia was silent.

"Speak! I'm asking you something."

"No. Yes. He's like a good grandfather. To the child and to everyone. Comes in and shakes his cane. Not to hurt anyone. Just like that. For fun. Then he starts looking through his pockets. For you a gift, and one for you. An anniversary or a birthday. Spends money. Sits down and makes himself comfortable. Speaks like a common person—one forgets he's a nobleman."

"A nobleman? Well, what else?"

"Nothing."

"And all this with both of you?"

Kasia did not answer.

"Have you lost all shame?"

"No. What are you talking about? I don't know what you mean."

"You know. I could kill you even though I don't have a weapon. I could throttle you right here and now. But I won't. All I want is the truth."

"I've told you the truth."

"You're pregnant by him?"

"Pregnant? No."

"You've completely forgotten me, haven't you?"

"I didn't forget. May God strike me! I thought of you every day. I lit a candle for you to Saint Michael. We knew you still had a year to serve and we've had bad times. People talk too, point at us. Someone put it in the paper. The women don't order new dresses but turn their old jackets inside out. Bobrowska got a needle through her nail and the nail had to be removed. She was afraid it was infected and the finger would have to be cut off. And then he came, a good person, and took her to the doctor. The doctor prescribed a salve and it healed. He took Bolek to school, bought him books, pens, a penholder, a briefcase, spoke to the teacher. This and that. Here are three rubles—to your good health. He isn't earning money now, but he saved it from the good years. A devoted person, even though he's old."

"And what else?"

"That's all."

"Is he there now, upstairs?"

"Upstairs? Yes, I guess so. He was supposed to come."

"I want to see him."

"Don't start a fight."

"A fight? If I wanted to, I'd squash him like a bedbug. All of you. But I don't intend to. I always hated that bitch Bobrowska, and you're a stupid peasant, worse than a cow."

"Don't say such things. God will punish you."

"Well, let's go!"

IV

Lucian opened the door and took in everything at once. Bobrowska, Cybulski, all the new things in the house. The windows were hung with embroidered curtains, the walls freshly painted. There was a cheap rug on the floor. Several prints hung on the wall: King Batory, King Sobjeski, a hunting scene with dogs. Cybulski sat on a new upholstered chair. Lucian recognized him. He had occasionally given Lucian a walk-on part. But in the years of Lucian's imprisonment, Cybulski had grown old, stout, potbellied. The hair on his big head was long. Dressed in an alpaca jacket, a soft collar with a wide, black silk tie, a golden chain across his silver-embroidered velvet vest, beardless and without a mustache, he looked at first like an old woman. He had a loose double chin with barely any neck. Large pouches, and beneath them smaller, wrinkled ones, hung beneath his olive-brown eyes. His pipe lay on a tray. Cybulski had apparently just finished telling a joke, for he was laughing, and all his pouches, folds, and wrinkles were shaking, and his silver-speckled vest was heaving. Bobrowska seemed both younger and older. She reminded Lucian of a warmed-over loaf of bread. Her hair was grayish, but her round face was less drawn than previously and it was heavily rouged. She was wearing a pink robe and mixing some batter in an earthenware dish. The first to speak at Lucian's entrance was the parrot. Emitting a shrill scream, the bird seemed to have recognized him. A frightened smile spread over Bobrowska's face. Kasia came in behind Lucian. Cybulski stopped chortling, wiped away his tears, and became grave and sad.

"Jesus Maria! Lucian!" Bobrowska cried out. She lifted the spoon out of the bowl and a chunk of the soft yellow mixture fell to the floor.

"Yes."

"How did you get here? Adam, look! Kasia! . . . Oh, children!"

"Don't spill the batter. . . . Yes, here I am. You didn't expect me, did you?"

"Oh my, whom do I see! Kasia, where did you find him? When were you freed? I can't believe it! As if fallen from the sky. Just today I was thinking about you. Kasia, you are a witness. I opened my eyes and said: 'Such a hot day and the

poor fellow can't even cool off there. . . .' Adam, you remember him? You gave him a walk-on part. What was the
play called? It's slipped my mind. Oh, what a surprise. When
did you get out? We thought you still had another year in
that hell."

"I was included in the amnesty."

"What amnesty? A miracle! How well you look! Magnificent! Kasia, why stand there like a dummy? Take this mess
away from me. I was going to fry some pancakes. You remember Pan Cybulski, of course?"

"Yes, certainly, I remember. I've had the honor."

"Well, why stand at the door? A guest in the house, God in
the house. And such a guest! If I'd known, I would have had
flowers. Made a parade for you . . . as they say. Oh, what
am I talking about? I'm completely confused. You look
young, like a young prince! . . . Kasia, why don't you
move? At least get a chair so he can sit down. Take this spoon
from me. Poor me, I've lost my head. . . ."

Only now did Bobrowska approach Lucian. She moved
mincingly, with half-outstretched arms, her glance one of
sluggish doubt, as if she did not know whether to embrace him
or not. Lucian backed away, saying: "Don't go to any
trouble . . ."

"How else should we greet each other? I stand here with
my head full of worries. I haven't been well, lately . . . arth-
ritis. . . . The doctors have told me to go to Czechocinek to
take the salt baths. . . . Suddenly he drops in like an angel.
. . . Well, where is the chair? Wipe it off, Kasia, he'll soil
his suit. How nicely you're dressed and how well everything
fits you! When you went away it was wintertime and God's
world was all snow and ice. Like my own heart. . . . You
look good, but a little sallow. Don't tell me you've already
eaten. I really want to fry these pancakes and I seem to remember that they are your favorite dish."

"I've eaten supper. I'm not hungry."

"Not hungry? Well, sit down, anyhow. My hands are a little soiled with eggs and flour. That's why I can't embrace you. Kasia, why don't you wipe off the chair?"

"With what? The rag is wet."

"Oh, you're such a child. Wipe it with whatever is handy. With your skirt. . . . Come closer. Don't try to tell yourself we've forgotten you. We talk about you, we two women and your little son as well. He's sleeping. He's already a grown boy. We've a new room, chopped through the wall of your alcove. That's where he sleeps and does his homework. Draws, writes—everything as it should be. I could kiss every one of his fingers. He's asleep already, the mischiefmaker. He's your son, your son! You men know each other, shake hands for me too."

"I remember the Count. He acted with us," Cybulski said in a rasping voice. He laughed as if he had made a joke. What began as a giggle ended in an asthmatic rattle with a falsetto echo as if he had two voices.

Lucian bowed. "Yes, I've had the honor."

"Certainly, you acted. Not any big parts, but you showed talent. What was the play called? An adaptation from the French, I think. In those days the theater still had a normal aim—to entertain the public, to educate and amuse at the same time. In our new era of empty positivism and so-called constructive work, they want to turn the theater into a university, a university of pedantic pomposity and false didactic with all the disadvantages of a university but minus its advantages. But what it tries to teach, no one knows, because it is all empty gestures and hollow phrases. One cannot, I say, teach merchants to keep their books in order and save capital if it isn't as natural to them as it is to the practical British or the money-minded Prussians. We Poles were always epigenous in every sphere, and as soon as we hear of a wedding somewhere, we try to dance at it. Our critics always burn their lips sampling foreign dishes."

Cybulski laughed. For a moment his face was radiant with a kind of joyful vindictiveness. He had, in the past years, suffered much from the critics. He had been forced out of the regular theater, and even the plays he had produced in the summer theaters were torn apart by the reviewers.

Lucian looked at him in surprise. "You are mistaken. Obviously you think I am someone else. I didn't have any roles. I was only a walk-on several times. . . ."

"Yes, you played. A walk-on? Elzbieta, this is a misunderstanding. You yourself recommended him. I remember as if it were yesterday. What was the part? An *amant!*"

And Cybulski again burst into laughter. His eyes filled with tears.

v

"You babble about art, you old dog," Lucian said to himself, "but your only comfort in life is an old bitch and a young peasant. . . . Someone shamed your swinish honor. . . . I remember when you yourself stepped on others. You came to rehearsals eating oranges and shouting: 'Begin again!' 'That's not the way to kiss!' 'A man betrayed doesn't speak that way!' 'That's not the way to walk!' 'That's not the way to stand!' Now the critics have knocked out your teeth and you've become softhearted." Lucian felt no anger toward him. This evening he had attained, he felt, an objectivity he had never known before. He was suddenly overcome by tedium. "Well, so he's sleeping with Kasia. Who cares? It's all a bore. Even more so than prison. . . . What is he, after all? A pompous windbag. One squeeze from me and he'd be done for. I could kill him simply by yelling."

He heard Cybulski say: "This cult that has formed around Modrzejewska is simply barbaric. She has talent, yes. But she isn't the only actress in Poland. Kochanska has more talent, and there are others equally gifted. This, my dear Count, is idolatry. They are engaged in a contest to see who can flatter best. May the ladies and gentleman excuse it. The expression is 'kissing the behind.' But why kiss a behind even if it belongs to a genius? Aren't all behinds alike? The mob must always have heroes, idols, and when none exists, one must be created. They take a dummy and put a laurel wreath on him—"

"It's all very clear," Bobrowska interrupted him, at the same time fussing with a pot. "The men begrudge each other, terribly! And whatever bit of praise they have must be lavished on a woman."

"There's a system in this," Cybulski continued. "Wickedness, that's what it is. They raise one to the skies, the better to flatten the others. From the Christian standpoint this is simple idolatry."

"Who takes Christianity seriously?" Lucian asked. "Isn't the Pope himself a sort of idol?"

"Well, my dear Count, let's not go too far. Without the Church it would be worse, much worse. I'm an old man already with one foot in the grave, as they say, but somewhere within me there's still a desire to devote my last few years to our faith. The Church must have a leader; otherwise it becomes a headless institution like Protestantism. Even the Jews have a miracle rabbi, a sort of elder priest of the Sanhedrin, or whatever they call it these days. In religion, one law is supreme: if you sin, you've sold your soul to the devil. When you repent, God will forgive you. But in the theater there's no law. That's the horror of it. You produce a play, put work into it, knowledge, your best efforts, and an ignorant puppy makes a joke of it. With one smear of his pen, you're finished. These people have no code in their death dealings. They are like those ancient Chinese rulers, boys of five, who would pick names out at random, and have the bearers beheaded. In Poland, my dear Count, the anarchy of primitive man rules."

"You, my dear Adam, take opinions too seriously," Bobrowska interjected again.

"Too seriously? What do theater people have besides opinions? What's left of my life but reviews? I have pasted everything in a scrapbook and that is, so to say, my estate. A writer leaves behind books, a painter—pictures. What remains of us? Time devours us like a wolf."

"And what remains of all other people?" Lucian asked, just to say something. "I have but one ambition: to live in the present. After I die, they can throw me to the dogs."

"And how can one live in the present, surrounded as one is by evildoers? I don't sleep well, my dear Count, and I have time to think. What separates these people from the underworld? They have the same morals, perhaps even worse. What the others do with a knife, they do with a pen. Throw me to the dogs after death? They throw me to the dogs while I am still alive. Not only me. Today one man devours another. It's a system. You lie down to sleep and I'll bite off your ear. . . . It hurts? Don't scream, because it's not manly. Where does it all come from? From man's abandonment of religion. I myself was an atheist in my younger days. We toyed with so-called progress. But one may shudder at the results. Your sister, my dear Count, has reached heights. I envy someone like her more than all the Modrzejewskas and Kochanskas or whatever they call themselves. Your son, Bolek, is a decent boy, pleasant, good-hearted, and with a mind of his own. Well, how did all this come about, if I may ask? One survives everything."

"Yes, one survives. In prison we say: 'Sooner or later you get out: either on two feet or in a coffin!' "

"Well, we should celebrate this occasion. Unfortunately I'm not permitted to drink. Health reasons. But we must have a taste of something nevertheless. Elzbieta—"

"Yes, I'll get it. There's still some vodka left from last time. Well, I'm not prepared at all. Where did Kasia go? Probably to get Bolek. She shouldn't wake him. It's not healthy for a child. Why don't you say something, Lucian dear? How was your day?"

"Oh, just a day. In the morning I was there and now I'm here."

"May I ask if you've already seen your sister?" Cybulski said after a while.

"Yes, she was waiting for me at the gate."

"Indeed! A marvelous person. Elzbieta and I are, so to say, old friends. Maybe even before the Count was born. Oh, what have I said? Women are, after all, always young. They never grow old, ha, ha. . . . There were all sorts of disagreements between us, but we never broke off completely. I mean—our friendship. What she did for Kasia is virtually noble. Pure altruism."

"Please, Cybulski, don't praise me."

"I'm not praising. There's good in all of us. I've always dreamed of rising above all the filth in my old age, of saving a few thousand rubles and settling on a small estate. As soon as one is surrounded by trees and sky and hears God's birds, the city, with its false ambitions and imagined accomplishments, disappears. But some accursed souls must suffer this stench to the bitter end. Everything, as they say, slipped through my fingers. I spent all my money. I didn't understand that thrift can be a great virtue, not for philistines, but especially for people like me. Well, these days I direct plays for the summer theaters and I'm not even sure it will continue. They want to take everything away, down to the last drop."

Bobrowska clasped her hands together. "Oh, Adam, what's happened to you today? You're usually so gay."

"Occasionally these things must come out. You, Count, must excuse me. It's time I left."

"What's wrong with you, Cybulski? I'm about to make pancakes."

"No, I just don't feel right. My stomach. Give the guest your pancakes."

Kasia came in from the alcove.

"I'm going, Kasia, my love."

"Why? It's not late yet."

"I didn't sleep much last night. That happens sometimes. My dear Count, don't take offense. I'm an old man, and the foolish things I've done and do are a result of loneliness."

"Yes, I understand."

"God meant man to be miserable, particularly in old age." Cybulski rose.

"Well, where's my cane?"

"Why run away? Kasia, hand him his cane. Take a droshky, absolutely!"

"Yes, I'll take a droshky. Well, we'll be seeing each other. Would you like to come to the theater, Count? It's actually in a garden, but a theater is a theater. There's one trouble with the open sky—no gallery, except perhaps for the angels. . . ."

And Cybulski again began laughing and raised his cane as if to poke someone.

"Good night!"

VI

"What happened? Why did he run away?" Bobrowska asked when Cybulski's footsteps had died away. "He's so sensitive! Old age has suddenly hit him. It's not time so much as the insults he's received. He worked for so many years and suddenly they spit in his face. Well, the spitters themselves won't rule forever . . ."

"If he went off on account of me, I'm sorry," Lucian said, knowing that he wasn't sorry and was speaking without conviction.

"On your account? Why? No, he suffers. He's an abandoned old man. At least he has a little money. . . . He's not entirely a pauper. Usually he's gay. He even jokes too much. Well, tonight is your night, Lucian. Kasia, why hide in a corner? Go to him, sit next to him. Don't be embarrassed. After all, you're the mother of his child. . . ."

"Bolek's sleeping. Shall I wake him?" Kasia asked.

Lucian placed his chair so that he faced Kasia. "No, don't wake him."

"Do you know what? I'll go off somewhere," Bobrowska offered after a pause. "I can let this batter go. Unless you want pancakes, Lucian?"

"Me? No."

"It won't spoil. I'm due at a customer's. I'll be back in a couple of hours and meanwhile you can talk things over."

"Where are you going?" Kasia asked distrustfully. "Who is the customer?"

"Oh, what's the difference? You don't know all my customers. Don't think I've told you all my secrets. I have a little pile somewhere, ha, ha. . . . One thing, children, don't argue. Lucian, she hasn't done anything to offend you. I say this sincerely."

"Nothing?" Lucian said. "What more could she have done other than enter a brothel?"

"What are you saying? He's an old man. Tell him, Kasia, tell him. Why should he think God-knows-what?"

"I've told him."

"What did you tell him? Well. . . . People like you, Kasia, spoil things for themselves. I want nothing. I'm not young any more. A little cheerfulness and a good word— that's all I care about. Cybulski is an old friend, even from the time that Bobrowski, may he rest in peace, was living. He loves Kasia like a daughter. He once kissed her on the fore-head, but that's as far as it went."

"She herself says he slept with her."

Bobrowska stared with crooked, tearful eyes. "She said that?"

"Yes."

"Why did you tell lies?"

"I didn't say that."

"You did say it!" Lucian said. "Don't take back your words!"

"I'm not taking them back."

Bobrowska made a gesture as if to roll up her sleeves. "What did you tell him?"

Kasia was silent.

"Did he sleep with you or not?" Lucian asked without anger and with an expression of disgust.

Kasia's face became downcast. "In the beginning."

Bobrowska glared at her. "If that's true, then the two of them have fooled me."

"I didn't fool you. You knew about it. You talked me into it yourself."

"*I* talked you into it? Well, that's the gratitude one gets from people like you. He became sick and couldn't go home. He had to sleep here. That night he was more dead than alive. When did all this happen? Unless when I went out of the house. Of course, you're no minor. You already had a child by then. I talked you into nothing, and I don't want you to spread slander about me. A peasant remains a peasant. If you want to confess, go to the priest. I tell you what! Both of you go, and take your child. I haven't the strength any more for such mixups. If this is the reward for kindness, I'd rather be left alone with four walls."

Lucian stood up. "I'm going."

"You can take her along. I rescued her from the dregs. You went to prison and she was left with the boy at God's mercy. Her father, Antek, drank. He helped out with an occasional ruble, but as time went on, he gave less and less. His own woman deserted him. Everything fell on my head. She learned to sew a little from me, but she's no seamstress, can barely thread a needle. For what she's cost me, I could have hired a skilled seamstress. Isn't that true, girl?"

"It's not true. You sent me on all sorts of errands and I never saw a penny. Papa, Antek, paid. The Countess, Lucian's sister, sent money and you used it to buy a machine."

Bobrowska flared up. "Is that so? You filth, you ungrateful wretch! You lousy bitch! I owe you something, do I? Lucian, you did me a great favor. You went off to kill a man, and you left this bitch with me. Well, I've had enough. If you feel, you pig, that I've used you, go away and never come back. I'll be frank about what concerns you, Lucian! With people like you, one never knows. I don't want any problems or complaints. You're both young, but my spirit wants peace. Cybulski is good to me, a friend, as they say, from my youth. He also can't take troubles. He changed when you came in. His heart is weak—"

"If he has a weak heart, let him go to a doctor and rest under an eiderdown instead of chasing after women. And don't be afraid. I won't come again."

"You'd better take Kasia and your son with you. With things as they are, she'll only be a burden to me."

"Where can I take her? I don't have a home."

"Take her. You need a woman. At worst, she can be your maid. There isn't any work now anyhow. I hardly have enough for myself. After all, you made her unhappy. It's your child, your flesh and blood. This, I hope, you won't deny. I'll tell you the truth: Cybulski is clumsy. He's like a cripple. He lives with people, but they exploit him. He was about to move in, but now he'll be afraid to, poor thing. When you came in, he grew white as chalk. He began to talk as if it were a funeral."

"What was he afraid of, the old son-of-a-dog? I wouldn't kill someone like him."

"See, you're starting already. Kasia, why do you stand there like an idiot with your mouth open? I'm not throwing you out, but you'll have to go. Understand, it doesn't have to be this very night. I'll go out and you talk it over."

"What have we to talk over? Perhaps he has nowhere to go himself," Kasia said, and seemed frightened at her own words. "If you don't want me, I'll get a job."

"Who'll give you a job with a boy? They investigate you."

"I'll find something. At worst, I'll go to my papa's. He won't drive away his grandchild."

"A fine home for a child! Well, you're the parents and I'm a stranger. I love him, he calls me Grandma, but everything has changed. What do you say, Lucian dear? Or maybe I shouldn't address you informally any more?"

"Speak as you please. I'll take Bolek away from this house. You needn't worry. But I must have a few days."

"A few days won't make a difference."

"Well, I'd better go," Lucian said.

"Already? If you want to spend the night here, you can. It's all up to you. I can go away somewhere, or make myself a bed in the workroom."

Kasia suddenly took a step forward. "No, it isn't necessary."

"Are you ashamed?" Bobrowska asked.

"No, I don't want to!"

"Well, I won't force you."

"She is in love with the old man," Lucian said, feeling both disgust and amusement. He went to the door, raised the latch, and spoke. He seemed to spit the words out between his teeth: "I'll take the child, but I never want to hear from either one of you again. If you should run into me on the street, cross over to the other side. You're worse than dead to me!"

He slowly closed the door behind him and descended the rotting steps. On the other side of the gate, Lucian paused for a moment. His eyes narrowed and he muttered: "Well, I've survived this too." The taverns were already closed. Across the way, near a gate, a whore in a red shawl loitered. Lucian took his watch (the same one that he had worn that Christmas night) out of his vest pocket and looked at it under the street light. He could go home to Felicia, Zawacki, the children, or to the address given him by Wojciech Kulak. But he had no desire to go to either of these places.

TWO

I I 🏛

1

Clara lay in bed, propped up by three pillows. Her hair was white, her face jaundice-yellow. Louisa too had turned gray, and Felusia had already begun to attend a gymnasium. For the thousandth time Clara scanned a bundle of letters that had also turned yellow. She read bits here and there. Louisa brought in some medicine and a glass of water. Clara took the medicine, grimaced, and drank the water. For two years she had been suffering from gallstones. She had been to several doctors, but her condition had worsened. Three specialists, in a consultation, had decided that an operation was necessary. But it was a dangerous one. Who would take care of Felusia if Clara should die? The girl had a rich brother, but what a pity it would be if she had to spend her adolescence in Sasha's wanton house. Perhaps Alexander would take her to live with him in New York, but he now had another wife and a child. He had finally succeeded in becoming a doctor. Although he did not write to Clara, he kept in touch with Felusia and sent her an occasional present. His name and address were printed on his stationery. He lived on a street called East Broadway. After her second adventure with Mirkin, Clara had received what in effect had been a final letter from him. In substance, he had written: "I want to forget. I beg of you—don't open old wounds."

Well, Clara had failed. Twice she had been on the point of marrying Alexander, and each time it had been Mirkin who had interfered. Mirkin was dead and he had not even mentioned her name in his will. Nor had his fortune been as great as had been supposed. It was thought that his secretary, Yasha, had robbed him. Clara had long since decided to blame no one. All her mistakes had been of her own doing. Besides the men whom she might have accused of having wronged her—her father; her first husband, Grisha; and Boris Mirkin—were all dead. Calman was an old man. Running into him in the street one day, she had barely recognized him. He seemed shriveled up. He had shuffled along, supporting himself with a cane, and looked like a beggar. As for Alexander, it had been *she* who had treated *him* unfairly.

When one lies ill in bed and no one comes to visit, one must think about something. When there is no future, the mind turns to the past. Occasionally Clara would ask Louisa to bring her the albums which she had kept since her girlhood. But indulging in nostalgia brought her little joy. Only now could she see how much mockery there had been in the notes and compliments of her fellow students and the Russian officers who had done business with her father. But Zipkin's letters still rang true. Even his reproaches were genuine. How he had struggled on his arrival in New York! What resentment he had had against the city! He had tried to settle in Oregon, in California, and had planned to return to Europe! At one point he had even been close to suicide. "What use is my life now that I no longer have any ideals, no hope of improving the human condition. I long for you, Clara. I know that it would be bad for me to be with you, but without you I am as if dead." "My only consolation is reading. There is a large library here where one can read free. I read so much, I'm afraid of ruining my eyesight." "Oh, Clara, if you were only here and we could walk together in Central Park on Sundays, or go to the country for a weekend." "Here, Clara, one can travel from the Atlantic to the Pacific, from parts of Canada that lie close to the North Pole, to Argentina, which is not far from the South Pole!" His letters were full of impossible propositions—that they live in a cabin in the woods, or settle somewhere in British Columbia, that he become a hunter in Mexico or Brazil. These dreams ended when he became involved with a schoolteacher; she and Sonya helped him through medical school. And finally he became what he had planned to be from the beginning—a doctor.

Clara tried to visualize America, New York, East Broadway. How did things look there? Were the houses like those in Warsaw or Paris? And the trains that "ran above the rooftops"? What were they like? Was Central Park similar to the Saxony Gardens? Clara imagined Alexander living in a house twelve stories high, overlooking Central Park. An express train ran above the level of the roofs, and Americans, Negroes, Chinese, Spaniards, and Jews milled about in the street below. Everyone was shouting. New York was a masquerade ball, an eternal carnival. Alexander wore a top hat and spoke English. He stepped out on his balcony and looked at the Atlantic Ocean. Ships from different countries floated by—from India, China, Japan, Europe. On the docks, tea, coffee, sugar cane, and furs imported from Siberia by Mirkin's children were being unloaded. Ladies rode by in carriages. Gentlemen tipped their top hats. Sailors went in and out of a small house with red lanterns. The sound of music, laughter, dancing, shouting, came from within. There were the great Broadway theaters, the circuses, the cabarets, the restaurants, and the Metropolitan Opera, where the most famous singers of Europe performed.

Yes, if she had not been foolish she might be there now in that glittering part of the world, in that house on East Broadway. She saw herself sitting with Felusia and Alexander in the balcony and through binoculars inspecting Central Park, the Atlantic Ocean, and various islands. After dinner, Felusia would do her homework and Alexander would take Clara to the opera. Then they would return home to bed. How did a

New York bedroom look? In New York, she would not be suffering from gallstones. Zipkin would have diagnosed her illness at an early stage. It wouldn't have happened at all; heartbreak had made her sick. She had read in the newspapers that women remained young in America. Sixty-four-year-old women carried on with young men while receiving alimony from their millionaire husbands; four hundred dollars a week. . . . Even Sonya, a naïve Sonya, had become rich in Columbus's country. Her husband, Yackiewicz, the former socialist, had opened a ladies' clothing factory. A childish thought occurred to Clara: did such factories have tall chimneys?

What was the use of dreaming? She was in Warsaw. Whatever Sasha did not give her, she did not have. Felusia was growing up without a father. Clara was ill. Dying? She didn't fear death. But what about afterwards? What happened when the soul left the body? Did heaven and hell actually exist? Would devils place her on a bed of nails or hang her by her breasts? Would she fly through wastelands pursued by snakes and lizards? Clara had more than once considered doing penance. But how did one repent? She wished she had asked Calman. Sasha had promised to say Kaddish for her. But could he be relied on?

Clara closed her eyes. She placed Zipkin's letters beneath her pillow. The doctor had spoken to her frankly. He wanted to operate but was uncertain of the outcome. She had developed a weak heart.

11

When Clara was well and mingled with people, she seldom dreamed. Now that she had been bedridden for weeks, dreams attacked her like locusts. Even before her eyes closed, they began. Again she was with Grisha, her father, Alexander. At times she imagined herself living in a palace with Calman, but instead of being her husband, he was her father-in-law. The palace became confused with Alexander's house in New York.

Jampol and New York became one. Russian officers marched under the elevated trains. There was a ball. Clara danced more gracefully than anyone. Her feet were light, without substance. Suddenly she rose from the floor. All the dancers stopped, stared, pointed. Clara floated in the air, slowly, at an angle like a bat. The music played on. Through the open windows the Atlantic Ocean could be seen, its waves roaring and splashing. They rose so high it was hard to see why they didn't inundate the shore and flood Alexander's drawing room. "God in heaven, I'm flying!" Clara said to herself. "One can fly without wings. . . ." Clara opened her eyes and saw by the clock that she had been asleep five minutes.

Louisa came in—short, gray.

"Your medicine, madame!"

"*Merci beaucoup.*"

"Would madame like a glass of tea?"

"Not now. In the bookcase there is a thick book with a lock. Would you please get it for me?"

"With the gold-tooled back? The prayer book?"

"Yes, how do you know what it is? It's in Hebrew."

"Oh, madame, I know everything."

Louisa brought the siddur that Calman had given Clara as a wedding present. It had been gathering dust for years. Clara had often wanted to throw it away or give it to a synagogue but somehow hadn't done so. The prayers were translated into Yiddish. She had studied Hebrew as a child and so she knew the Hebrew characters. She began to read a prayer: "God Almighty, I, Thy servant, stand before Thee with a broken heart and on shaking knees to pour out my prayer to Thee. Who am I to open my lips to Thee? I am only flesh and blood, steeped in sin, befouled by countless transgressions. But Thou, Father in heaven, are full of forgiveness and mercy, and Thou dost not disdain the supplications of a pauper—listen to my cry, Father, collect my tears in Thy gourd and remember that we are only dust, a dream that vanishes, a shadow that dissolves and a flower that withers. It was Thou, Father, who breathed a soul into our nostrils and gave life to our limbs. We are truly the instrument of Thy hands. . . ."

There had been times when Clara had laughed at such words. She even used to mimic women making the benediction over the Sabbath candles. God forgive her, but she had even done so in front of Gentiles. But now Clara could no longer mock the holy words. True, the language was old-fashioned, but the content was true. Isn't man sinful? And doesn't he truly resemble a shadow that vanishes or a flower that withers? How much Clara would have given to know that there was indeed a God in heaven. But according to her father, heaven was empty. A balloon had risen high above the clouds and its passenger had seen nothing but space. Alexander had told her the same thing. The earth, he had claimed, had existed for millions of years and no one had created it; it had torn itself away from the sun and had gradually cooled. After death man was no different from a cat or dog: the worms ate him and he vanished. If that were so, then what was the point of life? Wouldn't it be better not to have been born? . . .

Clara put the book away and turned her face to the wall. How long would this continue? How long would she have to endure this pain? Would anyone accompany her hearse to the grave? Sasha traveled frequently. When she died, he might be somewhere in Russia. Would someone notify Alexander? She would be buried near the cemetery fence and no one would know she had ever existed. And what if they *did* know? What good would it do her if she were buried in the first row and had a marble monument with her name engraved on it? If man was no better than a dog, let him be forgotten.

III

But Clara improved, recovered almost completely. The doctors warned her to maintain a strict diet: eat on time, chew well, and avoid fat. Thank God the pains and pressure had stopped. Louisa no longer had to heat a brick and place it against Clara's stomach. Clara got up, dressed, and immediately began to eat whatever she pleased. Why should a fat piece of meat be worse than a lean one? How could the stomach tell whether something was boiled, broiled, or fried?

During her illness, Clara had come to a decision. When she thought she was dying, she had worried continuously about Felusia. What would become of the girl without either father or mother? Clara had determined, should she get better, to take Felusia to Alexander. In New York, Felusia would have a home, perhaps even go to a university for women. In addition to wanting to provide for her daughter, Clara had for a long time yearned to see that fabulous country. She had no intention, God forbid, of taking Alexander away from his wife. She would buy a round-trip ticket for herself and leave her daughter behind in New York. The question was what to do with Louisa on her return. Clara had discussed everything with the Frenchwoman and she had agreed to remain in New York with Felusia for a few years. If Zipkin did not want to take the girl into his home, Louisa would find a job and visit the child on her days off wherever Clara settled her.

Clara burst into tears at Louisa's devotion. The American climate might be advantageous for gallstones. Perhaps Clara herself would remain a year or two. She no longer had any ties in Warsaw. Sasha was a grown man. He had neither the time nor the patience for Clara. Months passed without his coming to see her. Why should she remain on Berg Street and pay nearly thirty rubles a month rent?

She wrote a long letter to Sasha. He immediately came to pay his mother a visit. Sasha was of medium height, broad, and wore sideburns and a mustache. He had left his grandfather's house to Celina and had had one built for himself not far from the manor. The estate was now leased to him for the next ten years. He had even forced his brother-in-law out of the mill. Mayer Joel had moved to Warsaw and opened a flour store. Sasha rang the bell. Louisa, having opened the door, tried to kiss him but was pushed aside. She stank of garlic. Besides, how long could one go on kissing Nanny? The floorboards creaked beneath him as he walked. He glanced into a mirror, saw that a lock of his black hair lay across his forehead, and pushed it back. He wore an English suit and shoes made by the best shoemaker in Warsaw. He had a diamond stickpin in his tie, and diamond links in his cuffs. A two-thousand-ruble ring sparkled on his left hand. He opened the door to his mother's bedroom.

"Sashenka! . . . Dearest! . . ."

Sasha could hardly endure his mother's kisses either. He placed his foot on a chair and said: "When do you go? How much do you want?"

"Heavens, just look at him! Look at how quickly he wants to get rid of me! Sit down. Eat something."

"I've eaten like a hog. I must go soon."

"Where? I thought you came to see me."

"Yes, but . . . I have a hundred errands. Do your doctors permit you to go?"

"I haven't asked them."

"Well, you're a mature woman."

"You look splendid, but a little fat."

"I'm always hungry. I'll give you two thousand rubles. Will that be enough?"

Clara's eyes grew moist. "What a question! I don't need that much."

"I don't want my mother to want for anything. If it isn't enough, send me a cable."

"God keep you well."

"Stop blessing me. You're not a grandmother yet. What are you trying to do—take Zipkin from his wife?"

"Are you crazy? With this head of white hair? I want Felusia to have a father. I wrote you about everything."

"Well, so be it. With a sister in America, I'll have an excuse to go there. One needs someone to visit. Travel first class. Do you get seasick?"

"How do I know? I've never traveled on the ocean."

"Well, in a good cabin one suffers less."

"If only I could live to see you married," Clara blurted out. Sasha was silent a moment. "You want to be a mother-in-law, do you?"

"I want you to live like an adult, not run around like a boy."

"What difference does it make? Whether I sleep with one woman or ten, my health is good."

"Please, my child, don't talk like that."

"Mother, the world is meaningless. Everyone is false, greedy. Why be tied down when it's possible to be free? If I told you how I live, you'd laugh."

"What's there to laugh about? I understand love, but promiscuity is no good."

"Why not? It's insane to live with one woman, stagnation. Actually, the more there are, the better it is. Women are arrogant, but when they know they can be changed like a pair of gloves, they behave like lambs. I'd rather have one suit and fifty women than one woman and fifty suits."

"Where did you learn to talk like that? You're really a good person. You just don't know what love is. When you fall in love with the right girl, and she with you, you'll know what you've been missing. Where are you off to?"

"To the daughter of a general."

"A widow?"

"No, she has a husband."

"That's terrible. Does it pay to risk your life?"

"I don't risk my life. I carry a revolver. Life must be exciting. If not, it isn't worth a cartridge of powder. . . ."

IV

Clara wasted no time. She applied for a passport and gave her apartment to Sasha. He visited Warsaw frequently. Why should he pay for hotel rooms when four rooms with all conveniences were available? She took Felusia out of school and hired an English tutor to prepare her for the visit to her father in New York. Clara intended to surprise Zipkin and so she did not let him know she was coming. Everything moved smoothly and quickly. As soon as the passports arrived, Clara and Louisa began to pack. There was actually no one to whom she had to say goodbye. Her aunt, Celina's mother, had died. Clara was not friendly with her neighbors. She kissed Sasha and wept. "If I should die on the way," she said to him, "hire a Jew to say Kaddish for me."

"Don't worry, Mama. You'll live."

Sasha was leaving for Russia and could not accompany his mother to the station.

Clara, Louisa, and Felusia rode in one droshky, their luggage followed in another. Clara had bought round-trip boat tickets at an agency on Nowa Senatorska Street. The travel agent had telegraphed ahead to reserve hotel accommodations in Berlin, where they were scheduled to spend a night. Clara was astonished. It seemed only yesterday that she had been lying in bed making plans, and now she sat in a second-class compartment of the Berlin Express. Since the train was en route to a foreign country, even the Russian conductor was courteous. At every large station, newspapers, magazines, chocolate, and cookies were brought to the passengers by vendors. Felusia sat glued to the window. It was a mild autumn. The sun shone, birds that migrate at the beginning of September had gathered in the fields, preparing to leave for a warmer climate. At the border, customs officials scarcely searched the luggage. Felusia spoke to everyone in French. In recent years Clara had begun to worry about every little thing. She had consulted fortune tellers, had had gypsies read her future in cards. But now she took everything lightly. She no longer suffered pain after eating. Her gallstones seemed to have evaporated. She was not even disturbed at the fact that they were arriving in Berlin on the eve of Rosh Hashana.

They spent the night in Berlin and early the following morning left for Hamburg. Russian and Polish newspapers had recently been waging a propaganda campaign against Prussia. Russia and Prussia were engaged in a tariff war. The papers were filled with the savagery of the German police, the Junkers, the students. Clara observed only the civility of the Germans. They bowed, addressed her as "Gracious lady," concerned themselves with her comfort, and she tipped everyone lavishly. Felusia was showered with compliments. They were sailing on the *Blücher*, and the ship's boarding was equally pleasant. Clara occupied one of the most spacious cabins. It contained two beds and a sofa, and there was even a toilet. A mirror hung over the sink. The desk was supplied with stationery.

Clara went out on deck. The hold of the ship was open, and cranes loaded barrels, crates, trunks, enormous sacks wrapped in mats and banded with hoops. It was hard for Clara to imagine a ship taking so much cargo into its hold. She could see the passengers on the decks below and they looked nervous and unkempt. There was kissing, crying, embracing. Clara heard Yiddish spoken. In first class, however, decorum prevailed. Ladies promenaded in expensive dresses and jewelry, fanning themselves as if at a ball. Men walked about in top hats, smoking cigars. A general had come aboard to say goodbye to his daughter. Three huge Englishmen strolled by with a thin, freckle-nosed girl. A long-haired, stout man in a cape kissed the hand of a woman he called Countess. Clara had thought that the ship would set sail as soon as the passengers were aboard. But it remained docked for hours. The sun sank in the west. Flames ignited the muddy waves. Fire and water blended miraculously. The ships in the harbor belched smoke, blew their stacks. Waste poured from portholes. Sailors climbed ladders, pulled heavy ropes, shouted. Seagulls cried and circled the ships. The harbor smelled of coal and rotting fish. It seemed strange to Clara that this ship would carry her directly to New York, to the city that only a little while before had seemed like a dream.

The anchor was raised, hawsers loosened. At the sound of a

hoarse whistle, Clara clapped her hands over her ears. The houses, churches, spires, and chimneys of Hamburg began to recede. Windows reflected a purple sunset. The first stars appeared. They seemed to rock together with the ship. The horizon opened up. Lighthouses came into view and ships anchored in the sea, as if forgotten by God and man. A young man approached Clara, offering her binoculars. The ocean grew vaster, wider, and ships swayed on the waves like ducklings. Louisa came to get Clara. An official behind a counter was distributing numbered tickets for the dining tables.

Clara had read about ocean voyages in books. In them the ocean had raged, pirates had attacked ships, sea monsters had swallowed people. But the *Blücher* was like a hotel. Clara combed Felusia's hair and tied her braids with ribbons. In the magnificent dining salon they were served dishes rare in Poland: lettuce, salt-water fish, oysters. At an adjacent table, a magnum of champagne was being opened. Louisa, who was seated opposite a Frenchman, had begun a conversation with him. *Mon Dieu*, he came from the same section as she! She had known his uncle! There was still a France in this world! People still spoke French! Clara, whose school French was limited, conversed with two Hungarian sisters who were going to visit their uncle in Chicago. They spoke German and Clara managed to make herself understood in Germanized Yiddish. They assured Clara that her German was perfect. . . .

Clara had taken along lemons and sour drops to prevent seasickness, but the night passed calmly. The following day was sunny. It was not until lunchtime that the sky grew overcast and the sun rays like axes severed the clouds. A cold wind began to blow. The waves, all gold, silver, and green gall, grew higher. They rose like hillocks, spread like pitch, seethed, and churned. The ship began swaying. Felusia's complexion had turned green. Clara dragged herself out on deck in a fur jacket and muff. The wind whipped her skirt, drove her backwards and forwards. Salty spray filled the air. Clara had read somewhere that one must not permit oneself to succumb to seasickness. But her stomach turned and an unsavory taste filled her mouth. She stood at the rail for so long, gazing at the turbulent foam, that she vomited, recognizing the taste of yesterday's salad. . . .

v

Clara and Felusia were both sick. The storm raged on. Waves like tremendous hammers pounded the sides of the ship. Felusia lay in one bed, sleeping endlessly. Clara, in the other, was unable to close her eyes. From her bed she could look out directly on the sea. The sky was scaly with clouds, some of which were suspended like watery curtains over the desolate scene. The waves mounted so high that Clara thought the ship must be inundated. Watery mountains charged forward, black and angular, melted boulders, lava from a cosmic volcano. They came in multitudes, white, green, and black, veined and foamy, row upon row, like supernatural armies, ready to destroy and swallow. The *Blücher* rose, the sky began to unwind, and Clara's bed seemed momentarily suspended in space. Soon everything descended and the waves retreated: devils driven off by an incantation, ready to begin their wicked game again. The sea raged all day and night. Whirling shapes rose from the water, skipped across as if of their own free will, and disappeared again in the cauldron. The engines pounded, making the cabin tremble and vibrate. The ship's whistle kept blowing, long and drawn-out warnings of peril. Fortunately, Louisa did not become seasick. She brought Clara and Felusia food and made lemon juice for them. She also kept Clara abreast of all the scuttlebutt: what the captain had said, what the ladies wore at each meal. Most of the passengers were ill. The two Hungarian sisters no longer appeared in the dining room. She and the Frenchman were the only ones left at their table.

During the day it was bad enough, but at night Clara's anxiety became unbearable. Felusia sighed in her sleep. In the dark, Clara prayed to God. If only Felusia would come out of it safely! Clara's seasickness brought on a gall-bladder attack. The pain moved from her stomach to her right shoulder. She became feverish. The ship's doctor gave her ineffectual medicines. In Warsaw, Louisa had heated bricks and applied them to Clara's stomach, but here it was difficult to do anything. Clara groaned, sometimes crying out like a woman in labor. When the cramps ceased, she listened silently to the tempest. Drown? Be eaten by fish? A wet grave—would this be her fate?

Clara dozed and awoke. The wind howled. The bed swayed. Clara held on to the bedposts to keep from falling out. They squeaked, as if about to break loose. Running footsteps were heard in the corridors. There was a slamming of doors. The steamer moved with unusual slowness, as if in final effort. Despite her fear, something in Clara yearned for the catastrophic end. She would be spared the agonies of dying slowly. If there were a God, let Him find her in the depths of the ocean and cast her into the Gehenna she deserved.

After four days the storm abated. Felusia had recovered, but Clara still remained in bed. It was only the day before the ship docked in New York that she was able to dress and go to the dining salon again. The room seemed to have grown larger and less populated. The passengers appeared strange to her, as if they had boarded the ship in mid-ocean. Clara noticed with amazement that Felusia had matured in these few days. She behaved with more poise and already made efforts to adapt herself to foreign ways. Clara had grown unaccustomed to walking and the floor seemed to recede as she stepped forward. She was compelled to hold on to Louisa to keep from falling. Clara saw that Louisa and the Frenchman, a large-boned individual with a shock of gray hair and a dark mustache, had become more intimate during the voyage. They conversed and laughed. He poured wine for her, even helped her cut her steak. When later Clara questioned her, Louisa confessed after some hesitation that she and Monsieur Dujacques, a widower, planned to get married when they reached New York. She insisted that she would continue to feel like a mother toward Felusia. . . . Louisa swore that on the night before they left Warsaw she had dreamed she was being married, had seen herself being led to the altar, and that her bridegroom had looked exactly like Monsieur Dujacques. . . .

The sea was now as calm as it had been wild before. The crests of the barely rising waves bore bunches of seaweed. Men and women who had been confined to their cabins now came out on deck thinner, paler, wearing clothes that had been saved for the last part of the voyage: plaid shirts, shawls, capes. Interrupted friendships were renewed. Each told the other of the miseries he had endured. The air grew warmer. Flying fish rose from the water. Dolphins, like great mice, leaped out of the waves. A steward brought out deck chairs and blankets. Older women allowed themselves to be tucked in and took up their interrupted knitting, discussing migraine headaches, rheumatism, and cough remedies. Sitting among them, Clara found herself unable to enter into their conversation. It was not only that they were speaking German rather than Yiddish, but that something within her separated her from the rest. These were settled people. They had husbands, sons-in-law, daughters-in-law, grandchildren. They knew precisely where they were going and how long they would stay. Clara's life was planless. She was, however, too old to join the younger group. She observed with astonishment how freely the young men acted with the women, and how boldly the young women behaved toward the men. They laughed and giggled, already on an informal and even intimate basis. "What was so funny? Why did they laugh so hard?" Clara asked herself. Were they actually so happy? Did they think they would remain young forever? Several young Englishmen in caps and checked suits began to play shuffleboard. The women joined them. An elderly man with a monocle excelled at the game and several people applauded him. Felusia played with them and spoke to them in French.

Clara tried to rid herself of her bitterness but was unable to do so. She saw herself as a sinner but could not stand loose behavior in others. Her thoughts kept turning from the vanity of life to the unknown entity called God. Even Felusia detected a change in her.

"You've grown so old," she said to her mother. "No one believes you're my mother. They think you're my grandmother."

VI

It was raining when they docked in New York. Clara, Louisa, and Felusia went through customs—a huge shed full of baggage and officials—and came out into a street paved with broad stones. Now it was covered with puddles and horse manure. Everything was wet: the brick-red houses with their fire escapes, the storage buildings, the horse-drawn trolleys, the crowds of pedestrians jostling about. In the distance Clara saw the train that seemed to be traveling over rooftops. Actually it moved over an iron bridge supported by thick pillars cemented into the pavement. Everything here seemed strangely old and worn, as if it had been in existence for hundreds of years. The rain fell at an angle, in sheets of spray, and through the watery net the city rose gray, straggling, all metal and stone, flat-roofed, small-windowed, full of chimneys, smoke, and dreariness. The first-class passengers, who had been allowed to disembark before the others, got into hansom cabs, whose drivers wore oilcloth raincoats and wet top hats. A relative had come in a carriage to meet Monsieur Dujacques and he asked him to drive Clara, Felusia, and Louisa to their hotel.

They rode through streets lined with brownstone buildings that had narrow entrances instead of gates. Looking through the carriage windows, Clara marveled. Was this New York?

Compared with Berlin and Paris, it seemed like a small town. In the puddles of the gutter floated bits of paper, cardboard, and rags. Clara had never seen so many broken umbrellas. Drenched pedestrians jumped over ditches, bending under the rain. Huge express wagons stood beside a watering trough. Everything seemed strange. They passed a barbershop. Through the shop window could be seen men lying on chairs, wrapped in sheets like patients prepared for an operation. A sign indicated facilities for baths as well as haircuts. Restaurant patrons sat in a row on high stools next to a counter. The carriage passed by factories where workrooms could be glimpsed in which both men and women were busy at machines, handling pieces of material. There was a brightly lit confusion and bustle within, a kind of chaos Clara had never witnessed. Even the noise differed from that of Berlin or Paris. It was hard to know where the hammering and crashing came from. Iron bars jutted from unfinished houses. Sodden posters and half-torn placards hung on fences. A Negro walked along, protected from the rain by a sack thrown over his shoulders. In a meat market a butcher in a bloody apron sawed at a bone. Other markets and stores came into view. In their windows hung bundles of dried mushrooms, strings of garlic, cheeses bound in cloth. Everything was jumbled together: onions and oranges, radishes and apples, sea fish, lobsters, mussels. In the midst of it all, the sun came out, turning the day summery and humid. The carriage pulled up to a hotel. A porter quickly picked up Clara's bags. The desk clerk smoked a meerschaum pipe and spoke in German. The three ladies climbed a narrow, red-carpeted stairway. Their rooms smelled of dry wood, bedbugs, and insecticide. Their luggage was brought up. They were in New York. . . .

God in heaven, from her earliest childhood Clara had heard about the wonders of America. But it was a city like all cities. The sky was above, not below. Clara sat at the window looking out. Lifting the lorgnette that hung around her neck, she looked through it at this once-distant country. Clara thought that if there was a life after death it would be like this—different and yet the same. Who was that giant carrying a sign? Oh, he was walking on stilts. He wore a red-and-white striped top hat. A clown from a circus? A peddler hawked his wares in a loud singsong. A crowd gathered around him. Was he giving things away? People grabbed up something, laughing. They were all so quick, so active, dressed garishly in bright colors or checks. Across the street, the entire window of a clothing store was filled with mannequins, dressed in silk, velvet, fur coats and stoles somehow different from the ones one saw in Warsaw. The crowds of women in front of the windows wore dresses and hats that looked new. Good God! There was a girl riding a bicycle! Why was everybody carrying so many boxes and packages? Yes, it was different. Louisa and Felusia were looking out the other window. Felusia kept shouting: "Louisa, Mama, look!" A street photographer was leading an animal along that was neither a horse nor a donkey, nor even a colt, although it resembled all three. There was a small saddle on its back. A man with yellow trousers and a feathered hat carried a parrot on one shoulder. A young man was selling cardboard marionettes that moved their arms and legs when he pulled a string. Adults as well as children seemed to play games here. Newsboys shouted. On a roof opposite, someone with a long pole was chasing pigeons.

"Well, Felusia, how do you like America?" Clara asked.

"Oh, Mama, it's funny!" she said and made a gesture that was completely like Alexander's.

Felusia was hungry and went with Louisa to a restaurant across the way. Meanwhile, Clara examined their rooms. She felt the mattresses, pulled out bureau drawers. In the hall there was a separate toilet as well as a bathroom with a long bathtub. Clara opened the taps and to her astonishment there was hot water even though she had not ordered any to be heated. From habit, she nevertheless rang for a maid and in a mixture of Yiddish and gestures indicated that she would like to have a bath. Replying in English, the maid smiled and ran the water in the tub. Part of an American newspaper lay on a chair. Clara could not read English, but she could tell from the pictures that they were advertisements for cosmetics, corsets, brassières, ways of removing unwanted hair, poison for cockroaches. One advertisement showed two pictures of the same woman: in one she was elderly, wrinkled, disheveled; in the other she appeared young, elegant, poised. Underneath were the words "before" and "after." Clara guessed their meaning. The thought that she too might become young again in this country ran through her mind. A new desire for life awakened in her.

VII

Everything took place more smoothly than Clara had anticipated. Louisa was invited to visit the family of Monsieur Dujacques and took Felusia with her. The weather turned cooler and Clara's fall clothes were more comfortable. She had already spent half a day in a beauty salon. She had been massaged, had had her hair dyed and set, her face made up. She had shopped for various trifles. In Warsaw Clara had bought a book of English phrases for travelers. She immediately began to pick up words, expressions. What was so difficult about being in America? For money, one could get anything. There were hansom cabs and coaches in front of the hotel and Clara got into one and asked the driver to take her to East Broadway. It turned out that the coachman spoke Yiddish. Clara burst out laughing when she heard his flat Polish accent. He was actually from Warsaw, where he had driven a droshky. As they rode along, he carried on a conversation over his shoulder. Did he know Warsaw? He had cut his teeth there. Berg Street? That was where the aristocrats lived! The very rich. Why had he left? He had been involved in a lawsuit. Why should he sit and wait until the anti-Semites threw him into jail? They wouldn't live to see that, the Russkies. May their flesh rot . . . their bones crumble! . . . He kept turning for a better view of Clara and almost ran down several pedestrians. "Whoever stays with those hooligans is crazy! America is a wonderful country. If one has a few dollars, it's paradise." English? One could learn it. Whom had the lady come to see? Relatives? She planned to go back? How foolish. It was good to be in Columbus's country. Everyone ate white bread, even the beggars. He was able to send his old mother a few dollars out of his small earnings. . . . "Whoa. Steady! Hey there, uncle, where do you think you're going? Are you blind? These pushcarts block up the streets and you can't get through. They're all Jews! In Warsaw they peddled in Goscinny Dwor, and now they peddle in New York. They make a living, don't have to have a license. Everybody works hard, but if one has a few cents, one is free as a bird. There are Jew-haters here too. They call Jews sheeny, kike. But you give it back to them. When two people fight, others don't interfere. There is a saying: 'Mind your own business! . . .' Hey! . . ."

The cab came to a stop. Fire wagons had appeared. The men did not wear brass helmets as in Warsaw. Here they wore black hats. They reminded Clara of executioners. Bells rang, the wagons flashed by, the horses in their brass harnesses straining from their reins. The driver turned to Clara. "They start fires, a curse on them. They carry out the merchandise at night and put a match to the building. If they're caught, there's trouble, but what won't they do for a few thousand dollars? When I came here, fire insurance was dirt cheap. Now it's sky high. If I ever caught such a fellow, I'd rip off his foot. The companies get rich but people's lives are endangered. Once a whole family was burned! The culprit himself was injured and that's how he was caught. He'll rot in prison, the lousy bum. He'll have to pray to God to come out in this lifetime. . . . Hey! . . ."

The traffic had become entangled: dray wagons, cabs, express wagons, even bicycles. Windows opened and heads were thrust out. Children played on the sidewalk. A small boy, stout as a barrel, with a stocking cap on his head, kept waving a short stick that reminded Clara of a rolling pin. Children screamed. The houses here had neither gates nor courtyards. Everything took place in the street. Laundry was hung on the rooftops. Garbage cans full of ashes were placed before the entrances. A heavy woman with painted cheeks, mascaraed eyes, and red stockings on her massive legs screamed at someone in a mixture of English and Yiddish. The driver leaned back toward Clara confidentially and said, "She's one of those, a streetwalker, a whore, may her mother's mother go to the devil. Don't want to work in America. Those loafers only live for sin. They're syphilitic themselves and make others sick. They have worms in their blood. A boy lands in their hands and his nose rots away. I have a wife and children, God give them health. The eldest is already in high school. At home we call it gymnasium. Who in Warsaw could afford to send a child to gymnasium? Here, Uncle Sam pays, each person gets the same as the next one. Each one is a citizen! . . . Here's East Broadway. What number do you want? There's a synagogue. There are plenty of religious Jews here. My own boy went to study at the Talmud Torah . . . I made a bar mizvah for him."

This street seemed more prosperous than the surrounding ones. The men wore top hats and the women were better dressed. A tall, gray-haired man in a cape and top hat exchanged greetings with someone. He raised a white-gloved hand and waved a cane with a silver head. He looked like a musician or an actor. Clara had seen a poster advertising Yiddish theater in New York. The cab stopped at a two-story redbrick house. There were three windows on each story and a stoop at the entrance. Yes, this was it. The number was painted in gold on the windowpane of the door, and a plaque announced: *Alexander Zipkin, M.D.* The coachman waved his whip and drove off. Here it was! And she had visualized a palace. Nevertheless, her throat contracted.

"God in heaven, if only I don't have an attack right here! If I only live to see him. . . ."

Breathing deeply, she calmed herself. Lifting the folds of her heavily ribboned dress, she climbed the stairs. "What is there to fear?" she said to herself. "He won't eat me. . . ."

She rang the bell. A girl came to the door. She looked like a maid and spoke English, but Clara replied in Russian. The girl showed Clara into a waiting room. Two other women were sitting there. One looked like a market vendor; the other, who wore glasses on her crooked nose and a bonnet, was probably a rabbi's wife, Clara thought. There was an aquarium with goldfish in the room. A landscape hung on the wall. A tiny garden with two naked trees was visible through the window. There was an odor of cabbage cooking which penetrated from the kitchen. Shakily Clara selected a magazine. She tried to look at the pictures, but her eyes refused to focus on them. The page turned green, gold, and the lines of print lifted as if drawn taut by a string. . . . The rabbi's wife coughed. The market vendor sighed. Clara hid her face in the magazine. From the other side of the door she recognized Alexander's voice, which had grown somewhat deeper and hoarser.

VIII

When the market vendor entered the office, she stayed for a long time. Clara heard the voices of both doctor and patient. Zipkin spoke in Yiddish. It was the first time that Clara had heard him speak Yiddish, and she was surprised at his Lithuanian accent. For a moment it made her want to laugh. She raised the magazine higher to make sure her face was covered. Leaning against the arm rest of the chair, she threw back her head and tried to relax. "Nothing good or evil can happen to me any more," ran through her mind. The door opened; the market vendor left and the rabbi's wife went in. From the threshold Zipkin said something about a teaspoonful after breakfast, lunch, and dinner. "What shall I say to him?" Clara thought suddenly. "I must not humiliate myself. I'll tell him that Felusia is here, nothing more." Through the magazine, Clara sensed Zipkin looking at her. She turned her hand to make it appear smaller. . . . The rabbi's wife stayed even longer than the market vendor. What was he doing? Why was it so quiet in there? Was he performing an abortion? Clara smiled at this ridiculous thought. The woman was undoubtedly a grandmother. . . . For a while, Clara stopped thinking. A child's wailing could be heard from another part of the house. Clara imagined that she heard the angry hushing of a woman. The room was too warm and stuffy, too full of dust and charcoal fumes. Clara began to fan herself. Perhaps the door would never open again. He would remain with that woman—two petrified mummies. At that moment the patient came out. Behind her, Zipkin gave instructions on how to use an inhalator. He imitated the sound: "Ah-ha. . . ." Clara shifted the magazine a little so that with the corner of her eye she could examine the lower part of Zipkin's body: a white smock, checked trousers. His shoes seemed unusually large. Did he have such large feet? She put down the magazine and saw everything as through a haze. The doctor's voice said: "Please come in."

Clara stood up, her feet numb. She looked at him. It was Zipkin, but older, his hair no longer thick. At the top of his closely cropped head there was a bald spot sprouting fuzz like swamp grass. His brows had grown together and he squinted myopically. Two wrinkles bordered his mouth, indicating the impatient bitterness of one who does things against his will. He had not recognized her! She wanted to cry. Perhaps she should not allow herself to be recognized at all. The office was furnished as simply as the waiting room. A desk, two chairs, a lamp. A stethoscope lay among the papers. There was an eye chart on the wall. Zipkin again said something in English and

Clara coughed to dispel the dryness in her throat. She addressed him in Polish. "Please excuse me, Doctor, I speak no English. . . ."

There was silence. They both sat down. Though he said nothing, Clara knew he had recognized her voice.

"Am I mistaken?" he asked tremulously.

"Yes, it's me."

He did not get up. He lifted his brows, in an expression both dumfounded and indifferent, as if he no longer wanted anything to happen. A strange thought ran through Clara's mind: He is disappointed that I'm not a patient . . .

"Really, this is a surprise," he said in Polish that already had a foreign tinge.

"Yes, isn't it?"

Again they were silent. Searching blindly in her pocketbook for a handkerchief, Clara inadvertently brought out a mirror, which fell into her lap.

"What has happened? Why didn't you let me know you were coming? God!"

"I don't know. Your daughter is here too."

"Felusia? Where is she?"

Clara named the hotel at which they were staying. "Louisa is here too."

Zipkin could not speak. Standing up, he glanced toward the door. For a while his tall figure towered over Clara. After some hesitation he sat down again. He looked at her—and she at him. Shoving aside a stethoscope, he said: "Quite a surprise."

"I hope I'm not inconveniencing you."

"What are you saying? I thought I'd never see you again." And his mouth twitched.

They began speaking, haltingly, incoherently, about the ship, the journey, where had she embarked, when had she landed, and as they made small talk a connection began to form mysteriously between the past and the present. The changes that time had brought to their faces, voices, and figures seemed to disappear. A hidden pencil retouched wrinkles, filled in crevices, smoothed everything. Zipkin grew younger and assumed his former boyishness and the Don Juan arrogance that had so appealed to Clara. In Clara's eyes the old flame again became ignited. Her face again grew impudent, passionate, vulgar, and at the same time Semitically gentle and maternal. It all happened within several seconds. "It's the same Alexander—why did he look so strange to me at first?" Clara wondered.

"Yes, it's the same Clara!" Zipkin decided. He rose and opened the door to the waiting room as if to convince himself that no new patients were waiting for him. He also glanced at another door that was covered with green drapery and that obviously led to his private quarters.

IX

"What made you come to America?" he asked, realizing at once that his question was rude, but unable to withdraw it. Clara thought it over for a moment.

"It's quite simple. Felusia is your daughter and she needs a father. One greeting card a year doesn't satisfy her. She goes to school and all her friends have fathers. It's different when a girl, God forbid, is an orphan—" Clara stopped, the last sentence had come out clumsily. Zipkin lowered his head.

"Just lately I've been thinking of you. Constantly."

"Constantly?"

"Yes."

"I thought you'd completely forgotten me."

"No, Clara, I have forgotten nothing. I tried to make myself forget. What else could I do? After what happened between you and Mirkin, I decided everything was lost."

"Mirkin is no longer alive."

"When did he die? I don't hold any grudges. That is the way you were and you couldn't change. You do know I'm married."

"Yes. I heard a child crying. Was it your son?"

"Yes, my son. He's a nice child. My wife is from Hungary. She helped me complete my studies."

"How is Sonya?"

"Sonya is wealthy. Her husband owns a factory, and she has three children."

"Do you see her?"

"Not very often. She's a devoted mother. Her husband, Yackiewicz is his name, has forgotten all his former dreams. I myself am not in the movement, but I still sympathize with it. There are many socialists and anarchists here. Their headquarters is in this neighborhood."

"I imagined New York would be entirely different."

"What did you imagine? It's the same world and the same people. They keep coming from Russia in shiploads. It never occurred to me that you might come too."

"I've only come for a visit."

"For a visit? For how long?"

"I don't know yet. It depends."

Zipkin covered an unfinished prescription with a blotter. "Well, at any rate you're here now."

"Yes, Alexander, I'm here. Although it seems to me that I'll wake up at any moment and find myself back home. I've been very ill. I almost died. But I'm better now. I had a severe gallbladder attack and as I lay in bed, I decided not to leave Felusia an orphan. How was she guilty? Each person must be punished for his own sins, not for those of others."

"Yes, that's true."

"After recovering I determined to make this trip. When one accepts death, there's nothing more to fear. It all happened so quickly. You remember Sasha, of course. He was your pupil, after all. He took over his grandfather's, my father's, contracts and is even more successful than he was. He's well loved and received by the most important people. The generals ask his advice about matters that have nothing to do with provisions. He has an unusual intellect and is almost too smart. I'd be happy if he accepted life without philosophizing. But apparently he takes after me. Anyhow, I told Sasha everything and he helped me. I can't tell you how kind and generous he is. A real tycoon!"

"Is he married?"

"No, if only he would get married!"

"Why? As you see, I'm a doctor here on East Broadway. Fate worked out this way."

"Are you satisfied?"

"Satisfied? Yes, I bear no grudges against anyone. My goal was Western Europe, not America. But it's a free country here. One can say what one wants to and write what one wishes. The President is criticized more than the bath attendant at home. But when it's legal, it doesn't matter. Why push against an open door? I received Felusia's photograph. When was it taken? She looks splendid."

"Yes, when you see her, you'll realize that she makes up for both of us."

"Why do you run yourself down? I'm not, as you can see, wealthy, but the house I live in is mine and I have my practice. Also, I'm resigned," Zipkin said, astounded at his own words. It had never occurred to him to think of himself in this way before.

"Why do you say you're resigned? You have your profession and your family."

"Yes, but—I had aspirations once. What satisfaction is there in treating these women? My wife is a decent person, but she's Hungarian and somehow that puts her in another world. They seem to think the way we do, but they're different. They're so neutral. Everything is so clear to them, so simple. They have none of our doubts. The Russian and Polish cultures are combined in me—a crazy mixture. You didn't marry again?"

"Marry? You know I didn't."

"How should I know? It's been years since I heard from you."

"You didn't want to hear from me. You didn't even want to know the other side of the story."

"The facts spoke for themselves."

"The facts? There are some things, Alexander, that one cannot judge unless one knows all the details. In France a woman committed a murder and a jury unanimously freed her. They even showered her with flowers. When they learned how much she had suffered, they saw she was a saint. Thus far, I haven't killed anyone. If I destroyed anyone, it was myself. If I had stayed with you, you might have become a tailor instead of a doctor."

"Am I to assume that you did it for my sake?"

"No, I'm not saying that. What's the difference? The past can't return. If only it could! If only I'd been as wise at eighteen. You wrote letters that seemed to drench me with ice water. Felusia was a child, and Mirkin came along and turned my head with his tales of wealth. I mustn't speak ill of the dead, but I've never met a greater liar. He fooled himself, that was the worst part of it. I don't say I acted cleverly; when I thought of it later, it seemed as if he had cast me under a spell. Only God knows how many tears I shed. I became dangerously ill. You asked if I married again. You married, not I. Perhaps while you were accusing me so bitterly you already had your Hungarian fiancée."

Zipkin lowered his head. "In that case, the blame is on me."

"No, I don't blame anyone. I paid dearly for my mistake—the highest price!"

x

"Kubuś is still in Warsaw, isn't he?" Clara inquired.

"Yes."

"Do you hear from him?"

"Seldom."

"Did she marry again?"

"Sabina? Yes, she did."

"Well, why not? People take care of themselves. No one wants to remain alone in the world. Alexander, I don't want you to think I came to ask you for favors, or to saddle you with Felusia. I can see that this is not the home for her. I had imagined something altogether different. Louisa is getting married. Imagine, she met him aboard ship. She has already promised to take Felusia into her home until my plans are clearer. She herself is too old to have a child. One doesn't realize how attached one's employees can become. I can ask you for support for our daughter, but I haven't fallen so low. I only want one favor of you: that Felusia gets to know her father. I don't want her to feel like a neglected orphan. Come and see her. She's yours. I have made peace with my fate."

"Where are you staying?"

Clara again told him the name of the hotel.

"Why there of all places? Well, it's all one and the same. My wife is very jealous," Zipkin said, lowering his voice, "although she has no grounds for suspicion. She's religious too, keeps a kosher kitchen and so forth. But I've remained an atheist. She has all sorts of idiosyncrasies and I don't want a scandal. She's capable of eavesdropping on a patient. If you want to continue our conversation, I had better come with you to your hotel."

"Why not? Felusia isn't at home. She went along with Louisa. I thought it would be better if we talked things over first."

"Yes, we'll take a carriage. Some doctors have their own and drive themselves. But I didn't want to become a coachman, and to hire one is too expensive here. Everything is different in this country. Everybody is democratic, or that's what they call it. All traditions have been upset here. If I'm called to a patient, I walk or I take the El—that's the city train. You must have seen it. Wait, I'll tell my wife you came to take me to a patient."

"If you wish. Perhaps if you're so afraid it might be better if you didn't come?"

"I'm not afraid. You don't wear the mark of Cain. Don't think I'm such a henpecked husband, but I simply want to avoid arguments, and I don't want to hurt her either. You can't imagine how people like her suffer."

"I know, I'm not made of wood, even though you may think I'm a slut. I'd like to ask you one thing: who wrote that letter?"

"Which letter?"

"The letter about my being with Mirkin."

Zipkin grew pale. "I don't know. It was anonymous."

"You once wrote that it came from Warsaw."

"No, from Paris."

"Do you still have it?"

"Perhaps. But I'd have to look for it."

"And I, idiot that I am, suspected my poor child, my Sasha. In what language was it written? In Russian?"

"Yes."

"Well, it must have been Mirkin himself, or his secretary, that charlatan. You must certainly remember him: Yasha Vinaver."

"Yes, I do."

"I don't know what he had against me. I never did him any harm."

"Then you're only troubled by the fact that he informed against you. Your own conduct doesn't bother you."

"My own conduct concerns only God and me, no matter how close you and I may have been. I can't even describe to you what happened. Even if I were to tell you, you wouldn't believe me. I once thought that no one can be fooled, and especially that I couldn't be, but Mirkin deceived me from the beginning. Perhaps I should not tell you this. I don't need to defend myself before you. He was impotent, and I knew this. Not from him—he played the role of a great lover— from a doctor who treated him. Yes, there are doctors who reveal their patients' secrets, especially after a glass of wine. That's why I agreed to go with him. He promised to buy shares for me that would make money. He promised me the sky, but it was all nothing but lies. Sick as he was, he associated with whores. Yasha Vinaver swindled him. He was a disgusting creature, but Mirkin continued to employ him. Believe me, Alexander, from the day that we first became intimate, I never stopped loving you and longing for you. I am prepared to say this before God when I'm called to my judgment. You may be a freethinker, but some power must have placed obstacles in our way. Some perverse spirit has trailed me since my childhood. You may think I'm crazy, but what I saw with my own eyes cannot be denied."

Zipkin frowned. "What did you see?"

"I can't tell you now. We'll talk again. When you know the whole truth, you'll agree with me."

"I want you to know one thing, Clara: I'll never take you seriously again."

"Take me as you like. . . ."

"Wait, I'll be back in a moment."

Zipkin rose. Suddenly he placed his hand on Clara's cheek. Clara caught hold of his wrist and kissed his hand. It happened quickly and unexpectedly. He opened the door behind the green drapery and left the room. Clara sat with her head lowered. Though Zipkin's hand smelled slightly of perspiration, it had awakened her desire. All the feelings she had tried to extinguish in the course of the years had returned with his touch. "I love him! I must have him even if it kills me," she said to herself.

12 ⌂

The rain dashed hail-like against the roof. It had been pouring
for three days. Fortunately the house stood on a hill. Below, in
the valley, the puddles looked like small lakes, and on the
naked branches reflected in them an occasional withered leaf
clung obstinately. The birds that had twittered the first afternoon were now silent. From time to time a crow cawed. As
the rain drummed on, a smoky mist rose over the puddles, so
that the surrounding tangle of brush and plants looked as if it
was smoldering. When a window was opened, there was a
smell of skunk and rot. Cold pervaded the rooms. Alexander
kept feeding the parlor stove chunks of wood and thin logs.
Sitting before the fire, one felt one's face burning while one's
back remained chilled. During the day, a murky light came
through the dripping windows. There was a road a short distance from the house. The whistling and puffing of locomotives could be heard coming from tracks some distance away.
But nothing could be seen except crooked tree trunks and the
dripping sky. The man from whom Zipkin had rented the cottage for a week had told him that there were wild animals in
the adjacent woods. In case of emergency, they were provided
with two hunting rifles. Moldy books were stacked on the
shelves. There were portraits of Civil War officers on the
walls, hooked rugs on the floors, and the patchwork quilts

covering the beds were mosaics of bright materials that Miss Clark, a spinster and the former owner, had sewn together during the long winter nights. Miss Clark had been dead for eight years and the property now belonged to her brother's son, a railroad official who lived in Croton-on-Hudson. The family used it only in the summer.

To go there in mid-autumn had certainly been an act of folly, but Clara had accepted the fact that everything she did must meet with failure. Zipkin had once spent a summer in this area. He had lied clumsily to his wife, telling her that a former patient of his was dangerously ill and Zipkin was the only doctor he would trust. Zipkin had sent a telegram to himself and made his wife send the reply. Felusia was staying with Louisa. Alexander had withdrawn some money from the bank, and he and Clara had come out for a week to pay off old debts of love and say things long unsaid. There was nothing to do in this retreat but lie in the broad bed under double covers. There wasn't even much of anything to eat. The nearest store was some distance away. Zipkin had stocked up on bread, cheese, sausage, butter, and eggs, thinking that they would be able to augment their supplies. There was wood and kerosene in the cupboard, and a bushel of apples picked in a nearby orchard. Zipkin and Clara had arrived on a mild October afternoon. It was an Indian summer day, balmy, the air filled with gossamer. But overnight the weather had changed. Zipkin was afraid that the rain might turn to snow and leave them stranded. All sorts of difficulties could ensue. His wife might become anxious and try to communicate with him. The local police would discover that they were not man and wife. The neighboring farmers were God-fearing Yankees. Yet Zipkin had taken the risk. Life with his wife was too monotonous. He had not been able to forget Clara.

At night in the dark, Clara's hair seemed black again. She told him everything, withholding nothing about Grisha, Calman, Smirnoff, Mirkin. She confessed and begged his forgiveness, enumerated her sins, and clung to Zipkin with renewed passion. How odd human nature is! That which hurts in the light, pleases in the dark. Jealousy becomes a source of pleasure. Clara's stories of unfaithfulness increased their passion. He questioned her, anxious to know, probing every detail. She even invented depravities to satisfy him. She in turn asked to hear about his experiences and he described them to her. She insisted on knowing everything about Sabina, about his present wife, and all his other women, the peasant girls on the Radziwill estate and the whores to whom he had gone with his fellow students at the university in Kiev. Alexander and Clara embraced, talked. Would they be able to live separately again? Clara argued that if he had been able to leave Sabina, why not this Hungarian frump? And if Sabina had been able to find another husband, why couldn't Lisa? He could give her his house and go away with Clara. She had a little money, some jewelry. Sasha would help her out. Alexander could practice elsewhere, in California, in Argentina, in South Africa, even in France or Italy. They had their daughter, that would be their treasure. Instead of hiding in some freezing hole, they could live together and be happy. "How much longer, dearest, do we have to live, after all?" she insisted. "As long as we remain alive, let's be together. Why spend our nights yearning for each other? Do those who languish for love gain paradise? . . ." Clara spoke and pressed her face to Alexander's breast. She had only articulated what he had been thinking. He had again made a mistake. Lisa was frigid. Sleeping with her gave no satisfaction. She only worried about their child, fretted about her own health. Her thoughts revolved around her housekeeping, her washing, her economies. In their first year together he had barely managed to communicate with her in broken German. Later they had switched to a stilted English, for both of them a language without flavor, without associations.

Clara, ill as she was, still seethed with passion. Her obscenities were blended with mysticism, her solemn amorousness was tinged with irony. She could act as silly as a fifteen-year-old or speak like a person with one foot in the grave. She jabbered in a mixture of Russian, Polish, and Yiddish, described all manner of experiences, related her girlish fantasies. Even while discussing death, she managed to inject lust. When she died, she would leave him her pearls and he was to present them to the woman who replaced her. She forced him to promise not to mourn her when she died, but to go to bed with another woman right after her funeral. Strange how this type of nonsense could arouse him! This treacherous witch with her gray hair and gallstones brought back his youth. But could he, for the second time in his life, desert a home and family? Could he trust her? The fervent promises he had made to her were just part of a game. The vows he had sworn to her had to be broken. Behind the intoxication of kisses and the endearments lurked a sober mistrust.

During the night there was lightning and thunder. Wind shook the panes. The chimney whistled. Branches broke from trees. Zipkin imagined himself a Robinson Crusoe who had been shipwrecked with Scheherazade. But the storm would not last forever, and Scheherazade would run out of stories. He was not prepared to abandon his house, which was almost paid for, his faithful wife, his son, who bore his father's name (Berish had become Bernard), and start life all over again with an aging adventuress. He still remembered those months in Paris when Clara had returned to Warsaw and he had haunted the boulevards and eaten watery soup at the free kitchens of the Alliance Israelite. . . .

11

"If you don't want to marry me," Clara argued, "let me be your mistress. I'm worth that much. I am, after all, the mother of your child. I'll rent an apartment in New York and whenever you can you'll come, and when you can't I can always imagine that I'm still in Warsaw. That apparently is my fate."

"You mean you want to settle here?"

"I don't know what I want. What did I do in Warsaw? I ate my heart out. I was a lost soul. Here, at least I know I exist. If you can't come every day, you'll come twice a week, or whenever you can."

"I have so little time."

"What do you mean by little time? One needn't be the prisoner of one's wife. You always came to me from someone else. It used to be Sabina. Why not Lisa? If there were no Lisa, someone else would come along. This is what I've made of my life!"

Clara began to weep. Zipkin kissed and consoled her. The rains had stopped, but the sky remained overcast. A dense, milky fog enveloped tree trunks and bushes, floated in huge seal-like shapes over the horizon. If one wandered only a few steps from the house, one might lose one's way. The sleepless nights had left Zipkin exhausted. At home he never lay down during the daytime, but here he napped. Yes, it was good to be with Clara. But she too was worn out. She looked withered. There were double rings, blue and bluish-green beneath her eyes. In the mornings, when she arose, her face was wrinkled. She tried to cook something, but the stove smoked. She walked around in a bathrobe, slippers, and Zipkin's overcoat draped across her shoulders. For the first few days Zipkin had not even looked at the books. Now he began to read. The novels in the library were all trash. Because there was nothing else of interest, Zipkin chose a book on occultism. At first the subject bored him, but gradually he became absorbed in the case histories. Was it possible? Could there be a grain of truth in them? The corroborations of many witnesses were presented. They all began the same way: as skeptics, who had to be won over. Zipkin read of one medium, a Mrs. B., who when in trance spoke in the voice and accent of a male Susquehanna Indian. This dead one-time chief could read minds and foretell the future. He was so omniscient that he could rap out on a round table the answers to anything asked of him. During Mrs. B.'s séances little flames lit up the darkness. Faces appeared, there were cold breezes, trumpets blew by themselves, mysterious hands composed of unfamiliar matter moved chairs about, lifted dishes, even playfully slapped someone's face or pulled an ear. Zipkin grimaced. He recalled that he had heard of similar black magic from the peasants on the Radziwill estate, as well as from his own parents. A dibbuk had entered the body of a girl, the daughter of a chandler. She chanted the Torah, recited the Talmud, uttered chapters of the Scriptures perversely, divulged the sins of influential citizens, defamed their wives. They had tried to exorcise the phantom by blowing the ram's horn, by excommunication. They used a fire pan, amulets, but the evil spirit continued to mock and blaspheme. The weak hands of the maiden lifted a rock so heavy that three men together could not have lifted it, and rolled and juggled it up and down as if it were a pebble. . . . "Why should people all over the world concoct such lies?" Zipkin asked himself. And why were these stories all so similar?

He discussed it with Clara and she insisted that these stories were true. She swore that she herself had witnessed how a table had indicated the number of coins each person present had in his wallet. And while she was still living with Calman, a fortune teller had predicted that a dark man would come into her life and that she would bear him a child. During her illness in Warsaw, a gypsy who read her fortune in cards had told her that she would take an ocean voyage. Clara nodded her head.

"Why do you think, dearest, we are here now? Because for years I called to you and you answered me. I heard your voice distinctly. You were calling: 'Clara, Clara . . .' "

"It's all illusion. We simply missed each other."

"It's not that simple. One has a soul, and souls yearn for each other. You won't believe me, but Grisha still comes to me in my dreams."

"Why shouldn't I believe you? I still dream about old Count Radziwill."

"Sometimes, Grisha is angry with me. He's beaten me too. I

used to wake up with a dead man's bruises on my arms and breasts. Lately he's been kind to me. Perhaps because the time of my departure is growing closer. . . ."

"Nonsense!"

"Dearest, it was predetermined that we meet. When I saw you in Mirale's room on Zielna Street, I knew you were the one . . . Everything within me glowed. . . ."

The first part of the week passed swiftly. Now the days grew longer. Zipkin and Clara had petty squabbles. They dressed and, braving the foul weather, crept along the muddy road until they came to a country store where they bought provisions. On the way back, it began to pour, and they were soaked through. Night fell and there was nothing else to do but go to bed. They covered themselves with every blanket they could find. Their bodies were warm, but their feet remained cold. Their talk about love, passion, and longing had become repetitious. Clara fell asleep murmuring. She awoke with a backache and stomach cramps. Zipkin heated a brick for her in the stove. She had taken the medicines brought along from Warsaw, but they hadn't helped her. The lovers slept fitfully. The night split into many parts. The mattress sagged, the pillows were hard, the bed linen coarse. Zipkin smoked. Clara kept puffing on his cigarette. She made him keep his hand on her belly because it soothed her.

"Now you can see what a wreck I am," she said.

"No, darling, I love you."

"What sort of love is this? No, I'd better keep quiet."

"Clara. You know it's all your fault."

III

Clara awakened him with a kiss. He opened his eyes and she called out: "*Mazel tov*, it's snowing!"

He sat up and saw that, outside, the gray of yesterday had changed overnight to a bright whiteness. The winter birds chirped. The frost glistened in the sunlight. The surrounding landscape that had disappeared behind the fog during the rainy days could again be seen. In the distance a roof with a smoking chimney indicated that they had been closer to their neighbors than they had imagined. Zipkin felt a boyish delight in the first snow of the year. Hurrah! It was winter! He embraced Clara. He thought of the winters on the Radziwill estate, and the later ones in Kiev: the skating, the sleigh rides, the fur coats, the supper parties. Who in America could understand how gay it had been back there? The students and the young ladies would pile into a sleigh, and the driver in his bearskin coat, felt boots, and cowl-like fur hat would urge the horses on. They sped up and down the hills. The young people giggled and snuggled together. Even though they belonged to the middle class, they shared many of the pleasures of the highest aristocracy. Later they drank tea from samovars, ate preserves, smoked innumerable cigarettes, and held discussions until three in the morning. Both boys and girls worried about the fate of the world. The fathers, though they visited the rabbis of Hushatin and Turisk on the holidays, were tolerant of the times and sought educated husbands for their daughters. The mothers, who still wore wigs themselves, helped their modern daughters arrange rendezvous. Each new poem that appeared in a magazine was a matter of importance. Each article merited a debate. Every idea or social movement brought to mind Siberia, the Shlisselburg Fortress, flight to Europe, and fantasies that hummed in the wind, droned in the telegraph wires, and formed on the windowpanes along with the frost patterns. But what did all these dreams matter now? The "honeymoon" week was over and, since Zipkin had not yet decided to leave his wife, it was time to return to the city. Zipkin and Clara ate their last meal together. Zipkin brought in cold water from the well, washed, and dried himself. Nine days before, he had been anxious to come here, but now he was eager to return. He clowned like a boy. He went half naked into the snow, which was full of bird tracks, tried playfully to pour a pail of water over a flock of crows, who fluttered their wings and cawed. He threw a snowball at the window.

They had to walk to the railroad station, because there was no one from whom they could rent a sleigh. It hadn't even been necessary to lock up the house; merely closing the door was sufficient. This was not an area for thieves. Zipkin carried both their suitcases. They passed snowed-in farms, crooked shanties, houses with smoking chimneys. If it were not for the smoke and the barking dogs in the dog houses, one might think no one lived here. The depot was empty. The train to New York had just left. As in Russia and Poland, there was an odor of tobacco and smoke. A fire burned in an iron stove. Various notices were pasted on the plastered wall. A kerosene lamp hung from the ceiling. A single fly that had survived the autumn flew about, buzzing. Zipkin seated himself on a bench, smoking one cigarette after another. Clara tucked her hands into her muff. Through the dirty windowpanes could be seen freight trains carrying coal, logs, planks. They moved slowly, their sides and doors inscribed with indecipherable names.

Men came in, knocked tobacco from their pipes, addressed Zipkin just to make conversation, saying it was cold, that it had come early and wouldn't end quickly. (Later Zipkin translated for Clara what they had said.) The Americans looked neither like squires nor like peasants. They were a type of individual not seen in Russia: a blend of landowner and intellectual. There was a boyish good nature in their eyes, a readiness to shake the hand of any stranger, a willingness to laugh, a desire to do a favor. They weren't swathed in furs like the Russians, nor were they as broad of bone, or as heavy. Long legs extended from beneath their sheepskin jackets. To Clara, they were another race. Even the dogs they led seemed more civilized than the Russian hounds. A telegraph key could be heard clacking. The depotmaster looked like an ordinary man. No policeman asked for papers.

Afterwards, Zipkin and Clara sat with the other passengers in a car and rode through snowy spaces along a river. The conductors walked back and forth. It began to snow again. Sheets of snow rose in the wind, whirled about, flew over half-frozen waters. The sky blended with the river. Mists drifted by. The forests were white. It could as easily have been part of Russia or Poland. Zipkin stared out the window. He seemed unable to satiate himself with the sight of snow. Clara shut her eyes. Well, if that was how it was going to be, so be it. Each day she lived now was a gift from God. He wanted to remain with his wife? Let him do as he wished. Clara had become resigned. She would rent an apartment somewhere and take care of Felusia. If he came, he came. If not, too bad. Clara surrendered herself to melancholy. Men did not know what love was. Clara opened her eyes. It had been light a moment ago; now night was falling. The snow had taken on a bluish cast. Alexander sketched in a notebook. They stopped in a village, and the train remained there for some time. Someone carried a bundle of straw brooms into the train. A stout woman in a fur coat and a velvet hat got off. Someone carried her basket and a small valise. Her plump, red face wore an expression of self-assurance that one never saw in European women. The train started again, the snow became thinner, falling at an angle, beating sharply against the windows. As they rode along, the frost drew all sorts of trails, sprays, needles, and blossoms on the panes. The locomotive whistled, its stack belched smoke. Huge areas fell away without village or house —a white desert. "Where are the peasants, the fields?" Clara wondered. "Where does the food come from? One doesn't see any farms." Clara remembered stories of Indians. Perhaps they lay ambushed in caves and forests, prepared to attack the train. And what happened to the souls of the dead here? Was there an American heaven and hell or did they return to the Old World? What strange thoughts came to her.

Zipkin took her arm fondly. "Aren't you sleeping? I thought you were. In fifteen minutes we'll be in New York."

13

Mirale's son, Karl Frederick, had died of an inflammation of the lungs. Ezriel and a handful of young people from the "Proletariat" circles walked behind the hearse. There had been a row about the burial. The Jewish cemetery would not accept the child for burial because he had not been circumcised. The Catholics did not want him in their cemetery because he had not been converted. After much difficulty, permission was received from the Evangelical cemetery to bury him there. One of the group tried to give a eulogy during the funeral, but his words could not be heard amidst the thunder and rain. Among the mourners were Esther Eisner, a woman they called Carola, and a stout man called Bleiweiss. Ezriel learned that one of the young men who used to visit Mirale on Zielna Street had committed suicide—no one knew why—and that Stefan Lamanski had become an outright agent of the government abroad and was spying on socialists in Switzerland and France.

After the funeral, Ezriel gave much thought to all this. What had become of his parents' progeny? Their daughter was an exile in Siberia. One grandson lay in an Evangelical cemetery. Another was a settler somewhere in Palestine. Ezriel himself lived with a convert. And what about that young man who had put a bullet in his brain? Couldn't he wait for the inevitable revolution? Or had he lost faith in it? Had he feared arrest? Suicides occurred often in revolutionary circles.

And how could Stefan Lamanski have become a Czarist spy? Was this his revenge on the comrades who had been suspicious of him? Or was he still being falsely accused? It seemed that, among the rationalists, one found the most irrational people. They could not explain why they did things, involved themselves in tragic love affairs, risked unnecessary torments. It occurred to Ezriel that the new literature had also become puzzling and undisciplined. From time to time he read a current novel or poetry in a literary magazine. The authors preached, wrangled, criticized, constantly wrote about suffering, darkness, fate, but Ezriel couldn't see what they were getting at. Like the suicide, they implied a great deal but were never explicit. Well, and what about himself?

One evening as Ezriel walked along Marshalkovsky Boulevard (he had decided to walk a verst each evening) someone called his name. It was Esther Eisner. She still looked attractive, though she was beginning to show signs of middle age. She had grown stouter and there were lines on her round face. She was elegantly dressed. Ezriel would have liked to avoid this meeting. Who could tell? Someone might be following her: Warsaw was full of spies; every janitor was an agent. Ezriel was not entirely without guilt. The government files contained a record of his association with a self-education group. They also knew about his sister. However, it was not natural for him to run away from someone who had greeted him. It was already late spring—Esther's hat was decorated with many flowers—but the weather was cold and rainy.

"Are you too famous to recognize people?" Esther Eisner asked coquettishly. "It's true that I've grown old, but that's not my fault."

Ezriel gave her the compliment she had asked for, expressing the reverse of what he observed: the years had had no effect upon her, she had remained eternally youthful. . . . Esther laughed, thanked him, took his arm. After a while, she released it. She began to ask if he had heard from Mirale, and interrupting herself, she said: "Oh, I forgot to tell you the most important thing."

"What is it?"

"They've killed Stefan Lamanski."

Ezriel felt himself grow pale.

"Who did it?"

"Someone."

"How?"

"With a bullet."

Ezriel's throat tightened. "You know my views."

"No matter how you look at it, he deserved it. It's a shame he was spared for so long. He informed on your sister. You can be sure of that."

"Yes, that's what they say."

"He did enough harm in his lifetime."

"Perhaps."

"What's wrong? You seem to feel sorry for him."

"No, but—it's painful nevertheless."

"Spies must be exterminated," Esther said. "I bless the hands that killed him."

"Would you have done it?"

"If I had had the chance? Surely. A *provocateur* is worse than a dog."

After a long silence, Ezriel asked: "Is there still anyone left of your family?"

"My parents are dead."

"What was your father? You told me once, but I've forgotten."

"Why do you ask?"

"No reason."

"He was a fine man. At first he had a store; later the poor man became a Hebrew teacher."

"A Hebrew teacher?"

"Yes, a Talmud teacher. He was a Hassid of the Kozhenitz rabbi."

"How many spies did *he* shoot?"

Esther laughed.

"You ask such strange questions. You're in a bad mood today. If I've upset you, I'm sorry."

"No, you haven't upset me, but what has become of us Jews in the span of one generation? At least we used to avoid bloodshed."

"Are you turning pious? It's a life-and-death struggle. What has all this to do with Judaism?"

I I

At first Olga tried to persuade Ezriel to get a divorce. There was no difficulty in obtaining one's freedom from an insane person. But she finally wearied of his procrastinations. Apparently he did not want to divorce Shaindel, nor did he want to become converted. Olga and Ezriel began to live together. Neighbors and acquaintances were unaware of the fact that they were not married, or at least pretended to be. To everyone, Olga was Mme Babad, but on her documents she remained Bielikov. He remained a Jew, while Olga and the children—Natasha and Kolia—belonged to the Greek Orthodox faith. Each time she and Ezriel considered taking a trip, there were complications because of the different surnames on their passports. They could not stay together at a hotel. But Olga realized that anger would solve nothing. Eventually she hoped to rescue Ezriel from his environment. When their affair started, he had been a poverty-stricken doctor on Nowolipki Street, with a practice consisting of market women and peddlers. In the hospital and clinic he had worked for groschen. There hadn't been a decent piece of furniture in his house, not even a rug. Shaindel had left everything in a state of confusion when she had entered the asylum. Olga had arranged for Ezriel to move to Marshalkovsky Boulevard, furnish an elegant office and apartment. Misha had been so neglected by his disturbed mother that he had been near a breakdown. He wept, raged, and suffered cramps. Olga had restored the boy to health. She had urged Ezriel to interest himself in hypnotism. Although Ezriel was misanthropic and isolated himself, Olga had convinced him that it was important to cultivate the friendship of the better families by inviting them to social functions. She had made him understand that windows needed curtains, floors rugs, walls pictures. Ezriel had retained the Jewish feeling of abnegation for worldly needs. He knew nothing about plans, budgets, lived for the moment, practiced no economies, paid interest to usurious moneylenders. In the end he had had to admit that it was Olga who had brought him a wealthy practice, secured him from need, and helped him gain a reputation.

But, as the saying goes, the more things change, the more they remain the same. Basically, Ezriel was no different. Seized with despair in the midst of a party, he would go and lock himself in a room. He said the wrong things, told patients how little he knew and how unadvanced medicine was. Women patients complained that Dr. Babad did not greet them when they met in the street, and walked by without tipping his hat. The neighbors had similar comments. He now owned a coach and employed a coachman, but whenever he went somewhere on foot, he lost his way, even on his own street. Instead of going in the direction of Krolewska Street, he would head toward the Vienna Station. No matter how many umbrellas and rubbers Olga bought for him, he managed to leave them behind somewhere. He hypnotized those who suffered from insomnia, constipation, stomach pressure, but neglected his own illnesses. No matter how often Olga spoke to him, she always had the feeling that he was concealing something from her. But what was it that tormented him? Was he secretly ill? Was he longing for Shaindel? Was he a victim of the so-called *Weltschmerz* that was being discussed in the literary magazines?

At least Olga was sure he loved her as a wife. In moments of excitement, he kissed her, embraced her, made up funny and endearing pet names. He could become childlike, optimistic, openhearted, and perform all kinds of foolish tricks. He himself admitted that he was like those lunatics who went from depression to exaltation. He switched from moods of pennypinching to extravagance; he would isolate himself, and then suddenly he would join her and the children, and share in their games. No matter what happened between Ezriel and Olga during the day, there was always a truce at night. There had developed between them a harmony, a ritual of symbols, a private language. Ezriel more than once remarked to Olga that sexual inspiration had within it all the symptoms of insanity. Their nightly caprices had laws of their own, an irrational "logic." During the day they avoided any talk of the fact that they were living together illicitly. But at night it was a favorite topic of conversation. In the dark Andrey was resurrected, Olga was again a Jewish girl from Lithuania. She spoke Yiddish, using idioms and expressions that she thought she had forgotten. Everything became jumbled together: life and death, Lublin and Vilna, Jewishness and apostasy, chastity and wantonness, tenderness and evil. At moments of orgasm Olga saw strange images, monsters. No matter how often Ezriel asked her about them, she could never explain the meaning of these visions. They became accustomed to this nightly intimacy and daytime remoteness. Essentially, Ezriel remained for Olga, odd, secretive, treacherously alien, just as Andrey had once been. The bit of happiness he gave her barely balanced the scale of pleasure and pain. The slightest conflict was enough to upset it.

His daughter, Zina, hated Olga and did not conceal her feelings. This twenty-year-old girl, just out of the gymnasium, treated Olga as if she were not the lady of the house. Zina came and went, slammed doors and gave orders to the maids. She had planned to study abroad after obtaining her diploma, but instead remained in Warsaw. She resembled her father, was tall, golden-haired, with a skin like porcelain. She was considered a beauty, but Olga did not find her attractive. Zina's life was empty. Not only was she at odds with Olga, but she seldom exchanged a word with her father. She dressed shabbily, kept her distance from young men, had no friends, read cheap books, and was not interested in anything worthwhile. She had studied English and Italian, but what good were languages to a person who did not speak for days on end? Ezriel more than once chastised her, but she had placed a seemingly insurmountable barrier between them. She avoided him, made impudent replies, and talked of moving out. When at home, she would lock herself in her room, and ate alone. Above all, she had no fixed schedule for anything, whether it was eating, sleeping, reading, or studying. Ezriel was able to understand others, but his daugher remained a riddle to him. Was she a melancholic? Was she possessed by some *idée fixe?* Did she silently suffer for her mother? Olga had her own opinion of her stepdaughter: Zina was simply a spoiled brat, egoistic, sullen, indifferent, heartless—an enemy in the house. . . .

III

Sunday mornings Olga took Natasha and Kolia to church. She did not want her children to grow up atheists. Her churchgoing also served to emphasize the fact that although she lived out of wedlock and with a Jew, she was nevertheless a devout member of Greek Orthodoxy. The governess took care of Ezriel's son, Misha. On the fourth Sunday of each month, Ezriel would visit Shaindel.

Between Blonya and Prushkov, not far from where he and Olga had once spent a few rainy summer days, Professor Przeborski's sanatorium for the mentally ill was located. At first Professor Przeborski did not want to accept Shaindel: she showed signs of religious mania, made scenes about the impurity of the food, and prayed in Hebrew. Even in an insane asylum there is a "dominant culture." Some of the emotionally disturbed were, in their own fashion, anti-Semites. But because she was the wife of a psychiatrist and because Ezriel had engaged a private attendant for her, Professor Przeborski had allowed himself to be persuaded. With the passage of time, Shaindel had improved. Her suicidal tendencies seemed to be in check and she no longer talked to herself or paced endlessly back and forth with folded hands. She was now in the state that psychiatrists call chronic melancholia, where there is a measure of improvement and an adjustment to circumstances. The prognosis was not a hopeful one, because the patient was not young enough and because she knew that her husband lived with another woman, but Shaindel's condition had become stabilized.

She now had her own room in a small house in the section reserved for the less critically ill. She was treated with opium, chloral, Turkish baths, massages. Twice daily her attendant took her for a walk in the garden, or she went out alone. People at the institution had become accustomed to the sorrowing woman with black, sad eyes, and a sparse beard sprouting from her chin, wearing a sagging gray dress, and a kerchief over her head. The attendants, male and female, called her Mama. Her private attendant cooked for her in kosher pots, and food was sent to her from Blonya. On Passover, she ate matzos. On Rosh Hashana and Yom Kippur, she was taken to worship at the women's synagogue in Blonya. She was often seen seated on a bench outside her cottage, knitting a sweater she never finished. On Fridays, this disturbed woman lit five candles in a brass holder: for herself, Ezriel, Joziek, Zina, and her youngest, Misha. In Blonya, in Prushkov, in all the surrounding area, everyone knew about her. Jews said that she was sane and that her husband, a charlatan, had committed her to the sanatorium so that he could carry on with others. . . .

The coach arrived, Ezriel stepped out, and Shaindel came to the door. Her attendant, Mrs. Shumkin, a lame woman who came from Lithuania and was the widow of a surgeon-barber, greeted Ezriel, said a few quiet words to him, and limped away, leaving husband and wife together. Ezriel approached Shaindel.

"Good morning, Shaindel."

"Good year."

"How are you?"

"As you see."

"May I come in?"

"Why not?"

The room contained a bed for Shaindel and a bench-bed for Mrs. Shumkin, a dresser and a commode. It resembled a room in Jampol. Even the smells were those of Jampol: a blend of onions, chicory, mold. A cat sat on a footstool. Shaindel sat down on the edge of the bed and Ezriel on the bench. He placed two packages on the table—gifts for Shaindel and for Mrs. Shumkin. Shaindel sat, bent over, tense and shy. Old age had come to her early. Her face was wrinkled and warty. The patches of hair that strayed from beneath her head-kerchief were streaked with white.

"You are better, yes?"

"So-so."

"Misha is a fine boy."

"Eh? Yes."

"He sends you his love."

"I thank him kindly," Shaindel said, as if quoting from a primer.

"Zina sends her love too."

Shaindel thought a while, "Already engaged?"

"No."

"What is she waiting for? She's already eighteen."

"You're making a mistake, Shaindel, she's twenty."

"How is that possible? Well—"

For a long time they were both silent. Then Ezriel said: "Mrs. Shumkin tells me that you aren't eating enough."

"I eat. How much can one eat? I'm not hungry."

"If you eat, you'll become stronger."

"What do I need strength for? My life is finished."

"Is Mrs. Shumkin a good cook?"

"Too much salt."

"You can tell her to use less salt."

"I tell her. Does anyone listen to me then? Do I count for anything? I am less than this filth." And Shaindel indicated the dirt under her nails.

"I'll tell her."

"Don't tell her. She'll torture me even more. She's made a pact with the Gentiles. She winks at them and sleeps with them. A wanton woman."

"You just imagine that, Shaindel. She's no longer young. She's crippled too."

Shaindel laughed. Her eyes became mad. "She's pretending, she's pretending. When no one looks, she walks straight. If someone winks at her, she runs like a girl. She was pregnant and miscarried. She buried the infant with a spoon."

"What are you saying? She's a woman in her fifties."

"Well, what of it? When is the Pentecost?"

"In three weeks. I gave you a calendar."

"They stole it from me."

"Who?"

"They steal everything. It's a pity—your money. She steals all my things. She tears out pages from my prayer book, to keep me from saying a Jewish prayer."

Ezriel stood up. "Show me. Let me see."

The prayer book was on the table. Ezriel began to leaf through it. All the pages were there from beginning to end. He said: "Not one page is missing."

"They're missing."

"Which pages are missing?"

Shaindel did not reply. It was hard to know if she hadn't heard or had pretended not to hear. She closed her eyes, placed her wrinkled hands in her lap, and sat in secret agony. For a moment she smiled mockingly as if to say, "How easy it is to deceive a man!"

Ezriel asked: "How do you sleep?"

Shaindel seemed to shrink. "I sleep if they let me."

"Who doesn't?"

"They don't let me."

"Who, Shaindel, who?"

She looked at him painfully. "Leave me alone!"

"Shaindel, I'm your husband. I want to help you. I'm a doctor, too. Who doesn't let you sleep?"

"They don't let me—go, go away. I will be dead soon."

THREE

14

In the homes of the Marshinov Hassidim, the young men whispered among themselves. Reb Shimmon's Hassidim, the deserters, had won a victory over Marshinov. The rabbi's son, Zadok, had put on the short coat of the heathen—had become depraved. His father, Rabbi Jochanan, was growing more and more feeble. The rabbi was seldom strong enough now to go to the study house to pray. Warsaw doctors insisted that the rabbi should move to Otwock, or go away to the mountains. They ordered him to eat fatty foods, but the rabbi could not even tolerate lean food. He could take nothing more than a glass of milk and an egg cookie. On the Sabbath, he tasted a sip of wine, a crumb of Sabbath loaf, a bit of fish, a sliver of meat. Reb Jochanan had become emaciated, skin and bones. His face was white. His beard and sidelocks had turned gray early. Only his eyes remained shining. The rabbi was studying the Cabala: the Zohar, the Tree of Life, the Covenant of Rest, the Book of Piety, the Book of Creation. He sat all day in his prayer shawl and phylacteries like an Ancient. He had separated himself from Tsipele, no longer even slept in her room on Friday nights, which were the nights of union. Mendel the beadle related strange tales about Jochanan. He had almost ceased going to the place where even the Czar goes on foot. When he prayed, or studied, a heat emanated from his body that was not of this world. Once it happened that Mendel picked up the cushion of a chair in which the rabbi had been sitting as he recited the Song of Songs. The cushion was so hot that Mendel had almost burned himself. Mendel swore by his beard and sidelocks that in the dark a pale light shone forth from the rabbi's face. He slept no more than two hours out of the twenty-four and in his sleep his lips continued to murmur. Mendel had listened and had heard the rabbi whisper holy names in Aramaic. Honest Jews who were known not to exaggerate bore witness that they had seen the rabbi perform miracles. He would reach for a pen (the rabbi wrote with a goose quill) and it would be drawn to his hand like a magnet. The pages of the books he read turned by themselves. Everyone who visited the rabbi's study agreed on one thing: his body smelled of myrtle and clove—the aromas of the Garden of Eden. Hassidim who had given the rabbi their lists of requests would emerge from his study pale with astonishment. On one occasion the rabbi had read out the name of a child, and although the father had requested that the rabbi pray for the boy so that he would be diligent in his studies, the rabbi instead prayed for his complete recovery from a current illness. The Hassid had not even heard from home that his child was sick. Later the father received a telegram saying that the child had been ill. He had recovered at the exact hour of the father's audience with the rabbi. Another time, a father came to the rabbi complaining that his son was rotting away in the Czar's barracks because he refused to eat the non-kosher food. The rabbi lifted his shoulders in surprise. Barracks? His son was not in the barracks, he told the astounded Hassid. How was that possible? The father had just received a letter from him. Several days later the father learned that his son had deserted his regiment and had stolen across the border. Once, the parents of a schoolboy who had suddenly lost his sight came to Marshinov. All the specialists had given the boy up. The rabbi listened to the parent's story and ordered that the boy's eyes be bathed with tea. Within a week his sight was restored.

Oddly enough, the rabbi himself was not aware of his powers. He asked Mendel the reason for the large crowds that came to him, not only for the holidays, but on weekdays as well. When Mendel replied that it was because of the miracles, the rabbi looked puzzled. For the first time since he had become rabbi, he grew angry at Mendel: "What miracles? Which miracles? Don't talk foolishness! The Almighty," the rabbi said, "needs no miracles. He carries out His will through the laws of nature." Tsipele related to Calman examples of the rabbi's powers. A letter had arrived from her daughter, Zelda, who was living with her father-in-law in Wysoky, to say that she was pregnant, blessed be the Lord. When Tsipele went to the rabbi to give him the good news, he already knew it and wished her *mazel tov*. Tsipele's hands and feet had grown numb. There had been no visitor from Wysoky in the past weeks, and Zeldele had kept the matter secret because of her fear of the Evil Eye. How then had the rabbi known? Another time, when Tsipele had brought him a letter, he had begun to read its contents while it was still in the envelope. He had suddenly realized what he was doing, grown shy, and stopped. Tsipele told her father about these incidents and wept: it was too much for her to live with such a saint. She was afraid of his holiness.

"Father, he has completely estranged himself from me!"

And a muffled cry came from her, as she concealed her face in a batiste handkerchief.

Calman grew sad. "God willing, in a hundred years you will sit with him in Paradise."

"Papa, I want him here!" Tsipele cried.

Over the years, much had happened. Calman had moved away from the estate. He had not even gone to live in Jampol but had settled in Warsaw. His in-law, Reb Menachem Mendel, Ezriel's father, had died a few weeks after having been operated on for cataracts. Tirza Perl, his widow, had gone to the Holy Land. She wrote that she prayed at the Wailing Wall, at the shrine of Rabbi Yehuda the Hassid, and at Rachel's grave. She had seen Uri Joseph, Ezriel's son, who lived on the land, had become a colonist. Tirza Perl sent Calman a present of a bag of Palestinian earth as a token of gratitude for having paid her fare to the Holy Land. Calman had taken over Reb Menachem Mendel's flat on Krochmalna Street. Here everything had remained the same: the table on which Reb Menachem Mendel had studied the Torah, the bench, the Holy Ark, the books in the bookcases. Many matches had been proposed to Calman, but he had not remarried. His white beard had grown sparse and he wore long sidelocks. His teeth had gradually fallen out, but what were teeth? Enemies that caused pain. He wore spectacles and needed a cane, but his powers had, thank God, not yet entirely left him. He cooked his own oat grits. He shredded a chunk of bread and ate it with borscht. On Fridays he carried his own Sabbath pot to the baker, and invited a guest for the Sabbath meal as well. The Society for the Care of the Sick still prayed on the Sabbath at Reb Menachem Mendel's house, and Calman became their beadle. A few days a week he slept at sick people's homes to help out. His children, his grandchildren, his business got along without him. But the sick needed him, and Calman had read in one of the holy books that a person belonged to those who needed him, not to those whom he needed. It certainly wasn't easy for Calman to stay up nights, to sit in stuffy rooms, carry bedpans, or listen to the sighs and complaints of the sick—nevertheless, he daily praised God for having been sent the blessing of doing charitable deeds.

But since his son-in-law, the Marshinov rabbi, was not well, and his daughter had begged him to come to her, he had left everything and gone to Marshinov. If it counted as a good deed to visit an ordinary patient, surely it meant infinitely more to be with a patient who was a saint. On the other hand, one could grow angry at an ordinary sick person who did not heed the doctor's orders. One could even administer medicine to him forcibly. What, however, could one do with a saint, who didn't care about his health? Calman had countless times determined to reprove his son-in-law, to caution him to follow the doctor's advice. Yet whenever he found himself in the rabbi's presence, looking into his face, he became as if paralyzed. This was not Tsipele's husband, but an ancient sage. Outside the rabbi's door it was the mundane middle of the week, but in Jochanan's room it was Yom Kippur at all times. Candles burned. It was as if the sun shone there with a festive light. The warmth was like the inside of a Holy Ark. The glory of God reigned over Reb Jochanan's countenance, over the braid of his prayer shawl, over each fringe of the ritual garment. One actually sensed the awe of angels, the fire of the seraphim, the flapping of wings, the secrets of heaven, the presence of God's host. Even a fly on the wall did not seem common. How was one such as Calman to open his lips there? Jochanan conducted himself simply. He stood up before Calman and said fondly: "Peace on to you, Father-in-law! How is Father-in-law?" and presented a hand that burned like a living coal.

II

The Hassidim told wondrous tales of Reb Jochanan—the enlightened Jews could not stop relating the wonders of Zadok. Those close to him swore that this was no young man but lightning itself. One could not believe half the things reported of him if one hadn't witnessed them. When Zadok decided he wanted to learn French, he read a Polish-French dictionary three times over from A to Z. After the third reading, he remembered each word. Once through the grammar and he knew every rule, every exception. In this fashion he studied Greek, Latin, even English and Italian. He enrolled in the Warsaw University's faculty of mathematics, but it was little more than a formality. The other students were like kindergarten children compared to him. The professors invited him to their homes, discussed mathematical problems with him as with an equal. Zadok became a frequent visitor at the home of Professor Dickstein, an assimilated Jew. He hadn't up to that time tasted non-kosher food, although he already went about with his head uncovered and drank tea and coffee in the homes of the assimilated Jews. In addition to mathematics, Zadok studied physics, chemistry, biology, philosophy, and just about everything else that was offered. When Zadok visited his uncle, Dr. Babad, Ezriel was astounded. The young man knew anatomy and physiology. His professors warned Zadok not to spread himself so thin, but Zadok only laughed. One had to be aware of everything. There was room in the brain for the knowledge of all the ages. On the contrary, the more one knew, the easier it was to remember.

Zadok's assimilation was the talk of Hassidic Poland. He had been married at sixteen when he had still been pious. Reb Joshua Walden, his father-in-law, demanded that his daughter, Hannah, divorce her heretic husband, but Hannah wouldn't hear of it. Zadok now dressed in modern fashion and Hannah no longer wore a wig. Zadok still had five years of board due at his father-in-law's, but he and Hannah moved into a flat in the Old City. The assimilated elders of the Warsaw community voted Zadok a subsidy. He also did some tutoring in a wealthy home. Hannah, the pampered child, secretly accepted money from her mother, but what was money to Zadok? He went to bed with books and arose with books. In the hundreds of years that the Jews had studied nothing but the Talmud, the Gentiles had produced an Archimedes, a Euclid, a Copernicus, a Galileo, a Newton, a Pascal, and a Darwin. The Jews had stuck to ancient Talmudic precepts and the Gentiles had built railroads and steamships, had invented the telegraph and the telephone, designed microscopes and spectroscopes. They had harnessed the forces of nature. Each day Zadok discovered new wonders: Mendeleyev's table of atoms, Lobachevsky's non-Euclidean geometry, the findings of Faraday and Maxwell, Helmholtz and Hertz. Because the Jews had remained voluntary prisoners of their ancient legends, they had forfeited an ocean of knowledge that could not be drained. In Poland there were few scientific publications, but from Gebetner and Wolf, dealers in foreign publications, Zadok had obtained the most recent German books and periodicals that dealt with the very latest achievements and experiments. He did not read but scanned. He leafed through a book or magazine so rapidly that those who witnessed it hardly believed that he could have managed to read a line. Later, when they discussed it with him, it was clear that he had absorbed everything, and missed nothing. . . .

But where did all this secular learning lead? Evenings, Zadok liked to go over to his Uncle Ezriel's house on Marshalkovsky Boulevard and talk. With his Uncle Ezriel, Zadok could speak rapidly, cut his sentences short. They discussed Spinoza, Kant, Hegel in the same way as the Mishnah and the Gemara. Zadok had not lost the Hassidic gestures, the clutching at the beard, which he had already shaved, the wrinkling of the brow, the nail-biting. When he became excited over Fichte's *Ego and Non-Ego*, or about Schopenhauer's "blind will," he was capable of overturning a glass of tea on Olga's best tablecloth. Olga made no secret of the fact that she could not stand him. This genius brought into her splendid home the cackling sound of Yiddish, the manners of Grzybow Place, the chant of the synagogue. Even when he kissed her hand in the manner of a gallant, his nose interfered. Olga remarked sarcastically that he kissed ladies' hands as if they were his ritual garment. She had an even more serious complaint: each time Zadok came, he left Ezriel disturbed and melancholy. Despite Olga's grumbling, Ezriel continued to encourage Zadok's visits. Zadok intrigued the male guests who came to the Babads'. They asked him complicated questions, to which he replied in the wink of an eye. Within half a minute he multiplied two rows of six figures, and calculated square and cube roots with ease. He was always asked how he did it. How could a brain work so swiftly? Did he actually calculate with such speed or did the answer come to him automatically? It was something to talk about and argue over. Zadok made the evenings interesting. In addition to Zadok's lightning mathematics, there were always the discussions about hypnotism.

Ezriel had, at first, as good as rejected hypnotism. The sessions that he had witnessed at the hospital had not convinced him. He could not see where hypnotism could be effective as a cure. He had tried hypnosis on Shaindel, during the time when she was still at home, but the results had been negative. The entire concept of forcing one's will upon another's seemed to Ezriel irrational, a sort of modern abracadabra. For if staring into someone's eyes and repeating words could work, why couldn't Reb Jochanan's good wishes, or the Evil Eye of a witch? Mesmerism was bound up in Ezriel's mind with spiritualism, mind reading, clairvoyance, and other such occult matters that had nothing to do with science and were more likely to awaken old superstitions than to heal. Deep within him, Ezriel felt that all spiritual diseases, even the so-called functional ones, were organic and had to do with the structure of the brain or its chemical processes. Could words and glances alter cells and tissues? The more Ezriel doubted, the more he studied these matters. Investigations into this subject were being conducted all over Europe, although France —Nancy and Paris—remained the center. Slowly Ezriel began to believe that this was indeed a factual force, not some sort of fancy. Bernheim, Charcot, Janet were not charlatans. Feldman's demonstrations in Warsaw were not hocus-pocus, not hallucinations. He himself had witnessed cases of hypnotic catalepsy, lethargy, somnambulism. He had seen hypnotized patients shiver from alleged cold, perspire from nonexistent heat, react to suggested hallucinations, carry out post-hypnotic orders. There could be no thought of chicanery or make-believe here.

It wasn't long before Ezriel himself began to use hypnosis on his patients. He practiced on Olga. He reached a stage where he could rid her of a headache over the telephone. Olga had for years suffered from insomnia and Ezriel had hypnotized her so that she could sleep. He would seat his subject in an armchair, request her to make her mind as empty of thought as possible, to think about nothing. Then he would instruct her to stare at the lid of a silver watch which hung on the opposite wall, and he would begin to speak: "Your lids, dear lady, are growing heavy; they will soon close. Your gaze is tired, misted over. Your arms and legs are sinking; a weariness is coming over your limbs; you barely hear my voice; you're growing sleepy; you can't keep your eyes open any longer . . ." At times he would place his hand on the patient's abdomen. . . . His patients actually fell asleep, carried out his suggestions. Despite the fact that he had achieved hypnosis so often that there could no longer be any question of his ability, his own doubts of his performance persisted. Each time he hypnotized a patient, he could not help being suspicious that he or she might be playing along with him.

III

It was odd that Zadok not only allied himself with the extreme assimilationists but went even further than they. On a visit to Ezriel, he clutched at his chin and argued with his uncle in a Talmudic-like chant: "If you believe that everything the rabbis scribble in their commentaries was given to Moses on Mount Sinai, then conduct yourself according to *The Beginning of Wisdom*. On the other hand, if you are a freethinker —what does 'Jew' mean? In nature there is no such specie as Jew. All these labels—Jew, Gentile—aren't worth a fig."

"The fact that Moses did not speak to God is no indication that He does not exist," Ezriel interrupted.

"And supposing He does exist, what of it? Since we do not know what He wants, why compound nonsense with more nonsense? Where is your logic, Uncle Ezriel?"

"My logic is that the spiritual development of man is as much nature as physics or embryology. Since Judaism does

exist, that means the powers that be want it to continue exist-
ing."

"One can say that about every religion."

"That's true."

"What about the religions that have disappeared?"

"They were intended to disappear."

"Then perhaps our time has come?" Zadok asked.

"Even an incurable patient calls a doctor. No one dies willingly."

"What about those who commit suicide? Their desire too is
rooted in nature."

"They are the exception rather than the rule."

"What is an exception in nature?" Zadok pinched the spot
where a sidelock once grew. "The universe is not a grammar
book. In nature as in mathematics, there are no exceptions."

"Who says that nature is mathematics."

"It's certainly closer to mathematics than to grammar."

"Let the suicides kill themselves, I want to live, both as an
individual and as a nationality."

"In that case, you should do what Joziek did, emigrate to
Palestine."

"You're right about that."

"But if you don't believe, what tie do you have with the
Jews of Yemen or India? Nationalism is nothing but inertia.
The Jew has built his entire existence on a legend four thou-
sand years old."

"This legend you refer to gives me sleepless nights. What
about the pogroms we suffer? They are something concrete."

"The reason for pogroms is that we have remained as Haman described us: 'There is a certain people scattered abroad
and dispersed among the people in all the provinces of thy
kingdom; and their laws are adverse from all people; neither
keep they the king's laws,' " Zadok began to chant in the tune
of the Book of Esther. "We want to be everything at once:
Russians, Jews, Frenchmen, Turks. We want to be an amalga-

mation of all the nations. If one lives in Poland, one should be a Pole, not stand with one foot in Warsaw and the other in Jerusalem."

"What is your solution? Conversion?" Ezriel asked.

"Wallenberg is right: you cannot live in someone else's country and consider his daughter taboo, his meat impure, his God an idol. So long as men separate into groups, there cannot be a group within a group."

"You talk like the anti-Semites!" Ezriel said.

"Maybe they are right?"

"And what if the socialists were to take over thirty years from now?"

"Then humanity would become a single entity and there would be no place for either Jews or Gentiles."

"That means that I must now become a Gentile, so that in thirty years I will become an internationalist."

"History is dynamic. Have you read Hegel's *Phenomenology?* The spirit is dialectic. I, myself, Uncle Ezriel, am a hedonist. When man does that which brings him pleasure, he is following the right path. Jews suffer, an indication that theirs is the wrong path."

"Poles suffer too. It would be better to become a German or an Englishman."

"If I could, I would surely do so."

"As an Englishman, you'd be drafted to fight the Boers."

"If I had no choice, then I would fight."

"The English demand that you fight with zeal."

"Who would care what they wanted."

"Is that your philosophy?"

"It's Spinoza's."

"What about the Jew who enjoys his Judaism?" Ezriel said.

"Only the pious enjoy it. What can your Judaism mean to you, Uncle?"

Olga knocked on the door. "Tea is ready."

Ezriel and Zadok went into the dining room. The samovar

stood on the table around which Natasha, Kolia, and Misha were already seated. Natasha, now a girl of fourteen, was a fourth-form student in the gymnasium. She was tall, slim, with a turned-up nose, black hair, and dark eyes. Her mouth was too large for her face, and the boys called her "frog." Kolia was eleven. He was the image of his mother: black eyes, straight nose, and long chin. His hair was cut short in military style. He wore a student's jacket with brass buttons and a high collar. Misha, too, was going to school. He resembled Shaindel. In the short time since Olga had left the room to summon the men, Misha and Kolia had located a piece of string and were playing a string game, "Etel Betel." They were taking turns removing the string from each other's hands, each time forming a prescribed pattern called "water," "cymbal," a "broom," and so on.

Olga put her hands to her head. "Again they've got hold of that dirty string! Go wash your hands."

"Ma, it's not dirty."

"Go wash your hands, I say!—Wait!"

Olga went into the kitchen and returned with a wet sponge and towel. Natasha smiled wisely like an older sister as the boys' hands were being washed. Kolia stuck his tongue out at her, and Misha began to laugh. Ezriel poured tea for Zadok and himself. The children added granulated sugar, but Ezriel and Zadok bit into pieces of lump sugar. The cook came in and out of the room as she served cookies and cake. She wore a white apron and a cap over her blond hair. Olga glanced at Zadok: "Well, Pan Zdzislaw, how are things going?"

Zadok started. She had interrupted his private thoughts.

He replied in flowery Polish with a Jewish accent. "Thank you, honored lady. How can things be going? One stumbles along. We have discussions, but what comes of our words? At times I envy the animals who carry out their functions silently. Animals, like nature itself, know only deeds, therefore an animal can no more make a mistake than a rock. A pebble showed that Aristotle was wrong. I'm referring to the experiment on the leaning tower of Pisa."

"Are not words deeds too?" Ezriel asked. "Isn't our intellect a part of nature? Why should a stone be infallible and our brains continue to make mistakes?"

"What is Uncle trying to say? From the pantheistic point of view, there are no false ideas, only crippled ones. All errors are subjective."

Olga rapped on the table. "They're starting again! Talk about something the children can understand."

Natasha suddenly spoke up. "Papa, animals can make mistakes too. If one puts duck eggs under a chicken and she hatches them, she thinks the ducklings are hers—is that not a mistake?"

"I want to say something, too." Kolia raised his hand like a pupil in class.

"See how talkative they are all of a sudden," Olga said, half reproachful, half smiling.

"What do you want to say, Kolia?"

"When we were in Wilanow, at Madame Malewska's, the boys dug a trench and put a kerchief over it. The cat did not know that there was a hole beneath it and fell in."

Misha burst out laughing. "Oh, how funny!"

"How about their arguments?" Ezriel asked.

Zadok had apparently already been thinking about something else. He raised the lids over his large, black eyes, made a grimace, and began to scratch his left temple. "The cat? Ducklings? I don't know if one can rightly call these happenings errors. Properly speaking, an error occurs only when one has made a mistake about a definite fact. The hen and the cat do everything by instinct. It only means that instinct is not perfect either, and that is known. The hunter places a wooden decoy in the water or simulates bird calls to fool his prey. But let us imagine that animals are capable of thinking and making mistakes—what does that have to do with our discussion?"

"If error is possible, then sin exists. If sin is possible, there is no determinism and there is room for absolute ethics and religion. Maybe man has to discover God in the same way that he discovered America or gravity?"

"Well, there they go again! Children, drink your tea. Misha, don't puff your cheeks out," Olga ordered. She turned to Ezriel.

"Pan Zdzislaw is right. If one does not know, one should not speak. It's better to believe without philosophies. One cannot find God through reasoning."

"Certain truths have already been found, eternal truths, that are forever valid."

"What truths?"

"The Ten Commandments."

Zadok jerked his head as if to dislodge a fly. "What sort of discovery is that? The struggle for existence is a biological law. According to Malthus, wars are necessary. The entire history of man is filled with wars. The very Bible that says 'Thou shalt not kill,' orders the killing of men, women, and children."

" 'Thou shalt not kill' means within one's own group."

"In what way is one's own group better than other groups? These are all social laws. It's the same to nature who kills whom. For thousands of years bulls have been slaughtered and nature has kept quiet. Can it be possible that mankind will have to account for all the bulls, calves, and chickens it has slaughtered? Why should a human life be so dear to nature?"

"Because man suffers more. He can foresee suffering. He does not live exclusively in the present."

"And if he suffers, does that make him privileged? Nature would not care if man had remained a cannibal."

"According to you, Zadok, one is permitted to make pogroms . . ."

Olga shivered.

"I beg you, stop this babbling!" Olga said sternly. She had countless times asked these yeshiva scholars not to conduct their futile discussions. But no sooner did they get together than the wrangling would begin in a Yiddish-spiced Polish. They argued like the impractical idlers in a House of Study. Zadok, for all his bad manners, at least had a modern outlook, but Ezriel still clung to the glorification of the moldy Judaism of his origin. He had somehow remained entangled in its fanaticism. Above all, Olga wanted to avoid talk about religion, since the household was mixed. In the school which Misha attended, he had to leave the room when the priest came to give his lesson. The children absorbed all sorts of nonsense. Each time Kolia and Misha quarreled, Olga was afraid lest Kolia call Misha Jewboy. She considered Ezriel's reference to pogroms at the table tactless. Whose fault was it if stupid peasants allowed themselves to be agitated into savagery? Why expose the children to such horrors?

It suddenly became so still in the dining room that Misha could be heard sipping his tea and tapping his spoon against the glass. Kolia grew serious. Natasha turned her head away. Ezriel drank and drew his brows together. He realized the logical weakness of his arguments. His father had applied the same type of reasoning. "If what you say is so, then this is an unbridled world!" he would insist. Well, maybe the world was unbridled? Perhaps one was permitted to stage pogroms? . . . It seemed strange that Zadok, who had so recently abandoned piety, had been able to make peace with life, while Ezriel still became indignant at every evil deed. Each time he read a newspaper, he was dumfounded. It only contained reports of beatings, slaughter, attacks on innocent people. The Russian Jews were chased from the cities, driven from the villages. They fled to Poland, and the Polish press ranted against the "Litvaks." All of Russia was one skein of injustice. The police were corrupt, the courts were crooked. Criminals occupied seats in the most exalted Synod. The Poles, victims themselves, nevertheless behaved most severely toward the Jews. The Jews, on the other hand, did not live honorably. Competition was ugly and each grabbed only for himself. Palestine?

They couldn't all emigrate to Palestine. The Turks had already forbidden Jews to purchase land there and the Arabs resented them. Assimilation? No one wanted this raggedy crew outside of a few paid missionaries. Socialism? How would it come about? Who would bring it about? It would again be a case of violence, murder, evil. And what assurance was there that the socialists would be saints? They were already divided into factions and fighting among themselves.

No, this slaughterhouse could not be cleansed with more blood. This was clear to Ezriel. But with what, then? And what was his role in this mire? To be a swine at the trough? To grab for himself as long as it was possible? To send Kolia and Misha to the university and raise two more lawyers? To get Natasha an officer for a bridegroom? . . . In all the years that Ezriel had studied, had wrangled with himself, he had believed that he was destined for something higher. He had been dazzled by such words as culture, humanity, progress, civilization. Now the awakening had come. He had been left without a belief, without an ideal, without hope. His youth had passed. The work grew ever more difficult, the expenses higher. He did not speak of it to anyone, but he spent sleepless nights pondering these "eternal questions." "Why am I living? What am I doing here? What is my mission? What is my duty?" he asked himself again and again. "Or does man not have any duty? Is he simply a cow that needs to graze until he dies or is killed?" Yes, Zadok was right: according to logic, and according to science, might was right . . .

"Why are you letting your tea get cold?" Olga asked.

15

I

Olga had a stroke of luck. Wallenberg had kept his promise, and left her seven thousand rubles in his will. For a long time Olga had wanted to build or buy a villa. It was a residue of nostalgia for the time when she had lived with Andrey in Druskenik near the Niemen River. All respectable Warsaw doctors had their own summer homes. More than thirty years had passed since the Uprising, but Poland was still full of bankrupt nobles, whose dilapidated manor houses could be purchased at a low price. Olga consulted brokers and began to look for a country house. Ezriel himself yearned for some property outside the city. He wanted to get away from the noise. What better escape was there than fields, lakes, and forests?

The agents soon became active and every Sunday Olga insisted that Ezriel accompany her to look at some property or other.

The trips themselves stimulated Ezriel. Warsaw was crowded, dusty, noisy. The houses kept growing taller and the sky narrower. But as soon as one left the city, one saw God's world: a broad sky, distant fields. Storks circled in the blue as they had in Jampol or Turbin. Time seemed to have stopped. Creatures quacked, chirped, twittered, whistled, each had its own tune. Ezriel again heard the sound of the cuckoo as on that day in Otwock, on his last visit to Miriam Lieba. Looking at the properties disturbed Ezriel as much as it pleased him and he would have signed any contract. Olga, more knowledgeable, haggled over prices, found fault with the plumbing, the building, even the grounds, and asked all sorts of questions about taxes and mortgages.

It seemed to Ezriel that nothing would ever appeal to her. But, finally, she found what she wanted. Not far from Warsaw, between Zakroczym and Nowydwor, near the Vistula, there was a small estate, of some hundred acres, mainly pasture land for cattle. At the river's edge the soil was entirely sandy, but the property included a large orchard of apple, pear, and plum trees, as well as gooseberry and currant bushes. There were forty cows (with meager udders), several horses, a pair of goats, even some hogs; and, in a half-muddy pond, carp and wild ducks. The squire, a drunkard, had neglected everything, but the old villa had a foundation of stone and was as solid as a fortress. Poplars that dated from Napoleon's time shaded the windows. The estate included stables, barns, sheds, storage huts, and an ancient structure for drying cheese. The price was modest, but there were mortgages and some renovations would be needed. The old peasants working there had once been serfs. Olga didn't hesitate for long. She left a down payment and settled with the debtors. Ezriel put in everything he owned and even borrowed money from a bank. He had high hopes. If worst came to worst, he could move out there, isolate himself from the world, and live off the land. The estate was bought in both their names.

Ezriel suggested that they postpone the renovating, but Olga was impatient. She engaged a crew of workmen. The roof needed repairs, stoves had to be replaced, a road paved, a second well dug. They needed new furniture. Olga had promised Ezriel that she would not borrow any more money, but once the work of renovating the house had begun, she couldn't stop in the middle. They were soon forced to take out another loan. One day Ezriel had money saved up for a rainy day, and the next he was in debt and paying interest to banks and usurers. He maintained two households, one in Warsaw and the estate in Topolka. Overnight he had become burdened with maids, male servants, and old Gentiles who were crippled with rheumatism and whom he had to provide with a sort of pension. As if to spite him, he had fewer patients, since most of the rich women whom he treated were vacationing.

Ezriel sat in his office and spent every free moment adding up figures. The first few weeks showed that there would be no revenue from the estate. The farmhands demanded higher wages. The grass became sun-scorched and the cows gave little milk. The fruit was stolen from the trees or they were picked clean by the birds. The peasants had all sorts of privileges: they had the right to fish in the pond and chop wood in the forest. It was probably necessary to hire a steward, but all stewards drank and stole. The peasants' dogs were wild and Ezriel was constantly being attacked by them. Even bathing in the Vistula wasn't easy, because of the river's stony bed, and the peasants had warned him that not far from shore was a whirlpool that could engulf the best swimmer. Some of the neighbors told Olga that it was advisable to keep rifles on hand because of bandits. There were other neighbors who turned out to be anti-Semites.

The illusion that one could find peace and serenity in the country did not last long. As a rule, Olga gained weight during the summer, but this year she became as emaciated as a consumptive. She had made a mistake but refused to admit it. Her children and Misha were in Topolka for the summer, but Zina had stayed in Warsaw. Olga wrote to Ezriel daily. Sometimes she sent him telegrams. She needed all sorts of supplies. The workmen procrastinated, did their jobs badly. The plumber's estimates had been inaccurate. The government demanded overdue taxes. Everyone seemed to realize that Olga and Ezriel were amateurs. Olga, who until now had been sympathetic toward Poland, began to be resentful. One Sunday night Ezriel and Olga were awakened by the sound of shots fired close to their bedroom window. Who had done the shooting and why, no one knew.

11

Before calling in his first patient, Ezriel paced nervously back and forth for a few minutes in an effort at self-hypnosis to bolster his confidence. These people came to him for courage, and like a false prophet he soothed them. "Peace, peace," he said. A loved one had died? Well, one must keep on living. One feared death oneself? How unhealthy. The main thing was to enjoy life as long as one could. One had been betrayed by one's husband or wife? One's children were selfish? One was going broke? Or approaching old age? Life was tedious? It was all a matter of nerves. All one had to do was get a grip on oneself. Other doctors prescribed remedies, but Ezriel tried to cure with false encouragement. That morning when he opened the door to the waiting room he saw Esther Eisner sitting there.

Ezriel called her into his office. "Well, who has been shot now?"

Esther looked at him gravely. "Your sister is in Warsaw," she said quietly.

"Mirale?"

Esther's voice grew even softer. "She has escaped from Siberia."

"I see."

"She must leave the country at once."

"Where is she?"

Esther gave him the address. Then she shook his hand and left. There was only one other patient, whom Ezriel quickly dispensed with. He was due at the Jewish Hospital that afternoon, but he telephoned that he could not come. Standing at the window, he looked out. He had an odd feeling—as if Mirale had returned from beyond the grave. How old was she? . . . How long was it since she had opened the door in the Hassidic House of Study in Jampol and said: "Come home. Your future father-in-law is waiting!"

He would need money. Mirale was probably penniless. He stood beside the bookcase, took out a book, looked into it, and replaced it. Then he picked up a pen and wrote some figures on a sheet of paper. "How have I accumulated such expenses?" he wondered. He glanced at his mail, which consisted almost entirely of bills. The Jewish community demanded their taxes. Joziek, in Palestine, had married. He wanted to become his own master and asked his father's help. Topolka was a real burden. Olga had written that she was in trouble. And so it went. As soon as Ezriel deluded himself that there was a slight respite, some new complication arose. Some force was toying with him, placing difficulties in his path, as if to thwart all his earthly hopes. He walked along the hall and heard Zina murmur something in her room. The girl should have been in Topolka in the fresh air, taking care of Misha, but she chose to spend the hot days in the city, atoning for what sin? Could she too not make peace with the world? What was bothering her? She had no religion. She had been raised in a secular atmosphere. He felt like going to her and asking the familiar paternal question: "What will become of you?" But instead he waved his hand, walked down the stairs and into the street. A new house was being built nearby. Municipal workers were repairing the pavement and the tracks of the old horse trolley were exposed. There was a smell of lime, fresh dung, big-city heat. The visit to Mirale had its dangers. One could not know. Perhaps she had been allowed to escape to see whom she would contact. Ezriel was hot and sweaty. Rather than take a droshky, he walked, now and then looking back to see if anyone was following him. For some reason the police were out in force. Had some dignitary been assassinated? Was a funeral for some revolutionary scheduled? It would be both foolish and tragic to end up in prison for no reason at all. He suddenly realized that he was praying to

God, promising a donation to charity in return for his safe-keeping. "God Almighty," he thought, "save me from falling into their trap. And help Mirale, too. She has suffered enough. . . ." He stopped, wiped his forehead, and said to himself: "I do believe in God and in the power of prayer."

Ezriel had not been to Dzika Street for a long time. Ragged young men stood about, talking and smoking cigarette stubs. Dray wagons carrying loads of iron pipes rolled across the so-called cat's-head cobblestones of the street. The noise was deafening. At the gates to the courtyards, vendors sold rolls, bagels, baked apples, peas, beans, licorice, and halvah. Porters carried overstuffed baskets or pushed carts. Ezriel remembered when this had been a quiet section. Now there was a sign on every window, behind which machines wove, spun, cut, rolled. On Gęsia Street, clerks stood in front of stores, inviting the passers-by in. Little hotels and restaurants had sprung up everywhere. A man with long hair, a broad-brimmed hat, a black ribbon tie, obviously an intellectual, walked by. A Hebrew teacher? A revolutionary? It was in this neighborhood, somewhere in Krasinski Park, that the young radicals had their meeting place. At the gate to the house he was looking for, Ezriel glanced back for the last time to see if he was being followed.

Slowly he walked across the courtyard. He had been foolish. He should have brought along his instrument bag. In case anything happened, he could explain that he had been called to attend a patient. But where was the patient? . . . Below, to the right, there was a Hassidic study house. Through an open window half-covered by curtains, Ezriel heard the singsong recital of the Talmud. He glimpsed a white face, a skullcap, the cornice of a Holy Ark, the flame of a memorial candle. "Perhaps I should go in and remain there. I have two hundred rubles with me. I'd have enough for a year and a half. I once lived in Warsaw on two rubles a week. I could sell my watch, too. . . ." The fantasies began to multiply. Olga would search for him for a while and finally give up. Mirale would go abroad even without his help. Olga would remain in Topolka. Zina would have to find herself a job. But it would be a pity for Shaindel. Shaindel would undoubtedly be transferred to the Jewish Hospital. Misha would remain with Olga, without a father. She had grown fond of him. Or perhaps Mayer Joel would take him in, or Rabbi Jochanan. . . . And what would he do? Sit and study. If he had to run away, it would not be to Topolka. If religion was opium, as they say— it was the opiate most suited to the Jewish soul. Jews had been dreaming over the pages of the Torah for two thousand years. These were noble dreams at least, not bloody nightmares. . . .

He saw the number he was looking for and knocked on the door. Soon he heard footsteps and someone asked: "Who is it?" "The sewing-machine salesman," Ezriel said, repeating the password Esther Eisner had given him.

III

The door was unbolted. A dark woman with upswept hair held at the back with a comb confronted him. "Please, come in!"

He walked through a dark corridor redolent of kitchen odors and dirty laundry. Ezriel heard a voice singing a lullaby: "Ah-a-Ah-a-Ah-a-Ah—" The little one at least, Ezriel thought, needn't fear the police. He was led through a dining room where a young man sat at a table, his sleeves rolled up, fussing with some sort of mechanism. "Is he making a bomb?" No, it was only a wall clock. They came to a door, the woman knocked and then pushed it open. Ezriel saw a small woman, middle-aged, almost old, wearing a black skirt and a gray blouse. Her hair, a mixture of black and gray, was combed up into a tight knot. For a moment he did not recognize her. Suddenly he realized that it was Mirale. Yes, it was Mirale, but completely changed. Her face was wrinkled, red as a frozen apple. "It's you," he said.

"Ezriel!"

They embraced. Beneath the sleeves of her blouse her arms were thin and bony. She said in Russian: "Your sister has grown old."

"Mirale, why do you speak to me in Russian?"

"I've forgotten Yiddish. . . ."

Nevertheless, she began to speak in Yiddish. Seating herself, she indicated a chair for him. "Has she grown smaller?" Ezriel asked himself.

He continued to look at her. This was Mirale, his younger sister. Her fingers were bent. One of her nails had grown horny. A bone jutted from her wrist. Her throat was as wrinkled as tissue paper. They had made sand pies together, had played house. Ezriel's eyes dimmed. When had her R's grown so hard, he wondered. At first her words made little sense. She stammered, spoke of their parents, asked whether the anniversary of their father's death was being observed. She mixed broken Yiddish with Russian. Her speech sounded like a Litvak's, Ezriel thought. Mirale related how long it had taken her to make the trip to Warsaw, how many weeks she had been dragged along in carts and sleighs. She mentioned the names of Russian cities, villages, and spoke of how the peasants had helped her. "You won't believe it, but once they hid me in a wagon, under a sack of oats, in a chest like a coffin. I breathed through a hole. It was so frightening. But it's difficult when one must urinate. Well, I'm stronger than I thought. I survived everything. . . . They believe I can do more for our cause abroad, but I doubt it. . . . I'm neither a speaker nor a writer, just an ordinary woman. . . ."

"How did you manage to stay alive?"

"I managed. You almost never answered my long letters, but you did send money. Thanks for that."

There was a pause while they looked at each other hesitantly, estranged by time. Ezriel felt as if Mirale by some miracle had become the elder. He even felt a kind of jealousy of this weak woman who had chosen her path and followed it unwaveringly. He detected a bit of sisterly sarcasm in her tone when she said, "Well, you're a real doctor."

"Yes."

"What happened to what's-his-name?"

"Zipkin?"

"That's right."

"He's a doctor in America."

"Another doctor? Well, and what about—what was her name?"

"Vera Charlap? She died."

"I was still around then. No, I was in prison."

"Rose Berkowicz committed suicide."

"Why? Well, such things happen. In Siberia suicide is quite common. Especially among the men. She was a fool, that Rose Berkowicz."

"I thought her intelligent."

"No, a chatterbox. Couldn't forget either her gymnasium or her father's tannery."

"Do you still believe in the revolution?"

Mirale looked serious. "I believe."

"Here in Poland everything has come to a halt."

"Oh, I don't know about that. How can an ideal be stopped? The worker is still enslaved. The peasant is still hungry. The bourgeoisie persecutes everyone. You should see whom they're sending to Siberia! Civil servants, teachers, and petty officials. There aren't enough soldiers, and women or peasants with sticks are sent to guard the prisoners. Ah, what this degradation has led to!"

"It's always been the same."

"No! The masses are losing patience. The peasant is embittered. The boil is ready to burst."

"Where will you go?"

Mirale thought for a moment. "As yet I don't know. Wherever the Central Committee sends me. I'll be in touch with someone today. I'll probably get my orders tomorrow."

"How's your health?"

"So-so. I have rheumatism, but that's not fatal. The important thing for me is to get across the border."

"How much money do you need?"

"I don't know. You're always willing to help."

"You're my sister."

"Yes, but you've become an aristocrat. What happened to your wife?"

"She went out of her mind."

"Why? She was such a happy person. Naïve, but lively. Esther Eisner told me about it. Esther's remained a child—still uses the same phrases. Who's the woman with whom you're living?"

"A doctor's widow."

"Well, she exchanged one doctor for another. We really didn't live in Siberia. Time stopped for us. But the railroad strikes show that the people have awakened."

The woman who had opened the door for Ezriel knocked and brought in two glasses of tea with cookies. She looked as if she were performing some holy rite during which one must not speak a word. Pious Jewish girls once served yeshiva students in the same way. Ezriel thanked her. Mirale looked at her somewhat mockingly. "Thank you for the trouble. . . ."

Like an old woman, Mirale took a piece of sugar, dunked it in the tea, then bit off a piece. "Is it chalk or something?" she asked.

Ezriel also bit off a piece. "Why chalk? It's sugar."

"There's no sweetness in it."

"What are you saying?"

Brother and sister exchanged glances. "I seem to have lost my sense of taste. It's from all the traveling. There was a little too much of it. Well, I'm resting now. I still don't know how I'll get to the border. How far is it from here to Mlava? I'll have to ride in a cart. In Germany, I'll be able to take the train."

"You seem tired."

"Yes, I am tired. When I look at you, I see that you resemble Father. You're different, but still—you also have something of our Grandfather Abraham Hamburg about you."

"Yes, Mother used to say that too. It always struck me as ludicrous. You look like Mother."

"Yes, sometimes I frighten myself. I say something and I feel as if it were Mother's voice, even though I speak Russian, not Yiddish. I only had occasion to speak Yiddish a few times. This insane government exiled a completely innocent Litvak from Slutzk, a worker, and he had a hard time with Russian. He was so funny. Really, rather common. He had brought along his phylacteries and prayed every morning. He knew nothing about the movement and only wanted to know when Hanukkah and Purim and Passover fell. There was no Jewish calendar. It was known that I was a rabbi's daughter and so people came to me with questions about religious matters."

"What happened to him?"

"He grew sick and went out like a candle."

"How many victims has the revolution already swallowed up?"

Mirale paused for a moment. "I don't want to argue with you; no matter what you may think, people must have food and clothing. A regime that can't take care of its people must be overthrown."

IV

Only the next day did it occur to Ezriel that the piece of sugar's tasting like chalk to Mirale was a symptom of illness. She must have typhus. It was impossible for him to take her to a hospital, because the police were searching for her, so she remained in the same small room in an iron bed. Ezriel was her doctor. Soon in delirium, she chattered in Russian, Polish, and Yiddish. She raved about having been sentenced to hang. Another woman who was being hanged with her had kept the noose from being tightened. Mirale leaped from her bed, determined to flee to the border. The Central Committee was expecting her. The success of a railroad strike in England was at stake. There was a spy in their midst who must be silenced. "I'll shoot him down like a dog!" Mirale screamed.

Comrades soon came to inquire after her illness. Though leeches had already gone out of style, doctors still relied upon bleeding. When the leeches were applied, Mirale suddenly asked: "What are they, capitalists?"

Ezriel told Olga nothing of what had happened. She arrived in Warsaw sunburned and angry. Why hadn't he come to Topolka on his days off? What had he been doing all alone in hot, dusty Warsaw? The way she spoke of her burdens, one might have thought she was working like an ox. Yet she intended to give a ball and had already set the date. She had invited all the landowners and officials in the district and had included Wallenberg's children. The ball would be expensive but would further Ezriel's career. She had all sorts of plans. A squire owned a forest not far from Topolka. They would obtain permission from him for their guests to hunt in his woods on the day before the ball. For the women, she would arrange an excursion on the Vistula. Natasha must meet young men. As for Olga, she was not going to spend her entire life behind a stove. Having settled in Topolka, they should make the most of it. She was full of enthusiasm and was furious because Ezriel reacted with indifference.

"I can't lead your sort of life," she announced. "I want to be a cosmopolitan, not a rabbi's wife."

Ezriel explained to her that the ball would cost hundreds of rubles and increase his debts, but Olga answered, "If you weren't so impractical, everything would be all right." She used the Yiddish word *batlan*, and enumerated half a dozen doctors who were rich, owned villas, bought their wives expensive pearls, and charged twenty-five rubles a visit.

"You may give ten balls if you like, but I'll neither pay for them nor attend them!"

"Is that your final word?"

"You can count on it."

"Well, no is no. But I have no intention of living in a convent."

She announced that she would sell her last piece of jewelry if necessary to pay for the ball. It suddenly occurred to Ezriel that she had chosen the eve of the Ninth Day of Ab for her party. It was a leap year and so the Ninth Day of Ab came late.

Ezriel had no choice. He had to tell Olga that Mirale was in Warsaw.

"Do you want to be arrested?" Olga cried out in anger.

"Shall I let my sister die?"

"There are other doctors in Warsaw. What do you know about typhus? You might do her harm."

Since Mirale's illness was approaching its crisis, Ezriel spent the night at her bedside. It was hot, but the window had to remain closed, covered by a curtain so that no light could be seen in the courtyard. The janitors were all informers and reported every trifle to the police. Mirale, covered by a feather quilt, lay weak and flushed, her eyes closed. Her hair had grown dry. She tossed, trembled, breathed laboriously. Ezriel wiped away her sweat. How helpless medicine was in such cases! How ironic it was to survive Siberia and later to perish because of some bacteria! Mirale, warring against the autocrats, was now battling inner forces that wanted to destroy her. War everywhere, war in the forests, in the city, in the field, in man's body. She wanted to free the peasants and the proletariat. Like their father, she campaigned against the company of Satan. But what would come after victory? Not redemption, not saints who benefited from the splendor of the Divine Glory, but lots of newspapers, magazines, theaters, cabarets. More railroads, more machines. . . . Did it pay to die for newspapers, theaters, machines? And would anyone remember what the Mirales had done? . . .

V

After her illness, Mirale was so weak she could not stand on her feet, and had to learn to walk all over again. It was not safe for her to remain in the room on Dzika Street. One of the Committee members of the second "Proletariat"—the authorities had liquidated the first—had a house near Falenica. Mirale was taken there and planned to stay through the holidays. The house belonged to a comrade, Jan Popielek, a machinist in a steammill in the Praga suburb.

Ezriel bought some especially nourishing food for Mirale and decided to bring it out himself. In the horse-drawn omnibus to Praga, he sat beside the window, looking out. Warsaw was full of dirt. A stench arose from the gutters. The farther one went from the center of the city, the more old-fashioned the buildings became. The houses in Praga were ancient. Even the people seemed to belong to another generation. Their clothes dated from the time of King Poniatowski. On benches, outdoors, cobblers worked on boots, wrinkled old women with white hair wandered about in torn shawls and wide aprons reaching to the tips of their shoes. Their paws extended, dogs crouched and yawned. Cats sat on low, mossy roofs. A paralytic, wearing thick socks instead of shoes, lounged on a bench near a fence. A church bell rang. A catafalque arrived from somewhere. A number of old women grouped themselves around it, made the sign of the cross, and whispered to one another.

Then Ezriel saw something so unusual that he could not believe his eyes. Not far from a factory, near a wooden lamppost, stood his daughter Zina speaking to a man in high boots and a cap. "I'm imagining it!" Ezriel said to himself. His bus came to a stop. Yes, it was Zina. Ezriel barely restrained himself from calling to her. Had she become a streetwalker? He felt himself grow red. He arose as if about to get off. Suddenly Ezriel understood: Zina was a member of the "Proletariat" group. He sat down again, dumfounded. He would have expected any nonsense from her, but not this. She was such an egotist. Why should the workers and peasants concern her? He asked himself how it could have happened that he had never even suspected her of joining the organization. To be so completely fooled! He felt ashamed for himself, for her, for Olga. Who knew what she might be keeping at home? She might have placed the whole family in danger!

He rode to his destination and left the package for Jan Popielek. Then he took a droshky home. Zina probably was no longer a virgin either. The comrades believed in free love. . . . He sat there dazed. She read Alfred de Musset and Baudelaire, admired Byron and Leopardi! Had all that been a pose? She had been in a dark mood the last few months, had attacked the suffragettes and educated women. But she had taken the courses she had planned to take, and spoken of becoming a nurse. She had found a pupil to tutor. One thing should have made him suspicious: she showed no interest in clothes and was content to wear Olga's discarded jackets and coats. What else should he have expected? His daughter barely knew the Hebrew alphabet. He had taught her everything, except Judaism. He himself had shown her how to escape one's heritage. At the gymnasium she had attended she had not liked the few Jewish pupils and had been proud of looking like a Gentile. . . . She had actually expressed hostility toward Jews on several occasions. And this was his daughter, the granddaughter of the Rabbi of Jampol. How had it happened? Ezriel had to laugh. Every week he read articles on education in the Hebrew magazines, and he had raised an ignoramus. The writers of the articles themselves did not give their children a Jewish education. They were all the same— the Hebrewists, the lovers of Zion, the radicals. Ezriel reminded himself of a saying in *The Best of Pearls:* "The children are the secrets in the hearts of their parents." The children testified to the hypocrisy of their fathers. . . .

Arriving home, he immediately went to Zina's room, but found it locked. He got the key, opened the door, and began to look through the bookcase. There was no trace of illegal literature. He searched in the drawers of the dresser and desk, even lifted the pillow on the bed. Suddenly her mattress seemed overstuffed. He lifted the sheet, found papers inside, hard objects. He felt like a policeman searching someone's house. He got a knife, tore the mattress open, and found it filled with pamphlets and handbills. Suddenly Ezriel spied a bundle wrapped in paper. It was so heavy he could barely lift it. Inside he found a gun and cartridges. It was the first time in Ezriel's life that he had touched such an instrument of destruction, and its weight astounded him. He didn't know how to handle it and was afraid it might go off. Sweat appeared on his forehead. What did one do with such a weapon? Where could one hide it? If he were caught with it, he would rot in jail or die on the gallows.

16 ⛪

I

On the eve of the Ninth Day of Ab, the huge, blazing sun was
beginning to sink behind banks of clouds that looked like
glowing coal. In Nowydwor and Zakroczym, the benches in
the Houses of Prayer had already been placed on their sides as
a symbol of mourning. In the menorah, only a single candle
burned. The last meal before the fast, bread with ashes and a
hard-boiled egg, was being prepared in Jewish homes. The
men and women would soon remove their boots and shoes and
remain in their stocking feet before reading the Book of Lam-
entations. But at Olga's, preparations were being made for a
ball. Many of the guests had arrived early that morning to
hunt in Squire Sadowski's forest. The women had gone row-
ing on the Vistula, which was as smooth as a mirror. In the
kitchen, food was being cooked in huge pots and kettles. Outdoors on a spit a whole pig was roasting. It had been slaughtered the day before, by Antony, one of the servants. Ducks
and geese were browning in the ovens. The cooks were preparing appetizers and desserts. There were odors of meat and
fish, chicken-fat dumplings and noodles, parsley and paprika,
cinnamon and saffron, pepper and cloves. Olga came in and
tasted each dish: one lacked salt, another spice, a third herbs.
The dining-room tables were already set with linen cloths and
napkins, silver, porcelain dishes, and crystal glasses. Decanters

and carafes, filled with wines and liqueurs, reflected the colors of the sunset. In the drawing room, everything had been readied for dancing. The musicians had tuned their instruments. The piano stood open. Ezriel had not come.

Olga did not dare to calculate the cost of her party, but at least the important guests were there—Wallenberg's daughters: Pani Malewska with her husband, and her younger sister, Pola, with her; a retired general dozed in a chair under a tree; a colonel in the artillery, the county natchalnik, the military natchalnik, the natchalnik of the post office, some officers, and nobles from the surrounding neighborhood, were out hunting in the woods; even a priest had come. In front of the house were britskas, phaetons, and several carriages. Coachmen and lackeys lounged about, talking and eyeing the peasant girls who were helping out in the kitchen. An old cow with a shrunken udder had been slaughtered. But other cows grazed in the pasture, twitching their tails. The poultry population of Topolka, however, had suffered almost complete decimation. The garbage trench behind the kitchen was full of the bloody heads, feet, wings, and innards of fowl and attracted hordes of flies. Although the sun had barely set on the horizon, a three-quarter moon accompanied by a bright star had appeared in the sky. As it grew dark, Olga began to worry about the hunters, who had not yet returned. However, they soon arrived with their booty: several rabbits, a pheasant, a few wild ducks. The dogs ran along wearily with lowered muzzles, several of them limping. The hunters carried their double-barreled shotguns like canes. Some stopped at the well to wash. Others went to their rooms to change. Natasha, who had made friends with a young lieutenant, sat with him on the balcony. They were poring over her autograph album, reading the verses that her girl friends and even boys had written in it. Although he had used the verse for all his girl acquaintances, the lieutenant pretended to think a moment, then wetting the tip of his pencil on his tongue, wrote:

*"Deep within me
I feel your gaze.
Your charm
disturbs my soul—
Graceful as a young doe,
you move away—
But what will I do
now you are gone?"*

Suddenly there was the sound of screaming. A boat had overturned in the Vistula. The women were drowning. There was a tumult among the men. The hunters threw down their guns and hurried to the shore. At the river, the men shed their uniforms and swam quickly to the boat. Luckily the water was not deep and everyone was rescued. Servants brought cognac and dry clothes to the shore. Some of the women laughed—others cried. There were guests who felt that the ball should be postponed, but the orchestra began to play and the fireworks were set off. Several officers shot their guns into the air. A kind of Bacchanalia ensued. Everyone got drunk. The dinner turned into bedlam, with some of the guests sitting, others standing. The orderlies, who had helped in the rescue, mingled with their superiors. One officer who had lost a boot danced about in his socks. The same women who earlier had filled the air with their screams now laughed hilariously. Ivanov, a military doctor, begged the guests to seat themselves at the table. Olga could barely control her tears. At last there was a semblance of order. Dr. Ivanov drank a toast to the hostess and everyone shouted "Hurrah" and "Vivat." After dinner there was more dancing in the salon.

Dr. Fyodor Petrovitch Ivanov danced with Olga. He was in his fifties, a giant, straight as a board, his hair gray at the temples, his face square. He had a snub nose and blue eyes that were set a bit too far apart. He wore a decoration seldom awarded to any but professional soldiers, for he had taken part in several expeditions to Middle Asia. He was born in the Urals and had been exiled to Poland because he had been involved in a duel with a high-ranking officer. Dr. Ivanov, a bachelor, had brought with him from Russia a woman companion. It was known in the area that, although he did not take bribes, Dr. Ivanov was lenient with the Jewish draftees, especially the young Hassidim with their sunken chests and curved spines. They were sure to receive the blue or white certificates of rejection from him.

In the years of Olga's mourning for Andrey, and later while she was living with Ezriel, who could not endure the sight of a strange man's arm around her waist, she had avoided dancing and had practically forgotten how. Besides, new dances had come into fashion. Nevertheless, she danced with Dr. Ivanov. He led her like a dancing master, guiding her attentively. He exuded strength and military discipline. Ezriel always transmitted his unrest to her, his complexities, his guilt feelings. Because of him, she had become nervous about everything. He had tried to restore her spiritually to a world to which she did not wish to return. After all the preparations and mishaps, it was relaxing to dance again, to allow herself to be led by someone who knew exactly how to conduct himself. A short distance away, Natasha was dancing with the lieutenant who had written in her album. How many times had she danced with him?

II

Despite its ill-fated beginning, the ball was a success and the guests danced until dawn. Olga had renewed relationships with old friends, received invitations, obtained innumerable compliments, from men and women alike. The Polish nobles, who usually became sullen in the company of Russians, had for the moment forgotten the old grudges. Olga had danced three times with Dr. Ivanov, more than was fitting, and he had suggested calling on her in Warsaw. The sun was already shining in the east when the last guest departed. Olga went up to her bedroom, fell upon the bed, and still in her ball gown, slept until eleven. As a small girl, she had fallen asleep in the same way on Passover nights after asking the four questions and drinking the traditional four goblets of wine.

The following day there was a great deal of packing and commotion in Topolka. Natasha and Kolia had to return to their respective gymnasiums, Misha to grammar school. It was necessary to clean up after the guests and to prepare for the trip home. Olga had various errands in Zakroczym. Only when she reached town did she realize that it was the Ninth Day of Ab. Having discarded their shoes as a symbol of mourning, Jews walked around in worn slippers and shabby capotes; boys aimed thorns at their elders' beards. The women went about unwashed and with saddened faces, dirty kerchiefs covering their heads. Through the open doors of the houses, Olga saw old Jewesses sitting on stools nodding over threnodies. Disheveled girls bustled about in the kitchens. Though the world had moved forward, in Zakroczym they were mourning a temple that had been destroyed two thousand years before. Many of the stores were closed; others did business but were half shuttered. Olga made her purchases and found that, despite the fact that it was a fast day, she still had to bargain so as not to be overcharged. From the back rooms there emerged little boys in feather-covered gaberdines. They had pale faces, untidy sidelocks, and soiled fringed garments. They stooped as if with age, and persecution already showed in their eyes. Through the open doors, unmade beds with their soiled linen were visible. There was a stench of rotting objects and chamber pots. Multitudes of flies buzzed over every dish of food. Dust covered everything. So this is the Judaism for which Ezriel yearns. He came from this and wishes to return to it! "But it's not for me!" Olga said to herself. "Not for me or my children!"

On the way back, Olga rode past a cemetery. She had forgotten the Jewish customs. Wailing women lay stretched out on the graves. Olga ordered her coachman to stop for a moment. Apparently there was a funeral in progress. A crowd of Jews, their heads bowed, were gathered around a grave. Someone was reciting Kaddish. She told the coachman to drive on. Flowers decorated the graves in Christian cemeteries; here everything was naked, sandy, desolately Asiatic. "I hate it, I hate it like death itself!" Olga murmured to herself. "I would rather die than return to this filth!"

Leaving Topolka was not a simple matter. It did not pay to hire a steward. There was an old peasant caretaker, but one could not depend upon him. Olga was afraid that the cows would not survive the winter, or that they would simply be slaughtered. The peasants were digging potatoes, but there could be no thought of selling them. The money Olga had invested brought her nothing. She was puzzled that she could have been so mistaken and blamed Ezriel. A man who does not know the right way himself confuses others. Topolka would not be a loss in other hands. If it were lived in year round, it might even be made to yield a profit. But when one had to worry about every ruble in Warsaw, one could not maintain such a property. Landowning was not for Jews. That was it. If someone like Dr. Ivanov owned Topolka, he would turn it into a paradise.

On the following day Olga, the children, and a maid seated themselves in a carriage. Behind them was a wagon containing their luggage. Once more they passed through Zakroczym. Jewesses sat on the porches of the houses darning socks. From the House of Worship the words of the Torah could be heard. A boy with long sidelocks, carrying a prayer book, walked by. Kolia pointed to him and said, "That's a Jew."

"Papa said I'm a Jew too," Misha said.

"That's right, you are."

"Why don't I have sidelocks like him?"

Natasha laughed. "Give yourself time."

"What is a Jew?"

"Judaism is a religion."

"Is it true that Jews are devils?"

Natasha and Kolia both laughed. Olga looked at them sternly. "It isn't true, Misha dear. Jews are people like everyone else."

"Why do the Jewish boys leave class when religion is taught?"

"Because the Jewish religion is different."

"What is the Jewish religion?"

"Oh, the same, only a little different."

"The Jews don't believe in God's son," Kolia interjected. "The Jews killed God."

"Can God be killed?"

"Stop this nonsense," Olga said, growing angry. "Children shouldn't speak about religion."

"Why not?"

Natasha smiled, but Olga saw that her mind was full of other things. The girl had fallen in love with the lieutenant who had written in her album.

"Well, it can't be helped. It happens to every woman." Olga had an odd sensation, as if in the last few weeks the ground beneath her had collapsed. The night before, she had suddenly awakened and had been unable to fall asleep again. A childish thought had occurred to her: a bed was only a pair of boards and how easy it would be to fall out! Olga knew she was being foolish, but in the dark the idea assumed an uncanny importance. She had climbed out of bed and placed chairs on either side of it. . . .

17

I

In mid-October, Shaindel died. A telegram had arrived stating that she had been taken ill. Ezriel went to see her at once. She had pneumonia in both lungs. Ezriel and the doctors at the institution did what they could, but it was impossible to save her. She died on the ninth day of her illness, and for the final five days of her life Ezriel sat by her bedside. Calman was unable to come to her funeral. He had been operated on for a rupture and was in the Jewish Hospital. Tsipele and Jochebed came to the town of Blonya, where Shaindel was buried. Jochebed looked like an old woman. Her daughter and two daughters-in-law had come with her. Kaile, the maid, accompanied Tsipele. During her illness, Shaindel had shown no signs of insanity. She had spoken rationally and groaned like a sane person. Her staring eyes reflected a fear of impending death. She made Ezriel promise to have Misha say Kaddish after her, but she never once mentioned Joziek or Zina. The day before she died, Shaindel asked Ezriel to recite the prayer of confession with her. He had no prayer book, but remembered the words of the daily prayer, "We have trespassed." He quoted the words to Shaindel and she repeated them after him, attempting to smite her breast with an emaciated hand. Shaindel knew by rote the prayer said before going to sleep and the one used for candle lighting. She lay in bed, mumbling the sacred words, dozing off, waking, and muttering them again. On the last day, a surgeon operated on her. He cut away a piece of her rib to draw the pus from her lungs. But it was too late. Shaindel opened her eyes and with her last breath said to Ezriel: "Did you have something to eat?"

The Burial Society in Blonya wanted three hundred rubles for a cemetery plot. Ezriel did not have that much money, but Tsipele, the rabbi's wife, pawned her earrings to help him. In Blonya, there were no followers of the Marshinov rabbi, and the society exacted a high price. Until the funeral, Shaindel's corpse, covered with a black cloth, was kept in a poorhouse. She was laid out on the floor, with her feet toward the door. At her head, which rested on a sparse bundle of straw, burned two candles in clay candleholders. The women from the Burial Society sat on a bench and sewed a shroud. The sheet out of which it was made was not cut with scissors but torn and basted with large stitches. The women quickly fashioned a pair of long drawers and a cowl. On the very stove where they heated the water with which to purify the corpse, the poorhouse women cooked groats for their children. The ceiling was as black as in a bathhouse. There were pallets of straw on the floor, and some cripples rested on them. After the cleansing, Shaindel was placed on a stretcher, and four men carried her to the cemetery, which was a long distance away. It had begun to snow. Jochebed was led by a daughter and a daughter-in-law. Tsipele supported herself on Kaile. Ezriel had wanted to bring Misha along, but the youngster happened to have a cold. The snow became heavier. From time to time the carriers halted, switched shoulders. At the cemetery, the grave-digger promptly began to dig the grave. Ezriel stood numbed. How long ago was it that he had become her bridegroom. He relived everything—the Simhath Torah when Shaindel had worn a gourd with candles and had pulled him by the sidelock and called: "I am the Queen of Jampol"; the writing of the articles of engagement at Calman's estate; the invitation to the in-laws, during which he and Mayer Joel had had a debate about a dibbuk; the wedding. It seemed only yesterday that it had all happened. But in this time Shaindel had managed to bear children, to become insane, to spend years in an asylum, and to die. Tsipele's sniffling was replaced by a choked weeping. Jochebed made old-womanish utterances in a wailing singsong: "Already, all finished!" she cried. "Cut down in her prime, woe unto us! She was the most beautiful in the family! She shone like the sun. Why did it happen? She was a pious woman, a sainted soul! Mother, you know that she is coming to you. Holy angels, guide her! She should not know punishment! She has already had hers. . . ." From time to time, Jochebed cast a murderous glance at Ezriel. She had remained angry with him, convinced that it was he, the heretic husband, who was responsible for Shaindel's death.

The gravedigger sighed and dug. The earth had already begun to freeze. A worm wriggled in the mud. Two planks were laid on the floor of the grave. Shaindel was lifted and placed between them. Then she was covered with earth. The gravedigger recited the passages from the Scriptures. Ezriel said the Kaddish. An earthen mound remained and snowflakes fell upon it. Several strange women had followed the funeral. Ezriel only now noticed them. They stood there, stooped, mumbling, wrapped in thick shawls, with clods of mud clinging to their shoes. Some wrung their hands, others thrust them out for alms. A crow, on the tip of a birch, looked out over the graves, over the tombstones, over the fence, into the white distance. Mrs. Shumkin, Shaindel's companion, was also there. She had limped the entire distance, leaning on a cane. She said to Ezriel: "You should know no more sorrow! . . ." and burst into tears. She had, apparently, become accustomed to Shaindel, to the asylum, to its personnel.

Customarily the seven days of mourning are observed at the locale of death. But neither Tsipele nor Jochebed were able to stay. The rabbi was ill and Tsipele did not want to leave him alone. The two sisters hired a sleigh and left for Marshinov. Ezriel returned to Warsaw. There were moments when he was inclined to believe in the immortality of the soul, but that ditch, those chunks of clay mixed with roots and earthworms, had severed the flimsy membrane of his faith. Where would Shaindel's soul go? Into the atmosphere? The worm was well off, born right in the grave. Ezriel's sorrow did not diminish after the funeral. A part of his life was in Shaindel's grave. He remembered her complaints that he was driving her to madness, when she first began to be ill. Perhaps if he had remained a proper Jew, she would still be alive and healthy. "Well, I'm full of sin and don't even have the will to save myself. . . ." Ezriel was debilitated through lack of sleep, and numb with grief, yet within him an imp argued: now he would no longer be burdened with the expenses of maintaining Shaindel and her companion. He would be able to repay the debts that had accumulated because of Topolka. His own thoughts disgusted him. He spat and said to himself: "Ghoul! . . ."

At home he was met with another tragedy. Olga, weeping, threw herself on his chest. For a moment he was surprised, thinking she was overcome by sympathy. Yet he knew that Shaindel's death could not have affected her so. He soon learned that her sorrow had nothing to do with Shaindel. Natasha, who was barely sixteen, had run away with the sublieutenant she had met at the ball. She had left a letter for her mother. Olga handed it to Ezriel. Natasha wrote that she loved Fyodor more than her own life and was going with him to the city where his regiment was stationed. She loved her mother, Ezriel, Kolia, Misha, even Malvina, the maid, but without Fyodor she could not take another breath. A moment without him was worse than death. . . . She asked her mother not to search for her and not to advise the police. She would marry Fyodor when they arrived at their destination. She was actually his wife already.

Natasha concluded her letter with a whole row of dots and dashes.

11

Through Dr. Ivanov, Olga learned that Fyodor had been assigned to a regiment somewhere in Tashkent. Olga could have had the young officer brought up on charges before a military court and gotten her underage daughter back by force. But she did nothing. The girl had disgraced her and was not the same Natasha as before. Olga wept. Natasha in her letter to her mother had promised to write, but many weeks had now passed without a word. Had she married her seducer? Was she dead or alive? Ezriel consoled Olga as best he could, but she would not be comforted. She had sacrificed herself for the girl. Was this her gratitude? It wasn't easy to hide the facts. Natasha's classmates came to inquire about her. Kolia cried because he missed his sister. Misha wanted to know where she had gone. Olga was compelled to find new excuses for the neighbors. Natasha had gone to a foreign school to finish her education. But what school? What was her address? The girls concocted a story that Natasha had been kidnapped and sold into white slavery in Buenos Aires. Olga telegraphed the garrison in Tashkent. There was no reply. She began to talk about going after Natasha. But supposing she found her? She could no longer live at home. She might even be pregnant, or infected with venereal disease. Nor could Olga leave Kolia and Misha alone. There was no one to take care of them. Olga had been prepared for the fact that Natasha would eventually marry, but the girl's elopement was a blow from which Olga was unable to recover. She considered her life finished; there was nothing left to hope for.

During the daytime, Ezriel was busy. His practice was not large, but he still worked both in the Bonifraten and in the Jewish Hospital. After Shaindel's death, his expenses had grown smaller, but he was still in debt. He owed several thousand rubles for Topolka. Olga began to practice economies in her housekeeping. Now that Zina had moved to a furnished room after quarreling with her father, and Natasha had eloped, the apartment seemed as if emptied by a plague. If anyone spoke, there was an echo. Olga compared herself to the father in Slowacki's poem, "The Father of the Plague Victims." Kolia was too old to play with Misha and wandered around like a lost soul. Olga trembled over him more than ever. Who could tell? Perhaps some dark force would snatch him away too? She became too attached to him and could no longer conceal her concern. Ezriel warned her that she would only cause damage to the child by such an attitude. Ezriel and Olga sat together over lunch like mourners. The maid brought the food in silently. Olga had lost her appetite. The large pots no longer seemed suitable for their small family.

At night, both Ezriel and Olga slept badly. They dozed off and awoke. The clock in the dining room seemed to tick more loudly than usual, chiming out the hours and half hours. Sounds that had previously gone unnoticed now bothered them: the trembling of the windowpanes in the wind, the squeaking of furniture, the footsteps of the tenants in the apartment above, the ringing of gate bells by late homecomers. Somewhere in a closet, under the floor, they heard a rustling. At first they suspected a mouse, but it wasn't a mouse, and no matter how much Ezriel and Olga racked their brains they could not figure out exactly where the sound came from. One could imagine it to be a time bomb that might explode at any moment, or some mysterious creature that had stolen in and was undermining the foundation of the house. Olga talked and talked. How could she go on living? She had lost all faith in the world. What use was Topolka now? With whom would she go there in the summertime? It seemed to her that behind her back everyone was laughing maliciously, talking about her, enjoying her disgrace. But was she guilty? Had she not raised Natasha properly? Topolka had brought her nothing but misfortune. If not for Topolka, Natasha would now be sleeping in the next room. Perhaps all this was a punishment from God? Or else Andrey had punished her because she had replaced him with another.

Olga also blamed Ezriel. His worrying and doubts were contagious and had disrupted the family.

For the hundredth time, Ezriel observed that misfortune drew people to religion and mysticism. Olga lay awake through the nights, seeking an answer. Were these afflictions her punishment for being converted? Although she had never been very devout, neither had she been a heretic. Only a year before meeting Andrey, she had still fasted on Yom Kippur. But when Andrey had been forced to become a Christian because of his position, how could she have remained Jewish? And did God care whether one worshipped Him in Russian or Hebrew? Was it possible that God actually sat in heaven and judged everyone? Even if it were so, she had suffered enough. Perhaps she should go to a fortune teller? She knew of a medium who foretold the future and helped find lost objects.

Although Olga in the past paid little attention to Ezriel's arguments, she was now eager for his opinion. Did he truly believe God wanted people to pray in Hebrew and wear earlocks? Who had heard God say this? Didn't all religions speak of God? Was it possible that God demanded something different from each race, each era? In the name of God people had hanged, slaughtered, burned others. How did Ezriel account for that? And what about animal sacrifices?

Ezriel explained that he neither believed in revelation nor had faith in religious traditions or dogma. Man must continuously seek God. The entire history of man was one great search for God. But in addition man must also serve God. When he ceased to serve God, he served tyrants. Undoubtedly Judaism had come closest in the search for God. Christianity and Islam were both products of Judaism. Jewish suffering had produced a spiritually superior type. For two thousand years the Jew had not been in power and had not carried a sword. Even the current endeavor of the Jews to return to the land of Israel was unique. In the passage of two thousand years, hundreds of nations had become assimilated into other cultures. But the Jews still struggled to return to the land of their ancestors. This fact alone proved that the Old Testament contained divine truths.

III

Natasha wrote from somewhere in Samarkand that she had broken with Fyodor. He had gone back on all his promises and refused to marry her. She would have perished long ago if a wealthy merchant, a widower, had not taken her in. He was not young, had married daughters himself, but Natasha intended to become his wife so that her child would have a father. Olga wept. So this was what had become of her little girl! The merchant wasn't even a Russian, and had an Asiatic name. Her little Natasha was pregnant with a bastard. At seventeen, she would become the stepmother of two women older than herself.

Ezriel did not even attempt to console her. He had his own troubles. Mirale was now ill with consumption. She had succeeded in getting out of the country to a sanatorium in Switzerland. Zina had disappeared; months had passed without a word from her. The number of his patients decreased and they refused to pay his former fees, as if sensing that his spirit had weakened. The banks demanded payments and interest on loans. At night, when he could not sleep, it seemed to him that he could almost feel the hands of destiny upon him. What was being demanded of him? Was he about to die? He felt that some further blow awaited him. At the Bonifraten Hospital, the chief doctor started an argument with him. It concerned a trifle, but they exchanged angry words out of all proportion to the incident. It became clear to Ezriel that the hospital authorities wanted to get rid of him and were only looking for an excuse to do so. But why? Was it the recent rise in anti-Semitism? There were only two Jewish doctors on the staff. In astonishment Ezriel saw his former friends becoming his enemies. Even the nurses grew insolent. What was happening? Had someone made a false accusation against him? He couldn't even defend himself or tell Olga about it. There was nothing to tell.

Ezriel waited. Perhaps he was imagining things. Had he developed a persecution complex? Intrigues had also started at the Jewish Hospital. Incidents occurred that could not reasonably be explained. Occasionally an insane patient would attack a doctor, but this now began to happen to Ezriel too frequently. The patients taunted him, threatened him. It seemed that the wishes of the sane were being turned into action by the insane. But what could be the explanation for such a turn of events? Was it chance? Was he himself unwittingly the cause? Did others see something in him that he did not see? Olga experienced similar torments. She complained that the storekeepers were becoming impudent to her. They let her wait while they served customers who had arrived later. They packed her purchases carelessly and overcharged her for the merchandise. Neighbors who had always exchanged salutations with her pretended not to see her. Even good-natured Kolia suffered. His fellow students beat him and called him insulting nicknames. The teachers gave him poor marks unfairly. To top it all, Misha became melancholic. Ezriel could not fit these facts into any sensible theory. He was still a believer in causality.

Olga began to indulge in all sorts of irrational conjectures: perhaps there was a curse on Topolka; perhaps Zina had cast a spell on her. Ezriel grew angry. Since when had she become so superstitious? But Olga did not cease talking, partly to him, partly to herself. How could Natasha have committed such an outrage? It was not in her character. And where had Olga's eyes been? Why had she permitted this Fyodor to seduce Natasha behind her back? No, the thing wasn't that simple. An Evil Eye had been cast upon her. The Jewesses of Zakroczym looked like witches. The old peasant women at Topolka had eyes like hawks. Had they sneaked some magical herbs into her food? Devils existed. She herself had seen a house haunted by an evil spirit. She had known a girl who had been cursed by her stepmother and had grown a mouth as crooked as a frog's. Olga thought of her own mother; perhaps her mother's spirit was offended with her. She had never lit a candle on the day of her death. Her mother had died in a leap year, and they had never known exactly when the anniversary fell. Suddenly Olga conceived a new idea. She accused Ezriel of denouncing her to the Rabbi of Marshinov and because of that the rabbi had cursed her. These saints were filled with hate and revenge.

Ezriel made fun of all this nonsense, but something of what she said remained with him. He observed, as he had many times before, that latent madness in the human brain always showed up in a crisis. Primeval fears had not vanished. There existed in everyone a hidden desire to worship idols, to perform black magic. The Book of Deuteronomy constantly warned against such dark propensities. Whoever its author was, he apparently knew that fatalism was the most profound malady of the soul.

Ezriel felt that he was on the brink of disaster. Perhaps it would be best to leave the city temporarily, or even forever—to go off somewhere. As the Talmud says: "To change one's place is to change one's luck." Ezriel thought of Palestine. Joziek was not religious but he had remained a Jew. Now he even wrote in Hebrew and signed his letters Uri Joseph. He had married a Jewish girl. His children would be educated in Hebrew schools. On the spur of the moment, Ezriel decided to visit Joziek. He would see his son and witness at first hand what was being done in Palestine. Suddenly Ezriel understood the reason for all the recent incidents. Providence expressed itself in events. The forces that moved the most distant stars and the tiniest microbes had ordered his departure. Like the patriarch Abraham, he had received the commandment: "Get thee out of thy country." He knew it would be impossible to make anyone, even Olga, understand his reasoning. Nevertheless, he did not doubt that he had found the only solution.

18 ⌂

Herr Nelke was the proprietor of a combined beer hall and restaurant on Fourteenth Street. A widower, he lived in the downstairs apartment of a house he owned on Tenth Street and Avenue B. He rented his upstairs apartment to Clara. She occupied three thickly carpeted rooms hung with tapestries on which were embroidered such German proverbs as: Rise early, Work diligently, Save money. There were also portraits of Herr Nelke's parents, both stout, he in a top hat and wearing side whiskers, she in a high coiffure with bangs. Herr Nelke himself had side whiskers and smoked an amberstemmed pipe with a porcelain bowl. On Sunday mornings, he attended the Lutheran church. When he returned home, he played a few old German songs on a zither. Later his guests arrived. They drank beer, ate the sauerbraten and dumplings prepared by the old servant, Frau Hanse, and conversed in thunderous voices. Each Sunday Clara feared a fight would break out among them. But it never did. They left early. In a corduroy jacket and gold-embroidered vest, Herr Nelke would stand in front of his house calling after them: *"Auf Wiedersehen, grüss Gott, danke schön."* Herr Nelke was both a devout Christian and a socialist. The disputes among his guests concerned articles in the German socialist newspaper. It was through an advertisement in this paper that Zipkin had found the apartment for Clara.

There wasn't a single Jew living in the neighborhood. The horse-drawn streetcar would bring Zipkin directly there. Felusia began to go to school. Herr Nelke's "dear departed wife" had left a spinet and Clara was permitted to use it. She also had kitchen privileges and for a small compensation received lunch from Frau Hanse. A milkman left milk at the door. Food was delivered from the grocery. A nearby butcher provided not only meat but also German veal sausages, ham, and knackwurst.

In the beginning, Alexander kept his promise and visited Clara twice weekly. In the interim Clara studied English at the public school, knit a jacket for Felusia, read Russian and Polish library books, and looked for bargains at the stores. Once in a while, just to pass the time, she took the El uptown, passing factories, billiard parlors, various shops, offices, restaurants, and dance halls. There were empty lots and unfinished buildings on some streets. In this scattered city that seemed to be growing in all directions, Clara thought everything unusual. Her fellow passengers wore outlandish clothes. The locomotive shrieked, the wheels screeched. It seemed to Clara that at any moment the train would plummet down onto the stores, stables, express wagons, the masses of people wandering through the cold, the snow, mud, and horse droppings. Here and there, she could see a Negro, a Chinese. Clara felt that everyone here had been exiled to a sort of American Siberia. Everybody hurried: the working men and women at their machines; screaming newsboys; pedestrians. Clara closed her eyes, letting herself be carried along. It was miraculous that she always returned in one piece from these trips.

Later that winter there was snow such as Clara had never seen before. It fell heavy as sand. The tracks of the streetcar that led to Zipkin's house were buried. As soon as the snow was shoveled away, another storm came, to be measured in inches by the newspapers. The days grew as dark as during an eclipse, the nights dense and black. The city was disease-ridden. Zipkin's wife and child became ill. He suddenly found himself with more patients than he could handle. Clara's disenchantment with America increased. There were no cafés where ladies could sit down and read. The theaters were far from where she lived. Clara had nothing in common with the neighboring German women. In the evenings, no light could brighten the city's murkiness. Clara's only consolation was an occasional letter from Sasha. But even these were delayed by storms. Alexander's visits brought her more anguish than pleasure. As soon as he entered he would announce that he couldn't stay long, nor could he eat the meal she had prepared. Despite his gifts to Felusia, he seemed to have little affection for her. After she retired to her room, he would drum with his fingers on the table and peer at his watch. Even his kisses and endearments were full of impatience.

No, this wasn't what Clara had dreamed of. This bustling New York wearied her more than Jampol. Numerous divertisements were available, exhibitions, balls, and dances, but a lady could go nowhere unescorted, especially when she knew little English. It might have been easier for her had she lived in a Jewish neighborhood. The Jewish immigrants amused themselves by attending the Yiddish theater, lectures, discussions, celebrations. Even in wintertime, the Jewish quarter was congested. People converged in groups outdoors, talking as if it were summer. There were employment offices, tea parlors, and cellar restaurants where home cooking was served while musicians played. Fraternal societies held meetings. The stores remained open late. Barrels of herring, sour pickles, sauerkraut stood in front of stores. Home-baked bread, buns, challah, bagels, poppy-seed rolls, and cakes were sold from pushcarts. In the delicatessen stores, people ate hot frankfurters and mustard. On East Broadway, the crowds streamed down the street in groups. They all seemed part of one family. Each ship from Europe brought socialists, bearded and long-haired revolutionaries who made speeches about the struggle for freedom. New "greenhorns" arrived daily from abroad. Every home had a room or two rented out. Every third housewife prepared homemade meals for boarders. Yeshivas and cabarets, kosher restaurants and travel agencies, wedding halls and matrimonial bureaus abounded. Prostitutes hailed men to their rooms—sextons called them to a quorum in the synagogue. In the shops, the workers sang both liturgical and socialist songs. In the evenings, boys and girls danced in the narrow, gaslit rooms. Everyday was a holiday. But Clara was not a part of it. She wandered about the snowy sidewalks alone. Not once did she pass Zipkin's house on East Broadway at night to see if the lights were on behind the curtains.

11

The cold hung on. Felusia had gone to visit a school friend. She was learning English rapidly and becoming Americanized. She was making every effort to rid herself of her Polish accent and even went so far as to mock her mother's halting English. Clara had gone out to shop one afternoon. She needed wool for a cap for Felusia and a Christmas present for Frau Hanse. In his last letter Sasha had asked his mother to send him a photograph. Clara needed other small items as well: a darning needle, underwear, garters, a feather for a hat. Clara put on her fox fur, warm overstockings under her galoshes, and thrust her hands inside a giant muff. She spent about half an hour in a large store on Grand Street, then she walked to a restaurant on Delancey Street, where she ordered a meal of tripe, consommé with groats, boiled beef, a piece of honeycake, and tea. She had found everything she wanted except the right kind of feather. She rummaged through hat stores and remnant stalls. Then she visited a photographer, who posed her in a carriage to which a wooden horse was harnessed. Usually Clara knew which streetcar to take home, but she was in an unfamiliar neighborhood. It was evening and it had grown colder. People walked rapidly, emitting vapor from their mouths and nostrils. Horses slipped on the ice and the teamsters shouted. Fire wagons went by in a blasting uproar. Clara stopped various people and asked for directions, but they all contradicted each other. She had come out on the Bowery and was advised to take the El. She climbed the stairs and waited for the train. The wind lifted her hat and she had to hold it by the brim with both hands. The cold penetrated her heavy clothing. Her forehead smarted, her nose felt wooden, and her eyes teared. There must have been an accident. She waited fifteen minutes and when no train arrived went down to the street again. She had to warm herself somewhere. Her hands were stiff. Her eyebrows prickled. The snowflakes on them made everything rainbow-colored. Suddenly Clara caught sight of a jewelry store. It was still open. She decided to go in and get warm. She might even purchase a trifle. A dense fog formed before her eyes. Men were standing behind counters under bright lights. One man was fussing with a jewelry box. Another was looking through a magnifying glass. Clara wanted to say something in English, but she seemed to have forgotten the little she had learned.

Suddenly she heard a familiar voice, speaking in Russian. "Do my eyes deceive me? Can it really be Clara Danielovna?"

Clara trembled. In the glare she saw a man with a black mustache, in an unbuttoned fur coat, a light suit, and a *papacha*, a Russian fur hat. Clara wiped her face with a handkerchief and said: "Yes, I am Clara Danielovna."

"Clara Danielovna!" the man cried. "If this is possible, then anything is! I recognized you! . . . What a coincidence! Can it be, madame, that you don't recognize me?" He clapped his hands together.

"My eyes are tearing from the cold. Who are you?"

"Sit down, Clara Danielovna, give me your packages. Oh, this is unbelievable! Mr. Schwartz, we will postpone our matter until tomorrow. But you look frozen. To see you here, of all places! I don't know whether you remember me: I'm Yasha Vinaver," he said suddenly in a lower tone.

Clara's heart leaped. Yes, she had recognized him. It was Yasha Vinaver, Mirkin's secretary. The man who had written that calumnious letter about her to Alexander. She glanced toward the door, ready to flee, but he had already taken her packages. He was much stouter, but it was the same man, the same square face, the same Mongolian eyes. His nose was as square as a wooden peg. He was, apparently, well off. He wore a gold watch chain on his vest and a ring on his finger. Clara seated herself on a chair. A young man brought her a glass of water. She drank it and thanked him. The cold began to recede from her hands and feet; her fingertips tingled. She placed her muff on the counter. The proprietor too spoke to her in Russian, and she explained that she had lost her way. He smiled sympathetically. "We are people, not animals. It could happen to anyone. Besides, you are a friend of Gospodin Vinaver."

"Clara Danielovna, God must have directed you here!" Yasha Vinaver said, bending over her. "Who could imagine that you were in New York? Suddenly a door opens and in you come. Like a vision. As I love God—a miracle! One of those things that cannot be foreseen. . . . Why were you wandering about in this blizzard? I beg you, Clara Danielovna, come with me to have some tea so that you can warm up. Then I will see you home. On a night like this, it's a tragedy to get lost."

Only now did Clara find her voice. "I'd like to go home. That's all."

"Well, where do you live? I'll get a cab for you. Ah, what a strange meeting. Such a coincidence!"

They went out into the street, but there wasn't a cab or sleigh in sight. Just then a streetcar appeared, headed east. Yasha Vinaver helped Clara in. He paid their fare, threw the tickets into the glass receptacle, and obtained two transfers.

Later they would have to take a streetcar going uptown. Clara sat down. Vinaver was still carrying her bundles.

"I believe you married that physician—what is his name?"

"No, I didn't marry him," Clara replied dryly.

"No? Then what are you doing in New York, if I may ask?—Ah, a foolish question. I'm really so surprised to see you that I talk nonsense. This is my fourth trip here on business. I deal in jewelry and fur. The jeweler in whose store we met is one of my customers. You know undoubtedly that Mirkin died?"

"Yes, I know."

"Lived, as they say, like a fool, and died like a fool. He was a decent man, but without sense. His wife is scum, she's still alive, I believe, and the children take after her. I used to argue with him: 'Boris Davidovich, come to your senses!' This business of chasing after women in his old age was not good for him. What did he need them for? And a man his age should have written a will, not left everything to his enemies and a fig to his friends . . . but man is foolish . . . well, may he rest in peace. He had his good side. And what about you, Clara Danielovna? You won't believe it, but I've been thinking of you lately. Where is she, I thought. What became of her? There was a terrible storm at sea when I was coming over. I was sure it was the end and then one thinks all kinds of things. Such an unexpected encounter! We will be getting off soon to change streetcars."

III

The other streetcar came promptly, and they got in. Clara wanted to return the money Vinaver had spent on her fare, but her purse lay buried somewhere in her muff and she couldn't get it out. What a strange situation: for years she had imagined revenging herself on this man who had ruined her life, and now he was escorting her, sitting beside her like a cavalier.

"Clara Danielovna, what became of your doctor? Did he get married?"

Clara felt a stabbing in her side. "Gospodin Vinaver, I am grateful to you for getting me home, but I am not the fool you imagine me to be."

Yasha Vinaver's face grew grave. "What do you mean? What are you talking about, Clara Danielovna?"

"Doctor Zipkin showed me the letter you wrote to him. I know your handwriting very well."

"What letter? What handwriting? I don't understand, Clara Danielovna."

"You understand very well. The letter you wrote from Paris to Alexander Zipkin. You maligned me, although you gained nothing by it."

"Really, Clara Danielovna, I don't know what you mean. There must be some misunderstanding. I never wrote any letter to Zipkin about you. You're confusing me with someone else."

"I'm not confusing you with anyone. There were times when I could have shot you or thrown acid in your face. But my anger is spent. When one grows older, one realizes that it doesn't pay to make too much of a fuss about anything. But you slandered me, Gospodin Vinaver, made an accusation just for the satisfaction of hurting me. Why?"

"Did what? When? Honestly, Clara Danielovna, I don't have the faintest idea—"

"Don't pretend to be a simpleton. You sent a letter to Alexander Zipkin telling him I was with Mirkin. I have the letter at home and it's in your handwriting. If you like, I'll show it to you. You even used indecent expressions. To me that piece of paper is an example of human baseness."

"No, no, no, I'm a victim of a false accusation. How can you be so sure that it is my handwriting? I'll tell you what we'll do. We'll go to the most reputed handwriting expert in New York and let him decide. If he says it's my handwriting, I'll pay a penalty of five thousand rubles. No, I'll do better, I'll jump off the Brooklyn Bridge. If you like, I'll make these statements before a notary. I won't leave the country until this matter is cleared up!"

"But, God in heaven, it's definitely your handwriting!"

"Let the professionals decide. I've committed sins, but I've never denounced anyone, particularly a woman. And where would I have gotten Zipkin's address? It all reminds me of the blood accusation of Damascus. I don't want to speak ill of the dead, but couldn't it have been Mirkin?"

"I know his handwriting."

"Well, the truth will out, as they say, like oil on the water. I'll stay here until I clear myself even if it takes months. Meanwhile, I swear to you by everything holy that I never wrote anything about you to anyone. I would have had to be not only a scoundrel but insane to have written such a letter."

"I don't understand."

"You don't understand, but you blame me. Is the letter signed by me?"

"No, it's anonymous."

"Anonymous? Then why pick on me—why not someone who would have been directly interested? After all, your business was with Boris Davidovich, not with me. It's true that sometimes your conduct did not seem correct to me, but I'm not God, nor am I, as the saying goes, God's Cossack. If I hadn't been discreet, who knows how many families would have been broken up. I am, as you know, a bachelor, and no one hears more about what goes on in family life. Partly because we know how to keep quiet. God, if I were to tell all the things I know! Believe me, Clara Danielovna, if you accused me of killing someone, I wouldn't feel as hurt. It is, pardon me, like spitting in my face!"

Clara sat without speaking for a while. "I don't know what to say," she finally stammered.

"I must see the letter tonight!"

"Very well. It's late, but come to my apartment. I have no intention of using the letter in any way."

"What do you mean, using? It's a question of honor. Duels are fought over things like this. There are wrongs a person can commit and still remain at peace with himself, and there are other deeds that make one's life worthless. Every person must retain his self-respect. I believe that Mirkin, with all due respect to him, forged my handwriting."

"Why should he have done that? I didn't try to deceive him. I told him quite frankly that everything was over between us and that I was going to Alexander. He even said that if I left he would follow me."

"Why didn't he? I knew that you were making a mistake, because Boris Davidovich had a big mouth. But it isn't in me to meddle in someone else's business. He seemed very confused in his last years. But why he should write such a libel is beyond me. Anyhow, I'm innocent. None of us will live forever. We'll all stand before God, and I don't want to, as the saying goes, carry someone else's sin in my satchel."

"If you're innocent, I apologize."

"No, that isn't enough! Near what street are we? Ah, we're only at Fourth Street. It's true that you were always nasty to me, but what can one do when one is looked down upon? I, too, have my pride. But I would never deliberately harm anyone."

Clara lowered her head. "I'm afraid I've made a terrible mistake!"

"Well, we'll soon see."

For a time they were both silent. Then Yasha Vinaver took out a cigar, placed it between his lips, held it there awhile, and withdrew it. "What actually happened, Clara Danielovna?"

"I lost everything."

"You had a daughter?"

"I still have her, thank God, she's here with me."

"And the doctor married?"

"Of course. What else should he have done after a letter like that?"

"Well, I'm not guilty. God is my witness. I have no wife or

children to swear on. But I did have a mother once and I swear
by her bones that I am innocent!"

"I believe you."

Clara covered her face with her muff.

IV

It disturbed Clara to take a strange man to her apartment at
this late hour. It was enough that Zipkin came to see her.
Herr Nelke and Frau Hanse knew that Dr. Zipkin was Felusia's
father. Vinaver's visit might arouse their suspicions. They
might even tell her to move out. Fortunately, Frau Hanse did
not open the kitchen door, as she customarily did when she
heard footsteps. Felusia was already asleep. Clara tiptoed into
the bedroom. The letter was in a dresser near the girl's bed.
Clara opened drawers in the dark, felt around for papers..

"God, the things that happen to me!" Clara thought. "For
years I've borne a grudge against someone without reason. If
he only knew what I had wished upon him! . . ." If not Vinaver, it had to be Mirkin who had tried to destroy her. But
why? Why were people always so hateful to her? Clara went
into the living room. Vinaver's fur coat and hat were lying on
the sofa. He was sitting at the table. Only now did Clara notice the gray at his temples and in his mustache. He had lost
half his hair. Yes, he too had aged. The light-colored English
suit and the pearl stickpin were of little help. Clara put the
letter down in front of him. He quickly took out a pair of
pince-nez and placed them on his nose. She stood off to one
side. He read, removed the glasses, held them awhile between
his fingers, then put them back. He drew an envelope from his
breast pocket and looked from it to the letter. Doesn't he recognize his own handwriting, Clara wondered. He stood up
and seemed to weigh both papers. Then he began to read the
letter again. An expression of astonished absorption spread
over his face.

"Well, what do you think, Gospodin Vinaver?"

"I don't know. I don't know anything yet."

"What do you mean?"

"It looks like my handwriting."

Clara barely kept from bursting into tears. "How is it possible that you don't remember what you did?"

"I don't understand. Clara Danielovna, I am a lost man!"

"Perhaps you didn't write it. How could you possibly have forgotten?"

"Look here, compare the handwriting. I swear to God I remember nothing. Unless someone forged my handwriting."

"Perhaps someone did?"

"Who? Boris Davidovich wasn't capable of it. I'll take it to a handwriting expert anyhow. This is unnatural."

And Yasha Vinaver again snatched up the envelope and the letter, wrinkled his nose, and stared at them. He moved closer to the lamp. For a while, he contracted his brows as if about to detect an error. But instead his face again reflected confusion and astonishment. He said: "If it was copied, it was the work of a master."

Clara moved a step closer. "No matter what it is, I see you regret it, and that satisfies me."

"It may satisfy you, my dear, but not me. When a person does something, he should remember what he did. But I don't remember anything. I swore by my mother's bones, and I would never knowingly have lied on such an oath."

"You simply forgot. One does many crazy things when one is young," Clara said, trying to justify his action.

"I wasn't so young. And why would I have done such a thing? Perhaps Mirkin dictated it to me? But I remember nothing, absolutely nothing. No, it can't be!" Yasha Vinaver's tone changed. "It's some kind of misunderstanding, a terrible thing. Truly, it's a mystery. Clara Danielovna, I am completely confused!"

"What is your father's name, Vinaver? Unfortunately, I've forgotten it."

"Moisey."

"Jacob Moiseyevitch, I see that you are an honest man, and I forgive you. It happens that sometimes we do a bad thing and it flees from our memory. I've suffered enough as a result of this piece of paper, and I don't want anyone else to suffer because of it."

"Yes, but how did it happen? It's entirely out of character for me. It's as if someone were to come to me and say that I'd cheated a widow. Clara Danielovna, the light isn't very good. Would you be kind enough to light another lamp or a candle?"

"Yes, but I don't think you'll solve anything."

"Do me a favor and light another lamp. This is terribly important to me."

"Very well. I'll light one, but don't be so upset. It was all fated. It was destined that my life be bitter. You were only the messenger. . . ."

"Please light the lamp."

Clara went to light a kerosene lamp. Her heart seemed to twist as she fussed with the wick, the disk, the globe. The lamp shook in her hand, the flame rising in its chimney. With a final effort she placed the lamp on the table. Yasha Vinaver again busied himself with the letter, then turned up the lamp wick, panted, and mumbled to himself. He burrowed in his vest, took out a jeweler's lens, and skillfully tucked it beneath his eyebrow. He stared stubbornly at the yellowed piece of paper with the experienced eye of a professional. For a while he remained motionless. Then he smiled, but instantly he grew grave again. For a moment Clara thought that perhaps this was not Yasha Vinaver, who had had a lot of hair and as far as she knew had been a man without conscience. This man was half bald.

v

Yasha Vinaver removed the loupe from beneath his eyebrow. His eye seemed changed. Clara was sitting opposite him.

"Clara Danielovna, I know everything now!"

"Yes?"

"This is   handwriting, but it is not my style. Boris Da-vidovich, may he rest in peace, must have dictated this letter to me, that's why I had forgotten it. He dictated thousands of letters to me. Clara Danielovna, come closer and I'll show you what I mean. No, stay where you are. I'll come to you. Each phrase is typical of him. The very first words: 'Esteemed Doc-tor, be informed that—' is not an expression I use. I call people by their names, not titles, and as far as I can remember, he wasn't even a doctor then, only a student. Read further on: 'Your beloved is a slut, reveling in Paris with a lover.' That's not my style. Absolutely not. He was fond of that word, 're-veling.' I never used it, nor the word 'slut.' Never! The entire sentence structure is incorrect. I don't claim to be especially educated. I only went as far as the fourth grade, but, as the saying goes, I've developed a style. Even if I were writing to a peasant, I wouldn't be vulgar. The pen is, to me, a holy thing. But here the language is uncouth. He must have dictated it to me with many other letters, perhaps at night, following a hard day, and I simply forgot it. See what it says here: 'She's behav-ing wantonly with others as well.' That is disgusting, the lan-guage of scum! Clara Danielovna, I could deny having had anything to do with this. One doesn't go to jail for this sort of thing. But it is a question of truth. I am as much responsible for this letter as I am for all the other inanities he made me write for him. In this case I was nothing more than the lackey you once called me in a letter to Mirkin."

"I called you a lackey?"

"Have you forgotten?"

"Absolutely."

"You see? One forgets. I happen to remember: 'What the pen writes, the ax cannot chop off!' I too was angry and hurt for a long time afterwards."

"I really don't remember."

"Yes, time tends to wipe out the things we do that are alien to our nature. Clara Danielovna, I have not been lying, although technically I did write the letter. It's the intent that matters. Let us read on: 'She writes passionate letters to you, but considers you a simpleton.' "

"No, don't read any more! I can see that you're right! I should have seen it immediately. He used that expression often."

"I'm glad you understand. It's really scandalous."

"Scandalous! He broke all his promises to me and ruined my life as well. And all this on the threshold of the grave. The fool."

"Yes, as I mentioned to you, Clara Danielovna, despite his cleverness, he was without insight. He came, may he forgive me, from a low-class background. His father was a blacksmith. Clara Danielovna, he died owing me wages. Some of his tricks would make your ears ring, but it's too late to discuss them."

"How late is it? I'll go down to the kitchen and make some tea."

"No, Clara Danielovna, I beg of you, don't bother."

"At least have some cookies or fruit."

"No, thank you. Why did he do it? In a way it's a compliment. He was jealous of you. But even if he didn't want something, he'd always spoil it for others. Once we went fishing. There was no sense taking the fish home and I suggested giving them to the boatman or throwing them back while they were still alive, but no. Later, he just left them on the beach. That's how bullheaded he was."

"Why did you say, 'Even if he didn't want something'? He wanted me very much. Too much. You know that quite well."

"I know nothing of the kind. If he had wanted you, then he could have had you."

"You know very well, Jacob Moiseyevitch, that Mirkin was impotent."

"Is that so? No, I didn't know it. I thought it was quite the opposite."

"What do you mean?"

"Well, this isn't fit for a lady to hear, but he was a lecher to the very end. I was compelled to witness his behavior."

"What did you see? Well, I'd better not ask."

"Clara Danielovna, I don't get involved in the affairs of others—on principle. And I keep my opinions to myself. The doctors had warned him against sexual excesses and against overeating. His heart was surrounded by fat, but he called them idiots. He was made of iron; he might have lived another ten years. As a boy, he had helped his father at the anvil. That was Boris Davidovich."

"That doesn't mean you know everything about him."

"The less I know, the better. God is merciful. . . . Clara Danielovna, what about you, if I may ask? Do you live alone?"

"Only with my daughter."

"Why is that?"

"Oh, I am a fool too. Everyone is a fool in his own way. Alexander married a Hungarian spinster. She simply bought him by helping him through the university. But I, foolishly enough, longed for him. Jacob Moiseyevitch, one mustn't judge, one dare not. If years ago someone had described to me the kind of woman I've become, I would have called her an idiot. I was deathly sick and thought my time had come. I wanted my Felusia to get to know her father. She used to ask about him. My son, Sasha, is, thank God, wealthy and respectable, my only source of comfort, unbelievably good to me. I told him my troubles, kept no secrets from him, and he said, 'Mother, go to New York!' I left him my apartment. He has a house in Jampol that is virtually a palace, but he has business in Warsaw. To be brief, I came to America and Alexander fell at my feet. He was unhappy with his wife, she did not understand him, and all the rest of it. I decided to wait it out here, and we see each other when he can tear himself away from his patients, and right now there's an epidemic of grippe. That's how it is."

"A bad situation, Clara Danielovna. You're still attractive. You deserve a better fate."

"Thanks for the compliment. But one gets what one deserves. I have no resentment against anyone but myself. What do you do?"

"Well, my situation is, as they say, a good one, but—one grows older."

"Wouldn't it be fine for women if men grew younger!"

"Well, if you can still joke, matters could be worse. It's when one is satisfied that the worm begins to gnaw. I live in Kiev, but I'm on the road most of the time. I'm a merchant of the First Guild. I have a warehouse in Kiev and numerous employees. A relative keeps house for me. After Mirkin's death I decided it was time to stop serving others and strike out on my own. He didn't leave me a penny, although for years he spoke about making me rich after his death. Anyhow, I was lucky. I went into businesses I knew nothing about, but I had, as they say, a little common sense. I've been all over Europe and even traveled to China, and in America they know Vinaver too, at least in trade circles. I'm staying at the Astor House with the millionaires. But one gets depressed—especially on this last trip across the Atlantic. I nearly went out of my mind."

VI

"Why did you never marry?" Clara asked.

Yasha Vinaver smiled. "The old question. I happen to be distantly related to Boris Mirkin, may he rest in paradise. I began to work for him when I was still young and we had many adventures together. He would always say: 'Don't get married. Take me as an example of what happens.' His wife was a real witch. In those days he was still living with her, and I had a close view of family life. He was having an affair with a druggist's wife and it was really funny. 'Every woman has her price,' he assured me, and his words have stayed with me. He always insisted that it was best to have an affair with a married woman, and that's how it turned out for me. Often I doubted my success, but how does the saying go: 'Even a rabbi's wife will listen.' I remember one incident with the wife of a lumber merchant. She behaved very affectionately toward him. She used to drape her shawl across his shoulders and, when he coughed, bring him hot water to soak his feet. A handsome female. The merchant and I did business together and we were neighbors. When the merchant had to make one of his trips to Vilna, his wife packed for him, putting in all sorts of medicines and a jar of raspberries. I stood at the window and watched as he seated himself in the britska and she fondly kissed him goodbye. Suddenly my door opened. She came in without even knocking. 'Jacob Moiseyevitch,' she said, 'kiss me!' Those were her words! I could scarcely believe my ears. She burned like a flame—"

Clara raised her brows. "There are all kinds of people."

"Well, such experiences make one lose one's faith. Meanwhile, the years went by. I traveled with Mirkin and shared his life. You couldn't drag a lady through that kind of muck. Family life was impossible for me. Now I'm not young any more. A woman my own age doesn't attract me, and a young woman would deceive me as sure as that lamp stands on the table. And why not? As long as they don't believe in God, why should young blood deny itself? And what would I do while traveling? You should see how our traveling salesmen behave. Still, they demand faithfulness from their wives."

"Well, if that's how it is, you mustn't complain."

"Right. But at times loneliness overcomes me. I work, travel, run around, but for whom? I don't know why, but the sea makes me melancholy. The waves roll and rush, but where to? Usually I make friends, but on this voyage everyone was seasick, especially the women. Suddenly I had the most profound feeling of depression! I wanted to jump into the sea."

"Why?"

"Well, I don't know. Moods accumulate storms of their own."

"I understand. How long will you be here?"

"Several weeks."

"How do you spend your time?"

"Quite well. But I'm often unhappy. Clara Danielovna, what's the sense of your life here?"

"Who knows?"

"Why not let me take you to the theater or a concert? After all, your doctor isn't free every evening."

"No, he isn't. He has his family. I could go out sometimes, but I don't understand English."

"They have something here called vaudeville. There are also cabarets where ladies may go."

"Yes? Well, it's possible. I held an unreasonable grudge against you."

"When does your doctor come?"

"No definite time, that's the trouble. But we don't have a contract saying that I must sit here and wait. When he finds me, he finds me—if he doesn't, he doesn't. You said you wanted to jump into the ocean. You're a man and can go anywhere. I sit here as in a dungeon, and at times I feel like laughing. I've imprisoned myself just so that he can drop in for a couple of hours. But why am I telling you all this?"

"I'm your friend."

"Friendship. Love. They're words. Everyone is out for himself. First I hated you and now I'm baring my soul to you. I can't quarrel with Mirkin. He's dead."

"Do you believe in another world, Clara Danielovna?"

"I don't know, Jacob Moiseyevitch. Why?"

"One has thoughts. For example, what possibly could the soul of Boris Davidovich be doing in heaven?"

"Perhaps chasing women there too?"

"Most likely. Well, I'll be going."

"Thanks very much, Jacob Moiseyevitch, for bringing me home. You saved my life."

"Well, it wasn't that bad. Perhaps it was ordained in heaven that we should meet here and clear things up."

"Why do you keep talking about heaven? You're still a young man. You'll stay on earth for a long time."

"Who can tell? No one knows what tomorrow will bring. Both my parents died young. There was a time when a man my age was considered old. I always remember my grandfather with a white beard, but when he died he was barely sixty. At times I regret not having a child."

"Well, for a man it's never too late."

"Oh, yes, it is. Good night, Clara Danielovna, forgive me. I'll come to see you."

"Yes, do come. You'll be a welcome guest."

"I wouldn't want to meet your doctor, though."

"Why are you afraid of him? He's not a jealous type. Besides, if you come during the day, you'll never meet him."

"Good night. Thank you."

Yasha Vinaver left. Clara held a lamp at the head of the stairs to light his way down. Returning to the apartment, she paced back and forth across the living room, casting two shadows. A huge head wobbled on the ceiling. For a while Clara shrugged her shoulders as if arguing with someone. "Well, what shall I do now? I'm not even sleepy, I'll read this book." But she had no desire to read it. "Why the devil don't I get old?" She wished Zipkin would suddenly walk in. She would tease him about Yasha Vinaver. But Zipkin was at home yawning. Well, all was lost. Let old age come and put an end to everything! . . . Clara went to the window. The night outside was frozen desolate. Stars blinked in the sky. Clara began to pray: "Dear God, I've had enough. . . ."

19

I

At winter's end, Clara returned to Warsaw, taking Felusia with her. Zipkin had come less and less often. Clara had yearned for Sasha, for her apartment on Berg Street, for Warsaw itself. The idea of sitting on Tenth Street and straining her eyesight for Alexander had become ever more painful. Instead of being helped by the American climate, Clara had suffered from stomach trouble, from her gall bladder, from nerves. Neither Zipkin nor the other doctors in New York whom she had consulted had been able to help her. Why then should she stay and be sick in a strange country? In the few weeks that Clara and Yasha Vinaver had seen each other, a friendship had developed between them. Yasha Vinaver had taken her out among people, to theaters and restaurants. He had insisted that he loved her, even proposed marriage. Clara had made it clear that she loved only Alexander. But the contrast between Yasha Vinaver's and Alexander's behavior toward her made her realize how badly Zipkin had been treating her. He had never had a free evening for her, had never brought a friend to visit, had kept her isolated like some cheap mistress to whom one came when one needed her.

Yasha Vinaver, who had returned to Russia, assailed Clara with letters. He intended opening a Warsaw branch of his business and made numerous suggestions. Would she accept some light employment with him and agree to live with him? He was not Mirkin, did not need ten women at once, nor did he want a woman merely for her body, but for companionship.

While still in America, Clara had tried to play Yasha Vinaver against Alexander. She had shown him Vinaver's letters, but this had only estranged Alexander further. He had insulted her and for two weeks had not come to see her at all.

Once, when Clara had berated him for being so cold toward Felusia, Zipkin had replied: "I don't know whether she's my child or not."

"You should be ashamed."

"You lived with two men!"

There had been only one way out—to go away. When Alexander heard her decision, he tried to dissuade her, but Clara said: "You can always come to Warsaw."

No, this was no longer the same Alexander. He was older, stouter, more settled. He had grown fond of his wife and was apparently afraid of her. He always came to Clara in a state of fear, and actually they had not spent a night together all winter. He remained distant toward Felusia. Clara went to a travel agency and bought a ticket for Felusia. She had left Warsaw on the night before Rosh Hashana. Her ship was scheduled to sail from New York on the last day of Passover. She was accustomed to traveling now, had packed her things and was ready. She had written to Louisa, who had settled in a town near the Canadian border, but she had received no reply. She said goodbye to Herr Nelke and Frau Hanse, her only acquaintances in New York beside the milkman, the grocery-man, and the Chinese laundryman. In the final days before her departure, Zipkin had tried to convince her that she was being foolish, that he would act better toward her. He had even promised to take a trip with her during the summer and take care of Felusia, but Clara replied: "If you love us, leave her and come with us."

"You know that's impossible," Zipkin had said.

At two o'clock in the afternoon, Clara had been driven to the ship. Alexander came later to see her off, carrying packages, one for her and one for Felusia. The ship wasn't due to leave for several hours and Alexander came to Clara's stateroom. Felusia, who had learned English, had made friends with an American girl of her age on the ship, and the girls had gone out on deck.

Alexander sat down and said to Clara: "We haven't really had a chance to talk things over."

"If you have anything to say, there's still time."

"Clara, I love you."

"*Mazel tov*. If this is love, then I'm the rebbetzin of Jampol."

"Clara, you don't understand me."

"What is there to understand? You had your chance."

"Clara, I'm in a dilemma."

"I've heard everything. You couldn't even manage to come to see me once a week."

"Clara, everything is too complicated."

"Why do you tremble so before her? The ship will be sailing soon. If you have anything to say—then say it. If not—"

"Clara, I'll miss you."

"Well, then, get to know the taste of it. I lived twelve blocks away from you. It was I who came to you, not the other way around. Now if you come to Warsaw, I'll know that I'm worth something."

"It may happen."

"Then come quickly or it may be too late . . ."

Zipkin lit a cigarette. "Clara, why did you take this trip with Mirkin?"

"That story has a white beard."

"I can't forget it. Each time I think of it, I feel sick."

"Well, feel sick then. What's happened can't be changed."

"You don't even regret it."

"No, I don't regret it. I regret nothing."

"Now you're going to that informer, Yasha Vinaver."

"What of it? You've earned it. I'll tell you something, Alexander: I don't love that man. He disgusts me physically. But if he is persistent, I'll live with him."

"In that case, you're a real whore."

"Yes, that's what I am. Keep well, Alexander, have a happy family life."

"I'm going."

"Enjoy your sleigh ride."

"You're the worst woman I've ever met."

"Thanks for the compliment!"

"I don't intend to desert an honorable woman for filth!"

"Stay with her! I don't envy you the pleasure."

"*Adieu*, slut!"

"*Adieu*, idiot!"

Zipkin, white-faced, turned to leave.

"Come here, give me a kiss," she said.

"No, you bitch. . . ."

Alexander ran out of the cabin. He left his cane behind and did not return for it. Clara took it to Europe . . .

11

The trip back was as calm as the first crossing had been stormy. The days were balmy. When the ship stopped in England, Clara went ashore for several hours. A Jewish woman, a Mrs. Bachrach, with whom she had become friendly and who was on her way back to Berlin, accompanied Clara. She showered Clara with attention and even proposed that Clara come to live in her house. She had two rich sons in America and told Clara that she was returning to Germany because she wanted to be buried alongside her late husband when she died. How peculiarly humans behaved! Clara told this elderly woman everything, all her secrets, all her sins. The woman consoled her. Yes, Clara had made mistakes, but Dr. Zipkin seemed a heartless man. He deserved losing her. He would come to Warsaw and fall at her feet. Clara was astonished at herself. It

wasn't like her to place her trust in strangers. She had always
been so proud. Suddenly she was possessed by a feeling of
freedom. She smiled, and was smiled at. In all the years during
which Clara had been involved with Grisha, Calman, Zipkin,
and Mirkin, she had been filled with fury, with a bitterness
that she had almost been able to taste. She had only been concerned that no one get the best of her. Now that was all gone.
Her table companions grew friendly with her. How had it all
come about—had a curse finally been lifted from her, Clara
wondered.

Between meals, Clara sat in a deck chair. She was as usual
knitting something for Felusia and would occasionally glance
at the waves, the sky, the blue edge of the horizon. Who could
tell? Perhaps she would not have suffered so much had she
known how to be good from the beginning. She should never
have dared to say all those terrible things to Calman, or to be
unfaithful to him! And since she had been in love with Alexander—what had been the sense in becoming involved with
Mirkin? In all her cleverness, she had disregarded life's most
elementary rule: do not unto others what you would not have
others do unto you. But would she be able to redeem herself?
Should she return to America, throw herself at Alexander's
feet, and tell him she could not live without him? Sasha had
written that his father was ill. Perhaps she should find some
charitable work to do: helping the sick or the poor? Clara's
thoughts swayed in rhythm with the waves. Often Madame
Bachrach sat with her, embroidering a tablecloth and relating
stories of her relatives, of doctors, of spas. Once such family
tales would have bored Clara. But now she was interested in
Madame Bachrach's anecdotes and even asked for more details.

As far as Felusia was concerned, Clara both loved her and
had begun to feel some resentment toward her. On the one
hand, Felusia kissed and comforted Clara when her mother
complained about her life. On the other hand, she often be-

haved as if she were ashamed of her. She had begun to criticize
her mother's taste in clothes and tell her to lower her voice when
she spoke. When Clara attempted to express herself in English,
Felusia would make fun of both her Russian accent and her
mistakes in grammar. Although it had not occurred to her to
use the word, she indicated in many ways that she thought her
mother was vulgar. It seemed heartless that Felusia cared little
about her father, whom she might never see again. The only
person she really missed was Louisa. She said quite openly that
she would have liked to remain in America with her former
governess and Monsieur Dujacques. She now disliked Russia
and insisted that she would not go back to a Russian gymnasium. She would go only to an English school in Warsaw or, if
that was not possible, to a French one. Young as she was, she
had managed to make the acquaintance on shipboard of passengers who ignored Clara and who seemed to express an unspoken pity that so refined a young lady should be saddled
with such a mother. Sometimes it seemed to Clara that the girl
could hardly wait for the time when she would be old enough
to free herself from her mother entirely and live her own life.

The days went by one way or another, but at night Clara
was afraid. She had left Alexander. With every beat and turn
of the engines, she was leaving him farther behind, and she
already longed for him. He had been an infrequent visitor in
New York, but he had come. What would she do in Warsaw?
Yasha Vinaver? She no longer had the strength for a new
affair. She couldn't love another man. Why had she fled?
Why hadn't she bought a house in New York and tried to
settle down? Alexander apparently was beaten too, or he
would not have abused her so. It was possible that he had been
telling the truth: he really was in a dilemma. . . . "Well, if
worse comes to worse," she thought, "I'll go back. I'll spend
some time in Warsaw, see Sasha, then leave again. . . ."

The ship docked in Hamburg. Clara stayed the night there
and then took the train to Berlin, where she spent three days

with Frau Bachrach before taking the express to Warsaw. She had grown accustomed to spending nights in trains. Felusia lay down in their compartment. Clara dozed sitting up. The clacking wheels helped her sleep. She heard the locomotive whistle through her dreams. At the border, the customs officials searched her baggage, turned everything upside down, but Clara wasn't troubled by it and did not argue when she had to pay duty. She hadn't spent much money in America. She still had a considerable part of the two thousand rubles Sasha had given her. In the morning, the train arrived at the Vienna depot in Warsaw. Clara thought she could detect the special odor of Warsaw air. Everywhere there were swarms of soldiers, officers, policemen. All Warsaw seemed to be one big barrack. She rode in a droshky to Berg Street. When she opened the door of her apartment, she realized with astonishment that her son had not used it during her six months' absence. The windows were closed, the shades lowered, the beds made. A thick coat of dust lay over everything. Before going away Clara had left everything in order, but in her last-minute hurry she had dropped some orange peel in a basket in the kitchen. She now recognized the peelings, which had become blackened and shriveled as if petrified. Clara began to laugh and cry at the same time. She had crossed oceans, been happy, had suffered, and here lay the orange peelings from a piece of fruit she had eaten just before leaving. Felusia began to sneeze from the dust. The janitress came up, complaining that Pan Jacoby had never come and that she had not had a key to let herself in to clean up. The woman went up to the sink, turned on the faucet, and after a snort, a thin stream of water black with rust began to trickle out.

III

Sasha came to see his mother, but his visit was short. On that very day, he was scheduled to leave on a trip. He told her that his father was sick, had a growth in his stomach. Sasha scarcely spoke a word to Felusia. He had never recognized her as his sister. She was the daughter of his one-time tutor, a disgrace to the family. Clara went to Krochmalna Street to see Calman, but he was away at his daughter's in Marshinov. The rabbi's days were numbered, Calman's cleaning woman told her. Warsaw became too warm and Clara would have liked to be in the country but could not decide on a place to go. Yasha Vinaver had unexpectedly gone to St. Petersburg, and she was annoyed with Sasha, who had become gross and sullen and had developed a brutal look about his mouth. His hair was as wildly wavy as that of a gypsy, and he told his mother depraved stories about his affairs with officers' wives, about a quarrel with a colonel, and about a Russian woman whom he had made pregnant. He talked like a libertine, boasting of his conquests and deceptions.

Clara tried to admonish him, but he laughed and replied: "You have no right to preach morality!"

"But I am devoted to you."

"The devil won't take me, and if he does, it'll be too bad."

"Remember that my life depends on you!"

"Each of us is responsible for himself. . . ."

Before leaving, Sasha again showed Clara his pistol and bragged what a skillful shot he was, always hitting the mark. She was in a state of anxiety when he left. "What has happened?" she asked herself. "Have I developed scruples or has he become baser?" His showing off revolted her. When he told her about cheating the officers who were commissioned to buy provisions for the soldiers, Clara had been disgusted. How casually he had related it! Didn't he understand that soldiers worked hard when training and needed to eat their fill? What else did a soldier have besides his bowl of groats and portion of meat? Clara reminded herself that her own father had sold inferior products. She recalled arguing with Calman when he had been her guest in Jampol: "Everyone cheats . . . if you

want to be a saint, Reb Calmanke, donate a scroll to the synagogue as my Aunt Sprintza did. In business, one can't be softhearted . . ."

"How could I have been so callous?" Clara wondered. "Oh,
it's all my fault—Sasha drank evil with my milk. . . ."

Several days passed. Clara had been in touch with an employment agency and they had promised to send her a maid,
but so far no girl had appeared. In the evening, Clara prepared
supper for Felusia and herself.

Clara paced back and forth across the parlor. Zipkin's cane
hung on a hook in the corridor, and Clara suddenly felt like
examining it. Perhaps there was some inscription on it that she
had overlooked, or it might be hollow, containing a letter or a
piece of jewelry. . . . She walked toward the corridor but
froze after two steps. A strong pain shot through her left
breast. Her heart, her arm, her shoulder ached. Her breath
failed. She struggled back to the parlor, fell into a chair, and
remained sitting there, stricken, unable even to cry out. Her
head drooped to the left, her brow grew moist. She wanted to
call Felusia but the girl would be frightened, and besides her
voice seemed muffled. "Well, it's the end! God in heaven, take
pity on me!" Clara prayed. She had pills for such an emergency, but they were in a drawer of her nighttable. The pains
grew even more piercing. Suddenly the doorbell rang. It rang
again and again. Someone began to knock on the door. Clara
tried to rise, but her knees buckled. The slightest movement
cut her like a knife. She heard voices. There seemed to be two
people outside. The knocking and the ringing grew even
stronger. Suddenly Clara saw Felusia. The girl had been
awakened and stood there in her nightgown and barefoot.

"Mama!"

"Open the door," Clara groaned. "I'm sick."

"Mama! Mama!"

"Quickly! They will help me . . ."

Felusia went to the door. Clara saw the woman from the

employment agency and a stout Gentile woman with straw-like hair and red cheeks.

Felusia began to scream: "A doctor! A doctor!"

"A miracle!" Clara thought. Clara mumbled to the agency woman, asking for the pills from her nighttable. The maid brought a glass of water and the agency woman ran to fetch a doctor. The maid suggested an ambulance, but Clara managed a protest: "I don't want to die in a hospital," she said.

A doctor, who happened to live nearby, gave Clara a sedative, and she was carried to bed. The pains were no longer so sharp, but she was left with an unusual fatigue, a feeling of heaviness, as if her body had already become a dead weight. "At least I will die in bed, not in a chair," Clara thought. She no longer feared death. If only her suffering would end! . . .

A few days passed. Once, when Clara opened her eyes, Sasha stood beside her. An old man with a dirty white beard, a sallow face, long sidelocks, thick brows, entered. "Did they bring me a rabbi?" Clara wondered. Then she recognized him. It was Calman! She was overcome with joy. "He has forgiven me! . . ."

She whispered to Sasha that he would be left without a mother. . . . Then she grew silent. God above, she had already experienced all this. She remembered everything: Calman's serge capote, the fringes of his sash, Sasha's summer suit, the medicine bottles, and the half orange on the chair. She had witnessed this whole scene in her dream that night, years ago, when she had returned to her aunt's apartment after her first night with Zipkin. . . . A mystical sadness overcame Clara. Her final days had been revealed to her years before. The half orange glistened in the afternoon sun, red as wine, and the seeds and veins could be seen exactly as in her vision.

Calman leaned over her, and his braided sidelocks hung down in a straight line. "How are you?"

Clara replied: "Well, as you see. . . ."

IV

That evening, Clara thought the end had come. But days went by and she lived. Sasha arranged a consultation of specialists. Besides the maid, Clara was attended by a nurse, who had worked at the Jewish Hospital. Once again Clara began to feel better, regained her appetite, even wanted to get up, but the doctors forbade it. With the fountain pen she had obtained in America, Clara wrote a letter to Sabina, Alexander's first wife, and sent it off with the maid. For a long time Clara had wanted to see her. After all, her son, Kubuś, was Felusia's brother. Perhaps, since Clara was on her deathbed, Sabina might relent and come to visit her. Sabina had married a wealthy merchant, a Pan Max Mandelberg, and probably no longer felt so embittered. Clara begged Sabina to come, to forget past wrongs, and if possible bring Kubuś along. Felusia was his sister, and a sister is a sister whether the rabbi has spoken the marriage vows or not. Clara signed her letter: "The dying one." The maid returned with the reply that Sabina would come the following day.

Before writing to Sabina, Clara had sent a lengthy cablegram to Zipkin, informing him of her heart attack and asking him to take Felusia into his home and if possible to come for her. A telegram was also sent to Kiev to Yasha Vinaver's office, with a request that it be forwarded to him wherever he was. Within twenty-four hours she received Vinaver's wired reply that he was on his way to Warsaw. Somehow or other, Esther Eisner, Zipkin's old friend, had learned of Clara's illness. Although her hair was almost all gray now, Esther was still associated with the radicals. The second "Proletariat" had been all but liquidated. The two new socialist parties were at war with each other. Innumerable groups and programs had emerged, but it was difficult to tell what exactly each one represented. One heard the names Mendelsohn, Rosa Luxemburg, Dashinski. Jewish labor circles wanted to form a separate party. In Russia, the social democrats had moved even further away from the Narodowolces, or Social Revolutionists, as they now called themselves. But Esther Eisner, still a seamstress, remained on good terms with all factions. She came with her friend Carola and a large bouquet of flowers. Clara would meet Esther on the street occasionally and had once ordered a dress from her. Tears came to Clara's eyes when Esther arrived with the flowers. She remembered their first meeting years before in Mirale's room, the same night she had met Zipkin.

"Now all good things come . . ." Clara said.

Calman recited prayers in her behalf in the House of Prayer. He had sent a note to the rabbi in Marshinov asking him to pray for Clara and came each day to inquire after her health. Zipkin sent a cablegram saying that he would take the first available ship. Yasha Vinaver had interrupted all his business transactions to come to her. He had brought not only flowers but a whole basket of delicacies that Clara was not permitted to eat: caviar, lox, pastry, liqueurs, and delicatessen. Now in midsummer, he wore a white suit, white shoes, and a panama hat he had bought in New York. His many-colored tie had a diamond stickpin in it.

Kneeling at Clara's bedside, he cried: "Clara Danielovna, you must get well, do you hear?"

"Well, if I must, I must," Clara replied sarcastically.

"Clara Danielovna, you're still young. You still have many years before you."

"God will be interested to learn that."

He seated himself beside Clara's bed and refused to stir. He told her about his travels, his business affairs, his acquaintances; he spoke of his longing for her. Sasha came, and Clara introduced Jacob Moiseyevitch to him.

Vinaver said: "You do not know, Sergei Calmanovitch, what a mother you have!"

"I know, I know. But tell me."

"A remarkable woman. Still beautiful. Clever as the day is long."

"Do you hear, Mother?"

"Yes, I hear. Where were all these words before?"

The doctor forbade Clara to talk too much, and Yasha Vinaver finally left her and seated himself in the living room. He had tipped the maid and the nurse, and they served him tea. He tried to be on fatherly terms with Felusia, but the girl stayed in her room most of the time. She seemed to regard her mother's illness as sham, another of her self-indulgent whims. Vinaver smoked a fat cigar and conversed with Esther Eisner and Carola. They said that the current regime could not last very long, that the people would revolt.

Yasha Vinaver remarked: "One company of Cossacks will scatter them like mice."

"Louis XVI had an army too."

"Cossacks are not Frenchmen. When they charge on horseback with bared sabers, heads roll . . ."

"Why is that idea so pleasing to you, Gospodin Vinaver?"

"Who says it pleases me? But we must have order. The Bible says that when a slave gets to be king the earth trembles."

"Let it tremble, then," Esther Eisner interrupted, "and let all the tyrants tremble too . . . Their end is coming . . ."

"As far as I'm concerned, let it come. I'm no tyrant. But have you ever traveled on a train whose staff was about to strike?"

"It wasn't very comfortable, was it? It will get even less comfortable, Gospodin Vinaver. This is only the beginning . . ."

The front doorbell rang. Sabina had kept her word and had come to see Clara, although a day later than she had promised, and without Kubuś.

V

Each day Clara grew stronger. She wanted to get up, but the doctor said the danger was not over. Yasha Vinaver had put aside all his business affairs. He spent entire days with Clara, and even nights, sleeping on a sofa. He read the newspapers to her, discussed politics, the theater, opera, the stock exchange, advised her to buy certain shares that would bring big dividends and that he had bought for himself. Frequently he suggested that she come to live with him as soon as she recovered. He would marry her, adopt Felusia. Clara kept saying it was too late, but, deep within her, hope stirred. Who could tell? People did get better. She was not yet old. Wasn't it a miracle that even in her present state a man was in love with her? A man like him could get a young woman. Yasha Vinaver chattered away and Clara closed her eyes. This endless babbling was his greatest defect. She was not accustomed to a man who said whatever came into his head. He was like a gossipy woman. But, in her condition, could she be fussy? She began to regret having summoned Zipkin, who would only upset her. But she did want to see him, and it was good to know that he was willing to come.

Sabina turned out to be sour as vinegar, exactly as Zipkin had described her years before. Dried out and wrinkled, she wore expensive clothes, but they looked as if they had come from a trash heap. Sabina asked all kinds of questions about Alexander but said things to Clara that almost caused her another attack. How could she be sure that Felusia was Alexander's daughter and not that other man's, what was his name? And even if she was Alexander's, Kubuś was a legitimate child, who could not be brought face-to-face with a bastard sister. Besides, he also had a brother in America. As far as Sabina was concerned, that chapter of her life was closed, and she did not want to reopen it. Sabina would not even sit down. She stood there in her hat and gloves, poured out her quota of bitterness, and left, without even a good wish for Clara's recovery. It seemed to Clara that the woman had left a bad odor behind her. She told the maid to scent the air with perfumed paper.

Visitors continued to come. Celina, her aunt's daughter and her father's widow, came from Jampol with two of her girls, Clara's half sisters. Celina had not remarried after Daniel Kaminer's death. She and her numerous children were supported by Sasha and partly by the rent she obtained from Daniel Kaminer's house. The time when Celina spent half her days lolling in bed had passed. She had lost her looks. She had become a sloppy matron, with sad, weary eyes, and legs swollen from difficult childbirths. The girls were pretty but starved-looking and unmannerly. Clara was afraid they would soil her apartment. They sat in the kitchen, eating. The maid complained that they snatched food from the pots. Although Celina had come to ask about Clara's health, she did nothing but complain about herself and her family. She opened Clara's pantry, her dresser, handled each dress, petticoat, and pair of drawers. She rummaged about, asking Clara whether she still needed this or that article of clothing. Clara presented her with everything. Celina took the delicacies Yasha Vinaver had brought, storing several small items in her bosom, the rest in a basket. Clara said jokingly that perhaps Celina should leave quickly, because sometimes the one who comes for an inheritance ends up paying for the funeral.

Celina took offense. "But it's all for your little brothers and sisters."

"Yes, I know."

Celina and the two girls left with armfuls of packages. Even though she reproached herself, Clara felt that these children of her father's old age were strangers to her. In her will, Clara had left everything to Felusia. The maid, this time, needed no orders to use scented paper. She washed and scrubbed after the Jampol visitors, and even complained that the girls had left fleas behind.

Sasha had to return to Jampol on business. After several

days, Yasha Vinaver too began to attend to business transactions. He tol   lara that he would have to go abroad but had postponed his departure until she was fully recovered.

"I don't know what you see in me, Jacob Moiseyevitch," Clara said, "a sick woman, no longer young."

"What am I, a stripling?"

"You could get a young girl."

"I've had young girls."

"Or are you so anxious to become a widower?"

One evening, when the twilight remained blue for a long time and Clara's face was bathed in shadows, Yasha Vinaver confessed that he had fallen in love with her when she had been with Mirkin. Mirkin had maligned her, had related that she had indulged in all kinds of perversions. It had made Yasha hostile, but these feelings had soon been transformed into a kind of love. During the nights she had been with Mirkin, Yasha had been unable to sleep. He had tried to convey his feelings to her, but she had answered disdainfully. She had constantly emphasized the fact that he was a mere valet. Once, when all three of them had been playing cards, Clara referred to the jacks as valets, lackeys, bootpolishers, and glanced slyly at him. It had made him so furious he had sworn he would have his revenge by making her fall in love with him and become his mistress.

"Was that why you sent the letter?"

"No, Boris Davidovich dictated it to me."

"No, Jacob Moiseyevitch, Mirkin did not dictate it to you. You wrote it yourself."

"No, really."

"Yes, you did."

"I swear before God I didn't."

"Well, all's fair in love and war," Clara quoted.

For a long while they were both silent. Then Clara said: "If I recover, I'll let you have your revenge."

VI

But Clara grew worse. She suffered a second attack, and the doctors said they could do nothing more. She sank into a lethargy. She lay there sleepy, spent, unaware of the passage of time. She dreamed incomprehensible dreams. She was, at the same time, in Warsaw and America; she was both on a train and on a ship. The train rode into the ship and Clara wondered: "How is it possible? Unless tracks had been laid across the water. It must be a dream. I must be close to death. . . ." It occurred to Clara that she must say confession, but she forgot about it immediately afterwards. She remembered that Alexander was coming to see her and imagined herself with him. It seemed that he had made a mistake. Instead of coming to Warsaw, he had gone to India, or China, among savage tribes who were ruled by a khan, a caliph, a maharaja. The sultan wanted to marry his daughter to Alexander, but Alexander refused. He was determined to come to Clara. He had bribed the eunuchs, but someone had informed on him—Yasha Vinaver! Now Clara would no longer believe anything he said. But how could Alexander be in India when he was sitting at her bedside talking to her? He still acted as though he were devoted to her. "Well, it is all in my head."

"My dear lady, let me apply this compress!"

The nurse placed a cold compress on Clara's breast and gave her some medicine. Clara could barely swallow it, she had lost all desire for food and drink. What she had just experienced was strange indeed. She had lifted her right hand, but it remained lying on the bedspread as if there were two of them. The hand she had raised was transparent; through it she could see the clock, the upholstery of the chair, the tiles of the oven. "Did I imagine it, or was it really so?" She looked down and could see through the blanket. "Has anyone noticed what is happening to me?" No. She had two heads now, and the second one tore itself free from the first. Was her body a shell for another body? Or was this her soul? "Am I dying? Or am I dead?" No, she was still alive. The maid lit a lamp. Jacob Moiseyevitch was reading a newspaper. "What wa he reading with such absorption? Why was he so preoccupied?" Clara felt like laughing. She had often dreamed she was flying. But this was no dream. For a while she left her bed, the same Clara, but weightless and ethereal. She soared across the room. God above, she floated over the table, the chair, over Jacob Moiseyevitch. She glanced at the paper and read the headline. Someone had resigned. She hovered over Jacob Moiseyevitch and his newspaper, then over the headboard of her own bed. Great God, she was staring at herself. She looked down and saw another Clara, sick and pale. Was the other dead? No, she still breathed. But Clara had no pity for her. She was as indifferent to her as one is to cut-off hair or the trimmings of fingernails. The other person was not herself, but a garment. Could she fly farther? Clara moved and passed through the wall. She was outdoors and saw windows, balconies, trees. There was a moon in the sky. She wanted to go farther but something held her back. Pulled by an irresistible force, she penetrated the walls back into the room and was drawn into the other Clara, who was gasping for air.

"Clara! Dearest! Clarachke! . . . Mama! . . . "

Clara opened an eye. "What is it?"

Something was being poured into her mouth. Something damp was being rubbed across her brow. She smelled the odor of vinegar and valerian drops. Clara realized that she was dying but had been brought back to life. For a long while she lay quietly, feeling all the pains and pressures of the flesh: the bloated belly, the paralyzed intestines, the heavy heart that beat weakly as if it were hanging by a thread. She wanted to speak, but the words would not form. She gathered her strength and murmured: "What's in the paper?"

Everyone grew quiet, exchanged glances. Then Jacob Moiseyevitch replied: "The Minister of the Interior has resigned."

"Show me the paper."

Again those present looked at one another. Jacob Moiseyevitch brought the paper and held it for Clara to see. She recognized the huge letters and the name. She had not been
dreaming. She had actually soared over Jacob Moiseyevitch's
head and the *Courier Paranny*. She smiled, closed her eyes, and
felt lighthearted. Suddenly she opened them again. Next to
the stove, figures materialized. She recognized them all: her
father, mother, aunt, grandparents. Their faces glowed, casting a light that dimmed the lamp on the table. A joy such as
she had never seen before exuded from them. Who was that—
Grisha? They looked as if they wanted to approach her, but
could not. Clara wanted to speak to them, but her lips would
not open. She shut her eyes, but they were still there. Her
mother smiled. "How is it possible that I can be her child?"
Clara asked herself. "She is still so young. I could be her
mother . . . "

That night Clara died. She wasn't laid on the floor, as is
customary among the pious, but was left in her bed. Her face
was covered with a silken shawl, and two candles were lit. Felusia had been sent to stay with the wife of an officer, a friend
of Sasha's. The whole night through, Jacob Moiseyevitch sat at
the bedside of the dead woman. He found Clara's prayer book
and after some hesitation began to recite Psalms in the melodic
chant he had heard as a child from his father, mother, grandfather. He did not understand Hebrew, but somehow the words
themselves had substance. From time to time he lifted the
cover from Clara's face. Did she know he was sitting there?
Did she hear his voice?

As hour after hour went by, the corpse became less and less
Clara. The nose grew longer and acquired a Semitic curve, as
if during her lifetime Clara had been able to keep it in check.
The mouth fell open and Jacob Moiseyevitch was no longer
able to close it. An eye opened and the pupil within looked out
blindly. It was no longer Clara but a shape, a fragment of eternity.

20

Summer passed, and autumn, and winter settled on Warsaw.
The city was progressing—it already had electricity. Soon, it
was said, it would be possible to telephone from Warsaw to
Lodz, or even all the way to St. Petersburg or Paris. News of
technological discoveries appeared almost daily in the press.
But, in spite of all the achievements, Warsaw was still knee-
deep in mud, full of ragged, hungry people. Many additional
houses had been built, entire streets rose from the ground, and
the congestion grew worse. Families huddled in damp, dark
basement rooms, and rents kept going up. The liberal Dr.
Marian Zawacki had published a series of articles in a popular
medical journal in which he cited statistics showing that,
thanks to industry and new developments in medicine and hy-
giene, Poland's population had grown to a point where there
were more mouths than bread. With the exception of the current year, in which the population growth had, uncharacteris-
tically, fallen off slightly, if it should continue at the same rate
there would be a permanent crisis—in short, hunger. Reminding his readers of the Malthusian law, Dr. Zawacki called on
Russia, too, to throw off its medieval superstitions and give
some serious thought to birth control, as England, France, and
all the civilized countries had done. A Catholic journal
promptly published an article attacking not only Dr. Zawacki

but all liberals, suffragettes, socialists, and atheists. And for good measure, the writer included the rich Jews who took up every new cause and tried to foist Western European decadence on Poland.

Through one of the vagaries of fate, while Dr. Zawacki was occupying himself with this polemic, a tragedy was taking place in his own home that he would surely have called medieval. Felicia's brother, Lucian, who had been living with the Zawackis for several months, had suddenly disappeared. He left the house one afternoon in early October and never returned. Felicia had worried and wept for several days before she finally notified the police. Their search was futile. She advertised in the Warsaw newspapers, but nobody responded. In utter desperation, she finally visited a clairvoyant and medium, a woman called Pani Chmielska. Pani Chmielska attempted to call up Lucian's spirit and, when it would not come forth, came to the conclusion that he was not yet "on the other side." After consulting a crystal ball, she announced that Felicia's brother was alive. He was living either in Warsaw or in its vicinity and would return to her. To convince Felicia, she called forth the spirits of Count and Countess Jampolski, who assured their unhappy daughter that Lucian was indeed alive but was enmeshed in a love affair from which, with God's help, he would presently untangle himself. The medium had drawn all the curtains, then seated herself at a table with Felicia and gone into a trance. The voice that had come out of the darkness through some horn or tube was not Chmielska's but a man's. It was the voice of an old Polish general who had fallen at the Kosciusko uprising. During the séance, Felicia was aware of a cool wind passing over her. Something or someone touched her neck and patted her cheek. She had no doubt whatever that Chmielska had actually made contact with spirits. What troubled her was the propriety of consulting such a person. Should she have come? Wasn't the Chmielska woman a kind of witch? The church denounced spiritualists and their ilk in the strongest terms and called them agents of the devil. Marian, on the other hand, laughed at them, dismissed them as charlatans. Felicia decided to say nothing about the visit either to her husband or to her confessor. It was the first time she had ever withheld a sin from the priest, and she was tormented by pangs of conscience. She again began to suffer from insomnia.

Lucian's disappearance had its effect on the children as well. Wladzio, who was preparing to enter medical school the following semester, complained that the newspaper stories about his father were making things difficult for him and that he was being snubbed by the more aristocratic student groups. He now spoke of going away to study in Krakow, or even in France. It was widely known in Warsaw that his mother was Jewish and his father had served a prison term for murder. One student had even discovered the name of Wladzio's grandfather, Calman Jacoby, and had taunted him to the point where Wladzio challenged him to a duel. Only the last-minute intervention of other students had averted what would have been certain bloodshed. The boy was heard to say he would be relieved if his father never returned.

Lucian's daughter, Marisia, had grown fond of her Tatuś. He kissed her, fondled her, brought her presents. Now she had settled into a mood of despondency. She had grown silent, morose, and cried in her sleep. Oddly enough, Janina, too, had changed since Lucian's abrupt departure. She and Marisia had shared a bedroom, but now it was as if a black cat had run between them. Janina moved into a tiny back room, though it was unheated. The only one not too deeply concerned about Lucian's disappearance was Dr. Marian Zawacki. Lucian, he said flatly, was a psychopath, a maniac, a criminal, and it would be better for the entire family if he kept away. While living at the house he had never lifted a finger. All he had done was to jabber, boast, sleep, and stuff himself. Marian had given him a manuscript to copy, but Lucian had never got beyond the first page. The fact that his children had turned out decent and hard-working, Dr. Zawacki took as convincing refutation of the claims for heredity made by some scientists. In his own household, three children were being reared who belied the myth of heredity and offered solid support to the case for environment and education.

Dr. Zawacki had been taking on a steadily increasing burden of work. He kept regular office hours at home, was associated with two hospitals, and made outside calls in his carriage. He wrote medical papers, contributed to an encyclopedia, had written a book, and was active in numerous associations. The lamp in his study was seldom turned off before two in the morning. He had been considered for a professorship at Warsaw University but had ruined his chances because of his liberal opinions. Nevertheless, he was still held in high esteem. He had several times attended the Governor-General at his palace. He was personal physician to many members of the Polish aristocracy on the highest level. Marian Zawacki, the son of a shoemaker from the Old City, had come far. Felicia, his wife, was aging and had long since lost her feminine appeal, but Marian Zawacki was still in love with this wilted woman. She was as devoted to him as a mother. She was an excellent housekeeper. Their adopted children afforded him as much joy as if they had been his own—more, perhaps, because he did not worry about them so much.

One night when Dr. Zawacki was at work on an article on the pathology of the heart, he heard soft footsteps outside his study door and then a knock. It was Janina, wearing slippers and a robe over a long nightgown. Zawacki looked at her in surprise.

"Not asleep yet?"

"I'm sick, Father."

"What's the matter?"

"My heart."

"Your heart? How do you know it's your heart? Because you live in a doctor's house?"

"It's beating."

"It's supposed to beat. Come over here."

He held the stethoscope against her breast. "You're healthy as a cow," he growled. "Go to bed."

11

Janina was in her senior year at the gymnasium and was due to graduate the following summer. But suddenly she began to get low grades. She had begun her studies late. The other students called her "matka," mother, because she had once blurted out that she intended to have twelve children when she married. The teachers often joked with her too. To the teachers, she was Panna Janina, the oldest girl in the class, set apart from the younger girls by her high bosom and wide hips. A peasant's daughter, she had never taken readily to studying. Now she seemed to have lost all incentive to learn. Felicia talked about getting her a tutor. Zawacki called her into his office one evening to test her on trigonometry. The girl had no idea of the difference between a sine and a cosine. He took a sheet of paper and a pencil and had her bring her compass and slide rule. Quickly he drew angles, lines, and figures, all the while chiding Janina with mock ferocity. Soon he was denouncing the entire Russian educational system, and his anger became genuine. In Western Europe, educators were working ceaselessly to modernize teaching methods, to make learning more practical, more accessible, more inviting—whereas in Poland hardly anyone was even aware there had once lived a man named Pestalozzi. Zawacki showed Janina how simple these mathematical concepts were in essence. Sine, cosine, tangent, and cotangent were not some weird abracadabra but expressed values and relationships that a child of eight could understand.

As Zawacki warmed to his theme, his voice rose and Janina's face turned redder. She was uncertain how much of his criticism was directed at her personally, and she had to struggle to hold back her tears. He can help me, she thought. Should I tell him the truth? He was shorter than she, but this smallish man with the creases in his forehead and the two clumps of gray hair around his pate had money, power, knowledge, wisdom, while she had nothing but a thick head and was, in addition, sinful. She had lost her innocence. She had given herself to Lucian, her father's murderer. And this was the third month that she had missed her period. Oh, she had betrayed everyone: God the Merciful, her blessed father, the good, noble people who had taken her in, Marisia, Wladzio, everyone. There was only one way out for her—death. No, she would not tell him, Janina decided; better perish. She picked up the papers and instruments with trembling hands and returned to her room. Her feet felt like two blocks of wood, so heavy she could barely lift them. At the threshhold she stumbled, nearly fell. Had he noticed anything? Did he have an inkling? "Oh, God, let death come to me! Let it come now! Deliver me from this shame!" In her room she collapsed on the bed. "What has Lucian done to me?" she moaned. "What has he done? Far better if he had sent me where my father is! I deserve this punishment. Death is too good for me. I should be cut to pieces and have vinegar poured on the wounds. At least if I had enough courage to go to confession —but I can't. I can't. I contaminate my soul, the Church, Holy Communion." Janina had a small bottle of iodine she had bought at the chemist's. But was this enough to poison herself? Maybe she should hang herself? Or perhaps she should go up to the attic—where she had committed the sin— and throw herself out the window? But no—why sully the street with her bloody remains? And why put the Zawackis to the expense of buying her a coffin and paying for her burial? The best thing would be to throw herself into the Vistula. There the fish would eat her, and then her soul would go to hell.

She was sobbing silently and she put a towel over the pillow so as not to wet it. Yes, she must do it, before the Vistula froze over. Should she leave a letter? Should the Zawackis know who was responsible? And what of her own family? She had a mother, sisters, brothers, and they were all so proud of the education she was getting and of the fine house in which she was being reared. And—what of him? Where was Lucian? Did he ever think of her? Was he sorry? No. Men like him did not suffer from the pangs of conscience; they bragged about their conquests. Sleeping with her, he had said things about her father—she didn't remember the exact words—but he had seemed to be boasting! Could anyone imagine such monstrous behavior? And who would believe that a girl like Janina could stoop to such debauchery! Embracing her father's murderer, listening to his evil words as he defiled her body! Kissing the lips that blasphemed God, man, everything holy. Was there a more debased person in the whole world? Lucifer himself could not conjure up anything more heinous.

Her weeping became convulsive and she put her fist in her mouth to keep the noise from penetrating to the other rooms. Gradually it subsided and her tears dried. She lay in the dark, silent, tense. The details of the "courtship" came back to her in a rush: the way he had kissed her in the corridor, whispered compliments, bitten her earlobes; the alluring stories he had related, all calculated to inflame desire—about the uprising, the apaches of Paris, about Stachowa, Kasia, Bobrowska; about Miriam Lieba, his Jewish wife who had died in Otwock. Gradually, she had let herself be won over. Then he had promised he would take her to California, Corsica, on ocean voyages; they would start a new life, a new family. He had brought her to a state in which she could think only of stealing every possible minute to spend with him. She resorted to outrageous ruses as easily as if she had been born a cheat. She had taken risks that she now saw were insane, such as going to bed with him in an upstairs room, the door of which did not close properly, while Felicia was entertaining guests in the salon. She had been seized by a whore's lust. And what was she now? Was she any better? If anything, she was worse. And afterwards, when she had begun to reproach herself— and him—he had simply left without a word. He must surely be prowling around Tamki with Wojciech Kulak's fine friends, probably carrying on with ten other women. Or, who knows? He might have gone back to Bobrowska, especially since Kasia was there too.

All at once Janina remembered something. The day before Lucian left, he had been reading a newspaper in the attic—and she remembered him saying, "So the old dog finally croaked." He was referring to Cybulski, Bobrowska's lover. She was sure she remembered Lucian mentioning that the old director had been living with those two. In that case there might be an address in the paper. A hazy plan, born of desperation, was taking shape in Janina's mind, one of those straws a drowning person clutches at. It occurred to her that the newspaper must still be upstairs, because the little room had not been touched since then. She sat up, listening, holding her breath. Even though she was about to end her life, she wanted to see him just once more, to say to him the things she had been saying in her mind a hundred times a day.

III

Before leaving for gymnasium in the morning, Janina told Felicia she was going to visit her own family that evening. Felicia was somewhat surprised because Janina usually went to visit them on Saturdays, but she made no objection. Felicia was well aware that the girl was suffering, but attributed it to her poor grades. In school that day Janina did not hear a single lecture. The graduation certificate which once had seemed so important had lost all value. The wisdom, the knowledge the professors were attempting to impart seemed so remote! One of them with gray sideburns and a red face was lecturing on logic, explaining something called a syllogism. To help the class remember the rules, he recited a short Latin verse, one word of which remained in Janina's mind—Barbara. What had Barbara to do with it, she wondered. At recess Janina slipped into a toilet to avoid talking to the other girls. Two girls went into an adjoining compartment together and Janina could hear them tittering, saying dirty words, she imagined. Well, they could do that, they were still virgins. . . . She left right after her last lecture, not waiting for Marisia, who was in a lower class. The gymnasium was on Marshalkovsky, and Janina headed toward Swiętokrzyska. From there, by way of Bagno and Panska, she would come out on Iron Street.

Janina had found the newspaper, and Cybulski's obituary notice had the address she was looking for. In recent weeks, the item said, the deceased had been living at the home of a friend, Elzbieta Bobrowska, widow of the actor, Vicenty Bobrowski, who had appeared in a number of character roles under Cybulski's direction. Janina set out to find Lucian.

It was still daylight when Janina left school, but the winter twilight descended rapidly. It had rained in the morning, but in the afternoon it grew cold and the rain had turned into sharp snow, thin as needles. The sky, hanging low over the tin roofs, was a rusty yellow, and the snow came down in gusts as big as blankets. On Swiętokrzyska, a man busied himself with a small portable stove. He was selling baked potatoes, a sure harbinger of winter. A tiny trail of smoke was struggling to escape from the little chimney. Porters stopped to warm their hands. Their eyes had the fixed dullness of those with nothing left to hope for. An old washerwoman came into view, stumbling under an enormous bundle of wash. It was hard to see how she could keep from falling under such a load. "I'm not the only one," Janina thought. "Others are suffering too. Why hadn't that occurred to me before?" She looked around for someone to give alms to, but the beggars seemed to be avoiding the outdoors because of the weather. If only there were a church where one could kneel before a holy figure! Janina began speaking to God. Words, phrases she had heard from Felicia came to her lips: "Oh, Thou, who art full of compassion! Thou seest my sorrow, Thou knowest my weeping heart! True, I have sinned, but I was bewitched, blinded . . . Holy Mother, what am I to do?"

The snow grew drier. The snowlike needles landing on Janina's fur collar no longer dissolved but clung to it, forming a white ridge around her neck. The street had emptied out. Janina was now walking on crackling, salty whiteness. Around her, everything had turned white: the sidewalks, the balconies, the chimneys. A Jew with a snow-covered black beard passed by. Wearing a long caftan and broad boots, he was pushing his way through the driving snow. Where could he be going? To his church, she was sure—whatever they called it. He must pray too. In a small shop behind a counter sat an old Jewess with a bonnet on her head, knitting a sock, her fingers deftly working the four needles. Did she know her good fortune? She had a husband, and her children were legal, not bastards; she had no need of examinations or matriculation. A tall man appeared from nowhere carrying a pole with a flickering flame on top of it—the lamplighter? Or was he an angel bringing fire from heaven? The street sloped sharply at this point. Janina passed a cluster of little shops where shoemakers, tailors, and tinsmiths lived and worked. A man with unkempt, wiry hair, his face smeared like a chimney sweep's, was tugging at something with a pair of pliers. I mustn't look at him, Janina thought. The child may be born with a defect! And she smiled faintly at this first blossoming of her motherly instincts.

At last she was on Iron Street, but there were still difficulties. There were no lamps in front of the houses as in the better neighborhoods, and the numbers were obliterated by the snow. Her eyelashes were thick with snow and the light from the street lamps came to her in slanted rays, like fiery straws. Finally someone pointed out the right house and she turned in at the gate. A dog lunged at her, but she shooed him off with her schoolbag. A slovenly girl came out and emptied a bucket of slop water right at Janina's feet. In answer to Janina's question, the girl gestured toward the outside staircase and pointed up. The steps were rickety, and Janina made her way up cautiously. She knocked on the door, but there was no answer. She pushed it open and instantly someone screamed, "Shut it! It's not summer!"

A stout woman stood at a table, pressing a dress. The room was lighted by a naphtha lamp. A parrot began to screech. Janina saw everything in swirling spirals and circles.

"Stay where you are! I'll brush the snow off." The woman grabbed a broom and brusquely swept over Janina's shoes. "What brings the young panna here in such a blizzard?"

"Are you—are you Pani Bobrowska?"

"Sure, who else?"

"Excuse me, but—" She could not bring out another word.

"Well, talk. The iron's getting cold. What do you want? Do you want to have something made?"

"Excuse me, please, but would you know a—a Count Lucian Jampolski?"

"I knew it!" The woman stamped her foot triumphantly. "Just as if my heart could talk. What did he do, make you a belly?"

Janina felt a sharp pain and began to back away.

"No need to run away. I'm a plain woman, and I talk plain words. Take off your coat and sit down. Warm yourself. I have an experienced eye, that's all. Nobody has to put a finger into my mouth. Here's a stool, get up close to the oven. If I can help you, I will."

There was a lump in Janina's throat. Her fear was blending with a long-forgotten submissiveness, relief at being able to share her burden. She managed a barely audible "Thank you."

"Get them off, get them off. You'll go out and catch cold, on top of your other troubles. I'll be finished in a little while. That's it, put it down on that bench. This Count of yours is a brute, a criminal, the worst scoundrel in Warsaw. How did you ever fall into his claws? You look like a decent child."

"*Proszę, Pani—*"

"No, no. No crying. I'll just finish this jacket and we'll talk. Awful weather, isn't it? You should have worn galoshes, taken an umbrella. Put down your books. Nobody will bite them here."

Bobrowska took a mouthful of water from a mug on the table and sprayed it on the garment she was pressing.

I V

Janina talked and cried. She blew her nose and wiped the tears away with her handkerchief. She did not touch the tea Bobrowska placed before her. Bobrowska listened intently, now and then clapping her hands in a gesture of exclamation.

"Great God!" she finally burst out. "The victim's daughter! Put the father six feet under and ravished the daughter. Gave her a bastard. Is there anything more despicable in the whole world? This man has no heart but a stone! There's no God-given soul in this creature, but a devil. The devil incarnate. These good people took you in, together with his children, the children he had with that Jewish consumptive. Oh, my dear, I'm sick! It is not to be believed! No conscience! A mad dog, a ravenous wolf! And how could you go to him after what he did to your father? Yes, yes, of course. Those sweet words, that smooth tongue. Oh, he knows how to do it all right, he knows how. When he wants something, that Satan, he's soft as butter. I know him well. I wish I didn't. Runs around making bastards. He's blackened my face, too. He was a friend once, in and out all the time, eating my bread. I got him parts with Cybulski, may he rest in peace, and how did he thank me? Gave me a bad name, got dragged into court on account of him, smeared in all the papers. Went off and did a hellish murder—and left me with a sweetheart and her bastard. Her mother—I mean Kasia's mother—saved him from the gallows, and he violated her daughter. It's a habit with him, he ruins the whole family. I'm honest with you—I don't see how anybody could go to bed with her father's murderer, but it's done, and that's all there is to it. You can't get your virginity back— No, no. I'm not blaming you, I can't throw stones at anybody, God knows. But as long as you've come here, you have to open up, as if it was to your own mother."

Janina exploded into a new flood of tears. "Where—where is he?" she sobbed.

"Where is he?" Bobrowska laughed raucously. "That's a good question. He stopped by when he got out of jail, but I sent him to the devil. I sent that Kasia packing too. She's around here somewhere, in service, and the boy is with her father, an irresponsible drunk. I'm sorry for the child, but what could I do? I couldn't have her in the house any more, not with that fine lover of hers moving in as a permanent guest. If he's staying away from you, child, you'll never find him. Either he's out of the country somewhere—and good riddance—or he's moved in with some of those low-lives he got to know in jail. And even if you found him—then what? What would you do, pour salt on his tail?"

"Please, Pani. What should I do?"

"Well, enough crying. If you were a common girl, I would say, have the baby. With so many bastards running around, what's one more? But in your station you can't go around with a belly. Can't see much yet, but soon it'll show and then you'd be disgraced. How long since your last period?"

"The third month."

"Then there's still a chance. I know a woman who could do the job for you. A scraping—she scrapes it out and that's it. It's risky, and it's a sin—if that bothers you—but what can you do? They would drive you out of the house, and your own mother—the disgrace would kill her, or she'd put an end to herself. It's done quite a lot now. Used to be very seldom, but now all kinds of fancy ladies go to have it done. God cursed us women. It costs money, and there's some danger. But the one I'm telling you about is trained—what's it called—a trained accoucheuse, worked in a clinic at one time. It costs twenty-five rubles, but you won't get a bloodclot there. You go home, lie in bed a few days, and nobody's the wiser. She makes one condition: if something should happen—after all, you could break a leg just walking across the street—you have to keep your mouth shut. Why aren't you drinking your tea?"

"Thanks, thank you."

"Well, wipe away the tears. You fell into a garbage pile and you have to scramble out. You'll know better next time— maybe. Do you have the money?"

"Money? No."

"You have to pay twenty-five rubles. In advance. And you have to drive home in a droshky. Once you get home, you'll find some excuse: you're not feeling well, you fainted, something like that. It's not hard to pull the wool over people's eyes. If I had the money, I'd give it to you, or lend it to you; you'd pay me back, and if you didn't, it wouldn't matter either. But I have nothing myself. Do you have any jewelry or anything?"

Janina was feeling more at ease. She had stopped crying, removed her beret, and eaten the bowl of grits and the slab of bread Bobrowska had served her. She listened to the older woman and was surprised at her own readiness to confide in this total stranger. Yes, she did have a ring with one stone, and some earrings. Pawn them? Yes, she was willing to pawn them, but wouldn't the pawnbroker suspect her? He'd be sure to think she was a thief. Anyway, she had no idea where to find a pawnbroker— As she talked, her own words sounded strange to her. In this one evening she seemed to have grown more mature. She was naming things that a short time ago would have caused her revulsion. To her own ears she sounded like the wives who used to visit her mother for a heart-to-heart woman's talk. Even her voice sounded different. Was it possible? Could she have changed so much in so short a time?

"Why should he suspect you?" Bobrowska was saying. "You're grown, a young lady. Just don't wear that cap, or carry those books. The best thing is to go to a Jew. The Jew doesn't care who you are, or where it comes from, all he wants is his profit. He looks at what you bring under his glass to see if it's real, then you get your money and a receipt that says you have to pay him interest until you take your stuff back. If you don't pay him the interest, he has a right to sell your jewelry."

"Where can I find somebody like that?"

"Plenty of them around. There's one not far—right on Iron Street."

"Will I get twenty-five rubles?"

"If your stuff is worth five times as much."

"But when can I do it? I attend gymnasium."

"You can forget about the gymnasium!"

"How? I can't just go to them and say that—it costs plenty of money, too."

"Well, I can't help you there. God knows I don't have to get involved in these messes. You're a complete stranger to me. I could have told you to go tell your sad story somewhere else, but that's the way I am. If I see somebody in trouble, it catches me here—even if it's a total stranger, even a Jew."

"Could you possibly—would the pani find it possible to pawn the things for me? I'm so clumsy."

"When? How? Much more likely they'd suspect me. I have no jewelry. Used to have. Nothing left now but this little crucifix. When do you want to do it? The sooner the better. The longer you wait, the riskier it gets."

"Yes, I can see that."

"What in blazes do I have to get into these things for?" Bobrowska burst out in self-reproach. "Don't I have enough troubles of my own? Eh—go on, go on, finish your grits. At my age it's time a body had a little rest, that's all, as God is my witness, it's time."

Bobrowska rose, then sat down again. In her lap on one side she placed one hand, knotted into a fist; in the other she held Janina's empty teacup.

V

It was late Saturday night. Dr. Zawacki, Wladzio and Marisia had gone to the theater. Felicia refused to go. She disliked all those frothy French comedies that mocked God, the church, family life. How could people listen to the profanation of everything holy on Saturday night, then calmly go off to church on Sunday morning, Felicia wondered. How do they reconcile that loose, trivial talk with Holy Writ? Dr. Zawacki pointed out that, in the first place, everyone was attending the theater nowadays, even priests. Furthermore, all that lofty verbiage in the Scriptures simply had no relevance to daily life. The French comedies, frivolous though they were, were truer to reality than pious preachments. But Felicia was not to be swayed.

"I'd rather read a book," she said.

Zawacki had asked Janina to come too, but she'd had to go to visit her mother. She had left early, right after lunch, explaining that an uncle of hers, from Plock, was visiting her family and they were having a party for him. Felicia had never heard the girl mention an uncle in Plock, but she couldn't keep the child from visiting her mother. Janina was looking so pale, so preoccupied lately. The gymnasium was putting too much strain on girls these days, Felicia thought. They had to know the history of every Czar, every Ivan, from the very beginning. They were stuffed with figures and calculations that would be of no earthly use to them. They were taught everything, except how to be pious Christians, faithful wives, and capable housekeepers. This new pedagogy was ruining the young people, no doubt about it. The children were learning greed, egoism, godlessness, and indifference to their elders.

Felicia was in her boudoir, reading a history of Christian martyrs. It was an old edition, with gold-tipped pages and rare woodcuts—an heirloom handed down by her grandmother to her mother. But her mind kept straying from the text. Where

was Lucian, she wondered. In what mire was he wallowing?
How had such a son come to her parents? She had just received a letter from Helena, in Zamosc. Helena was the
mother of five children. Felicia's eldest brother, Josef, who
had gone to England after the uprising, already had a grandchild, a little girl with an English name—Catherine Joan.
From his meticulously detailed letters—sent once a year, before Christmas—Felicia noted how much Polish he had forgotten. He included numerous Anglicisms and expressions
that, although written in Polish, sounded foreign. Even his
handwriting seemed different. Who knew if he was still a
Catholic? He had married an English girl, and those Protestants knew precious little about true religion. Felicia's eyes
drooped and she dozed off. Almost immediately she was
dreaming—a brief but extraordinarily vivid dream. There
were lighted candles all over the room. On the table lay a
coffin. Nuns were reading from their missals in buzzing under-
tones. Girls came into the room—Felicia shuddered into
wakefulness. She crossed herself. Oh, dear Jesus! Oh, Holy
Mother, have mercy! Mercy! She wrung her hands in anguish. She had seen everything so sharply: every candle, every
wick, the silver stripes on the coffin, the nuns' black habits; she
had even smelled the sweet scent of wax and incense. What
sign was this? What new ordeal? Had she previewed her own
death? But no girls would be paying their respects to her.
. . . She felt suddenly cold. If only there were a prie-dieu,
like the one her parents had! In her prayers she invoked the
martyred saints she had been reading about. She crossed herself over and over again. Lost in her devotions, she became
dimly aware of an insistent ringing—the front doorbell!
Could they be coming home from the theater already? The
clock showed only a quarter past ten. An accident? Her hands
shook so, she was barely able to stand up. She hiccuped, and
acrid saliva filled her mouth. God in heaven, if it's a calamity,
let it happen to me! I offer myself as the sacrifice! I gladly give
the victim the years left to me! Felicia heard the maid go to the

door. She wanted to run into the corridor herself but was stopped by fear. What was taking so long out there at the door? They were carrying a body! "Oh, Jesus, give me the strength to withstand this new trial. May your name be blessed unto all generations!" At that moment the door to the room was opened, and Janina was led in. The maid was holding her by one arm and a stranger, a coachman, by the other. She was white as chalk, but she was alive.

Felicia was both alarmed and relieved. "What happened?"

The coachman raised his head. "She got sick in the droshky."

"Quickly, put her down on the sofa," Felicia commanded, an angry edge to her voice. "What's wrong with you?" she cried. "You're going to live, do you hear! You're going to live! I have given you my own years. Run for a doctor, quickly. I'll telephone the first-aid station."

Dr. Zawacki had had a telephone installed in his office some time ago, but Felicia had never used it until now. She trembled every time it rang. She was convinced there was some diabolical power, or magic, in all these newfangled mechanisms. She rushed to it, but the study was dark. She hurried to the kitchen for matches and could find none. She picked up the naphtha lamp and carried it back to the study. It shook so much, she feared it would fall out of her hands and start a fire. The flame rose and the glass enclosure wobbled. She managed to set it on the table and went to the wall where the instrument hung. She lifted the receiver, as she had seen her husband do, and attempted to bring it to her ear. But it was the speaking end she was trying to listen to. She tried to reverse it but became entangled in the cord. She heard a squeaky murmuring.

"Quick!" she screamed. "Emergency! This is Madame Zawacki, the doctor's wife!"

The voice at the other end was shouting something, but Felicia was unable to understand a single word. The coachman! Maybe he will understand them. She ran back to her boudoir, struggling with each step to keep her balance. Janina was lying on the sofa with open eyes. Her coat had been removed and blood showed through her dress.

"Dear man! Can you use a telephone? Quick! Call the first-aid."

"My horse is freezing."

"Help me, please, please help me! I'll pay you. Magda, bring some water. Here, take this and cover your horse."

She tore a small plush tapestry from its position on the divan and held it out to him. He started to put his hand out, then withdrew it.

"In the name of heaven, will you go to the telephone! Magda, show him where!"

"I can't be talking on any telephone. She's bloodied up my carriage. I have three rubles coming."

"We'll pay you, we'll pay. Where's my purse? Jesus, help me! Child, what is it? What happened? Did you fall down? Were you run over—answer me! Oh, great heaven—"

The coachman pushed his cap back. "Nobody ran over her, ma'am. It's just that she's about to give birth. That, or a miscarriage. Better get a midwife, d'you see?"

21 ⌂

1

It was an afternoon that same winter. Felicia sat in her boudoir as she so often did, browsing through her history of Christian martyrs. Zawacki was seeing patients in his office. Felicia scanned the pages, stopped to contemplate, and now and then forced her drooping eyelids to stay open. Thank God, Janina had not died (perhaps because Felicia had made her a gift of her early years). But Felicia would not keep her in the house, nor could the girl continue at the gymnasium. Zawacki had found her a post in a hospital where she was to enter a nurses' training course to earn her keep. The whole affair had been a blow to Felicia and a disaster for the children. Felicia's thoughts often reverted to her dream. Was it possible that a *fatum*, a predestined event, could be reversed? Suddenly she heard the soft sound of a key turning in the front door. Or was she imagining it? Then the sound of rapid footsteps approached and the door of her room opened. It was Lucian, dressed in a short jacket, high boots, and the peaked cap favored by laborers and underworld habitués. He was sporting a short beard. He removed his cap and said, "Well, here I am."

"Why didn't you ring? Did you pass by the patients?"

"I didn't care to talk to that garbage," he said, referring to the maid.

There was a time when Felicia would have greeted such an

unexpected visit with delighted surprise. But since the Janina incident, she had reached a point where nothing in this world could any longer surprise her. It would not startle her if Marisia were to do the same thing Janina had done, or if Wladzio were to follow in his father's footsteps, or if she discovered that the doctor had a mistress.

"Well, you're alive."

"Yes, I'm alive. Don't think I've come to stay. I wanted to say goodbye, that's all."

"You're leaving?"

"Yes. For America."

"You had better watch out for Marian. He might do something foolish."

"Something foolish? I'm armed. If anybody as much as musses my hair, he gets a bullet in his head."

Felicia shuddered. "Stay away from him!" she said. "He's a good-hearted man, but he has a temper. He doesn't mean any harm. He really loved you like a brother. He's older than you are, too."

"How much older? Nobody loves me and that's the truth. I hate everybody and they all hate me. I'm a hounded beast. I must get away from this accursed Poland. Everybody wants to ruin me here."

Felicia felt as if all her strength had ebbed away. "Who wants to ruin you? You are your own worst enemy."

"Enough of this grandmotherly twaddle! I didn't come to be preached at. I need money, that's why I've come."

"Thank you for being so honest."

"How much can you give me?"

"What I have, no more. I can't take anything from Marian. How much do you need?"

"Five hundred rubles."

"I'll give you my pearls. Pawn them. But they're worth much more."

"How much more?"

"Twenty times more."

"I'll bring you the ticket, or pawn them yourself, if you want to. Where's that Janina?"

"Not here any more."

"Where is she?"

"What do you want with her? Haven't you done enough harm?"

"Tell me where she is!"

"I don't know. In some hospital. Training to be a secular Sister of Mercy."

"What hospital?"

"I don't know. I don't know! What do you need her for? Leave her alone. You're leaving anyway! You've caused us enough trouble as it is."

"What trouble? You sit warm and cozy by the oven while I rot away. You lay under your counterpane while I was fighting that damned Ivan. I rotted in the woods, ate grass. I could have married well too, and driven around in a carriage. I could have knuckled under to the Russians like all the swinish traitors, all the lackeys of Ivan!"

"Little brother, what good are words? Poland is sunk in darkness. Only God can help us."

"What God? There isn't any God. We could have helped ourselves if we weren't a nation of mice, lice, and roaches. I don't want to be a Pole any more, you hear me? I want to go to America and forget this evil-smelling country. There one has a right to be a freethinker too. I'm sick of having to live with all these lies, all these fairy tales about the Redeemer, the Holy Mother, the rest of that foul cant. Mary was an adulteress, plain and simple. Jesus was the bastard of a Jewish carpenter, *that's* the true story!"

Felicia shook her head sadly. "What is it that ails you, little brother? What hurts you so?"

Lucian grimaced. "Everything, that's what! What kind of swinishness is all this life anyway? We're born in slime and blood, we suffer through a few years and are chewed up by the worms. The whole thing disgusts me! What good are these cursed children of mine? They'll croak too. Marisia will surely betray somebody. Wladzio is a young brute, but—I don't like anybody. Maybe you, a little, but you're an old woman already. You look seventy. Are you sick?"

"Does it make any difference to you?"

"No difference at all. I walked in and thought I was seeing Mother. How old are you?" Suddenly his tone changed. "Felicia, I must get away!"

"Well, I can't keep you back."

"You know what ails me? Everything. I'm hungry, poor, persecuted, sick."

Felicia became alarmed. "Are you sick?"

"It's not important."

"Is it serious?"

Something like a smile crossed Lucian's face, an illusion caused perhaps by the fact that one of his eyes was bigger than the other. He stood opposite her, pale as the snow outside, gray streaks in his beard, a high forehead, deep wrinkles, his hair half gone. There was a vague smirk on his lips, something like drunken mockery. Felicia scanned his face, seeing things that only an elder sister would notice: some of their father's characteristics, a suggestion—a faint intimation—of some feature of their mother's, and in his expression much of what he looked like as a child, when Felicia had played with him. He seemed on the verge of saying something funny but couldn't decide whether to utter it or not.

Finally he said, "It's not exactly the fashion to admit it, but I have what is politely termed a 'social disease.'"

"It can be cured."

"Yes."

Felicia covered her face with her hands. Lucian walked over to the window. She lowered her hands and regarded him. He hadn't looked so old from the front, but seen from behind he had more than one aspect of middle age. A shoulder drooped. The hair on his neck stood out like silvery bristles. The feet encased in the long boots seemed unevenly matched. All at once Felicia felt a resurgence of strength in her limbs. She stood up and walked over to him.

"Take that jacket off. You'll catch cold."

Lucian did not turn around.

"Lucian! It's still not too late."

He turned quickly. "Give me the pearls!"

"You'll get them. They're yours. You need a doctor."

"What kind of doctor? Your stinking husband? I must go."

"Why? Where to?"

"I have to, that's all. Leave me alone."

He thrust his hand into his trouser pocket. Felicia sensed there was a revolver there. He looked at her with a maniacal stare that was at the same time inexplicably childish, like a little boy with a new toy. "He's liable to shoot," Felicia thought. Strangely enough, she had no sensation of fear, but something like a spasm of inward laughter shook her. "Is this what they are, the murderers, the wicked, the sinners, the seducers? Is this how they look? A boy, a foolish boy! A child playing with a gun!" A verse from Luke flashed through her mind: "Forgive them, Father, for they know not what they do." She touched him on the arm. "Take your hand out of your pocket."

He recoiled from her touch. "I'll shoot her too," he thought suddenly. "She suffers too much. I'll let her have it right in the forehead." He stood staring at her with a kind of insane haughtiness, with the pride of one who has reached the very depths. "I'll soon find out if there is a God or not. . . ." As if he had articulated his thought for her to hear, she said, "Foolish boy. There is a God."

And she started for the door, to have a talk with Marian. All at once it became clear to her that, despite his anger with Lucian, Dr. Zawacki would help him.

11

Lucian spent that evening with Felicia and Marian. Venereal diseases were not Marian's specialty, but he examined Lucian and gave him some medication to alleviate the pain and arranged for him to see a specialist, one of Marian's colleagues, the following day. Lucian even saw Wladzio and Marisia for a while. All three adults sat in the dining room talking till late. Marian spoke of the recent achievements in medicine and reiterated his belief that man has no soul. What we call soul is nothing more than brain and nerves. Man is a machine, Zawacki insisted, a complicated machine, but a machine. All of nature, in fact, is a machine—the solar system, the cosmos, every leaf on a tree, every flower in the flowerpot. The textbooks distinguish between physics, chemistry, botany, zoology, cosmography, but in nature all these forces work in unison. Felicia protested, but Lucian sided with Marian.

"What's wrong with me?" he asked Marian. "Is it my physics or my chemistry?"

"Your illness is functional."

"What exactly do you mean?"

"The machine is sound, but there is a loose screw."

"Do you think it can be tightened?"

"All you need is a wife and a profession."

"What can I turn to now?"

"First, get well. If I were you, I'd study pharmacy."

"Study? At my age?"

"You're not that old. You might find a well-to-do wife."

"Well, brother-in-law, you're an optimist."

"No. Women have perverse natures. They like a charlatan." And Zawacki winked, to show he intended no offense.

Lucian had already bathed. He had tea with raspberry juice and kissed Felicia before going off to bed. He was seized by a deep tenderness for the sister to whom he had brought so much shame and suffering and who forgave him everything. If there could be one such person, then why not the whole human race? "Could her physics or chemistry be so different from mine?" Lucian thought. "We're brother and sister." He entered his room. He had a home again, at least for the time being. For a long while he sat on the bed, astonished at his own life, at all the traps he had been lured into, all the tribulations he had suffered. "How had it all happened? Why?" he asked himself. "Did some demon take possession of me?" There must be an end to the farce! He stared at the toes of his boots. "I'll simply stay here, that's what I'll do. I've had enough. Absolutely. Permanently. I'm cured—cured." He undressed and placed the revolver in the nighttable drawer. He drew up the covers and fell asleep at once. He slept deeply, without dreaming, for several hours. Suddenly he woke, opened his eyes wide, sated with sleep. He sat up, looking into the darkness. The burning pain of recent days had stopped. He began to think of Janina, who had come to this house as a result of his killing her father and who had been driven away because of an equally impulsive action on his part. "Has she forgiven me?" he asked himself. "Yes, she has. And she loves me. A pity she has no money," he thought suddenly. "She could have been the well-to-do woman Marian had suggested. I could become a pharmacist, and she the pharmacist's wife and assistant. We would measure out dosages together behind the counter." Lucian smiled to himself. "And I was all set to run off to America or put a bullet through my head. It's simply nerves. I no longer have the strength for this kind of life. The few years left to me I must spend in peace."

No sooner had this thought struck him than he was assailed by the extraordinary feeling that he had no time left at all, no years, no months, not even a few days. He had reached the farthest shore. He sat motionless, listening to his innermost being. He had no cares, no desires, no need for sleep, no wish to be awake. "What is the matter with me?" he asked himself. "Has there been a sudden change in my chemistry?" A sickening tedium enveloped him, a dreariness such as he had never known before. He opened his mouth to yawn, but what came out was a belch. A pharmacist, of all things? Study? He wanted to laugh. America? On a ship? To those Yankees? Insane. Insane. The aches, the ambitions, the concern with people fell away from him. He had gorged himself to satiety. Suddenly it came over him that living itself was a corruption —sleep again? Wake again? Eat again? Bah! Go to the doctor? Phew! Enough! Something in him was running down. Something in his mechanism was grinding to a stop, like a machine chugging spasmodically on the last drop of fuel. He seemed to be inhaling clouds of gas; he was full to the bursting point. He tried to visualize a future, but his imagination was paralyzed. He could only turn his thoughts backward, not ahead. But even the past had lost all color, all taste. There was nothing left but words, names: Marisia, Stachowa, Kasia, Bobrowska. He made an effort to visualize their faces but could no longer remember what they looked like. Soon the names, too, slipped away. A strange process was taking place in his brain cells. His memory was fading from minute to minute. Bobrowska became Chrobowska. He knew this was an error but was unable to correct it.

He opened the drawer and took out the revolver. "Yes, now is the time!" a voice said. "There's nothing left for you." He fumbled with the heavy thing in the dark, his hands weak, as if asleep. He could barely make out which end was the muzzle and which the handle. Well, it is the end! God forgive me! He comprehended something, not with his mind but with some nameless sense. He had completed some mission and was being called back to where he had come from. He coiled a finger around the trigger, then brought the muzzle up to his temple. For a time he sat nodding, almost dozing, with his eyes open. The muzzle slipped down to his cheek and rested against his chin. He was not really Lucian any more. He was involved in an action which he could neither comprehend nor describe in words. He was becoming one with something he had never previously known, not even in a dream. He listened to it as it whirled, loosened, and dissolved—a substanceless body, a thinking entity without meaning. The barrier between interior and exterior had dropped away. "Is this death?" he asked himself. "But I am still alive." His insides seemed to have stopped their motion. He was seized by an urge to vomit, to spit out his entrails. He could no longer endure the weight of his flesh. It was the end! In the final seconds, his mind was still engaged in some thought that he could not grasp. It was as though he were speaking a language he could not understand. "Now!" a voice commanded. It was an order that could not be ignored. He had a last act to perform. With the dregs of his strength, he raised the revolver and pulled the trigger. It was as if a blade had parted his skull: there was no pain at all.

The next morning Lucian was dressed in fresh clothes and placed in a coffin. Felicia collapsed, but Marisia and Wladzio stayed with the corpse. Zawacki was without religious belief, but Marisia started whimpering, demanding a proper Christian burial for her father. Candles were lit in all the sconces and candelabra. The coffin, uncovered, was placed on a table. Two nuns—one young and one old—came from Felicia's church and stood by the coffin reciting the Office for the Dead. At nightfall Felicia had regained her strength and was led into the salon. She recognized everything—the silver-striped coffin, the dripping candles, the nuns, the odor of wax and incense. Lucian's head was swathed in a bandage and rested on a silk cushion. It was no longer Lucian but a stranger with unfamiliar features—sunk in a silence that had an element of alarm in it. It seemed to Felicia that the silence was screaming. Nevertheless, a solemnity filled the room, as though it had been turned into a church. "Where are the girls?" Felicia asked herself. The door opened wide and Janina entered with two other girls. Janina's weeping sounded almost like laughter. She ran screaming to the coffin and sank down beside it.

"I love you! I love you! What have you done? What have you done?"

She threw herself on the coffin, covering it with kisses.

"Ei—ei," she wailed, "ei—eeei . . ." It was a dirge sprung from the village, from generations of peasants. It had in it something of the strangled whine of a wounded beast. The two girls with Janina were fellow students from the hospital.

Felicia stood in stony silence. "Is it all determined in advance? Is man nothing more than a toy? Had this end been predestined for Lucian?" Something in her emptied out. She folded her hands. She could not even cry. Dr. Zawacki came up to her.

"Why did he do it? Such a hothead," he said.

"Be still, Marian."

"You must go back to bed. You're pale as wax." He took her by the wrist, held it, and strained to listen for her pulse. It was irregular and slow, as though deliberating whether to go on or stop.

22

I

Ezriel had an unexpected visitor. Among the patients in the foyer there was a woman dressed in mourning. One of the first to arrive, she apparently wished to wait until everyone had gone. Each time Ezriel opened the door, she indicated with a black-gloved finger that he should take the others before her. Finally, she came into his office and raised the heavy veil from her face. Ezriel saw an elderly woman, wrinkled, with white hair and sad eyes. There were silver hairs on her chin and her mouth was sunken. Yet she conveyed an air of faded elegance.

"You do not recognize me, Doctor, but I recognize you," she said.

"I'm terribly sorry."

"I am the wife of Dr. Zawacki . . . Perhaps you'll recognize Countess Felicia."

"Yes, of course! Now I remember you!"

"I remember your wedding. I stood beside the wedding canopy."

"My first wife is dead."

"I know. Occasionally I read *The Israelite*. I saw the obituary."

"Yes."

For a while they were both silent.

"And how is Dr. Zawacki?" Ezriel asked then.

"Don't you know? Marian is gone."

"When?"

"Doesn't the doctor read the newspapers? He is gone. He got up one morning hale and hearty and suddenly passed away."

Again there was a pause. People perished like flies. He had grown afraid to inquire about anyone.

"I am sorry," Ezriel finally said. "Dr. Zawacki was a good physician, and what's more important, a decent human being."

Felicia nodded her white head. "Yes, a great man. In his own fashion, a saint."

"This world is nothing more than an inn—we are all guests."

"True."

Felicia took out a handkerchief and wiped her mouth. "Doctor, I'm not a patient. First of all, I'm not sick, and even if I were, I wouldn't visit a doctor. I have come on a private matter."

"I'm at your service, gladly. Please sit down."

"Dr. Babad, I know you will laugh at me, but I'm accustomed to that. The doctor knows, of course, that my brother, Lucian, left us of his own free will."

"Yes, I know everything."

"He came home from prison sick, beaten. We wanted to help him, but he was doomed. He put an end to himself. He left two lovely children, your late sister-in-law Miriam Lieba's children. I hear that the children's grandfather is still alive, but he doesn't want to know them, and they are not interested in him. Our society is filled with prejudices. Doctor, this is what I came to tell you. Since Lucian's death, I have more than ever become involved in occultism, or spiritualism. I feel it is a part of the Christian and even of the Jewish religion. How can a religion omit the immortality of the soul? After Lucian's death, I threw myself wholeheartedly into this belief. I know all the arguments of the skeptics, and I don't blame them.

There are doubts in all of us, but when we see the truth it becomes sinful to doubt. I'm neither insane nor untruthful. I've seen spirits, talked with them, touched them with these hands. It's as true as I'm standing here."

"Yes, please continue."

"Doctor, I have no desire to preach or to try to convince anyone, but I pity those who are at the spring and do not drink. It's better for some people never to be enlightened. Most of them are afraid. They prefer to believe in the devil. . . . I came to see you, Doctor, to bring you greetings."

Ezriel raised his head. "From whom?"

"From Miriam Lieba. At the last séance, she sent them. She also said she had met her sister, your wife."

Ezriel bit his lip.

"Doctor, I know what you think, but her voice was as clear as yours is now. The dead live absolutely."

"If only it were true."

"It is true, Doctor. A daughter knows the voices of her parents. I've spoken with them innumerable times. They've told me things no one but I could have known."

"Well, I'm listening."

"Doctor, I know how busy you are. But I'd like to suggest something. We're very exclusive and don't invite just anybody. Cynics would disturb our group. But I believe you're searching for truth. The late Miriam Lieba spoke about you often. She praised you immensely. It would be a great joy for her to contact you."

Ezriel smiled briefly. "She must know my address."

"Oh, Doctor, by all that is holy, don't be sarcastic. These matters are too serious."

"I'm sorry, madame, but I find it hard to believe that a woman who is dead and decomposed can speak and send greetings. How can she speak when her vocal cords are silenced? And if her spirit lives, why does it speak only during a séance? Even if one accepts the fact of spontaneous revelation, these mediums are known to be thieves and scoundrels."

"How can you be so sure? I admit that there are swindlers, but you find them in all professions. Pani Bielska, the leader of our group, is a woman of extraordinary powers."

"What powers? How did they come to her? I'm drawn to religion, but I can't stand fanaticism and lies, or those who take advantage of the lonely and disturbed. If a trace of Miriam Lieba exists, why reveal itself to some Pani Bielska? Why not to me, or to her sisters? Where is the logic?"

"Doctor, our terrestrial logic cannot explain everything."

"Well, I can't believe in all these phantoms. I can accept the fact that Miriam Lieba's soul is in paradise. Everything is possible with God. But that Miriam Lieba's soul should reveal itself and send me greetings from the other world only when a bunch of charlatans turn off the lights is too much."

"Well, Doctor, I'm sorry. My intentions were good."

"I don't doubt it and I thank you heartily. If your belief is helpful to you, I don't want to take it away."

"You can't—my eyes have seen and my ears have heard. After Lucian's death, I was a shard. About Marian's passing I cannot even speak. My poor head seems to be an anvil for God's hammer. The blows began when I was still a girl. One catastrophe followed another. That in itself was the hand of Providence. I would have gone out of my mind if not for this consolation. I won back everything: my parents, Lucian, Miriam Lieba, and my husband. They show their love for me, guide me, and teach me to stand all trials. I know I'll soon be with them and I look forward to that day. Wladzio and Marisia no longer need me. I once adopted a girl, but, thank God, she is studying to become a nurse. But my poor brother left another son, an illegitimate child, and he worries me the most. The doctor perhaps remembers—"

"Yes, I do. He had a boy with some servant girl."

"Kasia. That's the mother's name. His name is Bolek. The mother has remained a creature of the dark. She works as a maid. A certain Bobrowska tried to teach her how to be a seamstress, but the girl could not master the trade. I am still puzzled how my brother could have had dealings with such a common woman. Now a son has grown up who isn't of our class. I sent Bolek to gymnasium, but he ran away. He became a waiter and isn't even good at that. He keeps coming to me for money and is forever involved in unsavory affairs. He's my brother's child and a grandchild of the Jampolskis. His father and grandparents can't rest because of him—he doesn't let me die—"

"Then he has a function in this world."

"It's not a joke."

"I know. My dear madame, there is such a thing as heredity. Despite all denials, it is one of the strongest influences in our lives."

"Why didn't Wladzio take up these odious ways?"

"The law of heredity remains a mystery. More mysterious than all the mediums and their black magic."

"I believe that every drop of semen contains a spirit."

"Then every man carries within him millions of spirits."

"Yes."

"Perhaps. I myself, madame, am thinking of visiting Palestine, even settling there. Tell my sister-in-law about it. Perhaps she will come to say goodbye to me."

"Why Palestine, if I may ask?"

"I don't know why myself. I have a son there. Something is driving us Jews back to where we came from."

"Well, and at the same time you are a rationalist?"

"I am no rationalist."

"I read about the emigration of the Jews in *The Israelite*. They are fleeing the Czarist pogroms, but clearly it's all part of God's scheme. But I assumed that it involved only those interested in agriculture. Is it possible to practice medicine there?"

"I hope so. Why not? But Jewish culture cannot integrate with other cultures. We must either become complete Jews or perish."

"That's true."

"What is it like in the other world? Have the Jews assimilated there?"

"Oh, Doctor, if you didn't remind me of my husband I'd get angry. He had a similar sense of humor, but behind it all he was a mystic. He passed away like a saint. His ideas are changed now. He keeps telling me that the truth is to be found only in evangelism, and not in worldly knowledge."

"What do the Jews, the Mohammedans, the Buddhists, the Brahmins do in the other world? Can there be various religious truths?"

"I don't know, Doctor. I am only in contact with Christians. The spirits are not all the same, either."

"It seems that way. According to you, madame, the other world is just as confused as this one."

"God has many mansions."

11

A short time after Clara's funeral, Calman had to be rushed to a hospital. His urine was blocked. He was operated on, but days passed and he wasn't able to sit up. Jochebed came to see her father daily. The Society for the Care of the Sick, whose members prayed at Calman's house, and of whose congregation Calman was one of the beadles, sent men to sit at his bedside. Jochebed suggested that Calman have a room to himself, but he did not want to isolate himself from his fellow men. It was difficult to put up with the noise, the smell, the groans of the other patients, but was man born to indulge himself in pleasures? The nurse put up a screen, and Calman put on his prayer shawl and phylacteries. He had brought along a prayer book, a Pentateuch, and *The Beginning of Wisdom*. Calman asked for no dispensations from the Almighty. He had lived out his allotted span. Whenever he had a free moment, he said his prayers and read his books. Sasha visited his father and brought flowers and other gifts, but Calman ordered these trappings taken away. The cookies and chocolates were distributed among the patients. Sasha promised to say Kaddish after Calman, and Calman nodded his head. Calman knew well enough how Sasha was living. Calman looked back on his life. Wealth had come and gone. He had buried two of his four daughters. His son-in-law, the Marshinov rabbi, was at death's door. Ezriel was living with some converted woman. Calman had been charitable, but not sufficiently so. He could have provided for many men with his possessions, but instead he had yearned for new tracts of land, new leases. He could have married a respectable woman, but had become enamored of Clara. Well, soon he would have to give an accounting of himself! Behind him he left Gentiles, irreligious Jews, generations of base individuals. . . . He thought about Zelda. Would he be allowed to be with her? She had died pious. Who knew to what heights her soul had risen? He would be punished. There was one consolation: God was merciful. He knew the measure of man, that he is ashes and dust.

People all around Calman were dying. A patient asked for a glass of tea and, soon after, he was lying still and the orderlies took him to the morgue. All night long a young man had been screaming. In the morning he fell silent. Here, in the hospital, man could be seen in proper perspective—a pile of bones. But was man entirely responsible for his follies? He had to eat, have a place to live. As long as he breathed, passion filled him. The younger doctors eyed the nurses. Wandering among the dying, the nurses smiled, flirted, and giggled in the corridors. To the left of Calman lay a heretic Jew who told Calman he knew Ezriel. Todros was his name, Todros Bendiner. Ezriel had once lived in his house at 19 Krochmalna Street. But in recent years Todros had been living in a home for the aged. He was suffering from cancer of the spleen. His face was yellow as saffron, but he said to Calman: "Your psalter was not written by King David."

"By whom, then?"

"It's a collection of many writings. They were first assembled during the time of Ezra."

Calman wanted to remonstrate with him, but checked himself. Instead, he asked: "Do you believe in nothing?"

"Man is no more than an insect."

"An insect is also created by God."

"And who created God?"

"Well, enough of that!"

Todros also read, not holy books, but secular ones. Students came to visit him: young men in short coats, clean-shaven, bare-headed. They discussed politics and world affairs, used Hebrew expressions but looked like Gentiles. Calman wanted to ask the doctor to change his bed but was afraid that Todros would be offended. Well, he would soon see, soon know the truth. There was a God. The world was not mere chaos. From the hospital window, sky and clouds could be seen. Birds flew about. An orderly had opened an upper portion of the window. A yellow-specked butterfly had flown in. Such a tiny thing and able to fly! Where had it been all winter? It had certainly had a mother, and she in turn had had a mother, generation after generation of butterflies. . . . Could all this have happened without someone watching? Was he, Todros Bendiner, wiser than the Almighty? "Father in Heaven, forgive him!" Calman prayed. "The temptations are great." Tears came to Calman's eyes. He wept for this wise scholar who had wasted a life and spent his waning days with idle books, jokes, and foolish students.

Several more days went by, but Calman was unaware of their passing. One morning he opened his eyes and saw that Todros's bed was empty. Someone had removed the bedding. A small woman in a nurse's cap, with freckles across her face and a pointed nose, was spreading a fresh sheet over the matress. Calman wanted to ask her about Todros but did not have the strength to speak. Besides, he knew the answer. Where did one go from here? The sun was shining. Some of the sick people conversed. Others groaned. A young man had been discharged, and his neighbors congratulated him. Calman wanted to sit up but could no longer do so. His body had become too heavy, his distended belly was filled with pain. Nauseating odors rose from his stomach to his mouth. He wanted to say the Prayer upon Arising but was too weak even for that. "Woe is me, I'm powerless," Calman thought, "but once I was a powerful man. . . ." He closed his eyes and no longer wanted to open them. He felt that he had ceased to be Calman and was becoming something else, a tangle of dreams, sayings, visions. He opened an eye, and the sun no longer shone. Ezriel was standing over him. "Father-in-law, how are you?"

Calman moved his lips, but no words came. Yet he remembered that Shaindel had died and that Ezriel was planning to visit the Holy Land.

III

A strike was brewing in Lodz and someone was needed to smuggle in revolvers and ammunition. Zina volunteered. The arms were packed in two valises. The cartridges were to be wrapped around her body. She stripped and an expert woman smuggler wrapped Zina from loins to knees with the "noodles." Zina could scarcely move. But what could be expected of a "pregnant" woman? Pretending to be in the final stages of pregnancy, she even painted some flecks on her face. Her stomach was padded with a pillow, in which another pair of pistols were placed. The woman, who was supposedly Zina's mother, took her by droshky to the Vienna depot. There, she placed her "daughter" in a second-class carriage. She carried a novel and some knitting for the "infant." An officer gallantly gave her a seat by the window. An elderly woman began to confide her own experiences, about how she had an urge to eat eggshells and the lime from the walls. Zina could barely keep from laughing. The child, whom the old woman discussed with such fondness, was now an officer somewhere in the Caucasus, probably one of those reactionaries and despots that the revolution would have to shoot. The conductor came in and

Zina gave him her ticket. A huge gendarme, with a chest full of medals, looked in, nodding at Zina. The bell rang three times and the train began moving. The "mother" shouted after her: "Remember, daughter, take care of yourself! . . . Be careful!"

"Don't worry, Mother, everything will be all right!"

Zina hid her face in her novel, but she was thinking of her father. How could he have been taken in by this new nationalism of the vicious Jewish capitalists? He had read and studied, had once belonged to a self-education group, and had kept in touch with her Aunt Mirale until she had been exiled to Siberia. How could he not see that the world was divided into exploiters and exploited? Wasn't he aware of Russian despotism? Didn't he know how imperialists achieve their aim? How could he ignore the condition of the Russian peasant, the Polish worker, and occupy himself with old wives' tales from the Bible? Should Jewish masses desert everything and go to Palestine, where the so-called philanthropists would exploit them in the name of a newfangled nationalism? And who would praise him for his sacrifice? An invisible God? But hadn't Dostoevsky been a Slavophile? Wasn't Tolstoy making a fool of himself? Weren't all universities filled with professors who knelt before every religious statue and kissed the priests' hands?

Zina sighed. She was hot. Her skin burned. The woman had bound the cartridges too tightly about her. They clung together like an armored plate, pressed against her loins, her belly. She was sheathed in a hot mass of metal. God in heaven, if they went off, she would go up like a human torch! And what then, eh? The masses would struggle, triumph, exult, and she would be a pile of ashes. . . . They would not even remember that there had been an individual called Zina. Well, but there was no other way. Someone had to make a stand. A struggle had to be launched against such injustice! . . . Zina had a piece of chocolate in her bag and a couple of cookies. She took out a piece of the candy and ate it. She kept mopping her brow with her handkerchief. She had never known that a person could sweat so much. Streams ran down her back, her sleeves. Her face and head grew even hotter. She began to suffer from thirst. How could she have forgotten to take along something to drink? Suddenly she had an urge to urinate. "Mother, my insides are turning over." She felt a piercing and burning in her stomach. Had she eaten some spoiled food? No, she would not go. She would sit there for the few hours the trip would take. In her torment Zina attempted to read, but the type danced before her eyes. The page became blank, spotted. Ethereal circles danced among the letters. "If only I don't faint. No, it mustn't happen. I must keep control of myself! Thousands of lives, hopes, ideals depend upon me! . . .

"Be strong, Zina! Be strong!" she mumbled to herself. "God in heaven, have mercy upon me!" some part of her cried. She caught herself praying and was astounded. "Oh, I don't know what's going on inside me! I must get up! . . ."

She attempted to rise, but her legs seemed to be paralyzed. She tried fanning herself with her book. Hammers seemed to be beating at her temples. Her heart pounded. Fiery sparks flashed before her eyes. Bells rang in her ears. Her mouth filled with a tasteless fluid. Did they know what was happening to her? Why was the old man staring? And the officer? "Oh, Mother dear, I am lost . . ."

Leaning forward as if to vomit, Zina fell on her face. The old woman cried out. The officer jumped up, trying to lift Zina by her shoulders. The cartridges tore loose and began to roll out from under her dress. There was pandemonium in the car. Other passengers came running, mostly military men. "What's that?" shouted a colonel with a red beard. The onlookers restrained their laughter. Cartridges kept falling out of Zina's clothing. Water was brought. The train was halted. Two gendarmes appeared from the next car.

IV

The one person who could probably have saved Zina was her Uncle Sasha. Sasha had taken over his mother's apartment after Clara's death. The maid and Felusia were still there. Since Zipkin in the end did not come, Yasha Vinaver had arranged to take Felusia to him. Ezriel rang the doorbell, and the maid answered. He asked for Sasha, but he was not in town. The maid told him that the master had not slept at home the past two nights. Without a mistress, the apartment was in disorder. The maid seemed to have visitors in the kitchen. They were laughing. On the way down, Ezriel ran into Esther Eisner. She had come to see Felusia, but Felusia was not at home either. Esther Eisner had already heard that Zina had been arrested. Her arrest had disrupted the organization, and further arrests were feared. A short distance from the house, Ezriel and Esther met Yasha Vinaver. Esther introduced Ezriel to Yasha, who immediately began to eulogize Clara.

"Doctor, to you she was, how shall we put it, a stepmother-in-law. But she was very close to me."

"Where did you meet her?"

"In Berlin, America, Monte Carlo, under various circumstances, but she was always a woman. You understand, Doctor? A woman! One hundred percent! . . ." And Yasha Vinaver snapped his fingers.

"Are you really taking Felusia to America?" Esther Eisner inquired.

"I wrote a long letter to Dr. Zipkin. If he consents, I'll adopt her. I haven't any children, and I'd like to have a daughter of my own. I'll place her in the finest boarding school. One can't live all alone. Impossible! . . ."

"A fool!" Esther Eisner exclaimed after Yasha had said goodbye and left them.

"There's room for people like him in the world too."

Esther Eisner recommended an attorney to Ezriel, but what

could an attorney do? The least Zina's sentence could be was three years in prison, and she could even be sentenced to hang. Someone influential was needed, someone who was friendly with the authorities and could have the matter quashed before it came to trial. Ezriel went to Jampol. Perhaps Sasha was there. Ezriel hadn't been there for years and found the town unrecognizable. Buildings had been put up, stores opened. There was even a depot. Young men walked about in short coats. There was a lumber warehouse where Calman's store had once stood. Ezriel passed Jews and Jewesses, but no one seemed familiar. Where was everybody? Probably dead. Finally he recognized a water-carrier. Ezriel hired a britska to take him to Sasha's house.

He passed what had been Calman Jacoby's estate. The sky, the cornfields, the cornflowers at the edge of the road, the birds—had all remained the same. The peasant women who kneeled beside the seedbeds, pulling out weeds, seemed the same as ever: the same calico dresses, the same blond braids. The storks flew in the same circles. Every cricket made the same sound it had made when Ezriel was a boy daydreaming about Shaindel. A bee suddenly landed on Ezriel's sleeve. Two butterflies, both the same color, with twin markings, fluttered next to each other. The air smelled of earth, manure, summer aromas. Cows grazed in a pasture. One cow lay down, weary of nibbling grass, dribbling saliva. The great eyes which were all pupil stared wonderingly about. To Ezriel they seemed to be asking, "Where have I come from? Why am I a cow? . . ."

The coachman, a youth in a leather-visored cap, turned to Ezriel: "Does the gentleman want to see the master?"

"Yes. Pan Jacoby."

"He can't be at home."

"Where is he?"

"Sometimes at the barracks. Mostly in Warsaw."

"I've just come from Warsaw."

"We never know where he is. Disappears and shows up again like magic. Gee-up! . . ."

"What about the lime quarries? Exhausted?"

"Altogether! . . . The older Jacoby died."

"Yes, I know."

"Whoa! . . ."

Sasha was not at home. A Gentile woman suggested that perhaps the master was at the barracks. Ezriel looked at her and knew—instinctively—that this was no maid but a mistress. Bluish circles ringed her eyes. Looking at Ezriel with the curiosity of a relative, she dragged out her words. "Yes, the master does come home, but I couldn't say when. He might come today or tomorrow or the day after tomorrow. One never knows. Who should I say has called?"

"Dr. Babad."

"Aha."

"I'll try the barracks."

"Yes, maybe the master is there, maybe somewhere else. Only God knows." And she sighed.

"I understand."

Sasha wasn't at the barracks either. Or, if he was, Ezriel couldn't find out where. There was no one to ask. In the large parade ground, a sergeant-major was drilling soldiers. Cavalry horses were being groomed, their sides curried with combs and brushes. Officers strolled back and forth. Two soldiers carried an empty kettle on a pole. Bayonets gleamed in the sun. The soldiers shouted coarsely, attacking a dummy, piercing it, turning the bayonets as if to gore its intestines. There was an odor of hay, sauerkraut, leather, and sweat. Everything was the same, even the putrid odors. But the young soldiers Ezriel had run after as a young boy were now old men or dead. Ezriel wondered sorrowfully about Zina. What were her thoughts in prison? The afternoon sun warmed him. Meanwhile, the coachman went to fetch water for his horses. Ezriel put his arm over the horse's neck. It stood there, this creature of God, silently, with bent head, drooping ears, hanging tail, its eyes full of humility. It seemed to Ezriel that the horse was saying: "One is born, and one must die. Everything else is unimportant. . . ."

v

Sasha was visiting not far from the barracks. Lydia Michalovna, an officer's wife, was sitting in a rocking chair, knitting a tiny sacque. She was of medium build, a trifle overweight, with a high bosom. Her hair would not lie flat but stood on end like the hair of Negresses in the illustrations in textbooks. She had a round forehead, a Russian nose, black eyes, and full lips. Lydia Michalovna was only twenty-seven but looked older. In the next room in a cane crib a child of four was sleeping. A maid sat at its bedside. In the courtyard an orderly was chopping wood. Lydia Michalovna's bedroom was filled with knickknacks. On the sofa, which was covered with cushions, lay a huge doll. On a side table were three gold-tooled leather albums, one on top of the other. Lydia Michalovna had just celebrated her birthday, and presents were heaped everywhere: little boxes with colored covers, bottles of perfume, bonbons, books, and vases filled with flowers. Everyone in the officers' club agreed that Lydia Michalovna was not pretty, but nearly all the men were attracted to her. The women gossiped about her, swore that she cuckolded her husband, who had gone into debt for her and paid exorbitant interest. A few days before, he had fallen from a horse and dislocated his shoulder. He was now in a military hospital in Warsaw, because the local company doctor was an alcoholic and considered incompetent. Lydia Michalovna was a favorite subject of discussion for the officers' wives. What did men see in her? A young officer had mentioned that Lydia Michalovna had an unusually white skin, a statement that caused both merriment and malicious gossip. Everyone knew that Sergei Calmanovitch Jacoby, the Jewish contractor, was a frequent visitor at her house, but since it did not disturb her husband—what business was it of theirs? The women had something to chatter about during the long summer days when their husbands were occupied with their duties, or at night—playing cards.

Lydia Michalovna rocked herself as she knitted, and from time to time raised her black eyes questioningly to Sasha, who walked to and fro in his high boots. His hands were restless, and as he moved about, he kept touching things. He went over to the clock, held the pendulum for a moment, then swung it to the left. His hair was unruly. He wore a blouse with a tassel like a student or a revolutionary. He stopped before a round mirror in an ornamental gilt frame and began making faces into it. He moved his lips, his brows, his nose, like an actor rehearsing a role.

Lydia Michalovna suddenly flared up: "Will you stop running around like a wolf in a cage?"

"Well, speak, I'm listening."

"Sit down. I can't shout. Today you are wilder than usual."

"I'm not wild. These summer days drive me crazy."

"Why blame it on the days? Darling, it can't go on like this!"

"Well, I've heard that before. You're repeating yourself. It's second nature with women. You've said it and I've heard it."

"I beg you, don't 'thou' me. Not now. I wasn't born for this sort of life. I don't care about people talking. I swear by everything sacred that gossip bothers me less than the barking of a dog. But I must feel right with myself. It doesn't concern me that others have no respect for me, but I cannot lose my self-respect."

"Empty phrases. All the ladies talk the same nonsense. Truly amusing. What is respect? Respect for what? We are all animals."

"I know, I know, but I cannot go on in this way. I can make peace with the fact that I have a lover, but he must conduct himself like a lover and not chase every petticoat in sight. I can share with a wife, but not with every peasant woman in the village. I haven't fallen that low yet."

"What's all this foolishness? With whom are you sharing me? Unless you're jealous of Hanka?"

"I can't stand the sight of her. She looks at me like a bleeding calf. If she is nothing to you, as you say, why don't you send her away? The longer she serves you, the worse it will become."

"I've sent her away a thousand times, but she won't go. She'll throw herself into the well, and I don't want any scandals. Girls like her are capable of anything."

"Maybe you're afraid that she'll throw acid at you?"

"I'm not afraid. I'm not afraid of anything. When I saw them put my mother into the grave, I decided that this world is nothing but a plague and we're all a bunch of worms. I'm ready to put a bullet through my skull. That's the truth."

"You're ready to shoot yourself, but you chase after every woman. Everyone is talking about you. It will end in disgrace, if not catastrophe."

"What are you? A gypsy? A seeress? I'm risking my skin, not yours. Besides, you know I don't beg anyone for anything. It's all the same to me: yes-yes, no-no."

"Why do you speak like that? You're still young. Truly, this sort of fatalism is bad. When you began—when we began, you were different. Then you spoke like an idealist."

"Idealist? I told you frankly I wanted you. I desired you. I still do. Everything else is garbage."

"It isn't garbage. We're getting older. What will you be like at forty, if you feel like this now?"

"At forty I'll be lying with my head down and my feet up."

"But why? Why? You're healthy and capable. I don't want to throw myself at anyone, as God is my witness, but we could be happy. What I have with Kostia is no life at all."

"What's wrong with him? No one could be better than he.

He's diligent, devoted, tolerant. I'm the third lover you've had, and—"

"What do you mean, the third? You know that's not true."

"I'm not lying."

"Well, I'm not going to bicker with you. I mention something and you make a mountain out of it. You may think what you will, but I'm not a cynic. I would have been a good wife if Kostia had been different."

"Well, I must go."

"Where are you going? What's the matter with you today?"

"You're making me nervous. You used to behave like a woman. Now you preach like a priest. I'm tired of your admonishments. If I live, I live, and if I croak, I'll be dead. If you think I'm too cynical, I can leave you alone. From today on— from this moment on. *Adieu!*"

"Where are you going? God in heaven, I didn't mean to insult you. Don't you believe that a person can love?"

"Love, not harass."

"Well, I pity you. Don't run away. You're liable to wake my child. Your mother did well to die. . . ."

Lydia Michalovna remained sitting in astonishment. She had turned pale. The last words had slipped out as if of their own accord. Sasha had an urge to slap her, but he thrust his hand into his trousers pocket. After a while he left without saying anything. He walked past the living room and went outside. For a while he lingered on the threshold.

"Well, let her go. To blazes with her! . . ." He walked several more steps and stopped again. "What in hell does she want? Why do they all make these terrible predictions? They hate me, that's the truth. Females hate every man they can't dominate and step on and that's what they call love. They are leeches. I'd rather have open hostility."

Sasha headed for the barracks. He stopped, picked up a stone, tossed it aside. Purposelessly, he strayed from the path.

He came to a swamp where frogs were croaking. He toed the slime aimlessly with the tip of his boot. The sun was setting in the west. Dusk began to fall. Gnats droned, chased each other in a whirl. Shadows skipped over the grass as if cast by invisible beings. "What is wrong with me? What torments me so?" Sasha asked himself. "It's gnawing at me so that I don't know which way to turn. . . . And what is the point of all this talk? What does she want of me? Something, after all, is tormenting her too. . . ." It suddenly hit Sasha that in the space of a short time he had lost his mother and father. "God in heaven, I am an orphan, I am all alone in the world!" he thought. "She is also an orphan. . . . We are all orphans. That's why we want to creep into one another. . . . That's why women want to hang on to someone, to cling. . . . Well, I won't have it! I'll spit on the whole lot of them! . . . I'll leave this whole mess, and go to the other end of the world! . . ."

Sasha had an impulse to throw himself into the mud.

"I'll simply kill myself. That will be my end! . . ."

23

Hannah, Zadok's wife, celebrated Rosh Hashana the way her
parents did at home. Zadok insisted that it wasn't necessary:
no one had yet been to heaven and seen people judged, the
Book of Judgment open itself, the angels shiver, the good and
bad deeds recorded. He argued that as long as Hannah had
taken off her wig and broken away from Jewish fanaticism,
she might just as well be consistent. But Hannah would not
listen. It was no great sin to go wigless. Among the Litvaks,
even rabbis' wives went around with bare heads. But Rosh
Hashana was Rosh Hashana. Hannah had reserved a pew in
the synagogue. She baked Rosh Hashana challahs, bought apples, honey, a live carp, carrots, grapes, and everything that
was needed for the holiday. On Rosh Hashana eve she made a
benediction over the candles in the silver candlestick her father, Reb Joshua Walden, had given her as a wedding present.
Since they were celebrating the holiday, Zadok invited his
Uncle Ezriel to join them. Hannah insisted that the holiday
traditions be followed to the letter. They each took a wedge
of apple and honey and said: "God grant us a good and sweet
year." Then, before eating a spoonful of carrots, they recited:
"God grant that our merits be many."

Zadok sat smiling at the head of the table, but from time to
time he grew pensive. It seemed outlandish to be sitting here in

an apartment in the Old City, while in Marshinov his father presided at the table. Thousands of Jews were assembled there. The court was full, the walls of the House of Worship were straining. No small thing, the Days of Awe in Marshinov! If Zadok had remained pious, he would at this moment be sitting at his father's right hand. Thousands of eyes would be looking at him, the heir-to-be. In his imagination, Zadok saw a forest of fur hats, sidelocks, beards. His father's following grew larger from year to year, but Zadok, his son, had joined the "enlightened." It was good after all that Hannah had insisted on celebrating the holiday. With candles lit and a white cloth covering the table, it was more pleasant even to read the *Courier Warshavsky*, or some German almanac. In the traditional holiday loaf, the fish, the chicken soup, there was some semblance of Marshinov. And his Uncle Ezriel was there with them discussing the Talmud. They were splitting hairs over laws, not for any practical purpose, but just to show that they still remembered.

From time to time Zadok imitated the chant and gestures of his former teacher. Hannah, who was busy carving the chicken, called out: "Don't make fun of Jewishness."

"I'm not making fun. Each nationality has its own nonsense. Take the ram's horn, for example. It undoubtedly stems from the Stone Age. It was originally used as a call to war. In the days when the Temple still stood, the mouth of the ram's horn was edged with gold and there were silver trumpets on either side of it."

Hannah opened her eyes wide. Her hair was bound up in a delicate scarf. "Trumpets? That's impossible."

"Yes, it's the truth. Ask Uncle Ezriel."

"Yes, that is so," Ezriel said.

"I never know whether he's fooling me or not. He tells me all kinds of stories. He can talk anything into me. But I know one thing: a holiday is a holiday. The Gentiles have their holidays too."

"Right as rain."

Hannah grew tearful. "Oh, Uncle Ezriel, I long for the way it was at home. At our house Rosh Hashana was beautiful! My mother had a gold dress with a train which she wore only on Rosh Hashana and Yom Kippur. When she put it on, the room lit up. She had a golden chain, so thick—an old-fashioned one, with a lock. It was a gift from Grandmother, may she rest in paradise. Papa prayed in the study house, but Mama had a seat in the synagogue, right near the east wall. She has a prayer book with a silver clasp. When I think of my sister Tilly standing near my mother, and of me here, all alone, in the city, I feel like crying—"

And big tears formed in Hannah's eyes. Zadok laughed. "Now she's bawling!" But he immediately grew serious.

Hannah went into the kitchen. They could hear her blowing her nose.

"Blood is thicker than water," Ezriel said.

"What should we do, Uncle Ezriel? How long must we hold on to this? There must be an end sometime."

"Zadok, it's not good."

"What is not good, Uncle Ezriel? The generations must go on. Epochs change; the Old Slavs had their religion too. They were idol worshippers. They served Baba Yaga, or some other idol. Now they are Christians. If everyone stuck to the old ways, there would be no progress."

"To the Slavs, Christianity is progress. But where is our progress? We had a spiritual life, now we are spiritually naked."

"Something else will work itself out. We are living in a changeable epoch. The times when we were the chosen people are over. Some of our laws are rooted somewhere in India. They have the same taboos about menstruation. Our system of kosher and impure foods probably stems from the African Negroes. Honestly, Uncle Ezriel, we have nothing to be so proud of. We have even borrowed the Ten Commandments from Hammurabi."

"According to the Bible critics, we have nothing at all of

our own. The entire Scriptures are one amalgamation of borrowed legends. Borrowed from whom? It's a big lie."

"It's the truth. They are borrowed, and why deny the
truth?"

"And even if it is true? A cellar with poisoned air is just as
real as a garden, but one suffocates in it. Second, since one cannot know *das Ding an sich*, and what we call reality is subjective, actually a dream—one can choose the kind of reality one
wants. Why throw away gold and keep mud? Since a coal and
a diamond are one and the same, why not remain with the
diamond?"

"Because diamonds are useless and coals make factories run.
Uncle is mistaken. According to Kant, reality is not a dream.
Schopenhauer derides the second edition of the *Critique*, but
actually the second edition is the true Kant. Kant is not Berke-
ley."

"Whatever he is, reality is not known."

"Why are you planning to go to Palestine? Olga has spoken
to me. You're embarking on a disastrous path."

"Why is it so disastrous? I no longer believe that I can help
the sick. I cannot swindle people. My father existed on six rubles a week and I can manage on the same."

"Are you serious about this?"

"Entirely. What is called nerves is a moral illness. I cannot
forget what my mother, may she rest in peace, used to say:
'Satan has a new name: nerves.' Our grandfathers and grandmothers were not nervous, although they were hounded and
tormented. Evil for them was not a sickness but a temptation."

"Would you call paranoia a sin and a temptation? Really,
Uncle, I'm shocked. But why go to Palestine? If you want to
become a pious fanatic, you can do that right here in Warsaw.
And what will happen to Olga? She won't go with you."

"Is that what she said? She changes her mind every day.
She's bringing Misha up to hate Jews and everything Jewish. I
cannot allow this. Even if all religions are false, why reject

one's own and accept somebody else's? Just because Ivan is strong and we are weak?"

"The world belongs to the strong."

"I cannot live in such a world. I cannot kiss the fist that hits me."

"They will beat you there too—the Turks, the Arabs. Are you going to leave Olga?"

"I cannot bring up children who will spit on me when they grow up. Plain and simple. They are already beginning to spit. Kolia keeps telling Misha that we are God-killers. When they quarrel, he calls him 'dirty Jew.' "

Hannah entered from the kitchen. "What are you two whispering about? It's a holiday. There is a God in heaven, there is. He is leading the world, not your philosophers."

11

A large crowd had assembled in Marshinov for the Day of Atonement. But only several score remained for the Feast of the Tabernacles. How many Hassidim could, after all, fit into a tabernacle? Although the rabbi was sick and constantly feverish, he spent the night inside the tabernacle on a bed made up for him there. The Warsaw specialists, who had long ago advised the rabbi to eat fatty foods and go to a sanatorium, had given up hope of his recovery. The Marshinov doctor, Ząbek, had let it be known that the rabbi's condition was hopeless. He was in the last stage of consumption. He had grown extremely emaciated and his face had a corpselike pallor. He coughed weakly, spat blood, had suffered several hemorrhages. His fingernails had split, his beard and forelocks had grown larger, thicker, a mixture of gray and white. His intimates knew the rabbi suffered from a catarrh of the intestines as well and that his urine was not clear. The rabbi drank half a saucer of milk each morning and ate nothing but an occasional spoonful of groats. But Reb Jochanan had remained Reb Jochanan, constantly refreshing himself in God's service. He continued to attend the ritual bath, maintained fasts, and studied holy books. When he recited the Torah, the rabbi's pale face flushed and his eyes grew brilliant. Even Dr. Ząbek admitted that divine powers kept the rabbi alive. His senses had become keener than ever before.

Although the rabbi had scarcely eaten all week, on the night of Succoth he made a benediction over the wine, tasted a sip of it, a bit of the bread, a bite of fish, a drop of chicken soup, a sliver of meat, a spoonful of carrot stew. He sang the table chants and gave a sermon. Hassidim remarked that such interpretation of the Torah had never been heard before. He revealed holy secrets. He seemed like an angel of God. The tabernacle was a permanent one, all that had to be done to use it on the Holy Days was raise the roof with pulleys, so that the worshippers sat under the ceiling of branches that replaced it. The boys from the rabbi's yeshiva hung lanterns constructed of melons; paper kites; clusters of grapes, apples, pears; a pomegranate left from Rosh Hashana; and birds made of eggs blown hollow from the branches. Marshinov maidens, daughters of the Hassidim, draped the walls of the tabernacle with blankets and embroidered throws. At night the table was covered by a festive cloth, on which was placed a braided loaf protected by a napkin, and a carafe of wine with a benediction beaker. And when Tsipele made the benediction over the candles in the silver candlesticks, the tabernacle seemed transformed into one of the mansions of paradise. The melodies of the Hassidim could be heard over half of Marshinov late into the night. The next morning, Kaile, Tsipele's maid, said to her that in the middle of the night she had looked out her window and seen a glow emanating from the tabernacle. By this time the candles had gone out. Afraid of fire, she had gone down to look through the draperies. There was no fire, but the light shining from the rabbi's face lit up half a wall. It faded as she stood there, and her knees had given way from fright.

The first two days of Succoth in Marshinov passed with great joy. The rabbi performed in a state of ecstasy: blessing the citrus fruit, waving his palm branch. There was dancing in the tabernacle too. The Hassidim who had been invited to the tabernacle were served wine. On the second intermediary day, Tsipele came to give the rabbi his medicine. The rabbi was not alone. He was studying with his youngest son, Gadele, already a grown boy. Now that Zadok, his elder son, had become worldly, Gadele was to be the rabbi's spiritual heir. The rabbi's son-in-law, Pinchus, Zelda's husband, the son of the Wysoker rabbi, was also there.

Seeing the bottle of medicine, the rabbi grimaced. "After the holiday."

"The doctor said you should take it every day."

"Not necessarily."

Suddenly the rabbi remarked: "Speaking of doctors, what's new with Ezriel?"

Tsipele was astounded. For years, ever since Shaindel had become insane and Ezriel had gone to live with a convert, the rabbi had not mentioned his name.

"Who knows?"

"His father, Reb Menachem Mendel, was a just and pious man."

"Yes."

"A pity. . . ."

Two hours later, as Tsipele sat reading at the window, a carriage drove into the courtyard and a tall man in modern clothes stepped out. Tsipele paled when she recognized Ezriel. There was a child with him. Mendel the beadle informed the rabbi that the doctor, Reb Calman's son-in-law (he did not want to call him the rabbi's brother-in-law), had come from Warsaw to extend his greetings.

The rabbi smiled. "Send him in."

Ezriel and Misha entered. Approaching him, the rabbi extended his hand.

"Peace be with you, Rabbi!"

"Peace to you. Welcome!" the rabbi exclaimed.

"The rabbi recognized me?"

"Yes, of course, Ezriel."

"This is my son, Moishele."

The rabbi bent down toward the child. "So, Moishele. Are you a good boy?" And the rabbi pinched his cheek.

Misha didn't answer him and the rabbi asked again: "You're a mischief-maker, eh?"

"Rabbi, he doesn't understand Yiddish," Ezriel said in a hollow tone.

"Well, one can serve God in any language."

"Rabbi, I brought him here. I want him to become a Jew."

Tears flowed from the rabbi's eyes. "Well, well . . ."

"Rabbi, I can't stand it anymore!" Ezriel cried out, his voice breaking.

Taking out his handkerchief, the rabbi dabbed at his eyes.

"Did you see the truth?" he asked.

"Not completely. But I saw their lie," Ezriel replied.

"It's all the same."

III

During his student days and later when he practiced medicine, Ezriel had kept mostly to himself. The Christian students did not mingle with the Jewish ones. The Jewish students ignored each other to avoid becoming a segregated group. In the hospital and at the clinic, he had kept his colleagues at a distance, because, first, Shaindel did not want to know their wives, and also because they were not the kind of people with whom he could be intimate. They played cards, gossiped. Many of the doctors were involved in organizational activities, most of these supported by the assimilationists. Here in Marshinov, Ezriel felt for the first time in years that he was not alone. Addressing him in the familiar "thou," aged Hassidim recalled his father, Reb Menachem Mendel of Jampol. Reb Shimmon, the Stiktiner rabbi, had died and Mayer Joel, who had gone over to Reb Shimmon, and his sons-in-law returned to Marshinov. Young men and boys called Ezriel "Uncle."

Usually, a large crowd did not assemble for the last two days of the holiday. But this time a great number of Hassidim came. Some were curious to see the heretic who had returned to Judaism. It seemed odd that Zadok, the rabbi's son, had become an atheist, while Ezriel had repented. Tsipele wept when Ezriel came to see her. Her daughter gazed at him lovingly. Gadele trailed alongside Uncle Ezriel, eager to converse with him. Everywhere people went out of their way to greet him. Jews grasped his hands, reluctant to let go, gazed at him warmly. Each person wanted to hear for himself why Ezriel had forsaken the enlightened ones, the materialists, the philosophers. The women of the court took over the care of Moishele. They taught him Yiddish, pampered him, guarded him, kissed and petted him. Each day was filled with delight. Ezriel prayed in the study house, said the blessing over the citrus fruit, and helped Misha do the same. He ate with Misha in the tabernacle. The boy seemed to revive. He grasped the Yiddish words with unusual rapidity, played tag and hide-and-seek with the children.

Ezriel realized how isolated he had been all these years. He had formed no real friendships. No one had been interested in him. Here in Marshinov, he was at home. He could drop in everywhere, everybody spoke his language, had known his father, and even his grandfather, Reb Abraham Hamburg. He was treated like a prince who had returned from exile.

In recent years, Ezriel had grown accustomed to finding in everyone symptoms of neurasthenia, hysteria, or simply chronic dissatisfaction. Rage and pride showed everywhere. He read frustration, thwarted ambition, unfulfilled lusts in all eyes. People never seemed to have enough possessions, or they studied insatiably, or needed more and more love affairs. Ezriel had concluded that this was human nature, since he, too, was no different. He had accepted Schopenhauer's philosophy that human life oscillates between lust and tedium. The conception that everything was blind will, the result of blind forces, attracted him, although his reason rejected it. Every play, every novel, every chapter of history, every newspaper article led to the conclusion that all was futile and must end tragically. Even Olga's parties, the dancing, the drinking, the jokes, the flirting arose from melancholy. Everyone was trying to forget himself.

In Marshinov, there was joy. Eyes shone, faces glowed. The glory of God must have descended upon these Jews, the Talmudic scholars, the students of Hassidic study houses. Ezriel did not see in them the symptoms of uncertainty, overindulgence, impatience. He stood, on the seventh day of the Feast of Tabernacles, in the House of Prayer and looked around him. What he saw here was completely contrary to the textbooks. According to the sociologists, poverty was the cause not only of sickness but of crime. But these Jews were a living denial of all these theories. They did not enjoy fresh air, did no exercise, nor did they eat the food recommended by modern physicians. They stooped when they walked, shuffled their feet, spat on the floors, never used forks. Most of them wore patched satin capotes, ragged skullcaps, shabby shoes, torn stockings. They earned their precarious livings from halfstocked stores, tutoring, matchmaking, or brokerage fees. They sighed as they prayed. "Woe is me . . . Dear Father . . . woe and double woe . . ." This was no privileged class but an assemblage of paupers, less secure than the peasantry and the proletariat. They had been driven out of Russia, were the victims of pogroms; writers had vilified them, called them parasites; anti-Semites had manufactured false accusations against them. But instead of becoming degenerate, sinking into melancholy, drunkenness, immorality—they celebrated, recited the Psalms, rejoiced with happiness that could only come from the soul. No one here was in despair over the pogroms, as were the Jewish intelligentsia all over Russia. They placed their faith in God, not in man, evolution, or revolution.

IV

On the night of Simhath Torah, Misha carried a flag and a red apple with a candle stuck into it. He stood with the other boys on a bench and chatted in a mixture of Polish and Yiddish. For the first three years of his life, Misha had spoken Yiddish with his mother, and the language was not completely strange to him. Tsipele had bought him a skullcap and a sash. He knew how to make a benediction over bread, water, or a cookie. The procession of men carrying the scroll of the Law passed the boys and they stretched out their hands, touched its mantlet, and brought their fingers to their lips. Even girls had come into the House of Prayer. Simhath Torah is a holiday when rules are relaxed. After a while, Ezriel was called to carry the scroll. The beadle sang out his name in the traditional chant: "Arise, Reb Ezriel, son of our teacher, Reb Menachem Mendel," and the entire assembly looked toward him. When Ezriel walked past Misha with the scroll, the youngster jumped off the bench he was standing on and followed his father. Ezriel let him touch the Tree of Life, the post around which the scroll is wrapped, so that he too would be helping to carry the Torah.

Ezriel asked him quietly: "Do you want to remain here, or go back to Warsaw?"

"Remain here," Misha replied.

"For how long?"

"A thousand years."

The Hassidim sang and danced. The boys joined in with their high-pitched voices. The girls clapped their hands. The main festivities began on the following morning. Ezriel had forgotten that Jews could rejoice so heartily. Although it was forbidden to drink before the day's prayers were ended, Hassidim took a sip after the morning services. The beadle warned the tipsy descendants of Aaron that they would not be permitted to make the priestly blessing. But they paid no attention to him. Youths carried flasks in their pockets. They started playing pranks, tied together the ritual garments of two elderly Hassidim, hid someone's prayer shawl, or skullcap, or replaced the Succoth prayer book with the one used during the High Holy Days. Their elders scolded: "Pups! Ignoramuses! Tipplers! Where are you when there's no wine?" And the boys answered back: "What's so important about being old? A billy goat has a white beard too." "Heathens, you'll be thrown out of here!" an elderly Hassid said, smiling broadly. But even as they joked, not one of them missed an "Amen." When the reader, during the recital of the Eighteen Benedictions, made the mistake of praying for "dew" instead of "rain," everyone laughed. The rabbi smiled to himself. After the singing of "Unto thee it was shown," all the scrolls of Law were taken out of the Holy Ark. There were perhaps twenty scrolls both new and old. Some had ragged mantlets decorated with crowns and fescues; the coverings of others were unornamented save for the ancient dates embroidered on them. Because the Holy Ark was left empty, a lighted candle was placed within it.

Ezriel had forgotten these customs. Each prayer had its melody, its nuances and accompanying sighs. Holding the scrolls, the Hassidim danced, singing the chants of Marshinov. Too weak to carry a large scroll, the rabbi held a small one. He put his face to it, kissed it, buried his cheek in the velvet of its mantlet. Feebly, he began to sing. The Hassidim pushed forward to kiss his Torah. Dancing and swaying, he leaned down so the children, Misha among them, could reach it. Everyone watched, knowing the rabbi was in constant pain and that his days were numbered. Barring a miracle, he would never see another Simhath Torah. They smiled and wept. Singing, they wiped away their tears. They danced singly and in small groups. Holding up scrolls of the Law, two old men danced facing each other. What else did the Jews have beside the Torah? But what else was needed? After the procession, all but three of the scrolls were replaced in the Ark. There followed a kind of auction for the honor of being "the groom

of the Torah" and "the groom of Genesis." "One ruble!" "Ten
gulden!" "Two rubles!" "Two and a quarter!" "Three!
. . ." The beadle banged on the reader's lectern and called
out in a festive singsong, "Three rubles once, three rubles
twice, three rubles for the last—" "Four rubles!" cried a
hoarse voice. It was like a marketplace, but the House of
Prayer needed money for the winter. The walls were peeling.
Immediately after selling these honors, the reader began the
recitation of "And this is the blessing." Each man and boy, all
but the smallest, was called up separately to make the benediction. The smallest children were summoned and came running
in a group. They were all covered by the same prayer shawl.
Misha was among them. The reader made the benediction
with them, in his deep voice, the children repeating in their
thin, piping singsong: "Blessed be Thou who hath chosen us
among all nations and given us the Torah . . ." "This is the
true chauvinism," Ezriel thought, and smiled to himself. They
had chosen themselves. In every epoch they had been roasted
alive. In every generation there was another excuse for exter-
minating them and their holy books. Hadn't they crucified
Jesus, used Christian blood in their matzos, defiled the holy
water, desecrated the wafer? These Jews in the House of
Prayer deserved destruction for many offenses: for being capitalists (wasn't that a joke?), they were strangers (merely
eight hundred years in Poland). What were they not? Chau-
vinists, reactionaries, petty bourgeois, fanatics, jargonists, bar-
barians. Every "ism" spelled doom for them. But their real
crime was that they tried to lead sanctified lives, without wars,
without adultery, without mockery or rebellion.

But could their behavior serve as an example for others?
Could their conduct become what Kant calls a maxim? Yes, it
was possible. Humanity could abolish warfare, divide the land
so that there would be enough for everyone. Each group
could have its language, its culture, its traditions. But one
thing all would have to have in common: a belief in one God
and in free will; a discipline that would transform all man's

deeds into serving God and helping one another. In a divine existence, there are no neutral activities. Everything must exalt, purify. But such things could not be brought about forcibly, nor could the Messiah be compelled to arrive.

v

There had been a time when Ezriel had assumed that he knew a good deal about the eccentricities of the human mind. He had been accustomed to hear his patients chatter irrationally, contradict themselves, accuse or justify themselves. He had also thought he knew intimately the workings of his own brain. But in the past weeks Ezriel had realized how plural man's thinking could be. The simultaneous existence within one of both an evil spirit and a good one, as described in the Holy Books, was apparently a profound psychological truth. Even while Ezriel was in Marshinov praying, studying, dancing with the Hassidim, and teaching Misha Judaism, something within him continued to worry about his patients, about Olga and Topolka. Something insisted that his piety would end with the holidays and his return to Warsaw. He argued with himself that a materialistic existence was bad and that religion was a remedy for all ills. But could he believe as these men did that every law, every custom had come down from Mount Sinai? Could there be anything more contradictory than a penitent who remained a heretic? Or even one who doubted? He was reminded of a passage in Proverbs: "None that go unto her return again"—which, according to the Talmud, referred to heresy. The essence of religion, as interpreted by Ezriel, was a wholeness, an unblemished faith. But could anyone who had read the Bible critics and understood the evolution of ideas revert to religious innocence? These Jews believed that the Torah came to them directly from heaven, but Ezriel knew it had been written by various writers at different times. In Genesis, light and darkness were two separate entities. The sun was apparently not the source of light but a lamp that added light to and brightened an already existent source. The stars were an addition to the moon. The sky was a dam or sluice that prevented the waters of heaven from inundating the earth.

In the same Torah that contained "Thou shalt not kill," there were commandments on how to liquidate entire nations, how to plunder, burn, even rape. Leviticus was full of magic and taboos similar to those found among savage tribes in Africa and Polynesia. Could Ezriel learn from the Torah the divine and absolute truth? What was he doing here in Marshinov? Why was he deceiving these people?

He had drunk wine with them and danced with them, but he had done so without real faith. "Am I a hypocrite? Have I taken leave of my senses? Am I simply a self-murderer, as Olga calls me?" He bit his lips. Perhaps among Jews he was an exception. But among Christians there were millions like him, after all. They studied Darwin and attended church. Not only had the church and state been separated in some countries, but within their own psyches the Gentiles had established a difference between religious and scientific truth. Was this possible? There could be only one truth: either the world was created in six days or it had developed over millions of years; either God had parted the Red Sea or he had not; either Jesus had been resurrected from the dead or he had remained dead. Was Ezriel capable of basing his life on contradiction?

Simhath Torah fell on a Friday. All day Ezriel went from one kiddush to another. He drank with the others, dry wine, sweet wine, mead with nuts, beer. He nibbled on strudel, flat cakes, tarts. At Tsipele's house he had partaken of cabbage with raisins and cream of tartar. He was sated, tipsy. But in some recess of his brain, he had remained cold-sober. No, he was incapable of building his life on revelations. He could not rely on the hearsay of religious authority. Perhaps there had been no Moses, no miracles. The Torah was merely a book. All religions were dreams. God was eternally silent. If He existed, was there a method for finding Him? How—a priori, a posteriori? Or should He once and for all be identified with nature, as in Spinoza's conclusions? So many had tried to show proof of His existence and had proven nothing. The Kantian elephant had borne a mouse.

Yes, for the Hassidim, it was Simhath Torah. Evening approached. At sundown the women hurried to make their benedictions over the candles. Kaile, Tsipele's maid, prepared the Sabbath stew and sealed the oven with dough. Soon they would see in the Sabbath, singing: "Come, my beloved." It was the Sabbath when the reading of the first section of Genesis comes round again. But did this have any connection with the outside world? Could Ezriel accept this life, forsake his career? He had fled because his life was not turning out well. Would it be more fulfilled here? What would he do when everybody returned home after the holidays? Why had he come in the first place? Had it been to escape estrangement, impiety, a daughter who hid a revolver under her mattress, a wife who arranged balls for lechers and oppressors, patients who deceived their husbands and wanted only to have more enjoyment at someone else's expense? Or to find the way to a mute God whose nature is unknown, whom one does not know how to serve, and even whether any service rendered Him is appreciated. He, the Almighty, had kept silent in times of idolatry, slavery, wars, plagues, tortures. He had disposed of all men in the same fashion: those who worshipped Him, and those who rebelled against Him. On the other hand, if God did speak, what would happen to free will? His father, peace be with him, had been right: God cannot reveal His purpose if good and evil, faith and denial are to remain hanging in the balance. Moral life depends on this doubt. Man must discover God through temptation and suffering, exactly as he had discovered that one could be poisoned by toadstools and that a serum distilled from cowpox could cure smallpox. Everyone sought God, every race, every savage tribe. Mankind could not exist without this constant search, as he, Ezriel, had so often pointed out to Zadok.

In the evening the Jews went back to the House of Prayer. Candles and kerosene lamps were already lit. The floor had been swept and strewn with yellow sand. The Hassidim chanted the Song of Songs. The reader stood before the lectern and began: "Oh, come, let us exult . . ."

VI

On Sabbath night, Ezriel went into the rabbi's study and remained there for two and a half hours. No one in Marshinov recalled the rabbi spending so much time with anyone before. Mendel the beadle, who placed his ear to the door, heard only mumbling. It wasn't like Ezriel to speak his thoughts to someone else, to reveal his torments, but this time he held nothing back. He sat opposite the rabbi and it seemed to him as if every word he uttered stabbed the rabbi like a spear. From time to time the rabbi grimaced as if in pain and clutched at his breast. Ezriel frequently asked if he should stop, but the rabbi replied: "Continue, continue!" Ezriel spoke frankly: What proof was there that the Law of Moses was true law? The other religions had their own laws. Where was there proof that God existed? And if He did exist, yet never indicated what pleased Him and what did not—why was there punishment? Could a king who did not issue laws to his subjects punish because the laws were not obeyed? From the rabbi's expression, Ezriel knew he was blaspheming. It was cruel to torment a saint who had given his life to his religion and was now close to death. What could the rabbi tell him that he himself did not know? Ezriel grew afraid lest the rabbi rebuke him, abhor him as a heretic, and drive him away. At times the rabbi's face grew mournful and baffled, at others there was the trace of a twinkle in his eyes. His sidelocks dripped perspiration. The candles in the holders grew smaller. Shadows danced on the walls. Several times Mendel the beadle peeped in, but the rabbi waved him away. From time to time, the rabbi had a coughing spell and spat into a handkerchief.

When Ezriel grew silent, the rabbi asked: "From whom are you descended on your mother's side?"

"Mother was a pious Jewess."

"I know. Was she also descended from pious men?"

"Yes, Rabbi, from Rabbi Yom Tov Heller."

"So? You are a grandson of saints."

"What shall I do, Rabbi?"

"Do no evil."

"Is that all?"

"It is much."

"What shall I do about my wife, Rabbi? I told you about her."

"Yes, I heard."

"Shall I leave her?"

"If you can."

"And if I cannot?"

"Then wait."

"What shall I do with Moishele?"

"Leave him here."

"Rabbi, I don't know what to do."

The rabbi smiled. "One does, nevertheless. At least don't cause anyone sorrow."

"Shall I put on phylacteries, live like a Jew?"

"Yes, as well as you can."

"Even though I don't believe in the Law of Moses?"

"The saints also doubted. As long as the soul dwells in the body, it can never be totally sure of anything. God willing, we will all see the truth."

"And meanwhile?"

"Meanwhile, don't harm anyone, or yourself either."

"Shall I remain a doctor?"

"Doctors are necessary."

"I have kept nothing from the rabbi."

"Everything requires God's help. Even with free choice, the grace of God is necessary. Even free will is mercy."

"What must be done?"

"One must pray for mercy."

"Even without faith?"

"There are no total unbelievers. The body is blind. But the soul sees, because it exists in this world and the other. Without the body, there would be no such thing as free will. That is its reason for being."

"It's good to hear this, Rabbi."

"Why worry? It's God's world. Everything comes from Him. The evildoer certainly harms—but there are remedies. There is no reason to despair."

"What shall I do to deserve mercy?"

"Perform kind acts. You have already done something noble in saving Moishele."

Ezriel wanted to say a few more words, tell the rabbi about his intention to visit Palestine, but the rabbi stood up, extending his hand. "Go in good health. God knows everything . . ."

"Thank you, Rabbi."

"The body is a vessel for pain, that is why it rebels."

Ezriel went to his room. Moishele was already asleep. Ezriel got into bed but could not fall asleep. The rabbi's words echoed in him. It was wonderful, that this saint who imposed such mortifications upon himself was so lenient with others. The real difference between a saint and a wicked man suddenly came to Ezriel: both weighed everything morally, but the saint made demands on himself, whereas the rogue made demands on others. Ezriel fell asleep and dreamed of Olga. He awoke trembling and lustful. Perhaps she no longer loved him.

He began to consider the reasoning behind asceticism. Why were there so many recluses, fakirs, monks, nuns? Why were the revolutionaries prepared to die for their beliefs? In this egotistical world, why were there so many candidates for martyrdom? He himself was about to renounce a woman who loved him, and a career, to assume an existence of suffering. Why? Because the soul yearned for as much power as the body. It craved freedom from material bondage, but could not achieve it. Even to acquire some freedom, the soul must struggle constantly. Jewishness is based on compromise between body and soul, not on war between them.

What the rabbi had tried to tell him was simply this: "Don't force yourself. It is better to do a little with good will than a lot by compulsion."

VII

Sunday morning, Ezriel went into the House of Prayer and put on his prayer shawl before praying. Many of the Hassidim had left the previous night or at daybreak, but several quorums still remained. Ezriel put a phylactery on his bared arm, and the other on his forehead, then wound the thongs around his fingers in the form of the Hebrew letter Shin, the initial of Shadai, the holy name, and intoned: "And I will betroth thee unto me for ever; Yea, I will betroth thee unto me in righteousness, and in judgment and in loving-kindness and in mercies. I will even betroth thee unto me in faithfulness and thou shalt know the Lord."

"What words! What a lump of auto-suggestion to swallow on an empty stomach!" Ezriel said to himself. Customarily in the morning Ezriel glanced at the newspaper. A pogrom had occurred, a flood, a strike, a demonstration. He would turn the page and read about murders, suicides, arson, thefts. In the House of Prayer, each day began auspiciously. He finished his prayers and went to say goodbye to Tsipele. Moishele had already eaten breakfast. Tsipele told Ezriel that she would engage a tutor for the boy for a few weeks before enrolling him in a cheder. Zelda, Tsipele's daughter, was staying in Marshinov and would help keep an eye on Moishele. Tsipele's children were already grown, and it would be a pleasure for her to raise another child, Shaindel's child, her father's grandchild. Ezriel wanted to leave her money, but Tsipele grew angry. "I don't need money!"

"It costs money to bring up a child."

"Pish-pash! He'll cost me a million. . . ."

"Moishele, do you want to stay here?"

"*Tak*. Yes."

"Mind your aunt."

"Yes."

Ezriel wondered why the child wished to stay. Olga had been like a mother to him. Kolia had played with him. But he'd raise a fuss if Ezriel tried to take him away. Moishele was holding a slice of ginger cake and drinking milk. He was at home with Tsipele already. They had bought him a gaberdine and a cap worn by cheder boys. He was mixing Yiddish words with his Polish. Ezriel left pocket money for the boy and rode to the train. The depot was filled with Hassidim. He should have traveled with them third-class, but he purchased a first-class ticket. He had to be able to think in the two hours it would take to get home. What was Olga doing? He had been away from home less than a week, but it seemed as if months had gone by. The train arrived. The Hassidim pushed forward with their packs and satchels. Ezriel watched them. They were almost all small, disheveled, with stooped shoulders, ruffled beards, and spoke with outlandish gestures. During the train's long wait, they shouted, ran about from one car to the next, became entangled in their long capotes, behaved so boisterously that the Gentile passengers laughed at them. Ezriel heard one Pole say to another: "A wild rabble, eh? . . ." Yes, here they were a rabble, but, only an hour before, they had been priests in a temple. Would the world ever understand this? They were completely lacking in that ornament the Gentile world called dignity or pride. Everything fine in them was concealed. Externally, they were almost caricatures.

The Hassidim came up to him, bustled around him, and for a while he was tormented by shame of his brothers. He was disgusted with himself! He was ashamed of Jews! This was what the Enlightenment had led to! . . . He decided to sit among them. He entered a third-class wagon. The bell rang for the third time. The train started. The benches were taken by

Gentile passengers who had gotten on at earlier stations, and the racks were filled with suitcases. The Hassidim stood in groups. Some tried to sit on their own baskets and traveling bags. They spoke, gesticulated, clutched their beards. One Hassid grasped another's lapel, trying to make him understand the rabbi's words. A yeshiva boy took a bottle of schnapps out of his basket and invited others to drink with him in honor of some rabbi's anniversary. Since there was no water with which to wash one's hands, the Hassidim wiped their palms on the windowpanes. Ezriel was also offered a sip of schnapps. He said the benediction, and they answered "Amen." They expressed the hope that he remain a Hassid and that he not, God forbid, be alienated from his ancestry. Two Gentile women began to giggle. A Gentile with blond mustaches spoke up. "Drinking, Jewboys, are you? You're drunks, eh? The Christian doesn't have a piece of bread to fill his stomach, but you scabheads, idlers, slurp vodka. They should do the same with you here as they've done in Russia: drive you out." "Where would you drive them to?" said a derby-hatted individual with black, piercing eyes. "Who would take them in, the vermin? The Prussians? They drop all their filth on us here in Poland. . . ." The Hassidim pretended not to hear, or perhaps they really didn't. They understood little Polish. Ezriel's impulse was to answer the Poles, but he knew that it was senseless. The Polish newspapers were growing more and more virulent against the Jews. Their wrath was aimed mainly at the Russian Jews, the Litvaks, who had been driven from the Russian provinces and were "Russifying" Poland. The Gentile in the derby continued. "They'll flood us, these devils! They'll do what they did to Egypt. They're chased like mice out of Russia, and here they spit on the Polish people and take away their bread. Create a food shortage. What are we supposed to do with this low rabble? Just look at them, folks: a wild horde! Worse than the Tartars! No manners whatever! . . ." "Hey, you, Jewboy, you've knocked down my satchel!" shouted a Gentile woman with a chirping voice.

"Pick it up, you lousy dog. . . . Oh, children, they're trampling my belongings! . . ." Ezriel picked up the satchel and put it back on the rack. "Yes," he said to himself, "in a first-class wagon I would have had rest, but this is the way it really is: we're a people without a home and we can't live with anyone. We remain alien, always the object of mockery and derision. Nothing has changed. Conditions are as bad today as they were a thousand years ago. Even worse: in those days, there was no 'enlightenment'. In those days, at least, Jews kept their faith. . . ." The conductor came in and began to search under the benches. Yes, a boy was actually concealed under one of them. The conductor pulled him out by his boots and one came off in his hand. The boy had long sidelocks, large black eyes. The bootless foot was wrapped in a rag.

"A thief, eh? . . . Where, you accursed ragamuffin, is your ticket?"

"I lost it."

"Lost it, eh? You'll sleep in jail tonight, you rascal! You leprous scab! . . ."

"Jews, we'll have to give him a hand," a young Hassid spoke up.

Ezriel paid the boy's fare. The conductor gave the boy back his boot. The Poles laughed, grew angry, twirled their mustaches. They whispered among themselves about Ezriel. With his European attire he did not belong to that crowd. Suspicious glances were cast in his direction. From time to time, Jewish correspondents from Western Europe came to Poland and wrote disparaging articles about the country for the European press.

VIII

Ezriel hired a droshky and was driven home. When he left the city, the sun was shining and it was still warm. Now, autumn had come. A mist hovered over Warsaw and from time to time a single drop fell from the overcast sky onto Ezriel's face.

The droshky reached the house. Ezriel paid the fare and started up the stairs. His name was inscribed on the brass plate over the door. At least he was still the master of this piece of metal. He rang the bell and heard footsteps. "Well, I mustn't be so nervous!" he said to himself. "I'll make my decision." Olga opened the door. She stood facing him—dark, slim, in a black dress and a new coiffure.

She smiled questioningly. "You're back?"

"I hope you recognize me."

"Well, come in."

He walked into the foyer and put down his valise.

"Where is Misha?" Olga asked.

"He's staying with the rabbi."

"Oh."

He opened the door to his office and glanced inside as if suspecting that someone had replaced him. In the living room, he hung his hat on the head of a little angel. It was a gesture to convince himself that he still lived here and could do as he pleased.

Olga followed him in. "You didn't even kiss me. . . ."

"From the way you spoke to me when I left, I thought everything was finished between us."

"What did I say? There were patients here, and I didn't know what to tell them. You're the talk of Warsaw."

"Let them talk."

"How does one just leave a child by himself?"

"He isn't alone. The rabbi's wife is his aunt. He has more relatives there than here."

"Well, I understand. After all, I'm a complete stranger to him. I only raised him. What will he do there, become a Hassid?"

"Go to cheder."

"Well, do as you see fit. I have nothing to say about it."

Olga stood near a rubber plant. As she spoke to Ezriel, she fussed with a half-withered leaf that was about to fall, as if trying to fasten the stem to its branch. She looked at him side-

long, smiling in a curiously embarrassed way. "Why don't
you take off your coat?"

He kept it on and sat down, resting his head against the
back of the sofa. A mood of tragic playfulness overtook him.
"Olga, it's bad!"

"What is bad, dearest?"

"Everything. I want to be a Jew and I long for this home. I
rode back in a third-class carriage and saw how the Poles feel
about us. We're well hated!"

"Who is loved? Why did you ride third-class?"

"I wanted to be with the Hassidim."

"If you're going to associate with them, you'll always run
into that sort of thing."

"Worldly Jews like us are hated even more. How are you?"

"Ah, I'm still alive. Did you think I'd commit suicide?"

"Why that, of all things?"

"You didn't even write one word."

"The letter wouldn't have come much earlier than I."

"Still—I hope you've decided what you want to do. If
you're to remain a doctor, you can't treat your patients this
way. You're not the only doctor in Warsaw."

"I know."

"Neither are you, as the saying goes in Yiddish, the only
male in Moscow."

Ezriel tensed. "What's happened? Has someone made you
an offer?"

Olga's face reddened. She paused a moment before she replied. "Yes."

"Who?"

Olga smiled, but her eyes remained sad. "I've told you
about Dr. Ivanov, the lieutenant colonel."

"Aha."

"He was in Warsaw and paid me a visit."

Her words shocked him. He grew pale with jealousy. "He
fell in love with you? Just like that?"

"Don't be so sarcastic. A man can still fall in love with me."

24 🏛

I

My dear Zadok (or do you prefer Zdzislaw?):

I know I promised to write you immediately, but six weeks have gone by since I left and I haven't until now been able to take time to write. What happened to Zina completely unnerved me. Perhaps I had no right to go and leave her in such a predicament. But, as God knows, I was unable to help her. I lowered myself before Sasha, when I finally located him, but all I got from him was impudence. He had sunk into deep gloom after the death of Clara and Calman. I had already liquidated everything and I had no alternative but to leave. I don't know what to write about first. I've been in Berlin, Paris, and have even seen the "Great Charcot," as he is called. I am now, as you can see, in Switzerland, in Bern. My sister Mirale is still in a sanatorium in Arosa, and I'm afraid that her condition is not good. She has sacrificed herself for the revolution, about which I hear talk here day and night. I cannot begin to tell you what is going on in the so-called Russian colony here, which consists ninety percent of Jews. A people that for four thousand years had lived with God and divine ideals has completely forgotten itself and its history of martyrdom. It has staked everything on a revolution that is likely to bring nothing but a blood bath. The tragedy of it all is that this handful of people are already divided into parties, groups, circles, all fighting and hating one another. Oh, how they hate! I don't deny that there are many idealists among them. My sister is one of them. And what drove Zina to all this? And what will happen to all of them when the guillotine begins to work? I was no less disappointed in the Western European idols. Charcot is a full-fledged tyrant. He screams at the doctors as if they were messenger boys. I saw his patients and God knows that neither he nor Janet can help them. They are the same unhappy people who came to me. One of them I actually recognized. They travel from Paris to Nancy, and from Nancy to Carlsbad or Baden-Baden. It is easy to hypnotize them. They are taken in by every fashion, every popular book, every new play, every blown-up scandal. We make too much fuss in Poland over this Western Europe! The Prussian governor is no better than our natchalnik. The stinginess and pettiness of the German hotel keeper is unbelievable. In Paris I encountered poverty and filth even worse than on our Krochmalna Street. The Alps are magnificent, but the philosophy lectures that I have heard here in Bern and in Zurich are just as tedious, pedantic, and false as the wisdom dispensed in Warsaw. In Germany, anti-Semitism is rife. Here, in Western Europe, I have seen what I have known for a long time: that the person who estranges himself from God seeks only an opportunity to hate. We hate in the name of patriotism, or class distinctions, party relationships, or simply because we live in different localities, or speak a different dialect. The professors make filth of one another. There is bitter combat concerning Kant in Germany. There is no greater accomplishment for the Prussian student than to drink scores of mugs of beer and fight duels. A youth who does not have a couple of dueling scars on his face is ashamed to go into a beer hall. Official Germany is permeated by an obsession for conquest, while France is consumed with a mania for revenge. Both are united in contempt and envy of England. Europe is full of plans, but all of them demand human sacrifice.

When I left Warsaw, I was still toying with the idea of settling somewhere in Western Europe. But here many things became clear to me. I am now fully determined to go on to Palestine. Do not think that I have any illusions. I know full well that the settlers there are no saints. How, in any case, can this or that part of the world solve human problems? Yet Palestine is for me the symbol of the return to my roots, the source of the ancient truths that for thousands of years people have tried to alter, emasculate, or drown in dogma. When I sat and listened to the celebrated Wundt, I realized that intellectuals would continue to present their philosophic, sociological, and psychological interpretations even if the whole world were to become Sodom. And how far are we from such a state? All this culture blunts moral feeling and destroys faith in the divine powers. Here, even more so than at home, megalomania is evident in every countenance. I mean, among the intelligentsia.

I have had moments when everything seemed black and I seriously considered suicide. But each time, as if by their own volition, my feet led me among Jews, the real Jews, the Jews who live with God. I found Hassidic study houses in Berlin and even in Paris. I cannot describe to you what a pleasure it was for me to encounter these Hassidim, to look at their faces, beards, eyes, to hear the words of the Torah. When one gazes at the Talmudic scholars, one actually sees eternity. What is Berlin to them? What is Paris? How wonderfully they have isolated themselves amidst all this madness! They do not even know that they are in Europe and that we are at the end of the "magnificent" and bloody nineteenth century. In their Houses of Worship, it is always the beginning. They do not boast of progress, nor do they build their hopes on a "new man" that this or that system will bring to the fore. These Jews are the true realists. They know that in all generations man is born bad and that he must work from the cradle to the grave merely not to become an evildoer.

I know, Zadok, that you don't agree with me, but I must tell you what I think. It is a riddle to me how men of my age, or even old men, can seek comfort in a future in which they will no longer be in existence. I have simply stopped understanding those people who hang their hopes on childish promises. I tell you, Zadok, that there is no worse nonsense than the optimism of the professors.

I don't have to tell you that I am going to Palestine with a heavy heart. Misha is with your mother. Olga and I are as good as separated. She is neither a Jew nor a Gentile. Like so many modern Jews, she has one desire: to forget her origin, to destroy her roots. I hope for her own sake that she succeeds. I am not in a much better position than she is, having no real faith and doubting everything, but at least I no longer have the illusion that our history can be obliterated. The power, whatever it is, that has kept us alive for four thousand years is still with us. I can deny God, but I cannot stop being a Jew—contradictory and strange as these words may sound.

I have heard nothing here about your father, and I hope it is not too late for you to go to him. I send you and Hannah my warmest greetings.

Your devoted, Ezriel

25 🏰

I

Zadok was letting his beard grow. A shortened capote still hung in the closet and each time he opened the closet door he looked at it. His father, Reb Jochanan of Marshinov, was on his deathbed. Zadok was prepared to hear the bad news any day. But to go to Marshinov clean-shaven and in a jacket was unthinkable. It would be a disgrace for his mother. Zadok's beard grew quickly and he looked like a Hassid again. He sat in an armchair, smoking cigarettes and skimming the stacks of magazines he had bought. Since his beard had begun to sprout, he had ceased attending classes and paying visits to his assimilated friends. He was supposed to receive some assistance from the community, but he had neglected to ask for it and the stipend had gone to a more aggressive student. Hannah was pregnant and walked about with a pointed belly and yellow flecks on her face.

It was summer, and whoever could afford it was away in the country. The sun beat down on the roof of their attic room. Odors of rotting fruit, sewage, and fried onions from neighbors' cooking wafted in through the windows. The children in the street screamed, threw stones, and hit pieces of wood with makeshift bats. Zadok glanced through the magazines and knit his brow. When his Uncle Ezriel had been in Warsaw he had not been so wretched. At least there had been someone to talk to. Simply because in the last few years his Uncle Ezriel had denounced all material values, Zadok had argued for materialism. This summer Zadok had reached a stage where he had become resentful of the science that his Uncle Ezriel had compared to salt water: the more one drank of it, the less it quenched one's thirst. Every aspect of it was filled with detail, but one could arrive at no meaningful total. Zadok had long since discarded metaphysics. The philosophers played with words as children play with toys. Uncle Ezriel had been right about that, too: today's man worshipped words as if they were idols. Zadok could derive no true satisfaction even from the exact sciences. Mathematics—the language of nature, as Kant described it—was nothing more than a kind of chess game. The axioms were not axioms but accepted rules. Lobachevski's and Riemann's non-Euclidean geometries destroyed any illusion that mathematics was a basic truth. The more Zadok considered Darwin's theory of the origin of species, the less it appealed to him. Even if life should be millions of years old, the species could not have developed without a plan. Every flower, every bird, every animal contradicted this theory. And where had the first cell come from? And from where did dead matter come? And what were laws? What sort of thing was a law? The moment one stopped thinking about everyday matters, one was immediately faced with the eternal mysteries. Zadok pulled at the hairs of his chin and grimaced. He had escaped from the Talmud, the Zohar, from the Shulhan Aruk; he had wanted to depend only on facts, on reason. But facts led nowhere: reason was bankrupt from the beginning. Truth remained veiled. Abroad? What could one learn abroad that wasn't known here? He received literature from Berlin, Leipzig, Bonn, even from Paris and London. Sitting there in his armchair in the Old City, he was in contact with the greatest minds of the world. But how much, alas, did the greatest minds know of the world? Not very much.

Hannah came in from the kitchen with her hair disheveled,

in a spotted apron and battered house slippers. "Zadok, bring up a bucket of water."

Zadok picked up the bucket and went down to the pump. This fetching of water had become a nuisance. In the few years that Zadok had lived in Warsaw, he had literally seen the growth of anti-Semitism. Gentiles who used to say "Good day" and remove their caps had stopped greeting him. Children who had grown up before his eyes had begun to ape and ridicule him. Girls laughed impudently in his face. The Polish press grew daily more malicious, constantly inventing new accusations against the Jews. Even the assimilated Jews were no longer immune to abuse. In Russia, there was no end to the pogroms. Jews were driven out of the villages. The pale of settlement where they were permitted to live grew smaller from year to year. And who was in the vanguard of all this? Not the hoi-polloi or the ignorant, but educated people with university backgrounds. In Germany, anti-Semitism was rampant among the professors. If education was not a remedy against the ancient practice of human oppression, then what was?

Zadok pumped the water. Around him stood a circle of Polish boys, aping his motions with the handle. "Hey, Jewboy, that is a pump, not your fringed garment! . . ." Zadok picked up the pail, spilling the water and wetting his boots. He had ceased sleeping nights and he was weak. He could barely lift the bucket. Lately Zadok had begun to worry about another matter: the eating of meat. How could one be opposed to violence and at the same time consume the flesh of innocent beasts and fowl? Could there be a justification for this? It was simply a matter of power. Whoever held the knife slaughtered. But he, after all, was against the right of might. He had already informed Hannah that he would no longer eat meat, but Hannah had answered him with a lament. Hadn't he made her life miserable enough as it was? Because of him her mother, brothers, sisters, and sisters-in-law would have nothing to do with her. She had no Sabbath, no holidays, no life whatsoever. Now he wanted to deprive her of meat as well. She wasn't able to cook two kinds of meals, meat and dairy. She had neither the money nor the strength for it. She was in the last months of pregnancy and was barely able to stand on her feet. . . . Hannah wept, complained, and made such a fuss that Zadok gave in to her. He would eat meat, if only she would keep still! But the meat didn't agree with him. Hannah bought giblets, heads, feet, entrails, livers. He felt that he was actually swallowing blood and marrow. It would have been possible to kill him, and cook him, in exactly the same way. How can those who torture creatures talk of justice?

Hannah was fussing in the kitchen. Zadok riffled the pages of his book. Maybe it would be better to go to Marshinov now. True, his beard was still too short and he had no side-locks whatever. But he could wait no longer. Suddenly he leaped to his feet. "What am I waiting for?" "Hannale!"

"What is it?"

"I'm going to Marshinov."

"Right now?"

"Right now."

"And you'll leave me alone?"

"Put on your wig and come along."

"I can't go running off like this. . . ."

Hannah promised that she would be ready the following day. Zadok went to the depot to inquire about the train schedule. During the trolley ride to the station, Zadok took account of himself. He had once been a devoted son. When his father had become ill, he had stained his psalter with tears. But since he had become a worldly man, he had become cruel. His father was spitting out his lungs and his son remained in Warsaw. He had not seen him in years. Days went by and he did not even remember that he had a father, let alone the state he was in.

11

Marshinov was quiet. The death of the rabbi had been expected for weeks. Two years before, Dr. Ząbek had said that the rabbi's days were numbered, but when God gave life, one lived. However, the rabbi was no longer able to rise. He saw only his intimates. He would glance into his Zohar, doze, awaken and return to the holy book. Still far from fifty, he looked like an old man. His beard was white and unkempt. His arm had become so scrawny it could scarcely hold the arm phylactery. He was white as a corpse and his eyes watered. It was no longer possible for him to tolerate a saucerful of warm milk, a spoonful of chicken soup. A sip of tea was all he could manage. Tsipele, not Mendel the beadle, served him everything now. Her face had become shrunken. Since Calman's death, she wore a kerchief instead of a bonnet. She had lost her sister Shaindel, and her father, and now her husband was dying. All she could do was to pray.

"Please, take a drop of milk! . . ." Tsipele bent over the rabbi. The glass in her hand trembled.

"Thank you, I don't need it."

"I beg you, drink."

"I can't."

"Woe is me!"

"Sh—there is a Creator."

"Why do I have so much misfortune?" Tsipele said, and burst into tears.

The rabbi wanted to console her, but his throat was too dry. What misfortunes? The soul was no man's property but an object left in trust. When the depositor wanted it back, one had no right to oppose him. And since the soul must return to the throne of glory, one must not damage or stain it. One must be confident that what God did was good. But the rabbi was unable to say this. He glanced fondly at Tsipele. When they were first married, she had occasionally shown some female vanity. She would laugh, joke, adorn herself with jewelry.

Blessed be the name of the Almighty, now that she was a grandmother she had cast aside all childish nonsense and her face was comelier, more Jewish, as her mother's had been, blessed was her memory. Yes, that's how it was: when vanity was gone, the fear of God took its place.

Tsipele bent lower. "Perhaps a sip of soup?"

"I cannot."

"Take your medicine!"

"I beg you, no."

Tsipele stood silently at his bedside. She muffled a cry, not wanting to grieve him. Then she left, wringing her hands. The rabbi closed his eyes. Although the shades were down, the light still bothered him. He had difficulty in praying. He lay there, yearning for silence. Even the chirping of birds in the garden disturbed him. He wondered if he had served the Creator properly. He had neglected his studies, had had evil thoughts, doubts about Providence. He was unworthy of being a Hassid and had been crowned a rabbi against his will. And how had he pastured his flock? He hadn't paid enough attention to the poor and to the children and the young men who had later been lost to the faith. He hadn't inspired the fervor of piety in them. His thoughts vanished for a long time: his attention slackened. Something bubbled in his breast, his back. He felt as if the last portion of his lung wanted to tear loose.

Fragments of thought passed through his mind, bits of Scripture raced by, disconnected portions of the Talmud, of the midrash, words in Chaldaic. Passages of the Torah, interpretations, holy names came to him. He feared that the devil was at work on him. Before a quorum of Jews, the rabbi had nullified the blasphemous words Satan might force him to say or think in his last hour. But who could know whether this nullification was valid? The rabbi felt a dull ache of the spirit. In all these years he had yearned for a vision, a sign from above. Saints had had revelations of the prophet Elijah. While still alive, they had ascended to the mansions of heaven, had seen angels, seraphim, cherubim. The saint Baal Shem-Tov, the miracle worker, had seen the Nest of the Bird and had spoken to the Messiah. Even less important saints, those of later generations, had been favored by visions. But he, Jochanan, was apparently not worthy of any grace from above. His sins blocked the way. If the eyes are not clear, they do not see. If the ears are stuffed up, they do not hear. If one is concerned with matters of the body, one cannot perceive the spiritual. He was even more afraid lest he find nothing later on. His soul might be incarnated in a cow, a wild animal, or a frog. Did he belong among those who were not worthy of seeing the face of the Shechinah? He thought of the arguments of the heretics: there is no judge, no judgment, no leader. A passage from the Book of Ecclesiastes came back to him: "The dead know not anything." How could Ecclesiastes have said this? And how was it that the immortality of the soul was not mentioned in the Scriptures? Perhaps the Sadducees, God forbid, were right? . . . "I'm losing my soul . . . I'm dying an atheist. . . ." Reb Jochanan began to mumble, "I am sinking —Father in heaven, have pity on me! Protect me! Not because of my merits, but because of my holy ancestors. . . ." Suddenly the rabbi smiled. "And what if I do sink into the abyss? Would this in any way lessen the glory of the Almighty?"

The rabbi opened his eyes. It was evening. There was a candle on the table. His wife bent over the bed. "You slept for a long time."

"Yes. . . ."

The rabbi remained in a dreamlike state, praying inwardly for the truth. Someone had entered and left. The candle went out, or was extinguished. The rabbi thought about darkness. It is nothing but the lack of light, the concealment of His face. Then what was there to fear? He was still there. Evil spirits? Let them be—they were necessary! Incarnation! So be it. Rabbi Jochanan saw his father, his face emerging from the ritual bath. Everything dripped, his beard, his sidelocks. Were there ablutions on high, too? His father spoke, but without a sound. The rabbi listened. So that's the way it was. Suddenly something fluttered. Opening his eyes, the rabbi saw a great light. What was it? Sunrise? Lightning? He lay there, his limbs numb. It was neither of these. It illuminated every beam of the ceiling, every corner of the room, the windowpanes, the bed cover. "And God said, 'Let there be light.'" "And God saw that it was good." The rabbi was witnessing Creation. Within one moment everything had become clear, all questions had been answered. The rabbi closed his eyes, but the light was still there: a radiance that shone neither outside him nor within him, but filled all space, penetrated all being. It was everything together: revelation, surcease from all earthly turmoil, the profoundest joy. "All is right, God is perfect!" something in the rabbi cried out. It was all so simple that he could not grasp why he had not known it before. How long had it all lasted? A minute? Seconds? Time itself had vanished. He had merged with eternity. He had only one wish left: to let those who had sunk into doubt and suffering know what he had seen. He stretched out his hand to knock on the wall, but his hand made no sound.

He lingered in this state until sunrise. He seemed still to be in his body. The stars dimmed. The morning star rose and faded. Opposite the bed, the wall turned purplish, but it could not interfere with that other brightness. This now was a reflection of fire. What the flesh saw appeared hazy: the sky, the sun, the trees outside, the walls of the chamber. The door opened, and Tsipele brought in a glass of tea, but she seemed to be enclosed in shadows. A young man entered. The rabbi knew that this was his son, Zadok, but it no longer mattered.

A few minutes later the rabbi rattled, the death throes had begun. The Hassidim tore their way in, to be present at the departure of the soul. The warden of the Burial Society placed a goose quill near the rabbi's nostrils, but it did not stir. Tsipele wailed. The rabbi's daughter, Zeldele, came running up with a cry. Pinchus, the rabbi's son-in-law, wept with a piercing sound. The rabbi's youngest son, Gadele, had fallen asleep, and Mendel the beadle went to wake him. Zadok spoke to no one and no one spoke to him. He just stood there. They opened the windows and said the Justification of the Law. They raised the body and put it on the ground. It had almost no weight. There was a smile on the rabbi's face. He was covered with a prayer shawl and two candles were lit at his head. His intimates went out to telegraph the Jewish settlements that Jochanan, the Rabbi of Marshinov, had died.